THE GOBLIN CORPS

ARI MARMELL
THE GOBLIN CORPS

THE FEW.
THE PROUD.
THE OBSCENE

an imprint of Prometheus Books
Amherst, NY

Published 2011 by Pyr®, an imprint of Prometheus Books

Cover illustration © Lucas Graciano.

Inquiries should be addressed to
Pyr
59 John Glenn Drive
Amherst, New York 14228–2119
VOICE: 716–691–0133
FAX: 716–691–0137
WWW.PYRSF.COM

15 14 13 12 11   5 4 3 2

Library of Congress Cataloging-in-Publication Data

Marmell, Ari.
    The goblin corps / by Ari Marmell.
        p. cm.
    ISBN 978–1–61614–377–0 (pbk.)
    ISBN 978–1–61614–378–7 (e-book)
    I. Title.

PS3613.A7666G63 2011
813'.6—dc22

                                                                2011009890

Printed in the United States of America

For George, Gary, Jason the Larger, and Naomi:
the original Demon Squad.

And with special thanks to Richard,
without whom Morthûl would not have been
the Charnel King that we all know, and . . . Well, know.

PROLOGUE

The flickering torches, sickly embers staggering atop loose bundles of rotting wood, no longer even pretended to hold the darkness at bay. Their illumination succeeded only in convincing the mind that countless unseen horrors lurked within the underground, artificial night.

Not that this was much of an illusion; countless unseen horrors *were* lurking in the dark. But here, deep in the rock beneath the Iron Keep, horrors were nothing new.

The flagstones gleamed dully beneath the glowing brands thanks to a perennial coating of luminescent slime, a revolting substance that even the greatest magics of the keep's master had failed to exterminate. The slow, steady slap of approaching footsteps was heralded by the nauseating sounds of that slime squelching beneath heavy boots.

He was known to the men and monsters under his command only as Falchion. Ice-blue and empty eyes peered through the narrow slits in a bucket-helm shaped of dingy steel. It tilted to one side, that helm—a gesture of revulsion, perhaps?—at the sight of an enormous brown rat, dripping with slime and less-pleasant substances, that clung to the bricks beside him. A glove of mail lashed out, and the low reverberation of iron on stone echoed throughout the chamber, almost masking the truncated squeal. The tiny corpse dropped to the floor, already forgotten, as its executioner continued calmly into the adjoining chamber.

"Careless, Falchion. Clumsy and careless." Nasal and whining, it was a voice capable of conveying little more than arrogance and scorn. "Are you really so dense that you still haven't learned how fragile this sort of incantation can be? The death of that rat might well have disrupted the entire—"

"Shove it, Havarren." Falchion assumed an easy stance in the far corner, crossing his arms with a faint grating sound. Those cold blue orbs flickered downward, glancing briefly at the rust-red mail that covered him from shoulders to hips. A single eyebrow rose marginally, as though he'd only now discovered that he wore the hauberk at all.

"'Shove it'? Really? How . . . common." The second speaker leaned forward, finally exposing his own face to the faint torchlight.

Falchion snarled behind his faceplate—a reflex that had become ingrained, triggered by nothing more than the man's proximity. Where Falchion was thick, corded, and well muscled, the other fellow was lanky to the point of emaciation. Thick blond hair cascaded to a near-perfect point just below jutting shoulder blades. His attire was vain, even foppish: bright ruffles and knee-high cavalier boots—tanned from the hide of something with more intelligence and fewer legs than anything so mundane as a cow—were complemented by an immaculately pressed violet coat and pants that were, to Falchion's perpetual dismay, worn tightly enough to accentuate, rather than conceal, what lay beneath them. And unlike the general himself, who wore at his side the heavy blade from which he'd taken his name, the other was armed only with a flimsy dagger, poor protection from anything more menacing than an agitated rabbit.

But then, Vigo Havarren possessed methods of protecting himself that had little to do with sharpened steel.

A caustic retort clung to the tip of Falchion's tongue, begging for release. Yet he clamped his mouth firmly shut as the chamber's final occupant approached the center of the room. He watched both men through pinpricks of unholy yellow radiance that sat where most human beings kept their eyes.

"General Falchion. Lord Havarren." The voice revealed just the faintest trace of an accent; whether this was natural or simply the result of a decayed vocal apparatus, Falchion never knew. "Gentlemen, the death of a rat is hardly going to interfere with one of *my* incantations. The death of two *sentient* entities, however, might well serve to *strengthen* the spell. Shall I find out? Or can I count on your silence?"

Havarren blanched. "Silence can be arranged."

Falchion just nodded.

"Good." The master of the Iron Keep stepped—*glided*, it seemed—to the large stone platform along the chamber's northernmost wall. The fur-lined hem of a cloak that had been a beautiful midnight blue when it was new—about four centuries past, give or take a decade—whispered across the flagstones. Somehow, it remained unmarred by the grasping slime.

A huge iron cauldron sat beneath a granite altar, a noxious blend of fluids bubbling within, heated without the aid of any visible flame. Virgin's blood, dragon's tears, spider's breath, essence of ghost, the heart of a newborn, and other reagents so rare that centuries of searching had been required for their acquisition—all splashed and burbled and flowed through the cauldron, agitated and stirred by the agonized thrashing of the live animals occasionally tossed into the pot by the lanky sorcerer.

"Havarren?" the master of the keep glanced up from the table, where he had been carefully arranging an additional assortment of rare and eldritch objects, enchanted tools, ancient amulets. "Time?"

The gaunt wizard briefly furrowed his brow in concentration. "Almost, my lord. You may begin . . . now."

The first of the priceless arcane objects was hurled into the cauldron. Instantly the vile substance began to glow, filling the underground chamber with the light of the noonday sun. Falchion flinched slightly—not at the sudden influx of illumination, but at the close-up view of his own dark master: Morthûl, the Charnel King of Kirol Syrreth.

Garments once of royal quality, now worn and tattered beyond hope of repair, shrouded a body unimaginable by any rational mind. Mummified flesh creaked like hardened leather with every move the Dark Lord made. The left side of his face was covered in that not-skin, frozen in a perpetual rictus; the right was nothing more than naked bone. That hideous, sickly yellow glow was most conspicuous in the eyes—but it leaked as well from the nasal cavity and between King Morthûl's teeth. Worms and maggots, beetles and roaches and less savory creatures all crawled about and among the Charnel King's clothes and patches of long-dead flesh, wandering between exposed bone and protruding ribs, every so often dropping from the empty sockets in a twisted parody of tears. A full head of raven tresses completed the horrific image, trailing from beneath a tarnished silver crown.

Falchion, general of the Charnel King's armies, shuddered again, a rare moment of self-reflection stealing over him in this most pivotal moment of a plan that had taken the Dark Lord centuries to implement. This, this was the man—the *thing*—to which he had sworn his loyalty and his life. It was enough to turn even the strongest stomach, to send even the most corrupt soul scampering into the corner to wail in terrified self-pity.

But Falchion was, above all else, a practical man. And if one man, however revolting, however many centuries dead, was about to conquer the known world—well, Falchion wanted to be on his good side, no matter what it took.

Morthûl's rotted form abruptly stiffened, as though rigor mortis had finally caught up with him. Then, with an explosion of voice somewhere between a sonorous chant and a low-pitched howl, the Dark Lord raised his arms, both fists—one skeletal, one wrapped in brittle skin—clenched tight. Unspeakable energies crackled around him, and a blinding wave of bile-green luminescence flowed from the cauldron into the Charnel King himself and thence upward, where it vanished through the room's cold ceiling. From there it would erupt to the surface and flow in writhing tendrils across the continent, seeking its targets.

Falchion saw Havarren bow his head and knew he was sending a mental signal of his own, an aspect of the ritual Morthûl was too busy to perform. Immediately, agents of Kirol Syrreth, lying in wait throughout the Allied Kingdoms to the east and south, moved out into the streets to do violence. Humans and goblins waylaid all who walked the roads so late, in a dozen cities across the land. In mere minutes a thousand lives, young and old, rich and poor, good and evil, were cut abruptly short. And for every life snuffed out in these darkest of hours, the Charnel King's spell was strengthened, his power grew.

It had taken Morthûl over two hundred years of laborious research, of perusing tomes so old they predated even his own birth, to master the magics he now manipulated. Three hundred more were spent in methodical search for the necessary components. Agents of the Dark Lord had combed the world from pole to pole, questing for items so rare that even the greatest wizards of the day scoffed at the notion of their very existence. And finally, tonight, it all came together in a few short moments of the most fearsome sorceries the world had seen in generations.

Across the continent, kings and queens and princes, emperors and dukes and popes—all who ruled, or might one day rule—collapsed in agony so exquisite that the gods themselves must have writhed in sympathy. The Charnel King's spell swept them up in its wake and slowly, utilizing their own bodies as a gateway, traced its way through the flow of time itself, performing subtle alterations not upon the current royals, but on their ancestors.

Still chanting, his fingers flitting as though mending a rent in an expensive fabric, Morthûl began rewriting the events of lives long passed. Slowly, over the span of generations, he instilled in each successive ruler a growing loyalty, an intense fealty to the lord of Kirol Syrreth. It took time: Seemingly endless minutes were required for the manipulation of each separate generation. But when the ritual finally reached its conclusion, just before the dawn, he would have conquered the world entire, without a single voice raised in protest, a single sword in rebellion. Once he had worked his way forward through the ages to those rulers living today, their fealty, their loyalty, their *worship* would be absolute, instilled by tradition that stretched back a thousand years.

The last of the dispatched souls dissolved into the power emanating from the iron cauldron; the last of the ancient relics sank in its depths, melting into the obscene mixture that threatened now to boil over the sides and onto the floor. The critical juncture was upon them. Moments more, and the damage would be too extensive to ever be undone, the point of no return forever passed.

Falchion, Havarren, and yes, even the Charnel King jumped at the thunderous crash of a steel door slamming into a rock wall—a sound swiftly overwhelmed by the clatter of feet dashing through the corridor. The half of Morthûl's visage that was capable of expression twisted.

Fear. For the first time, Falchion saw fear on the Dark Lord's face.

"Stop them!" Even that single hissed command was a strain on his body and mind, both of which channeled more sheer magic in that instant than any wizard in history.

A metallic rasp pierced the room, and Falchion stepped toward the corridor, blade in hand. He nodded briefly as Havarren appeared beside him, animosity temporarily forgotten.

But the determination Falchion saw etched across the wizard's features fell away as the first of the approaching figures strode determinedly into view.

"You! You're dead!" The arrogance in Havarren's tone was gone, drowned by an amazed and growing terror. "How . . . ?"

The regal figure actually smiled at Havarren's bewilderment. "My dear Vigo, surely you didn't expect *me* to be inconvenienced by *one* little dragon, did you?"

His name was Ananias duMark: one of the greatest sorcerers of this generation, beloved hero of the Allied Kingdoms, and perpetual thorn in Morthûl's side. He was also, Havarren knew, a half-breed, though little in his build or features, his rugged chin or earthy-brown hair, hinted at his elven heritage. He wore a simple robe of mahogany hue and carried a staff of that selfsame wood, intricately carved with a thousand runes.

A curse on his lips, the gaunt servant of the Dark Lord began a convoluted dance with his fingers, weaving the magics that would finally obliterate this cretin from the face of reality itself.

He never finished. A piercing shriek, deafening in the echoing chamber, sounded from the hall, and the first of the half-elf's allies leapt bodily *over* the new arrival and slammed into Havarren's chest, taking them both to the slimy floor.

A lock of fire-red hair fell across Havarren's face, and the musk of animals flooded his nostrils. This, then, would be Lidia Lirimas, scout and beast-tamer. Even as he tossed her from him with a surprising burst of strength, he couldn't help but scoff at his half-elven foe. Would the pattern never change? Each time it was the same damn thing: Every few years, duMark would wander the lands, assembling a brand-new band of "heroes" from the most worthy of that generation. It was such a cliché that Havarren felt the urge to laugh aloud.

Until, that is, his attempt to rise from the clinging slime was cut unexpectedly short. Lirimas, a second cry escaping her throat, spun on the ball of her left foot and brought her right heel across his face. Bone snapped with a brutal sound, and the mage once more collapsed.

A gleam of triumph in her bright blue eyes, the young warrior raised her slim-bladed sword high, determined to see Havarren's head cleaved from his body.

It would have gone better for her had she not been quite so focused. . . .

Even as he parried blow after blow from another of duMark's companions—a heavily built, dark-skinned man with a scraggly goatee and a head as bald as an egg—Falchion interposed himself between the woman and Havarren's crumpled form. He'd been overwhelmingly tempted to stand back, to focus on his own opponent and let the chips—and swords—fall where they may. But he knew that the Dark Lord valued Havarren's council, that he would be *perturbed* if the arrogant bastard were allowed to die.

So, since his blade was occupied at the moment, Falchion hauled off and slammed his mailed fist into the young ranger's face. Blood spurted between his knuckles, and Lidia's nose disappeared amid a spreading mass of pulped cartilage and bruised flesh. Not dead, perhaps, but quite firmly out of the fight, she collapsed backward in a heap.

The mage hauled himself to his feet, tossing a grudging nod of thanks Falchion's way. That simple gesture sent new spears of torment shooting through his fractured jaw. A growl deep in his throat, Havarren raised the back of his hand and wiped a smear of blood from the corner of his misshapen mouth—and if any in the room noticed that the blood was some odd shade other than red, or that it congealed too thickly to be normal blood, they assuredly dismissed it as a trick of the dancing, insufficient light.

It would almost, he thought bitterly, have been better to die than to owe his life to that—that imbecile! This was *not* something he could afford to have hanging over him. He needed to repay the debt, and fast!

Hmm. The bald man, dressed in leather leggings and precious little else, was giving the good general no small amount of trouble. His obscenely large axe hadn't yet penetrated Falchion's defenses, but a number of thin lines scored the general's hauberk, and the dark-skinned intruder showed no sign of tiring. With a nonchalant gesture, Havarren sent a stream of iridescent orbs hurtling from his fingertips, balefire summoned from the bowels of hell itself. A brief sizzling sound accompanied the stench of burning flesh, and the dark-skinned man collapsed with a scream, his back charred black by the sorcerous assault.

Falchion couldn't be bothered even to return in kind Havarren's own nod of thanks. With barely a sideways glance to acknowledge the aid he'd just received, he stepped toward the hallway, blade raised to meet the next invader.

Arrogant bastard. Should've let him die.

The gaunt mage tensed. Another offensive spell danced on the tip of his tongue; his hands glowed with the vile radiance of demon-spawned magics. Desperately he twisted about, seeking the face of the man who had started it all.

Too late. The half-elven interloper had reached the northern wall, his meandering steps having somehow carried him between the various combatants. He stood at arm's length from the incandescent form of the Dark Lord himself.

The Charnel King of Kirol Syrreth, though absorbed in his own magics, remained well aware of the world around him. His head slowly swiveled to stare directly at Ananias duMark. Within the greater aura of the ancient spell, his unholy glow left a luminescent streak as he moved, not unlike the slithering of an eel beneath the surface of a stagnant pond.

"I grow bored, Ananias." Morthûl's voice, distorted by the eldritch whirlwind surrounding him, seemed to come from the deepest corners of the room—as though the walking corpse had been but the mouthpiece of something greater, something darker, that no longer need confine itself to his form. "This spell you see taking shape before you is ancient, far older than you or even I could ever dream. Even at your best, you could never hope to disrupt it. And though you may have fooled the others, I know well that you're hardly at your best. Havarren's dragon did you more harm than you let on, did it not? Flee, Ananias duMark. Flee now, and you may yet escape my reach before the night is through."

It was a pure, unadulterated bluff. Truth be told, Morthûl hadn't the barest idea what duMark, or any other sorcerer, might or might not be able to do to the ongoing incantation. That worried him—but not so much so as the fact that every iota of his power was tied up in maintaining these most ancient of magics. If that damn half-breed *did* interfere, there wasn't a bloody thing Morthûl could do to stop him.

But even as the interloper lifted his hands, the Charnel King saw Havarren rising, bolts of cobalt-blue lightning arcing between his fingers, preparing to strike duMark down. The Dark Lord's rictus grin widened, and he felt the eldritch forces around him surge and dance, as though they, too, celebrated what was to come.

Morthûl's triumph, his euphoria, were short-lived indeed. At the sight of the half-elf's sudden smile, he felt his own expression falter.

Ananias duMark released his spell. No great, earthshaking magic was this, no enigmatic ritual from days of yore. Thin streams of pure arcane force, crossbow bolts shaped of light and willpower, sprang from his palm. It was among the simplest of spells, a beginner's trick, easily mastered by the lowliest apprentice, anger given form. So simple, so weak, it was absolutely useless against the various sorceries and enchantments that protected the Charnel King's undead form.

But then, it wasn't *aimed* at the Charnel King. The bolts flew true: straight into the air above the combatants. The Dark Lord's scream of impotent fury was lost amid the deafening cacophony of the crumbling ceiling.

Slabs of stone toppled to the floor, pulping anything that dared get in their way. Clouds of dust billowed upward from the shattered cobblestones, a raging storm somehow smuggled into the underground chamber. Thunder rocked the Iron Keep's foundations, echoes blending into echoes until they filled the empty spaces entirely, a physical presence as real as the ponderous rock. The marble altar disintegrated into a fine powder, the magics imbued within it lost as though they had never been. The cauldron, jagged stones already bobbing within its putrid contents, disappeared beneath an enormous chunk of ceiling. The tiny portion of the iron vessel not crushed beyond all recognition was bent so hideously that it would never again hold liquid. The nauseating glow that had permeated the room since the incantation began now faded away, the final moments of a strange and alien sunset.

It seemed as though the torrent of rock might never end. Surely there could be no more stone above their heads! Surely they must have reached the surface by now, and beyond, and still it came. But slowly, ever so gradually, end it did. The stone fell in smaller pieces, in shorter bursts. The impenetrable dust began to disperse, though sight remained a hopeless prospect, as the room's only torches were long extinguished.

And then the last, straggling portions of the ceiling had fallen, the last of the grit settled. Silence reigned, but for the occasional drip of unseen water.

Until, finally, something stirred.

Like a dog shaking off a light summer shower, Ananias duMark rose to his feet, small chunks of rubble cascading off him—or rather, off of the faintly glowing aura that surrounded him and had prevented him from becoming a permanent resident. Casually brushing the dust from his sleeves, he examined the substantial mountain of debris. Even a creature as overwhelmingly powerful as Morthûl couldn't conceivably have survived that collapse—not without the same sort of protective spells that had saved duMark himself. And the half-elven mage was quite certain that the king's godlike powers had been fully invested in the ancient spell. No, odds were good that the terror of a hundred generations was smeared across a hundred square feet of cobblestone.

Then again, this was the Charnel King of Kirol Syrreth and master of the Iron Keep, and "odds" meant precious little. DuMark halted himself halfway through a simple light spell, allowing the inky dark to wash over him. Only then did he once more scour the heaps of stone, searching for the faintest trace of that telltale yellow glow.

"Ananias . . . Help . . ."

The half-elf cursed under his breath. He'd completely forgotten . . .

With a strength born of desperation and fueled by arcane arts, duMark tossed stone after stone across the room, digging toward the source of that plaintive cry. He'd never have gotten so far—never have survived his many clashes with King Morthûl—without his companions, but they could be so bloody *inconvenient* at times.

There! More stone, its jagged edges stained with blood. The sorcerer quickly cleared enough space to see the dark skin beneath the rubble.

"Kuren?" he whispered, scraping away more of the detritus. "Kuren, are you all right?"

"He can't hear you." That same whispered voice, and now duMark could just make out a second form lying beneath the insensate warrior.

"Lidia?"

"Yes." The voice, and the breath behind it, were weak, injured, but alive, thank the Gods! "He—he dragged himself over me as the ceiling began to come down. I—I think he's alive. That is, I can feel his heartbeat. But he's bleeding badly, Ananias. His mouth is full of blood, and . . ."

But the half-elf was only half listening. His hands now glowing with all the magics he had remaining, he ripped the last layers of stone from atop his companions. For just an instant, something snagged his attention, and his head jerked to the side.

But it was only a hand, protruding from between two gargantuan slabs of rock. A hand possessed of long, slender fingers.

The sorcerer, despite his friends' condition, couldn't help but grin. Whether or not Morthûl himself was dead, there was at least *one* foe who wouldn't be causing duMark any more trouble. Momentarily satisfied with that, he turned back to his companions. "There's a great deal of damage, Lidia. Shattered bones, internal bleeding. Even this far from the epicenter, it's a miracle he survived this long. Any other human would be dead."

Any other, but not Kuren Bekay. Even as a child, he had proven exceptionally strong for his size—a natural attribute duMark's own spells, some years gone by, had magnified tenfold. The man could rip trees up by the roots, and it would take more than a stone hailstorm to put him down.

Probably.

"Let's get him out of here," duMark ordered, hefting the bulky soldier as though he were an armful of dirty laundry. A quick glance at Lidia, only now dragging herself to her feet, suggested far more eloquently than words could have done that Kuren was not the only one in need of aid.

DuMark met the woman's eyes with his own, refusing to look at the ruined mass that was the rest of her face. "Can you walk?"

"I can bloody well walk away from *here*," she told him, a horribly liquid tone to her voice.

"Good." The sorcerer glided across the broken, uneven footing. "Erris and Father Thomas are still upstairs, holding off the guards. We'll see if Thomas can provide a tincture for you, do something about the pain until he has the time to patch the two of you up properly."

DuMark threw a single, lingering glance behind him. Nothing but tons of stone. Nothing stirred in the rubble. It was finally over.

"And then . . . we can go home."

The door slammed shut behind them with a startling sense of finality, rather like the final page of a long and wearying book. And once again, the room was still.

The air shimmered as if observed through a sheen of rippling water. The very fabric of the room *parted*, and slowly, an inch at a time, Vigo Havarren returned to the chamber. At his sudden appearance, a faint illumination spread through the room, as though invisible torches shed their flickering light upon the walls.

The gaunt wizard was coated in dust and grime. Blood, or something that was *almost* blood, seeped from a dozen small wounds, and his jaw still hung crooked on his face. For a brief instant, Havarren simply stood, motionless, lost in concentration. A grating screech, a sudden crack, and his jaw popped roughly back into place. A single grunt was his only concession to the sharp pain that followed.

Gingerly prodding at his chin with the fingertips of his left hand, he knelt beside the right—which he'd deliberately left in the debris—and wished wistfully that it would prove as easy to fix as his jaw. Already, fleshy tendrils had sprouted from the stump where that hand once rested, but it would be weeks before the writhing mass again formed into anything resembling an actual limb.

Standing once more, Havarren scanned the room. A faint gleam of metal shone from the gaps in a small hill of stone, but he ignored it completely. The wizard neither knew, nor cared, if Falchion had survived. No, his concern was for—

The center of the chamber erupted, showering the already-devastated room with a flurry of jagged rock. A volcanic wave of balefire coursed from the floor, the sorcerous flame melting the rubble into so much slag. Havarren only barely levitated himself above the hell-spawned flood before the all-consuming tide could eat his legs out from under him.

A roar emerged from beneath the carpet of liquefying rock, the mingling wails of a thousand damned souls. Bursts of smoke broke through the eldritch flood, filling the room with the choking stench of sulfur. The walls began to glow with unnatural heat, and the gaunt wizard found himself wondering if even the Iron Keep could survive what was happening to its foundations. Tendrils of balefire climbed those walls, slowly metamorphosing into the questing tentacles of *something*: something unknown, unseen in all the worst nightmares of mankind. Almost tenderly they brushed the sides of the chamber, the touch of a lover—or perhaps the first inquisitive prods of a prisoner seeking escape.

Arms spread, riding atop the final, cresting wave, he rose. He set his foot down atop the ruined floor, and the balefire parted beneath his tread. Eyes blazing to outshine the arcane flame below, the Charnel King of Kirol Syrreth ascended once more from the clutches of damnation.

But duMark's assault had left its mark. The withered flesh that covered the left side of his body and face was cracked and torn away, leaving gaping windows to bone and muscle beneath. His finery was no longer threadbare, no longer worn: It was nothing but a thin cobweb of dangling threads. Roaches, maggots, and things unidentifiable swarmed across his body, writhing in panic, seeking shelter from the chaos around them. Many fell from him in a great deluge to sink and die in the hellfire below, but an infinite number appeared to take their place.

Quaking under a surge of unaccustomed fear, Havarren could do nothing but watch as Morthûl walked, unhindered, through the wrath of hell, stopping only when the pair of them stood face-to-face.

Slowly, as though it required no small amount of effort, the Charnel King spoke.

"I," he told his servant, his voice nearly too low to hear at all, "am *very* disappointed."

Vigo Havarren didn't believe in many gods, and he tended to despise those that he did believe in. But now, for the first time in his extremely long life, he felt an uncontrollable urge to pray.

Ananias duMark, greatest sorcerer of the Allied Kingdoms, emitted a sigh of sheer bliss as he slowly sank into the down-stuffed mattress. His robe hung on a peg across the small bedchamber; his staff leaned precariously against the wall beside it.

For the past month, ever since his final encounter with his ancient foe, duMark had daily driven himself near the point of collapse. Only within this last week had his arcane abilities returned to what he considered acceptable levels. Only now, finally, could he rest. Exhausted beyond human understanding, the wizard was asleep before his gently pointed ears hit the pillow.

King Dororam, his snow-white beard matted by the pillow upon which it pressed, bolted upright in bed, his heart pounding. Convinced, at first, that he had escaped a truly horrific dream, he had just begun to lie back once more when the hideous, earsplitting scream—identical, his sleep-numbed brain finally realized, to the one that had awakened him—echoed through the halls of Castle Bellatine. And it was only then, as he came fully awake, that Dororam realized his wife, the elegant Queen Lameya, no longer lay beside him. That it was her despairing wail that came to him through the dark. A chill of fear waltzed with improper cheer down his spine, and the aging monarch leapt bodily from his bed, his hand already reaching for the latch set in the thick mahogany door. . . .

Echoing the king of whom he dreamt, duMark jerked upright, face coated in sweat, throat aching from his lingering scream. Before the echoes of that shout had dwindled, the mage was striding across the room, hands reaching of their volition for robe and staff. Rarely, even in his hundreds of years of life, had duMark experienced a dream of such intensity, and even the most wet-behind-the-ears apprentice wizard would have recognized it for the dreadful premonition that it was. Even before the hem of the robe had fully settled around his feet, duMark was mouthing the incantation that would teleport him instantly to Castle Bellatine. But his thoughts were elsewhere, miles away from the spell that he knew by heart.

Gods help me. I should have made sure. . . .

He arrived in the midst of unadulterated chaos. Every servant and resident of the castle dashed hither and yon, spurred on by the call of some urgent duty, none knowing what he or she should actually *do*. One harried steward, though startled by the sudden appearance of the half-elf in the hallway, recognized the wizard by sight. Without a word of explanation, he quickly led duMark upstairs.

Over a dozen guards milled about on the landing beside the royal chambers, but they all stepped aside quickly as duMark strode past.

Queen Lameya, tears streaking her cheeks, rocked bodily back and forth in a chair in the center of the room, a low wail of anguish sporadically punctuating her sobs. DuMark had always thought of her as an attractive woman, despite her age. Now, however, grief's ungentle fingers had sculpted her face into a grimace of pain and twisted her hair from a distinguished gray to brittle white.

"My daughter, duMark!" King Dororam, who had stood behind his wife, hands upon her shoulders, stormed across the room, his gaze boring into the mage's own. Although a decade older than his wife, Dororam had grown up a warrior and had allowed neither body nor mind to deteriorate. But tonight, his hair was tangled with sleep, his well-trimmed beard matted exactly as duMark had dreamed. And the aura of fury radiating from him was enough to make even the sorcerer retreat a step—almost enough to hide the sorrow behind it. "My own daughter!"

DuMark quickly regained his composure. "Your Majesty," he intoned, bowing slightly. "Something has happened? I thought I sensed—"

"Happened? *Happened?!* Oh, gods!" And then he, too, allowed the tears to come, though the rage never once left his eyes.

Reluctantly, the captain of the guard—an older man, one who had served King Dororam for decades—stepped forward, his armor clanking and tabard swaying with each step. "My Lord duMark, Princess Amalia . . ." The old soldier swallowed once, audibly, and then rigidly suppressed his own grief, his own horror. "Princess Amalia has been murdered."

DuMark felt his knees go weak beneath him. Had the wall not been near enough to support his slumping form, he would surely have collapsed to the floor. *Why didn't I make sure . . . ?*

"What . . . ?" His voice was little more than a whisper, barely even a breath. "What happened?"

"We're not certain, my lord. One of the serving maids thought she heard a scuffle, and when she went to investigate—"

"They butchered her, Ananias," Dororam intoned, his hands seizing the front of the mage's robe. "Butchered my child like an animal! They didn't—they didn't even leave us a whole body to bury. . . ."

Slowly, gently, duMark removed the king's fists from his robe. "Your Majesty—I am so sorry. If there were anything I could do . . ."

Dororam's head shot up, that haunted look once more replaced by that burning rage. "It was Morthûl, wasn't it?"

DuMark nodded slowly. "I think it must have been."

The king's mouth twitched, his teeth clenched. "You told me he was dead, duMark."

"I truly believed he was, Your Majesty. But there's no other answer. Had he died, Falchion or someone else might have taken over, but they'd be far too busy consolidating power to worry about retribution. No, my king. Only the Dark Lord himself could have done this. I'm sorry."

Dororam stared for the space of several heartbeats. And then, without warning, he was striding across the room, his right hand clenched tightly about the hilt of the sword he had yanked from the captain's scabbard.

"Assemble the soldiers," he shouted to the guards around. "Assemble them all, and dispatch messengers to the dukes. We ride on Kirol Syrreth at dawn!"

DuMark, following on the king's heels, shook his head in protest. "Your Majesty—"

"*What?!*" Dororam spun, blade held at the half-elf's throat. "You are partially to blame for this, duMark! Would you withhold justice from me as well?"

It took no small amount of effort for the sorcerer to keep his annoyance from showing on his face. *Why are they all such fools?*

Carefully modulating his voice, duMark said, "Your Majesty, I share your grief. Were it within my power, I would hand you the Iron Keep this very morn." Carefully, he pushed aside the blade with the head of his staff. "But winter comes in a few weeks. In the peaks of the Brimstone Mountains, the snows are already falling. By the time they reached the borders of Kirol Syrreth, whatever remnants of your army had managed to avoid starving or freezing would find themselves stalled at the Serpent's Pass, unable to cross the Brimstone Mountains and easy targets for the Charnel King's troglodytes. What justice would *that* bring you, Your Majesty?"

It appeared, at first, as though Dororam were deaf to duMark's entreaty. But slowly, so slowly, the king's wrath dimmed just a little, and the arm that held the sword began to relax.

"What," he asked, his voice tight, "do you suggest?"

Internally, duMark sighed in relief. The others might have reacted poorly if he'd been forced to enchant the man. "Only that you wait. Delay your vengeance, my king. Shauntille is far from the only nation with reason to hate Morthûl. Use the opportunity that winter brings to send messengers to the others. Assemble the armies of *all* the Allied Kingdoms. With such a force at your side, even the gathered hordes of Kirol Syrreth cannot stand against you. And I personally shall ride by your side, to ensure that this time, the foul abomination stays dead!"

Thoughtfully, Dororam nodded. "It shall be as you suggest, Ananias. We will wait, and we shall assemble every fighting man this land has to offer. This spring will be the last thaw the Dark Lord ever sees.

Before I am through, not only the Iron Keep, but all of Kirol Syrreth will be thrown down!" The sword clattered noisily to the floor, dropped by nerveless fingers. With his rage diverted, the king of Shauntille found himself defenseless against an overwhelming tide of sorrow.

"And now, Ananias, if you'll excuse us . . . We have a daughter to mourn."

The half-elf bowed once and departed. As he marched through the carpeted passages of the Castle Bellatine, his mind worked at a feverish pace. King Dororam and his armies might be inconvenienced by a little snow, true enough, but duMark was the greatest sorcerer of the Allied Kingdoms, and it would take far more than a change of season to hinder *him*. He had sworn that this time Morthûl would truly fall—and that was one vow he was bound and determined to keep.

Like a fading mirage, the mage vanished from the walls of the great castle. There were preparations to make, and even a man so potent and resourceful had precious little time in which to make them.

CHAPTER ONE

BRUTE CAMP

Shadows danced in languid circles around the throne room of the Iron Keep. The impenetrable walls, adorned with an uncountable array of skulls from dozens of races, seemed to shift in the fluctuating light—and perhaps they did, guided by the fickle moods of their lord and master.

Upon his great marble throne the Charnel King sat, slumped forward, weighted down by the impossibly heavy matters pressing upon his decomposed shoulders. His right elbow rested upon the arm of the great chair, and his chin was propped on one skeletal fist. Leathery flesh, only partially re-formed from the damage Ananias duMark had inflicted, was twisted into a grimace of equal parts anger, boredom, and dejection. Had Morthûl been anything resembling a human, he might have been described as . . . melancholy.

Slowly, the hollow echoes of his footfalls puncturing the almost-sacrosanct silence of the chamber, Vigo Havarren approached his master.

"My lord?" The lanky wizard spoke quietly. "My lord, Her Majesty the Queen seeks an audience."

The Charnel King moved not at all. The faces embossed in the marble of the throne—dozens of hideous expressions, screaming in agony—looked far more alive than he. "I said that I would see no one. My loving wife included."

"Very well, my king. I—"

"For that matter," the Dark Lord continued inexorably, "I don't seem to recall making an exception for you, either."

"I—that is, Queen Anne expressly ordered me to seek an audience on her behalf. You've told us numerous times that, in your absence, we are to obey her as though she spoke with your voice. I thought—"

"You, Havarren, are not supposed to think. You aren't good at it." Finally, the master of the Iron Keep raised his head, staring directly at the blond wizard. "Still, you are here now. Has there been any progress?"

The mage reluctantly shook his head. "I'm afraid not, my lord. DuMark's spells have always been particularly potent."

Without further comment, Morthûl once more rested his chin on his fist and resumed the all-consuming task of staring into space.

Havarren imperceptibly shook his head a second time. Morthûl had most certainly taken his vengeance against Dororam, the monarch who had aided duMark and his allies numerous times in thwarting the forces of Kirol Syrreth. But a month and more, now, the Dark Lord's efforts had been spent in seeking the interlopers who had invaded the Iron Keep itself, the scum who had interfered with the Charnel King's ancient spell.

And for a month and more, those efforts had proved futile. Clearly, duMark had realized that his companions were in peril, had woven spells of cloaking and protection so tightly about them that even the combined efforts of Morthûl and Havarren had been unable to locate them, the many spies of Kirol Syrreth unable to unearth them.

It was all finally taking its toll. The collapse of his great spell, at what was supposed to be the culmination of all his work—combined, now, with his failure even to fully punish those responsible—had apparently sucked the heart from the Dark Lord. Morthûl had withdrawn ever further from the day-to-day aspects of ruling a land as large and strife-ridden as Kirol Syrreth. The various goblin races—unsteady allies at the best of times—were reverting to their natural rivalries. The human officers had kept the peace so far, but it was only a matter of time before their efforts must prove inadequate.

Worse still, word had just recently reached Havarren that King Dororam, enraged by the death of Princess Amalia, was assembling the armies of the Allied Kingdoms. Elf prepared to march alongside dwarf, halfling beside pixie, giloral beside human. Come the spring thaw . . .

Havarren, in the process of turning to beat a hasty retreat from the chamber, abruptly stopped short. So deeply had Morthûl withdrawn, the mage realized suddenly, that there was a better than even chance he'd not yet heard of Dororam's mobilization!

Nervously clearing his throat, Havarren turned back. "Umm—my lord, there is one other matter . . ."

Once more the half-naked skull tilted upward. "And that would be?"

The ancient evil listened, expressionless, as Havarren explained current events beyond the Brimstone Mountains. Even after the lanky wizard finished speaking, the Charnel King of Kirol Syrreth stared, as though he couldn't quite comprehend what he'd been told.

And then, slowly, Morthûl rose from his throne. The ancient garments draping his body fell in folds around him, delighted to be free from the confines of the marble corners. Even the profane glow seemed, ever so perceptibly, to brighten.

"Dororam seeks to challenge *me*? Here, in Kirol Syrreth?" A spasm of laughter racked the Charnel King's frame; dust and handfuls of squirming insects spattered across the floor, shaken from the folds of his clothes. Beneath that mocking laugh, Havarren heard clearly an undertone of fury at the hubris of a mortal who would dare stand against the Dark Lord himself.

"Come, Havarren," Morthûl commanded, already moving toward the door. "Let us see what my dear queen wants of me. And then, we have arrangements to make. I intend for Dororam to learn the folly of his actions."

Havarren nodded, falling into step behind his master. "You have a plan, my lord?"

"When do I not? But it requires careful timing. Havarren, summon my messengers. I want you to assemble a Demon Squad."

The mage nodded. "Any racial preferences?"

"No. Just make certain they're the best. I'll be asking quite a bit of them."

"Of course. And then?"

"Then? Then we see to the end of King Dororam and everyone fool enough to follow him."

Havarren grinned, a wide expression of sheer malevolence. There were certain aspects about his "employment" with Morthûl that he deeply resented, but it was nice to see the Dark Lord's old self again.

It meant that someone, a lot of someones, were going to die.

The isle of Dendrakis, from whose rocky earth the Iron Keep rose, lay secluded in the northwestern corner of the massive kingdom. Isolated from Kirol Syrreth proper by the Sea of Tears, it was a part of their homeland rarely visited by most inhabitants—human or otherwise—of that nation.

While it may have been the most important portion of the Charnel King's domain, however, Dendrakis constituted but the smallest fragment of it. Across the length and breadth of Kirol Syrreth, often in locales through which humans would dare not travel let alone dwell, goblin communities spread, a sporadic rash upon the earth. Gremlins and ogres, trolls and kobolds all made their homes here, in this last refuge from the sprawling mass of "civilization." Once, they had warred upon one another constantly, unmindful of all who got in their way. The human cities of Kirol Syrreth surrounded themselves with walls and watchtowers, leftovers from the days when any cloud of dust on the horizon could signal the advance of a goblin army.

The rise of Morthûl, centuries ago, had changed all that. But now, as whispers of his great defeat spread, the humans looked again to the horizon, awaiting the day when the growing chaos among the other races once more spilled over into indiscriminate bloodletting.

Many weeks south of Dendrakis, beyond the foul waters of the Swamps of Jureb Nahl, nestled in the shadows of one of Kirol Syrreth's many mountain ranges, sat Tarahk Trohm. An orcish stronghold, that sprawling settlement—like its twin, Tarahk Grond, so many leagues nearer the Iron Keep—was one of the largest nonhuman cities within the Dark Lord's kingdom. As such, and given its relative proximity to the Brimstone Mountains, its inhabitants were largely responsible for patrolling the nearest border.

One such patrol camped now in the thick forests just north of the Brimstone Mountains, having stopped for a leisurely noontime dinner. The sun shone directly overhead, though little of its light or warmth penetrated the canopy of leaves. Most of the broad-shouldered, bestial creatures sat around the cook-fire, laughing at crude jokes and feasting upon the slightly charred flesh of wild horses they had come across the night before. Some, more conscientious than their brethren—or perhaps simply more retentive—sat with their backs to any convenient tree, polishing their weapons with spit and old, stained rags.

And some, even in the middle of the day, stood watch.

"Cræosh! Join me by the fire!"

The orc so addressed, slouched in the bushes some twenty feet from the others, tugged his attention from the forest to glance back at his chieftain.

"I'm on watch, Berrat."

"Others can watch. Come."

Reluctantly, Cræosh straightened up. Although only about six feet in height—perfectly average, for his race—the warrior's shoulders were massive, nearly three feet across. Squinting red eyes, a sign of almost feminine beauty, peered from folds of swampy-green skin, and his shock-white hair was matted into three large tails by the careful application of mud and the blood of his enemies. A top-heavy sword, wickedly serrated, hung casually at his side, the leather-wrapped hilt permanently stained by the acrid sweat of his palms. Over hide tunic and breeches, the orc wore breastplate, greaves, and armbands that he'd melted down and reforged himself from metals scavenged across a dozen battlefields.

Casually, Cræosh wandered to the fire and slid to the leaf-covered ground, shoving a pair of smaller orcs out of his way. They glared at him, but neither felt brave (or foolish) enough to complain. With a forced grin at Berrat exposing a number of jagged yellow teeth, Cræosh ripped off a chunk of horseflesh and began to chew noisily, ignoring the sizzling rivulets that ran down his chin.

His companion returned a grin no less forced. Berrat was chieftain of his tribe, an influential figure in Tarahk Trohm. But Cræosh was

widely considered to be the best choice for the position once Berrat . . .
"stepped down." The brown-skinned orc was determined that his rival
would have no opportunities to replace him for a good long while. He
had called Cræosh to join him not from any sense of companionship, but
simply to keep a close watch on the warrior—and, frankly, to annoy him.
They both knew it, the other orcs knew it, and there was actually a dis-
creet betting pool among the patrol on when the one would finally challenge the other.

It would not, however, be today. Even as Cræosh raised the horse
haunch to his lips for a second bite, another orc—this one black-skinned
and boasting a ragged, scarred hole where his left eye once sat—dashed
from the concealing shadows of the trees. "Someone's coming!" he called
out before his boots had even skidded to a complete stop.

Instantly, Berrat and Cræosh were on their feet. "Take four," the
chieftain commanded his rival. "Go see. I will follow behind, once these
louts—" And here he took a moment to kick at a smaller orc who was
gathering his gear too slowly for Berrat's taste. Something snapped, and
the orc let out a pained yelp, but he did indeed start preparing a great
deal faster. "—are ready to go," he concluded.

"You, you, you—and you," Cræosh gestured with the steaming
chunk of horseflesh in his hand. "Follow me." Those he'd selected—
including Dækek, the monocular scout—fell in behind him. The
haunch of meat plummeted to the ground with a sticky plop as Cræosh
broke into a distance-eating jog that he and the others could, if necessary, maintain for a day and more.

The sound of their footsteps, pounding in rhythm, was an earthquake thundering through the woods. Over a ton of orc dashed through
the trees, sending small (and not so small) animals scurrying out of their
path. The trees had begun to thin considerably as they moved south, and
the Brimstone Mountains, though miles away, completely dominated
the horizon.

"There!" Dækek shouted, as his keen remaining eye spotted the intruder. Cræosh squinted even more than usual, attempting to discern . . .

"It's a gremlin!" he announced, voice harsh with disgust. "We came
all this way for . . ."

No, he realized, as they drew close enough to make out some detail. Not just any gremlin. This one looked as though he'd been to hell and back, and on a budget. His beige skin was bruised in a dozen places, lacerated in a dozen more, and thick blood matted his clothes. Although bald on top, as were most of his race, this gremlin had grown a full beard—and it, too, hung sticky with blood. His left tusk was missing, one of his spindly ears had been torn halfway from his head, and his right arm hung loose at his side, flapping horribly from the elbow down.

Given his druthers, Cræosh would have been just as content to ignore the gremlin's distress, if not kill him outright. But the strategically brilliant generals of Tarahk Trohm and Tarahk Grond knew that, come spring, the humans and elves and other such scum would attack. Where the gremlins quarreled, and the kobolds schemed, and the xenophobic hobgoblins drew back into Havicruess and locked the gates behind them—the orcs argued for order amid the chaos, for continued cooperation among the races of Kirol Syrreth. And so, for the sake of that order, Cræosh reluctantly went to the gremlin's aid.

Besides, *someone* must have done this to him, and Cræosh hadn't had a good fight in weeks!

The gremlin—barely four feet in height, and massing less than half of Cræosh's three hundred pounds—sobbed audibly at the sight of the huge orcs looming over him, though whether it signified relief or terror, the warrior couldn't tell. As though that sob had carried with it the last of his strength, the fleeing creature toppled forward.

Gruffly, Cræosh grabbed him by his tunic and hauled him upright. Cooperation was just fine, but he wasn't about to *coddle* anyone. "What happened?" he asked, his tone blunt.

"I—I—I, that is, I . . ."

Cræosh, fast running short of patience with the little sniveler, lifted him bodily off the ground with one arm and shook him hard. A few of the orcs winced at the grating sounds from the gremlin's ruined shoulder, though they weren't especially bothered by the moans of pain that accompanied them.

The large orc dropped his arm, and the gremlin's feet met the earth with a solid thump. "Now," Cræosh said amicably, "why don't you try that again?"

"Yes, sir!" The gremlin drew himself up into the closest approximation of a military stance that his present condition would allow. "My unit and I, see, we were patrolling near the Brimstone Mountains . . ."

Exactly what we *were supposed to be doing. Duplication of effort*, Cræosh thought bitterly to himself. *If they'd all just fuckin' talk to each other* . . .

"Well," the gremlin continued, unmindful of the orc's resentment, "we'd just about finished our morning rounds, when Ulev—he's our best scout, you see. Well, he used to be . . ."

Cræosh's jaw began to stiffen.

"Right. Umm, Ulev came running back, told us there was a small human caravan cutting through the foothills on the other side of the range. Well, of course, we all figure, hey, human caravan this far out, and Dororam's got all the armies tied down until spring, it's gotta be a merchant, right? That means stuff we can eat, things we can use or sell. So we all figure, hey, easy mark."

The large orc shook his head, the nostrils of his porcine snout distended in incredulity. "It didn't occur to you," he asked, his voice equal parts astonishment and disgust, "that a human caravan anywhere *near* our borders was probably well guarded?"

"I—that is, it's funny you should mention that . . ."

Cræosh snorted. "They slaughtered you."

The little creature nodded sadly. "Down to the last gremlin. I'm only here now because I had the sense to run when the human I was fighting tripped over a rock. A few of the bugbears were alive when I left, but the gods only know how they're faring by now."

Cræosh snorted again. "Gods," indeed! *What a primitive fucking people the gremlins are. . . .*

"We should go after them!" Dækek interjected. "Teach them to mess with Kirol Syrreth!" The others grunted their agreement.

But Cræosh refused. "Even if the bugbears managed to delay them, they're long gone by now."

It was now, however, the gremlin's turn to shake his head, and rather emphatically at that. "I don't think so, sir. You see, I'm not the only gremlin who ran, actually. We're really a pretty smart race, when it comes down to . . . Anyway, some of the knights rode in through some of the smaller passes, cut them off. I was a little farther ahead, but—well, if they saw which direction I went in, they might still be looking for me. I don't think they were happy about the idea of me getting away to report them."

Cræosh's ears perked up. "Knights?" That meant men who knew one end of a sword from the other. And Father knew how much he'd been craving a challenge!

"You." Cræosh pointed at one of the orcs. "Take the gremlin back to Chief Berrat. Have him follow along. The rest of us are gonna go find us some humans."

It was a deliberate affront to Berrat, and they all knew it. If the fight went badly, he wouldn't be so far behind that he couldn't bail them out; and if it went well, it would be over before he got there. In either case, he'd lose out on the lion's share of the glory.

As would Cræosh's "volunteer."

"Why do *I* have to go back?" he snapped unhappily. "Let Dækek go. He's faster anyway."

"Yes, he is. Which is exactly why I want him with me."

The volunteer growled. "I don't remember anyone putting you in charge! I—"

Cræosh's fist was a falling boulder. A bone-jarring thump was followed swiftly by a limp body sliding slowly to the grass.

Father, but that helmet hurt! Cræosh casually rubbed his knuckles. "Minor change in plan," he said, turning back to the squirming gremlin. "You wait here until he wakes up. *Then* you go with him to speak to Berrat."

"I . . ." The gremlin was looking astoundingly edgy. "That is, I don't really know that waiting around here is the best idea. I mean, I really ought to get back and report to my own superiors, don't you think? And besides, what if the humans get past—"

Words melded into a high-pitched wail as Cræosh casually reached out and grabbed the gremlin by his bad elbow. The screeching continued for perhaps thirty seconds before finally trailing off in an abbreviated gurgle.

"I'm sorry," the orc said mildly. "I was thinking about something else. Were you saying something?"

The ghost-pale gremlin frantically shook his head.

"Oh, good." Without further ado, Cræosh broke once again into that steady orcish jog, the other three following on his heels. There was no more time to waste with that Ancestors-damned gremlin, not when there were humans to kill!

It didn't take long to locate their steel-clad prey. Barely had they broken through a small thicket of trees, only a mile south of where they'd met the gremlin, when the ground began to shudder. From behind a small rise, a distant foothill to the Brimstone Mountains, they came: six humans riding enormous chargers. Encased from head to toe in polished plate, the knights gleamed in the midday sun, as though the orcs faced not a band of mortals but stars yanked from the firmament itself.

Cræosh wasn't impressed. Orcs, by and large, don't do awe; they have very little use for it. Out of long-ingrained habit, Cræosh offered a quick prayer to his Mother and Father, asking his Ancestors for their blessing in the upcoming battle. He knew, without checking, that his companions did the same.

"Six against four," Dækek grunted from behind, "and they're mounted. Hardly seems like a fair fight."

"Agreed," Cræosh replied. Ignoring the rapidly nearing warhorses, he put on a show of deep thought. "Should we give them a handicap?" he asked finally.

"What? Why? I *hate* fair fights!"

At a distance of perhaps a hundred yards, the knights reined in their mounts. Slowly, raising a hand, one of the humans—the leader, Cræosh assumed—rode forward a few paces. The large orc shrugged, setting his breastplate more comfortably on his shoulders, and advanced a handful of steps as well.

"Orc!" the human called loudly, his words carrying perfectly over the intervening distance. "I would speak with you."

"You would?" Cræosh shouted back in near-perfect Manspeak. "What do you call what you're doing now?"

Dækek and the others chuckled loudly. A low murmur drifted back from the other knights.

Their leader, however, appeared inclined to ignore the comment completely. "Surrender now," he yelled, "and I promise you a quick, easy release from your wretched lives!"

Cræosh raised his eyebrows, a gesture that meant basically the same thing in orcish culture as it did in human. "I'll make you a counterproposal!" he called.

"Yes?"

"Why don't you come and try to kill us the hard way, and I'll shove you up that horse's ass and feed him beans."

With a low bellow that would have done an ogre proud, the humans lowered their lances and charged.

Dækek and the others spread out, weapons coming free of their sheaths with a series of menacing rasps. Cræosh, however, simply set himself, his stance wide, his arms apart. The knights were wielding stout, thick lances, and that, to the orc's mind, was a *good* thing. There was something he'd always wanted to try. . . .

As he expected, the leader headed directly for him. Closer he came, and closer, and still the orc refused to budge. Slowly, an insidious grin spread across his filthy green face.

The lance was now mere feet from the orc's heavily muscled chest. And then, with a speed that was nigh incomprehensible, Cræosh sidestepped. Sidestepped—and grabbed.

It was a move that would have been, for even the mightiest of humans, absolutely impossible. But Cræosh's people, with the exception of the gargantuan ogres, are easily the strongest of the sundry goblinoid races. One unfortunate human was about to learn just what that meant.

Cræosh snagged the shaft of the weapon in both hands and jabbed downward, sinking the point deep into the soil. The dumbfounded knight vaulted into the air, held aloft by the lance's handle, which was locked professionally under his arm.

For a timeless instant, the tableau held: the plate-clad human a living pennant swaying in the wind; the orc, biceps bulging, both fists locked around the warped and bending lance. But of course, it couldn't last. Something was bound to give, and quickly.

It did. With an abbreviated scream, the knight slipped from the end of the lance and plummeted to the dirt, where he landed with a painful crash and a cacophony of clatters.

Casually, Cræosh released his grip on the lance—which, though wobbling frenetically, still protruded from the ground like some demented sapling—and strode to the battered warrior.

"How . . . ?" the human gasped, struggling desperately to regain his breath, unable for the moment to move. "It's . . . It's not possible!"

"You," Cræosh observed, "appear to be having difficulty breathing. Would you like some help?"

The knight's expression—now exposed, as the helmet's visor had been knocked askew in the fall—shifted in terror as the orc's foot slammed down hard beneath that helmet and crushed his windpipe.

They get younger every year, Cræosh noted, glancing briefly at the human's face. *Where's the honor in slaughtering children?* Then he shrugged, turning his attention back to the others. At least, at that age, the meat was tender. . . .

He snarled, all thoughts of food forgotten. Dækek was handling himself admirably; he'd already punched several holes through his opponent's armor with the jagged spikes of his morningstar. But the other orcs were more evenly matched, and even as Cræosh watched, one of his tribe went down hard beneath the largest human's hand-and-a-half sword.

With a thunderous cry, Cræosh charged, head down, shoulder forward. The knight, struggling to remove the massive blade from his opponent's corpse, barely had time to turn his steed to meet the sudden impact. Frantically he swung, determined to divorce the orc's head from his neck.

Cræosh ducked and then dove into the legs of the startled horse. Several loud snaps reverberated over the sounds of battle, and the animal collapsed, screaming.

The knight, abruptly pinned by one leg beneath his thrashing mount, struggled to yank himself free before—

Too late. A thin string of drool swinging from his lips, Cræosh reached down, grabbed the human's forehead in one hand and his jaw in the other, and twisted. A sickening pop, a gout of blood, and Cræosh was once again glancing around for more enemies.

But here, even Cræosh's years of battlefield experience proved inadequate. So busy had he been tackling the warhorse, he had perforce failed to notice another of his orcs dying beneath the blades of the two remaining knights. One of the pair went for Dækek, who had by then dispatched his own foe. The other had come for Cræosh—and by the time the big orc sensed his approach, it was too late to avoid the whistling blade.

And yet, just before his sword hit home, the human lurched, an expression of bewilderment stealing over his features. The blow landed, yes, but with negligible strength, failing even to bruise through the metal breastplate. Before the astonished orc, the knight collapsed, and only then did Cræosh finally spot the arrow protruding from the human's helm.

Arrow? But none of the remaining orcs were armed with bows. Who . . . ?

The surviving knight abruptly decided that discretion was the better part of survival. Spurring his horse into a gallop, he wheeled away from his confrontation with Dækek as fast as the powerful mount could go.

Straight into the same copse of trees from which the arrow had flown.

As the armored figure passed beneath the low-hanging branches, a silhouette dropped from above. Like a deranged monkey it bounced from tree limb to tree limb, hanging here from a fist, there from a foot, never staying put long enough to offer the human a viable target. With the accuracy of a circus juggler it tossed a gnarled club from appendage to appendage. Each time the creature attained a solid purchase on a branch it lashed out, club held tight in whatever hand or foot happened to be free. And each time it rang loudly, denting and mangling the protective shell of the knight's armor. Finally, after perhaps a full two minutes of such treatment, the human slowly toppled from the saddle.

For an instant more, the creature hung suspended, staring at its victim. Then, with a high-pitched keen, it dropped to earth and began carefully removing the knight's armor, intent on reaching the softer parts within. It was only when the creature was finally in full view that Cræosh noted the black leather breastplate that blended with its fur, or the bow and quiver strapped to its back.

"Bugbear," the orc muttered, shaking his head. He'd trained alongside the peculiar simian creatures before, but he'd never seen one in a real fight. He had to admit that its technique, though maybe a little primitive, was pretty damn effective.

This particular specimen sprouted unkempt red-brown fur, tinted so dark that in even the faintest of shadows it might as well have been black. Scars crisscrossed its shaggy form, roads of pain blazed through the foliage of its fur, and the predatory gleam in its recessed eyes said, as clearly as its actions, that this creature was a vicious, hot-tempered killer.

Good.

Hand hovering just above the hilt of his misshapen sword, Cræosh approached. He halted perhaps twenty feet away and cleared his throat. The bugbear's head swiveled toward him, bits of flesh and a small trickle of blood falling from his lips.

"Appreciate the hand, Nature-boy. Name's Cræosh."

"Jhurpess," the bugbear replied around a mouthful of raw knight.

Cræosh waited for more. Once it became abundantly clear that the only thing coming from the bugbear would be more chewing, he continued. "Not to sound ungrateful, you understand. But why, exactly, did you . . . ?"

"Metal creatures kill Jhurpess's friends. Orcs kill metal creatures. Jhurpess help orcs." The bugbear cocked his head. "Cræosh not very bright, is Cræosh?"

After a moment's contemplation, Cræosh decided—reluctantly—that there was precious little use in taking offense. Instead, he said, "Some moments are better than others. So, you were with . . ." He twisted, turning a puzzled gaze on Dækek, who was cradling his bleeding left hand in his right. "What was that gremlin's name, anyway?"

The other orc shrugged. "Don't think we ever got it, Cræosh. Scout's name was Ulev, though."

"Right." Once more, he faced the bugbear. "With Ulev's group?"

The bugbear paused, trying to connect the second half of the question with the first. When he finally succeeded, he nodded once. "Yes. Ulev was scout for Jhurpess. Ulev discovered metal creatures coming, so metal creatures killed Ulev." The bugbear shrugged philosophically. "Ulev not very strong. Not have lived very long anyway." Gesturing with what appeared to be a bloody femur, Jhurpess indicated the fallen orcs. "What about Cræosh's group?"

It was the orc's turn to shrug. "They died in battle—a battle that shouldn't have proved all that tough. Either they got careless, or they'd done something to anger their Ancestors. In either case, they've paid the price."

Jhurpess looked puzzled for a moment, his apelike face scrunched up tightly. Then he shook his head. "Cræosh not understand question. Jhurpess want to know if Cræosh want them."

"Want them?"

"Jhurpess still hungry. Humans not very filling."

Cræosh and Dækek exchanged looks. Orcs were known, on occasion, to consume their own fallen foes, but they'd rarely given much thought to others doing the same to them.

But then . . .

"Why not?" Cræosh said finally. "Dig in. Least we can do, I suppose."

The two orcs sat, taking a few extra moments to dress their wounds —or, more accurately, Dækek's arm. As Cræosh leaned over, holding the bandage in place so the smaller orc might tie it tight, he overheard a few choice whispered comments.

"Excuse me?" Cræosh couldn't help but ask. "A lice-infested, monkey-fucking *what*?"

Dækek shrugged, wincing at the pull on his bandage. "Sorry. I know it helped us out back there. I just . . ."

The larger orc grunted. "You're young. It rankles, realizing you just got your ass saved by an inferior. An animal. But we're *orcs*, Dækek. *Everyone's* an inferior. And a glorious death in battle's all well and good—I intend to make damn sure that's how *I* go—but not for a while, and not in some two-bit, shitty little scuffle. So deal with your pride.

Swallow it, choke on it, shove it up your ass, I don't care. But we're alive because of that lice-infested, monkey-fucking whatever. If that's the proxy the Ancestors sent to help us, then we'll thank them for it. You got me?"

"I got you. I think I—I . . ."

Cræosh had heard that sort of abrupt, mind-numbing terror before, but never in the voice of an orc. Senses screaming, he spun, hands raised to ward off whatever threat Dækek had spotted over his shoulder.

And froze, his jaw dropping nearly to his ankles. From the earth it rose, a nebulous figure, the stuff of pure shadow. Gleaming red orbs, burning embers in an otherwise empty face, were the shade's only visible features.

But while Dækek sat frozen in fear, Cræosh recognized it instantly for what it was. He'd never seen one before in his life, but he'd heard enough to recognize one of King Morthûl's messenger wraiths.

Which meant that the master of the Iron Keep had a message—*for him*. His apprehension would've needed either stilts or wings to rise any further.

For perhaps a full minute the wraith stared, hell-fire eyes burning into the back of the orc's brain. And then it was gone, vanished into the chilling breeze like the barest wisp of smoke.

"What—what . . . ?"

Cræosh didn't even look at his smaller ally. "King Morthûl had something to say to me."

"That was one of *his*?! But it didn't say anything!"

Cræosh finally turned, a startled expression on his porcine features. "It didn't, did it? But . . . I *remember* what it was supposed to tell me."

"Magic," Dækek muttered, and shuddered once.

"All right, that's enough!" Cræosh snapped. "I've given you some leeway here, but you're an *orc*, dammit! Quit your sniveling!"

Dækek straightened. "Sorry."

"And don't apologize. It makes your face break out." With that, the massive goblin adjusted the scabbard at his waist and began to walk.

"Where are you going?" Dækek called after him. "Chief Berrat should be here any minute now!"

40

"I know. Tell him I've gone to Timas Khoreth."

The one-eyed orc blinked in surprise. "What? But—that's *weeks* away!"

"That's why I'm starting now, isn't it?"

It wasn't just the distance, though. Timas Khoreth was easily the largest city in all of Kirol Syrreth—and a human one, at that. The goblin races weren't exactly welcomed with open arms by its citizenry.

Which meant that Dækek's next question, predictably enough, was, "Why?"

"I," Cræosh told him with a notable lack of enthusiasm, "was just assigned to a Demon Squad."

"Oh." Dækek paused, watching his commander's back. Then, "What about the bugbear? What do I do about him?"

"Nothing," Cræosh replied with a sigh, a truly uncharacteristic sound for an orc. "You see, he's coming with me."

The bugbear looked up, mouth full of half-chewed orc, and grinned.

It was a day no different than any other, and Timas Khoreth bustled with activity, unaware of the pending arrival of two new inhabitants. High in the watchtowers, guards chatted or dozed or threw dice, only half watching their assigned horizons. The great stone walls surrounding the city sat dully in the glare of the afternoon sun, casting a frigid shadow over the marketplace. Still, a bit of cold wasn't about to put a crimp in the activities of *this* city. The citizens simply threw on an extra layer or so and ventured forth to face the worst the world could toss at them.

Or the ungodly chaos of the market, which, some would claim, was the same thing.

On this particular cold afternoon, the center of town ebbed and flowed with a veritable tide of humanity. The noise was sufficient not only to wake the dead, but to send them scurrying for sanctuary—or at least sticking their fingers in whatever remained of their ears. Several thousand people crowded into a space that would have been cramped for one-third their number, pushing and shoving and shouting and grabbing, each concerned with nothing but the completion of today's errands. Only the occasional glimpse of a black leather jerkin or breast-plate among the uniformly drab populace, a blatant sign of the Watch's presence, kept the mob from degenerating into animalistic abandon.

For their own part, the mercenaries and soldiers of that Watch were rather more concerned with getting their own carcasses through their shift in one piece than in enforcing any particular brand of order. Any disturbance was met with club and bludgeon—and then with crossbow and sword, should they encounter even the least hint of resistance. It was an explosive, deadly situation, but the citizens ignored it as they went about their disorganized business. It was, after all, a threat they lived with day in and day out, year after endless year; scarcely enough to concern them now.

There was one in the marketplace today, however, for whom the general anarchy was *not* a familiar sight. Scuttling through the crowd, he glanced wide-eyed about him, mouth watering in anticipation of the opportunities.

He was called Gork by those outside his own race—an undignified epithet at best, but the closest most people could come to the strange bark that was his true name. At just a hair under three and a half feet, he was tall for a kobold. Although the pebbly, lizard-ish texture of his stone-gray skin prevented him from growing hair, his face and snout sprouted the occasional whisker, useful for feeling his way through small, darkened caves. His irises gleamed like a cat's in direct light, and were even more sensitive. (Only their massive cousins the troglodytes, and the Stars-damned tree-humping elves, could function as well in the dark as kobolds.) He wore ratty boots and a simple tunic, belted about the waist, that was clearly cut down from human-size. If the humans and other lumbering behemoths around him noticed him at all, they assumed he was just another scout or spy in the Charnel King's armies. Those were the only positions the diminutive, devious little sneaks ever held.

For his own part, Gork didn't tend to think of himself as a scout, or a spy, or any other formal title. Sure, he'd done that sort of thing, and he'd probably do so again once his clan was called once more to service. But that was basically a side-endeavor, a hobby, as it were. No, first and foremost, Gork was a thief, pure and simple. (Well, maybe not so pure.)

And here, in the lively market that was the beating heart of Timas Khoreth, there was opportunity enough to set any thief up in comfort for a good long while.

The only question now, Gork decided as he actually rubbed his rough palms together, was where to begin. And the answer to that very dilemma struck him like a bolt from the clear blue. Actually, it *was* a bolt from the clear blue: A glint of sunlight stabbed directly into Gork's beady little eyes. Although briefly blinded, the greedy creature was alert enough to rapidly assess the crystal that had sent the dazzling gleam from a merchant's carrel across the way.

It hung, spinning lightly in the breeze, from the drawstring of the merchant's coin purse. Pure quartz, just over an inch in length, it served no purpose other than sheer ostentatious display. It wasn't worth all that much—probably less than the contents of the purse itself—but it was far easier to get hold of, and should pay for a few diverting afternoons.

Gork maneuvered across the intervening road, silent as a thought—not, really, that he needed to be. The deafening discord of the marketplace was such that Gork could have sneaked up on the distracted shopkeeper even if he'd been accompanied by a herd of elephants, a marching band, and a jogging ogre with a bunion.

The merchant in question—a rather rotund individual, with thinning brown hair and a white cloak of softest fur—was currently haggling (read: arguing) with a young, cocky member of the watch. The soldier, clearly unaccustomed to anyone standing up to his intimidation, was loudly berating the shopkeeper over the asking price of a silver goblet, while the merchant, hands waving wildly in the air, rebutted with constant (and wildly inconsistent) pleas on behalf of the starving children they both knew he didn't have. It had long since degenerated beyond the point where either of them cared any longer about the goblet itself. This was a battle of will and wit between two men with far too much of the former and none of the latter, and was unlikely to conclude any time in the foreseeable future.

Gork breezed past them with naked blade outstretched. In a move so practiced it was all but invisible, he pocketed the crystal in one of the tiny pouches sewn onto his belt. And just that quickly, he was gone, carried away from the scene of the crime by the constant press of humanity long before the merchant could possibly discover he'd been victimized.

Humans, Gork chuckled silently to himself, would always be one of his favorite races. Big, clumsy, for the most part stupid—and, since Gork himself possessed little in the way of riches, always worth stealing from. A few rapid sidesteps carried him between two small buildings, out of the main thoroughfare and away from the largest concentration of shoving, unwashed bodies. Whistling a traditional kobold folk tune in a pitch no human could possibly hear, he began once more to scan the market, seeking his next acquisition.

His view was abruptly obscured as a large shadow fell across the mouth of the alleyway. Gork looked up—and up, and up some more—until his gaze met that of the black-garbed human standing before him.

There were enough dissimilarities in their features to make it clear that this was not the same soldier with whom the merchant had been bickering. Nevertheless, all humans looked enough alike to Gork that they might as well have been brothers.

"Is there something I can do for you, Officer?" the kobold asked politely. Or it sounded polite in his own ears, anyway. Humans never sensed anything but hostility in the gravelly tone of kobold voices.

"Oh, I think so," the human told him, smiling arrogantly down from above, a bothersome demigod. "I think you can hand me the crystal."

"What crystal?"

The soldier frowned. "Don't play games with me, you little shit. I saw the whole thing. See, you only got the thing because one of my platoon was distracting the fat guy. Way I figure, that entitles us to half."

Gork shrugged. "Can't give you half, can I? It wouldn't be worth nearly as much broken."

"Exactly. So you give it to me. I'll sell it, and then I'll find you and give you your cut."

Dragonshit, Gork thought. What he said, however, was, "Why not let me sell it, and I'll find you and give you *your* half? I've done this before, so I'll get a better price."

"*I'll* get a better price, because I'm human. People around here don't wanna deal with bugs like you." The frown, by this point, had deteriorated even further, bordering now on a full-fledged snarl. "Give me the crystal, you little . . ."

The man was already leaning down, fingers outstretched toward Gork's throat—whether to shake him up or actually choke him, Gork couldn't tell, and didn't plan to find out. With a vicious little growl, the kobold thrust out his snout and clamped down with his powerful jaws. Then, not waiting to see if the soldier's scream would draw other guards running, he spit the man's pinkie finger onto the ground and darted back into the crowd.

With a furious roar, the soldier came after him, shoving citizens and shopkeepers from his path; but for every pedestrian he was forced to manhandle, the lithe and tiny kobold gained precious seconds. A series of quick turns, a jump to the left here, a step to the right there, and it was done. By the time the enraged mercenary finally broke into the open, Gork knew that the man couldn't possibly see him. The human, cradling his bleeding hand, cast his glance over the constantly shifting crowds, seeking, searching . . .

All to no avail. With a last, frustrated curse, he made his way, somewhat more gently, back through the crowd, apparently only now thinking to return to the barracks and seek attention for his injured hand. Despite the open hostility burning in the expressions of many whom he had shoved, the crowd parted to let him pass. It was a scene that could, in other circumstances, have gotten very ugly in a very small amount of time.

But not here. Nobody in Timas Khoreth—nobody in Kirol Syrreth—would dare stand in the way of a soldier of King Morthûl.

From beneath the shadowed corner of a merchant's fruit stand, Gork tracked the soldier's progress. He let loose with a heartfelt sigh of relief, one that came all the way from his toenails—followed abruptly by a chuckle of sheer contempt. Were humans stupid, or what?

On the other hand, they were also really big, they carried lots of pointy objects, and there were a damn *lot* of them in this city. It would, the kobold decided reluctantly, be better for all concerned if he were to simply vanish from Timas Khoreth for a good long while.

Oh, well. The clan, camped in the browned grasslands outside the city, had been making noises about moving on anyway. None of the diminutive creatures enjoyed staying so near the Northern Steppes, not with the chilly nights and the ever-more-frigid winds. Gork would just have to talk to Hrark, the clan patriarch, and convince him that it was, indeed, time to be on their way. . . .

And thus were his thoughts occupied as he made his way from the hustle and bustle of the marketplace, sauntering between the looming watchtowers that flanked the south gates. He could feel the derisive glare of the guards on his back and head as he passed, and shrugged it off. Gork knew that whatever scorn the humans might heap upon him, he could easily return tenfold and still retain enough to choke a griffin.

Hrark's clan was encamped some miles to the west, and Gork happily occupied his mind on the long walk back by creating, listing, and categorizing all the reasons why humans were lower than dog shit. It kept him moderately amused, as well as oblivious to the weary miles, until he finally came within sight of the camp. Gork stiffened, senses straining, whimsy gone from his mind.

Many years and snows and bolts of lightning ago, it had been a thriving tree, covered in green leaves and waving gently in the brisk breezes. Now, it was an ugly, cadaverous claw, stretching toward the clouds, seeking salvation. It had been there, quite possibly, for centuries, as much a permanent feature of the landscape as the Brimstone Mountains to the south and east. Hrark had, in fact, chosen this very spot deliberately. The dead thing made it easier to spot the camp; many kobolds, accustomed to finding their way in the blackness under the earth, found life on the surface disorienting.

Gork had never had that problem, but he *was* somewhat dismayed to see the five large horses tied loosely to the decrepit trunk. Kobolds did not ride horses; simple geometry made it uncomfortable at best, often flat-out impossible. Ergo, the visitors, whoever they were, were not kobolds.

Gork dropped into a low crouch and crept, ever so slowly, around the encampment. Here he slid behind the tiniest of shrubs; there he vanished into a random pool of shadow. Carpets of dead vegetation and a ground liberally strewn with twigs might as well have been the plushest of carpets for all the sound he made. Finally near enough to hear what was happening in the center of the camp, Gork settled down behind a convenient hedge and watched. His fingers idly brushed the hilt of his *kah-rahahk* dagger: a hideous weapon, jagged and barbed across the flat as well as along the edge.

Hrark, patriarch of the clan and all-around bastard, was currently facing off with five of Morthûl's human mercenaries. His skin was touched with a subtle tint of blue, and it somehow made him appear harder than the other kobolds. The humans towered over the diminutive creature, looming dangerously in their midnight-hued leathers. The man in the center, a white-haired veteran with a long, lightning-shaped scar across his left arm, had the bearings of a leader—but he appeared to be present, at the moment, purely for moral support. The human doing the speaking (or shouting, as the case may have been), and the one to whom Gork's eyes and ears were instantly drawn, was a much younger man. A man with a bad disposition that might have been due, in part, to the finger with which he'd so recently parted company.

". . . rightfully mine!" Gork heard him screaming as he finally focused in on the conversation. "The little bastard took it, and I want it the hell back! You get me, you little son-of-a-bitch?"

Hrark peered up, squinting over the end of his snout. "First off, you towering turd, there's no need to scream at me. I can hear better'n you, with those stupid, tiny little rectum-looking things you call 'ears.'" The patriarch's own ears—large, triangular affairs that appeared vaguely canine—perked up at that, as though assisting him in making his point. "Second, I'd really prefer to hear his side of the story before I make any final decisions. I don't think that's unreasonable, do you?"

"I don't give a damn about reasonable!" the human shouted, having lowered his voice not one whit. Angrily, he thrust his bandage-wrapped hand in the kobold's face. "You see this? I lost a finger to that little shit! Reasonable be hanged, I want him!" His other hand lashed out, shoving the kobold back a few steps. "Are we clear?"

Hrark's face went cold, and the surrounding kobolds stiffened. The patriarch took a single step back toward the human, his jaws clenched. "You did *not* just push me."

It was at that point that the older veteran began to get the hint that, just maybe, they had overstepped their margin of safety. "Hey," he said, placing one hand gently on the younger man's shoulder. "Maybe we should—"

"Get off me!" Completely ignoring his commanding officer, the nine-fingered soldier advanced on Hrark. "I'll push you any time I feel like it, you—"

Two things happened then, damn near simultaneously. First, Gork noticed a pair of kobolds who had been skulking about at the rear of the crowd untying the horses from the blasted tree. One of them, all five reins clutched in his tight little fist, led them away while the other began brushing and covering the tracks with a small broom.

The second event was that Hrark, much as Gork himself had done, stepped forward and bit down. Only this time, since the human's hand was out of reach, the patriarch chose a target somewhat closer to his own level. Cloth and flesh ripped audibly. Hark retreated a pace, chewing thoughtfully, as the soldier collapsed to the ground, screaming in a painfully high-pitched timbre.

Everyone else watched the older soldier, who was torn between the need to avenge the rather excruciating injury done to his man and the realization that the kobolds currently outnumbered the humans by about six to one.

It wasn't the first time, nor would it be the last, that humans put far too much emphasis on size.

"Kill them all!" he shouted at the top of his lungs, ripping his sword from its scabbard.

Hrark barked, and the entire clan fell upon the humans, an avalanche of teeth and flesh and bad attitude. Kobolds jumped, dove, and even threw one another through the air—anything required to fasten a fist or a mouth upon their larger foes. Men toppled, overwhelmed. Tiny fists with tiny claws rose and fell, jaws bit down, and blood flowed freely from deep within the writhing kobold pile.

It was, Gork decided, safe to join in. With a joyous cry, he scurried up the blackened tree like a spastic cat, pausing on the very tip of the highest branch that would support him. Then, *kah-rahahk* in a two-fisted grip, he launched himself into space, coming down smack-dab in the middle of the wriggling mass. Taking only enough care to ensure that the flesh was not stony, he sank the dagger time and again into any target soft enough to accept it. Gouts of blood followed the blade each time he ripped it free, and he fancied he could hear the cries of pain, even beneath the deafening turmoil around him.

"Hey, no fair!" one of the nearby kobolds shouted. "He's using a weapon!"

"No points for Gork!" another voice called from the crowd. "Everybody else's bet is still good!" And with that, the speaker suddenly reached into the fray and yanked loose a flap of skin that appeared, just possibly, to be an ear. "Five points!" he called gleefully. His brethren ignored him, each intent on claiming his own share of keepsakes—as well as the money contained in the betting pool some nameless kobold had started while Hrark addressed their "guests."

A few more moments, and it was well and truly over. Skeletons coated in a thin fleshy pulp were all that remained of the humans, and even those wouldn't last long. Already, a "cleanup" crew was at work, hacking the bodies with axes and passing the severed chunks around the gathering. Anything edible would be gone within the hour, and the rest would wind up at the bottom of whichever river the clan next happened across. It was, all told, an efficient system; unsurprising, considering that this was hardly the first time they'd needed to make some of their "fellow" soldiers disappear without a trace.

Nor was it the first time that Gork had been responsible for that need.

"You!" The patriarch snagged Gork by the collar and yanked him out of the line where he stood with other eager kobolds, awaiting his portion of human. "Let's talk." Fingers locked firmly on Gork's tunic, Hrark strode swiftly away from the others.

"I certainly appreciate the assist, boss," Gork offered once they were out of earshot of the others. "If I—"

"Gork?"

The kobold swallowed. "Um?"

Hrark glowered at him. "I am looking for an excuse," he said, "to hurt you. A lot. You with me so far?"

"Umm, yes?"

"Good. Now, pay close attention; this is the good part. You listening?"

"Yes . . ."

"All right, we're cooking now. As of this moment, I am telling you to shut up. I am going to ask you some questions. You may answer those questions. Anything *else* you say will be the excuse I'm looking for. Is *that* clear?"

Gork looked around nervously.

"It's a question. You can answer it."

"Oh, right. Yes, boss, it's clear."

Hrark nodded, and then started twitching his snout, the kobold equivalent of the human head-shake. "I don't know what I'm supposed to do with you. Haven't we talked about this sort of thing?"

Gork decided, after a moment, that the question was more than just rhetorical, and thus presumably safe to answer. "Well, yes, but it wasn't my fault! They—"

"It's never your fault, is it, Gork?"

That one, the other kobold decided, *was* rhetorical.

And then, Hrark grinned. It was a twisted expression, curling back the snout, revealing the front teeth, and it was most assuredly *not* what Gork wanted to see. His own expression, already less than overjoyed, fell notably. He could feel his ears drooping loosely atop his head.

"Gork, my boy," Hrark oozed at him, actually going so far as to place an arm around his shoulders. "All trouble aside, that took skill, you know? What have you accomplished here today? Kept that little crystal from the soldiers, stood up for yourself, and that was a pretty spectacular leap you took into the fray earlier. You really are impressive, did you know that?"

Gork gawped at his patriarch, waiting for the other claw to drop.

"In short," Hrark concluded, "exactly the sort of kobold they need."

"They?" the other asked in a tight little voice.

"Oh, yes. 'You are so commanded,' the wraith said—or at least, I *remember* it saying, which isn't really the same thing, but close enough, 'to choose the best among you for assignment to the master's elite.' Congratulations, Gork. You're Demon Squad." The patriarch's grin stretched very nearly larger than his snout itself. "It's a great honor, of course. You'll be a hero when you get back."

Gork's world was very methodically crashing in around him. Demon Squad?! He was a dead kobold, pure and simple. "Great honor" his rough stony ass!

"Hrark . . . Boss. Couldn't you find someone else? I mean, battle isn't really my thing. . . ."

"Nonsense, my boy. You'll do fine."

"But they say that no one's ever survived a full tour of duty in a Demon Squad!"

The patriarch's eyes gleamed in the fading afternoon light. "That," he told Gork, his voice suddenly frigid, "is an added benefit.

"Pack your stuff and say good-bye to everyone. I think an hour ought to be sufficient, don't you?"

Finally, *finally*, Timas Khoreth hove into sight, a darker spot against the gleaming snows of the Steppes that began some leagues beyond the city. Cræosh was not, by nature, a sentimental orc. Hell, there *weren't* any sentimental orcs. But after weeks with the damn bugbear as his only companion, he felt an overwhelming urge to dash on ahead and kiss the very walls in thanks.

For his own part, Jhurpess squinted quizzically at the sprawling shape. "That it?"

As much as he hated the idea of a human city, Cræosh couldn't quite keep the grin from his voice as he answered, "Yeah, Nature-boy, that's it. Timas Khoreth."

"Oh. What 'Timas Khoreth' mean?"

The orc looked daggers at him. "It means the Khoreth of Timas. How the fuck do I know what it means?"

"Jhurpess just asking."

"And Cræosh just answering. Can we get moving already? It's been a long walk, and I need a drink."

The bugbear immediately started to reach for his pack.

"I mean something a hell of a lot stronger than water," Cræosh told him.

"Oh. Jhurpess understand. Cræosh want to celebrate arrival at city."

A brief pause. "Sure, something like that." The orc headed toward the towering city walls, his pace newly quickened.

After a moment's hesitation, the bugbear loped up beside him, moving on all fours. "Jhurpess enjoy last few weeks. Cræosh and Jhurpess going to be good friends in Demon Squad."

My other option was death, the orc reminded himself silently. *I can deal with a lot if it means I don't get dead.*

"Jhurpess not even care that Cræosh not very bright. Jhurpess a tolerant bugbear."

On the other hand, death has its perks. . . .

Jhurpess's tolerance was clearly a trait not shared by the black-armored humans standing post at the gates. "That's a first," one of them remarked loudly as the traveling companions approached. "A pig and an ape loose in the wilderness. Wonder how that happened?"

Cræosh reluctantly suppressed his temper. It wasn't worth getting into trouble in an alien city—and besides, his nose wasn't *that* piggish. Instead, he took a moment to examine the fortifications themselves, rising steeply behind the annoying soldiers.

This, despite its great size, was clearly a city designed with defense foremost in mind. The surrounding wall was close to twenty feet high, with large crenellations and dozens of murder-holes halfway to the top. The gates, flanked by a pair of watchtowers, consisted of massive oaken doors reinforced by a bar thicker around than Cræosh himself and supplemented by an iron portcullis. Cræosh was certain that the guards had ballistae, cauldrons of oil, and other such weapons close at hand. Even with an army of orcs, he'd hate to have to take Timas Khoreth by force.

Fortunately, he didn't have to lay siege to the damn place—and as for a particular trio of irksome guards, well, them he could deal with. He decided to be diplomatic about the whole thing, and rather than draw a weapon or even offer any retort, he simply continued on ahead, ignoring the fools entirely.

Orcs, it's worth noting, have a broader definition of diplomacy than humans do. It more or less amounts to "Anything other than killing you."

The guard who'd spoken, however, a bald fellow with just a few days' worth of beard, was clearly intent on making a scene. "Hey!" he shouted, stepping in front of the large orc. "Obviously, you didn't get the hint. Not surprising, really."

Cræosh glared.

"In words of one syllable, then," the human continued. "We—don't—want—your—kind—here. Is that sufficiently clear to you?"

"'Sufficiently' has more than one syllable, you leprous, brain-damaged goat-fucker."

The guard retreated a step, startled, but still determined to block their path.

"Look, I don't care if you *can* speak a civilized tongue. Timas Khoreth is a *human* city. That means *humans* live here. You people cause us nothing but trouble, and we've had it up to—"

"Jhurpess tired of this," the bugbear declared. Before Cræosh could even think about stopping him, the simian creature loped forward and backhanded the bald guard solidly across the face. The soldier's feet actually left the ground, and he spun for two full revolutions before crashing to the earth in a cloud of dust.

Had Cræosh hit the man like that, he'd have caved in the side of his skull and shattered the jaw completely. Bugbears aren't quite as strong as orcs, on average, so Jhurpess's blow merely snapped his neck.

The end result was pretty much the same, though.

Cræosh yanked his sword from its scabbard, cursing under his breath as the humans did the same. This, he figured, was probably not the most auspicious start to his new assignment. Briefly, he glanced at his irritating ally. He wasn't sure whether or not Jhurpess understood *why* they were about to be attacked by the entire watch, but the bugbear was smart enough to recognize the situation for what it was. One long hand snaked up over his shoulder, lifting the cudgel from its makeshift sling. Jhurpess pounded it once into the earth, launching a second dust cloud easily the equal of the first, and dropped into a simian slouch.

One of the other humans rose from where he had knelt to check on his fallen companion, his face a mask of rage. "You bastards! You killed—"

"What in the name of the blackest hell is going on here?"

Orc, bugbear, and human examined the late arrival. Another human—older than the others, to judge from the gray streaks in his chestnut-brown beard—approached from within the walls. He sat atop a gargantuan black warhorse, and his armor, similarly hued, was steel rather than leather. The symbol embossed in the man's breastplate, the silver crown of Morthûl, instantly marked him as an officer.

"Captain!" one of the soldiers called to him. "These—these creatures attacked us! They—"

The officer raised a gauntlet-covered hand, silencing the guard. Then, turning to face the heavily muscled orc, he asked, "Is this true?"

Cræosh shrugged his massive shoulders. "They didn't want to let us pass." He didn't point out that, technically, only the bugbear had committed any violence. He'd save that for later, if necessary. . . .

The captain turned back to the soldiers.

"He's an *orc*." The same soldier answered the unspoken question, as though it explained everything. "And he's got a bugbear with him!"

The captain nodded. "I'm not blind yet, soldier. Last I checked, we were all soldiers of Kirol Syrreth. Was I asleep when they changed the rules?"

"No, sir, but—"

"And didn't I specifically mention at last week's assembly that we were expecting a few, ah, *foreigners* because the general was assembling a Demon Squad?"

The guard snapped his mouth shut, unwilling to admit that he didn't know—because he'd been recovering from an unauthorized night on the town, and suffering from an equally unauthorized hangover, on the morning in question. The dead man lying on the ground, had he been able, might have admitted to a similar condition.

The captain shook his head. "You," he said, pointing to a passing soldier, one who'd been uninvolved in the altercation. "Show these two to the barracks." The soldier had been on his way to the mess hall for a much-needed lunch, but clearly knew better than to protest with the captain in this sort of mood. Glumly, he nodded, then gestured for the travelers to follow. The captain was still haranguing his men fiercely when they finally passed out of earshot.

And then Cræosh happened to glance over at his companion. The furry creature was staring back the way they had come, his mouth quirked dejectedly downward.

"What's your problem?" the orc asked.

"Guards take dead human away. What guards do with body?"

Cræosh thought for a moment. It'd been a while since his lessons on human culture, but . . .

"Bury him, I think. Why?"

"Because," the bugbear wailed, "Jhurpess *hungry*!"

Cræosh threw up his hands and moved to catch up with their guide.

It quickly became apparent, however, that even here, at the end of their journey, nothing was going to be simple. The orc had taken perhaps a dozen more steps when he and the human were both jerked to a sudden halt by the plaintive screech from behind.

Cræosh spun, one hand already grasping at his sword, to see Jhurpess crouched in the center of the road, arms wrapped over his head as though shielding his skull from a sudden hail.

Torn between outright exasperation and a certain reluctant sense of obligation, Cræosh stomped to the bugbear's side. He completely ignored the staring crowds that surrounded them, except for a single murderous snarl he directed at the humans nearest his odd companion. "What's the problem now?"

"Jhurpess not like city," the creature whined, refusing to uncover his head. "Too many! Too many!"

"Too . . . What's he blithering about?" the soldier asked over the orc's left shoulder.

"He's a forest-dweller," Cræosh snapped in sudden understanding. "He's not used to this many people." Then, in a much lower voice, he spoke directly into the bugbear's ear.

"Listen up, Jhurpess. You don't like crowds. That's fine, I can understand that. We all have our problems. I, for one, just happen to hate sparrows. Can't stand the little fuckers. Pathetic feathery little bodies, those—anyway, point is, you don't see me goin' around and throwing a conniption any time I see one. If you're gonna react this way every time the humans get a little ample, we're gonna have a serious problem, 'cause they're sort of common around here. Thicker than flies on a shit pie, really. You won't be much good to me, or the rest of the squad, like this."

"Jhurpess not want to be good to squad. Jhurpess want to go home, where it quiet."

All right, fuck this. I tried it the friendly way! The bugbear wailed yet again, this time in reaction to the orc's fingers digging harshly into the fur on the back of his skull and yanking his head back.

"I ought to kill you right here, you pathetic little weasel!" Cræosh snapped at him. "You're not a bugbear! You're a *teddy* bear!"

A growl sounded deep in the simian's throat, and Cræosh noted a single hand reflexively grasping at the handle of the massive club. *Good.*

"But if I did that, I might get King Morthûl kind of pissed at me— and whatever else you might have heard, I never met anybody *that* stupid." He lowered his own face, bringing it within inches of Jhurpess's own. The bugbear's breath spread over him in a noxious caress, and he forced back the urge to gag through sheer willpower alone. Obviously, there were still tiny bits of orc decaying between the creature's teeth.

"Just like he'd be angry at *you*," Cræosh concluded, "if you tried to back out of this now. You want that, Jhurpess? You want the Charnel King angry with your monkey ass?"

Eyes wide as bucklers, the bugbear shook his head as fiercely as the orc's grip permitted.

"Well, you know how to avoid that?"

Jhurpess blinked.

"By *standing the fuck up*, that's how! Take a good look around you! It's crowded, it's loud, it's smelly, it's annoying! See it, feel it, and then deal the hell with it and move on! You got it?"

The bugbear rose to his feet, head twisting this way and that as he tried to take in the entire scene at once.

"If it makes you feel any better," the orc added more gently, "think of them with plates under their asses and gravy on their heads."

Jhurpess stopped twitching. Slowly, a big grin settled over his features, and he actually licked his lips.

"Finally," Cræosh muttered, and turned his attention back to the guide. "Now, can we get to the damn barracks already?" *Before anything else goes wrong!* This was looking to be a *very* long assignment. . . .

Unless, he realized, they died fairly early on, like most Demon Squads he'd heard about. Considerably cheered, Cræosh lightened his step as the mismatched trio marched toward the barracks.

Gork watched, whiskers twitching in contemplation, as the hulking duo followed their reluctant guide through the market's heart. For a moment, it looked as though the bugbear was about to have a relapse of the fit he'd suffered on the way in. But before his orcish companion could say anything, the simian critter had abruptly straightened himself up. With a bellow that, from Gork's distance, sounded like "Get out of way!" he plunged through the mob, pushing, shoving, and—in a few cases—bodily tossing people from his path. Obviously, Gork realized with a sense of foreboding, the bugbear was too stupid to do anything in half-measures. Terrified or hostile—there didn't seem to be anything in between.

And these, unless he was very much mistaken, were his new teammates. *Dragonshit.*

Still, there was one distinct advantage to having so volatile an ally. It meant that, more often than not, everyone's attention would be on the bugbear and not on his far smaller, less conspicuous companion.

Much as it was now, for example.

Once more silent as a ghost, the kobold drifted into the crowd, alert for any opportunities that might—there! One man, knocked aside by the bugbear's passage, had just now clambered back to his feet, glaring and shouting along with the others. He seemed mostly uninjured, although his immaculately coifed black hair was now dangling in all directions and his soft green tunic was ripped along one sleeve. Even more important, though, was that his coin purse had been knocked loose when he fell. It hung now from the back of his belt, dangling by a single cord. A cutpurse far less talented than Gork could have performed the operation with no chance of discovery.

Or, to be more accurate, no chance of discovery *by the victim.* Gork's grasping fingers were perhaps half an inch from the pouch when a hand dropped down from the side and fastened on his wrist.

I'm slipping. That's two bystanders in two days who've spotted me. A high-pitched growl building in his throat, the kobold swiveled his head, scowling at the man who'd grabbed him.

Well, at least it wasn't one of the watch this time—or, if it was, he wasn't on duty. This human wore a typical peasant tunic, gray in hue, and brown breeches. Dull, sandy-blond hair topped his head, and duller brown orbs peered out from beneath it.

"You shouldn't be doing that," he informed the kobold, as though educating an ignorant child.

Gork, for his part, wasn't in the mood to be educated. "Get your hand off me before I eat it."

The human just cocked his head to the side as though puzzled.

Great. Not only was I spotted, it was the village idiot who got me. How embarrassing! Time to go.

He couldn't, due to the angle, quite get his mouth around a finger this time, so he settled for taking a small chunk from the edge of the man's palm. The ripping noise was satisfying to hear, as always, though the absence of any cry of pain was somewhat mystifying. Still, the man let go, and Gork began to back away. . . .

Aagh! Oh Stars, what was *that?! Gaaahh!* Snout twisted in revulsion, the kobold spit out the flesh on which he chewed, gagging to the point of dry heaves. It was a testament to the anger of the crowd that they stayed focused on the departing bugbear, rather than devoting any attention to the retching kobold in their midst.

Finally, as his stomach ceased trying to climb up his throat and his tongue ceased trying to climb *down* his throat, Gork saw just what it was he'd been trying to swallow.

Lying on the cobblestones beside him was a puddled mass of . . . Well, Gork wasn't sure *what* it was. A substance, fleshy but not quite flesh, quivered beneath the tiniest layer of a hard, thin material. *Chitin,* Gork realized abruptly. And the entire thing was coated with some off-yellow ichor that had the color and consistency—but most clearly not the taste—of custard.

"What the fu—?" Gork began to ask nervously of the man beside him. Only, even as he watched, the figure ceased to be a man at all. Over the span of perhaps twenty seconds, the stranger's head sank to the level of the kobold's own, the skin wrinkling horrendously as the body beneath it shriveled. The man's—no, the *thing's*—nose flattened and stretched, becoming nothing less than a snout! The skin retracted, tightening up so that it once again matched the size of the form that wore it, but it began also to harden, to shift in hue from an ugly human pink to a much more natural and attractive stony gray. Even the clothes twisted and writhed, altering size and shape to remain consistent with the being that wore them. Finally, Gork watched the creature's eyes fold inward, as though turning themselves inside out, and then pop open into reflective orbs that were the mirror image of Gork's own. Only the short sword the creature wore, which the kobold hadn't even noticed strapped to the human's side, failed to change shape.

Gork blinked in amazement at the kobold who now stood before him. The image was absolutely perfect—and it was blatantly obvious, now, exactly what the creature must be. "I know what you are," Gork told it.

The "kobold" nodded his recently acquired snout. "And does this bother you?"

The kobold shrugged. "I don't really give a damn *what* you are. What bothers me is that you soured my score."

"A pouch, no matter how subtly taken, will be missed the moment the former owner chooses to purchase something."

"So?"

The shapeshifter grinned, a strange, open-mouthed affair that didn't at all resemble the expression of a true kobold. "A more patient approach. You follow the man. Sooner or later, he will go somewhere unseen by others. A slit throat gets you the money as easily as a slit purse-string—and a body, despite its size, can be hidden for a lot longer than a missing . . ."

As he lectured, Gork ceased paying attention to his words. Instead, he listened to the tone of the creature's voice and watched the sharp gestures and the way he moved. Changing form was one thing; behaviors and mannerisms learned over a lifetime, something else entirely. It dawned on Gork that, with a few moments of study, he might just learn how to spot these creatures *regardless* of form. That, he decided, might just prove handy at some point in the—

His attention suddenly snapped back to the shapeshifter's words, and he didn't care at all for what he was hearing.

"What?! Someone as 'careless' as I am might *what*?"

The faux-kobold blinked at him. "Might, I was saying, prove detrimental to the squad as a unit. You *are* here for squad duty, yes? It seems unlikely that you'd be hanging around Timas Khoreth, let alone following the orc and the bugbear, otherwise."

"So what if I am?" Gork growled.

"So, I don't intend to trust my life to a creature without sufficient sense to kill his victims."

"Listen here, you faceless insect! I—" But the kobold's tirade was lost in the cacophony of the crowd, for the shapeshifter had already wandered away, his form warping once more, blending in flawlessly with all the other humans who, to Gork, still managed to look the same.

Gork growled a lengthy curse that had no equivalent in any language besides Kobold—but had something to do with the other's ancestry, various underground vermin, and a sharp stick—and drifted away from the marketplace. Not only had the damn shifter ruined his shot at the human's fat purse, but he'd delayed long enough that Gork could no longer even risk another attempt. If he was to arrive at the barracks in time, he had to be on his way. Muttering in his native tongue, he wandered the streets in the direction the orc and the bugbear had been taken.

He'd gotten perhaps four blocks when a voice called out from behind. "There, Officers! That's the one!"

Gork spun, one clawed hand reaching for the *kah-rahahk* at his waist—but he swiftly changed his mind upon seeing the half dozen guards rushing toward him, weapons already in hand. Instead, he raised his hands up by his ears in a clumsy imitation of the movements he'd seen humans make in the past to indicate (he hoped) surrender. "Is there a problem, Officers?"

Rather than answering, however, the largest of the humans simply grabbed him by the collar and dragged him forward. "Is this him?" he asked gruffly.

"Oh, yes, sir! That's most definitely the one!"

Gork stared in astonishment, his ears flattened against the sides of his head. It was the human from the marketplace, the one whose purse he'd almost stolen. But the man *couldn't* have seen him! Besides, he hadn't actually *taken* the damn purse! It didn't make . . .

And then Gork watched as the human gestured at the guards, describing—in detail—the kobold's attempted theft. Watched the sharp, alien tilt to the movements, listened with rapt attention to the faintest trace of accent . . .

"All right," the guard told him, "let's go."

Gork looked up, forcing his eyes wide. "But, Officer, I—"

Whatever else he might have said was driven from his lungs, along with the rest of his breath, by the soldier's boot slamming into his stomach. The kobold collapsed to all fours, hanging limp and offering no resistance as the guards lifted him bodily off the ground and began carrying him in the direction of what he assumed was the local gaol. Still, as he was hefted away, he had the strength to raise his head and meet the gaze of the "human" standing at the end of the street and watching them fade into the distance.

You, Gork projected at him silently, *are* so *going to die. If it takes a hundred years, I* will *kill you.*

It was not a vow Gork made often, or lightly, and it was one that he fully intended to keep. Assuming he ever got away from these damn humans. . . .

The orc sneered in revulsion at the cramped, filthy courtyard and the creaky, dilapidated buildings that surrounded it. Litter and dead rodents formed a patchwork carpet, and the structures were built of wood so rotted that Cræosh wouldn't have trusted it to support the weight of his own testicles. So far, nothing about the human city had impressed him, but this shithole corner of town was even worse.

"*This* is the barracks?" he asked finally.

"In a manner of speaking," the guide answered. "It's the *old* barracks. We haven't used 'em in years. Hell, we haven't even *cleaned* 'em in years. But this is where we've hosted Demon Squads before, and no one's told us that you lot get any special treatment."

Cræosh advanced on the soldier, hulking over him. "And what if we don't *want* to stay here?"

The human solider swallowed once, but held his ground. "Take it up with the captain, then. Not much I can do about it, is there?"

The orc debated ripping the man apart anyway—might have, in fact, had the next of his teammates not suddenly appeared from around a nearby corner.

"Oh, *shit*!"

At the alarm in his companion's voice, the bugbear immediately spun from where he'd been examining a small, hollylike weed that had cropped up on the far end of the courtyard (to see if it was edible, no doubt). As soon as he caught sight of the newcomer, however, he let out one of his high-pitched whines and covered his head with one arm—keeping the other fully extended, however, club in hand. Clearly, Jhurpess was prepared to cower *or* fight to the death, whichever proved most viable.

The figure loomed over them all, though it was substantially more slender than the broadly built orc. A thin layer of coarse fur, far shorter than the bugbear's shaggy coat, covered the creature from fore to aft in a spotted, patchy pattern resembling a bobcat's. Armor, leggings, tunic, and boots, all clearly tanned from the hide of a single gargantuan beast, made up the entirety of the creature's wardrobe—all except for a necklace of humanoid and goblin ribs. A huge snout protruded from the thing's face, something not unlike a wolf, or a coyote, or a hyena—and yet, not quite like any of them, either. Even as they watched, the horrible maw gaped in what could only be a hideous smile, exposing multiple layers of jagged teeth that actually flexed in and out when the creature spoke.

Or, presumably, bit.

A thin stream of drool trickled from its lower lip. In an abrasive, mind-numbing voice, interrupted constantly by the intake of a raspy, trembling breath, the thing said, "Pleased . . . to make . . . your acquaintance. I . . . am T'chakatimlamitilnog, of . . . the House of Ru."

"Ancestors," Cræosh whispered hoarsely. "What did I do to deserve getting stuck with a *troll*? And how do I atone for it?"

And then silence fell across the courtyard, except for the rasping breath of the troll and the rapid patter of retreating footsteps that were the only remaining evidence of the human who'd brought them here.

Slowly, being *very* careful to keep two arm's-lengths between them, Cræosh examined the new arrival. It—she? Yes, those were definitely teats hidden beneath the leather breastplate, and in multiple rows to boot. All right then. *She* was nearly a foot taller than his own six feet, and her slender body made her look even taller. He figured he was probably stronger, pound for pound, but damn, he didn't want to have to find out. Trolls were considered, bar none, the most cruel-minded, violent, vicious, and brutal creatures ever to serve in Morthûl's armies. In combat, or so he'd heard, they were more animal than sentient being, ripping apart their foes with an unholy glee. They casually perpetrated horrors too gruesome even for an orc's liking, and it was said that the concept of taking prisoners was completely foreign to them.

But what made them so wildly unpopular with the other goblin soldiers, and what inspired the decision to allow trollish units to fight alone, unassisted by the other races, was their attitude toward their fellows. Trolls had proved thoroughly incapable of grasping the concept of "ally" as it applied to any outside their own race. In a moment of anger, hunger, or even simple boredom, a troll's teammates were just as apt to end up dead, or even eaten, as anyone else. Cræosh found himself pondering the notion that he might just be better off, consequences or no, if he were to simply kill her now, before their working relationship became an issue.

Before he could come to a decision one way or the other, however, he and the troll were both startled nigh unto violence as yet *another* piercing scream burst from somewhere within Jhurpess's furry throat. More extreme even than that elicited by the troll's appearance, it was enough to convince Cræosh that they must be facing nothing less than a great dragon or the Charnel King himself. He twisted about madly, one hand groping again for his sword.

What he saw was certainly neither the Dark Lord nor a dragon. No, the creature approaching from across the run-down courtyard was . . .

"It's just . . . a gremlin," the troll rasped, her breath gurgling in the back of her throat as she struggled to make her bestial jaws form the words. "What is . . . the matter with your . . . bugbear?"

"You got me stumped," Cræosh told her. "But I sure as shit intend to find out." With that he advanced, reached out, and grabbed Jhurpess by the scruff of the neck. The bugbear didn't seem to notice, so intently was he staring at the gremlin.

Admittedly, Cræosh couldn't help but note, that *was* one disconcerting mother of a gremlin. At four feet tall, he was a giant among his own race, and his muscles literally bulged—which, in a gremlin's case, just meant that you couldn't actually trace the lines of the bones in his arm from twenty paces away. A thin mat of stubble, which constituted a full head of hair for his people, was just barely notable beneath the floppy, porkpie hat he wore crammed between spindly ears. He was well protected beneath a full suit of hardened leather armor, but it was a suit that had clearly been scrounged, piece by piece, from the field of battle, as not one component resembled any of the others. The gremlin had done his best to compensate for that particular mismatch by dyeing the entire suit a brilliant red that was enough to cause madness, blindness, or both. Even the moth-eaten hat and the wilted ostrich feather atop it had been colored to match. So all right, he wasn't an image of beauty, and he had obviously never even heard the word "stealth," but that hardly made him a figure to be *feared* (except, perhaps, for the possibility of going blind in his proximity).

"So what's the problem this time?" Cræosh asked, his impatience ringing clearly in his voice. "I thought we'd settled this whole collapsing-and-pissing-myself bullshit back in the market."

But this time, all the bugbear would do was whimper unintelligibly, and even being bodily lifted off the ground and shaken accomplished nothing. Finally, Cræosh dropped him back to earth with a grunt of disgust and left him in an untidy heap that more or less resembled a shag carpet sucking its thumb. The gremlin, newly arrived, opened his mouth to introduce himself—and stopped, staring openly at the quivering bugbear.

"I give up," Cræosh announced to the world at large. "On the one hand, I've got a friggin' troll, who's probably loyal enough that I can count on her not to eat me when anybody's watching. On the other, they stick me with a bugbear who makes a habit of crawling up his own ass and hiding whenever the wind shifts. And bringing up the rear," he added, pointing at the startled gremlin, "we have the incredible Walking Rosebud. This ain't a Demon Squad, it's a fucking side-show lineup." Since the bugbear had cowered out of reach, and the gremlin was several strides away, he settled for walking straight up to the troll— foolhardy as it might have been—and jabbing her in the sternum with a finger. "You can tell the boss, whoever or whatever he might turn out to be, that I'm going home. Have him send me a message when he's got a *real* squad together."

The troll grinned, and Cræosh was just about bowled over by a wave of hot, fetid breath. "Fingers . . . are stringy. But still . . . one of the tastiest parts . . . of an orc." She glanced down. "Are you . . . making an offer?"

Cræosh, who was *almost* certain she was jesting, yanked his hand back anyway, just in case.

The bestial creature laughed sharply, a grating sound that made the orc's ears hurt, and wandered over to lean against the nearest wall. Idly, she spun a *chirrusk*—a length of weighted chain with a razor-sharp four-pronged hook at one end—in a slow circle. The low-pitched whistling it caused as it whirled was extremely—and, Cræosh was certain, quite deliberately—annoying. Despite his threat, he did nothing more than mutter a few choice curses in Orcish and settle back against the wall; not, he made certain, the same one on which the troll was leaning

As though spring-loaded, the glowing gremlin popped up into his field of vision. "Hello!" he beamed, thrusting out a hand in a greeting custom that many of the goblin races had picked up from watching the humans. "It's really a pleasure to meet you! I mean, I've heard about these Demon Squads from time to time, but I never thought that I'd actually get the chance to be part of one! It's so exciting, isn't it? Oh, I'm sorry! Where are my manners? I'm Gimmol Phicereune. And you are?"

"Getting very annoyed," Cræosh responded.

"Ah. Yes, well, I can see how that might be the case, what with all this waiting and all. I mean, you'd think that they'd have someone ready to meet us. They called us here, right? Why, you wouldn't believe what I had to go through to get in the gate! They—"

Cræosh backhanded the small creature across the courtyard, remembering only at the last instant to pull his punch enough so that he wouldn't kill the chatty bugger. Then, actually sighing with pleasure at the newborn silence, the orc leaned his head back against the stone and resigned himself to patience.

Gork tumbled claw-over-cranium across the bumpy floor, coming up to his feet just in time to hear the door slam shut behind him with a ponderous sense of finality. Most of the guards were just doing their jobs, and thus went on the kobold's *secondary* mental list: that is, People Who Just Need to Suffer a *Little Bit*. The man who'd tossed him into the cell, however, was going on the Bad List, and would bleed severely at some unforeseen future point. Why, if Gork hadn't been the nimble kobold that he was, that impact with the stone might have damaged a lot more than his pride.

With a faint snort of disgust, he went to examine the various mechanisms on the door. Hmm. The lock itself should prove little more than an inconvenience. Would've been a lot easier if they hadn't taken his picks, but he had enough tools secreted about his person to get the job done.

The bar, though—that was a much more formidable obstacle. Gork was well versed in multiple methods of circumventing just such an obstruction, but those methods required specific tools, substantial time, or both. That he would be free of this cell, Gork had no doubt. Whether it would be in time to meet with the rest of the squad—or, for that matter, before the end of the month—was another question entirely.

"Kobold . . ."

Oh, dragonshit. Pupils dilating to pierce the darkness of the cell's far corners, Gork faced the cellmate he hadn't realized he had.

Larger than their gremlin cousins, the so-called hobgoblins were by no means the most fearsome of the goblin races. What they *were* was sufficiently xenophobic to make even trolls seem cuddly. They formed an army within an army, for not even Morthûl could convince them to fight alongside the other goblins, and Gork knew that his proximity to *this* hobgoblin was enough to cause the creature physical pain.

He knew, too, that there was only one way for the hobgoblin to make that pain go away. The kobold found his back pressed tight to the door, as though he could *will* himself through the wood.

The hobgoblin—filthy, half-starved, dressed in tattered rags, breath reeking of illness—reached out for him from the shadows, his hatchet-sharp features twisted in loathing. It was, Gork couldn't help but note in the portion of his brain that wasn't too busy gibbering in fear, much like the expression he'd once seen on a human soldier who'd discovered roach sacs in his underwear.

He tried to bite as the creature neared, but the crazed hobgoblin yanked his arm away from the snapping teeth. Even as the hobgoblin's fists closed around his throat, Gork thrust both hands outward, driving small claws into his attacker's stomach. But kobold claws, designed for scampering over jagged rock, were strong without being particularly sharp, and the hobgoblin's hide was more than sufficient to turn them aside.

It appeared, for what it was worth, that Gork needn't worry about choking to death, as the hobgoblin had something rather quicker in mind. The hand not already locked on the kobold's throat latched onto one scaly knee, and he lifted Gork clean overhead. Gork kicked the hobgoblin squarely in the temple with his free leg, once, twice, but though the larger creature staggered and swayed, he lost neither his balance nor his grip.

Gork tensed for a third kick, aiming this time at a bulging eye, and his entire world went white with agony as the hobgoblin slammed him bodily against the stone wall.

The back of his head felt numb—was, in fact, the only part of him other than his toes that *didn't* hurt—but the kobold retained just enough sensation to recognize the wet trickle of blood. The hobgoblin drew back, now aiming Gork at the wall head-first, apparently planning to use him as a squishy battering ram. Gork tried for one final instant to make his limbs respond, to struggle, to do *something*—and then the floor flew past beneath him, and the white of his agony faded away to black.

The fact that he awoke at all was enough to send ripples of surprise through the pool of liquid pain that was his brain. From beneath heavy lids, he saw the stone ceiling of the cell above him; through aching snout, he smelled the scent of someone cooking nearby. Carefully, Gork struggled to sit up, but toppled straight back down as his head and stomach tried to travel to opposite corners of the room. He rolled over, emptied said stomach across the stones—what was that, a fingernail?—and prayed to the Stars for a quick death.

"You're the best Hrark could do, huh? I'll have to have a few words with that little puke. *And* with the guards who tossed you in here in the first place. Ooh, have I got some plans for them!"

It was not the hobgoblin speaking. A new voice, then—a stranger. But the kobold just couldn't find the strength in him to sit up and see who the newcomer might be.

"Well, you'll have to do. Too late to find a replacement. I'm going to assume you've got your uses, though I'm buggered if I can see 'em from here. Better prove me right, though. Else . . ."

Gork weakly twisted to one side, hoping to catch a glimpse of the speaker in his peripheral vision, and encountered, instead, the charred corpse of the hobgoblin who had attacked him.

The proper response, Gork decided, was to throw up again. Which he did. Twice, just to be sure he'd covered all salient points.

"Great. All right, let's get that head dealt with. You've got a meeting to attend."

Gork felt a sudden pressure on the back of his skull, followed by yet another burst of pain. With no small amount of gratitude, he allowed himself, once more, to pass out.

It was perhaps two hours after the troll's arrival when Cræosh's well of patience ran dry. With a grunt of irritation, the orc slammed a fist into the wall behind him, knocking a loose chunk of brick to the ground. "That," he told his startled companions, "is it! I'm sick of this shit! If I wanted to stand around with my dick in my hands, it sure as hell wouldn't be with you all watching." Once more gathering his traveling pack, he pivoted toward the nearest street.

"Are you sure that's a good idea?" Gimmol called nervously, nursing the large bruise spreading across his jaw. "I mean, they're going to expect us all to be here, and if you've gone, they might . . ."

The gremlin's voice suffocated and died beneath the sheer malevolence of Cræosh's glare, though his jaw kept moving for some seconds afterward. With a nod of approval, the orc took two steps toward the road, only to come within a hairsbreadth of colliding with a brown-haired, dull-featured human.

"Watch it, you idiot!" the orc shouted, one fist raised to smash the obstruction from his path.

"Idiot?" the human asked with just the faintest accent. "Me? I'm not the one walking away from his assignment, am I?"

Cræosh snarled—but only a little, since the man did have a point. "Are you supposed to be our leader, then?"

"Perhaps I should be. But no. I'm a simple soldier, although maybe not as simple as some. I—"

"All right, you maggots, fall in! That means line your asses up! Now!"

Cræosh was irritated, impatient, and rapidly coming to despise the very notion of the Demon Squad. On the other hand, his mother had raised him a sensible orc—one who knew that you *never* argue with a disembodied voice. They never wind up attached to anything pleasant.

The troll already stood in the courtyard, the human having stepped up beside her, albeit not *too* close. Still grumbling, Cræosh moved to join them. Maybe now, they'd find out . . .

An enormous crashing sounded behind them, followed immediately by the bugbear's shrieking voice. "Red gremlin won't hurt Jhurpess now! Red gremlin won't hurt Jhurpess!"

Every face, even the troll's, went slack in shock. Jhurpess stood over the prone and bleeding body of the gremlin, Gimmol Phicereune, slamming his enormous cudgel again and again onto the prostrate form.

"What the fuck?" Cræosh whispered to the courtyard at large. The human shook his head slowly, and the troll continued to gawk.

"Stop!" The voice thundered between the buildings, somehow intensifying rather than fading each time it echoed. As though lifted by an unseen hand, the giant club—Jhurpess dangling from the narrow end—rose a dozen feet into the air. For a moment it hung, the bugbear swinging gently in the breeze, and then it dropped like a—well, like a giant club. Bruised only slightly but shaken to the core, Jhurpess rose,

casting a suspicious glance at both the gremlin and the club, and brushed himself off. Sullenly, his weapon dragging behind him, he moved to join the others in line.

"What in the name of the Ancestors was *that*?!" Cræosh demanded as the bugbear came up beside him. *They've assigned me a fuckin' lunatic! I didn't know bugbears had lunatics!*

Jhurpess stared at the orc as though *he* were the crazy one. "Cræosh not know?" he asked.

"Know *what*?! I swear, I'm gonna start breaking people if—"

"Bright!" the bugbear whispered fearfully. "Poison!"

It was the troll who picked up on it first. "Nature," she growled.

Cræosh pondered that. "Huh?" he finally rebutted.

"Bugbears live . . . in forests. Hunt there. Bright . . . fur or coloration . . ."

Cræosh finally understood. ". . . is often a sign of poison," he concluded for her. He turned back to the bugbear. "You," he told the hairy creature, "are *really* fucking weird."

"*Shut up!*" the voice demanded.

The orc grinned slightly. "I was wondering when he'd get around to that," he whispered to the troll. She just shook her head.

Slowly, as though trapped in quicksand, the gremlin began to drag himself forward. Blood caked his head and the side of his face, and edges of broken collarbone protruded through torn flesh. Still, the agonized creature did his best to obey the orders shouted down at them by . . . whatever.

He's determined, Cræosh noted silently, his opinion of the gremlin rising a tiny notch. *Gotta give the little shit that much.*

The garish red armor grew slowly brighter, as though the sun itself were staring at it, and Cræosh realized that the gremlin had actually begun to glow. Faint at first, barely leaking through mouth and nose, and then brighter, until the little creature was practically incandescent. As the astonished onlookers squinted, bruises faded, gashes pulled themselves shut, and the collarbone shifted back into something resembling its proper state with a sequence of horrible pops. The glow faded, leaving the gremlin to stand before them under his own power—far, perhaps, from the picture of health, but no longer in any immediate danger. His eyes wide, though not quite as large as the bugbear's, Gimmol took his place at the leftmost end of the line.

"*Get in there!*" the spectral voice shouted. Cræosh thought, at first, that the unseen commander must be talking to the gremlin, even though Gimmol had already done just that.

The air rippled. Like a fish leaping from a tranquil pond, a figure appeared before them. Smaller even than the gremlin, and covered in his own collection of fading wounds, he stood for a moment and brushed himself off, as though the teleportation had somehow soiled him. Then, glancing about with far more curiosity than fear, the kobold sauntered over and took up a stance beside the troll. Cræosh noticed with some amusement that the kobold was the only one who had not chosen his place in line based on height, something the others appeared to have done instinctively.

And finally, in a burst of sulfurous smoke, the mysterious officer made his own appearance.

It was all Cræosh could do to swallow his laughter. Dark gray skin covered a gargoyle's face and form. Two membranous wings sprouted from the creature's back, and rock-hard talons tipped its digits. Narrow cracks in the stony façade peered from above a draconic muzzle, and a barbed tail scratched idly at the empty air.

It also stood maybe twenty inches tall—although, because it was currently standing in midair, it remained at eye level with the orc.

"My name is Shreckt," the imp shouted. "And it is my unfortunate duty to turn the sorry lot of you into something vaguely resembling soldiers!"

The tiny demon began to pace, his feet clacking audibly on the nothingness on which he stood. "As of right now," he continued, "I wouldn't use any one of you to wipe my ass! But by the time I'm through, you're all gonna be worth something! You'll be soldiers, or you'll be fertilizer, and I'm fine with either!

"Now," he said, halting and turning to face the group, "before we go any further, let me get this out of the way. Invariably, some dumb fucker decides that, since I'm short, he doesn't have to listen to me. And that, you looming shits, ain't gonna cut it. So, any of you think you can take me? Now's the time to try."

Cræosh rolled his eyes, despite his complete lack of surprise, when Jhurpess stepped forward.

"Jhurpess can fight little thing," he announced, hefting his club. "Jhurpess will—"

Jhurpess, however, did nothing but scream as a bolt of lightning burst from the imp's tiny hand, crackling and sizzling its way down the courtyard, and slammed the bugbear halfway through the nearest wall.

"Anyone else?" Shreckt asked when the roaring, the thunder, and the sounds of falling masonry finally ceased.

Not surprisingly, there were no takers.

"Good." The imp gestured at Gork. "Help the monkey up."

"What?" Gork squeaked. "Me? But he—"

Shreckt raised a hand; the kobold immediately hurried over to the bugbear.

Jhurpess's fur smoldered, and even Gork's hand on his arm seemed to cause an inordinate amount of pain. Nevertheless, the bugbear struggled to his feet—using Gork primarily as a crutch, nearly shoving the kobold's head down into his own rib cage in the process.

"All right, then," the imp continued once the mismatched pair had limped back into line. "Here's the situation. I tell you to do something, and you do it. That, and that alone, is your life until I say otherwise. You will not speak unless I tell you to. You will not fight unless I tell you to. You will not think—well, that's probably not much of an issue. You will not eat, sleep, shit unless I tell you to. Any questions?

"Good. Names!"

"Gork!" the kobold piped up immediately.

"Jhurpess," came weakly, a moment later.

"Gimmol Phicereune," the gremlin announced next, "and it's a distinct pleasure—"

Cræosh reached past the human and smacked the gremlin on the back of the head. Gimmol shut up; possibly because he got the hint, possibly because it was all he could do to stay conscious.

"Omb Fezeill," the human said.

"Cræosh."

And finally, "T'chakatimlamitilnog, of the . . . House of Ru."

Even the imp looked taken aback. "Say that again?"

"T'chakatimlamitilnog," the troll repeated, snout furrowing in bewilderment.

"Right," Shreckt said after a moment. "'Troll' it is." His demonic visage swiveled toward Fezeill. "True forms during inspection, soldier."

For the first time, an actual expression crossed the human's face. "Is that really necessary?"

The imp's flinty face actually developed crags as his features scrunched up. "Is that really necessary *what*?!"

"Sir!" the man corrected. "Is that really necessary *sir*?"

"*Yes!*" the imp shrieked.

Slowly, the "human's" body began to warp. The squad watched intently—some in fascination, some in disgust, and one in outright hatred—as his true form appeared before them. Loathsome white flesh, vaguely akin to a maggot's, bulged from between segments of a dark gray chitin. The creature's eyes, protruding hideously from the sides of its head, only added to the insectoid image. Multifaceted, they stared, unblinking; Cræosh found himself confronted by a hundred tiny orcs contained in those alien orbs. A faint lump with gaping nostrils was the closest thing the creature had to a nose, and the mouth was full of jagged ridges made of something akin to bone. Its fingers were clearly built for grasping, for tiny barbs edged the digits from palm to tip.

It was, even for those used to supping with gremlins and fighting with trolls, more than a little repugnant.

"Doppelganger," Gork grumbled under his breath.

"Better," Shreckt said. "I expect you to look this way every time I call assembly." There was silence, then, except for the *tap-tap-tap* of the imp pacing across thin air.

"Gork!"

The kobold, still studying the doppelganger, just about came out of his skin. "What?!" And then, before the imp could draw breath to reprimand, he corrected, "What, *sir*?"

"You've had some, ah, problems with the local authorities."

Yes, sir! You were there, sir!"

"Indeed." Shreckt scowled. "For better or worse—worse, I expect—you idiots are my charge for the time being. And that means nobody fucks with you except me."

The imp actually rubbed his hands together. "Now, I've got a few *activities* in mind for the soldiers who arrested you. But we need to set an example, Gork. Did you get a good look at the man who accused you in the first place?"

The kobold hesitated a moment. Then, "I wish I had, sir. But I'm afraid not."

Shreckt's face fell. "No?"

"No, sir."

"Not even a glimpse?"

Gork shook his head.

"Drat. All right, then, that's it for now. You're billeted in that piece-of-shit building to your left. Between the roaches and the bird droppings, it oughta feel homey enough. Each and every one of you, equipped and ready to move, better be lined up in this courtyard at dawn tomorrow. You," he added, glaring at the bugbear, "get your ass to the infirmary. I'll be buggered if I'm healing any more of you myself today, and I expect you in top form in the morning." With that, and another puff of smoke, he was gone.

Slowly the group dispersed, milling about in various directions. A puzzled and vaguely suspicious expression on his once-more-human face, the doppelganger appeared at Gork's side.

"Why?"

"Why didn't I turn you in?" the kobold clarified.

Fezeill nodded.

"Real simple," Gork told him, his little muzzle twisted into an evil grin. "I don't *want* you in trouble with Shreckt."

"You aren't upset about what happened?"

"I didn't say that." Gork's grin grew wider, revealing jagged, yellowed canines. "You see, I want to deal with you myself."

The kobold delighted in the feel of Fezeill's gaze boring into his back as he casually wandered away in search of a bunk that wasn't *too* disgusting.

As ordered, they were all lined up like good little soldiers when the dawning sun finally broke over the horizon. (Although it must be noted that Gork, panting just a bit, had arrived with seconds to spare, and Jhurpess had simply bedded down in the courtyard once he'd returned from his side-trip to the infirmary). And, good to his word, Shreckt appeared but moments later. He carried a riding crop, cut down to his size, that he slapped against his leg as he marched back and forth across that same stretch of nothing.

"Good," he said with a grin. "You can follow orders. Not a bad start."

The imp took a moment to examine them each in turn. "You're here," he began, "as part of this squad, because you're *supposedly* among the best your races have to offer. Trained and experienced soldiers, or killers, or—whatever. So it would be redundant to try to train you further in any *conventional* capacity."

Cræosh didn't know about the others, but he was starting to get a twitchy feeling in the pit of his gut. Never, in all his years of war, had he heard of any "unconventional training" that didn't involve extreme discomfort.

"The Serpent's Pass," the imp persisted, "is the only route through the Brimstone Mountains large enough for an army. But Dororam might utilize the other passes to try to squeeze smaller groups of his people around behind our main defenses. Likeliest places for *that* are the northeast mountains, in the Steppes. So step one is to make sure that you 'elite' can function as well there as you can down here."

Cræosh winced. He *hated* the cold.

"Your first exercise, then, is straightforward enough. Survive four days in the tundra. Then we'll talk further."

The troll raised a clawed hand.

"What?"

"Four days . . . will barely get us . . . into the Steppes. Even from . . . here, it is . . . quite a long walk."

"True." Shreckt grinned malevolently. "That's why you aren't walking."

Cræosh had enough time for a single mental *Shit!* before they were surrounded by an abrupt puff of sulfurous smoke—and Shreckt, cackling maniacally, stood alone in the courtyard.

CHAPTER TWO

ELF CARE

"Something," Lidia murmured softly, "is bothering you."

"Is it?" duMark asked, spinning as his restless tread once again carried him to the limits of the small bedchamber. "What could possibly have given you that impression?"

The young ranger's lips quirked. "You're pacing like a caged orc, that's what. If I'd known you had this kind of stamina, I'd—"

The half-elf halted, one hand raised. "Do not even *think* of finishing that sentence."

The long-legged redhead matched her gaze with his, and he could see the wheels turning behind those eyes. It was she, however, who finally gave.

"Sorry, Ananias. I guess I'm still a bit sensitive about it all."

In the months following the assault on the Iron Keep, Father Thomas—longtime companion of Ananias duMark and chirurgeon of the finest order—had worked his hands raw repairing the damage General Falchion had inflicted. But while Lidia was no longer in pain, and she could breathe easily and smell clearly once more, there was little even the old man's skills could do for her appearance. He'd straightened the cartilage as best he could, but she still looked like what she was:

someone who had been punched in the face by a warrior wearing a steel gauntlet. The shape of her skull was disturbingly *off*, her nose uneven, the flesh around it permanently discolored. The loss of her former beauty had done nothing to diminish her fervor to fight for good, for freedom, and all the rest of it, but her companions were proving far less adaptable than she herself.

She could ignore it easily enough when it came from the others. From Ananias, after all they'd once been, it was a stab to the gut every time he looked at her—or, more accurately, refused to look at her.

Not that she'd ever show it.

Putting her own humiliation behind her, the ranger rose lithely to her feet and stepped in front of the pacing wizard, blocking the path he'd already beaten into the carpet.

"Had you actually stuck with one direction," she told him in response to his irritated expression, "instead of turning around each time you reached a wall, you'd be at the Brimstone Mountains by now."

"Pacing helps me think," he snapped at her.

"No. Pacing helps you *feel*. If you were thinking, you'd have come up with something already."

With a defeated sigh, the stately half-breed planted his rear on the bed. Only slightly self-conscious, Lidia sat beside him.

"He *must* know by now," duMark said—as he'd *been* saying, now, for days on end. "A blind leech with brain damage could see Dororam's armies gathering. So why hasn't he *done* anything?"

"Maybe your own efforts are distracting him? You said you had a few schemes working . . ."

"Not possible. They haven't progressed far enough."

Slowly, almost fearfully, Lidia extended a comforting hand and placed it on duMark's shoulder. She was, she realized with bitter self-loathing, absurdly grateful when he didn't brush it away. "It's not as though he's ignoring the threat," she told him, her voice calming. "You yourself told me that the patrols around the Serpent's Pass have increased fourfold. Why—"

"But that's not like him!" DuMark surged to his feet, allowing Lidia's hand to fall uselessly to the mattress. "Morthûl doesn't think defensively! Never has, never will! No, he's plotting something, all right. I'd bet my beard."

"You don't have a beard," Lidia told him curtly. "And what are you doing using a dwarven expression, anyway?"

DuMark glowered at her for a full minute. "Are you through?" he asked finally.

She shrugged, her bobbing shoulders making her red curls dance around her head. "For the moment."

"Good."

"Look," she said, heartily sick of the whole thing. "You're so hot and bothered because you can't figure out what Morthûl may or may not be doing? Why don't you find out already? What's your magic good for, anyway?"

The sorcerer shook his head. "The Iron Keep's not the sort of place you can just scry on, Lidia. The Charnel King protects himself against that sort of thing."

"So? When was the last time you took the easy way out?" *Not counting me . . .*

Slowly, a grin stole over duMark's features. "You know, Lidia, you might just have a point after all. I think I *will* go find out what his Bony-ness is up to."

"And how are you planning to accomplish that?"

"Well, I thought if I were polite enough about it, I might just find someone to ask."

Gork found himself screaming, just a little bit, as he materialized about fifteen feet above the frozen tundra and plummeted into the snow.

He screamed a lot louder when Cræosh appeared directly over him a moment later.

The orc, arms flailing, fell into the snow with a resounding whump. Grumbling mightily, he dragged himself to his feet and had barely vacated his self-made hole before the next of his companions (Jhurpess, it so happened) appeared from thin air above his head and plunged groundward.

Once the last of the Demon Squad had arrived—the troll, who was the only member of the group to actually land on her feet—Cræosh began examining his surroundings, trying to determine exactly how deep the shit they were in might be.

Very, was his first conclusion.

"It's fucking cold," was his second. "I think my testicles are somewhere near my throat." His companions, for whatever reason, didn't feel the need to comment on that particular pronouncement.

"Where are the mountains?" Gimmol asked, trying to look every way at once. "Didn't Shreckt say something about mountains?"

"Where food?" Jhurpess chimed in with his usual priorities. "Jhurpess hungry!"

"Jhurpess always hungry," Cræosh muttered. "Jhurpess better shut the hell up, or Jhurpess may find himself eating his club."

"For that matter," Fezeill said before the bugbear could respond to the orc's taunts, "where's the kobold?" He didn't actually *say "I don't want that little bastard out of my sight!"* but everyone heard it in his voice, even if they weren't certain why.

Cræosh's brow wrinkled. "You know, I didn't see him land."

"Must . . . have arrived before . . . you did."

But the orc merely shook his head at the troll's suggestion. "I dunno. I think I would have seen—"

Gork's head popped from the snow a few yards away. A murderous glint in his beady little eyes, the kobold literally dragged himself free and stalked toward Cræosh, brushing clinging clumps of white off him as he went.

"You—you stupid elephant! You nearly killed me!"

"Beg pardon?" Cræosh asked, stepping back out of sheer instinct. "What're you talking about?"

"*You!* It's all very well to be built like a damn brick when you're bowling people over or—or eating buildings, or whatever it is you do, but it doesn't help you *fly*, does it?"

The orc finally got it. "I, uh, landed on you, didn't I?"

"You're damn right you did, you monstrosity! You're lucky I didn't decide to *carve* my way out! You—"

Seeing the orc—and, for that matter, the rest of the squad—collapse into gales of helpless laughter was quite certainly not the effect Gork had been shooting for. With a final disgusted grunt, he spun on his heel and wandered some forty or fifty feet from the others, where he then proceeded to sulk.

"All right," Cræosh said, once he'd finally regained some semblance of control. "Our first step is to figure out where the hell we are. Then, we have to decide how to go about surviving this miserable place for four days."

"Why," the goblin lamented sadly, "couldn't he have let us pack some extra clothes?"

"Wouldn't be much of a test, then, would it, runt? Shit, *anybody* can survive the Northern Steppes if they're *prepared* for it." His brow, however, twisted in thought. "You were right about one thing, though. The imp *did* say something about mountains. Guarding the passes, and all that."

"There is . . . a mountain range off to . . . the east. I can . . . just barely see it."

Cræosh wandered over, squinting. "I don't see anything but snow, snow, and—wait! Is that—why, yes it is. *More* snow!"

Except for a quick sideways glower, the orc's sarcasm went ignored. "Trolls . . . have very good . . . sight. Better than . . . other races."

"*All* other races?" he asked distrustfully.

Was it his imagination, or was that actually a look of mild embarrassment stealing over the troll's features? "Still cannot match . . . elven sight."

"Well, don't take it so hard. You wouldn't *want* to be an elf. At least you're not named Bunnybugger or Treeface or something."

"I'm so . . . relieved."

"If you two would allow me?"

The orc and the troll turned as Fezeill stepped between them. As he passed, Cræosh could see the doppelganger's legs lengthening, his torso narrowing, his ears shifting beneath his hair. Even though he *knew* who it was before him, had watched the Fezeill take on an elven shape, the orc had to brutally repress the urge to murder the horrid creature on sight.

Finally, after a few minutes of staring through elven pupils, Fezeill said, "There is indeed a mountain range many miles to the east. But it's far, far too small to be the Brimstone Mountains."

"Well, that narrows it down, anyway," Cræosh said. He paused, dredging up old lessons in geography. "There's only, what, two or three ranges in the Steppes, right? So all we have to do is figure out which one it is, and we're set."

"Set? All it . . . tells us is where we are. There . . . remains the small matter of . . . survival."

"So we survive." The orc—who, despite his blithe façade was preventing himself from shivering violently through sheer stubbornness—signaled those who had lagged behind to catch up. "Let's move it, people!"

Gimmol, Jhurpess, and then, somewhat grudgingly, Gork, all gathered. "Move?" the gremlin asked, his face puzzled. "Where do we have to go?"

Cræosh pointed forcefully in the direction Fezeill-the-elf was staring. "There. Mountains."

"Oh?" Gork asked, voice still sullen. "And who decided we were going that way?"

His face fixed in a tight grin, the orc lifted his tiny companion from the snow, palming the kobold's head as if it were a melon. "*I* did. Any objections?"

"Mrmph," Gork reassured him.

"I'm so glad to hear it." *Thump.* "Any other questions?"

Jhurpess, Gimmol, and Fezeill watched the kobold stand up and once more dust the snow from his shoulders. As one, they shook their heads.

The troll, however, calmly returned his glower. "You are quite quick . . . to take over, yes? If I . . . *were* to object, what . . . would you do?"

Cræosh blanched internally, but he wasn't about to back down in front of the others. "Care to find out?"

The temperature dropped far enough to freeze the snow into solid ice. The rest of the squad stood as motionless as if they, too, had been frozen, terrified that the slightest movement might set one or another of their deadly companions off.

And then . . .

"Not . . . just now. I have . . . no objections."

Cræosh breathed a subdued sigh of relief.

"But if . . . I did, you would certainly . . . be the first to know."

In other words, the orc translated, *this ain't over.*

Well, he'd deal with that when it came up. For now, there was the pesky matter of survival, and standing around with their thumbs up their respective asses wasn't particularly conducive to that goal.

"Fine. Fezeill, we should keep a visual fix on the mountains. You'll stay in that form for a while, and——"

"I think not."

Cræosh snapped his jaw shut. "And why is that?"

Even as the doppelganger answered, he began to shift. "Because elves are just fine sight-wise, but they are somewhat lacking in the insulation department. As you said, 'It's fucking cold.'" By the time he had finished speaking, a second bugbear—somewhat lighter in hue than Jhurpess, though equally hairy—stood in the elf's place.

"Oh, great. Yeah, that's *just* what we need."

"I remain myself," Fezeill assured the frustrated orc. "I may gain my form's physical traits, but I retain my own mind. Mentally, Jhurpess is still quite . . . unique."

The true bugbear beamed at the unexpected praise.

"Whatever," Cræosh conceded. There wasn't time to argue. Already, his rich swampy skin tones were paling beneath the frigid bite of the tundra's winds. "Okay, then, troll. Looks like it's up to you and those superior peepers of yours. I need you to scout ahead, and——"

"Do not . . . call me 'troll.' I . . . do not call you 'orc' . . . do I?"

Damn it all, they *really* didn't have time for this! "Well, I can't just call you 'you,' can I?"

"My name . . . is T'chakatimlamitilnog . . . of the House—"

"Yeah, yeah, of the House of Ru. I got *that* part down, thanks. So what if we just call you Ru?"

"No. That . . . would be disrespectful."

Cræosh decided not to bother asking why. Instead he struggled to commit the convoluted name to memory. The name, unfortunately, was winning.

It was Gork who finally came forward with a suggestion. "How about 'Katim'?"

The orc shrugged. It sounded enough like *some* part of that damn name, to his ears if not her own. "How about it, *troll?*"

She scowled, her jagged fangs shifting about in their gums. "It is . . . crude." Then, however, she shrugged as well, the gesture a mirror image of the orc's. "But so . . . are you all. I suppose . . . it will do."

"Great. Well, now that we have *that* urgent issue settled . . . Katim, would you be so kind as to scout ahead? Ain't a one of us here who can see the mountains besides you." *And I doubt anything around here's so stupid as to attack a troll.*

Katim set out with a long-legged canter that quickly carried her to the limits of the orc's own sight. And there she stayed, idly twirling her *chirrusk* and waiting for her companions to get a move on.

Which, after no small amount of prodding from Cræosh, they did. Jhurpess and Fezeill loped ahead with relative ease, their four-legged gait providing extra leverage against the shifting powder. Gimmol, Cræosh, and Gork, however, were forced to rely as best they could on only two legs.

The orc gave up almost immediately on keeping the squad in any kind of military formation. Gimmol was, perhaps understandably, unwilling to get within fifteen feet of Jhurpess; and Gork, his short legs mired in the deep snow, simply couldn't keep pace with the others. Still, their footing solidified some as they moved from their landing spot, and soon the snow was packed tightly enough that the light kobold could stride across it. They made far better time after that, and when twilight began to fall, Cræosh himself could see the faint outline of the mountains, beckoning from the horizon.

By the time they caught up with Katim, the troll was already ensconced in a hollow between two "dunes" of snow, a hearty fire crackling away before her. Instantly, most of the squad dashed ahead, eager for the warmth of the dancing flames, arguing and shoving over the best spaces. Cræosh wandered past the fire, however, ignoring the sight of the two bugbears wrestling with one another. He saw the ass-end of the kobold vanishing over the top of a small rise and heard a moment later the thump of a fist landing and Gimmol's voice cry out in pain, but he disregarded that as well.

Instead, he settled into the snow beside the troll, pulling a chunk of jerky from his traveling pack and warming it in the fire. After several minutes of silence, broken only by the crunch of snow from the battling squad members and his own chewing, the orc finally faced his bestial companion.

"When I told you to scout ahead," he said around a mouthful of meat, "I sort of assumed that would include reporting back to us on occasion. We haven't seen hide nor fur of you in six hours!"

Katim twisted until her long snout was directly in Cræosh's face. Although the scent was enough to choke a swamp dragon, the warm breath actually felt good after a day of marching through the snow and frigid winds. "Did you . . . come across anything of note . . . as you walked?" The hideous rasp of her breath sounded even worse so close up.

"What are you, kidding? This is the fucking ass-end of Kirol Syrreth. The only thing 'of note' is the fact that my most important parts have all quit in disgust at the cold and gone home."

"That . . . is why I reported nothing back . . . to you. There is . . . precious little to report."

Cræosh nodded after a time. "All right, I guess you've got a point. But—"

"And you did not . . . tell me to scout . . . ahead. You *asked* me. Do . . . not get above yourself."

Whatever, Cræosh thought. What he said instead, at a much higher volume, was, "Fall in!"

It required a bit more than that—actually, it required him tromping around the small encampment and physically tossing almost every squad member toward the fire—but he eventually got them all assembled.

"We have preparations to make," he told them, "if we're gonna live through one night here, let alone four. And then we have to set a watch. Get to it!"

They got. Hollows were dug in the tightly packed snow, providing a surprising amount of shelter from the frigid nighttime temperatures—and, for that matter, a place other than the middle of the camp for the goblins to relieve themselves. After savoring its warming glow for a final few moments, they thoroughly doused the fire. No sense, Cræosh told them, of alerting anyone within twenty miles to their presence.

"I got first watch," the orc announced, once everyone was about ready to turn in.

"Watch?" Jhurpess asked, his voice perplexed.

Grimacing, Gork tugged on the bugbear's arm and whispered rapidly in his ear.

"Oh." Jhurpess blinked. "Something going to happen tonight?"

"I don't know, Nature-boy," Cræosh said. "It's just *in case* something happens tonight."

"Oh," he said again. "Jhurpess will go second, then."

The others shouted, barked, or muttered their own preferences. With all six of them, there would be no need for shifts of longer than an hour or so—a prospect particularly attractive to the kobold, who bitched long and loud about needing his beauty sleep.

The first hour passed uneventfully, or so Jhurpess assumed when he was rudely awakened by the orc's hard-toed boot in his side.

"Up and at 'em, Jhurpess."

Grumbling, the bugbear rose. His club carving a deep furrow in the snow behind him, he trudged along the featureless field of white until he was perhaps fifteen yards from camp. From there, he could easily see the entire squad. Satisfied with his brilliant selection of vantage points, the bugbear plopped down in the snow and promptly closed his eyes.

They didn't stay closed long. Jhurpess uttered a startled yelp as he was sent flying by a meaty blow to the side of his head.

"You fucking idiot!" Cræosh railed at him. "It doesn't do us any good if you go to sleep! You're supposed to stay *awake* on watch!"

"Jhurpess sorry," the simian creature said, rising again to his feet. "No one told Jhurpess about that part."

"No one told—Just how, exactly, did you expect to keep alert for danger without staying awake?!"

The bugbear shrugged philosophically. "Jhurpess had sort of wondered about that part. Jhurpess assumed it would be more obvious when the time came."

Cræosh winced in sudden pain, then wandered back to his hole. "And put the damn skull-cracker away, would you?" he called over his shoulder. "Anything attacks you from the open tundra, that bow of yours is gonna be a whole lot more helpful."

The bugbear waved happily in thanks, yanked the bow free of the rudimentary sling in which he carried it, and immediately set about stringing the primitive but powerful weapon.

It was only after the orc's vigorous snoring had begun wafting toward him over the prone bodies of his squad-mates that Jhurpess realized he had no idea how long an "hour" was. He was a creature of the wild, though, and a quick glance at the moon and stars told him exactly how long he'd been asleep. Well, he'd simply watch for that same duration, and then wake—umm—Fezeill. Yeah, that was it.

Although fully determined that nothing should slip past him, Jhurpess found his attention drawn more and more frequently to the gleaming stars overhead. With wonder in his eyes, the bugbear stared, dazzled, at their subtle twinkling. He was familiar with them, of course, having lived most of his life out-of-doors—but somehow, away from the constant frame of the trees and foliage, separated from him only by distance and the cold, crisp air of the Northern Steppes, they appeared larger, brighter. More real.

The familiar constellations were all there, exactly as every bugbear cub learned them. The Ogre, the Mother, the Wolf, the Deer, the Beetle, the Greater and Lesser Corpses, the Rotting Tree with a Thousand Beehives—all shone down upon Jhurpess, illuminating the night and giving the snow a ghostly luminescence.

But *something* was wrong. The bugbear glanced about, but saw nothing amiss. Sniffing, he aimed his nose into the wind, trying to detect something, anything. There was nothing save the icy wind, biting into his nostrils.

The scenery! *That's* what was bothering him! The moon and stars painted faint shadows across the canopy of white . . .

And those shadows were moving.

Jhurpess shrieked as it lunged from the blank expanse of snow. Huge, fur-coated arms reached with claw-fingered hands; an equally huge maw, more apelike than Jhurpess's own, gaped to sever the bugbear's head with a single, hideous chomp. So closely did the beast's coloration match the surrounding snows that it had stood invisible mere paces from Jhurpess's cleverly chosen vantage.

Every one of the bugbear's limbs thrashed and twisted as the creature slammed into him, and the bow—though useless, now, for its intended purpose—proved sufficient to deflect the blow that would have shattered Jhurpess's skull.

It was, at best, a temporary reprieve. Jhurpess found himself pressed into the snow beneath a bulk three times his own. Although he was, for the moment, safe from the ravaging claws and clashing teeth, the weight alone was enough to steadily drive the breath from his lungs. If it rose, it would maul him; if it stayed, he would suffocate. A mind far sharper than his own would've proved hard-pressed to find an escape.

But the creature rose! Air rushed into the bugbear's chest, sweet as baby's blood despite its deathly chill. A low-pitched growl in its throat, the monster lifted a meaty paw, ready to tenderize its dinner for good and all.

And Jhurpess's voice rose with it in a screech as shrill as his battered lungs could beget. For a single instant, the startled creature hesitated.

One single instant makes an astounding difference.

"Hey! Snowball!"

Jhurpess grinned at the sound of that voice.

"That's *my* bugbear," Cræosh continued as he neared. "You can't play with it."

The beast roared, a thunderous bellow that ceased as abruptly as it began when Cræosh brought his wicked blade up under the creature's chin.

The blow would have cleaved a human entirely in two, shredded the brain of an ogre, even cracked the bony carapace of a rock spider. But although the blood flew far and the beast reeled in agony, the hide beneath the fur prevented the sword from killing.

Ancestors! The orc retreated a step. He'd heard tales of the great yetis of the Northern Steppes, heard that nothing here save the ice dragons or the arctic eels were more fearsome, but he'd never have believed that *anything* could withstand such punishment! For a moment, the mighty Cræosh allowed himself to fear.

But only a moment.

Okay, so it had survived one of his mightiest blows. So what? It bled, and that meant it could die. By the time the others had appeared at his side, the last stirrings of doubt had faded. Cræosh was, once more, an orc.

A keening war cry rose to the uncaring heavens, and it took the startled Cræosh a moment to realize that it had come from the gremlin! "For King Morthûl! For the Demon Squad!" Gimmol shouted, eyes gleaming with fervor and anticipation—and then, glistening blade a shining beacon above his head, he charged madly in the wrong direction.

"Gremlins," Fezeill observed as the stunned party watched him go, "do not have particularly good night vision."

And then the yeti, blood already freezing solid around its gaping wound, was upon them with another earthshaking roar.

Cræosh parried madly, his blade barely fast enough to intercept those terrible claws on their course toward his own precious flesh. Fezeill, cursing in frustration, had clearly discovered that bugbear hands were not built to handle his thin-hilted sword, and was reduced to flailing awkwardly at whatever parts of the beast came within reach. Katim slowly circled the melee, a wickedly barbed battleaxe in one hand, *chirrusk* loudly spinning from the other. And Gork . . .

Where the hell *was* Gork? It only then occurred to Cræosh that he hadn't seen the little shit since the bugbear's wail had popped his slumber like a spit bubble. If he'd run out on them, Cræosh was determined to make damn sure the cowardly kobold regretted it.

The yeti lunged, jaws snapping shut just inches from Cræosh's face. He could actually hear the crack of small icicles of saliva shattering between the pitted fangs. He spun his blade up and out, determined to take advantage of such a tempting target, but the yeti jerked its head just out of range. Cræosh tried to follow up, but was forced instead to parry yet another attempt by the yeti to drag his stomach out through his navel.

Damn it all! All he needed was *one* opening, one break in the yeti's relentless assault, to slip his blade past those claws. . . .

And the Ancestors heard his plea. Gork erupted from the snow behind the raging beast, *kah-rahahk* clenched tightly in his left fist, and hamstrung it.

The tendons were too strong, and the flesh too tough, for Gork's attack to cripple the yeti—but it was more than enough to distract. Howling in pain and fury, the creature lashed down and back at the source of this new pain.

A second burst of snow and Jhurpess was there, war club held high. Howling and gibbering, he brought it down upon the yeti's shoulder, and the beast's screams grew even louder.

The constant whistle of the *chirrusk* changed pitch, and Cræosh winced as the wicked hook flashed past him, uncomfortably close. Katim twisted sharply, yanking on the chain, sinking the barbs deep into the yeti's flank. A quick gout of blood spurted—drenching Gork, who actually smiled at the sudden warmth—and then the troll hauled back on the weapon, dragging the staggering yeti toward her.

She dropped the chain to the snow and wrapped both fur-coated hands around the shaft of her axe. She stepped in and swung, even as Cræosh, sword held in a similar grip, did likewise. A metallic clang pealed across the arctic night as the two mighty weapons met in the middle of the yeti's throat. The great corpse toppled; the head took a moment longer, leaving a gory trail as it slid along the length of Cræosh's sword.

Katim nodded in the orc's direction as she bent to retrieve her *chirrusk*. Cræosh, puzzled, returned the gesture. It was *probably* just a sign of respect between warriors—at least, that's what it would have meant coming from another orc. But with trolls, who the hell knew?

Most of the squad was already tearing into the corpse, dividing and arguing over the best cuts of meat. Cræosh, however, moved some distance away from the roiling bedlam; there was something he had to do first, something he should have done the instant they'd arrived in the Steppes. Carefully, he dropped to his knees in the snow.

"Mighty Ancestors, long may your names be sung, we kneel on earth built upon your bones, supported by your deeds, to beseech your aid in the coming ordeal.

"Father, grant me your courage to face the foe. Mother, grant me your strength to strike him down. Ancestors, we pray only to be found worthy in your sight.

"Honor is victory. Victory is life. In your names alone, we strive."

Slowly, reverently, he rose, his spirits already lifted by the traditional prayer. Only then did he notice Katim, a few steps away, staring at him.

"What?" he asked belligerently.

"Foolishness," she rasped.

"Oh, yeah?" Cræosh's hand clenched on the haft of his blade. "You think the Ancestors are something to scoff at?"

"To attribute . . . your skill in battle . . . to others, that . . . is foolish. None but the living . . . may assist us in this . . . world. Still, you are . . . worthy." And with that enigmatic comment—and a revolting, equally enigmatic grin to go with it—Katim returned to the yeti.

"What," Cræosh asked the air around him, "was *that* about?"

He didn't expect the air to answer, of course, but it did. "You don't know much about trolls, do you?"

The orc scowled as Fezeill, still cloaked in the skin of a bugbear, appeared from the darkness. "Is *everyone* spying on me tonight?" he asked dangerously.

"Spying? Not at all, Cræosh. I was just keeping an eye on the most useful members of the squad. How would we have fared against that thing without you and Katim, hmm?"

Cræosh chose to let it pass. "What don't I know about trolls, then?"

"Ah, that. I've spent some time studying them, you see."

"Yeah, I'll bet. What's imitation the sincerest form of, again?"

But Fezeill shook his head. "Actually, we can't do trolls. I'm not certain why; something about the physiology, I think.

"Anyway, that's exactly why we make a habit of studying them. Anyone else, we can just walk among them unseen. But with the trolls . . ."

The orc nodded. "Know thy, umm, ally. So?"

"So the trolls do not worship their Ancestors, as your people do. Nor do they worship the Stars like the kobolds, or nebulous gods like the humans. They find such beliefs . . . Well, you heard it yourself."

"So what *do* they believe? And what did she mean by 'worthy'?"

Fezeill grinned—a tight, nasty expression that looked even worse on his current simian visage. "It means watch your back. Trolls believe that everyone they kill in this life serves them in the next. As will their victim's own servants, and theirs, and so on.

"*That*, my large friend, is why you can never fully trust a troll. They won't fight for anyone they don't respect, but the ultimate sign that a troll respects you is, inevitably, a heartfelt attempt to kill you, so that you may serve her after her own death. Something of a lose-lose proposition, wouldn't you say?"

Cræosh's mouth worked soundlessly. Finally, "I wish I could believe that you were fucking with me, Fezeill." He pondered for a moment. "How long do I have before she tries something?"

The faux bugbear shrugged. "Difficult to say. In your case, probably quite a while. Even trolls aren't so fanatical in their beliefs that they're liable to challenge King Morthûl's authority. She's been assigned to the squad, and for the time being, you're important to that squad. In fact, she'd probably risk her life protecting you, since she doesn't want anyone else claiming you first."

"Swell."

"But as soon as she decides you're no longer of immediate value . . ."

"I could try to take her now," Cræosh said. "Catch her before she's ready."

"She's a troll, Cræosh. She's *always* ready. Besides, you're safe for the time being. Why not wait and see if the tundra, or one of our future assignments, might not just do the deed for you?"

"I dunno, shapeshifter. I hate leaving a potential enemy at my back." Another moment, though, and the orc shook his head. "You're right, though. We need her, for now. Thanks for the tip, Fezeill. I owe you one."

Which, Cræosh mused as he strode over to join the others, *was probably the whole reason you told me.*

He found the subject of their discussion beside the yeti corpse, trying to lift the massive thing so she could get to the parts beneath. Impressive as her strength was, though, she didn't quite seem up to the task of lifting the gargantuan body.

"Allow me," he said, sliding up beside her. *Couldn't hurt to appear useful*, a small voice whispered in the back of his head. Brutally, Cræosh squashed it and put his hands on the thing's shoulders. "On three."

Between them, they had little difficulty in dragging the yeti to its feet, and once there, Katim was able to hold it upright under her own power. Cræosh moved around to the side and began stripping the flesh from a massive thigh with a hunting knife he kept in his pack. If they were to survive these four days, they needed all the meat they could—

"Hang on! I've got it!"

The missing gremlin came hurtling back out of the gloom, sword held point-first above his head, and leapt. He loosed another war cry as he hurtled through the air, and then slammed with a loud *thunk* into the dead yeti's chest. "I got it! I got it!"

Katim blinked once at the tip of the gremlin's sword that now protruded from the yeti's back. She reached down, picked up a small hunk of flesh she'd already sliced from the creature, and used it to slam the blade back through the corpse. A brief squeal came from the other side of the yeti as the gremlin fell, back first, into the snow.

"Did I get it?" Gimmol called out, lying where he had fallen. "Is it dead?"

"Oh, yes. It . . . is dead." Katim answered. "See?" And with that, she let the ponderous carcass topple forward. A second, much louder squeal was quickly drowned out by the earthshaking impact.

Cræosh looked up at her from where he'd been kneeling. "Was that strictly necessary?"

"No," Katim admitted.

He nodded. "Shitload of fun, though, huh?"

She smiled. "Yes." Then, "Why is he . . . even here?"

"You mean assigned to a Demon Squad? The best of the best?" The orc shrugged. "Maybe King Morthûl or General Falchion made a mistake."

"Ah. I look forward to . . . seeing what happens when you . . . tell them that."

They continued carving, scarcely even acknowledging the battered gremlin as he tunneled from the snow a few feet away.

"That hurt!" he whined at them.

"Doesn't it, though?" Gork asked as he sauntered past, a steaming hunk of liver in his fist. "There's a way to make it hurt less."

"Oh?" Gimmol asked pathetically.

"Yeah. Get out of the way." And then, chewing noisily, the kobold returned to his makeshift shelter. After another half hour or so of slicing and storing, the others did the same. Fezeill remained on watch, staring intently at the once-more empty tundra around them.

Whether it was sheer luck, the Stars, the Ancestors, or something else entirely, nothing further disturbed their sleep for the remainder of the night. Nor did much of note occur during the following day, either. The squad marched, and chewed upon various portions of half-frozen yeti, and marched some more, and squabbled among themselves, and marched again. The mountains had drawn notably closer as the afternoon slowly aged toward evening, but that was the only sign that the group had moved more than a few yards from their previous campground.

That all changed about an hour before sunset. Cræosh had just become thoroughly convinced that they were the only living things anywhere on this Ancestors-forsaken field of ice (the intermittent yeti notwithstanding) when Katim reappeared atop the next dune. The resounding crunch of her boots sinking deep into the snow as she approached was a tolling bell of ill omen to the orc's ears. If the troll was returning, rather than hunkering down and waiting, it meant she had found something worth reporting—and Cræosh was too cynical to even contemplate the possibility that it might be benign.

"What is it?" he asked before she'd even come to a complete stop. "What've you found?"

"A hut."

"A what now?"

The troll shrugged. "It seemed . . . rather strange to me . . . too. But see . . . for yourself."

The squad followed, retracing Katim's deep footprints, and sure enough, there it stood. It was a small structure of wooden planks, the sort that would have appeared fully at home in the center of any village—but it was here, plunked blithely down in the frozen wastelands of the Steppes. A cheery glow radiated through its windows, and a drunken serpent of smoke coiled from the brick chimney. There was even what might well have been a wind chime hanging before the door.

"This," Cræosh said, "is not making a whole hell of a lot of sense."

The others, perhaps awed at the orc's powers of observation, remained mute.

"So what now?" Gimmol asked from behind.

"We could go knock at the door, I suppose," Gork replied. "I'm sure whoever's there would love to see us. Probably has six extra places set for tea."

"Sneak in," was the doppelganger's suggestion. "Kill whoever's in there and take what we need."

"I'm leaning toward going straight through the door, myself," Cræosh told them. "That oughta catch anybody inside off guard."

"Have any of you . . . astounding idiots considered the . . . possibility that this might . . . be some sort of trap?"

Silence reigned as the members of the squad looked abashedly at one another, each silently accusing the others of not having thought of it first. Finally, however, a disgusted look settled over Cræosh's features.

"Trap for *whom*, exactly? How many people even know that we're way the fuck out here? And of those, how many give enough of a shit to want us dead?"

"Actually," Gork said helpfully, "it doesn't have to be a trap for *us* specifically. Maybe someone—"

But the orc, offering a single disdainful grunt, whirled away and stormed down the rise, bearing straight for the mysterious cabin. Jhurpess, Gimmol—and, after a moment of obvious reluctance—Gork all fell in behind, leaving only the doppelganger and the troll atop the dune.

"Where," Fezeill asked his bestial companion, "does one draw the line between bravery and stupidity?"

Katim smiled, revealing her shifting teeth. "Perhaps . . . one should draw it at the idea . . . of standing alone with a troll . . . after the comments you made . . . to the orc last night."

The false bugbear paled beneath his fur. "You heard that?"

"Trolls have . . . very good ears."

"Oh." A pause. "You know, the others might need us. I think we really should catch up before they wander in there."

"I thought you . . . might."

As they approached, a chorus of splintering wood suggested that Cræosh had not deigned to wait for their arrival. Fezeill drew near enough to the hut to see Gork disappear through the now-vacant door frame. With an exasperated sigh, the shapeshifter put on a burst of speed.

"Real subtle, Cræosh," Gork snapped as he entered. "That entry would do a rutting rhinoceros proud. What the hell did you think you were doing?"

The orc shrugged. "Picking the lock."

"Picking—*what*?"

"Yeah. Picking the lock. You see it, lying over there on the floor?"

"What's left of it, yes."

"Well, *pick* it up."

Gork wandered off in disgust as the two tardy members of the team finally made their entrance.

Cræosh barely glanced as the doppelganger and the troll joined them in the mysterious little structure. He was too busy examining his surroundings and finding himself vaguely repulsed.

The place couldn't have been more homey, in the most sugarcoated, clichéd sense, if it had been ripped from a human or elven bedtime story. The hut—more of a cottage, really—consisted of a single large space, separated into living room and kitchen only by a hanging curtain. Two small bookcases adorned the main chamber, each containing perhaps half a dozen large tomes. A sleeping cot stood between them, a small heap of blankets piled at the foot. Cursory examination of the kitchen revealed a marble-top counter and a larder well stocked with spices and garnishes, but little in the way of food. A small table, lightly stained with the rings of many a wet mug, sat in a niche beside the door. It was surrounded by six chairs that somehow looked comfortable despite rickety backs and tattered cushions. A trio of larger chairs, plush and well used, sat facing the cheerful fire that crackled away in the fireplace. . . .

Cræosh froze, cursing himself for not making the connection sooner. His senses screamed at him; his hand squeezed the leather of his sword hilt until it creaked.

Jhurpess, smiling contentedly, was muttering something about firewood as he methodically demolished several of the rickety chairs. Gimmol was sniffing each and every one of the spices, a strangely blissful expression on his face, and Fezeill was studying the volumes that lay on the shelves, though his disdainful snort suggested that he'd found nothing of interest.

Gork, however, was methodically checking the walls for hidden surprises, tapping and prodding at the wood, and Katim stood in the center of the room, shoulders hunched, idly fingering the shaft of her axe.

Cræosh gestured quickly to Gork when next the kobold glanced his way, and once the small creature had joined him, they both moved to stand beside the troll.

"You noticed it too," Cræosh began without preamble.

Katim nodded. "Something is . . . very wrong. I told you . . . we should not have . . . come here."

The orc nodded. "You might've had a point after all," he admitted. Then, "What about you, Shorty? You find anything?"

Gork scowled slightly at the—*ahem*, diminutive—but clearly decided that now was scarcely the time to object. "Not a thing," he replied, his small snout curled in frustration. "Not that I expected much. The walls are really too thin to be hiding much of anything. Still, this whole place worries me." He glanced over his shoulder. "I'll tell you, I'm *really* bothered by that fire."

Cræosh and Katim nodded in unison. "It took me a minute, too," the orc said. "Hell, it's such a natural part of the setting, you really don't even register it." As evidence, he gestured toward their other companions, obliviously going about their little tasks. "But if the fire's still burning . . ."

"How long until they come back, do you suppose?" the kobold asked.

Katim shrugged. "Could be minutes . . . or hours. There's no . . . real way of knowing."

"But it means we can't waste any more of our time," Cræosh added. "Okay, *listen the fuck up*!"

The other squad members straightened as though whipped, and the only sound in the room besides the crackling fire was the reverberating thud of one of Jhurpess's chair legs hitting the floor.

"For those of you who obviously shit their brains out with yesterday's breakfast," he said, glossing over the fact that it had taken him some minutes to make the same deduction, "we can expect company before too long."

At the puzzled expressions on the faces of both Jhurpess and Gimmol—although Fezeill looked more embarrassed than anything else—Cræosh added, "The fire's still burning, geniuses."

The final pair stared as one at the dancing flames.

"Now," Cræosh said, "you could all keep running around the place like your heads are on fire and your asses are catching, but it's not going to accomplish more than a little extra exercise.

"*Or* we can shape up, get into something resembling proper military procedure, and search this place from tail to tongue-tip. If there's so much as a termite in the rafters, I want to know exactly where he is, how long he's lived there, and if his daughters are cute. Move!"

The astounding thing was, they actually *did* work out an efficient system. Katim, who could easily reach heights that the others couldn't, took it upon herself to check the ceiling and the uppermost shelves. Cræosh, Fezeill, and (after a great deal of wasted explanation) Jhurpess began moving furniture, searching behind and under things. Gimmol sifted through the books, looking for items hidden within. And Gork . . .

Unlike everyone else, Gork lingered in the center of the room, head tilted to one side as though lost in thought. Finally, after several minutes—and just as Cræosh was about to yell something *really* obscene—Gork bent, lifted something off the floor with both hands, and walked over to Jhurpess.

"Here you go," he said, handing the bugbear the fallen chair leg.

The simian blinked. "Oh. Jhurpess thanks you."

"Don't thank me. I want you to drop it again. From the same height as before."

Another blink. "What?"

Gork sighed. "Stand up straight," he said slowly, "and drop it."

By now, the odd conversation had attracted some attention, and the others had all wandered over to see what, exactly, the little kobold had in mind.

Now utterly confused, Jhurpess dropped the chair leg. This time, most of the squad finally noticed what Gork had picked up on the first time.

"Hollow," Katim's voice rumbled at them.

"Sounds like it to me," Cræosh agreed. "Nice thinking, Shorty."

Grumble, grumble, *Shorty my stony ass*, "Thank you," grumble, grumble, *big hulking gorilla*, grumble . . .

"All right kits and cubs," Cræosh thundered. "Check the floor!"

And check they did, to the best of their individual abilities. Gork and Fezeill went back over the walls, the bookcases, anywhere the architect could have constructed a hidden lever or catch. Katim continued her search of the ceiling. But Gimmol simply stood in the center of the hut looking helpless, and Jhurpess—for whom "subtlety" meant "switch to a smaller club"—had simply begun tearing wooden planks off the floor. Cræosh stood by the door, hands crossed over his chest, supervising (by his definition) or just standing around uselessly (by everybody else's).

And of course, it was Jhurpess and his destructive urges who finally found the hidden chamber. The bugbear had just broken through into a large open space and was about to say something about it when, with a sudden splintering sound that *almost* drowned out his startled scream, the damaged floor around him gave way completely.

Cræosh blinked once as his hairy companion vanished from sight. In no great hurry, he turned to face the others, who were all staring at the jagged aperture.

"Tell me again," he asked, "why he's here?"

Gork shrugged his small shoulders. "Well, he *did* find the room. . . ."

Slowly, making absolutely certain to check the strength of the jagged wood, Cræosh and the others crawled forward and peered into the newly uncovered chamber.

"Jhurpess?" the orc called out. "You okay?"

"Jhurpess not happy!" came the response.

"No shit! Jhurpess not *supposed* to be happy! Jhurpess just went through the floor!"

Gimmol reached over and tugged on Fezeill's arm. "Is that sort of speech contagious?" he asked. "I'd hate to start talking that way."

"Don't worry," the doppelganger told him. "If you do, I promise I'll kill you quickly."

The gremlin shut up.

Cræosh tossed them a brief glare, but his attention remained primarily on the hole. "Are you hurt badly?"

There was a momentary pause. Then, "Jhurpess in pain. But not too bad, Jhurpess thinks." Another pause. "Cræosh didn't mean for Jhurpess to fall into hole, did Cræosh? Jhurpess was only supposed to *find* room."

Brilliant. "That was the plan, Nature-boy. Looks like it sort of fell through, though." Then, sensing the troll hauling back an arm in preparation to pound him something fierce, he quickly added, "Jhurpess, can you see any stairs or a ladder? Or any other way down?"

"Jhurpess can't see anything. Jhurpess lying in the dark."

Gork cleared his throat. "If I may?" The others watched as the kobold latched his claws into the thick wood and lowered himself headfirst. For a moment he just hung, sort of an irritable chandelier, and waited for his vision to adjust. Then, finally, "Yeah, there it is. Thick wooden ladder, plain as day. It's about—oh, ten feet to my left."

Several heads swiveled in that direction. "The fireplace," Fezeill muttered.

Cræosh nodded. "Obvious as a mama halfling's tits. Wonder why I didn't think of it?"

"Maybe," Katim rasped at him, "it's because . . . you aren't remotely as smart . . . as you think you are."

"And what, exactly, is that supposed to mean?"

The troll's snout wrinkled in an obvious parody of confusion. "Why are you . . . asking me? I'm . . . not supposed to be . . . the smart one."

"I hate to interrupt this little spat," Fezeill interjected, "but if I may remind the both of you . . . ?"

Cræosh nodded. "Right. Katim, you wanna go douse the fire?"

The troll paused a moment longer, and then, with a shift of posture that could only be described as a mental shrug, she strode to the brick fireplace. A brief examination, and then she simply lifted the large iron cauldron that sat beside the hearth and upended it onto the flames. They swiftly sputtered and died, and the temperature in the cottage fell rapidly. Curiosity writ across his bugbear face, the doppelganger wandered over to examine the area beneath the charred logs.

"Good," Cræosh acknowledged, and then redirected his gaze back toward the kobold legs protruding from the pit. "Hey, Shorty!"

Grumble. "Yes, oh ponderous one?"

"Can you see the catch from where you are?"

"Hold on . . . Okay, I see it. It's a primitive lock, really. Hatchling's play. Shouldn't take me—"

There was a sudden click.

"—or Fezeill," he continued, his tone chilly as the frosted windows, "more than a few seconds." He hauled himself back up to the floor. "You might want to let the shifter go first," he informed the others. "In case the ladder's rigged."

Fezeill smiled a tight little smile and proceeded through the hatch that had been hidden beneath the logs.

His safe trip to the cold dirt below proved that the ladder was not, in fact, rigged or trapped as Gork had feared (hoped?). The others followed, and though the rungs creaked alarmingly beneath Cræosh's weight, the entire squad managed the descent intact. Gork, his footing sure even in the murk, made his way to the fallen bugbear and retrieved several of the chair legs that had set the whole chain of events in motion. He brought them straight back to Cræosh, who, after a few false starts with flint and steel and a bit of oil, finally transformed one into a makeshift torch. The others looked around, at last able to see what, until now, only the kobold's superior night vision had discerned.

A pair of tables lurked in a far corner of the chamber, as distant from the ladder as the walls would permit. Both were draped with sheets, and it didn't take sight like Gork's or Katim's to note that something lay beneath each of those makeshift covers.

As the squad shuffled nearer, other details made themselves evident. The wall beside the tables held a large wooden rack, and upon that rack sat tools so twisted that even Cræosh shuddered to think what they might be for. Serrated saws and needle-tipped probes, curled lengths of wire and jagged pliers—and, perhaps most disturbing of all, a few simple knives and scalpels stored beside several lengths of tubing and a sewing kit.

"I would love . . . to meet the owner of . . . this hut," Katim whispered—although, given the limited range of her voice, her whispers really weren't all that different from her normal speech.

Cræosh found himself rather disturbed at the gleam in her eyes as she studied the implements.

But while the troll might have been fascinated, the others, even the normally unflappable doppelganger, found themselves ever more anxious to leave. Still . . .

"What," Gimmol asked, his voice far from steady, "do you suppose is under the sheets?"

Cræosh winced, though none of the others were in a position to see it. He had just about decided to simply pick up the bugbear—who lay sniveling in the corner, and should probably have been their first priority—and get the fuck out. But the damn gremlin had gone and asked the question aloud, and now the orc's pride wouldn't allow him to leave without checking.

Making a mental note to beat the snot out of Gimmol at the first opportunity, Cræosh plastered a confident smirk across his face. "Well, let's find out, shall we?" Then, before any of his more reluctant allies could even think about stopping him, he grabbed one sheet in each meaty fist and yanked.

The stench shambled across the intervening distance and embraced them all like long-lost relatives. Cræosh choked, Gimmol deposited his breakfast all over the floor with a revolting splatter—the effects of which actually *improved* the room's bouquet—and even the troll gagged. It was impossible that they hadn't noticed the foul, rotting odor before, impossible that the sheets could have smothered such a potent reek. Nevertheless, it had been completely hidden from even the troll's senses—an unnatural phenomenon that did nothing to improve either their confidence or their nausea.

One arm held defensively across his face, as though the stench might be warded off through determination and brute strength, Cræosh leaned over the leftmost table.

Why the fuck didn't I listen to Katim and stay the hell away from this hut?

Each table held a single corpse, face twisted in the throes of agony even Cræosh had never seen. One was an elf: young, not quite an adult, with chestnut hair and a road map of scars along his slender arms. Most goblins found elves hideous enough to begin with, but something about this one—his color, perhaps, or the vaguely puffy quality to his flesh—made him even worse. The other was a doppelganger, and if they had thought Fezeill's true form ugly, this one, with its shallow wounds and sunken features, was absolutely nauseating.

But while the wounds inflicted upon each were obviously painful, what pushed this beyond the pale as far as Cræosh was concerned was the tubing. Someone had connected the elf and the doppelganger with a series of hoses, running through a sequence of bellows and pumps. And suddenly the bloated, sickly skin of the elf, and the sunken, shriveled flesh of the doppelganger, made a sort of horrid sense.

It wasn't the torture itself that disturbed the orc to the core of his being—hell, he didn't know the doppelganger, and as far as the elf was concerned, he only wished he'd been here to listen to the screams. It was the thought of the twisted, cold-blooded mind that could have devised such a setup that worried him. Cræosh didn't think it probable that such a person would take kindly to trespassers, and he had absolutely no desire to find himself strapped to a table and sharing bodily fluids with Katim or Fezeill.

"Katim," he said hoarsely, "grab Jhurpess." Immediately, the troll's long strides carried her to the bugbear, whom she casually lifted to his feet with one hand. She did not, Cræosh couldn't help but note, take the time to berate him for ordering her about. It seemed that even Katim didn't care to stay any longer.

But Cræosh himself, despite his misgivings, remained morbidly fascinated by the tableau. Without conscious thought, he found himself reaching toward the elf. He wasn't certain what he intended to accomplish; perhaps nothing more than confirming, for his own sake, the reality of the twisted torture. The others fell into a deathly hush, their attentions fixed on the orc's fingers as they drew closer, closer . . .

The elf's hand twitched.

Five screams echoed from the underground chamber. Only Katim remained silent, though her grip on the bugbear had tightened so much that he might've been wailing in as much pain as terror. Those shrieks were swiftly followed by the sound of the world's smallest stampede as Gork, Gimmol, and Fezeill dashed for the ladder. Jhurpess would have joined them, had the troll not held him with an iron fist.

Cræosh had retreated from the table—but he, like Katim, was unwilling to leave this *thing* at their backs. He gestured shallowly at the troll and received a nod in return. Katim casually shoved the bugbear behind her and drew her terrible axe. Cræosh hefted his own weapon, and the pair of them moved to either side of the table.

And then Gork, whose vantage halfway up the ladder offered a view unavailable to the others, burst out laughing.

Attention torn between the abomination on the table and their obviously insane ally, the orc and the troll tried hard to watch both directions at once. The hysterical kobold was clearly having trouble breathing, and his sides heaved so hard that he would have fallen had not Fezeill—who was directly beneath him and most certainly did not want a kobold landing on his head—reached up with a lanky bugbear arm to steady his small companion.

Trying to keep watch on the sort-of-dead elf, Cræosh stepped nearer the creaking, overcrowded ladder. "And just what the fuck is so amusing about this?"

The kobold broke into all-new hysterics. But this time, he retained sufficient strength and presence of mind to point.

Katim and the orc both followed his shaking finger back to the elf's hand. The hand that had moved, despite all sense and all natural laws. The hand . . .

The hand that had a damned *stick* attached to it!

Cræosh roared with fury as he finally spotted the little wooden shaft—not much more than a sturdy twig—protruding through a tiny hole in the table and into the corpse's wrist. Still bellowing, the orc ripped the table from the floor and heaved it bodily over his shoulder. The crack of the wood was accompanied, in an almost musical harmony, by the fainter shattering of glass. Curious, Katim knelt beside the wreckage, inspecting the shards as they glittered, reflecting the flickering torchlight.

"Eep! Irp? Bedabedat! Biroo . . ."

"*What the . . . !*" Cræosh recoiled from another sudden burst of movement, then peered up at the ceiling, trying for a clearer glimpse of the gibbering creature that had just shot past him. It was tiny, he'd seen that much; shorter even than their diminutive Sergeant Shreckt. It too had wings, but they were clearly feathered, not leathery like the imp's, and the face was a great deal flatter. The high-pitched nonsense it had spouted as it passed resembled no language the orc was familiar with.

"Abroo! Bedara bruk!"

Cræosh scowled, though his blazing fury was rapidly ebbing into a simmering frustration. "Hey, Nature-boy! You feeling better?"

"Jhurpess hurt," came the response from atop the ladder. "But Jhurpess all right."

"Good. You feel up to using that bow?"

A moment later, the top half of the bugbear appeared, hanging from the edge of the fireplace hatch. "What Jhurpess supposed to shoot?"

"That!" The orc pointed his weighty sword at the creature, now firmly perched on one of the rafters.

"Eroo?" the strange little thing asked.

Jhurpess drew back the bowstring and let fly. The arrow sped across the room—and with a speed Cræosh would never have believed had he not witnessed it firsthand, Katim's *chirrusk* arced up and intercepted the missile.

The orc found himself struck nearly dumb. Nothing could have moved that fast! He wondered, with a sinking sensation in his gut, if he shouldn't have taken his own advice and tried to kill the troll when he had the chance.

But he wasn't about to let her *see* his worry. "What the fuck's with you?" he ranted, fists clenched. "Why'd you do that?"

"Because we . . . do not want to kill . . . the creature. It is . . . not a threat."

Cræosh blinked. "I thought trolls didn't take prisoners. I thought you didn't believe in mercy."

"We do not. But . . . this is not an enemy. It . . . is nothing more than an . . . animal. And I am . . . curious about it."

"Bejaba geroo! Urr urrup!"

"Pretty damn talkative for an animal, isn't it?" Cræosh said sullenly. But Katim would not be budged, and Cræosh was unwilling to force the issue.

"How come we didn't see it when we came in?" Gimmol asked, unable to look away from the corpses, perhaps still expecting them to leap up and eat him. "I mean, it's small, but there's not a whole lot of room to hide under those tables."

Cræosh directed his gaze, half questioning and half mocking, back at the troll. "Well? You're its new best friend. Why don't you tell us how chicken-dick managed to hide from us?"

"Rucha wamma burr!"

"Yeah, you heard me! Chicken-dick!"

Katim actually sighed. "Here." She handed the startled orc a small shard of glass.

"Oh." And then, "What the fuck's it mean?"

"It means . . . that there was a mirror . . . underneath the table. In . . . such poor lighting . . . it reflected the shadows . . . and made it appear that the space . . . was empty."

"Uh-huh. And that kind of premeditation—to say nothing of the fact that it was smart enough to puppeteer a damn *corpse*—doesn't make you think that, just maybe, the little shit's more than some dumb animal?"

"The 'little shit' could . . . not have moved the glass . . . by itself. If this *was* . . . premeditated, it was arranged . . . by someone else."

"Which reminds me," Cræosh told her, abruptly switching track. "Weren't we about on our way out?"

The ladder creaked even more loudly on their way up, apparently weakened by their combined weight (and undignified panic), but it held. When Katim finally clambered out onto the floor of the main room, Cræosh already had the others lined up in a vague formation and approaching the door.

The tiny winged creature shot from the massive hole, jabbering at them, clearly agitated about something.

"You sure you don't wanna kill the little fucker?" Cræosh asked.

Katim just looked at him.

"You suppose the owner's liable to be upset about Jhurpess ripping apart his chair?" Gimmol asked nervously.

"Oh, sure," Gork muttered. "He won't care in the slightest about the six-foot hole in his floor, but don't fuck with his chair. Tell me something, Gimmol, are your people always this swift, or are you a prodigy?"

"And just what," the gremlin asked, his face twisted in a scowl as fierce as he could produce, "is that supposed to mean?"

"It means that if you're representative of your people, I'm astounded that you exist at all! It's amazing to me that your species has the brainpower to remember how to breed!"

Hollering, Gimmol hurled himself at the kobold. The diminutive pair hit the ground and rolled, tiny fists flying like hailstones. The rest of the squad swiftly gathered; Gork and Gimmol would have been mortified had they seen the amusement plastered across their companions' faces.

Cræosh watched for a couple of minutes, until the whole thing stopped being funny. Then, growing bored of the spectacle and remembering that they were supposed to be fleeing the cottage, he grabbed a combatant's collar in each fist. He rose, dangling Gork and Gimmol like a pair of dejected kittens.

"Either put 'em back in your pants," he said, "or fuck and get it over with."

Despite their precarious positions, both pint-size soldiers managed to swivel toward the orc and give him a withering look of disgust.

"All right, then. Kill each other later. Right now, we're withdrawing."

"Don't you mean running away?" Fezeill asked from behind.

"Nah. Marching calmly is a withdrawal. Usually, if I'm running away, my hands are waving in the air and I'm screaming a lot." He paused. "Or is that sex? It's been so damn long, I can barely remember. . . ."

Katim grimaced and headed toward the door—or rather, the empty doorframe. She had gotten to within a yard or so of the entryway, in fact, when her egress was suddenly blocked.

"Umm . . . Cræosh?"

"Last time was back home in Tarahk Trohm," the orc was telling the largely uninterested—and somewhat disgusted—doppelganger. "Lovely shit-brown cutey, she was. . . ."

"Cræosh!" Katim called, somewhat more forcefully.

". . . Name of Mesharral, I think. . . ."

"*Orc!!*"

"What?! I—oh." Steel hissed against leather as his massive sword slid free of its sheath. Similar sounds followed as the entire squad drew steel, staring intently at the figure in the doorway.

He was markedly shorter than Cræosh, and slender as a reed. A dull gray cloak wrapped most of his body, and his features hid within the depths of his hood.

"I'm going to venture a guess, here," the stranger said in slightly accented Gremlin—which, of all the goblin languages, was most pronounceable to outsiders and served as something of a common trade tongue. His voice somehow conveyed the impression of song, even though his tone was neutral, even flat. "A boulder, obviously well traveled, came bounding across the tundra, crashed through my front door, and left this rather unattractive hole in my floor. Meanwhile, you good samaritans, concerned that there might be some poor unfortunates injured by said boulder, came racing in here to see if you could help. And now, upon realizing that there is little you can do, you were preparing to sneak back out into the snows, unrecognized and unthanked for your courage and generosity."

"How about that?" Cræosh asked. "He got it in one try! Can't put anything past you, can we? Well, since, as you were so good to point out, there's not much else we can do here, I suppose we'll just be on our way. Sorry about, um, the boulder and all. Squad, move—"

The new arrival held up a hand. "I think not."

Cræosh scowled. "You want to try to stop us? Are you stupid or just—no, you'd really have to be stupid."

The cowled figure snapped his fingers. With a resounding whine of old hinges, the hatch beneath the fireplace slammed itself shut. The crackling of wood, a sudden loud roar, and the flames were once again blazing away in the hearth, as large and as vivid as if they'd never been extinguished.

Jhurpess whimpered. Gork ducked for cover behind Cræosh. Gimmol appeared on the verge of passing out completely, and even Katim blinked nervously once or twice.

"Of course," the orc continued, "you could also be a wizard."

Though they couldn't see his face for the shadow of the hood, they were all quite positive the stranger smiled. "I could, at that."

"You fry us, mage, and you're gonna lose a good portion of your hut, too."

"There *are* other ways to kill you, orc. But the truth is, I don't want you dead. Sit, please."

There was a great deal of muttering, of reluctance, of suspicious glances in all directions; but what there was *not* was a whole lot of any real choice. The Demon Squad could do what the stranger asked, or they could fight their way past, and while Cræosh was pretty sure they'd come out on top, he was equally certain that not all of them would survive the attempt. No need to risk it. Yet.

Of course, after the bugbear's earlier rampage, the hut was now somewhat deficient in the chair department. Fezeill and Gimmol settled into the two plush chairs by the fire, leaving the surviving wooden seats for Gork and Jhurpess. Katim and Cræosh stood, she in the center of the room, he beside the gremlin's chair.

"Okay," he growled at the owner of the strange little hovel, "I'm as relaxed as I get without alcohol and nudity. So who the fuck are you, and what do you want?"

The figure pulled back his hood in reply. Dark tresses framed a slender face, sharp-featured and clean-shaven—and a pair of upswept, pointed ears.

"*Elf!*" Cræosh hissed, his body tensing. Fezeill, Gork, and Jhurpess were on their feet, ready to kill the foul, hideous creature.

Katim's *chirrusk* dangled from one hairy fist, but even as she moved to lunge, she drew to a halt, blinking.

"Are you not . . . kind of short for an elf?"

Cræosh scowled, though the troll's sudden reluctance was enough to stay his hand as well. "So he's a midget. What's the problem? Just means I'll have to bend over to yank out his entrails."

But now Gork, too, had picked up on it. "No, she's right!" he called out, as desperate to avoid this fight as he had been, just a moment ago, to start it. "Look at his eyes!"

The orc sucked in his breath. Every elf he'd ever encountered—every elf he'd ever *heard* of—had irises of woodland hue: greens, reds, and golds, for the most part. These eyes, larger than those of any elf he'd ever seen, had a reflective tint of deepest violet.

"But they're just myths!" Cræosh protested, his gaze darting from Gork to the strange elf. "Stories, wishful thinking maybe. They don't exist!"

"We don't?" the elf asked, his voice suddenly concerned. "Then what am I doing here?"

"No need to get sarcastic," the orc huffed.

"No," Fezeill added, gesturing at Cræosh, "that's *his* job."

Cræosh scowled at them both—then at everyone else, just because.

"We've run into them from time to time," Gork told them, his voice unusually subdued. "Kobolds, I mean. Nobody I know personally ever actually met one, though."

"'One'? Really now, kobold, is it so difficult to say it?"

"Dakórren," Gork finally muttered. "Dark elves."

The stranger made a face at that. "You've been cavorting with the eilurren, haven't you?"

"Eilurren?" Cræosh asked softly.

"Elves," Gork said. "That is, uh, 'light' elves. The normal ones."

The "nonnormal" elf was still going on. ". . . but I mean, really! 'Dark elves'? Don't you find that a little melodramatic? You've got humans fighting alongside you in the Charnel King's armies, but you don't hear anyone calling them 'dark men,' do you?"

"Jhurpess doesn't do *anything* with elves!" the bugbear protested once he could jam a word in edgewise. "And what 'cavorting'?"

"Meeting, playing with, socializing!" Cræosh snapped. "Generally being friendly! Which is why you have no idea what it means!"

Jhurpess began to pout. Cræosh ignored him.

"Fine, so you're dark elf, or dakórren, or whatever. That means exactly what to me?"

"So hostile, friend orc? We are not enemies."

"Legend says that you pseudo-faeries are one of the few races King Morthûl approached who refused to join his armies. If you actually exist, I see no reason to doubt that part of the story. So who's to say we *aren't* enemies, you pointy-eared bug-fucker?"

Katim rolled her eyes at the ceiling. "I see that . . . diplomacy is one of your . . . strong suits."

"What's wrong with pointy ears?" Gimmol whined at the same time.

Only the elf, it seemed, did not react adversely to the orc's comment. He smiled, a white, even-toothed smile. "You're alive, orc. Surely, that alone demonstrates my goodwill."

"Or your cowardice."

The smile slipped just a bit. "I could have stood outside and killed you through the open door before you even knew I existed."

"Don't think so, pixie. We're Demon Squad! We're ready for anyth*aaaarrgh*!!!" Cræosh flailed his arms, trying to catch the strange little creature who had dived from nowhere and plucked a tuft of hair from the orc's head.

"Rooo. Delaba wur! Ekee ekee!"

"Yes, I can see that," the elf said gently to the creature as it landed, quivering, on his shoulder. "Quite brave of you."

Cræosh shifted his near-perpetual scowl from the elf to the thing that had joined him. "You understand the little shit?"

"Oh, yes. Quite well." The elf's expression turned downright nasty. "Had your trollish ally not stopped you from harming him after his little game, you would have found my reception somewhat less cordial." And then, once again, the newcomer was all smiles, casually scratching the strange little beast—which was *purring*—under the chin.

"Did you know?" Cræosh demanded of the troll.

"Under the . . . circumstances, I felt the creature could . . . very well have been a . . . wizard's familiar. I thought it . . . safer to be sure."

"You coulda said something, instead of spouting all that 'Oh, it's just a pwecious wittle animal' horseshit."

"Why? I wasn't . . . sure one way or . . . the other. Look," she said, placing herself between the orc and the elf. "You told us . . . that you want something . . . from us?"

The wizard raised an eyebrow. "Did I?"

With a sideways glance that spoke volumes, Cræosh elbowed past the troll so he was once again standing at the fore. "Well, you said you didn't want us dead. For my money, they mean the same thing."

"Indeed." The elf snapped his fingers once again and then proceeded to sit comfortably in the large plush chair that hadn't been beneath him but a moment before. A sudden thump sounded behind them, followed by a brief whine as Gimmol's ass hit the floor. "Very well. My name is Nurien Ebonwind." He paused there, in case any of his "guests" wished to introduce themselves in turn.

"Ebonwind?" Cræosh sniggered. "Yeah, he's an elf all right. You have a brother named Twinklefart by any chance?" Gork stuck his snout in his hands and giggled.

Ebonwind sighed. "Forget it. Anyway, I find myself with something of a problem, and I believe you good folks can assist me with it. As I'm sure you can imagine, considering how much hatred there is between my own race and the other elves, it behooves us to keep as close a watch on their activities as possible."

"What 'behooves' mean?" Jhurpess asked. Cræosh smacked him.

"Unfortunately, the elves have grown adept at thwarting our spies. In the recent past, they have begun sniffing out our agents and intercepting our scrying magics with relative ease."

"How recent?" Katim asked.

"Oh, a thousand years, plus or minus."

Six pairs of eyes stared at him.

"Okay," Cræosh said, his fingers casually, perhaps even unconsciously, poking small holes in the back of Fezeill's chair. As he spoke, the orc constantly pulled the stuffing from within the cushions and shredded it, leaving a growing mess on the floor. "You got a problem. I sympathize, I feel for you, and all that rot. What the fuck do we do about it? And why do we bother?"

Ebonwind shook his head. "Patience is not one of your virtues, is it?"

"I try to make it a point not to have virtues. They itch."

"Of course. Very well, then. As you are doubtless aware, King Dororam of Shauntille is gathering the Allied Kingdoms to attack Kirol Syrreth once the winter snows have passed."

The squad members exchanged sharp glances. Sure, they'd heard the rumors, and most of them had assumed that that was why they were being assembled as a Demon Squad in the first place. Still, confirmation from an outside source was unsettling.

"I see that you have. Good. The elven nations, though not normally known for fraternizing with the humans—it means the same as cavorting, bugbear—*do* consider themselves to be one of the Allied Kingdoms. They are assembling their armies alongside the others, preparing to march."

Comprehension dawned like a summer's day. "And that," Cræosh finished, "makes them easier to keep track of."

"Exactly."

"So I ask again, what do you need us for? Even Gimmol here couldn't lose an entire army!"

"Why, thank you, Cræosh. I—hey, wait a minute . . ."

"True enough," the elf continued, ignoring the protesting gremlin. "But keeping track of what the elves are doing isn't enough. We need to know what they *will* be doing, before it happens. Once the elves have massed, they may decide to turn some of their might against *us*, should the fortunes of war permit. Or their absence from their homes could provide us with opportunities of our own. In either case, we must be ready. That's where you could be of great help, my friends."

Fezeill snickered. "I'm afraid I can't turn myself into an oracle, Ebonwind. And most of this so-called squad couldn't predict the number after seven."

He seemed oblivious to the various hostile stares that came his way—as well as to the sounds of the bugbear quietly muttering, "Five, six . . ."

"But you don't have to see the future," Ebonwind told them. "After all, what is it more than anything else that determines the movements of an army?"

Katim hissed, a liquid sound even less healthy than her normal rasping breath. "The movements . . . of the enemy."

The elf smiled, satisfied. "Precisely."

Cræosh actually laughed aloud, unable to believe what he was hearing. "You want us to spy on *Morthûl* for you? Report the movement of our own armies? I was wrong; you're not stupid. You're downright insane!"

Ebonwind tapped one finger against his cheek. "Are you so certain that I couldn't make it worth your while?"

"Worth? Pixie, you could hand me the entire fucking world on a platter, served hot with a nice side of cabbage and dwarf stew, and it wouldn't even come close to being worth it!"

"And are you objecting out of loyalty, Cræosh? Or fear of what might befall you if you accept?"

"Ain't any difference."

"I see." Ebonwind shook his head. "And the rest of you?"

"For once, the orc . . . and I are in perfect . . . agreement."

The rest of the squad nodded.

"Commendable, of course." The elf grinned once more. "And also unnecessary. I'm not seeking any classified information, just a slight advance on what the entire world would learn in two or three days anyway. That would give my people sufficient leeway to institute certain operations of our own against the eilurren—the 'normal' elves—with little chance of discovery. Actually, considering that the elves are a major part of Dororam's forces, it would be to your advantage to help us out. It would almost be bringing the dakórren into the war on your side. You could be heroes."

"And that's all?" Fezeill asked. "Just troop movements, nothing more?"

"That's all."

"And who's to say you wouldn't just pass that information along to Dororam?"

Ebonwind actually managed to look insulted. "What do I look like to you? Why would I possibly want to do that?"

Cræosh, however, was frowning. "I dunno, pixie. It still sounds treasonous to me."

"You aren't seeing the big picture, Cræosh! It's only treason if it brings harm to your nation. This . . . Why, this could be just the edge you need to ensure victory over Dororam's forces!"

That was a mistake. The orc's gaze went flinty, Katim hissed again, and even the kobold was growling softly.

"What's that supposed to mean?" Cræosh demanded. "You saying we can't handle a bunch of elves and humans on our own?"

"Not at all," the elf countered, obviously struggling to salvage the situation. "You can simply consider it some extra insurance." Then, before anyone could say anything further, he added, "And in any case, I would hardly expect you to undertake such a thing without suitable compensation."

"What compensation?" Jhurpess asked.

Ebonwind appeared uncertain as to whether the bugbear was asking for details, or for the meaning of the word. He decided to assume the former. "Oh, quite a lot. My people are *very* wealthy. We could pay more for this than you would see over the rest of your years combined.

"But more importantly, you must be aware that the potential opportunities for you all back home, should you survive Demon Squad duty, are enormous. Surely it wouldn't hurt to have a friendly wizard owing you favors, hmm?"

Cræosh absently scratched at his palms. It was, indeed, a tempting offer. It probably wouldn't do any harm, not if all he was asking for was troop movements a couple of days in advance. And if this was actually a dakórren initiative, as opposed to some personal gambit by Ebonwind himself, they were surely asking the same of others. Why shouldn't they be the ones to benefit?

Still . . .

"Oh, don't decide now," the elf said, clearly sensing his reluctance.

"The sun's long down. Why don't you all sleep on it, and we can discuss it some more in the morning? You're more than welcome to stay here, of course. It's much warmer than the tundra." And with no further ado, Ebonwind rose and slipped outside, seemingly oblivious to the cold.

He wasn't, not entirely. Even through his cloak, even through his magics, Nurien Ebonwind shivered in the freezing wind. But if they thought he was, so much the better.

Not that he actually needed to wait for their decision. The orc was far too suspicious to take him up on his offer, the bugbear was too stupid, the gremlin too ignorant, and neither the doppelganger nor the troll would trust their fate to an "inferior."

But one look at the kobold's face as he'd described their "compensation," and he knew he'd hooked one. And one, really, was all he needed.

"I do not . . . care for this at all," Katim said to the others as they gathered around the roaring fire. "We cannot . . . trust this elf, whether or not . . . he is dakórren."

"I tend to agree," Gimmol interjected. "Definitely not worth the risk. Do you have any idea what they say King Morthûl *does* to traitors?" He trembled slightly.

Cræosh nodded thoughtfully. "Fezeill?"

"I will admit that our host makes a most convincing argument. Nevertheless, I fear I have to side with the gremlin. It simply isn't worth it."

"Gork?" the orc asked next.

"Oh. Same here. Not a chance."

"Jhurpess?"

The bugbear scratched at his head. "Jhurpess not sure he understands what elf wants us to do."

Cræosh decided that, once again, ignoring the monkey was the wisest policy. "Yeah, I'm with you. And there are too many unanswered questions. Did he bring us here on purpose? I'm not prepared to believe we just *happened* to stumble across a dakórren wizard's hut in the middle of fucking nowhere. And there's gotta be other sources, *easier* sources, of the information he says he wants. Nah, the whole thing smells wrong.

"So, we'll go ahead and sleep here—no sense in letting a warm shelter go to waste—and we'll leave in the morning."

The troll cleared her throat; or at least, the others assumed that such was the intended purpose of the phlegmy sound that burbled from her gullet. "Are we willing to . . . trust that Ebonwind will not . . . harm us as we sleep?"

"Of course not!" Cræosh snapped. "I'm tired, I ain't dumb. We'll set a watch, same as usual." He twisted toward the bugbear. "And we stay awake this time. You got that, Nature-boy?"

"Yes. Jhurpess remembers that from last night. Jhurpess not stupid."

Cræosh opened his mouth to reply, and then shut it with an audible snap. Sometimes, it was so easy there wasn't really any point.

Gork, his snout quivering with anticipation, forced himself to wait just long enough to be certain that everyone else was fast asleep. It took every bit of self-control he had, the waiting did, but impatient as he was, one of the first tenets of kobold philosophy was that one never went behind someone's back in front of his face.

Kobold philosophy, it must be noted in passing, tends toward the convoluted.

Slowly, his footsteps landing on the creaky floorboards as silently as if they were sponge, Gork examined each of his companions in turn. As though his life depended on it—which, he realized nervously, it just might—he very gently prodded at them. Not enough to awaken even the lightest sleeper, only enough to confirm that they actually slumbered. Wiping his fingers roughly on his tunic—what, exactly, had Jhurpess *gotten* in his fur, anyway?—the kobold decided that the coast was as clear as it would ever be. Slipping through the open doorway, he made his way to their host. The elf sat casually by the front window, heedless of the cold, one hand again absently scratching the strange winged creature under the chin.

"I was wondering," the dakórren said without looking away from the frozen plains, "when you might decide to join me."

Gork's snout wrinkled in surprise. "You knew I was coming?"

A not-quite-smile twisted the corners of Ebonwind's mouth. "Does it really surprise you so much that I should?"

"No. That is, it did, but I suppose it shouldn't have."

"Come," the elf said, rising smoothly to his feet. "Let's move a little ways away, shall we? Then we can talk."

Amid the raucous orchestra of snoring and the multitude of twitching limbs, a single pair of eyes opened and watched intently as the smallest squad member sneaked his way outside. And they narrowed, not in surprise, but in the first stirrings of anger. The little bastard would be the death of them all! Best to wake the others now, confront him before . . .

No. No, that *wouldn't* be best, would it? A twisted grin appeared beneath those suspicious eyes. Cræosh and the others were too frightened of Morthûl to even *consider* Ebonwind's proposal, while Gork was too greedy to do anything *else*. But for the right person, at the right time, the options remained open. Gork's indiscretions were known, now. If it looked as though his little scheme might actually succeed, well, he'd be more than willing to share with a silent partner if it meant that partner *stayed* silent. And if not, if he appeared apt to bring the wrath of the Dark Lord down upon them . . .

The grin grew wider, teeth shifting within the jaw. If so, the Charnel King would surely be gracious toward the one who reported the traitor in their midst.

Feeling truly self-satisfied—and grateful, for the first time, that she'd been assigned to this bunch of incompetents—Katim watched in rapt fascination as the kobold and the elf walked into the frigid gloom, and wished only that she could hear exactly what they said.

As though it required the strength of a thousand gremlins, Gimmol struggled in vain to lift his eyelids. He didn't understand this at all! He hadn't been wounded, not unless something had happened as he slumbered. He wasn't in any pain—well, no more than the act of forcing himself awake every morning always caused. And yet, try as he might, he couldn't seem to open . . .

And then he screamed, an earsplitting banshee's call, as he suddenly realized the terrifying truth. His eyes *were* open; he just couldn't see! He was blind!

He screamed again, and again, and only then, as the last of them echoed away into oblivion, did he realize that his voice shouldn't be echoing at all. And his back . . . Why did his back hurt? It felt just like that night when he'd spent six hours in a gopher hole, trying to escape the notice of the troll war party. He . . .

"Hey!" It was Cræosh's voice, clearly unhappy, and it was followed by a sudden *clang*, one that shook the entire world. "Keep it the fuck down in there! I get *real* irritable before breakfast."

In there? What in the blazes did that . . . ?

He was inside the damned cauldron!

With a final shout that was half determination and half fear, Gimmol burst upward, flinging the iron lid halfway across the hut. Murder writ large across his face, he dragged himself over the lip of the huge pot—grateful indeed that no one had gotten around to lighting a fire—and dropped to his feet.

"*Who the fuck did that?*" he demanded, trying (without a great deal of success) to sound dangerous.

Cræosh began to chuckle. In a spreading wildfire of mirth, Fezeill, Gork, and even Jhurpess all joined in. Within moments, the entire squad was laughing hysterically, tears rolling down their cheeks.

All, that is, but two. Gimmol himself, of course, felt that the situation fell somewhat short of amusing; and Katim had also failed to join in the general merriment. His pride getting the better of his instinctive fear, the gremlin wandered over and seated himself beside the troll, who was currently sipping on a mug of what looked to be half-congealed blood. One whiff as he drew near, and Gimmol decided not to ask if it was, indeed, what it looked like.

What he said instead was, "I see that *someone* here has the good sense to take me seriously. When I get my hands on whoever did this . . ."

Katim nodded, mug held to her misshapen snout. "I think that would prove . . . most interesting indeed."

Gimmol glanced her way, but she seemed disinclined to elaborate any further. "Well, in any case," he continued, "thanks for not laughing at me."

"There was . . . no reason to laugh at you."

"Oh? You didn't think it was funny either, then?"

"I didn't say . . . that. There was no need . . . to laugh at you . . ." The huge trollish jaw gaped in a mirthful grin. ". . . because I already laughed . . . myself silly over it . . . last night when I . . . put you in there."

Gimmol backed away, his face ashen, as the room around him exploded into new gales of hilarity. Then, his lip quivering, he bolted outside.

Slowly, over the course of breakfast, the laughter settled down. "You know," Cræosh said thoughtfully, "maybe we oughta take it easy on the little puke. I mean, whatever else he may be, he's a teammate."

"You're right," Fezeill agreed, his voice thoughtful.

"Yeah," Gork chimed in. "I mean, better him than me, but . . ."

Katim nodded.

"We're agreed then," the orc announced. "We should stop picking on Gimmol." And then a nasty smirk split his face. "But we're not going to, are we?"

"Nope."

"Absolutely not."

"Wouldn't . . . dream of it."

"Good," Cræosh declared. "Who wants more yeti?"

They had just about finished breakfast when Fezeill glanced around. "Does anyone know what happened to our host?"

"Dunno that it matters, really," Cræosh answered. "I mean, we're planning to turn him down anyway."

"Granted," Fezeill said. "Still, I thought he'd wait to hear us tell him ourselves."

"Maybe he didn't need to," Gork suggested. "He *is* a wizard, after all."

"No," the orc told him, shaking his large head. "If he could have foreseen our reply, he wouldn't have had to ask in the first place. I . . ."

A small stomping sounded at the door. Even as they all looked,

Gimmol sulked in and tossed a scrap of parchment down on the table. "I found this tacked to the doorframe," he announced angrily.

Fezeill was the fastest of those who grabbed for it.

My dear guests,

I apologize profusely for running out on you in this manner, but I fear something has come up that requires my immediate attention. You are welcome to break your fast upon whatever foodstuffs you might find within my home.

"Too late," the kobold muttered.

I trust you have already come to a decision, one way or the other, but if not, you may look upon this as an extension of your deadline. Do not concern yourself with contacting me; when I have the opportunity, I shall find you. I will, of course, expect your final answer at that time.

Sincerely,

Nurien Ebonwind.

PS: The yetis are growing agitated about something. I'd advise that you not remain in the house for long after breakfast.

"Great," Cræosh muttered once Fezeill had read the missive aloud. "Just what we need. At least if he'd been here, we could've gotten it over with. I'll tell you something, I'm not looking forward to telling him no. As a rule, I don't imagine wizards take rejection all that well."

"What I am more . . . concerned about," Katim told him, "is that last . . . bit."

Fezeill nodded. "I agree completely. If the yetis are gallivanting about, would that not be a better reason to stay *inside*?"

"I'd have thought the same thing," Gork said. "Maybe—"

"Hsst!" The troll stood motionless, one furry hand raised in a call for silence.

And then the rest of them heard it, too—a faint whistling in the air. As though the sun had reversed its course, the morning began to grow dark outside the hut.

"Oh, shit!" Cræosh was already breaking for the nearest exit. "Incoming!"

The entire squad scattered like frightened roaches before the "-ing" had left the orc's mouth. Wooden shutters and cheap glass shattered as the hut's windows burst asunder with fleeing goblins. Katim had somehow compressed herself small enough to fit through the one, Gork had almost cleared the other before several hundred pounds of bugbear launched him the rest of the way through, and Cræosh had followed the "shortest distance is a straight line" theory and hurled himself through the nearest wall.

Just a few heartbeats after the Demon Squad had vacated the cottage, the entire structure was turned into splinters by the arrival of an uninvited boulder of the airborne variety. The ground shook as though the universe had sneezed, knocking Gimmol clear off his feet. Slivers of wood and shards of glass spun across the tundra. Cræosh, already bleeding from a dozen pinprick wounds, threw one arm over his face and dove into the snow. A series of thumps suggested that most of his squad had enough sense to do the same.

And then, as swiftly as it began, it was over. The crushed wood creaked as the boulder teetered a bit and then settled comfortably into the snow, apparently content with its new abode.

Cræosh rose, the sting of his various lacerations aching in the cold. The rest of the squad gathered around him, stained and speckled with the blood of similar injuries.

"I had no . . . idea," Katim said, "that yetis grew large enough . . . to throw something like . . . this."

"They don't," Fezeill announced authoritatively. "It isn't possible."

With a low growl, Cræosh reached toward Fezeill, palmed the back of his bugbear head in one ham-sized fist, and drove him facefirst into the boulder. With a sharp crack, the doppelganger—his nose bleeding a noxious yellow ichor—dropped into the snow.

"Feels possible enough to me," Cræosh said. "Anyone feel different?"

Oddly enough, no one spoke up.

"Fine. Now maybe it doesn't bother the rest of you that we nearly ended up flat as a dwarf at a troll orgy, but I happen to enjoy being six feet tall, and I damn well expect to stay that way." His mouth twisted as though he'd bitten into something distasteful. "I figure we've got us a few more minutes before the yeti—or yetis—show up to see how their little trick worked. And I'd really just as soon not get into a fight with someone who juggles small mountains. So what're our other options?"

"We could hide," Gimmol piped in, and then yelped as Katim lifted him off his feet from behind.

"Look around!" she snapped, her breath curling the hairs on the back of his head. "Where . . . do you think we could . . . possibly hide?"

The gremlin had to admit she had a point—and not just because she might eat his head if he didn't. Unless they all squeezed into cracks in the boulder, their options were snow and . . . Well, snow.

"Right again," Cræosh continued as the troll forcefully returned Gimmol to earth. "Which, as I see it, leaves only one choice."

"Withdrawal?" Fezeill asked sarcastically, slowly rising to his feet and gently probing his shattered nose.

"Nah," Cræosh told him as the first yeti howl sounded in the distance. "I was thinking more of running away."

Which, though he refrained from waving his arms and screaming, was exactly what they did.

Only once the motley band had vanished from sight did Nurien Ebonwind allow his concentration to lapse. A snowman melting in reverse, he materialized some several yards from the ruins of his house. His gray robe swirling about his ankles and his familiar perched on his shoulder, the dakórren examined the broken, splintered wood.

"Atiree eroo?" the little creature chirped at him.

"Yes," Ebonwind told it, "I'm afraid it was quite necessary. Yetis aren't known for their subtlety. Anything less than complete destruction might have raised questions." The elf sighed. "Ah, well. I can create another just as easily. Maybe somewhere warmer, next time . . ."

"Edabrelat! Ecci dibu."

"I know that, too. I *want* my call to attract real yetis. It should give the goblins something other than me to think about. I don't want them pondering certain questions just yet." Then, since the Demon Squad was probably still near enough to hear it, he let loose one more yeti wail for good measure.

"That's done then," he told his winged companion. "Let's be off, shall we? We've plenty left to do."

A word from the sorcerer, and they vanished once more, leaving only swirling, snow-flecked winds behind.

CHAPTER THREE

OGRE AND UNDER

The name of the village—if "village" was an appropriate term for the chaotic aggregate of buildings that had been thrown together in a small, unnamed hollow in the mountains—was Itho. From a distance, it was just another of the primitive communities that blemished the plains, the grasslands, and the forests that were the skin of Kirol Syrreth. Nothing, other than its peculiar location in the frigid wastes of the Northern Steppes, distinguished it from any of these others.

From a distance.

As one drew near, however, one might notice that the rudimentary wooden gates stood close to three dozen feet in height. Skulls, jammed atop many of the thick stakes and spikes that formed the defensive abatis, showed signs of violent, brutal death. A yeti skull topped the archway over the gate itself, glowering accusingly at the empty tundra as though blaming the snows for what had befallen it.

It wasn't the tundra's fault, of course. No, it was the yeti's own, for in his bestial, mindless hunger, he'd forgotten an important lesson to surviving the Steppes: Stay away from Itho.

Stay away from the ogres.

On this particular morning, the center of Itho bustled with activity that, while not so loud as the markets of Timas Khoreth, was more than sufficient to render an elephant completely sterile. Of course, in Timas Khoreth, the volume was due to hundreds upon hundreds of voices shouting at once. Here in Itho, where the entire population numbered less than eighty, it was due primarily to the fact that ogres are *bloody loud*.

Not to mention stubborn, prone to bickering, and stupid enough to give a bugbear fits. Which meant that *governing* ogres called for the absolute best that their race had to offer, and even then, most candidates didn't last very long. Itho's current "governor" had been in charge, nominally, for six months now. Not a historical record, but longer than average, which meant that *average* was something the ogre in question most certainly was not.

Her name was Belrotha, and as she emerged from the confines of her hut, she was actually feeling chipper. She took a moment to stretch her eleven-foot frame, admiring how her mottled, bruise-purple skin gleamed in the pink glow of morning. Then, scratching under her yeti-pelt tunic with a cracked yellow nail, she turned and tromped down the rise that separated her dwelling from the town proper. The sun glinted brightly, as she walked, off the large hilt that protruded from the furs on her back.

Several times she heard various greetings shouted her way, most of which she returned with a rotted, gap-toothed grin or a vicious snarl, depending on her current opinion of the individual in question. Some, as per usual, were citizens of Itho come to seek her advice, for in addition to being their nominal leader, Belrotha was hailed throughout the village and even beyond as the town's smartest ogre. (Not that the competition for the title was exactly what you'd call fierce.) Others, again as per normal, were unattached young males, determined to catch the fancy of such a beauty. That glistening, oily black hair; those wonderful, jagged teeth, two of which still resembled their original yellow hue; and those muscles! A true prodigy, Belrotha was a blessing on the town of Itho: smart, beautiful, and strong as a dragon's sphincter. (That last was an expression they'd picked up from an orc some years back. They'd liked it then, and they liked it even better once someone got around to explaining to them what "sphincter" meant.) Truly a divine creature, this one; a marvel among ogres, and a role model for all ogrelings to look up to.

"Belrotha!" a voice called from behind a nearby shack. "Me need advice!"

Reluctantly, the towering creature headed over. The one who'd called to her was older than average, which basically meant that he hadn't died before reaching middle age. Some few inches shorter than she, he found himself craning his neck upward. The posture made the turkey-turd green skin on his neck pale slightly.

"What you need this time?" she asked impatiently. "This second time you bother me this week, Worondek." In point of fact, it was the third, but since neither of them realized it, it hardly mattered.

"Me sorry," he told her, not sounding sorry at all. "Me need advice."

"Said that already."

"Yes." Worondek said. "Ladaviat ignoring her chores again."

"Hmm," Belrotha grunted. "What she supposed to work on this week?" Belrotha, in a flash of insight startling for one of her race, had instituted the policy of switching out tasks from week to week, ensuring that Itho's needs were met while never allowing anyone to get too trapped in a rut.

"Uhh, me not remember."

She grunted again. "Not important." Then she hauled back and slammed a fist into the smaller ogre's face. It was a blow that would have shattered stone or felled a small tree. Worondek merely lost his balance and a few teeth, and was quick to stagger back to his feet, ignoring the blood that streamed over his lips.

"That for always complaining to me," Belrotha said. "Need to learn to solve own problems."

"Okay."

"Call Ladaviat over here."

Worondek staggered away. Belrotha waited impatiently, arms crossed over her ponderous breasts, one sandal-wrapped foot tapping idly at the dirt road. It was only a few moments before the other ogre returned, his recalcitrant mate in tow, but she felt as though she'd waited forever.

"What you want?" Ladaviat huffed, unaware even that she ought to be worried. Then again, Ladaviat had never really gotten down the concept of "leader." It was her sort of ogre that kept Belrotha's presence from bumping up the race's average intelligence.

"You do chores," Belrotha told her sternly, her chapped lips parted in a snarl, "just like rest of us. You not do chores, all Itho suffer."

Ladaviat sniffed disdainfully. "And what you do if me say no?"

Belrotha cocked her head sideways. "Me kill you," she said matter-of-factly.

That, at least, got the other's attention. "What?"

The leader shrugged. "Chores still not get done," she added, displaying an uncommon amount of forethought. "But your food not get wasted either. Good trade."

Muttering, Ladaviat turned about and headed for the outer fence, presumably to resume her daily tasks, just as soon as someone remembered what they were.

With a satisfied smirk, Belrotha nodded to Worondek. "You wait until noon," she told him, "and then hit her on back of head with shovel. Then you tell her that for arguing with me."

The male nodded and then scurried off to his own duties.

"Belrotha! Come quick!"

Her shoulders slumped. Two emergencies before breakfast. Grumbling, she headed toward the town square. "What?!" she shouted, half hoping that if she sounded angry enough, whoever it was might decide to wait until after she'd eaten.

No such luck. "Look!"

Belrotha looked toward the main gate, following the young ogre's pointing finger, and her jaw dropped open. This, at least, was a *real* emergency.

It materialized from the morning haze beyond the gates. A pearl-white carriage, luminescent in the morning sun, ornately trimmed in gold—even the wheels were plated in the precious metal. Four pristine horses, equally white, were harnessed to the vehicle, pulling it smoothly—far *too* smoothly—across the uneven dirt and deep snows of the Steppes.

Belrotha gasped in shock. The carriage left no tracks in the snow! No hoofprints, no furrows, nothing!

"Bar the gates!" Belrotha shouted in a voice that came *this* close to causing an avalanche and rendering the whole situation well and truly moot. "Get . . ."

She stumbled to a halt, her tongue falling limp over her lower teeth. The massive bar that secured the gates of Itho—essentially an uprooted tree with the branches broken off, requiring four ogres working in unison to lift—disengaged itself from the brackets and *floated* gently to one side. The gates themselves drifted open a moment later, allowing a clear path for the phantom carriage.

This, Belrotha noted sourly, fell somewhere outside her previous experience, and she found herself at a loss. Her first instinct was to throw something heavy—a fairly common first instinct for her, really—but she realized, after a moment's intense thought, that whatever she hurled would probably float aside the same way the bar had done. Instead, one hand firmly on the hilt of her sword, she broke into a jog, determined to defend her people.

The carriage drew to a halt, still without disturbing a flake of snow, precisely between Belrotha and the gate. A strange figure arose from the driver's perch, sized somewhere between an above-average human or a below-average elf. He (it?) was wrapped in a deep-brown robe that trailed over his feet, and he wore the hood pulled over his head. Even his hands were covered in some sort of silken wrappings, functioning perhaps as makeshift gloves.

Without a word, or even a glance, for the ogres of Itho, the robed figure drifted from atop the carriage and gently opened the shining door. This, then, was the being who had dared to disrupt the smooth (ha!) running of Itho, and who would be the first to pay the price. An evil grin on her face and a half dozen equally pissed ogres falling in behind her, Belrotha marched on the carriage.

A march that faltered, staggered, and stopped completely as the inhabitant of the carriage finally deigned to emerge. The ground shook prodigiously as first Belrotha and then the others all dropped to their knees.

"Queen Anne!" Belrotha choked. "We sorry for not greeting you! We not know. . . ."

"Of course you didn't," Queen Anne replied, her voice gentle, lyrical. "How could you? Please, rise."

Queen Anne appeared to be a normal human female, beautiful (by human standards, anyway; Belrotha didn't see it, really) despite her age. Hair as dark as her husband's, save for a few flecks of gray at the temples, formed a veil about her head and shoulders. Her piercing blue eyes were bottomless pools. A velvet green dress, flared at the waist but cinched tight above, revealed a figure that women half her age would have killed for.

Or, rather, half her *apparent* age. There *were* no women half her age, for Queen Anne had stood at Morthûl's side since before he ripped Kirol Syrreth from the hands of old King Sabryen, more than six centuries past. Rumors offered a variety of explanations for her longevity: it was a hoax, and there had been multiple Queen Annes; she was a mannequin, made to appear living via illusions and/or cleverly placed mirrors; she was a vampire, feeding off the prisoners in the dungeons beneath the Iron Keep; or (as was most commonly accepted) her aging was slowed by a combination of her husband's magics and her own.

Slowed; but even with the aid of the great Charnel King, she couldn't halt time completely. When she'd first appeared beside him, she'd seemed quite youthful, scarcely past her teens. Now, it had taken her some twenty times longer than anyone else, but Queen Anne was finally starting to grow old.

All of this—or all of it that she could remember and understand—flashed through Belrotha's mind as she rose to stand beside the velvet-garbed queen.

"Come, Belrotha," the queen said. "I have a task for you to perform."

The ogre frowned. "This take me away from Itho for long?" she asked, trying hard not to sound disrespectful.

Queen Anne raised a single elegant eyebrow. "Is there no one else who can lead your people for a few months?"

"Yeah," Belrotha admitted, "but then me have to fight him when me come back."

The queen smiled broadly. "My child, if you return from this, I promise you'll have no trouble at all resuming whatever position you wish."

Not even Belrotha could miss the use of "if," not "when." But that was a *good* thing. Danger! Maybe battle! It had been so long since the Dark Lord's last campaign. . . . The ogre actually sighed in pleasure at the prospect of killing again.

"Me get to fight?" Belrotha asked suspiciously. No sense in getting too excited, just in case she'd misinterpreted.

"Oh, yes. Yes, indeed."

The ogre grinned stupidly.

"Step inside my carriage," the queen continued, "and I'll tell you more."

Belrotha came to an abrupt halt, scrutinizing the ornate conveyance. Yes, it was fairly large for a carriage, but . . .

"Uhh . . ." she protested.

Queen Anne smiled gently. "Go on. It's all right." On cue, the strange robed figure pulled the door open, bowing to Belrotha as she passed.

Still skeptical, the ogre crammed her head and shoulders through the portal, and froze once again. She actually took a moment to rub her eyes with her dirty, wrinkled knuckles.

The inside of the carriage was enormous. The room—and yes, it was actually a *room*—measured close to ten yards on a side, and the ceiling was high enough that Belrotha barely had to slouch. Several cushy chairs were scattered about, artfully arranged to look haphazard. Small tables stood alongside them, some of which were already topped by platters of steaming meats and huge mugs of anything and everything the ogre could have asked for. The carpet was a plush red, as were most of the cushions. All told, it was a room truly fit for royalty, and one that absolutely *could not fit* in the carriage.

The window adjacent to the door showed the buildings to one side of Itho's dirt road, and the window across the room showed the buildings to the other. But the road itself was only fifteen feet wide, and the room was over thirty. . . .

Belrotha squeezed inside, staggered to the only chair that looked sturdy enough for her seven-hundred-pound bulk, and slumped into it, holding her head and whimpering.

"You know where to take us, my pet," Queen Anne said to Brown Robe, who still stood by the door. She caressed the side of the hood with the back of her right hand, a gesture that might've been a lover's touch or the stroking of a faithful hound. Then she climbed into the chamber, and the carriage began to move.

The room rocked softly as they left Itho behind. It didn't do anything to detract from Belrotha's discomfort.

"How?" the ogre asked plaintively.

Queen Anne smiled. "A simple matter of the bending of space around a fixed position. The magic creates a confined area in which the *actual* size is not limited by the restrictions or the shape of anything else around it, although the *apparent* size remains subject to natural laws."

Belrotha stared, blinking, for perhaps a full minute. "Oh," she said finally.

The queen laughed, a beautiful, musical sound. "Come, child, I believe we were about to discuss the task I need you to perform."

Instantly, the ogre perked up. "Fighting?" she asked again hopefully.

"As I promised, Belrotha, as I promised. Tell me, have you ever served in a Demon Squad?"

Well, it was an honest mistake! Cræosh protested through the haze of pain that was the left side of his face. *The damn thing's so much smaller than the last one!*

None of which changed the fact that he was hanging limply in a yeti's two-fisted grip and finding it increasingly difficult to prevent the thing from popping his head off his body like a wine cork. Both his own hands pried at the fur-coated fingers, with precious little effect. His sword, which would've been *really* nice to have, was currently lying where the yeti had first smacked him in the face, some dozen feet away.

Where the fuck is the squad? Yeah, okay, maybe they were still finishing up with the other yeti—the big one—but there were *five* of them! It should *not* be taking this long. And if it took much longer, Cræosh would pay for his carelessness with a lot more than a bloodied face and a headache. . . .

And then the headache grew worse, as his ears were besieged by a scream unlike any he'd heard before. Cræosh could compare it only to the simultaneous castration of an entire pack of wolves. It rose, higher, higher, long past the point where most people would have burst a lung, or at least a blood vessel. In mirror image, he and the yeti that was throttling him both turned their heads, straining to see what new, sanity-shattering horror had appeared beyond the frozen dunes.

As though launched from a catapult, Katim soared over the top of the rise. Blood covered her snout, her armor, her axe, dripping a trail across the pristine white of the snow. And even as she landed the scream continued, reaching registers that Cræosh could scarcely hear. The yeti was practically writhing in pain.

Her feet barely touched the snow as she broke into her long-legged lope. In the blink of the orc's blood-gummed eyes, she was near, she was beside them, she was . . . Past?

Cræosh staggered and only then realized that he stood once more on his own two feet. And though those furry fists remained clasped about his neck, those fists were no longer connected to the yeti's wrists.

Prying the claws from about his aching throat, Cræosh lurched toward his fallen sword.

Her ungodly screech finally fading in the distance, Katim switched to a hiss of frustration. The yeti's flailing stumps were long enough, and certainly strong enough, to keep any sane opponent at bay, and the thing didn't look as though it would bleed out any time soon. Around and around she circled, probing for any opening with her axe, and wished her *chirrusk* wasn't still hanging, caught, in the thick hide of the other yeti.

But even worse, it was all so *useless*, a waste of time and effort. Yetis, so far as she knew, were just beasts. Cunning, quick to learn, but beasts all the same, not *people*. No matter how many she fought, how many she killed—and there had been quite a few, since their flight from the detritus that had once been Ebonwind's cottage—she was adding nothing to her stable of slaves in the world to come. Had this one not threatened to take the orc she'd already claimed, she probably wouldn't even have bothered. . . .

Steel glinted from behind the bleeding yeti, and all she could think was *Finally!*

Cræosh rose up and struck like an enraged serpent (albeit an injured, gasping serpent that could barely stand on its own two—umm, on its own). This time, the orc was prepared for the impossible resilience of yeti flesh. This time, he drove the sword into the beast's shoulder with every bit of strength he had left.

This time, Cræosh was also weak and shaky, and was rewarded with only a pathetic trickle of blood seeping through the fur. He actually wanted to cry as the yeti pivoted, the stump of its arm raised to deliver another crushing blow to the *same damn side* of his face!

But the Ancestors still had one benevolent eye turned his way. Katim's voice rang out in another soul-shriveling scream, and her axe struck true before the beast had even finished its spin. The musical sound of splintering bone tickled Cræosh's ears, and he exulted in the blood that splattered across his face in a warm soup.

The yeti toppled, jagged edges of bone screeching across Katim's blade. With a grunt of annoyance, the troll yanked a rag from her pack and began wiping the gore from her axe.

"Certainly . . . took your time," Cræosh gasped at her.

Katim looked up from her task. "I'm sorry, I didn't . . . hear you right. It *almost* sounded . . . like you said 'Thank you.' But . . . perhaps you better repeat it . . . just to be sure."

Cræosh grumbled. Then, "Thank you."

The troll shook her head. "Maybe you should . . . practice that more. It sounded . . . awkward."

The orc grimaced. "Now *I* didn't hear *you* right. That *almost* sounded like 'you're welcome.'"

"No, it didn't," she said, returning her attention once more to her blade.

With a grunt, Cræosh knelt and began applying snow to the

bruising on his face and throat. "Any more of those things show up," he said through a powdery white mask, "we're buggered so hard we're gonna be sneezing shit. You realize that, don't you?"

"I'm aware of that . . . Cræosh, although I doubt I . . . could have phrased it so . . . poetically."

"Yeah, well, you can be awed by my lyrical speech later, Carrion-breath. Right now, we can decide what the hell to do about—"

"Hey, guys!" Gork called from behind them. "We've finished stripping the meat off of . . . What the hell happened to you?"

"What happened to me?" Cræosh's voice was absolutely calm as he rose to his feet. "What does it look like happened to me?"

"Well, umm, that is . . ."

"It looks," the orc continued, "as though Katim and I fought a second yeti. By ourselves. While the rest of you were butchering one that was already dead. Or that's what it looks like to me, anyway."

Casually, he reached out and, once more palming the kobold's entire head, lifted Gork off the ground. "Is that what it looks like to you?" he asked.

For his own part, Gork clearly decided that Cræosh wouldn't have left his mouth free unless he actually expected an answer.

"You—uh, you did tell us that you could handle this one, Cræosh. Remember, we were fighting the big one, and you saw the little one on the dune, and you said, 'You guys finish this one off. I'll get the other one.' And then—"

"But you *did* finish the big one off. Why didn't you come help?"

"Well, Katim *did* go to help, didn't she? We, um, well, we sort of figured that, between the two of you, you could handle *anything*." He grinned. "And hey, you *did*!"

Cræosh dropped the kobold with a disgusted snort. "I guess you've got a point. But next time, I don't care if I'm fighting an elf or an ogre, a dog or a dragon. Once you've finished with yours, you make *sure* I've got things under control before you start in on something else."

"Ouch," Gork agreed, rubbing his head.

"Good." Then, raising his voice for the sake of the others, Cræosh shouted, "Get your asses over here!"

Fezeill, Jhurpess, and Gimmol appeared over the rise, each dragging several chunks of yeti that still needed to be butchered and salted. "Wow!" Gimmol yelped, catching sight of Cræosh's face for the first time. "What happened to you?"

Cræosh snagged a large haunch of yeti and proceeded to use it to hammer Gimmol into the snow like a tent spike.

"So," Gork asked—respectfully, as he eyed Gimmol's bright red plume, which resembled nothing so much as a flower poking up from the churned powder—"what's the next step?"

"Same as it has been," Cræosh said, tossing the slab of meat to Katim. "We take whatever we can use, and we get a move on before the rest of the pack gets here." Even as he spoke, a distant howl sounded on the arctic winds.

"Someone dig up the turnip," Cræosh ordered. "We've got to go!"

They went, but the cold, the shifting snows, and the beatings they'd taken in the day and a half since fleeing Ebonwind's house conspired to slow their progress to a crawl. Cræosh hadn't felt this bad since he'd been a teenager, the day after he'd been caught in bed with his father's favorite mistress.

"Look!"

Cræosh twisted his already-aching neck, seeking the cause of the gremlin's warning. An entire pack of yetis—six in the open, perhaps more out of sight—howled their rage from atop a distant dune. Far away, Ancestors be thanked, but in the squad's current state, maybe not far enough. It was to be a race, then, to see if they could keep ahead of the creatures long enough for Shreckt to call them home at the day's end.

Or rather, it would be a race for *some* of them. Jhurpess, however, took one look behind and finally came unhinged. His rapid, four-legged lope quickly carried him over the next rise, his shrill keening and uneven tracks all that remained to prove his existence.

Cræosh and Fezeill blinked at each other while the others stared in the direction Jhurpess had gone. Several times each opened his mouth as if to say something, closing it again when he realized that there wasn't a damn thing to say.

"Well," Cræosh said finally, "at least he's heading the right way." He pointed at the mountain range, the same they'd been pursuing since their arrival, now stretching across most of the northwestern horizon. "Sooner or later, he'll stop and wait for us."

Katim snorted once. "Assuming he doesn't . . . stumble into the Demias . . . Gap."

Technically, the infamous canyon was actually many leagues to the south (assuming the squad were where they thought they were, a fact of which Cræosh wasn't entirely convinced). But a handful of smaller crevices reached this far north and even farther, and for convenience, most of Kirol Syrreth's natives just called the whole chain by the name of the largest.

Cræosh just shrugged. "Either works for me."

Some miles and minutes later, the bugbear under discussion finally slowed to a brisk walk. It had taken some time, but Jhurpess had finally come to the realization that it wouldn't do him much good to escape the yetis if it meant his friends weren't here to help if something *else* popped up to eat him. And so, after a few bone-chilling moments of running through a list of everything that *could* pop up to eat him here—arctic eels, ice dragons, ogres, more yetis, blizzards (Jhurpess didn't actually know what a blizzard was, but he'd heard them mentioned in fearful tones, and assumed they were at *least* as nasty as yetis)—he finally decided to halt and wait for the squad.

The bugbear slumped down, legs stretched out before him, ass planted in the snow, and began digging shapes into the thick powder with a finger. He had just finished his third attempt at spelling the words "Demon Squad" when the snow beside him hiccupped.

Or that was the best way Jhurpess could find to describe it, anyway. As near as he could tell, the snow had simply bulged, as if something beneath it was trying to . . .

Dig its way out?

With a startled (if belated) yelp, Jhurpess shot to his feet. His gnarled war club was held fast in his hand, his fur-shrouded gaze fixed solidly on the ground. The snow bulged once more, and out slid a worm.

Jhurpess blinked. A worm? The bugbear might not have known a *lot*, but he knew well that no worm should—could—survive here. Any one of a thousand dangers made it impossible, the cold being only the most obvious.

The *least* obvious but, as it turned out, the most relevant, was a suspicious bugbear with a club.

Once more, Jhurpess began to settle himself into the snow, smugly satisfied with his quick and efficient handling of the situation, when a second worm appeared a few inches beside the gooey smear that was all that remained of the first. It was followed swiftly by a third worm, two millipedes, and a handful of maggots.

This, Jhurpess decided as he stood up once again, was moving beyond strange. One worm was a fluke; a whole mass of them was *wrong*. And "mass" was certainly the right word. Over the span of seconds, the writhing heap of worms, centipedes, millipedes, maggots, and the occasional grub had grown to the size of the bugbear's hand.

And then it *was* a hand! The crawling things actually formed themselves into a shape eerily approximating fingers and a palm. Jhurpess retreated slowly, fighting to convince himself that the resemblance was coincidental. . . .

A fight he lost when the fingers *flexed*, digging into the snow, and pulled. An arm—an actual arm, also consisting of various flopping and crawling and writhing vermin—followed. A second "hand" appeared a few feet to the left. And the snow around him was hiccupping again, in half a dozen spots.

Jhurpess was left with only two viable options. He could attack, despite his absolute incomprehension of what it was he faced, or he could run.

Another scream on his simian lips, Jhurpess leapt and brought his club crashing down on the head—or what looked like it might be becoming a head—of the first creature. The cudgel sank deep into the snow, leaving smashed invertebrates and pupae in its wake. One entire side of the club was coated in ichor and flaps of worm skin, and any coherent shape had been completely obliterated by the bugbear's blow. The worms and millipedes that had made up the hands and arms collapsed. Some burrowed downward, perhaps to join others beneath the snow; others writhed for a few seconds and then lay limp, apparently dead.

Jhurpess found his spirits rising. They might be unnatural; they might be revolting. But they were not, apparently, very tough. A grin settling across his features, the bugbear stepped back and allowed the other creatures to rise—six of them, if he counted right—and faltered, just a bit, when he finally saw them in their entirety.

Humanoid silhouettes shifted constantly, as though viewed through a heat mirage, as thousands of component creatures skittered and slithered across one another. Scores of the tiny creatures tumbled constantly from those "bodies," only to be reabsorbed on their way down. A thick ooze splattered, slowly but steadily, into the snow around them, exuded by who-knew-what.

And they had faces! No true features, not exactly, but shallow hollows where eyes and mouth should sit. Here, for a depth of perhaps an inch in each orifice, no worms crawled, no maggots twitched. It was just enough for an imaginative observer to fill in the features, and the expressions, on his own.

Jhurpess *wasn't* all that imaginative, but if he had been, he might just have realized that the creatures appeared to be screaming in silent torment.

The nearest swarm drew back its hand and whipped it forward, as though it was throwing something. Jhurpess assumed he was safe—the creature held no weapon, after all—right up until a few tiny projectiles smacked into his leather breastplate and landed, skittering and writhing, at his feet.

Jhurpess screeched at the handful of worms before him. He had no idea what the vermin would have done had they connected with something more yielding than his armor, and more importantly, he didn't want to find out.

Instinct had him grasping momentarily for his bow; but no, arrows probably wouldn't do much good against these "swarms." Instead, the bugbear dropped his club, reached into his pack, and brought out two of the chair legs he'd taken from the dakórren's hut. Wishing only that he had time to light them first—he had intended them for use as torches, after all—he hurled them both at the *thing* that attacked him.

The first, spinning wildly, careened off the target's shoulder, taking only a smattering of crawling creatures with it. But the second flew true. With a satisfying and surprisingly solid thump, it struck just above the hollow mouth, embedding itself deep in the creature's head and sending huge numbers of worms and centipedes tumbling free. The swarm-creature dropped to its knees, hands raised uselessly to clutch at the thing protruding from its "face."

The bugbear directed his attention at the next in line—and squinted, puzzled, as it just pointed at him. . . .

A brilliant blue gleam formed around the thing's fingers. Jhurpess barely had time to yelp before two needles of ice coalesced in the air beneath that hand and launched themselves his way. And then the bugbear was lying on his back in the snow, blood soaking the ground around him.

Magic! Not fair! Jhurpess struggled to rise, but his left arm proved unwilling to obey his frantic commands, and his right—though mobile—was uncomfortably numb. Thrashing the arm back and forth, impressing half an angel into the snow, the bugbear snagged the end of his club more by luck than intent. Using the massive weapon as a cane, he hauled himself to his feet.

They were coming! The swarm-creatures shambled inexorably forward, the nearest practically within arm's reach. Screaming stridently— he seemed to be doing a lot of that, lately—Jhurpess spun and raced back the way he had come, as fast as a two-legged gait could go. Looking back over his shoulder, he saw several of his pursuers lift their hands as though to cast another spell, but the rises in the tundra's snows swiftly blocked them from his sight. He whimpered, but he never slowed.

So they *definitely* should have run across the fuzzy bastard by now. Cræosh was starting to wonder, in a distant sort of way, if maybe Katim hadn't been right. Could Jhurpess have been so stupid, in such a blind terror, that he had barged over a rise of ice and snow to plunge into one of the ancillary canyons of the Demias Gap? Was his corpse even now scattered like lichen across some rock face?

Alternatively, had something just eaten his face?

Probably neither, but one could always hope.

The rising wind began to whistle as it whipped through the rocky crags of the mountains that were *finally* drawing near. Except no, Cræosh realized, that was no trick of the wind at all. Now that he was paying attention, he recognized it as a scream—and a very familiar one, at that.

Jhurpess appeared over a snow dune and charged toward the squad, running, for some reason, on two legs rather than four.

"Well, it's about fucking time, Nature-boy," Cræosh snapped. "Where the hell have you . . . ?"

Five heads swiveled, staring, as the bugbear continued past them without slowing even a little bit, vanishing again into the distance back the way they'd just come.

"Um," Cræosh finally observed, tearing the quilt of stunned silence that had settled over them.

"Should we follow him?" Gork asked.

"He was running from something," Fezeill said. "Perhaps we ought to go see what it is."

"No. He'll be . . . back. And we can let whatever . . . he's running from come to . . . us." Katim snorted in disgust. "Assuming it's . . . anything at all. Skittish . . . creature."

The orc was already sculpting a hollow in the snow, to serve as a makeshift chair. "'Skittish' is putting it mildly. I'm surprised Monkey-butt doesn't drop dead of shock every time his dick slaps his calf. And frankly, I'm sick and fucking tired of chasing his ass." He started to lean back, froze beneath Gork's and Fezeill's shocked stares. "What?"

"Slaps his *calf*?" the kobold demanded.

"Yeah." Cræosh sounded puzzled. "What about it?"

The others traded suspicious looks. "Is he messing with us?" Gork asked.

"I don't know," the doppelganger said with a shrug, "but I'm going over there to turn into an orc and find out."

Cræosh shrugged as they wandered away—*Who the hell understands these guys?*—and settled in, relaxing with a wide stretch. "Give a yell when Jhurpess shows up. Or whatever was chasing him, either way."

Jhurpess did indeed return only moments later, running as fast as two feet could carry him and howling loudly enough that Cræosh didn't need the others to yell. His sides heaving, his mouth panting out gusts that steamed in the cold air, the bugbear collapsed. Sprawled at his companions' feet, he stretched his arms wide, pointing both ways at once.

"Yetis! Worms! Yetis! Worms!"

Gimmol whimpered. "What's he talking about?"

Cræosh and Katim traded glances. "The yetis are that close?"

The troll shrugged. "It would seem . . . we didn't gain as much ground . . . on them as we'd hoped."

"And these worms he's blithering about?"

A second, identical shrug. "Whatever they are . . . they would seem to be heading . . . this way. Why not . . . just move off the trail . . . Jhurpess left and allow them . . . to meet each other?"

"Great idea!" Gork piped up. "Really, I mean it. Good luck!" And with that, the tiny creature dove into the snow and burrowed out of sight.

Fezeill shifted into a near–mirror image of Gork himself and followed. Soon two kobold burrows dotted the landscape, already fading from view as the snow caved in behind them. Jhurpess dragged himself to all fours and crawled behind a small rise.

Again, the orc and the troll exchanged looks. "I can fit behind the rise with Nature-boy," Cræosh said, "and I know how fast you can run. What about the strawberry?"

Katim glanced down at Gimmol, who gawped nervously back up at her. "I—I could dig!" he said frantically. "Maybe not as well as Gork, but—"

"No. Any part . . . of your outfit would stand out . . . pretty dramatically against the snow. Even Cræosh . . . couldn't miss it."

"That's right," the orc agreed. "I—Wait a minute!"

The ground began to vibrate before the argument could escalate. "Not much time," Cræosh told her. "Whatever you got in mind, better do it now."

Katim lunged, grabbing the gremlin by collar and crotch. Then, before the startled creature had even drawn breath to cry out, she took three running steps and flung. The gremlin soared like a very red eagle, screaming all the way, before he finally vanished behind a dune.

"Not bad," Cræosh complimented his companion. "Nice heft, good distance."

"Thank you."

"Could've used more of a spin, though."

"What . . . can I say? I'm . . . right-handed."

"Something to keep in mind, though."

The troll nodded. "For . . . next time."

And then, that more or less having covered it, they scattered.

It was a smaller pack, as such things go: just the same six that Cræosh had spotted earlier. Still, a half dozen pissed-off yetis was not something to scoff at. The apish brutes sniffed the air as they passed, searching this way and that; but whether it was the influence of the Stars, the Ancestors, or just the prevailing winds, they clearly detected no trace of the hidden goblins. They took a moment to study the trail of churned snow Jhurpess had left in his constant back-and-forth, roared in unison, and loped onward.

Another two minutes or so went by before the first of several heads and limbs appeared from the featureless white. "Are they gone?" Gork asked, scalp protruding from his burrow only enough to reveal his eyes.

"Yeah, they're gone," Cræosh told him. "I tell you, I'm starting to think this whole damn tundra is just plain unfriendly. Hostile, even."

Katim emerged from behind a hillock some distance away and jogged over. "Maybe they just . . . don't like you."

"Nah. I can't believe that."

"Try harder."

Gork, quite sick and tired of the pair of them, popped into the open. "How about this? You *both* rot! How does that grab you, huh?"

Several vicious glowers landed on the little creature, but the kobold was far too worked up to notice. "I mean," he continued, voice rising, "if it were up to the two of you, we'd already have died so horribly our mothers would feel it! We just had a pack—a *pack*—of yetis pass by so close that I'm amazed they couldn't hear my scrotum contracting in the cold! And they've just run off, in the direction we have to go—and where some other big worm-thing is probably waiting to burrow into our brains through our eyeballs! We're nostril-deep in dragonshit, and the two of you would rather strut around like rutting wefkoos than get dirty digging us out of it!"

Gork was gasping heavily by this point, even sweating lightly despite the chill—and not because of his sudden outburst. It had finally dawned on him, right about a sentence and a half ago, exactly who he was ranting at.

Cræosh advanced a single pace, wearing an odd expression. "Exactly what the fuck," he asked, "is a wefkoo?"

"Umm." It wasn't precisely the reaction the kobold had been expecting. He swallowed. "It's a small creature, about this high. . . . We, umm, we raise them as food stock. Kobolds, that is. Underground. We think they might be distantly related to birds, although they certainly can't fly. . . ."

"Preening creatures, are they?"

Gork nodded. "Unimpressive, though. Slower than rock melting, and not real bright."

"I figured." Cræosh took another step. "You feel better now, Gork?"

The kobold forced a grin across his face. "For the moment."

"Good. Then get your ass moving. Let's go see what's up with our furry friends and Jhurpess's worms."

Gork blinked, but he wasn't about to question the unexpected reprieve. He quickly fell in with Jhurpess and Fezeill as the squad set about tracking the yetis, and *back*tracking the bugbear.

Katim fell back to march beside Cræosh, who was bringing up the rear.

"I am somewhat . . . surprised," she said.

"What, that I didn't squeeze his head till it popped like a rotten grape?"

"I was thinking more . . . like a badger, but yes."

Cræosh decided firmly not to ask *why* trolls had an expression in their language for popping badgers. "Thought about it. Really seriously thought about it. Gork's useful, though, in his own way. And the fact is, the little turd's absolutely right. We've gotta have other priorities right now."

Katim grinned, a semifrozen tendril of drool dropping from her maw. "But as soon . . . as there are no other . . . priorities?"

Yeah, I don't think she's talkin' about Gork anymore. "I've fought humans, elves, and dwarves, soldiers and wizards, even a small dragon once, and not a one of them could kill me. You can be sure as shit squishes that I don't intend to let one of my own team do it." Deep within, a part of him cringed at so openly confronting the troll, but if there was fear in his soul, there was certainly none in his voice.

The troll's smile widened. "Are you so certain . . . I mean you harm?"

"I'm 'worthy,' remember?"

"Indeed you are. Look on the bright . . . side, Cræosh. For the . . . moment, we still have . . . *priorities*."

Cræosh wasn't certain how (or if?) he would have responded to that, had not Fezeill's voice come drifting back to them. "Mind your step up here," he called. "The ground's getting a little rocky and uneven. I think there's one of those chasms Katim mentioned off to the right. We shouldn't get too close."

The orc suddenly stopped short. "What's the problem . . . now?" Katim asked.

"Um . . . Which way did you throw Gimmol, exactly?"

The troll glanced about, taking her bearings, and pointed.

Ahead and off to the right.

For an instant, her jaw worked without the faintest sound. It was the first time Cræosh had seen her speechless.

"Oh," she said finally.

"Yeah," Cræosh agreed. "Oh."

Another moment of silence.

"Do we . . . actually care what happened . . . to him?"

"We don't. Shreckt might."

They dashed ahead, quickly overtaking Fezeill and the others. There was, indeed, a gorge—narrow but *very* deep—plunging away into the frozen earth, not far off their intended path. After a woefully inadequate explanation of the situation, Cræosh ordered them all to spread out and advance slowly upon the gorge, searching for a gremlin who might or might not already be a part of the landscape.

It was Gork who finally stumbled over him. The ground here sloped toward the chasm, gradually at first but dangerously steep near the edge. Several piles in the snow suggested that something roughly gremlin-sized *might* have landed nearby and then tumbled down the incline.

Or it could've just been the gusting wind. Gork had already climbed as far down that slope as he was willing to risk (not very), and was just about to haul himself back up when he heard whimpering.

Damn. "Gimmol? That you?"

"*Help!!!!*"

"I'll interpret that as a yes," Gork muttered, rubbing an ear. "All right, hold on!" *Stars dammit all, why'd I have to be the one to find him?* He gave serious thought to walking away, pretending he'd never found the annoying little scab, but the others had seen him come down this way to search. If he walked away empty-handed, and one of them found Gimmol later on, they'd certainly figure out what had happened—and then *Gork* might be the one lying broken at the bottom of the chasm.

So instead he dug into his traveling pack and hauled out a worn but sturdy length of rope and a small piton. Clearing away a patch of snow, he hammered the steel spike into the rock, wrapped the other end of the rope about his waist, and crawled down the slope on all fours.

And then . . . "Found him!"

Yeah, found. But *reaching* him, Gork realized with a snout-long scowl, was something else again. Back pressed to the rock as though glued, Gimmol lay at the very edge of the slope, inches above the chasm's lip. Only a protruding stone, onto which the gremlin had jammed his left foot, prevented him from sliding over the edge and plunging into darkness.

Steep grade, snow-wet stone, fingers numbed by the cold, and not a handhold to be seen. "You're *really* buggered," Gork told him helpfully.

Using the rope as a pendulum, Gork swung over beside the trapped gremlin and clung to the rock with his claws. Gimmol's eyes were tightly shut, but his twitch suggested that he heard the kobold coming.

For no reason the kobold could discern, a few streaks of the cliff face beneath Gimmol's precarious perch were not only free of frost but seared black, as though touched by a recent fire. "Okay," Gork said, studying the situation, "we'll get you out of here, but first I want to know—"

"Look down," Gimmol whispered.

"I already *know* it's a long drop!" Gork barked. "That's why I'm *not*—"

"Look! Down! Now!"

Muttering all manner of obscenities, Gork glanced downward. At which point he lost all interest in the peculiar scorching—and very nearly his hold on the rope as well.

"Oh, dragonshit . . ."

It looked rather as if a segment of the cliff face was moving, shimmering and shifting in the shadows of the evening. But the kobold's vision quickly detected what had probably taken Gimmol some time to perceive.

It wasn't the wall that was moving. It was the thousands upon thousands of worms, centipedes, and grubs that were swarming over it.

Gork's heart seized in his chest and his muscles went stiff; but the thought of lying helpless as ten thousand tiny bites stripped the flesh from his bones broke his paralysis just as swiftly.

"We've got to get out of here!" he squeaked, voice shaking.

The gremlin opened one eye. "Did you figure that one out by yourself, or did someone read it to you from a book?"

"You know, for someone in a spot as shitty as yours, you—"

"Hey!" Cræosh's voice wafted down from above. "Who's strutting now, wefkoo?"

Gork just sighed.

"Worms!" That wavering cry, of course, from Jhurpess. A momentary pause, presumably while Cræosh strained to see farther down into the chasm, and then . . .

"Shit on toast! Gork, get your ass up here!"

"What about me?" Gimmol screamed.

"We'll handle it! Gork, get up here!"

He obeyed, hugging the rope the whole way like a long-lost (and very tall) lover.

Cræosh and Katim lay belly-first upon the slope, as near to the edge as they could go without sliding. Yards away, on far more level ground, Fezeill and Gork awaited their next move. And Jhurpess . . .

Jhurpess hung, one-handed, from Gork's piton, now driven into the earth much nearer the quivering gremlin. But even with the bugbear stretched to his utmost, Gimmol remained a few feet beyond reach.

They might have tried the kobold's rope, but the worn hemp probably wouldn't support the weight of any member of the squad strong enough to haul Gimmol to safety.

"Hurry!" the gremlin moaned pitifully up at them. "They're so close I can hear them!"

Katim hissed once in irritation. "How sturdy is . . . your armor?"

The gremlin blinked in confusion, glancing at the scrounged, mismatched leather covering his chest and limbs. "What?" he asked finally.

Another hiss, with just a hint of aggravated growl sneaking in beneath it.

"It's all scavenged," Gimmol amended. "But it's real thick, and the straps are tough." He whimpered, trying not to look down into the chasm. "But it's not going to do any good against . . ."

The troll wasn't listening. With obvious reluctance, she uncoiled her *chirrusk* from her belt and passed it down to the dangling bugbear.

"If you drop that . . . weapon," she told Jhurpess, her voice tight, "you had better . . . be prepared to chase . . . after it."

"Jhurpess not drop weapon," the bugbear muttered, insulted. "Jhurpess knows what Jhurpess is doing!" Then he glanced down at the hooked chain in his hand. "Umm, what Jhurpess doing?"

Cræosh sighed loudly. "Use the damn hook!" he called before Katim could answer.

Comprehension finally dawned. "Oh! Yes, Jhurpess understands!" The bugbear tossed the haft from his free hand to one of his prehensile feet. Then, his entire face scrunched in what, on him, passed for concentration, he began to twirl the chain.

Cræosh looked over at the troll. "If he 'understands' this as well as he understood the concept of standing watch, we may be cleaning gremlin guts off your *chirrosk* for a week."

In lieu of any more meaningful comment, Katim snidely corrected his pronunciation.

Gimmol, having caught a glimpse of the chain in the bugbear's grasp, was clearly having a few doubts along similar lines. "Are you insane? He's going to kill me! I don't want to die here! I eeeyaaaagghhhhh!!!!!!"

The four-pronged hook came hurtling over the edge, flashing brightly but briefly in the sun, and the gremlin was absolutely certain that he was about to die.

But Jhurpess, for once, not only performed up to expectations, he exceeded them. The hook lodged not in soft gremlin flesh, but around the straps of the leather breastplate.

Gimmol's feet slowly rose from the tiny spur of rock that had saved him. He twisted slowly in the air, nothing but a single length of chain and the strength and skill (whimper) of the bugbear between him and the horror below.

And then he was falling!

It was a brief drop, barely a foot. He glared upward, determined to find some way—once he was back on solid ground, of course—to murder the bugbear for his carelessness. But the childish expression on Jhurpess's face suggested a panic akin to Gimmol's own. So what . . . .

Another brief jolt, even shorter than the first, and the gremlin realized with a growing sense of dread just what was happening.

The piton was slipping! Designed to hold only a curious kobold, it had performed admirably in standing up to the bugbear's weight—but now, between the swinging chain and the extra load of gremlin, it was right about ready to quit in disgust.

Gimmol did the only sensible thing: he screamed his head off in a girlish falsetto. This was too much for the panicking bugbear, and he too started screaming, loosing that now-familiar wail.

"Well," Cræosh snarled between clenched teeth, "that should make sure we attract any surviving yetis. Thanks, guys!" He pivoted toward Katim, but she was no longer there. She was, in fact, halfway down the slope already, her claws finding purchase in the stones that Cræosh wouldn't have trusted to support Gork, let alone the troll. Was she actually risking herself for *Jhurpess* and *Gimmol?* Had he misjudged her that badly? Had . . . ?

Oh. Of course. She was after her *chirrusk.* Never mind, then.

When the slope grew too steep for her claws and powerful fingers to prevent her from sliding, Katim drew her massive axe and, utterly unconcerned with any potential damage to the blade, drove it into the first crevice she could find. Metal screamed and sparks flew, but the weapon felt secure enough to hold. Then, as Jhurpess had done, she allowed herself to drop until she hung by a single hand above the chasm.

Grunting with strain, ignoring the sounds of Gork and Fezeill placing bets on what would happen, she twisted, stretching as far as her lanky arms would reach. . . .

There! She was hanging very near horizontally, her body forming a sideways cross, but she'd just been able to get a grip, not on the bugbear but on the piton. Muscles bulged, her snout twisted in agony—but slowly, so slowly, the spike slid fully free of the stone and began to rise, Jhurpess and Gimmol still hanging from it.

Everyone above, and the pair dangling below, held their breath. The troll's entire body quivered, and for a moment she froze, struggling and failing to lift the load any higher. She heard Cræosh shifting above, perhaps even looking for a way to help, but she knew he wouldn't find one.

But Katim wasn't finished. With a supreme effort of will, she again set the dangling pair in motion: not upward, this time, but side to side.

Jhurpess, clinging to the piton and the *chirrusk* with everything he had, whined once but otherwise remained silent. Gimmol, who wasn't using any of his own muscle to stay aloft, apparently felt justified in resuming his screams.

Back and forth, higher and higher, until finally the gremlin-end of the living pendulum, at its apex, reached Katim's own level. "Jhurpess," she rasped, voice nigh incomprehensible with strain, "haul . . . Gimmol up . . . a few more . . . feet. Then . . . when I . . . tell you . . . let go!"

"What?" the bugbear squeaked.

"Of the . . . *chain*, you . . . brainless imbecile! Not . . . the piton!"

"Oh." A very small, quiet voice now. "Okay."

A moment more Katim waited, summoning the reserves she would need to pull off this particular miracle. And then, a simple whispered "Now!"

The bugbear released the *chirrusk*, abandoning the screaming gremlin to his fate.

So much of this half-assed plan could go wrong. If she'd misjudged the remaining length of chain, or the height of the swing, or her own pain-dulled and cold-addled reflexes . . . If *anything* went wrong, they were dead.

Even as Jhurpess let go of the chain, Katim was once again hauling with all her might. The bugbear's weight was hardly negligible, but without the added load of gremlin, she managed to thrust him up toward her axe. Using it as a step, and jamming the piton into the wall as he went, Jhurpess scurried over the edge of the slope.

Katim didn't see it. The instant she was no longer holding the bugbear, she lunged, both arms stretched—one in each direction—boots scrabbling for just a few seconds of purchase on the same rock that had saved Gimmol's life.

She'd ordered Jhurpess to let go at the highest point of the arc, so when Gimmol had sailed off to her right, he'd also been traveling *up*. And that gave Katim the extra instants she needed. At the very last second, just before the gremlin plummeted out of reach, her fingers snagged the butt of the *chirrusk*'s handle. Katim shuddered in pain as the arm with which she held the axe dislocated itself at the shoulder, but she had him.

And her *chirrusk*!

Wrapping the chain over and over about her wrist, she hauled the gremlin up until she could grasp his collar, and then hurled him back over the lip of the canyon, trusting that one of her companions would catch him before he slid back down. And finally, though it took some doing with only one good arm, she hauled herself up and over the axe that she would never take for granted again.

For long moments, the squad just sat—*well* away from the slope—and gasped for breath. A loud pop and a howl of pain suggested that Katim had dealt, brutally but effectively, with her dislocated shoulder.

Gork wandered over to Gimmol, who lay faceup and panting, in the snow. "Hey," he said to the supine gremlin. "You owe me a new piton."

Gimmol punched the kobold in the testicles and then lay back, smiling, as Gork toppled over beside him.

Even Cræosh, anxious as he was to keep moving, recognized the need for a few moments' rest. As the minutes passed and the sun slid closer to the horizon, however, he decided they'd had long enough.

"All right, kits and cubs, naptime's over! Feet: On 'em!"

Jhurpess immediately climbed to his feet, and Fezeill was already standing—but Gork, Katim, and Gimmol just glowered, united in their sudden burning hatred of the orc.

Cræosh decided to try something unexpected and *reason* with them.

"Those yetis," he said, "are still out there. If they come back and find you all lying here like pimples on a dwarf's ass, they'll pop you accordingly."

"And we'll do any better if we're walking when they find us?" Gimmol asked sullenly.

But Katim, though wincing at every movement, was slowly standing. "I'd rather have . . . the option of running. And if we can . . . bring them together, the . . . yetis remain our best chance . . . of studying Jhurpess's worm . . . creatures in action." She very specifically turned on Gimmol. "Unless you . . . want the chance to . . . examine them again. Up . . . close and personal."

The gremlin quickly stood. Gork, cursing all orcs and gremlins, realized he was the only holdout and did the same.

Thankfully, they didn't have to go far. They'd followed the tracks for little more than another mile before they stumbled across the yetis.

Or what remained of the yetis.

"Ancestors!" Cræosh whispered. Gork muttered something similar invoking the Stars, and Katim just hissed.

Strewn about, the snow around them churned and bloodied by what must have been a ferocious battle, were five large corpses. Each had been chewed by hundreds, perhaps thousands, of tiny mouths. Most were stripped bare of skin, partially bare of flesh and muscle; one was nothing but a blood-encrusted skeleton. And the positions in which they lay—limbs splayed, jaws agape—suggested that they'd been very much alive even as they became something's banquet.

The squad swiveled as one toward the faintly trembling bugbear. "Jhurpess not like worms," he confided in them.

"No shit 'Jhurpess not like worms!'" Cræosh barked. "You *escaped* from these fuckers?"

The bugbear nodded. "Worms not run very fast."

Katim nodded. "Useful information . . . Cræosh. In case your . . . brilliant leadership and strategic . . . skills should prove . . . insufficient."

"All right, you listen, you dog-faced, flea-ridden—"

Fezeill screamed in a convincing imitation of a *real* bugbear and pointed a shaking finger behind them.

From the depths of the snow rose three figures, humanoid but blatantly inhuman. Their outlines writhed in the glow of the setting sun, while centipedes and maggots dripped from them in a horrible perspiration. Their features were nothing but gaping hollows, and their hands were raised, extended toward the exhausted goblins.

Cræosh glanced back the way they'd come, mouth open to order a retreat, and nearly swallowed his tongue. A fourth worm-creature had appeared from behind, but this was no more humanoid than Cræosh was a halfling. Yes, it had two arms and two legs, but it stood eight feet tall, and it was wider than three orcs side by side. In fact, it almost resembled . . .

"A yeti," Gork breathed from somewhere off to his left. "It's the damn yeti!"

He was right, the orc realized with a sudden surge of terror. Six yetis, but only five corpses. They must have arrived before the worms could do—whatever it was that they did—to the other bodies.

And . . . *Oh, Ancestors!* It meant that there were worse fates out on the tundra than death. The sun sat, mocking him, mere inches above the western horizon. *Damn, damn, damn! If the fucking creatures had just waited another hour or so, we'd have been away from this frozen hell and back—*

Four crawling arms rose, four wiggling hands opened, and a veritable storm of worms and centipedes hurtled at the Demon Squad.

Cræosh dove and rolled, coming to his feet well away from the wriggling projectiles now freezing to death in the snow. Unwilling to give his foes the opportunity to—was "reload" the right word?—he set his blade, took a single deep breath as he willed away his fatigue and his fear, and charged.

Close up, the writhing mass of component vermin was even worse, revolting on a purely instinctive level. He'd been told that King Morthûl sometimes gave a similar impression, what with the various crawling things infesting his half-dead body, but this was worse than anything Cræosh had heard about his Dark Lord.

He dealt with it—the fear, the revulsion, all of it—in typical orcish fashion: by trying to kill whatever it was that made him uncomfortable. The massive, jagged blade plunged through the roiling chest. A spray of dead and dying creatures, worms and centipedes primarily, spurted from the wound and splashed across the combatants' feet. The thing staggered a moment, and the vermin that formed the "flesh" near the injury wavered and twitched, *almost* falling free as though whatever magic held them in place had wavered.

A moment of weakness, perhaps, but a moment only. The creature straightened and shambled forward a step, moving inside Cræosh's reach, arms outstretched in horrid mockery of an embrace.

The sword, Cræosh noted sourly as he backpedaled, was clearly not the proper instrument for this particular endeavor. He knew that the things could be hurt, and he assumed that meant they could be *killed*, but it would take some special effort to make it happen.

A quick glance told him that the others weren't having that much better a time of it. Jhurpess bounced from foot to hand to foot, capering about his chosen foe in a spastic dance. His cudgel rose and fell, first in this fist, then in that, and each swipe crushed a sizable heap of worms. Cræosh wasn't sure if he could actually kill the thing that way or not, but as long as he could keep moving, not let it lay a grotesque hand on him, he had a shot.

Katim, naturally, had faced off against the swarm that had taken the form of the missing yeti, rather than any of the smaller ones. Her axe, presumably as useless as the orc's sword, still hung at her back, but her *chirrusk* was a steel cyclone, sweeping through the creature's form again and again, hurling the tiny creatures away by the score. With each whistling revolution, the faux yeti staggered, but again, Cræosh couldn't be certain if the damage was lasting.

The others weren't having even that amount of luck. Gimmol and Fezeill stabbed again and again, their short-bladed weapons proving all but useless, and Gork had once more disappeared entirely.

And then Cræosh's foe lunged, the hollow of its mouth agape in what could only be described as a silent roar, and the orc, parrying desperately, had no attention left to devote to the others. He could only hope that *someone* would come up with a bright idea of what to do next.

Gork wished desperately to the Stars that he had any idea of what to do next. Peeking from the lip of his latest burrow, he peered at the raging chaos and gave serious thought to just waiting it out. It wasn't cowardice that kept him out of the fight—well, not *just* cowardice—but rather an absolute conviction that his presence wouldn't make the slightest difference. His *kah-rahahk* wouldn't do any more good than Gimmol's short sword, not against enemies without solid flesh, let alone internal organs. He *sure* as hell wasn't prepared to *bite* the damn thing, and that didn't leave him any other options. . . .

Well, maybe *one*.

The vapors of an idea beginning to coalesce beneath his ears, and the kobold tore into his backpack.

Katim howled in bestial exultation as the worm-yeti finally lost cohesion, the entire swarm of vermin scattering beneath the weight and the wind of her spinning *chirrusk*. Like halflings fleeing a burning building—and yes, she'd seen it happen, so the comparison felt justified—the tiny creatures fled every which way, some burrowing into the snow, some freezing where they landed, some literally bursting in what must have been some sort of mystic backlash from whatever magics had bound them together. Her voice rose even higher as she cried her triumph for all the worlds to hear, for if these horrors could cast spells, as Jhurpess claimed, then they must possess intelligence—intelligence that would be hers.

Welcome it, my pets, she cooed internally, delighting at the thought of such a horror serving her in the next life. *Welcome it, and make it room. It will be with us all a very long time.*

She knew, though, that she had precious little time for celebration. Three more swarms remained, and the others were not doing so well as she. Jhurpess seemed to be having *some* effect, his thrashing club having taken its toll; the creature looked somehow smaller, less substantial than it had. But he seemed, too, to have hit some sort of plateau, a point beyond which he could not injure it further, could not land a final blow. He pranced around it, remaining a step ahead of the thrashing limbs, but that was all.

Cræosh had turned to the flat of his blade, wielding it as a cudgel, but the awkward grip and his previous yeti-dealt wounds were slowing him. He hadn't done even so well as Jhurpess, and though he fought hard, the eventual outcome was plain for all to see.

But he could stand a few moments more; it was Gimmol and Fezeill who most needed her aid. Even as she watched, the bugbear-wearing-doppelganger staggered, struck across the chest by a vicious backhand. He screamed, a sound more terror than pain, and began wildly grasping at his own chest. It took Katim a moment, from where she stood, to see that Fezeill was desperately yanking worms and centipedes from his own flesh! Her *chirrusk* spinning once more, the troll leapt upon the shapeshifter's writhing foe.

Good! Gork gasped in heartfelt relief as the troll hurtled through the air to drive her whistling chain through the thing's body. He'd have been mortified if he'd had to come to Gimmol's rescue *again*, and he *definitely* wasn't putting his stony ass on the line for Fezeill!

That left Jhurpess and Cræosh, though, each battling his respective foe, and the plan was as ready as it would ever be. A brief sigh, a final prayer to the Stars, and the kobold emerged from his burrow and began a squirming crawl toward the bugbear, scowling at the taste of wood in his mouth.

In his peripheral vision, Cræosh saw Katim's expression twist in rapture as the second worm-thing finally burst apart beneath her whirling chain. That left only the two, and damn, he hoped he could finish his off before Jhurpess did. That'd be embarrassing, if his was the last. . . .

And then the one he faced took a step back, for the shambling mon-strosities had clearly decided they were done playing fair. In perfect unison they raised their arms, and four glittering shards of crackling, semisolid fire shot from their fingers.

Katim was lifted from the snow and thrown back to the ground as two of the arcane missiles slammed into her. Wisps of smoke rose from her burned leather armor and scorched fur, and Cræosh smelled the aroma of roast meat. She climbed quickly to her feet, a snarl of fury rumbling from her throat, but she winced with every movement, every rasping breath.

The third flaming bolt struck the bugbear, spinning him in place, and the fourth . . .

Cræosh raised his sword, hoping to deflect the last one—it wasn't moving *that* quickly—but the damn thing *swerved around the blade!* A moment of searing agony, the world did a few quick somersaults around him, and the orc found himself lying sprawled some yards from where he'd started.

Rigidly holding his neck straight so that his ringing head would stay attached, Cræosh tried to struggle to his feet. And noted, with more confusion than pain, that his legs refused to cooperate.

Well, this is not good. And now he *knew* he'd been hurt worse than he thought, because he was clearly hallucinating! He hadn't *really* seen a flaming kobold burst from the snow. Flaming kobolds weren't native to the Steppes, were they? The snow—Cræosh actually found himself fighting back a giggle—the snow would put them out, right?

And then, mercifully, he passed out before he had the chance to say any of this out loud and *really* embarrass himself.

Gork was not, in fact, on fire—self-immolation would certainly have been an *unexpected* way to end the fight, but probably not the most effective one—but the torches he held in each fist most certainly were. He rose from his crouch behind the creature that had been battling Jhurpess, and struck before it even knew he was there.

The first blazing torch slid easily into the swarm. Charred vermin fell to the earth with a muffled *whumph*. Gork swung the second torch high, lunging on his tiptoes, and drove it into the creature's chin. Another instant of crackling and sizzling, and then the kobold was showered with dead and dying bugs.

Between the kobold's torches and the troll's *chirrusk*, the final swarm was gone in moments.

"Well," Gork muttered, extinguishing both torches in the snow, "so much for the easy part."

Katim dropped her gaze on him like an anvil. "Easy?"

"Hell, yeah!" He waved one blackened brand at the comatose orc. "Now we've got to get *him* back on his feet!"

Katim nodded slowly. "Indeed. That . . . could prove difficult. I—" And then, with a pained and rather puzzled scowl, she too collapsed at the kobold's feet.

"Well, shit." Gork waved the others over to give him a hand as best they could. In the distance, another pack of yetis howled their fury at the rising moon.

"Well, that was productive" the doppelganger said some time later, his voice so thick with sarcasm it threatened to freeze in the cold. "So what do you suggest we do now?"

Gork glanced up from the sprawling heap of orc and troll that lay before them, his jaw clenched in impotent fury. "I don't have the first fucking clue, Fezeill. Why don't you turn into a horse so we can carry them?"

"I can't do anything the size of a horse, kobold."

"No? You seem to be doing quite well as a horse's a—"

"Shut . . . up."

Everyone turned to the prostrate troll. "We thought you were unconscious," Gimmol muttered.

"That's because . . . you're all stupid," she said, glossing over the fact that she damn well *had* been. "Help . . . me stand."

It took the combined efforts of Jhurpess and Fezeill, but they did just that. Katim couldn't take more than a few steps without stumbling, but she was upright.

"We can't stay here," Gork pointed out. "Either the yetis or the worms could come back with reinforcements."

"I know. Is that . . . why you dumped the orc . . . and me in that rather . . . undignified pile?"

The kobold kicked the snow at his feet. "We thought that once we'd gathered you up, it'd be easier to move, or at least it'd keep you from freezing. . . ."

Katim raised a hand. "Spare me the . . . details. How do you . . . plan to move the orc?"

Gork, Gimmol, and Fezeill traded guilty glances. "Actually . . ." the gremlin began reluctantly.

"You were going . . . to leave him," Katim concluded. She laid just a touch of emphasis on *him*, making it damn clear that what she meant was *us*.

"Well," Gimmol said defensively, "it's not as though anybody likes him! And more importantly," he added quickly when Katim scowled, "we have to survive! That means we can't stay here! And—"

Katim growled. "We need him. We . . . wouldn't have survived . . . this long without him."

Fezeill snorted. "That, and if you let him die here, you can't claim *huurrk* . . ."

The doppelganger dangled, thrashing and flopping, from Katim's fist.

"Jhurpess thought Katim was injured," the bugbear said.

"*I* thought Fezeill was faster than that," Gimmol added.

Gork grinned. "And *I* wonder how long doppelgangers can hold their breath." Indeed, the bugbear face Fezeill was wearing at the time was turning an impressive, floral shade of violet.

Alas, his burning question would forever be unanswered. Katim opened her fist with a snort of disgust and then stepped over the gasping figure by her feet. "Jhurpess, throw . . . the orc over your shoulder . . . and let's move."

She recognized her mistake just a split second before the loud *thump* reached her ears. She briefly squeezed her eyes shut in pain, suddenly understanding the reasons for Cræosh's constant bad attitude. "Jhurpess," she said, steadfastly refusing to turn around. "I meant . . . *carry* the orc . . . over your shoulder."

"Oh. That does make more sense to Jhurpess, yes."

For the first time ever, Katim felt the urge to whimper. Still, it was less than half an hour until sundown, and then Shreckt would get them out of this frozen wasteland.

She could barely wait.

In the comfort of the gently rocking carriage, a cup of tea halfway to her lips, Queen Anne abruptly froze. "Oh, dear."

Belrotha, who was still, after so many hours, squirming about in search of a comfortable position that didn't wedge her butt painfully between the armrests of her chair, tensed. Her nerves were stretched near the breaking point already, so the consternation in the queen's voice was absolutely *not* what she needed to hear.

"What?!" she asked in as close to a squeak as an ogre could possibly get. "What wrong?"

"Nothing to concern yourself over," Queen Anne assured her with the faintest shake of her head. "Just something I had better deal with. We can't have them dying on us just now, can we?"

"Who? What? Huh?"

"Precisely, my child. Excuse me just a moment, please." And with that, the queen . . . shimmered.

Belrotha blanched. Queen Anne had, and had not, disappeared. A vague image—transparent and blurry, almost a soggy watercolor—remained in the chamber. But the strange apparition was utterly motionless, failing even to rock with the swaying of the carriage. The ogre hauled her knees up to her chest, causing the chair to groan in pain, and tried her damnedest to curl into a ball.

The moon had reached its zenith and begun the long descent toward morning by the time the squad arrived, limping and battered, in the craggy foothills. Shambling as awkwardly as the worm-men they'd battled, they stumbled into a tiny valley: little more than a crack between two steep slopes. It was cramped enough that every one of the goblins had either a protrusion of stone or someone's elbow poking them in the ribs, but the hills kept the worst of the frigid winds off them. They could probably have found a better location, if they'd bothered to look before it was already dark, but they hadn't.

They hadn't expected to need one.

After some minutes of panic, the goblins of the Demon Squad had tentatively decided that the "four days" must have included the final night as well. Shreckt would come for them in the morning.

He'd damn well better.

With a low groan, Jhurpess toppled face-first to the ground, allowing Cræosh to slip from his shoulder like a sack of elf giblets. The combined impact of orc and bugbear sent up a cloud of dust and snow thick enough to lean on. Katim, who had stubbornly insisted on walking under her own power the entire way, retained just enough dignity to *slide* to the earth beside them, rather than following them over in a near faint. And Fezeill hadn't fully recovered from his ill-fated attempt at kicking his breathing habit.

This left Gork and Gimmol responsible for making camp and setting watch, and since the kobold was already asleep by the time he thought to broach the topic, the gremlin kindly volunteered to take the first shift.

Aggravating, but it could've been worse. Gimmol was exhausted, sure, but he felt warmer than he had in days, and any tribulation was worth a few hours of silence and solitude. Gods and demons, could *none* of the uneducated cretins *shut up* for more than two minutes? It was enough to drive a gremlin mad! But while they slept, there was peace.

Until, of course, the apparition rose from the rock beside his sleeping teammates.

With a silence Gork might have envied, Gimmol crept nearer the phantom, fingering the hilt of what had, so far, proved to be a remarkably useless sword. The figure was transparent, allowing him a distorted view of the terrain beyond. It—she? It looked vaguely like a "she"—was facing away from him, but she appeared more or less human, dark of hair, garbed in flowing emerald green. He drew breath to call a warning, but she was already reaching down, running the back of her hand down Cræosh's jaw.

Gimmol's abortive shout became a gasp as the orc's flesh *rippled*.

That gasp, silent as it was, carried across the tiny vale. The apparition spun, and Gimmol raised his hands, prepared to do whatever he could to ward off the attack he knew was coming.

Except that it didn't. The tiny scraps of light cast by the dying embers touched the phantom's face, a face that Gimmol had seen in many a portrait throughout Kirol Syrreth.

"Queen Anne!" The gremlin dropped to one knee in a courtly bow, one far more elegant than his companions could have imagined. "Forgive me, I—"

"Have done nothing wrong." Her voice brought a touch of warmth to the frigid shadows. "You acted to protect your companions, as any good soldier should."

Gimmol nodded, emboldened by her indulgence. "Your Majesty, if it is not too presumptuous . . . What are you doing here? This is no place for—"

"Relax, my child. I'm *not* here."

Gimmol squinted. Yep; he could, at the proper angle, still see completely through her.

"I merely felt," she continued, "that you could use my assistance. This is my first gift to you." She gestured at the slumbering orc. His skin had ceased its strange, liquid motion, and the bruises and cuts, the abrasions and burns, had faded! To look at him, you'd think Cræosh hadn't seen battle in weeks.

Beneath Gimmol's marveling gaze, the image of the queen visited each of the goblins in turn, easing their hurts. She skipped only Gimmol himself, who had so far avoided substantial injury (despite his troll-powered flight).

"Who are we," he asked, his voice hushed, "that you would take such interest in us?"

The queen smiled. "Surely you have guessed that you are all important to my husband's plans for the upcoming war. Is that not reason enough to watch over you?"

No, actually it's not. Morthûl had too many minions at his disposal, some of whom weren't that much less potent, or frightening, than the Charnel King himself. The notion that he would send his queen to perform any such task was ludicrous. But Gimmol was far too wise to say so aloud.

"It is indeed, Your Majesty. But you said this was the *first?*"

"I did." The ghostly form began to fade. "You shall meet the other tomorrow. A pleasant night to you, dear gremlin."

"And to you." But Queen Anne was already gone.

His brow furrowed, Gimmol resumed his post. So lost in thought was he, he didn't realize how much time had passed until a half hour after his shift should have ended. Questions rolling around like marbles inside his skull, the goblin went to wake Gork for his turn at watch.

The dawn, punctual as ever, arrived precisely on schedule. Shreckt did not.

"I thought I saw her," a restored Cræosh commented to Gimmol over a breakfast of—what else?—yeti meat. "But I figured it was a dream."

"No dream," the gremlin said. "She was here, sort of. I talked to her, but she didn't seem particularly inclined to tell me why she'd come. She was nice enough, though, and she helped you guys out, so . . ." His jaw snapped shut abruptly as Katim smacked him in the head with a yeti femur.

"Nonetheless, you should . . . have woken us."

Gimmol nodded in understanding, clutching his head so it didn't fall off in the process.

"Okay," Cræosh said, pushing away the last of his own breakfast. "I think it's safe to say the little hell-turd ain't gonna show anytime soon. So either something's gotten real fucked up back home, and he can't come get us, or he's deliberately letting us dangle in the breeze."

"I know which one *my* money's on," Gork muttered.

The orc frowned. "For once, Shorty, I agree with you. Anybody know the best way to kill an imp?"

Katim snorted. "You try to kill . . . Shreckt, you are entirely . . . on your own."

"Cowardice, troll? That ain't like you."

"Suicide is not . . . like me either. Small or not . . . Shreckt is a demon. And attacking him . . . is most definitely . . . suicide." The corners of her mouth angled downward. "As is calling me . . . a coward twice. That was . . . *one.*"

Cræosh was saved the trouble of responding—or the humiliation of *not* responding—by Jhurpess. In a flash of fur, the bugbear was hopping up and down, slamming his massive cudgel against the rock so furiously that splinters of wood spun off across the campsite.

"What the fuck now?" Cræosh demanded. But Fezeill saw them too, now, and began backing away from the snow-slick hillside. "Worms!" he shouted, a finger pointing at the bugbear's feet.

And at the worms, the centipedes, everything the squad had hoped they'd left far behind, sliding through cracks and crevices in the stone.

"We're leaving!" Cræosh shouted, scrambling up out of the tiny shelter. It was, for once, an order that nobody felt the need to argue.

The goblins scrambled, spiderlike, up over the edges of the valley and broke into a chaotic run along the edges of the range. The faster pulled swiftly ahead—figuring that they only had to outrun their slowest companions, not the worms—and Cræosh felt no burning urge to rein them in. Once they'd put some distance between them and this latest mass of creeping death, *then* he'd worry about proper formation and military discipline. For now, he put his head down, pumped his legs, and made damn sure he wasn't last in line.

After some moments, when no trace of the worms remained in sight, Cræosh skidded to a halt. Katim stood ahead of him, peering thought-fully up one of the smaller mountains. "Sightseeing?" he asked irritably.

"Up there," the troll growled, oblivious to his irritation. "Look."

He looked. Some fifteen feet up the slope, a wide ledge—large enough for the squad, with room left over for the troll's ego—protruded from the stone. It looked, to Cræosh, as though the mountain were sticking its tongue—or perhaps a particularly wide finger—out at the world.

Yeah, brother, you and me both.

"Suggesting we fort up?" he asked.

The troll shrugged her fur-covered shoulders. "We cannot run . . . forever. Up there, they might . . . pass us by unnoticed, and . . . if not, the place is . . . defensible."

Despite himself, the orc nodded. "Provides a pretty good field of view, too. And yeah, I'll admit I'm not happy with all this running away."

"No? Then why . . . were you so quick to—?"

"Don't finish that sentence, Dog-face."

Katim chuckled.

"All right!" Cræosh yelled to the others. "We're heading up! Gork?" Ancestors damn him, where *was* the little . . .

"Yes, oh obstreperous one?"

Cræosh glanced upward. The kobold's stony head hung over the edge of the shelf.

Fucking show-off.

"I want you to check out the ledge," he continued, as though he'd fully expected to see the little shit up there. "Make sure it's clear."

"It's clear," Gork said. "Nothing up here but me and bat shit." Then, "Don't say it!"

"Wouldn't dream. Okay, boys and bitch, get climbing!"

Gork's report, they saw once they'd ascended, had been pretty accurate: just a flat expanse of stone, featureless but for large accumulations of snow and old guano. They settled in, alert for the tiniest sign of anything remotely abnormal.

But they were only looking *down*. Not a one of them noticed as, some distance above, a horse and carriage that could not *possibly* have navigated the narrow, winding mountain passes appeared from between a pair of crags. It drew to a halt, the door drifting open. . . .

"There!" It was Gimmol who first spotted them, rising from behind an outcropping of stone some few hillsides away. "Over there!"

"We," Gork said, strangely matter-of-fact, "are *a lot* dead."

Five enormous figures loomed from the rocks below: five writhing, wiggling, and very *familiar* figures. The worms, and whatever grotesque sorcery gave them shape, had finally finished with the other yeti corpses.

"We barely survived four!" Gimmol murmured, his voice suddenly hoarse. "And three of *them* were smaller!"

Cræosh hefted his sword, almost as though to parry the gremlin's despair.

Gork twisted toward his companions. "Hey, Gimmol, before we die, I want you to know something. All those times where I said I thought you were a fuck-up . . ."

"Yes?"

"I meant every word."

Katim rolled her eyes and shook loose her *chirrusk*, the clanking of the chain echoing through the peaks. She'd chosen a good spot, she knew these things could die, and dammit, she'd take at *least* one or two more to join her before the squad was overrun!

Even she had to admit, though, that given her druthers, this was *not* how she'd have chosen to go.

Focusing past the sounds around him as best he could—even the damned kobold, hard as he was making it—Gimmol peered over the ledge and chewed the inside of his cheek. He really, *really* hadn't wanted to have to do this, certainly not in front of the others. And hell, he probably couldn't do much, not against *five* of those things! But he had to try.

Sucking in a deep breath, the gremlin raised two empty hands, fingers spread. . . .

But someone else beat him to it.

The creatures had gathered in a fearsome pack, the nearest scarcely an arm's length from the slope, when the sun went away.

A small moon hung briefly in the sky, transforming day into dusk over a tiny patch of rock and ice in the midst of the Northern Steppes. Then it continued its arc, and it wasn't a moon at all but a gigantic boulder, jagged and uneven, ripped from the face of the mountain. It plummeted past them, near enough that the entire squad felt the wind of its passing, and crashed into the assembled creatures below.

The ledge—indeed the entire mountain, or so it felt to them—trembled at the impact. Dirt, snow, and rocks the size of Gork's head all sprayed up and out in a cheerful fountain. The goblins, all of whom had either been hurled prone at the impact or thrown *themselves* to the ledge at the sight of the boulder, covered their heads with their arms and waited for the detritus to cease its bombardment.

Cræosh, bleeding from a dozen tiny nicks, dragged himself to the edge and looked down. Nothing but greasy smears and a few writhing piles of freezing worms remained of the horrors that had pursued them.

And then, as he twisted to look *up*, a second impact shook the ledge. Above them all, impossibly tall, loomed a hideous, bruise-hued *thing*.

"Me Belrotha," it announced happily, beaming at them with a rotted, broken-toothed grin. "Me part of Demon Squad now. Queen say so."

Six faces turned toward one another, six pairs of wide eyes stared, and six voices rose as one.

"Okay."

Thoroughly sick and tired of wandering the tundra with no destination in mind, the squad remained camped at the base of the mountain—within easy reach of the ledge, just in case—for another three days. Boring, perhaps, but thankfully worm- and yeti-free, perhaps due to the presence of their intimidating, boulder-hurling new friend. And warm enough, given the cramped conditions.

Belrotha didn't say much to her new companions. Oh, she talked more than enough; she just didn't *say* anything. Cræosh and Gork swiftly began to wonder if the worms wouldn't have been the more pleasant option. Fezeill and Katim did their best to ignore her unless addressed directly. Even Jhurpess, one evening, sidled up to the orc's side and admitted, "Jhurpess not want to be mean, but Jhurpess thinks Belrotha might be kind of stupid."

But the ogre and the gremlin hit it off, oddly enough. "Probably," Cræosh noted sourly to Fezeill, "because she's too much an idiot to mind his prattling, and he's just thrilled someone'll talk to him."

And then, finally, just before evening on the third day . . .

"Fall in, you maggots!"

Instantly the squad lined up, their fury at the conniving imp warring across their faces with their immense relief at his arrival. Belrotha, who'd served in more than one unit, stood at attention with the rest when Shreckt appeared in a blast of sulfur.

The imp's gargoyle-ish jaw gaped open, prepared to bark another command—and open it stayed, as his gaze rose, and rose, and rose to meet the ogre's own.

"Umm," Belrotha muttered as the silence dragged on. "Me introduce self now?"

"Kneel!" the imp shouted. Instantly the ogre was on her knees, the

impact coating the little sergeant beneath a layer of snow rather like a soft down.

Cræosh snorted, and Gork and Gimmol both choked on guffaws that they knew better than to set free.

"Who the fuck are you?!" Shreckt screamed into the ogre's face.

"Me Belrotha."

"And?"

Belrotha blinked. "No and. Me just Belrotha."

Shreckt sighed. "What the hell are you doing with my squad?"

"Me part of squad now. Queen say so."

It was the imp's turn to blink. "Queen? You mean Queen Anne?"

The ogre frowned. "There other queen? Me not know about other queen!"

"Well, well," Shreckt said, shaking his head. "Ain't that a tickle?"

"Hey!" Cræosh butted in, his impatience getting the better of him (to no one's surprise). "You're three days late, you little—"

Shreckt's glare was burning, literally. His eyes blazed, and Cræosh noticed smoke rising from his armor.

"—officer," he concluded.

"Not at all," Shreckt said with a sudden and *very* unpleasant smile. "Actually, I'm a week early." Then, at their stunned expressions, "Well it wouldn't have been much of a survival test if it was only four days, would it?"

"Survival?" Jhurpess asked. "Jhurpess thought little sergeant said combat training."

Cræosh sneered. "Little sergeant lied his ass off."

The troll shrugged. "Are you really . . . surprised? Isn't that what . . . demons do?"

"All right, then," Fezeill said, resuming his true shape. "So you're 'early.' Why?"

Shreckt waived his riding crop under the ogre's nose. "Why don't you ask her?"

Belrotha looked about ready to panic. "Me not know. Me just got here, remember?"

"On the queen's orders," Shreckt reminded her. "And that's why I'm here, too.

"Survival training's over, you pukes. You've been assigned to Her Majesty directly. Until she or Morthûl says different, your asses belong to Queen Anne."

CHAPTER FOUR

A QUEEN SWEEP

The winds howled off the Sea of Tears, screaming across the walls of the massive citadel. Enormous slabs of black stone offered the structure its support, protecting those within from the elements. Across every inch of exterior stone, however, lay a latticework of black iron, filigreed into thousands, perhaps millions, of abstract designs and eldritch runes. Sometimes rain pounded upon the echoing metal; sometimes the lightning flashed, drawn from the clouds to the tips of the iron towers like a kobold to a merchant's purse. But always, *always* the winds shrieked as they wove through those tiny, uncountable hollows.

That, however, was the outside. Within the halls of the Iron Keep, silence reigned. Oh, there was movement aplenty, activity enough to put an anthill to shame, but it swirled and scurried in a constant, impossible hush. Seneschals—some living, some dead, and some to whom the question simply didn't apply—dashed to and fro as rapidly as the dignity of their office would permit. Messages were delivered, papers passed along to others, orders given, but no superfluous words, no casual conversations, were ever exchanged.

At every entrance and every major intersection stood guards, equally silent. The living were hardened, experienced soldiers, drawn from every race of Kirol Syrreth. The dead, who patrolled the halls in shambling formation, empty sockets gazing from iron helms, included not only goblins and humans, but elves and dwarves and halflings as well. In this reanimated, unfeeling mockery of life, former allies and enemies alike burned with fealty to King Morthûl where once minds and souls had thrived.

Vigo Havarren, who had traversed these halls a thousand times and more, ignored the guards as he blew past them, fascinated more by the architecture than the animate dead. From the lowermost stories, which were fairly mundane in scope and design, he passed into far more alien levels above. Here, many of the floors and walls were shaped of the same night-black iron as the keep's exterior, twisted into those same arcane designs. Some chambers were constructed *only* of filigree, allowing casual passersby to peer through the gaps in the iron to see what lay beyond; others, such as Morthûl's own chambers, were backed with walls of darkest stone.

Not even Havarren, for all his own mystical acumen, had ever discerned any master pattern to the runes in the iron, though he was certain there must be one. He recognized some *individual* glyphs, symbols of protection, sigils of power. Others he knew not: bent and twisted icons that coiled back upon themselves in impossible angles, refusing to obey the dictates of *geometry*, let alone any magic Havarren understood. Trying to comprehend the sheer amount of power that must flow through the Iron Keep with every second of the day made even the normally fearless wizard, chief servant of the Charnel King of Kirol Syrreth, shudder.

Squaring his shoulders, Havarren passed the final pair of skeletal guards and raised his hand to knock on the mahogany door. He wasn't even slightly nonplussed when the portal swung open before his fist had fallen. Accepting the unspoken invitation, he stepped across the threshold of King Morthûl's inner sanctum.

If the throne room of the Iron Keep, with its reflective floors and towering marble chair, was designed to impress, even intimidate, then this, the Charnel King's private audience chamber, must be intended to *disturb*. The shapes in the iron filigree wound over and around each other, sufficient to cause dizziness in anyone foolish enough to try following their twisting course. Worse, at various points along the wall roughly fifteen feet apart from one another, the iron bent *outward*, forming vaguely man-shaped cages. The inhabitants of those cages, had there been any, would be forced to stand; sitting, or even leaning against the bars, was made impossible by protruding barbs and the awkward angles of the cages themselves.

But there *were* no inhabitants. The cages, lacking any means of ingress, were purely decorative.

Or so Havarren chose to believe.

The floor was neither iron nor stone, but an unrelenting black, nightfall given substance. Occasional flickers of movement within, as though the floor were glass atop a malevolent sea, were yet another phenomenon that the wizard, despite his familiarity with the keep, had never been able to explain.

In the chamber's center sat the decayed master of the Iron Keep himself, not upon some great marble throne or a dais of bone, but in a simple, red velvet–lined chair. He leaned over a large desk, equally as mundane as the chair, perusing one of a hundred musty tomes that he kept in a library Havarren had never been permitted to explore.

For long moments, Morthûl continued reading, seemingly oblivious. He finally raised a bony hand and beckoned just as Havarren opened his mouth to announce himself. The sorcerer's approach startled a few dozen roaches and beetles, sending them scurrying across the upholstery and back into the folds of either the Charnel King's clothes or his flesh, depending on personal preference. Morthûl gestured a second time, leathery flesh creaking, and the book vanished from the desk.

"You requested an audience?"

"I did, Your Majesty. I felt you should know . . . That is, it seems that the Demon Squad you assembled—"

Although accustomed to the mercurial moods of his Dark Lord, Havarren was taken aback at the abrupt change. Morthûl was on his feet, his right hand seizing the wizard's tunic. The skeletal fingertips punched clean through the fabric, and several layers of skin for that matter. Save for a single wince, the gaunt mage knew better than to protest.

"What happened to my squad?" The pestilential breath crawled over Havarren's face as though it, too, carried the Charnel King's vermin.

My squad? Havarren filed the choice of words away for future examination. "Nothing's *happened* to them, precisely, Your Majesty. They're fine."

Morthûl released his aide, oblivious to the blood—or rather, the not-quite-blood—coating his fingertips. "So what *are* you telling me?" he asked more calmly.

"They appear to have been reassigned."

"To whom? And on whose authority?"

This is where it gets interesting. "Queen Anne, Your Majesty. To both questions."

One eyebrow—Morthûl's only eyebrow, in point of fact—rose. "Anne?" The Dark Lord shook his head, dislodging another handful of insects. "Why?"

"I couldn't begin to guess, Sire. This only happened two days ago. They've not even reached Castle Eldritch."

"I see." For another span, the dead king pondered. "Very well, Havarren. Do nothing for now. My wife is, ah, whimsical at times, but she knows better than to harm our cause. The squad must learn to deal with the unexpected, so let us see what she would have them do."

"Very good." The mage spun on his heel.

"Havarren."

"Yes, Your Majesty?"

"Do keep a close eye on them."

"Of course, Your Majesty."

She studied the meandering path of dirt and gravel that was Tiehmon's Way, lost in her own thoughts. Her ears and her hide twitched at the touch of cold winds, unpleasant reminders of the Steppes. Grimacing, she focused on the local scents of grass and mulch, soil and the dusty tang of the trail.

Tiehmon's Way, one of the many earthen highways that were the flowing arteries of Kirol Syrreth, had been her world for days now, and would remain so for days more. It perfectly marked the line of demarcation between the lush plains to the south and the frost-bitten scrub and dead foliage of the tundra-kissed lands to the north. It was also the main route between Timas Khoreth, where the squad had slept away their first warm night together, and the city of Sularaam, home to the rather ostentatiously titled Castle Eldritch.

Private residence, when she wasn't staying with her husband, of Queen Anne, the Charnel King's bride.

A small cadre of humans, garbed in the traditional black of Morthûl's army, appeared over a gentle slope in the road and cautiously marched past. Fingers nervously grazed against pommels, tightened on bowshafts, and wary squints brushed across her face. This, then, was the caliber of warrior the Iron Keep would send against the marshaled armies of the Allied Kingdoms? These frightened fools? It was enough to make a troll despair.

"Hey! Hound! You sniff anything out yet?"

On the other hand, cowardly humans were far from the greatest burden she had to bear.

"Of course she didn't!" Shreckt barked as the band caught up with her. "There's nothing to see on Tiehmon's. Which is what I told her when she asked to scout ahead!"

Katim refused to turn around. She'd gone "scouting" for no other reason than to escape the *constant prattle*, and now was wishing she'd gone even farther ahead.

Such as, perhaps, all the way to Castle Eldritch. If not beyond. Before she decided to off the orc here and now, and possibly the cub-sized sergeant right along with him.

The troll was rapidly losing what little respect she'd held for their "superior" officer. Even after he'd given them a full day to recuperate in Timas Khoreth—more than they actually needed, after Queen Anne's mysterious but reinvigorating visit—he'd scarcely even bothered to debrief them, asking instead for "the short version" of their experiences in the Steppes. He'd sounded only vaguely concerned about the odd worm creatures, despite their best efforts to emphasize how nasty the things were, and though he'd assured them that he would report their presence to General Falchion, he forbade them from wasting any more time worrying about it.

"Your assignment to Her Majesty," he'd told them, "supersedes everything else. Shut up and deal with it."

Since then they'd trudged along the dreary road, grasslands to the left, dead scrub to the right, and nothing but the occasional passing patrol to break the monotony.

"Training," Shreckt had explained impatiently on the second day, when Gork asked why there were so many soldiers on the road. The imp sat cross-legged in the air, his riding crop hooked to Belrotha's backpack so the ogre could tow him along like a pennant. "Most of those ass-licking mama's boys have never seen combat in a really *hostile* environment, so they're getting the training you *thought* you were getting."

The kobold had shaken his head. "But so many of them? Isn't that depleting our forces elsewhere?"

The imp had muttered something about it being "taken care of" and wouldn't talk any more on the subject, shouting at Gork to drop and give him eighty when the kobold persisted.

Katim, who'd been paying close attention to Gork during the kobold's shifts on watch, waiting in vain for Ebonwind to appear, knew it was more than curiosity that drove his questions.

Nor had Shreckt bothered explaining why he didn't simply teleport the lot of them to Sularaam. He'd given the order to march, so they marched. And—

"You didn't answer my question." Cræosh appeared beside her, shaking her out of her reverie. "Find anything worth mentioning?"

"I think that . . . Shreckt answered the question . . . quite adequately. This road offers . . . little worth reporting."

"Yeah, but I didn't ask *him*, did I?"

Katim was saved the effort of a response by the now-familiar (and now-despised) *"All right, fall in!"*

They did.

"Good!" The imp gave them all a quick once-over. "Gork!"

The kobold jumped. "Sir, yes sir, yes sir!"

Shreckt blinked. "One's enough, soldier."

"If you say so, sir!"

The imp's index fingers twitched. "Move ahead! Find us a camping spot!"

"Wha . . . Me, sir?"

"Did I st-st-stutter, soldier?"

"No, sir!"

"Then m-m-move!"

Gork moved.

Shreckt shook his head, then rotated it at an impossible, owlish angle, toward Katim. "The others'll be doing the scouting for a while, since I already know *you* know how to do it. Get 'em used to it now, when there's no real danger if they screw the pooch."

"Of course," Katim agreed, struggling not to gnash her teeth. There went her excuses for getting away from the damn orc *and* for keeping watch over the kobold, in one fell swoop.

Trolls believed in no higher power—no gods, no spirits, no Ancestors—but she couldn't help but wonder, as Gork vanished over the nearest rise, if she hadn't offended *something*.

It didn't take Gork long, since finding a good spot for a campsite in an open field isn't an entirely challenging prospect. He selected the area around a large tree some few hundred yards off the road. The grass was dying as winter solidified its hold on Kirol Syrreth—thank the Stars it hadn't started snowing on the plains yet!—but remained thick enough to sleep on comfortably. Yes, this place would be perfect; he—

"Hello, Gork."

"Ibriudra! Birri irugu!"

The kobold jumped, even though he instantly recognized the voice and the gibberish both.

"Ebonwind. Where . . . ? Oh, of course." He retreated a few steps so he could look up into the tree without straining his neck.

Sure enough, there the dark elf was, sitting comfortably in the branches. His gray cloak hung down in folds, flapping gently in the wind, and his peculiar familiar stood perched on a spindly bough.

"You building a nest up there?" Gork asked.

"I was under the impression," the dakórren said mildly, "that we had an appointment."

Gork snorted. "There's not much to tell you so far. Why don't you flutter off before the rest of the squad starts to wonder what's keeping me, and come back when I've got something worthwhile?"

"But Gork, I've seen the troop movements along Tiehmon's Way. Would you have me believe they're sightseeing?"

"Damn near. It's a training exercise, Ebonwind. It's not big enough to interest Dororam, which means it's not big enough to interest the elves, which means it's not big enough for them to react to, which means you can't react to them reacting."

"Tell me, Gork, do you always speak at such oblique angles?"

The kobold shrugged. "Call it a bad case of non-Euclidean grammar. Now go away so I can report back without being hanged, burned, beheaded, and castrated for treason."

"I must say, I'm disappointed, Gork. I do hope you'll have something more interesting for me the next time I make the effort of visiting you." With that he was gone, a single leaf, slowly falling from the tree, the only sign of his passing.

"Oh, sure," Gork muttered to himself as he headed back toward the highway. "Like it's my fault King Morthûl and General Falchion haven't ordered the army to gather around a campfire and sing songs. Dragonshit . . ."

"What the fuck took you so long?" Cræosh raged as he approached. "Shit, I could've found us a nice steamy spring in the tundra by now! What the fuck's out *there* to worry about? The grass too sharp for you?"

"You really wanna know, Cræosh? I had to relieve myself. That enough detail for you, or did you want shape, color, and texture?"

The orc actually backed down. "Well, I was just wondering, is all. It took you forever. . . ."

Gimmol snorted from behind them. "That's probably because he forgot how to do it. Are you going to be okay next time, Gork, or should I give you written instructions?"

"You pestilent, mewling little—"

"*Fall in!*" Shreckt, standing ramrod straight at about ten feet in the air, snarled down at the sullen squad. "All right, you assholes, that's just about enough! Do it on your own damn time! Gork!"

"Sir, yes sir, yes—"

"Shove a squirrel in it! I'm not in the mood. Did you find us a campsite?"

"Absolutely!"

"Then why aren't we there yet?"

With a backward glare at Gimmol, the kobold led them through the gently waving grasses.

If he noticed Katim's stare at all, he failed to recognize the gleam of suspicion within.

An invisible audience watched as the motley assemblage spread out a variety of sleeping rolls and blankets, many chewing on dried meats better left unidentified. Silently, somehow striding *atop* the blades of grass rather than bending them, the unseen spy approached—only to freeze, still some distance away, as the troll's nostrils flared.

No nearer, then, not now.

The watcher's attentions skipped over the kobold, wrapped and snoring in a burlap sack he'd made into a sleeping bag. This one he already knew.

The doppelganger, the ogre, and the bugbear were less than nothing; the one was too unobservant to notice if anything went amiss, the others too stupid to act on it.

The orc was a bit more alert, and suspicious by his very nature, but so long as they were careful, he'd not prove a threat.

The gremlin . . . Something about the gremlin rang false. He was a joke, plain and simple. He wasn't stealthy, he wasn't quick, and there was some question as to whether he knew which end of a sword was the dangerous one. All the worst human and elven stereotypes of the goblin races, rolled up into one strawberry-colored package.

But there *had* to be more to him! This gremlin had been assigned to a *Demon Squad*! Best of the best, and all that rot, even allowing for the usual exaggerations of propaganda. *Something* about this gremlin made him squad material, and that unknown, if nothing else, made him a possible threat.

178

Potentially, the imp was the biggest danger. His spells, his abilities, his diabolical nature all gave him a decent chance of penetrating any subterfuge he encountered. But he was also the squad's training officer, which hopefully meant he'd not be accompanying them on any future missions.

And then, there was the troll.

An invisible fist clenched tight. The damned hyena-faced, fur-coated bitch could ruin everything! If any one of the misbegotten assemblage were likely to detect him at exactly the wrong time, puzzle out what he was really doing, it was apt to be her.

She was already suspicious, of that he was certain.

"Ih? Niva ith ira. Adaba birru?"

"Yes, my little friend," Ebonwind whispered, voice too low for even the troll's sensitive ears. "I couldn't agree more. Doing it now would attract too much attention though—and besides, she *may* just want in on the deal."

"Diburi," the tiny creature avowed firmly.

"*Then* we'll kill her. We can afford a little patience."

"Ib eyda."

They awoke the next morning to find that someone had shit in Gimmol's hat.

The gremlin never could prove who did it, but given the previous day's arguments—and Gork's comment, over breakfast, that "I guess *someone* didn't need any instructions"—no one had any real doubt.

Shreckt had ordered Gimmol to store the thing until they reached the River Krom, where he could wash it thoroughly. The others had reacted primarily to laugh uproariously at the various spiky tufts that the gremlin called "hair," heretofore concealed beneath the hat. All in all, not Gimmol's best day.

It got a little better, however, on the *following* morning, as the entire squad awakened to the kobold's anguished screams. At some point during the night, someone had taken the thinnest of his wire lock picks and twisted them together into a useless knot.

Again, no one doubted who the guilty party might've been. But what Gork and the others couldn't figure out was *how* he did it; those picks never left the kobold's side, remaining in one of his many pockets even while he slept. And Gimmol just wasn't that stealthy. The mystery kept Gork brooding for the duration of their journey—which also had the unexpected but welcome side effect of heading off any further salvoes in this private little war.

And finally, after a march that lasted several lifetimes, the Demon Squad arrived at the River Krom where it emerged from the icy waters of the Sea of Tears.

The city of Sularaam sat on a small island in the river's headwaters. Ingress to the city was made possible solely by boat or by bridge, and those bridges were monitored *very* carefully. As the squad set foot on the eastern span, several of the ubiquitous black-garbed soldiers stepped forward, swords and halberds held at the ready.

"State your business in Sularaam," commanded a droopy-eyed fellow with a shaggy mustache.

Cræosh grimaced and Jhurpess fingered the butt of his club. But Shreckt floated into view and said, "Demon Squad. We're to report to Castle Eldritch."

And the guards stepped aside to let them pass.

"Jhurpess not understand," the bugbear confided quietly, falling into step beside the orc.

"Gee, *there's* a shocker," Cræosh said. "You don't understand? I'm flabbergasted. Tell Shreckt to stop the march so I can lie down." Then, as the furry creature stepped toward the imp, Cræosh yanked him back by the collar. "Never the fuck you mind. What don't you understand this time?"

"Guards here are nicer than guards at Timas Khoreth."

"Not nicer, hairball. More professional." The orc gazed approvingly at the great walls, the structured and orderly streets beyond. The armor worn by the patrolling guards was spit-shined, and several keeps stood within the city's center. "Timas Khoreth may have a garrison bigger'n my daddy's middle leg, but Sularaam's actually a *military* city.

"Um, you ain't gonna take two steps in there and collapse again, are you?"

"No. Jhurpess not do that anymore."

"Good."

There was a brief pause. "What 'Sularaam' mean?"

They'd barely reached the far side of the bridge when the carriage appeared. Hauled by four horses so pristinely white that snow would've stained them, it traveled so smoothly that it seemed to float over the cobblestones. The windows were curtained, preventing even an ephemeral glimpse of who or what lay within. The driver, too, was hidden, wrapped in a shroudlike brown robe, a corpse awaiting interment in some musty crypt.

Cræosh found his teeth clenching. He heard an almost subvocal hiss from the troll and saw the fur on her neck standing up.

"You feel it too?" he asked.

Katim nodded once, tightly. "Magic. Listen!"

Listen he did, and his hackles rose farther still. He heard the low roar of the crowd around, the muttering of his companions, the methodical whispering of the river—but the carriage itself rolled along as silent as a fog. If the great, gold-plated wheels made even the slightest thump, Cræosh sure as hell couldn't detect it.

"This," he murmured, "is less than good."

And then Belrotha stepped forward, her gargantuan hip bone knocking Cræosh completely out of her way. "Me see this before," she told them. "Queen Anne use it to find me in Itho." She frowned briefly as a thought, starving but determined, crawled across the open expanse that was her mind. "Hope Itho doing okay without me," she pouted. "Many ogres in Itho stupid."

"Embarrassing, isn't it?" Shreckt chuckled from atop the giant figure. "The ogre's smarter than you are. We're in Sularaam! Who else would've sent the carriage?"

Cræosh scowled. "Just being cautious, sir. You never know—"

"You never know. The rest of us know at least once in a while. Now shut up and fall in!"

They stood side by side in perfect military stance (the occasional glower at the tiny sergeant notwithstanding) as the carriage drifted to a smooth halt before them. The brown-robed driver immediately dropped—flowed?—to the ground and bowed.

"Greetings and good day to you, sirs and ladies. On behalf of Her Majesty, Queen Anne, I bid you welcome to Sularaam and wish you only the most enjoyable—"

"Stow it, lock it, shove it. Where's Queen Anne already?"

Katim grunted in exasperation. The rest of the squad—Shreckt included, for a change—stared at the orc in slack-jawed horror.

"Diplomacy," the troll rasped at him. "D—I—P—L . . ."

But the robed figure chuckled, the sound strangely muffled within the depths of its hood. "I take no offense, friend troll. Indeed, I was warned that some of your companions might prove impatient. If you will all kindly step inside, then, I shall happily take you to Her Majesty."

Cræosh looked askance at the carriage. "What are you, stupid?" he asked.

But again, Belrotha pushed past them, pausing only briefly as she reached the carriage. Then, with a sigh that resembled nothing so much as an earthquake on tiptoes, she pulled the door open.

The entire squad gathered around, gobsmacked at the opulent chamber.

"Me not like this," the ogre said to them, "but me do it before."

"Jhurpess want to go home," the bugbear wailed.

"How the fuck?" Cræosh asked.

"Has anyone here actually *heard* of grammar?" Gimmol lamented.

"I believe I can answer that," the robed driver said—responding, presumably, to someone other than the gremlin. "As I've heard Her Majesty explain it . . . *Ahem!* 'A simple matter of the bending of space around a fixed position. The magic creates a confined area in which the *actual* size is not limited by the restrictions or the shape of anything else around it, although the *apparent* size remains subject to natural laws.'"

The entire squad blinked in unison.

"Oh," said Gork.

"Yeah," Cræosh added. "What he said."

The imp, however, had had quite enough. "All right, quit staring, pick your jaws up off your damn toes, and get in the carriage! Queen Anne's waiting for us, and I, for one, do not intend to be the one to explain why we're late!" And just for emphasis, he sent a crackling blue bolt of lightning from his palm to slam, sizzling and popping, into the dirt by their feet.

There was something of a bottleneck as Belrotha and Jhurpess attempted to leap through the door at the same instant. As they *did* finally squeeze through, and as the bugbear resumed breathing on his own after only a few moments of treatment, there were no further problems.

Robe, as Cræosh had already come to think of him, watched as the various soldiers planted themselves in whichever chair they found most comfortable (and assuming they were large enough to remove whichever of their companions had chosen the same seat first). Then he said, "If you require anything during your ride, just pull on that rope there." He gestured toward a thick, knotted cord that hung down from the ceiling directly by the thick wooden door.

Um, door?

"And please do not attempt to open that door," he added, as though reading their minds. "It leads to Queen Anne's private chambers, and she has certain precautions in place to discourage unwanted visitors."

"Wait, wait, wait," Cræosh said, one hand half raised. "You telling me that the queen keeps a private chamber in her *carriage*?"

"She most certainly does not."

"But you said that door led to her chambers!"

"It does."

Cræosh decided firmly not to ask any more questions.

"Very well. If that is all, I must resume my post." Robe stepped outside, gently but firmly shutting the door behind him, and the carriage began to move.

"I," Gork told the room at large, "need a drink."

The orc nodded. "Make that two, Shorty."

Grumble, grumble, "Yeah, whatever," grumble. Rather sullenly, the kobold yanked on the rope. Then, at the rather resounding lack of a chime, he hauled on it again.

"Well, how about that?" he said, stepping away from the rope. "All this splendor, and they couldn't be bothered to keep the bellpull worki*aaagh!!*"

He staggered, one hand on his *kah-rahahk*, the other pressed tightly to his chest, as a black, shimmering *something* slid up from the floor. Vaguely human in size and shape, it stared into his eyes, its burning-ember gaze scorching a hole through the recesses of his mind.

"A—ba—dah? Wha . . . ?"

Cræosh laughed, though there was a faint twinge in his voice. "Relax, Shorty. It's one of King Morthûl's wraiths."

"Oh. Oh!" The kobold drew himself back up to his full height and swallowed hard. Twice. "What do you want?"

Silence, not so much a pregnant pause as a dead one. Then, "Well, yes, I did pull the rope. But I didn't hear—No, I guess I wouldn't know if—Nothing major, I just wanted—Listen, can I finish a bloody sent—" But the wraith was gone, dropping through the floor from whence it came.

"So?" Fezeill—in human form, at the moment—asked from the divan across the room.

"I'm not sure it likes me," Gork said.

The doppelganger and the gremlin exchanged looks of utter shock. "No!" Fezeill protested.

"Really?" Gimmol added. "How unreasonable!"

Gork glared at them both.

"You didn't answer the important question, Shorty," Cræosh said.

"Hmm? Oh, no, I'm fine, Cræosh. It just yelled a bit, I think. It didn't actually hurt—"

"No. I meant, is it still bringing my drink?"

Gork gave up and went to go stand in the corner. The wraith did indeed bring their drinks eventually, but the kobold's was warm.

The gently swaying room finally drifted to a halt, and Robe hauled the door open. "My friends and honored guests," he said, bowing low, "welcome to the Castle Eldritch."

Katim, who had remained standing by the door for the entire ride, was first out. She took two steps and stopped short.

184

The towering edifice had been home to the royal family of King Sabryen, a wizard of no small power in his own right before Morthûl overthrew him. Once the Charnel King realized that a bride and groom would require their own space if the marriage was to survive for multiple centuries—particularly when both were often involved in rather delicate experiments—he'd granted the old king's castle to his wife.

All this, Katim had known, but she'd never been here. She had assumed that the appellation "Eldritch" was pure melodrama.

A tangible sense of ages clung to the walls, suggesting not so much the passage of years as the passage of lives. A thick hedge of thorns served in place of a moat, but otherwise the castle's five towers appeared traditional enough.

Until one drew near enough to recognize that while the outermost buildings were whitewashed stone, the central towers were composed of solid white jade! That the thing didn't collapse under its own weight was a testament to the magics that gave the castle its name.

Robe ushered the bewildered company through a gate in the hedge, a second gate in the outer bastion—both gaping wide open—and into a well-landscaped bailey. A procession of minor functionaries, merchants, and petitioners flowed in a living stream (or perhaps a parade of ants) through those portals. Small but far more ornate portals of carved jade, allowing access to the interior of the castle proper, swung open at their approach.

Cræosh glanced at Katim as they passed through that last doorway. "I hate magic."

"You hate everything . . . you can't comprehend."

"So?"

"So it's a wonder . . . you can function at all."

Cræosh swallowed a retort. The damn canine had been snippy ever since they left the Steppes, but he reluctantly decided that the halls of the Queen's castle weren't the best place to have it out.

Despite the preponderance of doors and side passages, their brown-robed guide kept to the central corridor. Plush red carpeting cushioned their feet. Mounted suits of gleaming plate armor, joints welded shut, polished to a blinding sheen, stood three rows deep along both walls. Gork, his curiosity ever aroused—and his gaze flitting about for any smaller adornments that might not be immediately missed—casually sidled over for a closer look.

When he rejoined the marching squad, his face was so pale that even Jhurpess couldn't miss it.

"What bothering Gork?" he asked, his voice hushed.

"Just . . . don't go near the armor, okay?"

Jhurpess gave a halfhearted shrug and returned to picking the lice from his fur and flicking them into the thick carpeting. Gork shuddered once more, trying not to contemplate the agony and the terror those men must have felt *as their armor was welded shut around them*, trapping them helpless inside metal tombs. For the first time in his life, he felt a brief surge of sympathy for members of that disgusting, arrogant race.

He was also a little curious as to how Queen Anne had managed to keep the corpses from decomposing and stinking up her castle—assuming, he realized with another shudder, they were actually dead. Gork decided firmly not to think on it any further.

Mercifully, the corridor made a sharp bend to the left, leaving the horribly occupied suits of armor behind. Not that this hall was lacking its own warped splendors.

The walls were covered, end to end and floor to ceiling, in tapestries, murals, and friezes. Each was of the utmost quality, the work of master artisans, and portrayed a tranquil or pastoral scene, the world at its grandest. Here stretched miles of emerald forests, the browns and greens so rich that the passersby could almost have climbed the nearest tree and smelled the earthy aromas. There, depths of ocean stretched from towering cliffs, the white foam climbing halfway up the rock face before falling back to vanish in the waves. Verdant fields sprawled beneath the watchful gaze of a single pristine tower constructed atop a shallow hill. Every last one of them a landscape of peace, contentment, wonder.

Except for the rotting, bug-encrusted visage of the Charnel King, who appeared in each and every image. He strode regally through the forest, his long cloak leaving a trail of swirling leaves in its wake. He towered atop the seaside cliffs, arms outstretched, commanding the elemental tides. And the fleshy half of his visage peered, partially cloaked in shadow, from the upper window of the watchtower. The lord of all, gazing down on the very least of his holdings. A single beetle—a real one, no part of any image—crawled across the surface and vanished behind the fabric, as though the Dark Lord were somehow present even in this very hall.

Finally, they neared another set of double doors of a thick, rich wood, carved just as ornately as the jade had been. Even as Robe reached fabric-wrapped fingers toward the latch, they heard the sound of Gork dry-heaving behind them. Cræosh glanced back as they passed through the doorway.

"What's the problem, Shorty?"

"Don't look up," the kobold said, still gagging.

Cræosh, of course, immediately looked up, but he was already through the door, the ceiling of the hall blocked from view. "What's up there?"

"More frescoes of the queen's lord and husband," Robe said.

"So?" Cræosh asked Gork as the little creature stepped into the room.

Gork shook his head. "They're the erotic ones. . . ."

Cræosh had always been green, but not that particular shade. Resolutely, the orc determined to find another way to leave the castle once their audience was complete.

She sat upon a golden throne, atop a shallow dais and between two censers of pungent frankincense. Servants and seneschals stood at her side, and Robe quickly moved ahead and took up a position at her left shoulder. The audience chamber—a huge, egg-shaped place—was lined in more white jade and adorned with intricately etched marble pillars. A small line of petitioners—made up primarily of older, flabbier men who appeared to represent the city's successful merchant class—wound from the dais. A few muttered angrily as the Demon Squad moved past them to stand directly before the queen, but none protested.

"Ah, dear children," the queen greeted them, beaming down from atop her throne, "I'm delighted that you could accept my little invitation."

Invitation? Cræosh scoffed inwardly, but even *he* wasn't *that* undiplomatic. He dropped to one knee, hoping his companions would take the hint and do the same. "It was an honor, Your Majesty, to—" He gasped as a bolt of lightning (a small one, thankfully) arced into his side. Cræosh glowered at the imp, who was glaring right back, and promptly shut his mouth.

"My apologies, Your Majesty," Shreckt said—actually standing on the ground, for a change!—and spreading his arms wide. "Sometimes my charges speak out of turn. I command this squad, and I will speak for—"

"Tell me, imp," Queen Anne interrupted, "are you ranked so highly that you hold yourself aloof from matters of protocol?"

"Of course not, Your Majesty. I—"

"Then get on your knees before I have them cut from under you!"

The slight thump as Shreckt dropped failed to muffle the choked laughter that neither Cræosh, Gork, nor Gimmol could quite suppress.

"Now, my dears," Queen Anne continued, all gentle smiles once more, "you've been on the road for a great while. Relax, refresh yourselves, perhaps have a bite to eat. We will talk afterward, when you have made yourselves marginally presentable. Rupert will show you to your rooms." A simple gesture, bidding them to rise, and then her attention turned back to the next in the seemingly endless line of petitioners.

Robe—or "Rupert," apparently—gracefully drifted down from the dais's shallow steps. "If you will follow me?" Without waiting for a response, he flowed ahead, leading them not toward the hallway from which they'd entered (and thanks be for that!), but down a smaller passage that had been partly obscured behind one of the towering columns.

Two long corridors and a wide flight of stairs with an ivory banister led them to a smaller hall lined with modest wooden doors. Several loud clicks sounded as Rupert passed them by, and several doors on either side of the hallway drifted open.

"These are your quarters," the queen's servant told them. "Feel free to fight over them, but I assure you that each is absolutely identical to the others."

Cræosh popped his head through the nearest doorway. Acceptable enough, in a cushy, over-luxurious, human sort of way. A hardwood wardrobe stood directly opposite a large, four-poster bed (trimmed, the orc noted with no small amount of nausea, in fluffy pink). A large brass basin sat directly across from the door, illuminated dimly by the single flaccid beam of sunlight that penetrated the drape-covered window. (Cræosh allowed himself to note that these rooms shouldn't *have* exterior windows—they were somewhere in the very heart of the castle—and then chose to file that fact away in the abandoned recesses of his mind, right next to the door in the carriage and the frescoes in the entry hall.)

"Is the room satisfactory?" Rupert asked from over Cræosh's shoulder.

"You might do better," Cræosh snarled, willing his heart to cease pounding and his hand to unclench from his sword, "not to creep up on people."

Then, more calmly, "Yeah, the room oughta do fine. Don't know why Queen Anne wanted us to come here first, though. I'd just as soon find out why we're here."

"I believe Her Majesty felt that it might behoove you to make use of the amenities."

Cræosh finally turned to peer blankly into the shadowed hood. "Huh?"

"I can have the servants fetch some hot water as soon as you're ready."

"Why?"

Did Rupert actually sigh? "I see that you aren't fluent in Circumspect. Queen Anne feels that you and your associates could each do with a bath. Perhaps two or three."

Cræosh sniffed. "If you say so. I've always thought we orcs smelled kind of earthy, myself."

"Yes, sir. Earthy indeed. Quite fertile, even. Now if you'll excuse me, I'll have your water up in just a moment. I have to see about getting your ogre friend a larger tub."

The squad reassembled some two hours later, smelling a great deal less like last spring's compost. (Gork and Jhurpess were also rubbed raw, where the guards had been forced to hold them down and scrub them with wire brushes.) Shreckt, however, was absent, apparently having decided that his presence was unnecessary.

They sat around a lengthy table, polishing off a feast prepared especially for them. It's worth noting, in passing, that the chef on duty retired from Queen Anne's service less than a month later. He moved out into the country to spend the rest of his life raising cabbage, and he never told a soul what he'd been asked to prepare that evening, or why he occasionally awoke screaming in the predawn hours.

"So?" Cræosh asked the room at large, picking a fatty morsel from his teeth with a sliver of broken bone. "We're here, we're full, we're even clean. So when's the bill come due?"

"Queen Anne will tell . . . us why we're here as soon . . . as she feels it appropriate. You . . . will simply have to . . . try to remain patient." Katim snorted, then, obviously amused by her own words. "Or at least . . . fake it."

Cræosh grimaced, revealing the four or five other meaty chunks that he hadn't yet dislodged from his teeth. "I'm tired of being patient!"

Gork snickered. "How would you know?"

"How indeed?" Rupert asked.

Cræosh pulled a muscle in his neck trying to spot the new arrival. "Tell me something, Rupert, are you *looking* to get your fucking spine broken? *Stop sneaking up on me!*"

The hooded head swiveled. For the tiniest instant, Cræosh thought he might have caught the barest glimpse of what lay within those ebon-hued folds. His face pale, he shrank back into his seat.

"Listen to me, orc, because I have no intention of going over this again. You are Her Majesty's honored guests, and I have shown you the courtesy due you. But I grow tired of your little threats. The next time you feel the need to make one, I suggest you be prepared to *try* to carry it out.

"Now," he continued, his voice resuming its calm, modulated tones. "As you have no doubt been eagerly anticipating, Queen Anne wishes to see you again. She requests that you join her in her private gardens. If you'll kindly follow me?"

Curious despite herself, Katim fell into step beside the orc. "What did you . . . see?"

"Nothing," he said softly. "I saw nothing."

"Nothing? The hood . . . was empty?"

"No. No, you don't understand. I didn't just not see a face. I didn't see the inside of the robe! It was like looking into a pit, or the empty sky!"

"You realize . . . that what you are describing is not . . . possible."

"I don't give a dragon's rectum if it's *possible* or not. I know what I saw, and what I saw was *nothing*!"

"Well, you only . . . caught a brief glimpse. Most probably it . . . was simply a trick of . . . the shadows."

"Yeah. Yeah, probably." But he remained unusually silent for long moments after.

The others were not at all restrained by the same doubts that plagued the orc. Even as they walked, Gork found himself striding beside the bugbear, mostly because it meant he *didn't* have to walk beside Gimmol or Fezeill.

"You as worried as I am, Jhurpess?"

"What? Why Gork worried? Something Jhurpess not know about?"

Gork could practically hear Cræosh's voice responding with *There's a whole steaming shitload that Jhurpess not know about.* "Look, Jhurpess, the armor in the main hall, those—those tapestries . . ."

"So?"

"So I'm just a little nervous about what sort of flora someone of Queen Anne's proclivities might be cultivating in her private garden."

"Oh."

The kobold knew he shouldn't ask, but couldn't help himself. "You *do* know what flora is, right?"

"Of course Jhurpess know what flora means! Jhurpess born and raised in forest!" The bugbear sounded positively indignant.

"Glad to hear it."

"What 'cultivating' mean?"

The ponderous doors opened, allowing the brilliant glow of a warm summertime afternoon to radiate into the cold and gloomy hallway like . . .

Summer? The squad halted, gawking at the brightness beyond the beckoning doorway.

Then, shrugging in unison, they dismissed the incongruity as another of Castle Eldritch's little hiccups and stepped out into the sunshine.

Or rather, most of them did. Belrotha took one look at the gleaming sun and locked her fists on either side of the doorframe, refusing to be budged.

"Come on already!" Cræosh barked after a moment's pause. "Queen Anne's waiting, remember?"

"Me not care," the ogre stated flatly. "Me not going out there. It not summer outside."

"No, it's not," Gimmol assured her, placing one hand comfortingly on her calf. "But, well, this isn't really outside. It—it's a magic room, like inside the carriage."

"Not going."

"But Belrotha . . ."

"No. Took me many years of schooling to learn order of seasons. Not forgetting that now. Too confusing. If me forget how seasons work, me cannot lead Itho. Planting get all muddled. Me stay here."

"Oh, for the love of—"

Katim tapped Cræosh on the shoulder. "Let her stay . . . here then. She's not harming . . . anything. And do you really think . . . it's going to make that much of . . . a difference to her if she hears . . . Queen Anne's explanations?"

The orc nodded slowly. "Yeah, you have a point. You got a problem with that, Rupert?"

"I live but to serve. I have very few problems with anything."

Without a backward glance, save one from Gimmol, the squad continued into the courtyard, the ogre peering after them suspiciously from the safety of her doorway.

The garden occupied the entirety of the castle's inner courtyard. Full, thick rosebushes lined the entryway, their fragrance overpowering. Behind them were row upon row of colorful, exotic blossoms, ranging from the merely impressive to the truly fantastic. Had any botanist, sage, or druid been present, he would have been stunned to note four varieties of flower that were actually extinct.

A few birds, late for their winter migrations, took brief respite from the cold by finding a perch somewhere in the garden. Hedges and shrubberies crossed and meshed into an impenetrable thicket of branches and thorns at the garden's edge. Other, narrower hedgerows meandered through the courtyard, transforming it into a simple but elegant maze. These had been carefully arranged to draw the eye eventually to the queen's most impressive specimens, or to one of the few fountains and sculptures.

Cræosh, for one, could not have cared less. "So where is she?"

Rupert, who looked as though he was choosing his path through the hedge-maze at random, didn't bother to slow as he answered. "Fret not, my guests. The queen spends most of her time with the more unusual plants, at the garden's farther side. We will be there soon enough." And indeed, the dirt beneath their feet grew darker, the surrounding hedges brighter, as though this portion of the garden had been painted with a richer palette.

And there they saw the vines.

A deep, seaweed hue, they coated the far wall of the courtyard, a green and winding rash afflicting the stone. Into cracks, atop and around other nearby plants—it looked very much as if the entire wall were being consumed by some monster jellyfish.

Nor was the wall the only thing being consumed.

"I see you've met my baby," Queen Anne's musical voice lilted at them. She glided into view. Her velvet gown had, despite the soil that coated her hands, kept itself completely dirt-free. "Ivy is the pride of my garden, aren't you my sweet?" Cræosh could have sworn that the vines shivered in response to the queen's cooing.

"And him?" the orc asked.

Queen Anne glanced briefly at the corpse. He lay entangled at the base of the wall, the ivy growing not only around but through him. The rib cage alone was home to a dozen tendrils.

"Oh, that?" Queen Anne's gaze sort of drifted past the mangled cadaver, as though she'd failed to notice it. "Ivy requires extra care. As I said, she's very special."

"And what did he do to, uh, earn the honor of feeding your plant?"

"Do?" The queen sounded genuinely puzzled, and Cræosh decided that this, too, would have to be added to his list of Things Never to Ask about Again.

Jhurpess, too, was adding the ivy to his own mental list, a list he'd been keeping since he and Cræosh had first arrived in Timas Khoreth. An inventory of things the bugbear didn't like, it already included red gremlins, little gray sergeants, yetis, holes in floors, elven corpses, elven wizards, elven wizards' familiars, worms, chasms, brown robes, magic carriages, and—for reasons that no one in the squad would ever have been able to fathom—woodchucks. At this rate, the bugbear might have to learn how to write, or he was quickly going to lose track of everything he hated.

"You appear," the queen continued, focusing for the first time, "to have lost someone."

"Lost? Oh, no, we know exactly where she *oooff*!!"

Cræosh gingerly rubbed his side as the troll continued for him. "Belrotha was made . . . uncomfortable by the change . . . in seasons. She chose to . . . remain in the hallway."

"Oh, the poor dear. Well, I have to look in on my prize flower before I'm through for the day. Why don't you all walk along with me, and I shall explain what I require of you?"

"Prize flower?" Cræosh asked, moving well beyond Katim's reach before he again opened his mouth. "What's this one do, drink blood?"

"An intriguing idea, my dear child, but no. This flower doesn't actually do anything."

"Then what makes it so special?" Gork asked from the back.

"This flower blossomed on the grave of a man who had been interred alive; it absorbed his very life as he slowly died." She smiled at the looks of consternation on her soldiers' faces. "Metaphorically, of course. But symbolism is everything in magic, and a flower such as this can have great power when used correctly in the proper spell." Her eyes unfocused once more, as though she was staring at something just beyond the horizon. "I haven't yet found a use for it, but . . ."

She shook her head, causing her hair to bounce on her shoulders. "In a way, that is why you are here," she said, coming to a sudden stop.

Cræosh jerked to a halt, barely fast enough to avoid running directly into the queen. (Wouldn't have been diplomatic.) "The flower?"

"Not the flower directly. You see, I fancy myself something of a wizard."

Fezeill snorted—respectfully. Cræosh was going to have to ask him how he did that. "'Fancy'?" the doppelganger continued. "Your Majesty, save for King Morthûl, you're the greatest sorcerer in Kirol Syrreth."

"You are too kind," she said, beaming at him. "You may even be right. But whereas my husband's unusual nature allows him to draw most of his power from within, making use of ritual and components for only the greatest of spells, I, unfortunately, am bound by the limits of my frail human form. I require aid for a great many spells. Incantations, formulae, reagents. Hence, the flower.

"And hence, you. You see, I collect such items. Items of symbolic power, if you will. Even if I know of no spell for which I might use them, I keep them all the same. One never knows when one will need the proper ingredient, does one?"

"Who is 'one'?" Jhurpess quietly inquired of the kobold beside him. Gork sighed.

Katim, as usual, figured it out first. "You wish us to . . . retrieve one of these items for . . . you."

Queen Anne nodded. "More than one, actually. You see, my dears, war is coming. My husband is quite capable of providing for our magical defenses on his own, but it behooves us all to prepare for the worst. I, too, must stand ready to battle the wizards and magicians that march with Dororam, and thus, I must have access to my most potent magics. Unfortunately, my children, I also have responsibilities. So I cannot go and seek out the necessary items myself."

"Okay," Cræosh said before Katim could answer, "that's fair enough. But why not send Rupert? He seems, uh, capable."

"I need Rupert here, Cræosh. He is the best of my servants, my majordomo; he would be sorely missed. He also considers himself something of a bodyguard, and I fear dear Rupert would take it poorly if I asked him to leave my side.

"No, I need *all* my people here with me, to help prepare for the trying times ahead. And thus, you. When I'd heard that my husband had ordered a Demon Squad assembled and trained, it seemed the perfect opportunity for us all. I provide you with experiences to help prepare you for the struggles to come, and you can provide me with the items I require."

Cræosh frowned suspiciously. "What, exactly, do you mean by 'experiences'?"

The troll sighed. "She means, orc, that . . . we will be in . . . substantial danger while retrieving . . . these items."

The queen offered them a rueful grin. "It would hardly be training otherwise. And if it were easy, anyone could do it, could they not?"

Cræosh's lip twisted, but he bit back the urge to comment. Instead, he rounded on Katim and said, "And I thought you weren't gonna call me 'orc.'"

Katim blinked at him—and then her jaw opened as something Queen Anne had said finally penetrated. "Wait! The *king* . . . ordered the squad . . . assembled?"

"That is correct."

Five more jaws dropped. Demon Squads were a big deal, never assembled on whim, but they'd all just assumed it had been a military decision, from General Falchion or one of his underlings. To learn that the Charnel King himself had ordered them assembled added a whole new dimension to their experiences; one that made the smarter members of the group very, very nervous.

"So what do we do first?" Cræosh asked finally. "Dragon scales? The breath of a ghost? Eye of newt?"

The queen laughed, her voice melodic even in mirth. "You, my dear, have been listening to too many fairy tales. No, what I require from you, to start with, are the bones of a dead wizard. And not just any apprentice will do; he has to be a *true* magician."

Cræosh choked. "You want us to kill—"

Queen Anne quickly raised a hand. "I wish you to kill nothing. The bones of a mage long dead will suffice just as well as fresh ones. They might even be more appropriate for my needs."

"Oh." Cræosh found himself relaxing, but not much. "Still, we'd have no idea where to find—"

"You need not worry about that either. I know where to send you. I shall even undertake your transportation myself. All you need do is retrieve the bones themselves."

It sounded simple enough, and that worried Cræosh more than all the rest of it. "Okay," he said, his mind awhirl. "So where are we going?"

Queen Anne smiled. "Why, I'm sending you to Jureb Nahl."

From somewhere in the back, Gork moaned.

From its headwaters south of the Sea of Tears, the swamp of Jureb Nahl stretched for scores upon scores of sodden, stagnant, stinking miles. Nobody civilized lived there, and when the *goblins* say "nobody civilized," they *mean* it. The closest settlement, in the Grieving Mountains that bordered some of that foul marsh, was the kobold colony of Rurrahk. There, a certain Gork had been hatched and spent his childhood, and there, he'd heard the tales his grandsires told of Jureb Nahl.

He remembered enough of them to know that he really, really didn't want to go there.

This they claimed as absolute fact: Jureb Nahl hadn't always been a swamp at all. Two hundred years before Morthûl's rise to power, the area had been a grassy plain, perhaps the most fertile province in all Kirol Syrreth. The name Jureb Nahl referred, at the time, to a thriving community on the nation's western borders, known for commerce and learning. Even King Jarrom—grandfather of Sabryen, whom Morthûl would eventually depose—was known to visit, frequenting Jureb Nahl's great libraries. Had it been given another generation or two to grow, Jureb Nahl would have claimed its place as Kirol Syrreth's greatest city.

It was not to be.

The Grieving Mountains were, and are to this day, far less prone to activity than the great Brimstone Mountain range; nevertheless, some few of its peaks belch their fair share of smoke and lava. So it was on that long-ago morning, when the mountains heaved in the throes of tremors felt beyond the boundaries of Kirol Syrreth and one of the highest of the Grieving Mountains obliterated itself from within. Ash blackened the sky for weeks on end, and the Sea of Tears seemed coated solid with filth. Seemingly endless flows poured from the mountains and over the beaches, sending walls of steam sky-high, where they wrestled the waiting waters.

Jureb Nahl itself was far enough from the eruption to survive the initial blast, and its citizens were learned enough to persevere through the years of drought and famine that followed. But when the plains proved saturated with slow leakage from the Sea of Tears—when the people of Jureb Nahl realized that their lands had dropped, only a few feet but more than enough, below the water table—the people knew they were surely lost.

Still they did not surrender immediately. They dammed the worst of the torrents and rebuilt much of Jureb Nahl on the highest ground they had. All for naught; the waters continued to rise, turning the once-fertile grasslands into a sodden, saltwater marsh. And eventually, though their tears fell in quantity enough to cause a flood of their own, the last stubborn inhabitants of Jureb Nahl packed up and wandered away.

For a century the waters continued to rise, but eventually the bedrock beneath the Grieving Mountains shifted once again. The swamp was cut off from the Sea of Tears. Over the intervening centuries, subterranean springs in the roots of the mountains transformed the saltwater marsh to fresh, and such life as inhabits other swamps gradually appeared there as well. The birds and the bugs, the serpents and the toads—these bothered nobody at all. But other things—perhaps attracted by the ancient ruins and the lore that was said to survive within, perhaps just more of Kirol Syrreth's monsters—were said to dwell in Jureb Nahl. Only legends, perhaps, but the disappearance of many who wandered into the marsh was enough to give the place a bad reputation among the inhabitants of Rurrahk, and eventually all of Kirol Syrreth.

And this was where Queen Anne wanted to send them. Maybe it wasn't too late to go back to the Steppes?

"Your Majesty," Gork asked, obviously having trouble controlling his voice, "if I may . . . ?"

She smiled, her expression brighter than the impossible summer light. "You wish to know why I would send you to such a place."

"Well, yes."

She studied the flowers around her with a critical eye, poking gently at a few petals that apparently weren't doing what she wanted. "Somewhere within the swamps, my little one, there stands a tower. Once it was home to a wizard by the name of Trelaine, who hoped to unearth the knowledge of Jureb Nahl's lost libraries. He's long dead now, of course. Rumor has it he allowed an experiment to get out of control and blew himself into a thin yet meaty sauce. The tower has been abandoned for the long centuries since."

"But," Cræosh interjected, "if he blew himself up—"

"You should still find a sufficiency of his bones to serve my needs. I don't require much. Here." She reached out, offering a small bronze brooch in her cupped palm. The orc growled something awful as Katim lashed out and snagged the trinket before he could accept it.

Queen Anne didn't seem to care which of them held it. "I've had that made specially, to prevent any confusion. Between Trelaine's experiments and the hazards of the region, there could be a great many remains to be found. The brooch should differentiate the wizard's bones from any others."

"Back up a page and read it to me again," Cræosh said. "What hazards are we talking about, exactly?"

"I fear I couldn't begin to say, my children. I've never been." Then, at their expressions, she just shrugged. "If it were easy . . ." she said again.

Fezeill leaned over toward the gremlin and whispered, "I wonder if it's too late to request a transfer to something safer. Plague cleanup, perhaps, or dragon slaying."

Gimmol snorted. "Tell you what: *You* ask her."

Oddly, the doppelganger refrained.

"My little kobold," Queen Anne said suddenly, "would you step forward for just a moment?"

There wasn't any choice. Eyes threatening to bulge from his head— perhaps they, at least, could escape—Gork shuffled forward. "Y-yes, Your Majesty?"

"You know more about the swamps than anyone else here. You've seen them, have you not?"

"Well, not exactly, Your Majesty. That is, I grew up in Rurrahk, so I know the nearby mountains. But I've never actually been to the swamps themselves."

"Oh. Well, I suppose that will have to do. You'll have a short hike, but it's faster than walking the whole way."

Katim felt a sinking feeling in the pits of her stomachs, particularly the lowest. "You're going to . . . teleport us?" She'd hated letting Shreckt do it, and she trusted humans even less than she did demons.

Not that Queen Anne seemed particularly interested in her feelings. "Of course I am. We wouldn't want you to have to walk all that way, would we?"

"Umm." Cræosh hedged. "Actually, if it's all the same to you . . ."

The queen's face tightened, just a little. "Which, of course, it isn't," the orc said quickly, "or you wouldn't have brought it up. Never mind, then."

"That's better. As I was saying, though, Gork has the most direct experience with that part of the country. I'll need to pull the image from his mind in order to properly target the spell."

Gork actually yipped, a sound not unlike that produced by a small dog. A small dog who'd been goosed by a bear. "What?"

"Well, I can't well send you someplace I've never seen, can I? I could just pick a distance and a direction, but how would I know where to set you down, or what obstacles to avoid? Do you want to appear inside a tree, or under a mountain?"

"But . . . But . . ."

"Relax, dear one," she said, gently caressing his face. "Be at ease. I promise you, there will be no loss of memory, no damage to your mind. The process is completely safe."

"Well, okay . . ."

"Usually."

The queen placed eight fingers atop the kobold's head, tucked her thumbs under her palms, and began humming softly. Despite himself, Gork tensed.

"I'd suggest you not do that," the queen told him, ceasing her single-toned vocalization for just an instant. "I've been told that the pain isn't *quite* as excruciating if you don't fight it."

"Okay, I—*what*?"

It was, of course, far too late. It felt as if the fingers she'd placed upon his head had become ice and begun burrowing through his skull. Every muscle in his body tried to flex at once, threatening to rip itself free of bone and tendon. As though flipping through a book or a sheaf of scrolls, Queen Anne began with his most recent memories, reviewing his approach through the garden, his meal, his forced bath. No, this was far too recent. She skipped back through the years, ignoring some chunks, focusing on others, unaware or uncaring that every instant was an eternity of torment to the kobold. He didn't even have enough presence of mind to be grateful that she'd overlooked his collaboration with the dakórren.

Finally, as he drowned in a violently rolling sea of pain, he saw it: an image of the Grieving Mountains, clear as the day he'd first stepped into the outer world. He felt her grasp it, study it from all possible angles— and then, with a sudden rush of pressure, he was free. His ears clogged and popped three or four times in succession, and his head ached worse than it had after his coming-of-age ceremony, but already that pain was fading. Another moment, and it felt an exhausting, but already forgotten, dream.

He tried to think back, then, to his days in Rurrahk, feeling nostalgic for the first time in years, and instead he found himself reliving the battle with the first yeti in the tundra. "What . . . ?" He thought about that battle, then, and instead saw himself, at age six, picking his first pocket (a traveling merchant, if it matters).

"What did you do?" he screeched, forgetting for the moment to whom he spoke.

Queen Anne took no offense at his tone. "Your memories are a little scrambled," she said. "Some confusion, some absentmindedness. It's an unavoidable side effect. Don't fret over it, dear. Your mind will sort itself out shortly. A few hours, perhaps a few days at most.

"Now, my children, why don't you all go and gather whatever equipment or clothing you feel you might need? I'm ready whenever you are. Cræosh, Katim, please be certain Gork doesn't forget to pack anything important."

Hefting her pack over her shoulder, Katim moved down the hall, ready to join the others and get this damn fool errand started. Some strides ahead, the orc's door hung open, and as she passed, she saw him crawling around on the floor, peering under the bed.

Don't bother asking. Don't bother asking.

Katim sighed, and asked.

"Looking for my money," Cræosh told her, rising to his feet and twisting until a series of pops ran up his spine. "I figure, if she's gonna treat us like whores, we deserve to get paid what whores do."

"You refer, of course . . . to Queen Anne?"

"C'mon, Dog-face, you can't tell me you're comfortable with this. She needs special ingredients for her magics, she knows exactly where to find 'em, and she couldn't spare *anyone* to go looking until we came along? This whole thing smells worse than an ogre's afterbirth." He paused. "Or the dakórren's offer, for that matter. I'm getting tired of people lying about what they want from me."

"Perhaps you should think . . . of this as a compliment. Perhaps . . . she felt it was too dangerous . . . for anyone else available."

"And that's supposed to make me feel better why?"

Katim shrugged. "Yes, a similar thought had . . . occurred to me. And do you . . . know what I plan to do . . . about it?"

"What?"

"Nothing. You, of course . . . may tell Queen Anne where to stick . . . her orders, but I'd prefer . . . to be elsewhere at the time."

The troll resumed her walk, and was unsurprised when the orc joined her without further complaint.

And again, finally, she couldn't resist asking. "You hung around on . . . the floor in there just *waiting* . . . for one of us to come by and . . . ask, didn't you?"

"Pick up the pace, Dog-face, or we'll be late."

✳

The teleportation, despite the goblins' various misgivings, wasn't particularly unpleasant. Some of them might even get used to it.

Eventually.

The squad instantly scattered, backs toward one another—which was ostensibly safer than turning their backs toward *unknown* danger, but only just—and studied their new surroundings. To the north and east rose jagged foothills, spreading and maturing into equally jagged mountains. (Gork, alone among the squad, refused even to look at them.) To the south and west were patchy grasslands and copses of spindly trees that would eventually give way to the swamps of Jureb Nahl.

"All right," Cræosh said, satisfied that the immediate area was secure. "We're here, wherever the fuck 'here' is. Gork?"

"Oh." The kobold blinked away visions of his life as a kit in the winding kobold caves. "Right. We're exactly where Queen Anne said: foothills of the Grieving Mountains, a little south of Rurrahk, and about twenty miles from the swamp." The queen, he knew, could have dropped them nearer to the latter—but that would also have meant dropping them nearer to the former, and Gork had privately convinced her, with some impassioned pleading, of what a wonderful idea that wasn't.

Some of the others weren't so happy about it.

"Twenty miles?" Fezeill groused. "Really?"

"What's the matter, shapeshifter?" Cræosh asked. "You forget how to make feet?"

"Go to hell, swine."

Rather than allow either to press the issue, Katim and Gork pivoted as one and marched west. Fezeill watched them for a long moment and then folded in on himself. The result, when his body ceased writhing, was a long-tailed troglodyte. Distant cousins of the kobolds, they were a race known for their vicious temper—and for rarely appearing, except at the height of summer, outside the magma- and spring-heated caverns of the Brimstone Mountains. The broad, webbed feet and the rudderlike tail would, however, serve Fezeill well in the waters of Jureb Nahl.

But . . .

"Hey, lizard-breath!" Gork called. "You were the one bitching about how long a walk we've got. You wanna be cold that whole time?"

Two tiny slits peered at the kobold over a brown-scaled snout. "I wisssh to get usssed to the body," the reptilian thing hissed. "How often do you think I have to ussse this ssstupid form?"

"You sound like you're leaking," Gork said.

Cræosh shook his head. "Nah. Actually reminds me of a young lady I met a few years back. Huge gap, like you wouldn't believe, where her front teeth should've been. Ugly as hell and you couldn't understand half of what she said, but let me tell you, there are advantages to . . ."

Katim almost sprinted ahead, apparently determined to outdistance the orc's voice before she was subjected to the rest of that sentence.

"I believe," Fezeill said blithely as they gazed across the murky waters, "that the appropriate ressssponse isss 'Now what?'"

The Demon Squad had arrived at the outer reaches of Jureb Nahl just before dark the previous night. Staring directly into the setting sun, they'd been unable to get more than a cursory look at the place, and it had been unanimously decided—although neither Jhurpess nor Belrotha had known what "unanimously" meant—that they'd make camp there before dusk fell and head into the marsh come morning. Nothing worse than mosquitoes had disturbed their sleep, and they'd risen with the dawn, marched a few dozen yards farther west, and gotten their first really good impression of just what their task actually entailed.

"It ain't gonna be a whole lot of fun," Cræosh agreed. They were already up to their ankles in near-stagnant water; the filth and various aquatic vermin had already gone to work on feet and disposition both.

The ogre shrugged. "Me not see problem. Us just walk through water. Me get wet before."

"Prove it," Gork muttered, holding his nose.

"That's just fine for you, Belrotha," Gimmol said with substantially more courtesy, "but it won't work for all of us. I'd probably drown before you were in up to your waist."

"So me carry you?"

Reluctantly, the gremlin glanced at Gork, who was tapping his foot impatiently on the sodden ground. "What about him?" he asked, tossing a thumb over his shoulder. "He's even shorter than I am."

The ogre cocked her head. "Him not as nice as you. But me can probably carry both."

"You're all heart," Gork said.

"Jhurpess not want to get fur all wet and dirty," the bugbear wailed. "Jhurpess will smell bad, and prey will run away."

"Prey?" Cræosh asked. "You planning to hunt, Nature-boy?"

"Jhurpess hungry!"

"Now there's a surprise. Why don't you eat my—"

"*If* I may?" Katim asked in a tone that suggested she didn't really give a damn whether she might or not. "I believe we . . . were supposed to be accomplishing . . . something."

"Yeah, we're trying!" Cræosh barked. "If you've got an idea, now'd be a great time for it."

"What we need is . . . a skiff or a raft of some . . . sort."

Fezeill raised a scale-covered hand, a gesture more appropriate to a schoolchild than a troglodyte. "I don't mean to ssspit on your delusions, Katim, but even assssuming any of usss had the proper ssskills to build a raft—and any of you who think it'sss really as sssimple as tying a few logsss together are welcome to try it—I doubt we could make one big enough for Tree-trunk over here."

Belrotha scowled. "You make fun of me?"

"Not at all. Would you like me to?"

"What I had in . . . mind," Katim interjected yet again, "was for the rest . . . of us to make use of the . . . skiff, and for . . . Belrotha to pull it."

"Oh." Fezeill blinked. "Actually, that'sss not a bad idea. But we ssstill don't have a ssskiff."

"No." The troll's uneven teeth shifted and glinted in her evil grin. "But . . . it shouldn't be too hard . . . to find someone who does. Right . . . Gork?"

The kobold jumped, then frowned, and finally nodded. "She's right, actually. You won't find anyone stupid enough to go deep, but the very edges of Jureb Nahl aren't *too* bad. A few spots worth cultivating, plenty of snakes and gators to eat. Never any way of knowing exactly where, but there's always a few down-and-out folks eking out a living. Goblins and exiled kobolds, mostly, sometimes some humans. We used to dare each other to sneak out at night and steal from them, when I was a kit."

"Could take a while to find them," Cræosh said.

"Less time, and certainly . . . less discomfort than to cross . . . the swamp otherwise, wouldn't . . . you say?"

It actually took only a few hours' travel, paralleling the eastern edge of the marsh, to prove both Katim and Gork right. A rickety old shack stood upon a small rise, a few dozen yards beyond dry land. It looked to have been constructed with the castoff of other, better homes: the door hung askew, too small for the frame; uneven boards left gaps in the walls; and the chimney was so full of holes that no smoke would ever have reached the top.

"I don't get it," Gimmol said. "Why?"

The orc shrugged. "Kicked out of their homes, maybe. Criminals, or refugees, or just too poor to afford to live wherever they lived. Hell, some people are just fucked in the head; maybe they *prefer* being out here by themselves."

"Jhurpess would rather this to big city," the bugbear said.

Cræosh nodded. "See? Fucked in the head."

Katim snorted, studying the shanty. "Regardless, if they live . . . here, I can guarantee . . . they have some method . . . of traveling the waters."

Sure enough, even as they spoke, a gangly human appeared from behind the shack. He seemed to float, and it quickly became apparent that he stood upon a shallow-water skiff. A single pole provided propulsion, shoved over and over against the mud beneath the swamp.

"Wow," Fezeill said. "Built to order. Did sssomebody sssend word ahead with our sssspesssssifications?"

"All skiffs are pretty much the same, lizard-breath," Gork replied.

"Whatcha want?" the old man asked, the skiff drifting to a halt a few yards from shore. His eyelids danced as they tried to simultaneously narrow in suspicion and widen in fear. "We don' see many of your kind here. 'Cept for the little guy, there. See too many of his."

"No such thing," Gork muttered.

"Well, you're seeing us now," Cræosh said, ignoring the kobold and giving the man a good once-over. Most of the hair had fallen from his head, most of the teeth from his gums. An old battered tunic and breeches, just barely of sufficient quality for Cræosh to have wiped his ass with, was all that hid the questionable glories of his lanky, half-starved frame.

"We travel to . . . Jureb Nahl," Katim told him, deliberately ignoring the orc's frantic gestures to shut up. "We need the use of . . . your skiff."

"Do you now?" The old man rubbed a stubble-coated chin. "I suppose I can see my way to rentin' it out. Gonna cost you, though."

"Of course," Katim said, taking a step into deeper water. "How much?"

The human made a show of pondering. "Umm, well, I think twenty oughta about do it, don' you?"

Cræosh scoffed. "You'd better be talking *copper*, scrotum-face. I wouldn't—"

Katim's hand rose, clutching not her coin purse but her *chirrusk*. Steel gouged into wood, and the troll gave a fearsome yank. The skiff lunged toward her while the old man toppled backward into the water, his cries emerging as nothing but a stream of filthy bubbles. She leapt, clearing the skiff entirely, and hit the water on all fours. When she resurfaced a moment later, she did so alone.

It took a moment before Cræosh, or any of the others, could form a coherent sentence. "What the fuck was *that*?" the orc finally managed.

Katim emerged from the shallow water, yanked the *chirrusk* from the raft, and shook herself off like a wolf. "We need the . . . skiff."

"Yeah, but . . ."

"Squeamish, orc? That's . . . not like you at all."

Cræosh shook his head. How to explain? It wasn't the old man's death that bothered him, though he saw neither advantage nor honor in it. It was the casual way she committed even *unnecessary* murder. It confirmed his worst suspicions, and ensured many a sleepless night to come.

But of course, he couldn't come out and *say* that it made him even more frightened of the troll, could he? "It's just wasteful, that's all," he said finally.

Katim shrugged. "Shall we get . . . moving?"

The skiff was just large enough to accommodate the squad—minus Belrotha, of course—and not a one of them was happy with the rather intimate accommodation. Cræosh lashed a length of rope to one end, handed the other to Belrotha with a warning that he'd "better get the damn thing back in one piece," and they were off.

For about half a minute. Before they'd gotten more than a few ogre-sized paces, Katim tugged on the rope. "Stop here," she ordered.

The ogre glanced around, puzzled. "We not there yet."

"No. There is something I . . . have to do."

Cræosh began to ask what the hell she was about now until he followed her gaze to the old man's hut. The lunatic gleam growing in her eyes abruptly made all too much sense.

"Women and children, Katim?" he asked, mouth twisted in a grimace of disgust. "Great and mighty opponents, a fitting tribute to a troll."

"You wouldn't . . . understand, orc." Katim slid over the side of the skiff; the water, here, came up to about her ribs. "I won't be . . . long."

"No, you won't," Cræosh said. "Because you're not going."

"Oh? And are you . . . going to stop me?"

Every nerve, every instinct, screamed at Cræosh to back off. He *really* didn't want to take on the troll, certainly not on behalf of some scraggly humans. But there were *some* limits even to orc depravity, and no soldier went after the kids unless there was good reason; it just wasn't done.

Plus, and far more importantly, now that he'd made his position clear, he couldn't afford to back down in front of the others.

Ah, hell, it had to happen sooner or later.

Swallowing the bile in his throat, he too slid into the water. It would slow him, but hopefully not too much. "If I have to, troll, then yeah, why not?"

Katim smiled. "Priorities, Cræosh?" she asked, one hand grasping the haft of her axe, the other sliding toward that hideous chain.

"Yeah, right." The orc's fist closed over his own hilt. "Priorities."

Perhaps it *did* have to happen sooner or later, but it wouldn't be now.

A harsh tearing sound roared through the swamp as Belrotha ripped a rotted cypress from the mud. Tottering beneath the weight of the twenty-foot log, she took four unsteady steps and hurled it like a caber.

It struck—a wooded, waterlogged, wobbling bolt of lightning—directly atop the decrepit shanty. The hut disintegrated into flotsam amid a cacophony of snaps and splinters, and perhaps a scream or two.

"You—you . . ." The rest of the squad, had they not been equally dumbstruck, might have taken a moment to appreciate the sight of Cræosh at a loss for words.

Katim, however, managed to keep a hold on her vocabulary, if only just. "Damn you, what . . . did you *do*?!"

Belrotha shrugged. "Me solve problem."

"You *bitch*! You stupid . . . half-witted cretin!"

"No need to call names."

"Names? *Names*? You . . . idiot! They're no . . . good to me if . . . *you* kill them!"

The ogre shrugged again. "Me end argument? Troll and orc both alive?"

". . . Yes."

"Then us done here. You get back on raft before me have to put you there." The ogre bent low to meet the troll's gaze. "You not call me names again, either. Ogres in Itho used to call me names. Them stop when me tie them together and throw them off mountain. There not mountains in swamp, but me can—uhh . . . What word?"

"Improvise?" Gimmol suggested quietly from the back of the skiff.

"Yeah. That." Then, having said her piece, she stomped back to the skiff and fished the tow-rope from the water.

Cræosh and Katim stared at the ogre, then at one another. Then, as one, they sheathed their weapons and clambered back aboard the skiff. Belrotha grunted once, and they were moving once more.

After a few moments, Cræosh carefully maneuvered his way to the front of the raft. "Hey, Belrotha!"

"What you want?" she asked without looking back.

"What'd you find that was strong enough?"

"What?"

"To hold an ogre. You said you tied a few ogres together and threw them off a mountain. What'd you tie them together with?"

"Oh, that. Me not use anything. Me just tie their arms together."

"Yeah, but with . . . Oh." Cræosh stopped, finally getting it. "As in, you actually tied their *arms* together?"

Belrotha nodded, causing the hair on the back of her head to slap up and down, leaving greasy spots on her neck. "Yeah. Arms tied good, too. Almost got double knot, but me forgot how to make one."

"Oh," Cræosh said again. Then, "Ouch."

"Ouch," Belrotha agreed. "Me think it would hurt, too. Couldn't ask, though. Them not stop screaming long enough to answer."

Cræosh sat back on the raft and watched, lost in thought, as they passed between the twisted, moss-encrusted trees. By the time twilight fell, they'd moved far into the darkest depths of the swamp.

Somewhere ahead, across another several days of marsh, lay the ruins of Jureb Nahl. If even a quarter of Gork's folktales were true, Cræosh wondered if he might not've been happier if the troll had just filleted him and gotten it over with.

CHAPTER FIVE

FORWARD, MARSH!

ere in his private chamber, with no one about to see him, Shreckt kept his feet planted on the floor as he paced. Designed for people who were the size of—well, people—the room gave the tiny imp substantial space for his constant to-and-fro. Just as well, since if the walls had risked getting in his way, he might have tried blasting them with something.

How *dare* Queen Anne treat him that way? No matter how powerful she might be, no matter who her husband was, she was just a *mortal*, a paltry creature ruling a paltry kingdom in the ass-end of reality. Shreckt had been present at the fall of empires that spanned entire worlds, had danced on the graves of creatures that could have duplicated Queen Anne's most potent spells in their sleep!

He sighed, then, a heartfelt gesture—or it would've been if he had a heart. None of it mattered; not what he'd done, not where or even *what* he'd been, nothing. Here, in this world, he was bound to the form in which he'd been summoned, and to the whim of his summoner. Here, he was an imp in the service of King Morthûl.

And killing Morthûl's wife—even if he could somehow pull it off, with what little power he had available—would assuredly result in unpleasant consequences. So, with the utmost reluctance, Shreckt dragged his attention away from contemplating a dozen agonizing deaths for the Charnel King's slut and turned instead to more immediate problems.

Namely, that he hadn't been able to report back to King Morthûl, or to mention those worm creatures to General Falchion, since he got here. He'd fully intended to do so, once they'd gotten settled in at Castle Eldritch. Well, he was as settled as he was going to get, and the rest of the squad had already moved out on their next assignment, so now would have been a great time.

Except that he couldn't teleport!

He'd panicked into near-incoherence when he'd first tried, with a grand result of nothing for his trouble. He couldn't teleport to General Falchion, or to his own home in Timas Khoreth, or even—once he'd summoned up the nerve to try—into the throne room of Morthûl himself.

Once the imp had calmed down and taken stock, he'd finally realized that there was nothing wrong with him; it was something about the Castle Eldritch itself, perhaps a security measure on Queen Anne's part. And that left him in a new dilemma.

He could just ask her to lower the wards and allow him to depart. He could walk out the door and teleport from outside. But either option meant letting her know that he was going, and while there was no *inherent* reason she shouldn't know he was reporting back to Morthûl and Falchion, the Demon Squad had been assigned to her—and that included the sergeant. He wasn't sure how she'd take it if he started going over her head.

So he'd gone back and forth, mentally and physically, for days now. And just like that, he was sick of it.

Let the queen object! Let her try to stop him from reporting to King Morthûl. That would be just the leverage he needed to see her punished, if only moderately, for mistreating a demon of the Pit! Shreckt spun in the middle of a step and headed for the door.

It drifted slowly open before he'd crossed halfway across the room. Scowling, Shreckt drifted up until he stood at his customary height above the floor, the better to see and deal with . . .

"Rupert," he muttered. *The queen's homemade toy.* "Thanks so much for knocking."

The brown hood nodded. "And a good day to you, honored guest."

Shreckt chuckled. "Still performing, Rupert? The audience left a few days ago, and I ain't buying it one bit."

"No?"

"Nope. In fact, it's starting to irritate me. You could have said something about the wards, you know."

"We assumed that, as you *surely* wouldn't be attempting to do anything improper, you'd never encounter them."

"Ah." Shreckt took a few steps nearer the door. "And if I asked you to lower them now?"

"That would, of course, be up to Her Majesty to decide."

"Then let's go."

"Ah, yes. I'm afraid that won't be possible just now."

Your average human or goblin would have asked why, or made some protest. But Shreckt knew a threat when he heard it.

A bolt of lightning crackled from the imp's hands, blasted across the chamber, but Rupert was already moving. Passing *through* the wall and the heavy wooden door, he darted aside at the last instant, leaving only the trailing hem of his robe to be scorched, and then only lightly, by the levinbolt.

An invisible but all too tangible weight fell on the imp, smashing him to the floor hard enough to crack the flagstone. The breath blasted from his lungs, and if he'd actually been a creature that *needed* to breathe, he'd surely have passed out on the spot. He struggled to rise, but couldn't move so much as a wingtip. He calmed his thoughts, drawing upon a spell that would blast Rupert, however insubstantial he might be, into whatever afterlife awaited a creature never truly alive.

Nothing happened. The pressure pinning Shreckt to the floor had snuffed the flame of his magics as surely as the castle had thwarted his teleportation. For the first time in—well, ever—Shreckt began to fear.

"Queen Anne . . ." the imp croaked, straining even to speak. "She won't—"

"Queen Anne won't what?" The voice drifting through the doorway was soft, lyrical. A hem of green velvet glided into his peripheral vision, and he couldn't even turn his head to look. "Queen Anne won't allow this? Queen Anne won't be happy? My dear imp, Rupert does *nothing* without my order."

A muscle twitched at the back of Shreckt's neck. "Should have guessed . . . Too powerful for Rupert . . ."

"Yes, indeed," the queen said softly. "But with the right preparation, hardly beyond *me*."

"Squad?"

The hem shifted. "Are you actually concerned about them, imp? No, of course you aren't. You wouldn't know how. You're just hoping they'll last long enough to rescue you.

"Well, I intend no harm to your soldiers, Sergeant. But I can assure you, they will not be racing to your rescue. My tasks should keep them busy for quite some time to come; I doubt they'll even notice you're missing, or that they'll care if they do. And once those tasks are completed, I intend to be quite finished with you, so it's really a moot point, isn't it?"

Shreckt's view of the room shifted as Rupert lifted him from the floor. And while the imp had been frightened at the ease with which the queen had neutralized his magics, and frightened further still at the thought of becoming part of whatever twisted experiment or scheme she had in mind, he was *terrified* now. For Rupert had lifted him high enough to look into the queen's face, and he had seen a madness burning in her eyes with the same fervor as the Charnel King's own unholy glow.

King Dororam bent thoughtfully over the long table that ran down the middle of what had once been his study. He proudly wore a fine hauberk of chain; proudly because it had been crafted in his youth, but he remained able (albeit it with some huffing and puffing) to squeeze into it. He wore it every waking moment, along with the broadsword at his side, conditioning himself for the day when he would wear them at the head of his army as they marched on Kirol Syrreth.

His study, too, had been dressed for war. The books had been removed to the library, all save the treatises on battle and tactics, and the furniture replaced with a lengthy table brought from the soldiers' mess. Several immaculately drawn maps occupied that table, transforming the room into the strategic center for the upcoming campaign.

"I don't know, Theiolyn," Dororam was saying. "I don't think I can get a large enough force through that pass to matter."

The elf shook her head, coming close to smacking Dororam with her platinum-blonde topknot. "You misunderstand me, Dororam," she said in her melodic accent. "It is my own forces who will penetrate through this pass. We will serve as a diversion to draw attention from the larger force—yours—who will be coming through . . ." She jabbed a finger down on the map. "*Here* instead."

"Ah." Dororam glanced around at his compatriots. In addition to Theiolyn, the Speaking Prince ("prince" being a unisex title among the elven nations), the room was occupied by Thane Granitemane, a grim dwarf with a knee-length beard, who spoke for the assembled clans; Thizzwhff, one of the giloral Council of Chiefs, whose kaleidoscopic butterfly-wings were constantly bumping into everyone around the table; and the kings, queens, and/or regents of half a dozen other human nations. These sundry rulers were each accompanied by anywhere from one to four generals, ready to offer their own advice.

Only the halflings were absent, and that was because they hadn't anything resembling a government. When the others marched, any given halfling would either choose to march with them, or not.

"It has possibilities," Dororam said, staring at the map. "But if we move through here, we leave Thane Granitemane and his forces isolated."

The bearded figure snorted contemptuously. "We are dwarves, King Dororam. We fear little. Fighting on our own least of all."

"I don't mean to disparage your abilities," replied a large man with a handlebar mustache, one of Dororam's generals, "or those of your people. But if our main force on the Serpent's Pass doesn't draw the entirety of their resistance, you could find yourself not merely outnumbered, but surrounded. Are you certain that—?"

The door to the inner sanctum, one that was supposed to be guarded by a dozen soldiers, burst open, apparently struck by an invisible battering ram. A violent breeze swept through the room, ruffling hair and displacing several score sheets of paper.

His mouth locked in a scowl so stony it might have been etched onto his face, Ananias duMark stood in the doorway. The hem of his robe flapped in the fading wind, and one fist was clenched, white-knuckled, on his thick wooden staff.

King Dororam breathed a quiet sigh of relief. "DuMark," he said in greeting, "we were just—"

"Everyone else out!"

Most in the room were generals and kings, and certainly unaccustomed to being ordered about. Nonetheless, within two minutes, duMark and Dororam stood alone. The sorcerer crooked a finger, and the door slammed itself shut behind the last straggler.

Dororam's expression deepened into a scowl to equal the wizard's. "I give you *substantial* leeway, duMark," he said softly. "But you will not barge into my castle—my *home*—in this manner. You will not order about my guests, particularly royal visitors. And you will not—"

"Dororam, shut the hell up."

It was sheer astonishment, more than anything else, that compelled Dororam to comply.

"Good," the half-elf continued. "Tell me, then. Is it true?"

The king frowned. "Is what true?"

"Don't play games with me! Rumor has it that you sent a scouting party into Kirol Syrreth! Is it true?"

This, Dororam had not been looking forward to. "Yes," he said. "It's true."

DuMark collapsed into the nearest chair. "Dororam, when did you become such a fool? I asked you not to take any action. I *told* you that I have my own source of information, and my own efforts under way to hamper the Charnel King's efforts. Why would you risk interfering with either?"

The king shrugged. "You yourself told me that your source is less than reliable. I needed to confirm that you can count on his information *now*, before the war effort begins to depend on its veracity."

"As I recall, I also told you that my source would probably vanish completely if you acted too soon. If the Dark Lord figures out that we've an informant in his lands, he'll take steps. And despite my magics, a dead spy is of little more use to me than he is to you.

"Besides, I can assure you that even with his army's ongoing training exercises, the Brimstone Mountains are guarded well enough to repel any attack. You needn't have sent a party to learn *that*."

Dororam dragged over a chair and sat beside the wizard. "I'm not looking for a hole in his defenses, duMark. I simply want my men to corroborate for me that those exercises are, in fact, ongoing. If I can confirm that your source is accurate on *this*, I'll feel better about trusting it later, when it matters."

DuMark closed his eyes. *Gods, but the man can be such an idiot! Ever since his daughter died, he hasn't been his old self.* The half-elf had to stop himself from shaking his head in despair. *It's not as if Dororam's too old to make another one. . . .*

Well, what was done was done. "Your scouts understand their orders?" he asked.

"Absolutely," Dororam assured him. "They are to observe enemy activity near the borders only, and determine if the patrols are indeed less numerous than before. No incursions, no contact, and certainly no combat. Trust me, the Iron Keep will never even know they were there."

The trees—twisted, half-dead monstrosities groaning beneath the weight of mosses and fungi—obscured and even absorbed the sunlight far out of proportion to the amount of cover they provided. Even at the height of noon, the swamps of Jureb Nahl were brightened by little more than a diffuse, sickly gray luminescence.

Here and there the waters rippled as some animal moved beneath the ubiquitous layer of green scum. Rats clambered on clicking claws across the boughs. Huge spiderwebs lay draped over and around the trees, sometimes three or four at a stretch. And always, always lurked the alligators and constrictors, some big enough to be easily mistaken for logs until they opened maws bristling with dagger-sized teeth.

A constant drone jiggled within their ears, tickling at the fringes of consciousness. Insects sang mindless paeans to the world; the waters lapped and gurgled; birds hooted in the distance, falling silent only briefly as the goblins drew near. All were deadened and mangled into a single dreary tone by the weight of the air, still and humid despite the chill, giving the entire orchestra an eerie, dreamlike feel.

Then, of course, there was the constant miasma: the scent of dead and stagnant things, so pervasive that even the most bestial members of the squad struggled not to gag and resolved to burn their outfits once they'd returned to civilization.

But all of this, *all* of it, would have remained tolerable if they hadn't lost the bloody damn skiff!

It had been just after dawn on their third day in Jureb Nahl. They were debating the merits of stopping off on a small, moss- and peat-coated hillock and having a quick breakfast when the "hill" decided it had plans of its own.

Enormous tentacles rose from the water, lashing and pummeling, seeking prey for this strange wetlands predator. The goblins, save Belrotha, found themselves tumbling pell-mell into the water. Struggling to their feet, coughing pestilential gunk from their lungs, they'd found themselves facing what they could only refer to later, in Cræosh's words, as "a huge fucking hard-shelled swamptopus."

They'd succeeded in killing the damn thing—or, in other words, Cræosh and Katim had distracted it while Belrotha drove her massive sword through its body and then pummeled it into paste with a log, while the others danced around in the water and the clinging muck, trying to contribute and failing miserably—but not before the flailing tentacles had reduced the skiff to what would, in drier conditions, have been kindling.

And after all that, Jhurpess had pulled a face and announced that the thing didn't even taste very good.

That was three days ago, and since then, lacking any other recourse, they'd walked, waded, and (in the cases of the shorter members) swum through Jureb Nahl.

Hell no longer held any fear for the soldiers of this particular Demon Squad. After slogging through those green-scummed, vermin-infested waters, any or all of them would have cheerfully chosen an eternity in the worst depths of the Pit over one more night in the Ancestors/Stars/gods-damned swamp! The insects used the lot of them as an endless buffet of flesh and blood. The filthy, stinging mud had coated them (albeit, in Belrotha's case, only from the knees down), and the two shortest goblins had finally been forced to hitch a ride. Gimmol sat perched upon one of the ogre's broad shoulders; the kobold stood inside her backpack. Where he could, Jhurpess traveled via the branches above, but even he could not avoid the muck entirely.

Only Fezeill, in his scale-covered form, had escaped largely unscathed. The faux troglodyte had taken to scouting, and finally, *finally* he returned with the news they'd all been dying (and in some cases, very nearly killing) to hear.

"The ground ssslopesss upward jussst a mile or ssso from here," he said, his head poking up just a few inches from the surface. "I sssaw a few sssections of what appearsss to have been a ssstone wall. I believe that we've finally reached the ruinsss."

Cræosh's first instinct was to fall to his knees and thank the Ancestors, but he decided that such an act of obeisance could wait until it wouldn't submerge him completely.

The wall indeed proved to be one length of a larger ruin. Even better, it was constructed on a stretch of land high enough to stand completely out of the water. Sure, the air itself remained so choked with moisture that breathing and drinking were damn near synonymous, but still, it was something. Cræosh allowed himself a moment's respite, leaning back against the moss-covered stones and making some token gestures at wiping the worst of the sludge from his armor. "I am not," he announced, "looking forward to the trip *out*."

Katim, glancing about with narrowed eyes and flared nostrils, nodded absently. "Perhaps we can find . . . an old boat, or the materials . . . to construct another skiff. But I wonder . . . if we shouldn't first concern . . . ourselves with what we have here."

Cræosh righted himself and meandered over to stand between Katim and a thick cypress. "Oh," he said, peering past one furry shoulder. "Yeah, maybe we should, at that."

Portions of the wall, most of which were so dilapidated that they barely reached the orc's elbows, stretched into the haze in both directions. Great gaps revealed where over half of that fortification had long since crumbled into the wet and malleable earth. Copious grasses spouted from what had once been tightly mortared cracks. Molds and fungi coated the stones like a light dusting of snow.

Yet enough of the wall remained to show that it had once been a solid bastion. Surely these ruins must indeed be ancient Jureb Nahl itself.

The once-great town beyond that wall was equally pathetic. Some of the main roads remained visible, barely, as lighter stripes wending through the foliage. Walls and parts of walls were tombstones, marking the corpses of homes and shops and temples. One or two of the ruins retained their roofs, but most were nothing but sporadic bricks hidden among the weeds or trapped in the branches of ancient trees.

From where they stood, Cræosh and Katim could see the remains of the once-proud keep that had dominated the town's center, its four watchtowers piercing the sky above, allowing sentinels a clear view over what, at the time, had been open fields of crops. Several of the buildings actually looked to be in halfway decent shape, but heaps of craggy, broken stone were all that remained of two of those towers, while a third had been sheared down to a height of about ten feet by the rigors of past centuries. The northwest tower still stood, but open wounds gaped in the brick, and powdered mortar sifted earthward at the slightest breeze. The entire thing leaned subtly toward the sunset, and Cræosh didn't trust it to support the weight of a corpulent owl.

"If this dead wizard's tower is in the same prime condition as this one," he said, "I think we can count on going back to Queen Anne empty-handed."

"Or at least . . . empty-headed," Katim said. "*I'm* not going . . . to be the one to tell her . . . we failed. If she says . . . it's here, perhaps we should at least . . . look?"

"Okay, fine. So where in the name of my green and crusty orifice *is* it?"

The troll looked again at the watchtower. "If it were somewhat . . . sturdier," she mused, "it would provide . . . an excellent vantage point."

"Swell. And if Grandpa had been an ogre, Grandma would be hollow. You think your 'if' will support our weight?"

"Not at all," Katim told him. "But it might . . . support a kobold's."

Cræosh began to smile.

It was perhaps not all that surprising that Gork himself was less than anxious to test that idea.

"Hell no," was his actual response.

"Look, Shorty," Cræosh told him, "you're the only here who can do it."

"Then it doesn't get done."

"I'd ask Jhurpess, but he's too heavy to pull it off!"

"I'll pull something else off if you don't get off my case about—"

"Gork," Katim said, "try to be . . . reasonable."

"Okay, wait. You and the Great Green Pig want me to climb that . . . that death trap, and *I'm* the one being unreasonable? I think that squid-thing held you underwater too long, Katim. The only falling I plan to do any time soon is asleep."

"But—"

"Ask the doppelganger. He can be a kobold—sort of—and *he* can climb the damn thing."

"You're a far more ssskilled climber," Fezeill said smugly. "Regardlesss of form."

"So turn into something with wings and take a look around that way."

"Such as what? A giloral?" The troglodyte shuddered. "Even if I wanted to—and I'd rather bed an elf—it'sss a far cry from *having* wingsss to knowing how to ussse them. Not happening."

"Think of this as an opportunity to learn new skills, then."

Katim smiled, not precisely the reaction that Gork would have hoped for. "Listen, kobold, and . . . listen well. We cannot leave here . . . until we've found Trelaine's . . . tower."

"So we find another way to do it."

"We'd have to search . . . hundreds of square yards, perhaps . . . miles of swamp. Do you . . . want to go back in there?"

Little kobold teeth gleamed in the dim light. *"I'm* riding an ogre. *You're* the one getting wet and sticky."

"Precisely my . . . point."

Gork saw it coming and tried to duck away. Unfortunately, Cræosh had slinked around behind him during the argument, waiting for precisely that. The kobold screamed, thrashed, and bit down hard on Katim's arms; nothing helped. Shrieking and spitting troll fur the entire way, Gork sailed through the air toward the top of the leaning tower.

Oddly, though, his only *coherent* thought was, *If I hear so much as a single chuckle from Gimmol, I'll drown the useless turd.*

Even he had to admit—later, when he could think clearly—that it'd been a good throw. Katim arced him up and over the crumbling crenellations, rather than tossing him directly into the stone. (He didn't pretend it had been for his sake; she just didn't want to risk knocking the teetering thing over.) His landing was surprisingly gentle, and though the rock grated beneath him, sending more powder sifting out over the swamp, nothing actually fell.

For long and aching minutes, Gork lay spread-eagle atop the rickety stone platform, waiting for his heart to return to something resembling a healthy pace. Then he waited a few minutes more, until he could force himself to think about something other than slowly feeding Katim to a hive of rock spiders. *Then* he rose to his feet, taking mincing little steps, and examined the lands beyond.

He saw, first and foremost, that the trees and other growth thinned considerably to the north, until only an occasional gnarled and knotted trunk protruded from the marsh. Beyond them, a wavering phantom in the low-lying haze, stood a circle of great, rectangular stones—some standing on end, others lying horizontally atop them. The circle was incomplete, broken where the earth had eroded away and allowed part of the henge to topple into the swamp. Enough remained, however, for Gork to identify it—from tales he'd heard, and even a charcoal sketch he'd once seen—as a druidic circle, an altar to some god or power forgotten since before the rise of the Charnel King.

All of which might've been fascinating to a historian, but was useless to the kobold, since the circle was neither a wizard's tower nor of any immediate monetary value. And of that tower, there was no trace. Other than that henge of stones far to the north, he saw nothing but the thick trees and foul waters of the swamp.

"Fuck!" he shouted at the uncaring expanse. "Fuck, fuck, fuck!"

"Problem, Shorty?" Cræosh asked from somewhere below.

"Yeah, there's a problem! The problem is I hate this place! I hate this place, I hate this whole mission, and I'm not real joyously fond of any of you right now, either!"

There was a brief pause. "I'm gonna go out on a limb, here," the orc finally said, "and guess that you haven't found anything?"

"'Out on a limb,' he says," Gork murmured savagely. "Why doesn't he climb up here; I'll show him out on a limb. . . ."

Still muttering resentfully, the kobold began the arduous climb back to earth. It was certainly a near thing; more than once, he felt his grip giving way as mortar and stone crumbled beneath the pressure of even his tiny hands. Finally, however, he was low enough to drop onto the ogre's head—eliciting an abbreviated bleat—and from there to the top of one of the broken walls.

"So what now?" he asked, not giving Cræosh time to spew whatever smart-ass comment was assuredly forthcoming.

"I'd say we've got two choices," Cræosh said instead. "One, we comb this entire ruin, top to bottom, and hope like hell we find some clue as to where this goat-fucker Trelaine might have shoved his tower."

"That could take sssome time," Fezeill said. Then, as the weight of their disdain crashed down upon him, "I'm jussst sssaying . . ."

"The other option?" Katim prompted.

"Right. Option two is that we wander back out into the swamp and search aimlessly until we stumble over the damn thing or drop dead."

For a moment, no one spoke. Then, "I'll search what's left of the keep," Gork volunteered. "Hell, I've already seen most of it from up top, anyway."

The troll nodded. "I'll go with . . . him," she said. Then, at the naked hostility in the kobold's expression, she added, "We've already seen what . . . sorts of things live in . . . this swamp. It would be . . . foolish for you to wander off . . . on your own."

"Of course," Gork said through grinding teeth.

"Nature-boy can check the trees," Cræosh continued, gesturing vaguely upward. "I somehow doubt there's anything useful up there, but maybe he'll spot a building or something we can't see from the ground."

The bugbear smiled. "Jhurpess like trees."

"You don't say. Fezeill, you get to check *under* the water, see if anything's sunken but intact. Me and Belrotha—and Gimmol, I suppose— are gonna look through whatever other buildings are still standing."

He was off before he finished speaking, tromping through the broken walls. Belrotha followed a moment later, Gimmol trailing behind. Jhurpess and Fezeill headed toward the back end of town. Gork and Katim stood alone, by the dilapidated walls of the ancient fort.

"You try to toss me again," he told her, puffed up as big as he could, "you're going to lose a finger."

He anticipated a threat, a sarcastic remark, something, *anything* other than the knowing smile that crept almost sensuously across the troll's twisted snout. Shaken and not entirely sure why, Gork turned and moved toward the cracked walls of what had once been Jureb Nahl's beating heart.

Initially, other than rotted sludge that might once have been furniture, and a *whole lot* of vermin, the keep's main structure didn't provide much. While the outer walls had survived, the same couldn't be said of most of the interior.

It was only as they were departing what had probably been a barracks, picking their way through broken flagstones and clinging weeds, that something caught Katim's notice. Recognizing what might have been a hand protruding from beneath, the troll hurled aside a mess of sodden wood that had once been a bed, or perhaps a table, to reveal a partial skeleton, half buried in the soft dirt.

"What was it?" Gork asked, peering around her left knee.

Katim squinted. The skeleton was only visible from the thighs up, and a great portion of the rib cage appeared to have been shattered by a narrow object: a blunt axe perhaps, or possibly a gardening tool. The skull had also been partly crushed, this time by the furniture collapsing atop it, but she recognized the shape of a snout, shorter and broader than her own. . . .

"I think," Katim said slowly, "that this . . . might've been a troglodyte."

Now it was Gork's turn to peer closer. "You know, you may be right. I thought they only lived in the Brimstone Mountains. Too cold elsewhere, or something."

The troll shrugged. "I thought the . . . same, but here . . . he is."

Gork poked a hand into the soil by the skeleton. "Damn swamp! Things rot so *fast*. I can't tell if this skeleton's been here ten weeks or ten years."

"Does it really . . . matter?"

"Well, I'd sort of like to know if there's a bunch of troglodytes with sharp, pointy things waiting for me around the next tree."

"When you figure . . . it out, let me know. We . . . haven't checked the outer . . . structures yet."

The first one of those, another barracks, smaller and far more cramped, was even grimmer. Several rows of bunks stood rotting along the walls, half a dozen of which were occupied by the corpses of their former owners. Just to be thorough, Katim moved body to body, checking the remaining scraps of cloth and the smaller footlockers beside each bed.

"Can you tell what killed them?" the kobold asked nervously. "Dying of plague's not real high on my list of things to do."

"No plague," Katim reassured him, moving on to the fourth skeleton. *Could you even catch plague from bones?* She wasn't sure, and she wasn't about to admit her ignorance. "Two of the ones . . . I've examined have scoring or . . . scratch marks on the . . . neck. These men had . . . their throats slit."

"Oh. Good." A pause, then, "I wonder why? It's not like Jureb Nahl fell in a war or anything."

"My guess would . . . be that these men stayed behind . . . to guard against looting or . . . some such. I'd say . . . they didn't succeed."

"Nothing in the lockers, huh?" Gork asked disappointedly.

Katim had reached the fifth corpse. "Not a thing worth *aaaah!*"

Even as she recoiled, the kobold was skittering up the nearest decrepit wall, presumably fleeing from whatever had elicited her cry. She heard him calling out for help as he climbed. *"Belrotha! Cræosh! Jhurpess!"* And then, far more quietly, "Fezeill . . ."

It hung from Katim's forearm, mandibles chewing unmercifully through fur and hide and flesh. It was something akin to a normal millipede—if one discounted the fact that, judging just from the portion she could actually see, it had to be almost as long as she was tall. It must have been coiled tight within the corpse, or perhaps lairing in the mattress beneath.

Howling in fury, Katim retreated, dragging it from its hidey-hole. With her free hand, she yanked her axe from its thong. She had little room to swing, but between the sharpened blade and her own strength, she didn't need much. Laying the steel against the segmented chitin, she began to saw. The millipede thrashed, twisted, and then just *opened*. Yellow ichor spattered across the floor. The thrashing grew even more feverish as the thing went mad, unaware that it was already dead, and finally fell limp.

Even in death, the mandibles refused to release.

Grimacing against the pain, Katim shoved the tip of her blade along her arm, preparing to pry the creature loose, and collapsed as all sensation fled from her legs.

The wound wasn't that bad! she protested silently as she slid to the floor. *I've dealt with far worse—oh.* Realization hit her as her vision began to blur. *Oh, fantastic.*

Her last conscious image was that of the kobold dropping from the wall and racing toward her, blade held high. . . .

Her vision returned first, albeit poorly: she could barely make out basic shapes. What she first took to be ants or other bugs crawling across her legs swiftly erupted into a thousand white-hot pins, but she welcomed it nonetheless, for she'd feared the feeling might never return to her limbs. Her sight cleared, the world swimming into view, and her ecstasy faded somewhat at the various faces staring down at her. True, any lesser creature would be dead, but it galled her to have lain helpless before the rest of the Demon Squad.

"Well, well," Cræosh oozed, and Katim could smell the condescension in his voice. He was clearly planning to milk this for all it was worth. "Is trolly-wolly feeling all better after her nappy-wappy?"

Katim decided to test the movement in her tingling legs by kicking the orc in the groin. This elicited a single yelp, so high-pitched that the less sensitive members of the squad might not even have heard it. Without even seeming to have fallen through the intervening distance, Cræosh lay facedown in the dirt, knees bent, ass in the air, hands clutching at his privates as though someone were trying to steal them.

"A bit crude," Katim admitted in answer to the various expressions around her, "but I'm . . . afraid I'm not at my . . . best at the moment."

"Oh, I don't know about that," Gork said, gazing down at Cræosh with a beatific smile.

"What happened?" the troll asked.

Gork's grin vanished. With some obvious reluctance, he jerked a thumb in the direction of . . .

"*Gimmol?*" Katim sounded not only incredulous, but almost outraged.

The gremlin stepped forward and nodded shallowly. He presented a truly bizarre appearance now, with only scattered flecks of his bright red armor visible through a coating of mud. "I've made sort of a habit of studying natural substances," he told her. "Herbs and juices mostly, but a few animal toxins, too. I used these"—and here he held up a handful of dried stalks and leaves he'd removed from his pack—"to draw out most of the poison. You should be just fine in a day or so."

"Gimmol . . ." It took a moment for her even to remember how to say the words. "Thank you."

The gremlin beamed.

"If we're through ssstanding around admiring each other," Fezeill broke in, his tongue flickering wildly—on a real troglodyte, Katim would have assumed it to be a lizardly gesture of impatience, but coming from the doppelganger, she had no idea what it meant—"you'd better come with usss. Jhurpessss and I have found sssomething you should sssee."

✳

At the southwest corner of the long-dead town stood yet another thick copse of trees.

"Wow," Cræosh breathed, the air around him growing even thicker with sarcasm than humidity. (He tried to ignore the fact that, to his own ears, his voice still squeaked. *Fucking troll*.) "It's a big bunch of trees. I'm so glad you dragged me over here, Fezeill. All the *other* fucking trees in this swamp just weren't doing it for me."

"If you'd lisssten for jussst a moment, you jackassss, inssstead of running your mouth like a rutting ferret, you'd know that we found sssomething *inssside* the thicket."

"Oh. And that would be what?"

"Building!" Jhurpess said, unable to contain himself any further. "Jhurpess found big stone building! Many holes in roof and walls, but still sturdy." He frowned. "Jhurpess peeked inside, but Jhurpess didn't see anything worth eating."

"So what *did* you see?" Gork asked. "Even for you, 'nothing worth eating' covers a whole lot of ground."

"Oh. Just books," the bugbear replied, dismissing the very notion with a halfhearted wave. "Nothing interesting."

"Just books?" Gork repeated, not certain he'd heard right. "*Just books?!*"

The bugbear exhaled in what might actually have been a sigh. "What bothering Gork now?"

"We're trying to find clues to the tower, you stupid monkey! Maybe even a map! Where else are we going to find that but the library?"

"What library?"

"*A place with books!*" The kobold was actually screeching now.

With a grunt, Cræosh once more lifted the little soldier by his head and plunged him facefirst into the soft mud at their feet. Gork came up spitting, but it had had the desired effect: He shut up.

"Now," Cræosh said, "here's the way we're gonna play it. Fezeill, do you read?"

"Sssome," the not-troglodyte responded thoughtfully. "Doppelganger, Gremlin, a sssmattering of Hobgoblin. A decent amount of Mansssspeak, but sscertainly not any eight-hundred-year-old dialectsss."

"Gork?" Cræosh asked next.

"Barely a word."

The orc frowned. "Then why were you so hot about Jhurpess not rec-ognizing the library?"

"I, uh . . ." The kobold looked at his feet. "Maps and pictures could be helpful."

"Right." There was precious little point in asking either Jhurpess or Belrotha, so . . . "How about you, Katim?"

She nodded. "Manspeak, Gremlin, some . . . conversational Orcish. And, of course . . . Trollish. But I do not think . . . that I would have much better . . . luck with writing this old."

"Fuck!" Cræosh shook his head. He read both Orcish and Gremlin better than most of his fellow soldiers back home, but he had trouble with big words. He could speak Manspeak like a native, but he couldn't read more than a few snippets. *He* sure as shit wouldn't be the one to puzzle this out.

"So let me get this straight," Gork said, clearly getting worked up again. "We've actually found something that might just tell us where this damn tower is, and nobody here can *read* it?"

"Seems to about cover it," Cræosh acknowledged. Then, before the kobold could explode once more, he added, "Though as you said, if we can find a *map*, it doesn't really matter if we can read most of the words, does it?"

"It's a long shot."

"And your better idea is . . . ?"

"Um, so what are we waiting for?"

It was a mistake, and everyone knew it the instant the words left his mouth. Nobody was even a tad surprised when Cræosh, a huge grin splitting his ugly green face, answered, "We're just awaiting your report, Shorty."

From his seat on Belrotha's shoulder, which had somehow become his standard post, Gimmol watched the kobold wander away muttering darkly. He was such a joke to his companions that even after he'd treated the troll's wounds, no one had bothered to ask if *he* could read the books they might find. On the one hand, he was just as happy not telling them; the revelation that he'd studied ancient languages would raise questions he'd prefer not to answer. On the other, they had a job to do, he was as sick of this swamp as any of them, and he'd have loved to have seen the orc's smug face fall when he realized the gremlin was their best hope.

Ah, well. Maybe they'd get lucky and find just the sort of map Cræosh was hoping for. Chewing his cheek in thought, the gremlin continued staring into space long after the tiny scout had vanished into the foliage.

The structure, which Gork located after only a minimum of cuts, scrapes, and abrasions, was exactly as the terrible twosome had described it. A squat building, it was constructed of stone and clearly intended to last. Sure, there were gaps in the walls, and various vines crept through every tiny nook and cranny they could find, but overall it was in better shape than even the sturdiest portions of the keep had been.

The architecture was a little odd, though. The second floor was smaller than the first, leaving an open space, perhaps a balcony or something, above the entryway on the building's south side.

Those doors looked to be the only means of ingress, not counting windows on the upper floor and the sporadic holes in the walls. Standing proud despite the rigors of time, the double portal was some sort of varnished wood. The rightmost of the two doors was hanging open an inch or so, its latch and one of its three hinges having given up the ghost where the wood had not.

A thin smile passed over the kobold's face. He'd always wanted to try this, but traveling in the company of creatures so much larger and stronger than he, he'd never dared, lest he make an ass of himself. Here, however, with nobody watching and such a fragile, precarious obstacle . . .

Gork took several steps back, broke into a charge, and launched a massive kick (well, massive for him) at the loosely hanging door.

He frowned, standing on one foot, the other hanging in the air, at the peculiar sound. It hadn't been the crunch of splintering wood, or the door smacking open, or even bone breaking. It had sounded almost sodden . . .

"Oh, dragonshit."

The door hadn't budged at all. Instead, the rotten interior had given way, allowing Gork's foot to pass completely through. Where, by virtue of the clinging gunk and the long slivers formed from the door's cracking exterior, it was now firmly stuck.

The kobold found himself torn between the conflicting urges to laugh, to cry, and to scream, and settled for a compromise whimper. Gently, thanking the Stars for his tough hide, he began hopping side to side and rotating his knee, looking for an angle from which he could pull free with a minimum of splinters.

This went on for about a minute, perhaps longer. And then all thought of slow, methodical escape disappeared faster than roast elf at an orc banquet when something behind the door grabbed Gork's heel.

He only became aware of his scream when the shrill sounded echoed back to him from between the doors. Whatever had gotten hold of him let go just as swiftly, apparently startled by the kobold's outburst. Unmindful now of splinters, Gork yanked his leg violently from the hole and hobbled away. His calf bled shallowly from a half dozen spots, but somehow, that felt a small price to pay. He'd gotten a good seven or eight paces from the building and stanched the worst of the bleeding before his companions burst through the foliage.

"The fuck happened, Shorty?" Cræosh demanded.

Casually, Gork drew himself up to his full three-foot-five. "Well, I'd just gotten around to examining the front doors," he said, pointing at the large portals, "something that I don't believe Jhurpess or Fezeill bothered to do."

"We only made a brief examination," Fezeill protested. "We wanted to report back to the ressst of you immediately."

"Uh-huh," Gork said. "Whatever. Anyway, see that hole there? Toward the bottom? Well, I'd stuck my arm in there, trying to reach the latch, and I'd just about gotten it open, when something inside grabbed me."

"And that's when you screamed, you little pansy?" Cræosh asked.

"What? No, that wasn't me! I yanked my arm back, of course, and I guess I startled whatever was inside, because that's when *it* started screaming. I backed away from the door, and that's when you all came running."

Katim approached the doorway, giving the entire frame a good once-over. Her gaze passed over the missing hinge, and her nostrils flared as she sniffed at the hole. She said nothing, but Gork could see her fighting to hold back a snicker.

"All right, then," Cræosh said. "Let's see what you 'startled.' Belrotha?"

"Yes?"

"Knock for me."

The double doors crashed completely out of the frame and into the chamber beyond, where they landed as sodden lumps of rot. Cræosh and Katim were the first ones through, weapons drawn. The rest of the squad followed on their heels. And sitting on the ground before them, barely a foot from where the doors had landed, was . . .

"What *that*?" Jhurpess asked in bewilderment.

Not even half Gork's height, it was covered in soft brown-green scales. A tiny tail twitched behind it, accompanying the strange, seemingly random movements of the hands and legs. The little thing gawked up at them and began a high-pitched keening.

Cræosh glanced down at the strange little creature, then over at the doppelganger. *Yep, I was afraid of that.*

"This," he said glumly to the rest of the squad, "would be a baby troglodyte."

"But if it's a baby," Gimmol asked from Belrotha's shoulder, "where are its—"

The room echoed with a sudden chorus of hissing, rather resembling the war cry of an entire battalion of angry teapots.

"—parents," the gremlin finished lamely.

Katim cocked her head, listening to the approaching sounds. "And uncles, aunts . . . brothers, sisters, cousins . . . grandparents . . ."

"I think," Cræosh said, "that outside has suddenly become a much better option than inside."

The goblins bolted for the door and stopped short, plowing into one another just past the threshold.

"Yeah," Cræosh muttered, shaking his head, "I should have figured. That had to be next in the script, didn't it?"

Neither the squad nor the two dozen sword- or club-wielding troglodytes felt the need to respond.

Several of the reptile-men stepped aside, clearing a path from trees to library. A single troglodyte, limping dramatically and using a large branch as a crutch, slowly approached along the makeshift aisle.

"If we take out the leader," Gork suggested under his breath, "the others might surrender."

"Or they might decide to shove this building up our asses sideways," Cræosh said. "So shut the fuck up before they hear you."

The old troglodyte—and he *was* old, that much was obvious from the dull-hued scales that sagged loosely from his body—stopped just beyond arm's length. (Belrotha's arms, more specifically.)

At first, his attention remained riveted on Fezeill alone. He tilted his head and sniffed twice, even leaning forward to let his tongue flicker and twitch in the doppelganger's direction.

"You wear our form," he hissed in stilted, halting Gremlin, "but you are not one of usss."

Slowly, so as not to startle, Fezeill allowed his shape to shift for the first time in days. His scales melted away, quickly subsumed by the pinkish flesh that oozed around them like some horrible growth. Dirty-blond hair sprouted from his bald head, and he once again wore the human shape in which the squad had met him.

The troglodyte nodded once, as though he'd expected that. "You," he said then, turning to encompass the entire group in his stare, "are sssstrangers here."

"Really?" Cræosh barked back. "How could you tell?"

Apparently, troglodytes didn't entirely grasp the concept of sarcasm. "We have never ssseen your kind around here before. Therefore, you are sssstrangers."

"Okay, fine. So what now?"

The spokeslizard cocked his head. "You have invaded our home."

Various hands clenched on various weapons. Before the squad could do anything foolish, however, he continued, "But we have no wish to fight. You did not harm the little one; our enemy would not have been ssso merssssiful."

Cræosh decided that this was not the appropriate venue in which to clarify that they might well have killed the "little one"—lizard was good eating—if they'd had more time. "Yeah," he said instead. "Well, we ain't real interested in fighting you lot either. So what's the next step?"

"Ssstep?" Obviously, the old troglodyte hadn't mastered *all* aspects of Gremlin; he was glancing at his feet.

"No," Cræosh said, stifling an aggravated sigh. "I mean, what do we do now?"

"Ah. Now, perhapsss, you should leave our lands. Before we risssk any further . . . misssundersssstandings."

"Nothing better, Scales. Only problem is, we can't leave just now. We haven't found what we're looking for."

"And thisss would be?"

The orc threw a quick glance over at Katim and Gork, both of whom hesitated for a moment and then nodded in unison. Cræosh agreed; it didn't *seem* like it would do any harm to tell them. . . .

"A tower," he said then. "Some wizard's tower."

A wave of hisses swept through the crowd, and Cræosh wondered if they hadn't just made a rather sizable mistake. The old lizard quickly raised a talon for silence, however.

"There is one tower in the ssswampsss that we know of," the troglodyte said, "other than thossse in the ruinsss. Come inssside. We have papersss that might help you."

Alert for anything that even vaguely resembled a trap, the goblins returned through the huge entryway, footsteps echoing on, and squelching through, the warped, decaying planks that had once served as doors.

It was obvious that the reptiles had been making their homes here for some time. A rather pungent musk permeated the chamber. Several portions of the floor, corresponding with the ragged holes in the roof that Jhurpess and Fezeill had noted earlier, were coated in bird droppings. It looked as though the troglodytes had made some effort at cleaning them, and then largely given up. Huge bookshelves loomed along every wall, covered in mold and mildew. They contained only a few scattered tomes, and the heap of ash in the far corner was more than ample evidence of what had happened to the others.

"Well, this *was* the library," Gimmol said from his perch atop the ogre's shoulder. "I wouldn't lay odds on anything helpful having survived this long, though."

"That's just great, you little bug-fucker," Cræosh snapped. "Always the optimist."

"Oh, quit your jaw-flapping, you unevolved simian!"

The orc—not to mention the rest of the squad—was sufficiently startled by the gremlin's retort that he refrained from carrying the conversation any further.

The elderly troglodyte stopped at a makeshift table formed from planks of wood that had once been part of the bookcases and a stone base scavenged from the town's crumbling walls. Other troglodytes laid a long parchment scroll atop that table, unrolling it with reverential fingers.

What appeared from across the room to be a huge blot of green ink resolved itself into the very map Cræosh and Gork had wished for. The rise on which Jureb Nahl sat occupied one side, and the ancient cartographer had even attempted a rudimentary sketch of the town's layout. (Useless, now, thanks to the intervening centuries, but a valiant effort all the same.) Toward the north, a small circular design indicated the druidic henge Gork had spotted from atop the remaining watchtower.

And a few leagues beyond *that*, a solitary structure stood in what was, if not the *middle* of nowhere, then certainly within nowhere's borders.

"Sociable bastard, wasn't he?" Cræosh said. "Fucking wizards."

"What are these?" Katim asked, pointing to several charcoal notations. A large circle had been sketched around a portion of the northern swamps—including the henge and the tower, of course—and a few uneven scratches alongside probably represented a primitive dialect of Troglodyte.

"That," their elderly host said, "representsss the domain of our enemy."

"You mentioned that before," Cræosh said. "This enemy. Who is he?"

"They," the troglodyte corrected darkly, "not 'he.' The Rat Eaters."

The squad exchanged puzzled looks. "Rat Eaters?" Fezeill asked.

"Yesss. Rat Eaters. They wish to drive usss from these ssswampsss you call Jureb Nahl. But we have lived here many generationsss, sssince we sssplit from our tribe in the fire-mountainsss, and we will not be driven out again. There isss plenty of room for usss and the Rat Eaters both, but they are a cruel, ssselfish people. They invade usss often."

Gork elbowed Katim in the thigh. "That skeleton we found? Killed by these Rat Eaters, you think?"

Katim nodded.

Jhurpess, apparently, could contain himself no longer. "What wrong with eating rats? Jhurpess eats rats. Troglodytes do not eat rats?"

"We eat ratsss if we mussst, and many other foods besssidesss. But they eat *only* ratsss or other sssmall beasssts, only what they may ssswallow whole."

"Whole?" Katim's head rose from her study of the map. "These Rat Eaters . . . are serpentine from the waist . . . down?"

The troglodyte nodded.

"Humanoid from the waist . . . up, with scales finer and more . . . supple than yours?"

Again a nod.

"Nagas," Cræosh breathed.

"King Morthûl," Gork said, "is not going to like this."

"I thought his armies drove those slithering bastards out of Kirol Syrreth centuries ago!" the orc protested. More than a few orcish heroic tales stemmed from those battles, against the snake-men who not only refused to join with the Charnel King, but dared deny his soldiers passage through their lands and slew them in the dark.

"We also thought . . . there were no troglodytes outside . . . the mountains," Katim said with a shrug. "It would seem that Jureb . . . Nahl keeps many secrets."

And so does Queen Anne, Cræosh thought but dared not say. *Is that why she never sent her own people here? Did she know?*

"Thisss," the troglodyte said, breaking their reverie, "is the tower you ssseek."

"So?" Gork said, suddenly all energy. "What're we waiting for? Let's get this damn thing over with already!"

"I think not . . . Gork." Katim gestured at the fading lances of sunlight that penetrated the roof. "It is coming up . . . on nightfall. I suggest that we . . . find a place in town to camp and . . . set out at dawn. I have no . . . desire to traverse any more . . . of the swamp during the night . . . than I have to."

"Sorry, Shorty, but I'm with Dog-face on this one."

"You are too . . . kind, orc."

He ignored her. "Let's dig up a suitable—and by that, I mean *dry*—spot and—"

"You and your companions," their host interjected, "may ssstay here with usss. None of my people shall harm you, and a pair of my bessst warriors will guide you to the Rat Eaters' borders in the morning."

"Don't think we don't appreciate it," Fezeill said from the back, "but I'd very much like to know why you're being so helpful."

"I see you forgot to shape your current self a brain," Gork scoffed at him. "Isn't it obvious? We're heading into the heart of naga territory! You think they're going to let us just saunter on in and take what we please?"

The troglodyte offered a snout-twisting, tongue-baring expression that must have been a smile. "Your short friend is correct," he breathed at them. "If you are to ssssuccssseed in your objective, you mussst kill many Rat Eaters. Why should we *not* wish to ssspeed you on your journey?"

"Which means," Cræosh said, "they've got a much better reason to keep their word than break it. I say we take 'em up on their offer and stay here. But," he added with a pointed look at the troglodyte, "we set a watch anyway."

Cræosh's paranoia, while certainly understandable, proved unnecessary. The troglodytes were as good as their word, and unless one counted a barrage of puzzled looks now and again, the Demon Squad were left unmolested. The next morning, their hosts offered them a modest repast of various leaves, large insects, and unidentifiable hunks of meat—which only Fezeill and Gimmol seemed inclined to refuse—and then the limping elder once more approached, flanked by two of the largest troglodytes the goblins had ever seen.

"Thessse warriors will guide you to our borders," the old one said. "From there, however, you are on your own. We wish you fortune, but we will not interfere any further."

"Course not," Cræosh muttered at him. "Why should we expect any real help from *anyone*?"

"There is one other issssue," the troglodyte continued. "If the Rat Eaters capture you, they cannot know that we aided you. We mussst have your word on thisss before we allow you to leave."

"'Allow'?" Cræosh asked dangerously, subsiding just as swiftly when Katim elbowed him.

"All right, fine!" he wheezed, one hand gently massaging his ribs. "We swear, we promise, whatever. Can we go now?"

The reptiles made no move to go. "You *all* mussst ssswear," the old troglodyte told them.

One by one, they so swore. One or two of them might even have meant it.

Their "escort" proved less than helpful. They'd been trudging through the swamps for barely more than an hour before the guards halted.

"What, that's *it*?!" Cræosh was incensed.

"It," the smaller of the pair agreed in broken Gremlin. "End of our land. Rat Eaters from thisss. Go we now."

"Yeah, whatever. Tell the cripple I said thanks for nothing."

Without further comment, the troglodytes slid beneath the waist-high waters and were gone.

"Fuckers," Cræosh muttered.

With a great deal of groaning and lamentation, they continued. Jhurpess and Fezeill bitched the loudest: the former because the trees here were sparse, and thus he had to tolerate his precious fur getting wet and slimy; the latter because he'd decided that turning back into a troglodyte was unwise, in case they *did* run into the nagas, and was thus, for the first time, experiencing the biting, stinging swamp as the others had.

Still, though the next few days were miserable, they proved uneventful. The mosquitoes weren't quite so thick, and no great swamp beast rose up to consume them. (They did take a few moments to carefully scout a suspicious-looking hillock, but it turned out to be a genuine knoll. Belrotha stabbed it anyway, "just in case.")

Then, as the slow dimming of the afternoon sun heralded the close of another day, they spotted shapes protruding from the waters ahead. The indistinct forms eventually resolved themselves into the henge Gork had spotted earlier. Each of the slabs rose as high as the ogre's ribs, and though many were missing, more than enough remained to suggest the enormous ring they'd once formed.

And it was here, too, that the Demon Squad finally had their first encounter with the dreaded Rat Eaters.

CHAPTER SIX

NAGA HIDE

"This was a really stupid idea, Erik." The young soldier had to shout to make himself heard over the pitiful whining that permeated the overcrowded room. "King Dororam's gonna string us up by our heels."

"Shut up, Branden!" the one called Erik retorted just as sharply. "It's better than what old Bone-head would've done if we'd let the Iron Keep know why we were *really* here."

"Oh, sure," Branden muttered, glancing nervously at the two dozen civilians—hostages, really—that huddled miserably on the floor around them. "And the Charnel King won't have *any* problem with *this*, will he?"

Erik scowled, but made no other reply.

Other than the color of their hair—Erik's was blond, Branden's brown—and the fact that Erik was a smidge taller, there was little to distinguish them. Both were dressed in light traveling cloaks, both sported dull gray tunics and leggings beneath worn leather armor, and both carried plain arming swords at their waists. Each also struggled to retain the haughty mask of the professional soldier despite the parasite called "fear" that roiled in his guts.

They certainly had every right to be frightened. Branden and Erik were two of three commanding lieutenants for one of Dororam's scouting parties. They'd reached the Brimstone Mountains without incident and easily avoided the sparse patrols along the passes that led into the peaks themselves. Once actually in the mountains, however, the task had grown far more difficult. The Iron Keep assigned some of its best veterans to policing these passes, and the draconian troglodytes who dwelt therein lurked in wait to deal with anything that might slip past the patrols.

Challenging, to say the least, but Erik and his men were some of the best scouts of Shauntille, and they'd run the Brimstone Mountain gauntlet without once being detected. They'd advanced only a few miles into Kirol Syrreth proper, just far enough to determine that a large portion of the Charnel King's military was indeed unaccounted for. Whatever source informed King Dororam that the soldiers had been called north for drills and training was, it appeared, a reliable one. And that determination being made, the unit had fled back toward the mountains, making for the safety of the Allied Kingdoms.

And of course, it was at that point, with success close enough they could kiss it, that fate had pushed them down and laughed at them.

The unit had been spotted, not by roving orc patrol or trollish scout, but by a rag-clad goatherd following a stray kid over a small rise in the foothills.

For the sin of poor timing, he would have to die; Erik hadn't cared for the idea, but there was no help for it. They couldn't allow the Dark Lord to learn that an enemy vanguard had been spotted in his lands. His men had known it, too, and hadn't even awaited his command. Feathered shafts had flown, but the goatherd had already dropped his crook and his rogue goat and fled madly back the way he'd come. Feet pounding, the scouting party had given chase, over first one hill, then a second . . .

Erik had felt his stomach drop into his heels hard enough to bruise. There, nestled in a tiny vale, was an equally tiny village. Lights twinkled in windows; puffs of smoke rose languidly from chimneys.

It was barely a hamlet, home to fewer than fourscore inhabitants. The unit could take the lot of them—indeed, might *have* to, to keep word of their presence from reaching the Iron Keep. But Erik, who had performed some pretty heinous deeds in the name of duty and his king, was nonetheless unwilling to put an entire village to the sword.

All right, Plan B. If they couldn't hide their presence, they'd confuse the issue. Erik had given the order for his men to ride on the village, steal any obvious valuables, kill one or two of the menfolk—he could live with that amount of bloodshed, if need be—and generally do everything in their power to appear as raiders instead of spies. They'd be reported, sure, but the survivors would describe an attack by bandits, not a military engagement.

And so they'd charged, swords raised high, screaming like lunatics. Most of the villagers had run; a few had attacked with rakes and shovels (and been promptly cut down), and Erik and his men had been doing a pretty convincing job of banditry when they learned fate still wasn't through toying with them. One of the Brimstone Mountain patrols, apparently having spotted the commotion from high in the passes above, had appeared on the lone road leading from the village into the peaks. The unit's only viable escape route had vanished.

Erik, cursing, had tried to remember if he'd missed any major religious observances lately. He'd obviously pissed *someone* off.

Okay then, Plan *C*, and it was this to which Erik's friend and fellow officer, Branden, was so adamantly opposed. They'd take the entire village hostage! Erik would demand free passage and the right to keep the riches they'd stolen, in exchange for the townsfolk being left unharmed. It probably wouldn't get the unit out alive—Erik was certain that the Charnel King's men couldn't have cared less about their citizens—but even if it didn't, it would cement their identities as bandits. More importantly, every moment of delay was valuable; the instant the patrol had appeared, Erik ordered his three stealthiest men to flee, to make for the mountains by whatever routes they could find. *One* of them, at least, must escape to report back!

Now, most of the citizens were locked up in various shops or houses, while Erik, Branden, and three other soldiers watched over the largest single gathering in the town's only tavern. One townsman—the young goatherd who'd spotted them in the first place, in fact—was given a scrawled list of demands and sent to meet the oncoming patrol. Soldiers and citizens alike grew nervous as they awaited an answer.

Perhaps he was giving vent to a hidden streak of cruelty, or perhaps Erik, like most citizens of Shauntille, simply couldn't comprehend why the humans of Kirol Syrreth didn't just rise up against Morthûl. Whatever the case, he lost no opportunity to chip away at the hostages' hope of rescue.

"The soldiers don't care about you," he told the huddled citizens for the umpteenth time. "You watch! We'll probably have to kill a few of you just to make them believe we're serious."

"Erik," Branden said quietly, "maybe you should stop this. . . ."

"And once they do come," the larger man continued unheedingly, "it'll be without regard for how many of you go down with us. Hell, maybe they'll *deliberately* slaughter you, too. Weaklings and parasites have no place in the high-and-mighty empire of the Iron Keep, now do they?"

"Erik—"

"Shut up, Branden! I—"

His forehead plastered with sweat despite winter's chill, the third of the lieutenants—this one a slim, black-haired man by the name of Dale—slammed open the front door and stuck his head inside.

"They're moving!"

Erik straightened. "Attacking?"

"Don't think so, sir. They're not coming in at a charge, and they're splitting up. I think they're moving to block the other roads."

One hand on his chin, Erik nodded. It made sense; so long as they believed they were dealing with bandits, the soldiers of Kirol Syrreth had no reason to suspect that the path to the Brimstone Mountains was the only escape route the hostage-takers would consider.

A soft rumbling danced through the hostages, an indecipherable mishmash of whispers and sobs and sighs, from the moment they heard the patrol was moving. Erik slammed his foot down hard on the wooden planks, putting an abrupt stop to the sound.

"Shut up! All of you, just shut up!" He was raving now, his wide-eyed stare more than enough to convince his hostages and his companions both that he'd begun losing his grip on the situation. "You think they're coming for *you*? You think they give a damn about you? I told you, they don't! Whatever they decide to do, they'll just trample you down in the rush! Split your skulls if you get in the way! Nobody gives a damn about the lot of you! The soldiers out there don't, the rest of the army doesn't, and Morthûl sure as shit—"

"*You're partially right, Erik.*"

The young soldier's voice melted away, though his mouth continued to move. He spun wildly, seeking any possible source for that horrible voice. It was inhuman. It was *cold*, the winter winds outside given speech.

And standing as he was on the western side of the Brimstone Mountains, Erik had a horrible suspicion as to whose voice it might be. A wet stain began seeping down the inseam of his leggings.

"You . . . you know me?" It was, all told, a fairly stupid question, but the fact that he had enough presence of mind to string words together at all was little shy of miraculous.

"*I know you well*," the disembodied voice taunted him. "*Erik Kaleth, lieutenant. Officer in the armies of that warthog, Dororam. Fourth-generation career soldier, two sisters, one brother. Betrothed to a young woman back home who pretends ignorance of the whores you frequent, so that you in turn will not suspect what she's doing with said brother of yours. Shall I continue?*"

Erik's throat and tongue produced only a faint gurgle.

"*This creature was partly correct*," the voice said, and though there remained no visible sign of the speaker, everyone present knew that he had turned from the soldier to the huddled townsfolk. "*Sending in my soldiers to crush these insects would indeed have endangered you all.*" The invisible presence focused on Erik once more. "*And no matter what propaganda Dororam and Theiolyn and their ilk choose to spread, I do not casually slaughter my own.*

"*You brought this on yourself, you pathetic fools. For you have left me no choice but to deal with you . . .*"

The wooden floor bulged, the planks disgorging a swarm of twitching roaches and glistening beetles. They spouted upward in a geyser of thrashing legs and clacking mandibles. Soldiers and hostages shrieked in a single voice, united in terrified revulsion.

From the center of that horrid fountain rose a greater shape. Vermin poured from it in a living rain, revealing a worn yet regal robe, a silver crown, a dead and decaying figure that scowled with the one remaining half of its face.

"... personally," Morthûl concluded, revealed in all his profane splendor. "I believe this is yours." Casually, he tossed something at Erik's feet, where it landed with a sodden splat. It took a moment for the soldier to recognize that what he saw was three human hearts, partly melted and congealed into a single mass.

Erik had sent three men to sneak their way around the patrol. . . .

Branden retched across the toes of his boots, and Dale had begun, ever so softly, to cry. And Erik—Erik raised his blade, screamed his defiance at the Charnel King of Kirol Syrreth, and attacked.

Branden never knew if it was an act of sheer desperation, or if his commanding officer had finally slipped the final bonds of reason. Nor did he know why the Dark Lord, master of a thousand spells, chose to meet that attack with his bare hands. Perhaps it was an amusing diversion; perhaps he simply didn't consider Erik to be worth any greater effort.

The Charnel King's skeletal hand slammed into Erik's chest before the sword could fall. Branden saw leather freeze and shatter, saw pink skin turn white, then blue, beneath those fleshless fingers. The Dark Lord flexed, driving fingertips of bone into his enemy, and the skin did not tear; it *cracked*, sending slivers of frozen skin and blood to clatter around Morthûl's feet.

Nobody breathed, as though all in the room were as dead as Morthûl himself.

Erik gasped but otherwise didn't move at all, paralyzed in a mockery of combat by the unending cold of unhallowed graves.

A huge wood-roach, seemingly undisturbed by the cold, poked its antennae from the cuff of the Dark Lord's sleeve. Then, seeing a new environment to explore, it quickly scuttled over the skeletal arm and into the gaping wound in Erik's chest.

Dale finally threw up.

Other insects followed the first. After a moment's pause, even shaking his sleeve to ensure that no other vermin cared to make the trip, the Charnel King *pushed*. Frozen flesh shattered; ribs snapped like twigs. Branden cringed, unable to conceive of such pain, and actually felt relief for his friend when Morthûl drew back, holding Erik's blackened heart in his hand.

But Erik wasn't dead.

The side of the Charnel King's face that still wore flesh creaked audibly as it curled in a smile. "You led these men." He spoke almost affectionately in Erik's ear, though loudly enough for the others to hear. The profane yellow glow pulsed in rhythm with his words. "You will atone for your sins, Erik Kaleth, and theirs. Forever."

With one final sob, his last act of free will, the undead thing that was Erik Kaleth marched outside to await the orders of his new master.

"All of my citizens," Morthûl intoned solemnly, "may leave. Go to your homes, and do not emerge until tomorrow morning. Each of you will be compensated for the indignities you have suffered here today."

With a shuffling but quite rapid pace, the townsfolk fled.

Erik's heart cupped casually in his right hand, Morthûl rounded on Branden and Dale. "Your fate is less fixed," he said, his teeth dreadfully backlit by that horrid aura. "You are my enemy. You threatened my people. And you displayed a rather appalling lack of intelligence in going along with this idiotic scheme. But obedience and loyalty are virtues I admire, even when granted to foolish commanders and foolish kings.

"So I make you this offer. Cooperate. Answer my queries truthfully and I will allow you to go free. Refuse me, and serve your commander in death as you did in life."

A moment, perhaps so they could mull it over, and then, "Why are you here?"

Either some last remnant of nationalism pierced Dale's veil of terror or, more probably, he was simply so overcome with terror that he couldn't think straight. "We—we just wanted to take the town!" he sobbed at the Charnel King. "You—you know why we're here! You got our demands. You—"

It was Morthûl's left hand this time, the digits partially clothed in that same not-quite-skin. A rotting thumb broke three of Dale's teeth and sank through the roof of his mouth. Even as the man spasmed, his voice emerging in a choked gurgle, two more fingers invaded his body, his eyeballs bursting beneath them like engorged pimples. From where he stood, Branden could see clearly enough to note several wriggling things fall from the Charnel King's hand to slither down Dale's throat.

He doubled over, vomiting again—and racked with guilt that his only conscious thought was *Thank the gods Dale spoke first.*

"I don't care for liars," Morthûl said calmly. "Such lies invariably lead to a, ah, loss of face." And with that, the Charnel King tightened his fist and yanked, breaking free the entire front of Dale's skull.

Despite the various substances that spilled from the gaping hole, the faceless thing called Dale caught its balance before it toppled and shuffled slowly through the door. The bloody face landed on the floor with a hollow clatter.

"One opportunity," the Charnel King said, turning finally toward Branden, "and one only, to avoid the fate you have just witnessed. I am losing my patience. *Why are you here?*"

"We were scouting!" the soldier shouted, hysterical. "We needed to confirm that your armies were training, up north."

"Confirm?" Morthûl asked, a new edge to his tone. "And where did Dororam get this information that he wished to 'confirm'?"

"I don't know." Then, as the Dark Lord's hand twitched, Branden dropped to his knees, sobbing. "I don't know, I swear I don't! Please, I wouldn't lie to you! Not here, not like this! Please . . ."

Morthûl nodded slowly. "I believe you. It appears we have a spy somewhere in our midst." Slowly, clearly pondering, he began to turn away.

And then, as though he'd forgotten some bauble, perhaps his hat, the Charnel King suddenly stopped short and turned once more. "Oh, yes," he said, his tone such that Branden almost expected him to slap himself in the head. "You."

"M-me?"

"If I do release you, how do I know you'll not cause any further trouble in my lands?"

"I—I wouldn't!" *Gods, I'm* never *coming anywhere* near *here again!*

"No, probably not. You seem wise enough to learn from your lesson here today. Still, I must be certain. A brief test, then."

Branden's heart fluttered wildly. *Test?*

"A test of your obedience, and your fear. This should do." The soldier's eyes grew even wider and his stomach shriveled as Morthûl tossed Erik's blackened heart at Branden's feet.

"You may leave," the Dark Lord said, "as soon as you've finished. Unless you'd prefer . . ." He snapped his leather fingers, and Dale's open skull appeared briefly in the window, as though he were merely some curious passerby. "Do eat up, Branden. You've a long journey ahead of you, and you'll need your strength."

The Charnel King's laughter filled the room as Branden lifted the frigid mass to his tear-streaked face and slowly began to eat.

"I don't like it," Gork said from the wet tuft of grasses on which he was unrolling his blankets. "I think we ought to just kill the damn thing."

Fezeill nodded what was currently a human head. "For once, the kobold and I are in complete agreement. Who knows what it might do to us in our sleep?"

With a gruff sigh and a rustle of bedroll, Cræosh rolled over to face the griping duo. "That's why we set a watch, shapeshifter. Look, we've been over this. I'm all for kicking their scaly asses from here to Timas Khoreth and back again if they start fucking with us. But as of now, they haven't done shit, and we've got enough trouble without borrowing extra. I say, if they want to sit and watch us, let 'em stare till their eyes bug out. Doesn't hurt my feelings any."

"Yeah, *right now* they're just watching," Gork muttered. He cast a glance at Katim, currently crouched in the twisted cypress boughs above. "Let's see if they're so peaceful when it's me or Gimmol on watch."

They had, in fact, agreed to stand guard in pairs—save for Katim, who'd refused a partner, and since they were one short anyway, that worked out nicely. The purpose was in part to make it clear to the watchers that they were ready for anything, and in part to avoid leaving their fate entirely in the hands of sentinels as intellectually challenged as Belrotha or Jhurpess alone.

Cræosh, having clearly decided to ignore the kobold's bitching, was asleep instantly, his tectonic snores sending ripples through the marsh. It took more time for the others, but within half an hour, all but Katim were sleeping the sleep of the just (or at least the just plain exhausted).

They'd found the circle of stones atop a shallow rise, smaller cousin to the one supporting the ruins of Jureb Nahl. The ground was sodden, swarming with insects, and filthy as an orc's vocabulary, but in its favor, it offered a campsite that lacked the very real threat of drowning in one's sleep. In fact, with the exception of the night spent in the troglodyte-infested library, it was the most comfortable they'd passed since losing the skiff.

Or it would have been, had a strange pair of eyes not watched constantly from atop the stones. That lone naga, perhaps a sentry or a scout, had remained where they'd first spotted it, observing them with cold, black orbs. Unmoving and unblinking, only the occasional twitch of tail or tongue convinced Katim the thing lived at all.

It looked just as she'd described it to the troglodytes, as she'd heard in many a folktale. Half man and half snake, covered in squamous skin, possessed of ugly slits rather than a recognizable nose, and with a mouth far wider than any human's. It clutched a long spear in one fist, wore a blunt, axelike weapon on a leather harness. And still it did . . . Absolutely . . . Nothing.

Katim frowned, her snout twisting violently. Her fur stood on end and her mind gibbered at her that something was massively, horribly wrong.

To which she could only respond *Of course there is! But* what? *What am I missing?*

The troll took a deep, rasping breath, consciously relaxed her shoulders. Then, calm and casual as she could manage, she raised her head once more. She scanned slowly from left to right, her nostrils gaping as she scented the night air.

Her companions, snoring and drooling, were clumped at the base of the largest stone. From the edge of their camp, the ground sloped sharply, the hillock's edge plunging back into the depths of the swamp.

Katim shivered at that, a sign of fear that none of the others would ever be allowed to see. She dreaded the thought of that foul water creeping any higher, of reaching any point in Jureb Nahl where she couldn't keep her head above the surface.

A second shudder . . . Because Katim didn't know how to swim.

The troll gave herself a mental slap and returned her attention to her surroundings. The naga coiled, bathed in the rays of moonlight that penetrated the heavy clouds, atop the stones. It waited proud, immobile, as though the entire henge had been constructed solely to showcase the creature's magnificence.

Stupid, slithering, arrogant . . . Ah, shit . . .

Katim could've kicked herself as understanding finally dawned (though she felt more like kicking one of the others, truth be told). They'd spent so long studying the creature, watching for any sign of movement, of treachery, of danger—and that was the *point*. The thing wasn't just a sentinel, it was a *diversion*.

The troll drew her axe and sprang from the branches. And finally, the naga moved.

It spun toward her, hissing madly, tail thrashing, as she landed in a crouch atop the stone. The monolith teetered beneath her, but held. Its spear useless at such short range, the naga reached down with the speed (unsurprisingly) of a striking snake and yanked the peculiar club/axe thing from its harness.

Katim watched its eyes, saw them flicker aside as it moved to draw, extended her own weapon in that same direction to draw its attention even further . . .

And in that split second of distraction, hurled her *chirrusk* with the other hand.

Fast as it was, the naga probably could have dodged or parried the blow, had it not been reaching for its weapon. But it was, and it couldn't.

The serpentine head rocked back as the weighty hook slammed it across what would have been the bridge of its nose if it had one. Blood poured from split skin and from the nostril slits below. Katim took a single step and swung, deliberately striking with only the tip of her axe blade, slitting its throat rather than beheading it outright.

A second step and she *embraced* the toppling body, holding it immobile atop the tottering stone. It spasmed in her arms, spilling warm death across her breast and stomach, and finally hung limp. She allowed herself a brief smile of satisfaction—how many trolls could claim a naga in the next life's stable?—and then it was time to get back to work.

Still moving as silently as circumstances would permit, Katim gently lay the corpse down atop the stones, hung over the edge, and hooked the naga's fallen spear with her *chirrusk*. She hauled the weapon back up and, with some careful balancing and a few rasped profanities, used it to prop the body upright. It was clear from up close what she'd done, but hopefully it would be enough to fool anyone at a distance.

And there would, she was quite certain, be quite a few "anyones" showing up before long. She didn't know *how* the lone sentry had signaled them, but she knew, she *knew*, that it had.

Lying flat beside the corpse, struggling to ignore the reptilian musk and more casually disregarding the acrid stench of recent death, Katim waited. Patiently, long into the darkest hours, well beyond the hour she was supposed to awaken Gimmol and Belrotha for their turn at watch, she waited.

The waters off to one side of the hill rippled. It was a subtle movement, quiet and peaceful, barely more than a fish or a toad caressing the surface. Easy enough to miss, had Katim not been specifically watching for it.

It? No. *Them.* Three, if she had to guess by the patterns and the wakes slowly revealing themselves in the scum-covered marsh. Although she saw no sign of it, she was certain there must be a fourth, approaching the tree in which she'd first begun her watch. More than enough to slay the squad in their sleep.

Katim almost felt sorry for them. Her fist closed on the shaft that held the dead snake upright.

The first naga's head broke the surface. With a stealth Gork might have envied, it rose from the slimy water and crept up the slope, propelled in silent surges by its powerful tail. It clasped a long-bladed knife, a tool designed for murder, not battle. As it moved, it raised the knife and twisted it in the air: a signal, Katim realized, to the creature she'd slain. She reached out to twitch one of its hands and hoped the nagas on the ground were not awaiting a more intricate response.

Two more figures rose, swamp water flowing from them in torrents, and slithered after the first. She still saw no fourth naga, but an abrupt hiss from the vicinity of the tree proved its presence, and proved as well that they'd discovered she wasn't where she was supposed to be.

Rising into a low crouch, Katim yanked the spear from behind the corpse—unconcerned, now, with letting the dead thing fall—and cast. The lead naga, which had only just begun to turn in reply to its companion's hissed warning, fell to the earth with a sodden thump, the spear quivering obscenely between its shoulder blades.

The other two nagas froze for only an instant, but that was an instant too long. Grasping her *chirrusk* just beneath the hook, rather than by the handle at the chain's tail end, Katim dove from atop the stones.

The nearest of the nagas crumpled in a tangle of arms, legs, and tail, struck down by a ballistic troll to the ribs. Katim, who'd begun her roll before the mud could even stick to her armor, jabbed one prong of the *chirrusk*'s hook under the creature's chin even as she rose to her feet. Allowing the chain to flow through her fist and over her shoulder until she grasped the handle, she gave it a good solid yank. The serpentine creature literally left the ground as she drove the barbed prong up through its jaw and into its brain.

Katim moved aside, drawing her axe and allowing the *chirrusk* to fall. Warily she circled, watching for an opening, ears alert for any hint of the unseen fourth naga.

The one before her circled as she did, its blade held high, but even in its cold and unblinking visage, Katim recognized fear. The snake had been anticipating simple slaughter, not a duel with a troll. That knife wouldn't even slow her down, and the naga knew it.

The creature finally ceased circling, leaving its back to the slumbering goblins, and made a tentative stab that Katim barely even had to dodge.

Do they really think I'm that *stupid?* She had to struggle not to laugh. With no hesitation she spun, axe outstretched, and lopped the head off the fourth naga who'd been sneaking up behind her. It was, after all, the only reason the one she'd been dueling could have been foolish enough to put his back to the squad, no matter how certain it was that none had awoken. She allowed the momentum of her swing to carry her back around, so that she once more faced the remaining naga even before its companion's head had finished bouncing.

That, apparently, was the final straw. With a hiss that was actually more of a squeak, the naga spun and launched itself with its powerful tail, sliding into the murky waters beside the knoll.

Katim ground her teeth, and then shrugged. She certainly wasn't going into the water after him, but three dead in a minute—plus the sentinel from earlier—was certainly accomplishment enough. With a sharp crack (the loudest noise, in fact, of the eerily quiet skirmish) she retrieved her *chirrusk* from the body in which it was lodged. Come morning, when she could do so without waking her companions, she'd remove a couple of naga ribs to add to her necklace.

Then, satisfied with her efforts, she moved to wake Gimmol for his belated watch, eagerly anticipating the expression of shock on his face.

"Shock" was, perhaps, an understatement. Gimmol was still trying to make his jaw work when Katim went to sleep. The last sound she heard before drifting off was Belrotha asking the tiny gremlin, "How dead snake-men sneak up on us?"

And then she was being shaken by a calloused hand, and might well have lashed out if she hadn't recognized the scent of the orc's breath. "*. . . the fuck were you thinking?*" he was screaming as she came awake. "I don't give a pixie's ass if we're being attacked by crippled basset hounds! Something happens on watch, you wake us the fuck up! Jagged buggering hell, you yelled at Gimmol for the same damn thing, remember? What if one of them had gotten past you? We'd all be fucking dead, that's what!"

"And the downside . . . would be what?" she asked sleepily.

"Don't push me on this one, Dog-face!" And indeed, his tone lacked the usual undercurrent of suppressed worry that she normally found so amusing every time he spoke to her. "I got the whole squad behind me on this!" She spotted several movements in her peripheral vision that she interpreted as nods. "Well," Cræosh clarified, "except Jhurpess and Bel-rotha. But you know why, and they don't count. Don't fucking do this again!"

Best give them this one. "You're right. I . . . apologize, Cræosh. It won't happen . . . again."

The apology, which was about as sincere as a dragon's well-wishes, nevertheless accomplished what it was intended to. Namely, it stunned the orc into speechlessness long enough for Katim to get back to sleep.

She awoke once more, just as the horizon began to gleam with the approach of dawn, when Fezeill kicked her in the shin. "Get up!" he whispered, and she could tell by his voice alone that he'd once more taken the form of a bugbear. Instantly awake, Katim rose to her feet, looked swiftly around, and . . .

"Oh."

"Yeah," Cræosh said, his tone still more than a little irritated. "Seems your friends have come back to talk."

Standing in a rough semicircle in the waters beyond the hill were multiple distinct rows of nagas. Some were of a single dark hue, some mottled, some with patterns of bright colors in any number of rings, but they all boasted two features in common: They clasped weapons in their scaly hands, and they peered unblinkingly at the squad through cold, dead orbs.

"You've fought them," Cræosh hissed, struggling to suppress his ire for the time being. "What're our chances?"

Katim just shook her head. "I caught them by . . . surprise, and unprepared for . . . battle."

"In other words, you haven't got a fucking clue."

"In essence."

"Shit." He noticed Gork edging toward the deep shadows of the henge, doubtless preparing another of his disappearing acts. "Wouldn't bother this time, Shorty. You see those tongues? They're scenting the air, the way snakes do. Probably smell a mosquito fart in a hurricane; no way you're sneaking up on this many of them."

Gork muttered and held his position.

But the moments crept by as though trying to sneak away before they were discovered, and the anticipated attack failed to materialize. Just as the sentinel of the previous night had done, the nagas did nothing but stare at the Demon Squad, tongues flickering, occasionally hissing to one another but otherwise silent.

Although obscured by the thick cypress and hanging moss, dawn finally hauled itself, panting and heaving, over the eastern horizon. The nagas began to mill about, shifting aside. In unconscious echo of the troglodytes, they opened an aisle so that something might move through.

Something too big to be real.

Cræosh thought, at first, that it must be a dragon, and he felt his groin and his stomach clench. Then it drew near, and he wondered if maybe a dragon wouldn't have been preferable.

"Ancestors!" It emerged as a faint gasp, and a part of him was amazed he'd even gotten *that* out. Gimmol stood speechless once again, Gork was spouting an array of sounds in Kobold that could only have been the foulest profanities, Jhurpess was already scampering up the nearest of the standing stones, and even Katim's jaw had dropped.

It wasn't the naga itself; save for the red-and-black diamond pattern in its scales, it looked just like the others. It was, instead, the fact that said naga was curled up in a howdah atop the back of an alligator that had to measure no less than *eighty feet* from snout to tail-tip! It crushed plants beneath its tread, uprooted small trees, and shoved them aside as it passed. A pair of chains ran from the naga's left hand to a barbed metal rod lodged deep in the beast's mouth, but Cræosh couldn't imagine how *any* contraption could possibly control the thing if it decided it no longer wanted to be controlled.

"Any suggestions?" Cræosh whispered to Katim.

"This is exactly . . . the sort of thing we have the . . . ogre for."

The orc glanced back at Belrotha, then at the approaching monster. "I don't know. . . ."

But the alligator stopped some forty feet from the hill. It settled its body into the water and mud so that only its back and snout were visible. Letting the chains go slack, the naga raised itself up on its tail—a blatantly theatrical gesture, so it could loom over its audience.

"You," it hissed. "You ssslay many . . ." It trailed off in a sibilant breath somewhere between an actual snake and Katim's ugly wet rasp.

"Oh, great," Gork muttered from beside the slab of stone. "They talk like the damn trogs." And then, suddenly, his whiskers perked up and he began to smile.

Cræosh's hackles rose, but he didn't have time to worry about what the kobold might have planned. He advanced a step or two, enough to suggest he spoke for the squad, not far enough that he couldn't retreat to their sides. "Yeah, we did. But *you* were planning to murder *us*, Needle-tongue. Don't go getting all pissy about it now, just because we kicked your cloacae all up and down the swamp."

Gimmol's ears actually drooped. "We're staring down the gullet of an alligator the size of the Iron Keep, and he still can't even *define* diplomacy."

Katim, at roughly the same moment, asked, "What do you mean . . . *we*, orc?"

"Yesss, we attack," the naga said. "You invade home. We protect!"

"Oh, here we go again," Cræosh sighed. "All right, look, dammit! We aren't invading your home. We don't give a damn about any of you!"

"Then why here?"

The orc opened his mouth to reply—and Gork appeared before him from nowhere. "We're here because of the troglodytes," he said loudly. "The, uh, lizard-people."

A furious hissing swept through the assembled nagas. Even the alligator shifted pensively, though it may simply have been reacting to the noise. Cræosh couldn't decide between strangling the little shit or turning and fleeing like he was being chased by an amorous yeti.

"You?" the lead naga asked, its eyes dangerously narrow. "Friends of the invaders?"

"Friends?" Gork laughed. "They hate us!"

Cræosh, who had come to a decision and was raising a fist to beat the tiny creature into the earth, halted in midswing. *What's he doing?*

"Go on," the naga hissed curiously.

"They pretended to help us," the kobold said. "Told us where to find the tower we're looking for."

The snake-man nodded. "Tower. Yesss. We know tower."

"Right. Well, I heard them after dark, when they thought we were all asleep. They were talking about how stupid your people are."

The naga hissed again, violently.

"Way they figured, they could trick you into doing their dirty work for them. See, they didn't have to risk their precious hides killing us. They'd just send us here, and you'd do it for them. And if we killed a bunch of you in the process, hey, even better." He stepped forward again, to the water's edge. "They're sitting on their asses back there," he said, gesturing vaguely southward, "and laughing at you."

For a very long time, silence reigned. Then, "Tower you ssseek that way. Go nowhere elssse in our landsss, or naga ssslay. Yesss?"

"Yes," Gork agreed solemnly.

The naga yanked on the chain, and the giant alligator once more came to life. Without a word, the beast turned to the south and shambled away. In equal silence, the rest of the nagas followed suit, until the squad was once more alone in the swamp.

Only when they were absolutely certain that the very last of the nagas had passed from both sight and hearing did everyone present turn to stare down at the smug little kobold.

"I don't believe you just did that!" Gimmol said finally. "That was . . . That was . . . I don't even know *what* that was!"

"It doesn't bother you at all," Cræosh rumbled, leaning down to Gork's level, "that the people who you just sicced the snakes on were more than happy to help us out?"

"Maybe you'd rather have fought the bastards ourselves instead?" Gork asked.

The orc grinned, a nasty expression that revealed lots of broken teeth. "Calm down, Shorty. I was making an observation, is all. Quick thinking, actually. Good job.

"Now let's go find that damn tower while we have the chance."

Like everything else in this stupid swamp, actually managing that proved harder than finding a needle in a baby. They'd trudged and waded the rest of that day, and a good chunk of the next, until they stood at the borders of an open and empty expanse of marsh. The hillocks had flattened, the trees grown sparse, leaving what could almost be described as a plain of swamp, allowing them to see for miles in all directions except back the way they'd come.

And what they saw, in those many empty miles, was a lifetime supply of nothing.

"I don't get it," Cræosh said. "If that map was even remotely accurate, we should already see the damn thing."

"And is it only now . . . occurring to you," Katim asked pointedly, "that it might well . . . not have been?"

"You had doubts, you should've said something at the time, Dog-face. Doesn't do us a kobold's ass worth of good now."

"Hey!" Gork protested. Cræosh ignored him.

"What other choice . . . did we have? If I . . . *had* said something at the . . . time, we still would have had no . . . way to find the tower . . . would we?"

"Maybe not," Cræosh said, striding a few steps into the open marsh, waving his hands in frustration. "But this doesn't seem to have worked, either. Fucking waste of time. Maybe we should've—"

He never did tell them what they should have done, because he chose that exact moment—or perhaps, more accurately, that moment chose him—to disappear. Just like that, the orc was simply gone.

"What in . . . ?" Katim dropped into a combat-ready crouch, one that brought her snout to just above the water level. Jhurpess growled once, something between a roar and a whine. Belrotha, who started so violently that she nearly tossed Gimmol and Gork from their perches, started to look under logs and behind hanging curtains of moss.

And then, with a loud gasp, Cræosh's head broke the surface. Spitting great mouthfuls of the foul stuff, the mud-encrusted orc half swam and half staggered his way back to the squad.

"What happened?" Fezeill asked, his tone suggesting a bored curiosity more than any real interest.

"What happened," Cræosh told him, hacking and coughing sludge from his lungs, "is that some idiot decided to build a swamp on uneven ground."

Jhurpess and Belrotha looked at him blankly. "Someone *build* swamp?" the ogre asked. "Them not do good job. Swamp not good for anything."

Cræosh growled. Gimmol tapped the ogre on the earlobe. "I think that was sarcasm on his part, Belrotha."

"Sarcasm?"

"Yeah, sarcasm," Cræosh said. "It's like a sar-cave, but bigger." Then, before she could ask the next inevitable question, he quickly continued. "The ground drops off pretty dramatically. Fifteen or twenty feet, possibly a whole lot more. I decided not to sink all the way down to find out."

"Pansy," Gork muttered.

"So we're stuck?" Gimmol asked. "We can't go any farther?"

"Not unless everyone wants to swim the rest of the way. Fuck! Where's that damn tower?!"

"Maybe right here," Katim said thoughtfully.

"That's it, then," Cræosh announced to the squad at large. "The troll's gone. Lost her mind, taken leave of her senses. Brain-rot, I'd guess. Must've swallowed something when that 'swamptopus' dragged her under a few days ago."

"Are you quite . . . through?" Katim asked.

"Let me think. Yeah, for the time being, I think so."

"I'm so glad. What I . . . meant, as you might have realized if . . . you bothered to use your brain for . . . anything other than ballast, is that . . . the tower could be here if . . . it's fallen over."

"Of course!" Gimmol looked disgusted with himself. "It's obvious!"

"Is it really?" Gork spat back. "Perhaps you'd be willing to share your vast wisdom with us mere mortals?"

"Yeah," Cræosh said, somewhat less eloquently.

"Well, it's a wizard's tower," the gremlin explained. "It would've been built to stand up to about anything, so it can't just be gone, right?"

"If you say so," Cræosh said neutrally. "So?"

"But the ground around it wouldn't have the same magical protection, would it? That drop in the terrain that you, ahem, stumbled onto? If that was caused by currents and erosion and all that, it could have toppled the entire thing! It's why," he added, "most people don't actually *build* towers, or much of anything else, in swamps. I heard about this king, once, took him four tries to—"

"So it's here," the orc clarified, "just lying on its side under the water?"

"Quite possibly," Gimmol said.

"And wouldn't that suggest, Sir Genius, that it just might be completely filled with water? And thus pretty much impossible to navigate?"

The gremlin's face fell. "Well, I . . . That is, that would be a distinct possibility, wouldn't it?"

"Can I kill him now?" Gork asked plaintively.

"Wait your turn," the orc said, a nasty quirk to his lips.

"Excuse me," Fezeill interrupted. "While I must admit that I enjoy a platter of roast gremlin as much as the next doppelganger, I feel rather obliged to point out that Queen Anne isn't likely to take well to failure on our part. What say we find the damn tower already, and *see* if it's navigable or not?"

Cræosh and Gork both reluctantly agreed to hold off on spitting the gremlin over a fire, and the squad began careful exploration of the "cliff" that the orc had discovered. Fezeill resumed his troglodyte form—after demanding that the others keep *very* careful watch for nagas—and proceeded to search below. But it was Belrotha, with her added height, who spotted the first trace of the missing structure. It wasn't much, just a peculiar rippling and swirling in the otherwise predictable currents. She pointed it out to Gimmol, who in turn pointed it out to Cræosh, who proceeded to order the doppelganger-turned-troglodyte to check it out.

The grin on that reptilian snout, when he surfaced some moments later, brought a cheer from the assembled squad.

The tower was, indeed, lying flat on its side. The disturbance Belrotha had spotted was the edge of the platform that had stood atop that tower, its crenellations far enough from the main body that they came near to breaking the surface. But even the tower itself wasn't far beneath the scummy water, less so than the earth on which they stood now. All but Gork and Gimmol could have walked across it without getting more than their legs wet.

Fezeill had discovered, as well, that the stone appeared completely undamaged by the decades or centuries that the tower had lain submerged and that the place was windowless, lacking any means of ingress save for the main door at what had been the base, now about ten feet below the surface.

"I haven't examined the door itsssself that closssely," the fauxtroglodyte admitted as he climbed from the water. "The truth is, thisss form is not bessst sssuited for fine coordination." He flexed his thick fingers as though demonstrating.

Gork sighed deeply as the others looked his way. "All right, fine," he sighed, shucking most of his equipment. "But if anything down there eats me, I'm coming back to haunt the lot of you." Then, having made his pronouncement, he took a breath so deep it seemed to inflate his entire body, and dived from Belrotha's pack.

Navigating solely by feel and keeping one hand pressed firmly to the curved wall, the kobold kicked against the water, diving ever deeper. Finding the portal didn't actually take long, since it was right where Fezeill had suggested it would be. Even as his hand brushed the slimy wood, Gork felt a brief tingle beneath his skin. It wasn't precisely a static shock, though that was the closest equivalent his startled mind could come up with. It was more as though the door itself had *hummed*.

If he'd had the breath, Gork would've cursed. This was a Starsdamned *wizard* they were dealing with; of course he wouldn't rely on mundane defenses! Dammit!

After a moment or two, however, Gork had neither been slain nor transformed into some sort of rodent or amphibian. Focusing past the faint burning that was starting to tickle his lungs, he reached out to check the latch itself. To his expert fingers, it felt as perfectly preserved as the stone, without a hint of corrosion. *Magic. What a surprise.*

Hey, maybe Trelaine's spells preserved the interior, too! It might be completely free of water!

Of course, even if that were true, they still had to get in without flooding the damn place. . . .

Gork kicked upward, breaching the surface with a deep gasp.

"Anything?" Cræosh asked.

"Yeah!" The kobold repeated everything he'd learned—omitting, however, any reference to the strange sensation he'd felt upon first touching the door. If anything bad was going to happen, he wasn't about to get blamed for it.

He was splashing through the water with small yet powerful strokes and had gotten about halfway back to his companions when he felt the waves slapping against him and realized that he wasn't the only thing thrashing in the water.

"Uh, guys? There's something in here with me!"

Seeing Cræosh's eyes flicker past him and grow wide was *not* the most comforting response Gork could imagine to that particular pronouncement. "No shit! Get the fuck over here, Shorty!"

The kobold whimpered once and resumed his course as fast as his tiny arms and legs would move, not pausing even to glance behind him. He hadn't even realized he'd reached the squad until Belrotha's obscenely huge hand plucked him from the water. Gork began rubbing the muck from his face, trying to see what was happening around him.

"Move out onto the tower!" Cræosh was ordering loudly. "Even with the curve, it's more stable footing than this fucking gunk!"

Gork felt the ogre who carried him move to obey. With a final swipe of his hand, he cleared his vision, and then rather wished he'd chosen to remain blind.

The swamp called Jureb Nahl had disgorged its dead, and they didn't seem at all happy about it.

Well over a dozen bodies, bloated and putrefied by submersion in the swamps, circled in the water, their heads cutting the surface like sharks' fins. Some leered with hideous bulging lips and liquid-filled eyes, others with completely empty sockets. Their mouths all gaped in unending moans or nigh-silent screams.

"All right, we're gonna have to be quick about this," Cræosh said, not taking his focus off the surrounding waters.

"Quick about what?" the kobold asked suspiciously.

"Look, Gork, we don't know how many of these things there are, or if we can even kill them. We've got to get those damn bones and get out of here! They don't seem to swim too well, so they'll have to climb onto the tower to come at us, and that means only a few at a time. The rest of the squad's gonna hold them off while you and I go in there and—"

"You're insane if you think I'm going back down there, Cræosh!"

"You'd rather stay up here and fight, then? I don't think you're gonna have much luck trying to sneak up on these things!"

Gork cursed, loudly.

"All right, then. Let's—"

"No."

Cræosh pivoted to face the newest objection. "What do you mean, 'no?'"

Katim's snout twisted in a frown. "I mean that you are . . . not going with the kobold. I . . . am."

"Oh?" the orc sneered. "And why is that? Afraid this fight's not worth your while?"

The troll didn't rise to the bait. "It's true that I cannot . . . claim the servitude of creatures . . . already dead. But I was . . . thinking of more practical . . . concerns. This tower collapsed years . . . ago; there may be a . . . great number of narrow passages and . . . other obstacles. Gork cannot go in . . . there undefended, and in such an . . . environment, who here can . . . keep up with him better than . . . I?"

"Jhurpess could," Cræosh huffed. Katim ignored him.

"Decide faster, would you guys?" Gimmol said. "Those things aren't going to circle forever, and I don't think you want to be in the water trying to get that door open when they decide to attack."

And sure enough, the orc gave in. He might be a tad stronger than the troll, but he wasn't nearly so dexterous or lithe, and they both knew it. "All right, fine! But don't dilly-dally, okay? I don't know how long we can hold these things off."

Katim nodded. "We will hurry." *Don't think about the water. It's only a short climb to the door. Don't think about the water.*

Gork stood up, this time on Belrotha's left soldier, and prepared to dive. "You realize," he said, "that we could get down there and find that the whole place is flooded. Or that there's no way in *without* flooding it."

"Then we will deal with . . . it at the time." *Don't think about the water. Trolls do not fear.* "You go first and . . . open the door. I will be . . . right behind you."

"Got it." Gork took one last look at the hideous undead things, their circles growing ever smaller, and dove.

I will not fear. Fear is—

"Katim!" Fezeill shouted, pointing.

Several of the creatures had broken off their circling and begun moving, slowly but deliberately, toward the ripples and bubbles that marked the kobold's dive.

"If you're going, go now!"

Katim closed her eyes for just an instant, and dropped.

Terror surged through her as soon as her snout submerged, and she had to fight the instinct to take a startled—and lethal—breath. Taloned hands scrabbled across the stone walls of the fallen tower, seeking purchase to halt her descent. More by accident than design, the fingers of her right hand snagged in a crevice. There she hung, unable to make herself move, an easy target for the ghoulish creatures splashing and dogpaddling her way.

And then she felt something snag her leg.

The troll's entire body locked up, muscles pulling painfully against one another as she fought the urge to lash out in mindless panic, to drive her boots or her talons into whatever had gotten hold of her. Her mind filled with the image of those decaying monstrosities dragging her down, down, to slowly drown in the liquid blackness of Jureb Nahl . . .

No! I am a troll*! We do not fear!* Clenching her teeth so hard her protruding gums began to bleed, she forced herself to calm—and only then realized that whatever lurked beneath her wasn't grabbing at her leg so much as it was tugging at the hem of her pants. Katim relaxed and allowed Gork to guide her to the door, forcing herself not to struggle as he dragged her through the portal, now hanging open . . .

And felt her lungs empty themselves of breath in a single blast as she fell free of the water's embrace to land on the curved "floor" that was originally one of the walls of the fallen tower.

"What . . . ?" Turning a violent cough into a growled question, she twisted to examine the barren chamber. Above and slightly to the right, the wooden door hung open to reveal a veritable wall of swamp water, yet barely a trickle of the murky stuff dribbled in through the opening.

"It's as I suspected," Gork said. "Trelaine must've laid some pretty potent spells on this place. He probably just meant to keep his basement from flooding if the swamp rose in the rain, but—well, you can see for yourself."

Katim, still breathing heavily, rose to her feet. "I can indeed. It . . . seems that searching this place . . . will not be so difficult after . . . all."

"I don't know," Gork said, glancing around. "The floors and the ceilings are walls, and everything's gonna be topsy-turvy at best. Could make searching awkward."

"Then we'd best . . . get started, hadn't . . . we? The others are running . . . out of time."

"Yeah." A brief pause. "I'll pretend to care about that if you will."

Truth was, he'd considered leaving her out there to drown. Cræosh might have bought into her excuse about functioning down here better than the orc could have, but Gork didn't, not for one minute. He'd watched her in the water, knew damn well that she had all the swimming skills of a crippled brick. Something else had driven her down here. Probably the same something that had inspired her to keep an eye on him every waking moment, even when he was on watch and she was supposed to be asleep, since their days in the Northern Steppes. Yeah, he'd noticed, and yeah, it was pretty easy to guess why.

She knew about Ebonwind. Or, at the very least, suspected.

Obviously, Gork hadn't been as careful as he'd thought, back in the cottage. The troll must have spotted him leaving, must have watched as he made his pact with the dakórren and his strange little familiar.

Right now, though, he needed her. Gork would never have admitted it to the others, but the thought of exploring this place alone scared the piss out of him. And besides, she obviously hadn't said anything about Ebonwind to the others; hadn't tried to blackmail him, or cut herself in for a piece of the dakórren's promised reward.

So he'd watch her watch him, and see just what it was she had in mind before he decided what to do about her. Stars willing, it wouldn't come down to having to kill her. Just the thought of trying would've made his blood run cold enough to freeze the aforementioned piss absolutely solid.

"All right," he said calmly, pretending there was nowhere else he'd rather be than in a submerged tower, surrounded by irate corpses, searching for the bones of a long-dead sorcerer. "So where do we start?"

They chose the nearest room, through a simple door that had once marked the first landing on the spiral staircase. The mismatched pair were forced to crawl along and through the steps, scraping their palms and their knees, working their way forward through the floor of the second story. Gork found himself growing nauseated with vertigo every time he looked straight ahead to see the stairs spiraling over—no, away—and decided to keep his eyes on his claws. As it happened, though, the chamber was little more than a small closet, apparently having served Trelaine as something of a coat room. Broken coat racks and a few scraps of cloak covered the wall-turned-floor. After desultorily poking through the refuse, they moved on.

By the time they'd reached what had been the eighth floor—after having stumbled onto three guest bedrooms, a dining room, a kitchen (which had been unfortunately positioned above them, and the opening of which had resulted in a large pile of pots and pans falling onto the kobold's head), a broom closet, and a bathing chamber—they were both growing well and truly frustrated at the whole escapade.

"Who would've thought," Gork groused, "that some great and powerful wizard could possibly be this *dull*?"

"How many wizards . . . have *you* met in your . . . lifetime?"

"That's not the point at all," the kobold said, crawling ahead to examine the latch on the next door. He dug a wire from one of his pouches and began to poke at the mechanism. "The point is that I'm standing inside a fallen wizard's tower underneath a swamp, and I'm *bored*. What's wrong with this picture?"

The lock snapped open with a loud ping. Gork shuffled back, brushing off his hands.

"If you're that bored . . . I'm sure they'd love to have you . . . join them topside."

The kobold scowled. Katim, axe in hand, shuffled forward at a crouch and awkwardly kicked open the door. It fell inward with a crash, hanging down from the horizontal stairway on which they stood. She jumped inside, rising to her full height, the kobold close on her heels.

And then, in the light of the torch—which she carried while he was working on the locks, he while they entered each room—they saw what awaited them, and their spirits sagged. Katim's fists clenched tight, and Gork felt an overwhelming need to break something.

"*Another* storeroom? He couldn't possibly have even *owned* that much crap!"

"It would certainly . . . seem so, wouldn't it?"

"I *told* you all the interesting stuff would be at the top. I *told* you we should start there and work down!"

Katim growled something unintelligible, hunched back onto the twisted staircase, and crawled on ahead. Muttering and cursing, Gork followed, and almost ran into her as she stopped short at the gap in the wall leading to the next "level."

"Now this," she said, "may be . . . worthwhile."

His curiosity—not to mention his constantly bubbling store of impatience—now fully aroused, the kobold squeezed past. Doing so gave him a clear view of the door, sitting on the floor (which had once been the west wall).

"Oh, yeah! That's more like it." *Or at least more interesting.*

Gork had seen the insides of enough prisons to recognize that this thick, steel-bound monstrosity could only be the door to a cell. And in fact, it was held shut by a heavy wooden bar that fastened it to what was now the floor. Carefully he crawled over and peeked in the small window, twisting his head to peer between the bars.

"Do you see anything . . . worth going in there . . . for?" Katim asked.

Gork shook his head. "Can't tell for sure. There's a whole lot of seriously old straw piled against the far wall. Er, that is, the floor. Bunch of chains and manacles hanging from some of the walls—long suckers, too. And it looks like there're some bones sticking out of the straw, but I can't tell how many."

The troll dropped to all fours beside him and pulled the queen's bronze brooch from a pouch at her belt.

"You think we're going to find his bones in his own cell?" Gork asked skeptically.

"Probably not," Katim admitted, holding the brooch above the window. "But we don't know . . . what happened here. Would . . . you not prefer that we make . . . certain?"

"Fair enough. And I suppose he could've been holding a rival wizard captive, and that'd do us just as well. So how's that thing supposed to work?"

"I'm not entirely . . . sure. But it appears that we . . . are not close enough. It . . . is not doing anything . . . at all."

"That, or they're just normal bones and it's not *supposed* to do anything. Or you're doing it wrong." Gork quickly raised a hand in supplication as she cast him a sideways glare. "Okay, okay. Just kidding."

They stared silently at the bones below.

"Why don't we move on," Gork said finally, "and if we don't find anything elsewhere, we can come back?"

"I'd really prefer to . . . be sure, however improbable it . . . may be."

"And if I refuse?"

"Feel free to go on . . . ahead alone, then."

Sigh. "Fine. Move that bar, would you?"

With a grunt, Katim heaved. The bar slid from its brackets with a hideous screech, clattered to the wall/floor beside the door with a deafening clang. The entire door *flashed*, as though the sun had been hidden behind that bar, and then the light was gone—not counting the spots in Gork's and Katim's eyes—as rapidly as it appeared.

The door shuddered as something slammed against it, hard, from the other side.

"It occurs to me, albeit a tad belatedly," Gork said as they scrambled to their feet and backed away from the juddering portal, "that anything imprisoned in a wizard's tower might, uh, be magical enough to survive the centuries."

"A *tad* belatedly?" the troll snarled, obviously ignoring the fact that she hadn't thought of it either.

"Well, better late than never, right?" Gork asked. With a final earth-shaking thump, the door blew open.

The thing that emerged was pulled straight from someone's nightmares, possibly the same lunatic who had dreamed up the worm-folk. It hovered a foot or so above the ground, bobbing and swaying like a ship at sea. Its uppermost parts were a humanoid skeleton: grinning skull, collarbone, shoulder blades, arms—they were all there. Even a spine, a thrashing and twisting tail, hung from that skull. But beneath the shoulders was nothing but a spinning vortex of air, a whirlwind in miniature made visible by the centuries of dust and grime it sucked into itself as it spun. The spine lashed about, a whip in that wind, taking small chunks of stone out of the bricks wherever it struck. With an ear-splitting laugh that came from the midst of the raging winds, rather than from the mouth above, it lunged toward its "rescuers."

Katim's first thought, just before she brought her axe around to intercept it, was *Who the hell would create such a thing?*

Gork's first thought, as he glanced down at the *kah-rahahk* in his hands, was *What the hell am I going to stab with this?*

Even as he backed away from the hell-spawned creature, he watched Katim knock the first of its bony claws away with the flat of her blade, then bring her axe down straight into the rictus grin. Bone chips flew, and the skull howled in pain—or Gork hoped it was pain, at any rate—but rather than do the polite thing and drop dead, the creature only retreated a foot or so, striking with its other hand even as it moved.

The troll cried out, staggering back to slam against the nearest wall. (Floor? Whatever it was.) Gork's eyes tried their damnedest to pop from his own skull as her flesh contorted and a burst of wind—as dusty as the creature's own—flowed from Katim's wound and from her gaping mouth. She forced herself upright, choking something foul from her lungs, but her posture was stooped, and it appeared to Gork that the dancing axe was markedly slower than before.

Stars, what do I do? His own weapon wouldn't do a damn thing to a creature of bone, especially not one capable of laughing off a troll-wielded axe to the face. So far, the thing was focusing on Katim, but Gork had no doubt that if and when the troll fell, kobold was next on the menu.

And then, as his cheek was stung to bleeding by a small sliver of brick thrown loose by the whirlwind, he had an idea. It wasn't *much* of an idea, granted, but this didn't really seem the time to be choosy.

"Katim!" he shouted, gesturing wildly to attract her attention. "Down there!" He pointed to the door from which the beast had emerged.

Apparently, the creature didn't appreciate his interference. Skull and shoulders rotated atop the miniature cyclone so that the empty sockets and gaping grin were suddenly aimed at Gork. Before even the nimble kobold could dodge, those bony fingers reached out to score two deep scratches across his other cheek.

For an instant, it felt as though the tower had abruptly righted itself. The room spun, and Gork staggered sideways in a clumsy dance as his entire center of balance became, well, uncentered. His arms were dead weights at his sides, and he felt exhausted to the point of tears. He struggled to breathe and broke into a horrible choking fit, exhaling gust after gust of stale air. He felt the winds rippling through his body, flowing from his wounds and his orifices.

The thing spun back again, clearly recognizing the troll as the greater threat. By then, however, Katim had already darted by it— slamming her axe into its shoulder as she passed, for all the good it did—and dropped through the doorway.

Gork cowered, struggling to catch some measure of breath, and actually sobbed with relief when the thing chose to follow the troll rather than turn its wrath on him. Sometimes, it's good to be the little guy.

He watched as it drifted down into the sunken cell, determined to slay the troll first, and Gork gave serious consideration to just slamming the door. But he still wasn't certain he felt up to facing the rest of the tower alone; there was no way he could move that bar by himself even at full strength, let alone in his current condition; and if he tried and failed, it was purely a question as to whether the skull-thing tore him apart before Katim did.

Come to think of it, I wonder if Katim only went down there because she knew I couldn't move that damn thing on my own. . . .

Every inch a struggle, Gork lowered himself into the cell, slipping and tumbling the last few feet, and began creeping—lurching, really—along the wall. The cell's current floor was coated in a nigh-solid mass of ancient straw and an age's worth of dust and insect carapaces. Some were flung about by the creature's winds, but enough lay unmoving, ready to crunch beneath a careless foot. The kobold squinted, trying unsuccessfully to protect his sight from the stormy barrage. In fits and starts, fighting for every step, he drew near his goal. He just had to get there before Katim faltered. . . .

He very nearly did not.

Katim crouched in the opposite corner, axe bobbing wildly in a desperate attempt to hold the spectral thing at bay. Deep scratches marred both skeletal arms, and the creature's constant wail had risen in pitch, frustration now mixed with the hatred and fury they'd heard before. But still it came, clearly undaunted by the myriad wounds the troll had inflicted, and each time she drove it back. Stalemate.

But not for long. Her greatest efforts merely pained the thing, while it could kill with a glancing blow. She, for all her strength and trollish determination, would tire; and this odious apparition, she was certain, would not.

And speaking of odious, *where was Gork?* She'd gone where he indicated, assuming he had more of a plan than she did—in other words, *any*—but she'd seen neither hide nor, well, more hide of him since. If he'd trapped her down here without good reason, she would make damn sure she survived this monstrosity long enough to wring the little bastard's neck so hard that his spine popped out his—

A loud clanking, not unlike the fall of a lazy portcullis, sounded from across the cell. His outline blurred by the spinning detritus of the whirlwind, Gork faded into view behind the apparition. He staggered as he walked, as though weighted down by some unseen encumbrance. Well, all right, it was heartening (if only slightly) that he hadn't chosen to abandon her, but she wasn't certain how much good he'd do.

The kobold shrugged, and Katim saw a strange, shapeless weight fall from his shoulder. More clanking and clattering, and he bent down to lift whatever it was he'd dropped. Hands clasped together, he rocked back and forth, building momentum. Between the haze of the whirlwind and the constant blur of her own axe, she still couldn't see what he held.

And then, whatever it was, Gork heaved it into the air with the all the pathetic strength he could muster. Finally, Katim saw what it was, and she chortled with delight at her sudden understanding.

The heavy manacle, attached to the wall by its thick iron chain, hurtled across the cell and vanished into the spinning winds. The apparition didn't even seem to notice.

Katim stepped to the side, parrying a bony arm, stepped again, and again, always waiting for the thing to follow.

It jerked to a halt, somehow stumbling in midair, the chain taught behind it, tethering it to the wall. Again Katim choked back laughter; for a creature without flesh or muscle on its face, it was astounding just how confused it managed to look.

It was a neat trick, quick thinking on the kobold's part, but it wouldn't hold the apparition long. The manacle hadn't latched onto anything solid, but was held in place only by the spinning winds. Even as she watched, the thing yanked itself forward a few inches, two links of iron sliding obscenely from inside its "body." It reached down and clasped the chain in skeletal hands, tugging another few links free. In moments it would be loose once more.

But for those moments, its attentions and its deadly claws were directed elsewhere. Katim took a deep breath, summoned every bit of strength remaining to her, and swung her axe at the now-defenseless skull.

Bone cracked and the creature howled, but still it lived, still it struggled against the chain. Three more links; less than half a minute, and only the manacle itself would remain within the vortex.

Katim dropped her axe, shook loose her *chirrusk*, and leapt. She wasn't strong enough to make the doorway above on her own, but by hooking the weapon onto the stone lip she succeeded in hauling herself out, gasping and panting the entire way.

Like Gork before her, though of course she couldn't know that, she considered slamming the door and leaving her ally behind. But the troll couldn't be sure that replacing the bar would be enough to restore whatever magic had held the apparition at bay.

Which did not, she realized with a grin, make it useless.

Heaving the massive bar into the air, wincing as she felt muscles pull and threaten to tear in her stomach, she stumbled back to the edge of the cell-turned-pit, took an instant to orient herself, and dropped it end-on.

Beneath that plummeting weight, the creature's skull became powder.

The winds ceased as abruptly as someone blowing out a candle, allowing masses of straw, clouds of dust, chips of stone, and one corroded manacle to rain loudly across the floor. The bones themselves, including shards of skull, landed at Gork's feet. The troll watched as the kobold spent the next several moments gleefully pounding them into so much powder with the manacle.

He, like Katim, was obviously reveling in his newfound strength. When the creature died, the both of them felt an incredible rush of vitality; whatever the thing stole from them had now returned, and with reinforcements to boot.

"Well, that was fun," Gork said once he'd climbed his own way out of the cell and the pair of them had progressed back into the horizontal stairwell.

Katim snorted loudly. "Kobolds have a truly . . . odd notion of fun."

"Look on the bright side, Katim. It probably can't get any worse."

With a snarl, she backhanded Gork halfway across the hall. Trolls aren't superstitious, as a rule—their efforts to gather slaves for the afterlife aside—but damn it all, some things you *just don't say*.

"Actually," she said as he crawled his way back to her, "there *was* an upside . . . to us discovering that thing."

"Do tell," Gork said sourly, prodding at his jaw with two knuckles.

"If Trelaine had abandoned . . . the tower, he would surely have either taken . . . or destroyed that thing. Its presence . . . suggests that he indeed died here . . . as the rumors claim."

Gork wrinkled his snout. "Um . . . Yay?"

"Yay, indeed. While you're . . . celebrating, climb back down there and bring . . . back my axe."

As it turned out, though, the kobold's prognostications, however much they might have tempted fate, proved accurate. They encountered no further danger as they explored the last group of rooms: Trelaine's own bedchamber and bath. There remained, finally, but a single door left. Had the tower been standing properly, it would have led to the room at the absolute top.

"Of course," Gork grumbled, his words slightly slurred by a faint swelling in his bruised snout. "I knew it. I just knew it! Next time, we start at the top and work down!"

Katim couldn't resist. "Okay, I promise. The . . . next time you and I have . . . to search a fallen wizard's tower . . . for his bones, I will . . . listen to your advice."

Gork's left eyelid twitched. "I'm just going to go check that last door," he muttered darkly, setting his shoulders and pretending not to hear the troll's low chuckling behind him.

It was, they discovered, a most unremarkable door. It wasn't even locked. Very slowly, Katim edged it open with the tip of her axe. This was, or rather had been, the absolute height of Trelaine's abode. From all the tales Katim had heard of mages, the skeletal specter they'd faced was a well-heeled puppy compared to what they might find in here.

But the chamber, like the door, appeared mundane enough. Well, except for the fact that it stood right-side-up, despite the tower's horizontal orientation, but that discrepancy didn't bother them at all. At this point, such benign magics weren't even worth noting.

An old, dust-covered table stretched the length of the room, cluttered with crinkled parchments, bowls and pestles, and crystal vials. A wizard's laboratory straight from fairy tales, except for the other end of the table—perhaps a quarter of its length, all told—which was hideously blackened as if by some long-ago fire. That section was barren, suggesting that anything atop it had been hurled aside. Indeed, shards of broken glass, and chunks of metal melted into abstract shapes, were scattered across the floor nearby.

"Trelaine's accident," Katim said.

Gork agreed. "I don't see any bones, though."

"Nor do I. Let's . . . keep searching. They're bound to be . . ." The first of the swirling lights grabbed her attention and she peered upward.

"Oh, good," the kobold said, craning his neck back to follow her gaze. "Ghosts. I was just thinking that I hadn't really gotten my fill of dead things."

Roughly eight feet over Katim's head, where the ceiling sloped inward to form the tower's peaked roof, a ring of *something* spun through the air. Bursts of a pale luminescence—now an off-white shade of pearl, now of red, now blue—limned the apparitions in a faint aura, invisible unless one were looking directly at them. Gaping holes in the spectral forms vaguely suggested facial features, too lacking in detail to determine any expressions. They spun in an endless path, circumnavigating the room scores of times each minute. Although they moved too swiftly for an accurate count, Katim estimated somewhere between fifteen and twenty of them.

Hovering in the precise center of the phantom ring, a dancing marionette with an epileptic puppeteer, was a collection of bones. Even as they watched, the cracked and pitted skull rotated downward as if to stare at them, until it was knocked aside by a wildly flailing femur.

"I think I'll just go and see how the others are doing," Gork said.

Katim glanced down at the bronze brooch given them by Queen Anne. It, too, was glowing, nearly bright enough to wash out the ghostly radiance above.

"Those?" Gork asked.

Katim nodded. The kobold scowled. "Figures. What do you suppose *they're* all doing here?"

"Perhaps these are . . . the beings that perished in Trelaine's . . . experiments?"

"I suppose it's possible. Think they'll let us just take what we need?"

"Feel free to . . . ask them."

Gork, apparently, did *not* feel free to do that.

Slowly, keeping a weather eye above, Katim moved to stand directly beneath the floating remains. She yanked at a strap on her belt and allowed her *chirrusk* to fall into her waiting hand with a loud clank.

"I think, using this . . . I can jump high enough . . . to reach. I pull them . . . down; you stand beside me . . . and catch them."

"*What?* I'm not touching those things! No way! Not a chance. You can just find someone else to—"

Katim lifted the kobold off the ground by his collar. "And *I* am not . . . willing to turn around and leave . . . empty-handed after all the trouble . . . we've gone through. Do . . . you have a better suggestion?"

"Actually," Gork said, his whole face lighting up, "I do!"

More crawling, more banging of hands and knees, and more cursing in multiple languages finally brought them back to one of the storerooms on a lower—sideways?—level. There, after a few minutes spent searching, they located a large sack with only a few small holes worn through the fabric by the passage of time. Again with the crawling and banging, and they returned to the topmost room, where they commenced a slightly modified variation of Katim's plan. It took her a few tries before the barbed hook caught one of the bones at the proper angle. (Gork refrained from laughing at the sight of the troll bouncing up and down in the middle of the chamber, since he felt that his internal organs were perfectly fine where they were, thank you very much.) And once she'd snagged it, it briefly resisted her efforts to move it, as if it were jammed in place. With a final tug, however, she broke it loose; the bone tumbled earthward, and Gork caught it in the sack without difficulty *and* without touching the nasty thing.

It took time, far more time than they were comfortable spending, what with their companions (presumably) weathering the siege outside. Each bone had to be snagged at just the right angle, and some were too small or just the wrong shape for the *chirrusk* to hook. Once they'd gotten about half the visible remains, including the skull, they'd agreed that it would have to be enough.

Which, of course, led to even more crawling through those damned stairs.

It was sheer happenstance that Gork chose to glance back as they were roughly halfway back down/through the tower. Katim started at his sudden yelp, cracking her head on the steps. She'd been trying to navigate a particularly arduous twist in the spiral case and wasn't really in a position to turn and look. "What is it?"

"The ghosts!" Gork whispered. "They're following us!"

Katim cursed. "Are they . . . gaining?"

"No," the kobold said after a moment. "They seem to be keeping a set distance, actually."

"Let me guess. About . . . as far as they were circling . . . from the bones?"

"Uh . . . Well, yeah, about that."

She nodded and resumed her crawl. "If they start to get any . . . closer, by all means, yip."

Katim felt another surge of panic as they approached the door, hanging open, revealing the green-tinted wall of water beyond. Ruthlessly, she repressed it. The trip up, she told herself sharply, wouldn't be as difficult as the trip down. Once through the door, she could just climb the curve of the tower; shouldn't require being in the water more than a few seconds.

She hoped.

Thankfully, she discovered that getting *to* the door was the hardest part. The curve of the wall forced her to climb practically upside down, fingers wedged into tiny stones. Gork made it look easy—she almost reached out and knocked him off the wall, just because—whereas she nearly lost her purchase on three separate occasions. Each time, she found herself hanging precariously, and while the fall wasn't far, she'd have landed head- or back-first on the stone below.

But she managed, time and again, to retain her hold, to spur herself onward, and finally her fists closed on the doorframe, her fingertips suddenly soaked as they protruded into the murky waters beyond. Taking one last deep breath, she hauled herself out into the swamp.

Maybe the climb up was easier than the journey down, maybe it wasn't; but this time, Katim kept both her wits and her grip. It was less than a minute later that she clambered, soaked but otherwise unharmed, out onto the uppermost curve of the tower. She breathed deep, sucking in the fragrant miasma of the swamps.

And came damn near to losing her snout in the process, as Cræosh's blade missed her face by a matter of inches on its way to severing the claws from one of the waterlogged corpses. "Took your bloody fucking Ancestors-damned sweet time about it, didn't you?!" he ranted as he stomped past, sword falling as he methodically chopped inches off the undead thing's arm. "If I didn't know better, I'd think you wanted these things to finish us off!"

"It might have been worth it to . . . shut you up."

"Whatever!" The orc lunged and split a second corpse, one that was giving Jhurpess something of a hard time, down the middle. The bugbear, in turn, flipped *over* Cræosh, crushing the skull of the one Cræosh had been fighting. They exchanged brief nods and then turned to face the next in the seemingly endless wave. "Did you get it?"

"Yeah, we got it!" Gork shouted from his new position behind the ogre, keeping her tree-trunk legs between him and the enemy. "Not the whole skeleton, but it should be enough!"

"Great! Then all we have to do is find some way to get the hell away from here without being eaten, torn to shreds, disemboweled, or otherwise rendered nonhomogenous. Any ideas?"

"Well, now that you *ask*," Gimmol said from atop Belrotha's backpack, where he was launching a sporadic stream of crossbow bolts at the dead things, "no."

At which point, Jhurpess unleashed his familiar howl.

They thought, at first, that he might have been struck. But when they looked—those, at least, not so hard-pressed that they couldn't afford even to look around—the other goblins found themselves equally startled as the cowering bugbear.

"Ancestors," Cræosh whispered breathlessly. "What *now*?"

"Oh, yeah," Gork said from the lee of the ogre, "and there were these ghosts. . . ."

They rose from the water in an unbroken stream, a spout of glowing phantoms. Their moans grew deafening, disorienting, smothering the clash of battle and the ambient sounds of Jureb Nahl. Briefly they flowed toward Katim, as though intending to resume their orbit around the bones of Trelaine, and then they froze. Spectral heads rotated, surveying new surroundings for the first time in centuries. The shambling carcasses halted at the same time, some with arms raised in midswing. It appeared, for a span of heartbeats, as though the corpses . . . smiled.

One by one, the ghosts winked out. And each time, one of the bodies—finally and truly dead, finally at rest—sank from sight in the waters of Jureb Nahl. In but a few short moments, none but Morthûl's soldiers remained.

"What?" Jhurpess asked.

Belrotha nodded. "What him said."

Warily, Cræosh sidled over toward Katim. "Would you—either of you," he clarified, glancing at the half-hidden kobold, "care to explain what in the name of my middle testicle just happened?"

"Those ghosts," Katim began slowly, "seemed . . . to be drawn to Trelaine's . . . bones. They must have belonged . . . to these bodies out here." She actually shuddered with rage; to bind a soul to this world, to keep it from serving in the next, was unthinkable profanity! "Apparently, the souls . . . were trapped to bind the . . . physical bodies to this place. Bringing them . . . together seems to have freed . . . them."

"I suspected it might," Gork said. "That's why I suggested bringing them up here."

Katim glanced heavenward. She was starting to believe that there might just be some sort of higher power after all; Gork *had* to be somebody's idea of a practical joke!

"Okay, that makes sense," Cræosh said, his tone making it quite clear that it did no such thing. "If there's nothing else, let's get out of this fucking cesspool and back on dry land before something *else* goes wrong."

It was, though they'd never know it, fortuitous that they left when they did. Even at that moment, a combined force of nagas and troglodytes were dashing at top speed through the swamp, determined to intercept the interlopers before they left the tower. Gork, in his strange little way, had actually put a halt to endless years of warfare. As the nagas and their titanic alligator had launched their attack upon the newer inhabitants of Jureb Nahl, they and the troglodytes had exchanged a bevy of taunts and insults. Over the course of those insults, as each side listened to what the others were saying, the two sides had come to realize that they'd both been used—and in the naga's case, overtly deceived—by the conniving kobold and his allies. Furious, they'd agreed to put aside their own conflict, at least long enough to return to the nagas' territory and teach the mammals a lesson!

The squad was long gone by the time they got there, of course, but it seemed kind of silly to resume hostilities at that point. If the troglodytes and the nagas could work together on this, surely they could learn to share the vast expanse of Jureb Nahl? Perhaps even cooperate, for the betterment of both races?

The very next morning, someone hurled a racial epithet, the war resumed as fiercely as ever, and—to the best of anyone's knowledge—still rages to this day.

CHAPTER SEVEN

THESE AREN'T THE DRUIDS YOU'RE LOOKING FOR

"It's too soon, Your Majesty! Gods, you've already lost *one* squad in one of these asinine ventures. Are you *looking* to lose a second?"

Dororam, King of Shauntille, was largely unaccustomed to being spoken to in such a manner. And there had been a point, not terribly long ago, when he had appreciated Ananias duMark for just that reason: the wizard was clearly unimpressed, and certainly unintimidated, by rank. Dororam had always known that he could be assured of getting the man's honest and accurate opinions, unsullied by any sycophantic need to impress.

He couldn't say for sure whether he'd just grown tired of duMark's arrogance, or if the sorcerer's attitude really *had* grown more barbed and condescending of late. The practical upshot, in either case, was that Dororam was less inclined to be appreciative of duMark's attitude, and more likely to find it obnoxious.

"Ananias," Dororam began entreating for the fourth time, forcing his fists to slowly unclench, "we've been over this." *And over it, and over it, and over it . . .* "This source of yours does us no good if we fail to act on the information he provides. I will certainly admit, in hindsight, that Lieutenant Kaleth's mission may have been less than judicious—"

DuMark loosed a single bark of laughter. Dororam scowled. "I fail to see anything humorous in the loss of so many good men."

The half-elf sneered. "Had they been good men, Dororam, they'd not have been lost, would they?"

"Whatever the case," the king continued quickly, determined to keep a rein on his temper even if it killed him, "we miscalculated the risks. I acknowledge that, but I won't make that mistake again."

"Aren't you, though? You sent Kaleth and his men with orders only to measure the enemy's forces along the Brimstone Mountains, and look what happened." Actually, neither of them knew *precisely* what happened; when Lieutenant Branden had stumbled back into the capital, alone and broken, they'd been able to coax only a few details from him. But it was more than enough to tell them the mission had ended in disaster. "Now you suggest sending a second, larger unit—this time with explicit orders to engage the enemy—and you want me to believe you're not making the same mistake? Well, perhaps you're not, at that. This one's even more foolish."

"I would thank you," Dororam practically hissed, "to show me a *little* respect in my own palace!"

"Earn it, Dororam, and I'll show it."

Again, King Dororam managed—though it cost him no small amount of effort—to bite back a caustic retort. Instead, after several calming breaths, "You brought me word that the Iron Keep is now *expanding* its forces along the Brimstone Mountains. You told me that a great many additional watch posts and guard towers are to be placed at strategic locations along the border."

"True enough," duMark acknowledged, still scowling. "So?"

"So we cannot afford to let these watches stand. The bulk of our forces have to utilize the Serpent's Pass, and they'll be spotted days in advance. We've no way to prevent that. I *must* send a few units through the smaller passes, *in secret*. If we've no forces to harry Morthûl's defenders, he could keep our armies bottled up in the Serpent's Pass for weeks!"

"Elementary tactics, Dororam. I know all this."

"Then why do you object every time I come up with a plan to eliminate the sentries on some of the smaller passes?"

"Because it would compromise my source, as I've already explained." *If your foolishness hasn't already done so.* DuMark didn't utter the last bit aloud, but Dororam could see it written clearly in his expression. "If you'd just wait, perhaps until the spring thaw, that would be fine. As it is, launching any such attack, so soon after this information came to me, would be far too suspicious a coincidence. My source could learn he's been compromised, and we'd learn nothing more from him. Plus, if you strike too soon, Morthûl has time to reestablish those watch posts, and you'll have accomplished nothing."

Dororam threw up his hands. It was an argument they'd already had, and yet he couldn't stop himself from pursuing it as doggedly as an actor in a play. "I disagree, duMark. We'd be making a mistake by waiting. If we give the new deployments time to dig in, grow accustomed to their new terrain, they'll be that much harder to root out. Hit them now—and I mean hard, enough to wipe out the posts entirely— and we sow chaos in the ranks. It would take Morthûl time to draw off enough soldiers from other positions to reestablish those units."

"But he *has* time! Spring is still many weeks away, Dororam! You might clear the passes, true, but you could never hold them that long!"

"I can't," the king admitted, a sudden smile on his face. *Time to go off script.* "But Thane Granitemane and his dwarves certainly can."

The sorcerer actually blinked once in surprise. *Score one for the foolish human,* Dororam gloated. "The dwarves are involved in this operation?" duMark asked.

"Absolutely. Granitemane cannot spare enough of his people to *clear* the passes, but he *can* contribute enough to *hold* them.

"So it comes to this. My soldiers clear the passes now, while the Iron Keep's new units are being deployed. Once that's done, we fall back, allowing a platoon of Granitemane's dwarves to set up shop in the nearby caves. They remain there for the next few weeks, randomly eliminating any additional units Morthûl sends—all over the area, not just in the passes we intend to use. This makes it effectively impossible for the Charnel King to reinforce the Brimstone Mountains. And thus, it leaves the passes open for our secondary forces once our main armies hit the Serpent's."

"Whereas," duMark concluded, a grudging admiration in his voice, "if you wait until just before your armies march to take the guard posts, you run the risk of being unable to dislodge them."

Dororam smiled, a faint echo of the true camaraderie the two had once shared. "You see, Ananias? I'm not quite such a senile old man yet, am I?"

"No, Dororam, perhaps not quite as senile as all that. You could have told me of the dwarves' involvement earlier."

"I was working out the details with Granitemane." *And I want you to remember who's actually in charge here.* "I am also not completely oblivious to your own concerns, Ananias. Is this really liable to cause so many problems with your spy in Kirol Syrreth?"

"I hope not," the half-elf sighed, resting his chin thoughtfully on one hand. "If he does prove reluctant, I suppose I'll simply have to provide some additional motivation."

"I find myself," Gork said sourly as Cræosh abruptly loomed behind him, "starting to lose any real sense of motivation for this whole thing."

The orc snickered. "Ah, don't sweat it, Shorty. Hell, it's just a big, thick, ugly, black, twisted, nasty, evil forest. What could you possibly have to worry about?"

Gork's scowl suggested very clearly where the orc could shove his encouragement. And possibly the aforementioned trees.

The mismatched pair waited but a few short moments before the rest of the squad appeared. Her eyebrows raised marginally as she, too, surveyed the woodlands, Katim said, "There's still several . . . hours of daylight remaining. Are we planning to . . . continue on?"

Cræosh glanced sideways at her. "What do you think?" he asked, his tone just a bit snappish.

For another moment, the troll peered at the expanse of trees. "I'd suggest camping here," she said finally. "Rupert told . . . us that the forest would require . . . most of a day to traverse. I'd as . . . soon camp out here where I can . . . see a foe approaching, and enter . . . the trees at dawn."

The orc nodded. "My thoughts exactly. Thus, just in case you hadn't noticed the telltale clue that your feet aren't moving, we've stopped."

The troll grimaced. "Your wit, Cræosh, never . . . ceases to fail to astound me."

"I think," the orc said sullenly, after a moment of puzzling that through, "that we ought to make camp."

"I couldn't agree . . . more. Not with you . . . anyway."

Gork walked away, having neither sufficient interest nor sufficient patience to hear out the latest spat. Sooner or later, those two were going to kill each other; until then, he was sick of listening as they slowly worked their way up to it.

It had been constant in the weeks since Jureb Nahl. All the way back to Castle Eldritch, all during their rest and recuperation, all throughout the subsequent errands they'd run for Queen Anne—during which they had fetched her an array of peculiar leaves, the stone heart of a man who had been petrified by a basilisk, and finally a cobweb spun by a spider that had fed on flies who had themselves supped on the decaying corpse of a virgin faerie—the troll and the orc had bickered like an old, psychotic married couple. Gork was sick of them, sick of Queen Anne's peculiar needs, sick of the rest of the squad . . .

Sick of Nurien Ebonwind, who'd appeared to him three times during those weeks, pressing him for more on the Charnel King's armies. (At least the constant antagonism between Cræosh and Katim had distracted the troll enough for him to *have* these meetings.) Gork, who'd spent most of this time racing this way and that across Kirol Syrreth like a chicken whose head was about to be cut off, had snippily repeated the various rumors he'd heard.

"Look," the kobold had finally challenged the dakórren as he was about to depart their latest clandestine rendezvous, "it's not that I don't want the reward you promised me, but I've got to ask . . . You could get this same information from any soldier plucked from some craphole tavern. Probably better. Why do you keep coming to me?"

Ebonwind had smiled, his familiar had said something that might have been "Oopo vlimp," and they were gone.

Gork, not being an idiot, knew that meant one of two things, if not both. One, he was just *one* of Ebonwind's sources. Two, Ebonwind was, despite his protestations to the contrary, curious about a lot more than troop movements. Gork knew, or might know, or would know something that he *couldn't* get elsewhere.

I need out of this deal. Or I need to ask for more money.

And for that matter, how does he keep teleporting to me wherever I am, when even Queen Anne couldn't send us somewhere she'd never seen?

He'd been pondering his problems during another few days of precious downtime at Castle Eldritch when, without warning, Queen Anne had joined them one morning for breakfast.

"It's rather funny," she had said, her gaze ever so slightly unfocused, "that you ran across that druid circle in Jureb Nahl. As it turns out, you're going someplace similar."

Cræosh had grinned. "If you're asking us to bring back one of those damn stones, we're gonna need a few more ogres."

"Not at all, dear Cræosh. What I need, actually, is a religious relic."

"Well, that ought to be easy enough . . ." he'd begun.

"Symbolism, my dear, remember? Symbolism is everything in magic. Not just any religious icon will do, no, not at all. This must be the relic of a forgotten god."

For a moment, the entire table had been silent. Slowly, Gimmol had raised a hand.

"Yes?"

"Umm, Your Majesty? If you know of this god, he wouldn't exactly be forgotten, would he?"

The queen had sighed. "I meant, in this context, a god no longer worshipped, my little ones. 'Forgotten' just has so much nicer a ring to it, wouldn't you agree?"

"Great," Cræosh had said. "We're about to go charging off on some deadly assignment, and she's worried about theatrics."

"Symbolism," she had repeated once more. "Not theatrics."

"Whatever."

"This land," the queen had said, moving on, "was populated by a rather surprising variety of druidic religions before my husband set things right." The squad members had exchanged uncertain glances at that pronouncement, but felt it wiser not to question the queen's assessment of her husband's achievements. "Now, as best I've been able to determine, quite a few of these cults were wiped out completely. In most cases, that doesn't help us; druids are notorious for using plants as holy icons—holly, oak, berries, that sort of silliness—and that doesn't leave us much to retrieve, does it? But my understanding is that the Circle of Ymmech Thewl might have kept what we now require."

Katim's ears had twitched in recognition. "Ymmech Thewl? As in . . . the forest of Thewl?"

Queen Anne had nodded. "The same."

"*The* forest of Ymmech . . . Thewl?"

"No matter how you choose to enunciate it, yes."

Jhurpess had shrunk in his seat, clinging to the arms as though drowning in the chair. "Jhurpess not want to go to Thewl," he'd announced, fingers absently breaking small chunks off the edge of the table. "Thewl bad place. Jhurpess like to eat things, not get eaten by things." His brow wrinkled in puzzlement as a thought struck him. "What 'Ymmech Thewl' mean?" he'd asked.

Cræosh's fingers had reached, seemingly of their own accord, for the nearest sharp utensil. "Has anyone else noticed," he'd asked, "that we're being very deliberately sent into the darkest, most mysterious, and all around fucked-up nastiest places this kingdom has to offer? If you wanted us dead, Your Majesty, there are a lot more efficient ways to pull it off."

Queen Anne had laughed—a light, almost spiritual sound. "Why, I've nothing but the highest hopes for your survival *and* your success, dear one! I send you where the items I need are to be found. If they were not in such dangerous, unpleasant locations, they'd have been retrieved long ago, yes?"

Which, after a few more hours of studying what little was known of Ymmech Thewl's druids, and another gut-wrenching teleport to get them as near as the queen could manage, had led them here, to the forest's edge. And to another spat.

But they did, indeed, make camp on the outskirts, whittling away the remaining hours of the day: first by watching the verbal sparring, and then, when that got boring, Gimmol, Gork, and Jhurpess broke into a rousing game of Climb the Ogre. The contest grew rather more challenging when

Belrotha grew tired of the sport long before the others did. They finally stopped when Gork found himself lying on his back a hundred yards away, having missed impaling a tree trunk by a matter of inches.

Ah, well. It was getting dark anyway.

Nothing untoward happened that night (except that Gork spent most of his watch actually watching Katim pretending not to watch him, but that doesn't really count as "happening"). The same held true of their first few hours within the forest of Thewl itself. The place was foreboding enough, swaddled in a blanket of shadows, full of branches that reached like claws from bent and twisted boles, as though eager to grab an unwary goblin and shred him into fleshy confetti. But no danger actually manifested, nothing so much as a rabid squirrel or an irate rabbit. . . .

Actually, as Katim and Jhurpess both pointed out nigh simultaneously, there was no sign of *any* rabbits or squirrels, rabid, irate, or otherwise. No birds perched in the trees, twittering the day away with their inane songs; no deer bounded from clearing to clearing; no wolves lurked to thin out said bounding population. With a single exception, Ymmech Thewl appeared devoid of animal life. And that single exception—a huge, stone-hued snake with a head *on both ends*, that had curled around a towering tree and watched them with four unblinking eyes— didn't really make them feel any better about the whole thing.

Belrotha finally dealt with her unease by grabbing the snake just below each head and tying it around the tree in a simple but efficient knot.

It was a short-lived comfort, though—one that vanished the instant they found the body.

He'd once been human—that was clear enough. He lay facedown, just off the meandering strip of slightly thinner grass that Katim had laughingly called a game trail. His clothes were tattered, and a few scraps of leather suggested that he had once worn a small pouch but that it had been equally savaged. He appeared to have died desperately reaching for a walking staff lying just a few inches from his outstretched hand.

None of which would have troubled any of the goblins, really, were it not for the tree beside which the body lay. One of its thickest roots extended through the man's back, passing through him to join with its brethren under the soil. The corpse, Katim noted with a sniff, was quite ripe, far too fresh for *anything* to grow completely through the body, let alone an entire tree root. And Gork, kneeling down to see if the body held anything worth looting, went abruptly pale as he got a good look at the amount of dried blood on the skin and tattered clothing and realized the man must have been *alive* when the root punctured his flesh.

The tree stabbed him?! Gork felt a sudden need to lie down.

"Oh, it did not!" Cræosh snapped when presented with the kobold's theory. "You have any fucking idea how stupid that sounds?"

"Yes, I know very damn well how stupid it sounds!" Gork said, a hysterical tremor in his voice. "Of course it sounds stupid! It's the dumbest thing I've ever heard, let alone said! And as soon as you come up with a more plausible theory, I'll be absolutely thrilled to go along with it! So?" The kobold actually crossed his arms and began tapping his foot. "I'm waiting."

"It's simple," Cræosh said, gesturing toward the corpse. "Obviously he . . . Well, that is, the body . . . The tree . . ." He stopped, staring at the root protruding from the cadaver's back. "Or then again," he finished lamely, "perhaps not."

"Me know," Belrotha announced. The entire squad stared at her.

"Oh, yeah," Gork snickered. "This, I've *got* to hear."

"Simple," the ogre said. "Someone drop tree on human."

"Um . . ." Cræosh actually tilted his head. "You wanna run that by us again, Belrotha?"

"Me said, someone drop tree on human."

"That's what I thought you said," Fezeill groused, the words emerging as a growl from his simian mouth. (He'd decided, given their surroundings, that a bugbear's form was once again appropriate.) "Listen, you elephantine mass of ignorance, would you care to explain exactly *what* could have dropped a tree that size? I doubt *you* could even *lift* it!"

"You probably right," she admitted after studying the bole. "Me not think me could do it."

"And there's not much around that's stronger than you are, is there?"

"A few things. Dragon, maybe."

"I think," Gimmol said from his perch on her shoulder, "that most dragons have, uh, more efficient weapons than trees."

The ogre shrugged, practically dislodging the gremlin from his roost. "Me not know *what* did it," she said impatiently. "Me just making suggestion. You not like suggestion, you figure out for yourself. Me going this way." And with that, she turned and continued on her way.

"She's right," Katim said. "We're not . . . going to figure out what happened by . . . standing around guessing. Let's get . . . through this forest before we . . . find out firsthand."

"Scared, troll?" Cræosh smirked.

"No. Just not . . . stupid enough to stand around . . . waiting for more trouble. Are . . . you?"

"Whatever." But he stayed with the rest as the squad followed the impatient ogre.

Gork hung back just long enough for a final glance at the tree and the corpse. *Was* Belrotha's idea feasible? Could something huge have ripped up this tree and . . . No. The roots climbed smoothly from the surrounding dirt; Gork was no expert, but he was sure the tree had to have been growing here for a few decades, if not longer.

Which brought him back to his original theory, however laughable. With a sudden burst of speed, he ran to catch up to the others.

The sun had just begun its inevitable slide toward the horizon and the squad was finally approaching the heart of Ymmech Thewl when Katim and Jhurpess caught the scent of man on the breeze. A few quick hisses and hand-signals resulted in the rasp of drawn weapons.

He stood statue-still, some twenty yards into the massive clearing— a veritable island of grass in the center of the sea of trees. Although he was little more than a darker shape against the gathering gloom, his posture suggested that he was very carefully watching their approach. The goblins spread out, so far as the trees at the clearing's edge would allow, ready for any attack . . . but not ready for the man to raise a hand and beckon them onward.

"You must hurry!" he called, his voice young but reverberating with the ring of authority. "Night is falling!"

Cræosh—whose Manspeak was better than most of the others'—shouted back. "So what? You afraid of the dark?" They moved, albeit cautiously, out of the cover of the trees.

The human shook his head. They were near enough now to see his shoulder-length mane of brown hair, his plain robe (very similar to the one they'd seen on the body in the woods), and, perhaps most urgently, the dread scrawled across his face. "Not the dark! The trees! Come quick, before . . ." Even in the dying light, they saw his gaze rise and fix on a spot somewhere above and behind them. "*Run!*"

Naturally, they glanced behind rather than obey, and most nearly stumbled and fell at the sight. Towering shapes bent and swayed, horribly backlit by the falling sun. Limbs—uncountable, twisted, spindly—writhed like dying eels, the first wakeful stirrings of something that should never stir at all. And those looming things surged forward, carried ponderously but swiftly on creaking appendages. Cræosh's attention was drawn to the corpse of a human that flopped horribly along with them, impaled on one of those twitching limbs.

The goblins ran. They tore past the few sporadic trees between them and the human, and whether they merely scratched themselves on protruding branches as they passed or whether these, too, had come alive and grabbed for them, they could not say. It was a small miracle that not a one of them stumbled or injured an ankle as they followed the strange human.

He, too, was running from the unnatural forest. The surety of his footsteps and the even pace of his stride belied the near blindness he must be suffering as the day breathed its last. At the limits of his vision, Cræosh saw the man vanish with a sudden splash, and then the squad were near enough to see their destination.

In the center of this massive clearing, the river called the Precrene Flow split in two, traveling in tandem for perhaps a hundred yards before merging once more into a single ribbon of blue. The islet in the center, a hillock only slightly higher than the rest of the clearing, was home to a great henge of stones, almost a mirror image to the one in Jureb Nahl.

Almost. This one was in far better shape, missing none of the towering blocks. And this one, too, cradled a small stone structure in its center. It was toward this building that the human, having already emerged dripping from the Precrene, was fleeing.

Katim appeared to balk as they approached the banks of that narrow but swift stream, but the others hit the water without slowing, Belrotha scooping up Gork by his belt. The waters barely reached Cræosh's armpits, and that seemed to alleviate the troll's concerns, for she caught up with them an instant later. The waters were frigid, the current treacherous, but the goblins (save those being carried) kept their feet.

When they tromped up the banks on the other side, the brown-haired human was standing by a door that blended seamlessly with the stone wall, holding it ajar with one hand. "Hurry!" he called, waving frantically. "They don't often cross the stream, but it happens! Quickly!"

Under normal circumstances, most of them would have hesitated, suspecting some sort of trap. These were not normal circumstances.

However . . .

"Me not fit!" Belrotha screeched at them.

She spoke in Gremlin, since that was how the squad normally talked. The human may or may not have understood her words, but there was no misunderstanding her concern.

"Don't worry!" he shouted. "The building's just there to protect the stairs! There'll be enough room for her once we get below!"

Below? Cræosh shook his head, even as he shoved past Fezeill and into the minuscule edifice. *This ain't like any druid circle I've ever heard of.*

Sure enough, the interior of the building was devoid of features, save for a huge set of double trapdoors occupying most of the floor. Cræosh pointed, the human nodded confirmation, and the orc squatted to yank both open at once. They crashed aside, revealing descending stairs of carven stone, worn and pitted, coated with layers of dust that showed the footprints of recent use.

And they were indeed wide enough—and, after a short ways, deep enough—for Belrotha. She'd have to squeeze at first, just as she'd done to enter the building, but not for long. Satisfied there were no *obvious* traps, Cræosh plunged down the steps two and three at a time. An incredible cacophony of crashes and clatters and grunts above were signal enough that the rest of the squad followed. Those were punctuated by a single reverberating *boom*, presumably the sound of the human slamming the outer door. That, hopefully, would keep the trees at bay.

The trees. Cræosh felt an incipient headache and actually had to mouth the words a time or two, forcing them to sink in. *We were attacked by fucking trees! The orcs back home are* not *gonna believe a word of this. . . .* Cræosh wasn't afraid to die, at least not much, but being murdered by an abnormally ambulatory log was not how he wanted to go.

He also really, really didn't want to face Gork's inevitable "I told you so!" It might just result in bloodshed.

The human slipped by him on the wide stairs, startling him from his reverie. "Forgive me," the man said, nodding his head in the shallowest of bows. "I don't mean to be rude, but there's no telling what my companions might do if the first person into the room is an orc."

"Or what the orc might do," Cræosh said, "in reaction."

"Exactly." The human quickened his pace, disappearing around the staircase's gradual curve.

Cræosh immediately halted, stumbling as Jhurpess ran into him from behind. He waited another moment or so, just to be sure that their "savior" was out of earshot. "All right, quick assessment. How do we want to play this?"

"Isn't it a bit late for that?" Fezeill asked acidly. "If there's a trap waiting for us, it may be too late to escape it."

"Maybe," Gimmol said, "but the other option was staying outside. I didn't exactly hear you suggesting that."

The doppelganger scowled, but shut up.

"I don't yet see what purpose . . . a trap might serve," Katim said. "Though of course I . . . don't know who these people . . . are. I suggest we . . . continue, but very, very . . . carefully."

"We could just go down there and kill them all," Gork said. "I find that, on the whole, it's safer to trust dead people than live ones."

"Who said anything about trust?" Cræosh asked. "I don't trust *you* bastards; you can bet your last intestinal parasite I'm not gonna trust *them*." He pondered a moment. "Same time, though, I don't think we ought to kill them just yet. Might be they can tell us something about those trees. Or, for that matter, about the druids that used to practice here.

No sense in tearing around the place half-assed if we can get them to just take us where we need to go. Had enough of that in Jureb Nahl, thanks."

There was a general agreement to that one, so Cræosh resumed his trek down the winding stairs.

It led, after another handful of turns, to a wide archway. Stepping through, Cræosh found himself standing in a massive underground sanctuary. The walls were lined in wooden panels, except for four-foot-wide vertical strips of bare stone, positioned at intervals of roughly five paces around the perimeter. Said panels were intricately embossed with a series of patterns, suggesting layer upon layer of branches and leaves extending into the distance. The floor, too, was covered in wooden paneling, though bare of adornment. Flickering torches, scented with some sort of herbal mixture, were mounted to the stone, and a fire pit blazed merrily in the room's center. The smoke coiled upward to vanish somewhere in the dark.

"We were starting to wonder if you'd gotten lost," the human told Cræosh in a tone probably intended to be one of good humor. The orc decided, for the time being, to take it as such.

"Yeah, well, you know how confusing stairs can be. Up, down . . . So many choices."

The man's smile broadened, and Cræosh marginally relaxed. The human who had led them down here stood by the fire pit flanked by two others clad in identical robes. One was female, the other male, but otherwise Cræosh saw little to distinguish them. They were all pink and squishy.

Their guide waved elegantly at the pair behind him, starting with the male. The fellow thus indicated gave them a wide grin; combined with his unruly hair, the expression made him look like something of a yokel, or perhaps an amiable mop. "This is Josiah Gruder, my oldest friend and one of the staunchest of my brethren."

Brethren? Behind Cræosh's back, Katim and Gork traded wary glances, each feeling a sudden sinking in the pit of his or her stomach (or stomachs, in the troll's case).

"This," the human continued, now directing their attention toward the red-haired woman, "is Mina MacCray, a far more recent, but by no means less welcome, addition to our order." She offered them a shy half-smile.

First "brethren," and now "order." Katim growled, and Gork shook his head.

"And my name," he finished grandly, "is Alam Tyr." He bowed once more, with only the hint of a flourish. "I am the head acolyte of the temple of Ymmech Thewl."

Gork groaned aloud.

"What?" Cræosh asked, craning his head around.

"You," the kobold told him, "have the brains of a wildebeest."

The orc scowled, but Katim interjected before he could speak. "Think, Cræosh, if you . . . still remember how. What . . . are we here for?"

His scowl just deepened. "The relic of . . . Oh, shit!" He'd finally gotten it.

The head acolyte Alam stepped forward. "I'm sorry," he said, not having fully understood the conversation, which had, of course, been in Gremlin. "Is something wrong?"

Cræosh and Katim exchanged glances, and both nodded just slightly. They'd get more useful information if the acolytes knew why they were here.

They could always kill the humans later, if they decided they'd said too much.

"We were sent," the orc said, speaking Manspeak once more, "to find a relic of a forgotten god. But if you lot are here, the god ain't really forgotten, is he?"

"She," Alam corrected absently. "My particular sect personifies the World-Mother as female."

"Whatever. Point is, you worship her. Which means we're pretty well buggered."

"Kirol Syrreth had eighty billion druid sects," Gork muttered sourly, "and we just had to pick the one that's come back."

"Actually, quite a few of us have sprung back up in recent years," Mina announced proudly. "We're hardly the only one."

"But we *are* the one," Alam said, as though struck by a sudden revelation, "with so obvious and so famous a temple." He waved his hand upward, presumably indicating the small stone building in the circle above. "You came here specifically because you thought that this would be the best place to find such a relic." He frowned. "Alas, we no longer even have the relic that *we* need. . . ."

"Got it in one," Cræosh said. "But now, we need to get back and find some other place to look."

"That may not be quite as easy as it sounds," Alam said, his voice dropping. "I doubt very much that Gnarlroot and his minions will let you leave."

"Gnarlroot?" Fezeill asked from the rear. "That sounds like some floral blight."

Alam sighed. "In a way, I suppose it is." He wandered over to the nearest wall and placed his hand on the wood. "Let me start at the beginning then. Perhaps, when I'm done, we can help each other."

I truly doubt it, Cræosh thought. What he said was, "We're listening."

"All right. Hundreds of years ago, when the druids were a true power in this land, we—that is, they, my predecessors—wielded great magics. All the wonders of nature were theirs to protect, but also to control. They could summon weather at a whim, talk to animals with no more effort than you and I converse now. And every so often, they put the trees to work.

"It was one of the greatest of their spells, you see. Trees are quite strong, and they are capable of labors that hundreds of humans could not accomplish. How do you think they assembled the henges that make up so many of our sacred groves?"

"Right, trees. Got it." Cræosh sniffed. "So what the fuck happened upstairs? You not paying these guys enough?"

The acolyte shook his head. "When the Dark Lord came, so many centuries ago, he, um, *removed* most of the druidic sects. He felt they were a threat. In so doing, he also corrupted some of our holiest sites.

"That, in fact, is why we—and others like us, from other sects—are here now, in Kirol Syrreth. We seek to undo the damage caused so long ago."

"Should we be telling them all this?" Josiah asked quietly. "They *serve* the Dark Lord!"

"We have to work together on this, Josiah!" Alam retorted, then turned back to the squad. "As you are no doubt aware, war is coming."

"You know," Cræosh said thoughtfully, "I've heard that."

"We will not side with either faction," Alam said. "We have reason to abhor your Charnel King, certainly, but it is not our place to involve ourselves in such matters. We do not, however, have any wish to see the holy site we are working so hard to restore become a field of battle. And as you may have noticed, we are but a few days' travel from the Brimstone Mountains."

Another nod.

"We weren't sure what to do. The five of us are barely sufficient to fight off more than a small band of brigands, let alone legions of soldiers."

Five? The entire squad glanced uneasily about. They'd counted only three.

"And so, we decided—foolishly, perhaps—to attempt the great spell of old. We would have the trees themselves fight for us, as we could not."

Cræosh snorted. "You fucked it up big-time, didn't you?"

Alam nodded sadly. "I know not if we, in our ignorance, made a mistake, or if the Dark Lord's corruption twisted the intent of the spell. All I know is that what we got . . . was Gnarlroot.

"At first, he was the only tree to come alive. He was even helpful at first, albeit arrogant, rude, difficult to talk to. But after only a few days, he suddenly refused to do as we wished. He vanished back into the Thewl, and we thought he had just returned to his rest."

The young druid swallowed audibly. "He hadn't. Over the following days, other trees began animating. We caught occasional glimpses of Gnarlroot moving among them, although he never again came back to the ring itself. It was Josiah who first saw what was happening."

The other young man nodded. "I was out tending to the gardens when—when they surged into the river. Trees have no faces, I know. . . . But I'd swear there was murder in their expressions. The first of them took a swipe at me as I ran. I still have the scar on my back to show for it."

"We tried to dispel the magic," Alam broke back in. "We tried counterspells; we tried waiting them out; we even . . ." He blanched. "We even attempted a series of spells designed to slay all plant-life in sight. Nothing worked, and our situation was getting worse. It wasn't even just the trees anymore; Gnarlroot somehow started corrupting the animals as well."

Cræosh and Katim exchanged quick glances, remembering the two-headed serpent.

"Two days ago," Alam continued, "Emmet, the eldest of our order, went, we think, a little mad. He stole the Tree of Ever and fled into the caverns that hold the ancient altars, beneath this temple."

"What," Gimmol asked from atop the ogre, "is the Tree of Ever?"

"Our holiest symbol," the acolyte responded, somewhat startled to hear Manspeak from the gremlin. "It's a sculpture of an oak, perhaps this tall." He held his hands apart, one above the other. "It's made of petrified wood, you see. It's been a symbol of my order for uncountable generations. We use it to channel our magics. We could never have cast the tree animation spell without it. And without it, we have no chance of undoing that spell."

"Gnarlroot knows that," Mina said. "He knows that if he can get the Tree away from us, we can't stop him."

"You weren't doing a whole lot of good trying to stop him *with* the tree," Cræosh pointed out.

"I agree," Alam said. "And we think, in his own mind, that's why Emmet stole it. He believes he's protecting it from Gnarlroot. And perhaps he's right. I hardly think a walking tree could find its way down into the caverns. But it can't stay there! We believe we've found a way to reverse the spell. It's risky, and if it fails, we may lose our last defense against Gnarlroot. Nevertheless, we intend to try—but we need the Tree of Ever!"

"Wouldn't it help if all four of the rest of you were involved in this?" Gimmol asked. "I only see three."

"Yes, we are but three now. The final member of our order, Renard, left two days ago with a message for the other druidic sects. That way, if we fail, there will be someone to take our place in stopping Gnarlroot."

The squad, as one, began shifting from foot to foot. One or two of them even cleared their throats. "And, umm, exactly how was Renard planning to get past the trees?" Cræosh asked.

"He wore a charm that we hoped would repel the trees, and he traveled at the height of day. Gnarlroot and the others prefer the dark." Alam frowned. "Why?"

"We saw Renard in the forest," Gimmol told him. "The trees were, uh, neither repelled nor nocturnal."

"You're on your own," Cræosh confirmed. "No help from outside."

For a moment, the young druids all stood mute, fighting back tears.

"No help from outside," Alam finally repeated. "None, that is, but you."

"I'm sorry," Cræosh said, jamming a finger in his own ear and twisting. "I must have something trapped and dying in there. I thought I heard you say that you expected us to help you."

The acolyte didn't smile at all now. "That would be exactly what I said."

"Uh-huh. And exactly why are we gonna do that? Out of the goodness of our hearts? We have more than enough of our own shit to wade through without borrowing your ass to add to it. We are doing exactly one thing here, and that's leave."

"Really?" Mina asked, her tone suddenly condescending. "And what secret magics were *you* planning to use to get past the trees?"

Cræosh scowled, but Alam only nodded. "I'm afraid she's quite right, my friend. Gnarlroot was more than happy to let you in: more victims, you see. But I rather doubt he'll let you back out again so easily."

"We can be persuasive," the orc growled, but they could all see in his eyes that he knew they were right.

"Not here," the druid said. "I've no doubt that you're formidable indeed. But I want you to think about how hard it must be to chop down a tree when it's chopping back—with dozens if not hundreds of others waiting in queue. I don't think a force a hundred times the size of yours would have much of a chance.

"But if I were to have the Tree of Ever back in my possession, we could attempt the counterspell we've been working on. If it worked, Gnarlroot and his servants would return to their normal quiescent state, and you could go merrily on your way."

The goblins were being expertly and efficiently backed into a corner here, and they damn well knew it. Katim finally hissed, "Why have you not . . . gone below, then, to . . . retrieve the relic yourselves?"

"Or have you just been waiting for someone to conveniently show up and take all the risk?" Fezeill added.

Alam's face tightened, his mouth twisting in rage. "Don't you *ever* accuse my people and me of cowardice! Ever! We came here, to the heart of your lands, to restore this ancient shrine! We plan to stay, even with your war—*your* war, not ours—raging at our door!"

Cræosh quickly raised his hands. "Peace!" *For now, anyway.* "Fezeill didn't mean anything by that. He's an idiot. I've heard more intelligent conversation listening in on rutting warthogs."

The doppelganger opened his mouth to protest and then began hopping up and down and cursing as Gork punched him in the knee.

"But even discounting that," the orc continued, "it's a valid question."

"Yes, it is that," Alam said, calm once more. "The truth is, this building is not completely safe from Gnarlroot's minions. The three of us have to remain on constant guard. Our magics may not be much compared to our ancestors', but we're powerful enough working together. We must maintain the wards that keep the trees from tearing apart the building above. Were we to venture into the underground chambers, we might very well find this room filled with angry flora when we return, and we wouldn't be prepared to fight them off."

"So we get to go down there," Gimmol groused, "and find the relic, and then all you have to do is cast your spell?"

"I wouldn't say 'all,' exactly. But yes, that's the basic sequence of events."

"And what if your spell fails?" Cræosh asked. "You yourself said you didn't know if it was going to work. If it doesn't, we're still stuck here!"

The druid shrugged. "True. But they're better odds than you'll find any other way."

Briefly, the squad moved away from the watching acolytes and huddled in the room's far corner. "This shits," was the first thing out of Cræosh's mouth.

"I agree," Gork said. "I don't want to have anything to do with this."

Katim nodded, scowling. "And I despise . . . being forced to do . . . anything."

It was the orc's turn to nod. "Okay, so we're all agreed that we don't want to do this. So who's got the better idea?"

After a long, drawn-out moment of silence so still he could practically hear the roaches mating, he sighed. "That's what I thought. Here's another good one for you. Anybody think it's coincidence that this is happening now?"

"What—?" the bugbear began.

"If you ask me what 'coincidence' means, Nature-boy, I'm gonna break your leg."

"Jhurpess want to know what *Cræosh* means," Jhurpess pouted.

"Oh. I mean, of all the places we might have found the relic of a forgotten god, Queen Anne sends us to the one where the trees' bite is actually worse than their bark. What are the odds?"

"You think she knew?" Gimmol asked.

"I think she sensed a potential problem and saw the chance to kill two elves with one stone. Obviously, we're a lot more than the queen's errand runners." The orc sighed. "So now we get to be the *druids'* errand runners. Let's get this the hell over with."

Clearly unhappy, he trudged back over to the acolytes. "All right, where's the damn way down?"

Alam nodded. "It's right over here. I—"

"I'll show them," Josiah interrupted. "I'll go with them."

Cræosh and Alam turned as one to face the younger druid. "*What?*" Alam clearly wasn't sure he'd understood correctly. "Josiah, we need you up here! We—"

Josiah shook his head. "No, Alam. You and Mina can maintain the wards without me for a few hours. The one called Fezeill might be without tact, but he's not completely without sense."

"Oh, *thank* you," Fezeill gushed.

"We cannot ask them to go unguided, or to take this risk on our behalf while we stand up here and wait. One of us must go with them. My magics aren't as strong as yours or Mina's, so that makes me the logical choice."

"There's nothing logical about this at all!" Alam raged. "And I forbid you to go!"

Josiah smiled sadly. "And how, exactly, did you plan to stop me, Alam?" The head acolyte opened his mouth to reply, but no sound emerged. Josiah nodded. "We need the Tree, Alam. This is the best way to get it back. It, and maybe Emmet too, if he's come to his senses. I have to do this."

The older druid stared at him for a heartbeat more and then stepped back. "Very well, Josiah. Do as you feel proper. Mina and I will be waiting for your return." They clasped hands briefly, and then Alam moved away while the younger man approached the orc.

"If you and your people will follow me?"

"I don't know about this," Cræosh said. "Appreciate the thought and all, but I don't have time to be babysitting some tagalong down there. Why don't you just point us to the door?"

"Because the ancient druids kept a great deal of value in those caves, my friend, and they put powerful defenses in place to protect it. I may lack the power to bypass their magics, but I can *warn* you of them. Or would you rather face the magics of the ancient druids without that advantage?"

"Welcome aboard," Cræosh said.

Beyond the leftmost of several doors along the chamber's far wall, another stone stair delved even deeper into the darkness. It was smaller than the other, drawing a frustrated grunt from Belrotha, but large enough for them to make do. Josiah lit several torches from the brands on the wall, handed them out, and started down. Still unhappy and still lacking any choice, the goblins followed.

Something about this stair was different. It was colder, true, but that was probably just because of the greater depth. Somehow, though, it also felt more *isolated*, as though each step drew them farther from any semblance of the world they knew. Jhurpess, uncomfortable in confined spaces at the best of times, mewled and placed himself in the precise center of the stairway. His fingers drummed a nervous tattoo on the haft of his club. Gork, who had been about to sneak up behind the bugbear and scream, just to see what sort of reaction he would get, remembered the bugbear smashing Gimmol to a pulp so long ago and decided to save the prank for a cheerier occasion.

The steps finally stopped in a brief corridor—really more of a narrow room—that itself ended in an ancient wooden door. At least the ceiling was high enough for Belrotha to stand upright; let's hear it for ceremonial grandeur. "So what's behind the door?" Cræosh asked their native guide.

"Well," Josiah said slowly, "we know that there's a long cavern beyond, that eventually leads to the great altar itself. You'll see a couple more doors, one on each side of the passage. One leads to a ritual bathing chamber, the other to a series of changing rooms where priests donned their ceremonial garb once they'd been purified. There's probably not a whole lot of interest in either of them, but—"

"But Emmet could be hiding anywhere," Gork said.

The druid nodded. "Precisely."

"All right," Cræosh said. "Then let's get this door open and get on with it."

Josiah assured them, over and over, that however paranoid they were, the druids of old would never have warded the main entryway. It was used too often, there was too much risk of accidental harm. Nevertheless, Katim, Gork, and Gimmol had all gone over the door inch by inch before they were willing to let the others open it. And then, of course, when the young druid tried, he found that the portal was barred or barricaded from the opposite side. No amount of twisting the key or shoving at the door could make it budge so much as an inch.

Cræosh put a hand on the human's shoulder and pulled him away. "This," he told Josiah, "is why we carry a magic door-opener."

"A what?"

"You heard me. A magic door-opener. Belrotha?"

"Yeah?" the ogre asked.

"Open the door."

Josiah's shout of protest was completely buried by a resounding crash. Door, bar, brackets, lock, even part of the stone frame hurtled a few dozen yards, landed with a second crash, and skidded a few dozen feet more.

Cræosh blinked the dust from his eyes. The ogre was cupping one fist in the other and spewing a veritable diatribe (which, for her meant more than six words strung together) in her native tongue.

"Hey, you okay?" Gimmol asked, honest concern in his voice.

"Me got splinter in knuckle!" Another moment or two and she'd calmed enough to examine the wound. Gingerly, she plucked a sliver of oak the length of a sewing needle from her skin. "Lucky," she told the others. "It not go very deep."

Cræosh shook his head and proceeded into the corridor, dragging the benumbed acolyte behind him. It was the smell he noticed first: a strong scent, musky in a way, combining rot, mildew, and perhaps three or four hundred different types of mold and fungus. It had an edge, that aroma, stabbing at the upper nostrils. The sound of dripping water surrounded them, distorted enough by its own echo that they couldn't possibly pinpoint the source.

The cave—for indeed it was a cave, despite the ancient druids' attempts at carving it into a more friendly shape—was wide enough that the circle of torchlight barely brushed the walls. As Josiah had anticipated, each wall boasted a smaller version of the door Belrotha had just obliterated.

"All right," Cræosh said, once the others had followed them in. "I want . . ." He stopped as a sudden thought stuck him. "Josiah, which door is which?"

The druid blinked, staring off into the darkness where the formless wooden pulp that had once been a door had disappeared.

"Josiah!" Cræosh smacked him—very, very lightly, as they didn't want to kill him, not yet—across the face. The acolyte staggered, then shook his head.

"Oh! Umm, ceremonial baths on the left, cloakroom and changing rooms on the right."

"Okay." Cræosh mulled that over. "Right. Belrotha, you and Gimmol check out the bath. Everyone else, pick a dressing room. I want this place scoured fast so we can move on."

The ogre and the gremlin finished quickly enough, having found nothing at all of interest in the bathing chamber. A natural pool, glistening with very cold mineral water, sat in the center of the room, fed by a small waterfall—a "watertrickle," really—running down the far wall. A thin stone ledge ran around the pool about two feet down, and a ring of rotted wooden benches and stools circled it on dry stone. And that was it. They went to join the others.

Said others, it appeared, might have had a bit more luck. Three of the tiny cubicles—which Josiah laughingly called changing rooms, but which were, as Cræosh put it, "Not even big enough to get hard in"— had proven as boring and useless on the inside as they had appeared without. But Katim and Gimmol, who were searching the northern-most room and the southernmost room, respectively, each found a loose cloak peg on the wall. Both pegs were designed to rotate a half turn to the left, and both of them triggered a portion of the wall to slide open. The squad piled through the northern exit, eager to see what secrets might be stashed away in the hidden chamber. What they found, how-ever, was a walkway that did nothing more interesting than wind its way around to the southern of the two rooms.

"So what was the fucking point?" Gork muttered angrily.

Cræosh shrugged. "Who knows? Maybe it was a fuck passage."

The kobold blinked. "What?"

"For trysts," Katim explained. "Male goes to one . . . room to change, female . . . to the other, and they . . . meet in the middle."

"The druids would never do such a thing!" Josiah huffed.

"Yeah," Cræosh, Gork, and Katim all said as one. "Right." Disap-pointed at their lack of progress, they moved on up the corridor.

And with a single exception, that was the most interesting thing that happened for the next hour. They encountered said exception about a hundred yards into the cave, when Jhurpess stuck his head through a sizable crevice in the rock. Coming running in response to his startled— and avaricious—yelp, the others found gold. Once made up of an array of smaller ingots, it had been smelted into a single gargantuan block: a near-perfect cube, in fact, and just about a yard across! Had it been the source of the ancient sect's funding? A holy relic? An emergency stash?

The squad didn't know, and they didn't care. They just knew it was theirs now . . . Or it would have been, if they could only have taken it with them.

But alas, try as they might, they couldn't find a way to make it happen. Not even Belrotha could haul around a slab of gold that size, and they lacked both time and tools to carve it up. Finally, though it practically broke their hearts—and required them to literally drag Gork from the crevice, kicking and screaming—they left it behind.

More weary trudging through more darkened cave. Cræosh was giving real thought to grabbing the acolyte and literally tossing him ahead to see how much farther the passageway ran when they heard echoes from up ahead. Not the pathetic little reverberations that had played upon their voices and their footsteps to this point, no. These could only indicate an *enormous* cavern. Heartened, the goblins quickened the pace.

They became somewhat less heartened when the corridor came to a sudden end. Oh, it was a large cavern all right; the meager light they carried couldn't even begin to reach the far walls. What they *hadn't* counted on was the lake. The corridor simply halted, forming a small lip jutting out into the water. And from there, there was simply no place to go. They stood, exposed and uncertain, all but the furriest of them shivering in the damp chill.

Cræosh felt a growl congealing in his throat. He snagged Josiah by the front of his robe and yanked him around so they stood face-to-face. "As a guide," he said, his breath bringing tears to the acolyte's face, "you make a pretty good rock."

"There were supposed to be stepping-stones," Josiah whispered, his gaze flitting constantly between the orc and the sloshing waters. "That— that's how the druids of old crossed to their main altar. Stepping-stones."

"Maybe once," Katim said from the edge, staring out over the lake as best she could, "but . . . not anymore. I see nothing except . . . water."

"Fuck," Cræosh informed them. "Fuck, fuck, fuck, and maybe even fuck. What do we do now?"

"Well," Josiah began, "if you're willing to risk—"

The orc jerked the acolyte off his feet and held him dangling over the dark depths. "Listen, you little daisy-plucking candy-ass! If you even *suggest* swimming, you're the first one in the water—headfirst, with two broken arms. Even assuming we all knew how to swim, that water's colder than a vampire's tit! Plus, I don't have a clue what's taken up residence in there since this place was used last, and I'm not willing to trust that you do either." Slowly, he lowered Josiah back to the ledge. "Now. Did you have a suggestion?"

"No," the druid said, brushing himself off and straightening his wrinkled robe. "Not really."

"I'm so glad. Anyone else?"

For once, he didn't get the complete silence he expected. "Actually," Gork said, "I might."

You wouldn't think that you could *hear* the rolling of eyes, but that was the sound that followed, from several different angles. "And what would that be, oh wise one?" Fezeill asked.

"We just need another raft."

Cræosh's fist clenched. "And just where are we supposed to get that, you insipid little turd? Snap our fingers, tap our heels, and hope the cheerful fairies decide to help us out?"

"Not really," the kobold replied, "although it might be fun to watch." Then, as the twisting of the orc's face suggested that it might be time to get to the point, he continued, "But wood floats. Especially flat wood. And between the bathing chamber and the changing rooms, we've got over half a dozen doors that nobody's using."

"What?" Josiah asked weakly. They ignored him.

"I don't know," Cræosh said after a moment. "You don't think those doors might be pretty rotted through by now?"

But now it was Katim shaking her head. "They all appeared to be in . . . fairly decent shape when we . . . were examining them. I imagine the . . . druids used some of their . . . magic, or perhaps some . . . herbs and salves, to preserve their . . . furnishings." She shrugged. "It certainly couldn't . . . hurt to find out."

Fezeill snorted. "Funny how that sentence is invariably followed by copious quantities of pain."

"What 'copious' mean?" Jhurpess asked.

"It mean you copy something," Belrotha explained. "Dumb bugbear."

As they had no better ideas, and as neither the druid's protests nor the ogre's grammar lessons were worth listening to, they trudged all the way back and examined the doors more thoroughly. Sure enough, they were in surprisingly good shape, all things considered. Some rotten spots, some speckles of mold, but by and large they remained quite solid. If they could be secured together, they might indeed make a serviceable raft. Like a procession of ants, they toted the doors *back* to the ledge and began unwinding several lengths of rope.

"See, Fezeill?" Gimmol taunted. "You were wrong, back in Jureb Nahl. It *is* as easy as simply tying some logs together."

Again the doppelganger snorted. "You're not just an idiot, you're a *stupid* idiot. A guppy could capsize this thing. It wouldn't have lasted twenty yards in the swamp."

"Maybe," Cræosh said, digging a hole in the wood with a dagger so he could thread the rope through. "But the water here's pretty calm, and we'll be going really damn slow, and you're gonna shut the fuck up as of right now unless you got a better idea."

"*I* can turn into something that can swim here," the doppelganger said smugly.

"Yeah? If it's a mermaid, make sure she's stacked."

Fezeill lapsed into silence, quite possibly overcome with revulsion at the thought of becoming an object of orc lust.

But he did, much as Cræosh hated to admit, have a point. When all was said and done, their "raft" looked none too solid. They would have to lie on their stomachs, try to spread out the weight, attain *some* measure of stability. They'd have to make the crossing in multiple groups. And there was simply no way at all the rickety thing would support Belrotha's massive frame. They tried to make her feel better about staying behind—"The rearguard is the most important position," Gimmol told her—but even she wasn't *that* stupid. There was, however, not a damn thing to be done about it.

Leaving behind half the squad and a sulking ogre, the first group carefully boarded the raft and set out for the center of the lake, where, according to Josiah, their destination waited. They paddled in brief, unpleasant bursts as one or the other dipped a hand into the frigid water just long enough to provide some slight momentum.

The cavern was even colder than the corridors had been, and the icy spray sloshing over the sides of the makeshift vessel didn't help matters. Even the troll and bugbear found themselves shivering. Sporadic ripples nearby suggested the presence of something moving beneath the surface. It was, Josiah assured them, nothing more threatening than cave fish, and while they didn't precisely trust him on that, nothing came close enough to bother them.

Damp but determined, uncomfortable but unharmed, they arrived. Katim, Jhurpess, and Gork disembarked, while Josiah took the skiff back for the others. One hand resting idly on the haft of her axe, Katim began exploring the tiny islet.

It wasn't really anything more than the tip of a rock that either rested on, or protruded from, the cavern floor. Vaguely hexagonal in shape, it rose only a few inches above the surrounding waters; one good wave would have swamped it, had the lake actually produced any waves.

In the island's center, safe from whatever tiny tides the placid lake *might* generate, was a low-slung table. About as long as Cræosh was tall, it was carved from black marble and fused with the rock of the island itself. Definitely magic, for what Katim had first taken to be expert craftsmanship revealed itself, upon closer inspection, to be a true and seamless melding of the two types of stone. Etchings ran the length of the marble, nearly invisible in the feeble light. They appeared to be more primitive versions of the patterns in the wood upstairs.

And then, having deliberately examined everything else first, the troll turned to the islet's most prominent feature. Behind the table, or altar, or whatever it was, rose a ponderous statue of the same black marble. It was carved to resemble a human (or at least a humanoid), clad in robes not dissimilar to those worn by Josiah and the other acolytes. The face within the hood was a flat expanse of stone, reminding Katim of Rupert, Queen Anne's seneschal.

In only one way did it deviate from the human norm, in that it had three arms: two on the right, one on the left. The two "proper" arms pointed out and downward, while the third was held out before the statue, index finger pointing up. On its chest, beside that extra arm, were over a dozen lines of shallow scratches that might or might not have been deliberate.

As Katim could find no clue to aid her in deciphering whatever meaning or symbolism the statue was meant to convey, she quickly grew bored. And more bored still, when Josiah returned with the others, since Cræosh, Gimmol, and Fezeill insisted on repeating the examination she'd just concluded.

"And?" Cræosh asked when he was done. "What the fuck now?"

"Obey the statue," the acolyte said.

"What? Boy, if you don't start making some sort of sense . . ."

Josiah shook his head. "Hey, I've never been down here either, okay? I'm trying to piece this all together from ancient writings." He frowned thoughtfully. "Even back then," he said more softly, "the druids had enemies. The members of this sect constructed a hidden chamber in which they stored their holiest items, their most powerful magics, and a library that was said to equal, if not surpass, that of King Sabryen himself. If Emmet figured out how to get down to it, that's most likely where he'd be hiding."

"Great," Fezeill said, his patience obviously running as thin as the orc's. "How helpful. So how do we find it?"

"As I said, obey the statue. Sect writings say only that the statue points the way."

"Yeah," the doppelganger countered, "but it's pointing three different directions!"

Josiah shrugged. "I don't know, dammit!"

It was Katim's turn to grab Josiah by what was at this point becoming a very rumpled collar. "What about these?" she asked, practically shoving his nose into the markings she'd noticed. "Did the druidic sects not . . . have their own script?"

"I don't believe it!" Josiah whispered. "I haven't seen the ancient script anywhere except our oldest books!" Then, "Ah, give me a minute, if you please. It's been some time since I've had to translate this sort of writing."

Katim stepped away, allowing the young druid to go about his work. Somewhat impressed despite himself, Cræosh appeared at her shoulder.

"Nice thinking, Dog-breath. I thought those were just random scratches. The damage of years, maybe."

"One of the . . . many advantages of possessing . . . a brain," she said, choosing not to mention that she'd initially thought the same. "Perhaps you should . . . give some thought to acquiring one . . . the next time we're in town."

"I've got it!" Josiah announced, saving the orc the trouble of responding. "But, um, I don't know that it helps us. It's just a few random passages from our holy books."

"Great," Cræosh said. "Fucking nutcases, the whole lot of you. This is what worshipping gods does to a person. . . ."

"Read them to us," Gimmol suggested.

Josiah did just that, and yep, they sounded like the standard doggerel to be found in any of the human faiths. For a long while, the goblins and the druid milled about in silence.

"Well," the gremlin said finally, "it starts with a passage about your sect being the 'one chosen' to speak for the World-Mother, right? And that extra finger could mean one, too."

"One, two?" Jhurpess asked.

"No, not 'one, two.' *One, too*."

"Three, four," the bugbear continued, puzzled.

Gimmol shook his head.

"So . . . What?" Fezeill asked. "One of what?"

"Two other hands," Cræosh said. "We're supposed to pick one, maybe?"

Katim scowled. "This is awfully . . . convoluted."

"I'd have said stupid," Gork corrected.

But Josiah was shaking his head. "No, it makes sense. Instructions that nobody outside the order could puzzle out." He frowned. "There are two different references to the forces of evil as 'the right hand of darkness.'"

"Something to be avoided, then?" Cræosh asked.

"I'd think so, yes."

"Anything about *left* hands in there? Or left *anything*?"

"Not a mention."

"Good!" Jhurpess said, clearly having gotten tired of waiting around. "Then Jhurpess will go left!" Before anyone could react, the bugbear vaulted over to the left side of the altar and begun fiddling with the arm. With an ominous click, the pointing finger twisted in his hands.

The altar and the stone to which it was fastened slid aside on brilliantly concealed tracks, as smoothly as if they'd been oiled just yesterday. And that was followed immediately after by a deafening roar and a torrent of flame that towered all the way to the cavern's ceiling.

The smell of charred flesh and burnt dust assailed their nostrils; embers rained down upon the entire squad, singing skin and setting clothes and fur alight. Jhurpess avoided roasting into shriveled jerky only because the blast sent him staggering back into the lake, where his flaming fur was quenched with a loud hiss.

Katim followed with a quick dip of her own, putting out her own smoldering hair, though she kept a tight grip on the island's edge. The others hopped around the isle, beating the sporadic flames from their clothes.

The tower of flame died, and the altar slid back into place of its own accord.

"Of course," Josiah said, absently fingering a singed hole in his sleeve, "it might have meant the *statue's* left, not ours."

Cræosh, who had a truly impressive welt running down the right side of his face, stomped over and placed his nose less than six inches from Josiah's own. "I really," he informed the druid, "really, *really* want to kill you."

Behind him, a sequence of wet splats and some sniffling whimpers announced the return of the sodden bugbear to solid ground.

"So," Gimmol said with a feeble grin, "what now?"

What now, indeed? The missive on the statue had told them to make but one choice, and apparently it was going to hold them to that. A frantic check confirmed that the finger on the other hand refused to move, no matter how hard they twisted at it.

"Okay," Cræosh muttered. "Fine. So we do it the hard way."

"It would be a great . . . deal easier if we could have . . . brought Belrotha with us," Katim said.

"Yeah, it would be, but she ain't here. That's why it's the *hard* way. You up for this, troll?"

Katim's snout rumpled in a sarcastic grin. "Lead the way."

Since the fire had emerged from beneath the altar, the only possible location left for the *real* hidden passage was beneath the statue itself. It took them over an hour, with Cræosh, Katim, Jhurpess (singed and whining), and Fezeill (still in bugbear form) taking turns, but eventually they succeeded in reducing the sculpture into chunks so tiny that they'd have had to work out to become smithereens. One final blow from Cræosh and the heavy portal concealed beneath finally swung inward, dangling uselessly from broken hinges.

Of course, they weren't about to dull their blades against the stone. No, the tools they'd chosen were the arms of the statue itself, broken loose with the aid of Jhurpess's club. Josiah remained seated beside the altar, limbs sprawled, gazing in horror at the ruined sculpture.

The hanging trapdoor revealed only a series of metal rungs descending infinitely into the darkness. With a few more choice curses directed at the druids, at Gnarlroot, even at Queen Anne, they began to climb.

Fezeill went first, carefully testing each rung with his prehensile feet. He had descended well over thirty yards into growing darkness, the others following carefully behind (and, in some instances, panting with the exertion), when he suddenly halted.

"I'm not taking another step," he announced, "until we do something about the light."

"What light?" Cræosh asked from directly above.

"My very point."

"Heh. And just what exactly do you propose we do?"

"I don't care. Just do *something*."

Gork yanked a torch from Katim's pack, lit it, and let it drop. The flame flickered dramatically, but it didn't go out, and the plummeting brand halted not twenty feet below the doppelganger's toes, illuminating a rough stone floor. That, apparently, was enough to alleviate Fezeill's doubts, and the faux-bugbear quickly shimmied down the rest of the way, moving the torch and stepping aside so his companions might follow.

Cræosh was next off the ladder, his boots echoing against the stone. He lit a torch of his own off Fezeill's, but even the pair of them struggled to penetrate the gathered gloom. The orc cursed once, vilely even for him.

"All right! Everybody—and I mean *everybody*—grab a torch. I wanna see just what the fuck we've gotten ourselves into. That means you too, druid."

Entire constellations of sparks speckled the underground night as flint and steel scraped together, and the feeble glow of those first torches was quickly augmented by five more. And that, finally, was enough to let them see.

"What the fuck . . . ?" Cræosh asked eloquently.

"Oh, good," Josiah said. "We're here."

"Here" was a perfectly square platform of stone, perhaps forty feet on a side. In fact, it appeared to be the top of a squared pillar, for there was nothing but a deep, dark drop on every side. Equidistant between the four corners, a thin case of metal stairs descended from the platform. Each connected, about twenty feet out and fifteen down, with a stone catwalk. It, too, was a square, and it, too, had staircases descending from it. These reached beyond the torchlight, but Josiah assured them that they connected to *another* stone walkway beyond the first.

"So, um, 'concentric squares,' is it?" Gork said.

"Well, yes, basically," the acolyte admitted. "That's as accurate as anything."

"I see. And are *all* druids this insane? Or just ancient dead ones?"

"Uh . . ."

"What's down there?" Gimmol asked, gesturing toward the nearest edge. Given the catch in his voice, the others imagined that he was probably reliving his near-fatal plunge back on the Steppes.

"Down there—is down," Josiah told him. "To the best of my knowledge, not even the ancients knew. They used magic to hew this place from the rock, but even they had no real idea how far down it went. My best advice would be: don't fall."

"Gee," Gimmol said sourly. "Thanks ever so much. So much as one worm pops up, I'm gone so fast. . . ."

"So what's the damn point?" Cræosh asked. "What the hell is this place, and what the even more hell are we doing here?"

"Come with me to the outermost walkway," Josiah said, "and I'll show you."

They chose the northern stairs—entirely at random, for lack of any better way to decide—and crept with excruciating care across the narrow metal steps. Even Katim and Gork, either of whom could most probably have skipped down the stairs blindfolded, seemed oppressed by the seemingly infinite drop below.

There were, it turned out, three sets of rings—well, squares—surrounding the center platform. Gork was the first to reach the outermost. Peering out over the unguarded edge, he saw nothing but darkness, and a whole lot of it. Nothing below, nothing beyond—they might as well have stood in the center of an infinite void.

One that could not, frankly, have existed in the soft earth beneath Ymmech Thewl, but Gork had dealt with enough magic lately that he'd long since ceased to consider the laws of nature to be anything more than friendly advice.

"I think now would be a marvelous time for an explanation," Fezeill suggested. Everyone looked at Josiah expectantly. It took him a moment to answer, for he gawked raptly about; a few tears of wonder trailed down his cheeks.

"Symbolism," he said finally, in an unknowing echo of Queen Anne. "Both sacred and mystical. The four elements, the four winds, the four seasons. Earth, sun, moon, and stars. Childhood, adulthood, old age, and death. Most druidic iconography is circular, but the holiest, most important? Patterns of four. Oh, I'd never hoped to see this . . ."

Katim nodded. "And so, four levels of . . . squares. Four times four. How . . . primitive."

"Okay, yeah, symbolism," Cræosh muttered impatiently. "Great.

But all this"—and here he waved vaguely, as though the others could possibly have failed to realized what he was talking about—"seems just a little excessive."

"This was the heart of one of the greatest druidic sects," Josiah huffed, drawing himself up. "Such a shrine calls for nothing *less* than magnificence!"

"What's wrong with gold fixtures over a simple altar?" Gork complained. "I *like* gold fixtures. . . ."

"Somewhere here," the druid said, "is hidden the entrance to the repository of the ancients. We just have to find it."

It didn't take long, as this outer catwalk wasn't entirely featureless. At each of the four corners was a wooden door within a freestanding frame: a door that pretty obviously led nowhere at all, since they all faced out onto emptiness.

"Well, this," Gork said, his tone very similar to Cræosh's, "is starting to really chafe my buttocks."

"The ancient druids," Cræosh told Josiah, "were some sick bastards. This whole thing is the result of a truly twisted sense of humor. Were they *smoking* their holy symbols, by any chance?"

The acolyte, however, only smiled. "It's more magnificent than I'd ever imagined!" he whispered softly.

"Huh?" the orc asked.

"I agree," said Gork. "Huh?"

"Open the door," Josiah told them.

"Umm, hello? Anybody home?" Cræosh actually rapped lightly on the man's skull. "Anyone? There's nothing behind the door, human! I can bloody well see that *without* opening the damn thing!"

The druid would not be swayed, however. "Open the door," he repeated.

Gork and Cræosh both continued to stare.

"Which one?" Gimmol asked timidly.

"I doubt it matters. Patterns of four, remember? They probably all lead to the same place."

Gork and Cræosh continued to stare. Katim finally grew sick and tired of the lot of them, stormed over, and yanked the door open.

Instantly, the other two that they could see, way down the catwalks, vanished from their corners; the goblins could only assume that the fourth had disappeared as well.

"Of course," she said, gazing through the doorway. Beyond lay a brown-carpeted, smooth-walled corridor, albeit only a couple of yards long. Along the rightmost wall, in a shallow alcove, stood a statue, a smaller variant of the hooded figure above. At the hallway's end was yet another door, on which was carved a massive tree.

Slowly, one hand firmly on the hilt of his sword, the orc approached. He peered through the doorway, very slowly and very methodically taking in every detail of the short corridor. He then stepped to the side and stuck his head around the door frame and peered equally long at the vast emptiness.

"Have I mentioned lately," he inquired of the room at large, "just how much I'm growing to despise magic?"

Katim tapped him on the shoulder, waited until he moved aside, and shook loose her *chirrusk*. Sniffing furiously for any sign of deception that her other senses might miss, she tossed the hooked end into the passage. It landed with a muffled thump on the thick carpet, exactly as it should have done. Slowly she dragged it back, its barbs leaving deep furrows in both the shag and the thick layer of dust that coated it.

"Well," she said, "the floor certainly seems . . . real enough."

"Unless your hook thingy *did* fall through," Gork pointed out, "and an illusion just made it look like it didn't."

It was the druid who solved the dilemma for them by simply stepping into the hallway. "You coming?" he called back over his shoulder. "This has got to be the library! If Emmet's alive, he must be in here!"

Stepping as lightly as possible, with many a mistrustful glance at the floor, they crept in one at a time and followed. Despite the surfeit of dust, and the fact that this hallway hadn't been used in centuries (with the possible exception of a maddened Emmet), no mildew marred the walls, no rot perfumed the air. The corridor was odorless and ageless.

"Okay, boys and bitch," Cræosh said as he reached the second door. "Stay alert. One side, Shorty." The orc leaned back and launched a kick that a warhorse might envy.

Wood cracked, and the portal swung with a thundering retort. Immediately Cræosh leapt through, hands tight on his sword hilt, Katim on his heels and the others following after. What they saw was enough to impress even the least literate among them.

"Many books," Jhurpess said succinctly.

"Wow. I didn't know you could count to 'many,' Nature-boy."

Globes, drifting in lackadaisical patterns up near the ceiling, glowed without benefit of visible flame, shedding a painfully white illumination throughout the room. Walls that stood twice the height of the troll and stretched on for dozens of yards were lined almost to the last inch with bookshelves. A gargantuan hardwood table ran down most of the length of the room; it, too, had bookshelves built into it along the center.

And all these shelves were full to bursting: Leather-bound or wood-bound, neatly stitched or haphazardly stuffed into covers, small as a human's handspan to large as a heavy shield, and written in more languages than the entire squad had ever heard of. Cræosh hadn't thought there were so many books in the whole of Kirol Syrreth and the Allied Kingdoms combined.

Gimmol, with a faint squeak of ecstasy, made a beeline for one of the shelves across the room. The others, rather less taken by the sundry tomes, retained sufficient presence of mind to notice—even if it did take them longer than it should—that they were not alone in the great library. Sitting at the far end of the obscenely long table was an older human clad in robes similar to Josiah's. His hair looked as though it had once been a bird's nest until it was condemned for safety reasons, and if his cheeks had even seen a razor in weeks, it was only in artists' renderings. Trembling, bloodless fists clutched a small wooden icon, over which he was mumbling an endless stream of slurred syllables.

He spotted the goblins at about the same moment they spotted him, and he rose from his chair. His lips curled, and while Cræosh wasn't precisely an expert in spellcraft, it certainly appeared that the sounds he was making now were a whole lot more dynamic than his previous mutterings.

"Stop him," the orc snapped at Josiah, "or *we* will!"

The young acolyte advanced, one hand extended in supplication. "Emmet!" he called. "Emmet, it's me!"

The older druid seemed not to hear.

"We've been looking for you, Emmet," Josiah continued, slowly covering the length the table. "I've been looking for you. I couldn't have found you without the help of these kind folk." He grinned—a wide, exaggerated expression that did ugly things to his face. "Wasn't it nice of them to help me find you, Emmet? Thank the nice people, Emmet."

The hairs on Cræosh's neck stood tall and saluted as a thick blanket of dread fell over the library. Something was very, very wrong.

"Josiah," Gork called from behind the orc, "what are you doing?"

The acolyte ignored him. "And now that we've found you, Emmet, you have to go away. Good-bye, Emmet."

With the sound of wet parchment and a faint crimson spray, the young man's outstretched palm split down the middle. From within uncoiled a twisting tendril of wood and leaves. It whipped across Emmet's face as he tried to spin away; shredded skin and shattered skull glistened in the phantom light. Having passed completely through the old man's head, the branch continued onward, dripping with gore, halting only when the tip had firmly buried itself in a bookcase along the far wall.

For long seconds the old man's body stood—as though merely confused by what had happened—and the goblins gaped, overwhelmed and disbelieving. And then Emmet spasmed, legs and feet beating an impromptu dance across the rapidly reddening floor. His fingers unclenched, and the Tree of Ever toppled from his fists.

Even faster than before, the tendril ripped free of the bookcase and retracted toward the arm of the thing they had called Josiah. What remained of Emmet's skull blew apart, and the holy relic hadn't even reached the floor before it was snagged in digits of leaf and twig.

By now, the squad had shaken off their paralysis, minds finally catching up with their eyes. Expressions grim and weapons raised, they spread out across the library, alert for any twitch of that grotesque, impossible limb.

"So hostile?" Josiah asked, his grin growing even wider. The skin on either side of his mouth had begun to tear. "I thought we were friends."

"Gnarlroot, I . . . presume?" Katim rasped.

"Why, there's actually a brain among you," Josiah—Gnarlroot—said. "How remarkable."

"And Josiah?" Cræosh asked, stalling for time (and, frankly, for the faintest idea of what the hell to do). "What about him?"

Still the grin grew. Blood was leaking from the sides of "Josiah's" face, revealing the wood within. "So simple, really. A tiny scratch, back when the fools thought that *I* served *them*. I planted a seed, enough to begin the transfer of my newly awakened mind. He felt me germinating inside, felt every instant as I consumed his innards. I wouldn't even give him the freedom to scream. Emmet had by far the easier death." The grin faded. "But we do what we can. I'll not be so quick next time."

"Next time?" Cræosh asked. *Wait for it . . .* "You wouldn't have anyone in particular in mind, would you?"

"Well, since you asked . . ."

It was an obvious cue. Blades and blunt objects rose, and over half a ton of angry goblin converged on the druid-wearing tree.

They never reached him. The skin of Josiah's face finally split completely, peeling away in flakes resembling a layer of wax, and then the acolyte burst like an overripe melon. Cræosh was flattened by the concussion, and Gork and Gimmol both flew through the air to land painfully amid tattered pages. A monsoon of blackened, half-congealed blood coated the library. Scraps of sodden skin stuck to clothes and exposed flesh, tiny pennants flapping with every movement.

Fezeill, farthest from the carnage, was the first to blink the gore from his eyes, and the nigh-unflappable doppelganger stood stunned by what he saw. Gnarlroot, the *true* Gnarlroot, stood exposed in the midst of tattered rags that had once been Josiah's skin and clothes. It couldn't have fit inside an overweight yeti, let alone crammed itself into a human, but somehow it had managed. Covered in bark, spotted with leaves, yes, but this was no tree; it had no trunk, no branches in any normal sense of the word. Had some mad vivisectionist acquired an array of thick, rubbery tentacles—perhaps the limbs of an obscenely fat octopus—pasted bark all over them and tied them about the middle so they formed a single sheaf of limbs, writhing at the top and bottom, this *thing* might have been the result. It loomed over them, its uppermost tendrils screeching against the stone ceiling like fingernails on glass.

"Well," Katim said, her *chirrusk* beginning to hum as it whirled at her side, "this is not . . . the most promising event of the . . . day."

Half the library abruptly filled with wooden whips and bark-skinned spears. Katim jumped high, feet curled tightly beneath her, clearing the first barrage by inches. She swung her axe in a blow that should have severed one of those limbs before her boots touched the floor, but the edge only scraped across a surface far stronger than any armor. She retreated, weapons at the ready to parry.

Cræosh, too, had learned the hard way that his sword was nigh useless; his mightiest blow, though scoring a deeper wound than the troll's axe, had not even drawn . . . Blood? Sap? Whatever. Jhurpess's club rebounded harmlessly, and the rest of the squad's blades couldn't even penetrate the bark.

Gnarlroot, unfortunately, wasn't nearly so ineffectual. Here, a jagged needle of splinters drew a wail of pain from Jhurpess, left a ragged and bloody furrow down the bugbear's arm. There, a branch slammed Cræosh over the central table to land in a boneless heap on the other side of the room. Unsteadily, the orc dragged himself to his feet, but the side of his face was already turning a bruised and mottled brown. Katim's mighty axe and swiftly whipping *chirrusk* parried tendril after tendril, but she could deflect only so many attacks. It was only a matter of moments, and not many of those, before one would get through.

The Demon Squad was about to fall, and every one of them knew it.

And then Gimmol entered the fray. He'd extricated himself from the heap of ravaged books and stood at the rear of the library, forgotten not only by the foe but by his fellow soldiers. And no wonder. He was Gimmol the joke; Gimmol the useless appendage, the gremlin who'd been assigned Demon Squad duty either by some cosmic screw-up or by a superior so incompetent he probably needed a compass to find "up."

He'd hoped, despite the grief it caused him, to keep it that way. Gimmol had never wanted to stand out, never wanted to be anything but another gremlin. He'd already been disowned by his family, who couldn't understand how he could be . . . what he was. He'd spent his entire military career avoiding posts where it might come out, but somehow the Charnel King's wraiths had known. They must have; there was no other reason to choose him. And *still* he'd hoped . . .

Hell, he wasn't even that *good* at it, really. His greatest fear—well, second-greatest, after worry that one of his companions would throttle him in his sleep—was that the squad would come to rely on him, that they'd expect him to pull them out of a jam that was far beyond his capabilities.

But now, none of that mattered, not against a foe for whom all the squad's vaunted skills, their weapons of murder and mayhem, were meaningless. Gimmol took another step, raised his hands, and finally did what he'd been assigned to the Demon Squad to do.

Gimmol cast a spell.

Swords and axes and clubs froze in midswing; eyes went wide and jaws hung slack as a stream of crackling flame flashed from the gremlin's palm into the side of the thing called Gnarlroot. The unnatural bark refused to ignite, but the roar of pain—and yes, they all could hear it, of fear—was enough to shake the walls. Several of the more precariously balanced tomes fell from the shelves with a series of dull thunks, and the Tree of Ever tumbled from the branches to bounce from table to floor.

"How . . . how . . . ?" Gimmol grinned wide to see Fezeill at a loss for words.

"Well," he said, wiping a gathering film of sweat from his forehead, "you didn't think I was *just* the comic relief, did you?" And then he spun from the doppelganger-turned-bugbear to the stammering kobold. "And we won't be having any more misunderstandings about my hat, will we?"

Gork was saved the indignity of a reply by Gnarlroot's sudden and redoubled efforts to kill the lot of them. Clearly, the tree-thing was no longer playing; it wanted them dead, and fast. They were finally a real threat.

That, and the room was on fire.

Much of Gimmol's flaming burst had spattered from the unnatural bark, and quite a few of the nearest bookshelves were crackling merrily away. It was now an even bet as to whether the writhing tendrils could pulp the life out of the goblins before the thickening smoke suffocated the lot of them.

Frowning now, Gimmol sent a second bolt of fire into the murderous bole, and then a third. Each time the beast howled, each time it cringed, pained and clearly terrified, but the gremlin just didn't have the power to put the thing down. Sweat gushed from his pores, and not merely due to the rising heat; much more of this, and he'd be too exhausted to continue. . . .

"All right, the fire's not cutting it!" Gork shouted. "What else you got?"

"Lots," Gimmol retorted, flinching as another nearby bookcase went up. "But nothing that'll work even as well as the fire!"

"Nothing," Gork muttered, passing his *kah-rahahk* from hand to hand, desperately seeking some way to help. He saw the troll's muzzle whip around toward him, her hypersensitive ears perking up at his mutter. And somehow, without a word exchanged, he understood.

"Can you handle something . . . that large?"

"If you can get him there, I'll find a way."

With a quick nod and a shouted "Jhurpess!" Gork vanished into the billowing smoke and flickering shadow, the puzzled bugbear trailing behind with many a glance back at his beleaguered allies.

"Cræosh!" Katim roared. "Fezeill!" Even as she ducked a tendril, she pointed her axe toward three others that were thrashing across the table, reaching for the sorcerous gremlin. The orc scowled, but moved to intercept, the faux-bugbear at his side.

Safe behind a wall of armor and muscle, if only for an instant, Gimmol himself flashed a glance Katim's way. She pointed again, first toward Gnarlroot, then to the far end of the library. When the gremlin blinked in confusion, she sighed and charged, tucking into a roll beneath another swipe, and came up on the tree's far side.

Smoke curled around the chain as Katim spun her *chirrusk*, once, twice, and then slammed it into the burning bookcase. When she hauled it free, flaming wood and rapidly disintegrating books clung to the prongs. It wasn't much of a flame, but as she swung, Gnarlroot—perhaps disoriented by the gremlin's attacks—retreated a few steps toward the entryway. Again she pointed, and this time Gimmol understood.

A prolonged blast of flame followed—not so hot nor so forceful as the others, for Gimmol was struggling to conserve his remaining strength—but sufficient. Gnarlroot's nerve broke, if only briefly. Battered by eldritch fire, surrounded by ever-spreading quantities of more mundane but equally hot flame, the wooden creature decided to take the fight elsewhere. On scuttling limbs, it retreated from the inferno, into the abbreviated hall beyond the library. And there it stood, just beyond the door, free of the blaze.

And, for that matter, blocking their own exit.

"Great idea, Dog-face," Cræosh growled, his throat raw with smoke.

Katim hunched her shoulders, crouched to make breathing easier, and waved at the gremlin. Face set in a determined scowl, Gimmol advanced and hurled yet another flaming bolt (the last he could manage, in point of fact, without taking some time to rest up and recover). Gnarlroot flinched, the carpet in the hallway ignited, and the tree retreated farther, onto the stone catwalk beyond.

The catwalk, where nothing remotely flammable stood, where the creature could ward the door at its leisure and keep the goblins from escaping the choking smoke. As though making up for the lack of head to throw back, the uppermost limbs stiffened as Gnarlroot laughed.

"You fools!" No trace of Josiah remained in that hideous, grating voice. It was the sound of splintering wood, granted a vocabulary of rage and hate. "You've doomed yourselves! I do not tire. I do not weaken. I am relentless, inexorable! To you and all your pitiful kind, I am death! There is nothing I cannot do! *Nothing!*"

"Oh, yeah?" With an impossible nonchalance, Gork sauntered from the shadows a few yards along the ledge. He planted his hands on his hips and smiled. "Can you fly?"

From where he'd hung one-handed behind the open door, hidden by the passageway that shouldn't exist, Jhurpess flipped over the doorframe and launched himself screaming at Gnarlroot. In his other hand he held his great club . . .

A club wrapped in burning rags.

With thundering blows, Jhurpess drove the creature back, ever back. He bounded from foot to hand to foot, avoiding and sometimes even clinging to thrashing branches, never where Gnarlroot expected him to be. Gork would never admit it to another living soul, but in that moment, he was seriously impressed with the idiotic furball.

Still it wasn't enough. Gnarlroot teetered on the very edge of the seemingly infinite drop, leaning back from the flaming club, but *would not fall*. Branches scrabbled tight at the lip of the stone, and the terrible timber was already overcoming its instinctive fear, beginning to recognize that the flames on the bugbear's club were insufficient to do it much harm.

And then, howling at the tops of smoke-choked lungs, Cræosh, Katim, and Fezeill charged from the hall, carrying a blazing length of the great table between them, a makeshift battering ram. Wood splintered against wood, burning embers fountained across the assembled squad, and Gnarlroot, with a final desperate scrabble of branches, was gone.

From the gaping dark rose a horrible scream, failing even to echo in the great abyss, giving voice to the last fears of a life lived over the span of centuries. It was the death cry of a tree, and it carried within the pain and suffering and loss of epochs. Slowly, slowly it grew faint, ever fainter, and was gone.

The squad collapsed to the stone, careful to avoid the precarious edges, hacking up smoke and wincing as every movement pulled burned skin uncomfortably taut. Jhurpess shook the rags from his club and let them flutter after the tree into the gloom below.

"Think he's dead?" Gork asked breathlessly after a few moments of panting.

"I could toss you over and you could go see," Cræosh offered. And then, to everyone's shock, "But that was pretty good work, Shorty. Hell, all of you. Nice job."

"Don't get used to it; I'd just as soon not have to do it again."

Again to everyone's shock, the orc chuckled at that.

But Gimmol was paying the repartee scant heed. He sat and gazed at the mystical hallway, from which smoke still poured. Uncountable books, any or all of which might have contained priceless knowledge, secrets to be found nowhere else in Kirol Syrreth or even the entire world—all gone.

Only two items of any import had survived the conflagration. One was the Tree of Ever, which the gremlin had scooped up on his way out, while the others were carrying a burning length of table. It wasn't even warm, let alone burnt, by the fires that had raged nearby.

The other was the tome that had grabbed his attention when they'd first entered, the one he'd been examining when Gnarlroot revealed its true nature. That book sat safely, now, in Gimmol's pouch, where he'd shoved it at the first sign of trouble. And he couldn't help but wonder if he'd just been remarkably fortunate, to spot the codex among all the others, or if he'd been somehow *meant* to find it.

He'd need to do some reading before he revealed his suspicions to the group; this wasn't the sort of thing about which he could afford to be mistaken. But if he was right, if the hints he'd seen in his brief flip through the book were right, they were potentially in greater danger now than they'd ever been since the day they assembled in that Timas Khoreth courtyard.

And so, for long minutes, while the others rested and recovered from their recent ordeal, the gremlin read.

Belrotha was quite happy to see them, and Gimmol in particular, as they emerged from the lake cavern. They gave her a brief accounting of what had happened. *Very* brief, actually, since she proved completely incapable of grasping the concept that Josiah had been Gnarlroot, and she just looked at the gremlin strangely when they tried to tell her of his newly revealed powers. She expressed her regret that "Me couldn't be there to break nasty tree," and lifted Gimmol back to his normal post on her shoulders. That, in turn, made it easy for him to resume his study of the book, which had been interrupted by the end of the squad's "break."

Had anyone been paying any real attention to him, they'd have seen his expression grow more and more clouded as they climbed the stairs back up to the druids' main chamber.

Mina and Alam, the only remaining druids of Ymmech Thewl, glanced up sharply from where they knelt beside the fire pit. The head acolyte rose, a huge grin spreading across his face, as the squad appeared in the doorway.

"I don't know how you did it," he said, even going so far as to clasp Cræosh on the shoulders, "but the trees have all gone back to normal! Mina and I were just giving our thanks when you came in."

"Back to normal," Gimmol said thoughtfully. "Gnarlroot must have been the focal point of the spell. Without him, the whole thing collapsed."

"Yeah," Cræosh snapped, somewhat less than ecstatic despite their hard-won victory. "Swell."

It finally penetrated through the acolyte's haze of joy and celebration that something was wrong. He removed his hands from the orc's shoulders and stepped back. "Something troubles you, my friend? What could . . . ? Where's Josiah?" he asked, his thoughts finally focusing in on the moment.

"Funny you should . . . ask," Katim said sourly.

Cræosh nodded, and then gave the druid a shove that sent him staggering halfway across the chamber. "You sent the damn tree with us, boy!"

"Wh-what?" Alam was clearly confused.

"Are you deaf?" Cræosh shouted, one hand resting on his sword. "You want me to clean out your fucking ears for you? I said, you sent the damn tree with us!"

"What are you *talking* about?"

"Did you ever stop . . . to wonder," Katim asked acidly, "why you never . . . saw Gnarlroot after he animated . . . the other trees?"

"Well, yes," Mina said, stepping up to stand by—and if necessary, defend—her fellow druid. "But we assumed he was simply hanging back and directing them from afar."

"He was Josiah!" Fezeill shouted, having clearly lost patience with the humans, his allies, and the world in general. "Your friend was long dead by the time we showed up! He volunteered to help us so he could find Emmet—and that," he added, pointing at the Tree of Ever that Cræosh grasped in one beefy fist, "and then take it and kill us all!"

"You're lying," Alam snapped, his own fists clenching. "You're *lying*!"

Gork sighed theatrically. "You want proof? Why don't you go down-stairs—don't worry, we took care of the nasty things for you, it's per-fectly safe—and sift through some ashes? There might just be enough of Josiah's skin left for you to tell what happened."

"And how would we know," Mina asked coldly, "that you didn't kill him?"

The kobold shook his head. "You think we wouldn't come up with a more believable story if we were lying to you?"

The young woman opened her mouth to retort, but Alam put a hand on her shoulder. "No. No, maybe they're right, Mina. After all we've seen, is this really any less believable?"

"But Alam, Josiah of all people? I can't accept that."

"He had been quieter of late. Maybe . . ." The acolyte sighed softly. "Whatever the case," he said then, turning back to Cræosh once more, "Gnarlroot is dead. The trees have returned to their rightful place in the forest. And you have, indeed, returned to us the Tree of Ever. I am sorry that this tragic episode has cost us so many of our brethren. But either way, I thank you.

"I feel, however, that you should leave. Immediately. Mina and I have preparations to make for the coming conflict."

Slowly, Katim's head rose and she peered at the head acolyte intently. "I've been wondering about . . . something," she said. "You said that your . . . sect viewed the 'World-Mother' . . . as female. Each druid sect is . . . separate and distinct from . . . the others? Is that . . . correct?"

"It's a bit simplistic," Alam said, puzzlement in his voice, "but essentially correct. Why?"

"Each of you worships . . . nature, or your nature . . . gods, in dif-ferent ways."

"Yes," Alam said again. "But I'm still not getting your—"

"How will you and . . . Mina survive," she asked, ignoring the druid's confusion, "now that you . . . are alone?"

"The same we always have," Alam said, growing irritated at the stream of irrelevant queries. "Through hard work and faith."

"I hope you . . . succeed," Katim said with a meaningful—almost *sly*—glance at Cræosh. "After all, it . . . would be a true shame for your sect . . . to disappear. There would be . . . none left to pay homage to . . . your gods."

Cræosh grinned widely in sudden understanding, and nodded. Katim snarled and swung her *chirrusk*; Gork drew his *kah-rahahk* and lunged.

And that simply, the Circle of Ymmech Thewl was once again an extinct sect.

Jhurpess fell to his knees and began taking large, bloody mouthfuls of the nearest body, ignoring the occasional thrashing and feeble cries that suggested that Gork's strike might not have been instantly fatal. That fact didn't seem to concern the bugbear much; it always stopped once one got to the good parts. Cræosh opened his mouth to speak and snapped it shut at the sudden stream of vile curses coming, oddly enough, from the gremlin!

"What's the problem, Gimmol?" he asked. "Belrotha smack your head on the ceiling?" But while his voice was as gruff as ever, most of the others noticed the distinct lack of any pejorative; apparently, he was still processing the gremlin's newly revealed powers.

"We," Gimmol said, finally looking up from the large tome he held open before him, "are very, very fucked."

The rest of the squad—except Jhurpess, who was chewing too noisily to have heard a word of it—gathered round, staring up at the gremlin who sat upon the ogre's shoulder.

"What is it?" Fezeill asked.

Even in the face of looming crisis, Gimmol couldn't resist. "It's a book, Fezeill. If you practice really hard, you might even learn what to do with them."

Cræosh and Gork snickered out loud, and Katim stepped on the doppelganger's foot as he was about to retort. "Gimmol?" she rasped. "The problem?"

"This," he said, wiggling the book slightly, "is an ancient tome. I spotted it in the library because it was sticking out from the others. I think Emmet must have been perusing it at some point, maybe studying up on the different factions in the coming war. It's a treatise on necromantic magics."

Several pairs of eyes blinked in unison. He sighed theatrically. "Necromantic. Dealing with or having to do with death and dead things."

Heads nodded in understanding. "Necromantic magics are extremely rare," he continued. "Most races abhor it, and many wizards destroy such books and spells on sight. Here in Kirol Syrreth, King Morthûl has banned any wizards but his own personal agents from owning such a thing."

"Okay, so I can see how that might be valuable to you," Gork interrupted, "but why are you wasting *our* time with it?"

"I've come across a description of an ancient spell," the gremlin said, flipping back a few pages. "This section right here lists the various ingredients and components required for the casting of the ritual. 'The bones of a deceased wizard, a flower sprung from the grave of a man interred alive, a petrified heart, a relic of a forgotten god . . .' Stop me when this starts to sound familiar, people."

Katim's nostrils flared. "So Queen Anne is . . . casting a spell. This is . . . not a great surprise, Gimmol. We . . . suspected as much."

"Yeah," the gremlin breathed. "But it's her choice of spells that terrifies me.

"This spell is called the Rite of Twilight Ascension. It suspends the wizard between life and death. Permanently."

He nearly screamed in frustration at the incomprehension on their faces. "Don't you *see*?" he shrieked, his voice echoing maniacally in the corners of the lofty chamber. "We've seen the results of this spell! We *serve* the results of this spell!"

Understanding finally dawned. "You mean . . ." Cræosh began haltingly.

"Yes," the gremlin told them all. "This is the spell that made the Charnel King what he is.

"And Queen Anne wants to be just like him."

CHAPTER EIGHT

THE LIAR, THE LICH, AND THE BROWN ROBE

The dawning sun peeked over the sharp crags of the Brimstone Mountains, spreading its growing light over the kingdom of Kirol Syrreth. Over the mountains, over the doppelganger city of Grault, over the forest of Ymmech Thewl and its newly inanimate trees, the day crept. And then, reluctantly, it alighted upon the festering sore that was Darsus.

It was an ugly city, was Darsus. In the days of King Sabryen, it had been home to one of his army's largest keeps: a hulking monstrosity apparently built on the theory that there would be no need to fight if the foe was too terrified of the fortress to risk a siege. Jagged, toothy battlements sawed at the clouds, towers extended in directions that could serve no purpose but to demonstrate the insanity of the architects. The name of the place was long since lost, and much of the fortress itself had followed. What remained was a gaunt, skeletal thing, less a keep than a stone tree grown from the depths of hell. It was useless to have around, and yet none of the citizens of Darsus would ever contemplate tearing it down. There was too much weight behind it, too much history, too many ghosts of times long past.

But it wasn't that ugliness that made Darsus such an eyesore on the plains of Kirol Syrreth. Darsus was a human city, and could never compare to the twisted and alien towers of Grault, the sheer military-minded efficiency of the orcs, or the looming spires of the Iron Keep itself. No, it was that the city itself had begun to resemble that cadaverous keep, or the equally cadaverous king who ruled them now. Once a thriving center of commerce, travel, and trade, Darsus had fallen not to cataclysm and not to war, but to time. Merchants and traders drifted elsewhere, routes shifted to pass through Timas Khoreth or other cities, and Darsus withered.

Some few of its citizens acknowledged reality and departed, seeking new lives elsewhere. But many couldn't bring themselves to leave, to believe that the good times had truly passed. *Wait it out*, they said. *Wait it out, and things will be as they were.*

So many generations had passed since then that no one living in Darsus had ever actually experienced the "good times" that were surely coming back any day now. But it had become a religion, a way of life, and the citizens of Darsus today were no more willing to face reality and leave than their ancestors had been. And so Darsus continued on, a wound on civilization—an ugly, rotten little town of no means, no future, and no hope.

Well, no hope for most. As with everywhere else, a select few managed to thrive, even in the cesspool of despair that was Darsus. Like leeches or vultures, such people grow healthy as those around them sicken.

Sergin was just such a man. He'd always been one of the lucky ones. He was taller than average, although his rather extensive paunch and broad shoulders made him appear a little squat. His hair was greased black to hide the gray that everyone knew lurked beneath, and he had a perpetual squint.

Now while Sergin was neither a kind nor a generous man, it must be said in his defense that he wasn't particularly malicious, either. He was no happier to see the constant rot and ruin than anyone else, and he wasn't at all conscious of the fact that he was figuratively—perhaps even literally—feeding off the despair of those around him. Sergin was merely trying to survive, just as everyone else was; it was just that he was in a better position to do so.

Sergin was the proprietor of the Rusty Piton, Darsus's only remaining tavern, and that made him one of the richest men in town. His ale was weak and thin, his liquors of inferior vintage, his meals greasy and poorly cooked. A tavern like the Rusty Piton wouldn't have lasted a month in Timas Khoreth, but it was the only source of liquid solace available to Darsus's depressed masses, and those masses drank. A lot. On average, they spent more of their earnings on drink than they did on food. Sergin did his part to help; he kept his prices relatively reasonable, even going so far as to occasionally offer a free meal to the truly destitute. (Said meal served with murky water; alcohol, he *never* gave away.)

On this particular morning, Sergin was not a happy man. Last evening, he had unwillingly played host to a substantial brawl—not an uncommon occurrence, but neither was it an enjoyable one—and he'd lost several chairs, one of his best tables, and an uncountable number of tankards. It had been a profitable afternoon up to that point, one of the best that month; now, because that damn drunkard Lomis couldn't keep his damn hands off women with large brothers, the whole night was a loss. Maybe even the entire week.

Cursing under his breath, Sergin stomped out the back door of the Rusty Piton, a spent ale barrel loaded with garbage on each shoulder. He didn't bother to hold his breath anymore; most people couldn't set one foot in that alley without gagging or even retching outright, but Sergin had grown accustomed to the near-tangible stench. This alley had been his refuse pit for years now, and it had been cleaned out only on those occasions when it rained really, *really* hard. The miasma was enough to nauseate the roaches, and the rats' eyes watered constantly.

This, to Sergin, was a *good* thing. The walls of the tavern were thick, so the smell never troubled the paying patrons, and that scent kept the drunks from staggering into the alley to pass out. He *hated* when they did that.

And thus, when he tripped over someone lying not four feet from the door, nearly causing him to drop his barrels of refuse, it was enough to set him screaming.

"You bastard!" Sergin dropped the barrels where he stood, despite the fact that he'd just pulled something trying *not* to drop them. "You get the hell out of my alley, you hear? You get out right now! You . . ."

The bartender gasped as he recognized the body. He couldn't see the man's face, of course; but that shape, that shirt, that hair . . .

Lomis. It was Lomis.

Sergin began to kick him. "You bastard! You—you damn bastard!" Sergin, it should be noted, was not the most creative-minded of men. "You wrecked my tavern, you bastard! You owe me! Oh, gods, do you owe me! And I'm gonna collect every stinking copper, you hear me?" Another kick. "Every stinking one!" Kick. "Now you get the hell out of my alley!" Kick, kick.

Kick.

It was just about this point that reason began to slowly seep through the righteous rage enshrouding Sergin's mind. The owner of the Rusty Piton paused in midkick, staring down at the body. And body, he admitted reluctantly, is just what it was. Not even Lomis could possibly be so drunk as to have failed to notice the shoe-leather hailstorm. For a moment, the bartender felt the first surges of panic. Had he killed the man?

No. No, Lomis hadn't moved at all. Hadn't even twitched, not from the very first kick. The man had been dead before Sergin even entered the ally. The large barkeep breathed a quick sigh of relief, and then set about pondering what to do next.

Obviously, he would have to report this. Darsus didn't have a formal watch, but the council of merchants who made decisions for the city occasionally assigned their private guards as a part-time police force. (It had been they, in fact, who had finally broken up the previous night's brawl.) It was highly doubtful that they'd bother with any serious investigation into Lomis's death, but still, they'd have to be informed.

But first there was something else to do. The man was dead, and dead men, for the most part, are not known for paying reparations. Sergin would have to settle for whatever Lomis had on him at the moment. Probably not more than a few stray coppers, maybe a little silver if he was lucky—but it was *something*, and as far as the barkeep was concerned, it was morally his. Carefully, Sergin dug both hands into the tunic that covered the corpse's right shoulder and heaved him over. . . .

The naked, empty skull peered up accusingly at him as a small horde of maggots tunneled, squirming, through its running, viscous eyes. A thin dusting of blood dyed the sharp white of bone a stomach-churning pink. Here and there, some few strips of matter dangled between the ribs, swaying slightly as the body shifted.

Sergin felt his gorge rising and choked it back more by luck than by effort of will. Too stunned even to scream, he could only stare, paralyzed, at the hideous sight. So horrified was he at the gory thing that had once been a frequent customer, it took him a moment to notice the swarm of worms and maggots—coated in blood and other, less readily identifiable substances—that poured from the body. It was only when the first one, a bloated maggot coated in black slime, had begun to wriggle up his hand and into his sleeve that he finally reacted.

Now he did scream, a bellow of primal revulsion. Swallowing a second tide of nausea, Sergin shot upright and slammed his right palm over and over into his left arm, determined to crush or dislodge the creature before it climbed any further. He was rewarded, if such is the proper term, by a sudden moist pop—rather like squeezing a fermenting blue-berry—beneath his fingers.

But by then, several dozen more of the vile things had begun to climb him; many had already found their way into his boots, or inside the legs of his pants. And then, finally, he let loose a true, horrified, soul-wrenching shriek. No one came in answer, but in those final instants, he imagined that he heard similar cries from other nearby alleys.

Unspeakable things writhed against his skin, biting, digging, *tunneling*. He tried to flinch away, but there were dozens, *hundreds* of them now, all over his skin, in his hair, under his nails, filling his ears. Sergin felt himself topple, land amid the oozing refuse of the alley—and a thousand more crawling things that waited, impatient and hungry.

He was already mad by the time the bulk of the worms began to eat into his body, his throat, his face. When the end came, he was well beyond any capacity to feel it. For the others, for most of Darsus, the screaming would last for hours.

But then, Sergin always had been one of the lucky ones.

✳

"Well," Gork said, glancing pointedly back over his shoulder at the looming forest of Thewl, "we're out of the woods, so to speak. Where's this magical solution that was supposed to fall into our laps?"

Cræosh's lips twisted in a nasty scowl. "I didn't say we'd be handed a fucking answer when we cleared the trees, Shorty. I just said maybe something might come to us."

"Something might have," Katim pointed out helpfully, "if . . . some of us hadn't been too . . . nervous to talk about it on . . . the way."

As he'd been doing more and more often of late, Cræosh ignored her. It was his only option, really, other than violence, and he still wasn't ready for that.

"Fort Rheen's not really that far," Fezeill said. He was once again wearing his favorite human guise. "Why not head there first?"

"And then what?" Gimmol asked from atop Belrotha's shoulder. The gremlin still sounded on the edge of panic. "How's that going to help us?"

"And your idea is that much better?" the doppelganger snapped. "Even if we *wanted* to go there—and I assure you that none of us who remain remotely sane have any such desire—Dendrakis is clear across Kirol Syrreth!"

"I know that! It doesn't matter. He *has* to know!"

"How do you know he doesn't *already* . . . ?"

Cræosh turned a deaf ear. It was the same cycle they'd repeated half a dozen times back in the now-abandoned temple of Ymmech Thewl. In theory, he actually agreed with the gremlin: This sort of thing had to be reported. Where the consensus broke down was "To whom?"

General Falchion? That was Cræosh's vote, but Gimmol contended, and the orc had to admit he might have a point, that one of the general's own staff or messengers might let something slip to the wrong ears.

Sergeant Shreckt, then? They hadn't seen the little bastard in over a month, and even if they could find him, it meant going back to Castle Eldritch. Cræosh had ended that line of conversation with a "Fuck, no!"

(It had been then, incidentally, that Gimmol had revealed that the final component of the ritual was the soul of a demon. After a twenty-minute debate—read: screaming argument—about whether a demon could, by definition, even *have* a soul, they all managed to agree that Shreckt was the only feasible candidate. "That'd explain why we haven't seen him," Fezeill had observed casually. That had, in turn, opened up a whole new line of discussion, regarding whether or not it was worth letting the loathsome little imp die. They hadn't resolved *that* issue, either.)

All of which left only one other option, and most of the discussion since then had revolved around desperately trying to find a way to avoid it. *They had to carry word to the Iron Keep itself.* Cræosh could, just off the top of his head, think of about ten thousand things he'd rather do than report Queen Anne's activities to King Morthûl in person, many of which involved being disemboweled or boiled alive in various sticky substances.

And some of the squad, of course, still weren't sure why it was such a big deal. "Jhurpess not understand why this matter," the bugbear said—again.

"Much as I hate to set this sort of precedent," Gork added, "I agree with Jhurpess. I admit that King Morthûl's more than mildly horrible, but so what? So what if Queen Anne wants to be like him? Hell, if one of them's enough to scare the other kingdoms shitless, imagine what two of them can do for Kirol Syrreth."

"That's just it!" Gimmol was actually screeching. "It's too much!"

Katim winced. "Gimmol, tone it down . . . a little. My ears are about to . . . climb off my head and seek . . . their own way in the world." She reached up and poked him in one dangling foot with a talon. "Perhaps your head . . . might be willing to keep them . . . company?"

"It's too much," the gremlin said again—at a much lower volume. "You're making a common mistake, Gork. You see the Charnel King as a wizard who just happens to be dead."

The kobold shrugged. "It's what he is, isn't it?"

"Not by far. You ever wondered why this entire world isn't ruled by wizards? Why they don't just step in and make themselves gods?"

Another shrug. "I just sort of assumed they didn't have the power."

"Exactly. Even the greatest sorcerers can only channel so much magic, because the body and the mind can only handle so much without burning up. That's why you won't see any single wizard blowing up an entire kingdom, or mentally controlling thousands of people at once. A whole cabal working together might be able to do it, but most wizards don't trust their fellows enough to cooperate to that extent. Too many trade secrets.

"But King Morthûl doesn't have that problem. His body's *dead*! It's sustained by magic; it simply doesn't have the same frailties as a living one, and he's had *eight hundred years* to learn how to use that. King Morthûl can perform feats of magic that no mortal wizard could even contemplate, let alone achieve!" Gimmol's voice had been rising again; at Katim's snarl, he took a few deep breaths.

"It's as close to godhood as a mortal can get," he continued once he'd calmed down a bit. "In all recorded history, less than half a dozen mages who attempted the ritual actually succeeded; the strength of will required is enormous, even more than the sorcerous proficiency. Under other circumstances, I wouldn't worry about Queen Anne being able to pull this off—except that she's a stark raving loony, in case you hadn't picked up on the fact. She might start off cooperating with her husband, but it wouldn't last. How long do you think either of them could go on, trying to work side by side with the *one person* who posed an actual threat?"

Gork was finally starting to look troubled. "So wouldn't one of them just kill the other?" he asked hopefully. "We wouldn't be any worse off than we are now, right?"

Gimmol shook his head frantically. "You've never seen wizards go to war, have you? This would make all previous mage duels look like a children's squabble. I doubt Kirol Syrreth would survive. I'm not completely sure the *continent* would survive!"

"We'd hide," Gork said, very obviously arguing now for nothing more than the sake of being stubborn. "Kobolds are good at that. It's what we do."

"Not from this, Gork. If Kirol Syrreth goes, we *all* go with it." Gimmol paused a moment. "And besides, even if by some miracle you did survive, what would you come back to?"

Gork was trying very hard not to be convinced, but the others, even Jhurpess and Belrotha, had heard quite enough. "Okay, Gimmol," Cræosh said, "you've sold me. You're the mage here. What do you suggest?"

"There's no way I can take Queen Anne," the gremlin told them. "Ten of me wouldn't be powerful enough. The *only* choice we have is to tell King Morthûl and let him handle it."

"You're still assuming he doesn't know," Fezeill interjected. "That it wasn't he who assigned us to Queen Anne."

"He doesn't. He'd never take the risk. I'm *sure* of it."

Cræosh sighed. "I was really hoping for another way out of this," he told the world at large.

Katim's jagged, saliva-coated teeth gleamed in the setting sun. "There's always . . . suicide."

"Remind me of that when we get a little nearer to Dendrakis. I just might want to give it some thought."

For good or for ill, he would have plenty of time to think it over. All the way from Ymmech Thewl, in the shadow of the Brimstone Mountains, to the Sea of Tears from which the isle of Dendrakis rose, was pretty close to the entire length and breadth of Kirol Syrreth. Between terrain and distance, even accounting for the Demon Squad's stamina, reaching the Iron Keep would require . . .

"A month," Fezeill told them, having been the first to complete the math. "Maybe more."

"Well," Cræosh said philosophically, "we're fucked."

Gork frowned. "Are we? I mean, the Stars only know what Queen Anne might do with that kind of time, but we've got the Tree of Ever. Even assuming it now properly qualifies as a forgotten god's relic, it's not going to do her much good if she doesn't have it."

"No," Katim said, "we can't . . . count on that. If Shreckt *is* the . . . demon in question, it means that . . . Queen Anne has all the components but . . . one. Were I in her . . . position, I would not be sitting around . . . waiting for it to come to . . . me."

Belrotha cocked her head. "Little tree will go to her? What us here for, then?"

"You think she's got other feelers out besides us?" Cræosh asked, letting the ogre stew.

The troll nodded. "It would make sense, don't . . . you think? I'd say that we . . . can't afford to wait a . . . month on this."

"And our other option is what?" Gork asked caustically. "Do you suppose if we ask nicely enough, we might persuade time to wait for us?"

"Actually," Cræosh said, his face lighting up, "yes." He looked pointedly at Gimmol.

"Oh, no," the gremlin protested, thrusting both arms out as though to shove the notion away. "Not even the Charnel King messes with time. No way."

(Had Gimmol known the precise nature of Morthûl's recent ritual—the one compromised and thwarted by duMark and his allies—he might have chosen a different example.)

"I didn't mean it literally, Gimmol," Cræosh clarified. "Can't you just—I don't know—pop us over there?" He snapped his fingers for emphasis, the sharp retort echoing like a breaking bone. "Shreckt and Queen Anne do it all the time."

"I'm not Shreckt or Queen Anne," Gimmol said bluntly. "There's a whole steaming pile of things they can do that I can't." The gremlin scratched his temple, just beneath the brim of his hat. "Still . . ."

"Still what?" Fezeill prompted after a moment. "'Still' isn't very informative."

"I can speed us up a little," Gimmol said hesitantly. "We won't feel like we're going any faster, but we can cover the distance in a couple of weeks. Ten days or so if we *really* push it."

"Well, why didn't you just say so?" Cræosh demanded.

"Because it's harder than all hell, Cræosh," Gimmol said. "And because there's a price."

Katim scowled dangerously. "What kind of . . . price?"

"This sort of thing wreaks havoc on the body," the little wizard replied. "It's vaguely possible that a few of us might not survive the shock. Not *likely*, since we're all in pretty good shape, but possible. But even if it doesn't kill us, it's going to drain us. Think of it as aging a year or three over the next month."

Cræosh scowled. "I'm not crazy about that idea," he grumbled, "but I can spare a year or three. Most orcs don't make it to old age anyway. I'm a little more concerned about that whole 'not surviving thing,' though."

"I second," Gork said, actually raising his hand.

"I'll risk it," Katim rasped. "It's . . . extremely difficult to kill . . . a troll. I'm not . . . worried."

"Well bully and hot-shit for you," Cræosh muttered.

But in the end, their other options amounted to zero—a circumstance with which they were growing all too familiar. They roughly explained what was about to happen to Belrotha and Jhurpess. And then there was nothing left but to do it.

It took Gimmol three tries to get the spell right, and Cræosh was certain that the gremlin would dislocate his jaw with some of the harsh, alien syllables. When he finally *did* spit out the final phrase, the entire squad shuddered; a few even screamed. As though they'd taken a nice big slug of molten lava, a sudden heat blazed in their guts and radiated outward. Their blood boiled, their hair burned from the inside—or so it felt.

After only a few seconds, though, the burning faded to a tolerable level; not gone, alas, but easy enough to ignore.

"What now?" Cræosh asked, his voice sounding strangely high-pitched and tinny in his ears.

"Now we go," Gimmol said. "The incantation should last about a day each time, so I'm going to have to recast it. A lot." The gremlin sighed. "This is not an easy spell, Cræosh. It takes just about everything I've got. If we run into any sort of trouble, I probably won't be much help."

"That's fine. You just leave it to us."

The squad set out, and Cræosh was rather startled at just how swiftly the terrain flashed past to either side. It looked as though every step he took covered three or four paces' worth of space.

"Not exactly," Gimmol explained when he asked about it. "The size of your paces hasn't changed. You're just taking them a lot faster. Since your mind doesn't realize how fast your feet are moving, it *looks* like each pace is covering more distance."

"But we're just moving faster."

"Exactly."

Cræosh pondered that. "Wouldn't this be a huge fucking advantage in combat, then?"

The gremlin shook his head. "You're forgetting how much stress you're under. Yeah, you'd be a lot faster than your opponent, but a single blow would kill you. Combined with the rigors of this spell, even a minor wound might prove fatal. That, and you wouldn't really want to age a few years every time you fight someone, would you?"

Cræosh just grunted and began very carefully checking his path for rocks and roots. Given what he'd just been told, he absolutely did not want to trip over anything.

Dying from a skinned knee or a twisted ankle would be humiliating.

"I just thought of . . . something," Katim announced.

They'd halted for the night atop a small rise. It wasn't much—barely even a hill—but it was defensible, something that couldn't be said for most of the open plains here. They'd made good time, to have reached those plains already. At this rate, they would be at the shores of the Sea of Tears in less than another week.

"And that is?" Cræosh asked, his tone suggesting that he wasn't really all that interested in anything the troll might have come up with.

"We were so concerned with . . . reaching the Sea of Tears, we didn't . . . consider crossing it."

"Um, by boat. Just how stupid—"

"And how many ports . . . stand on the cost of the Sea . . . of Tears?"

"Just Sularaam," Gork interjected. And then, crushed beneath the weight of sudden realization, he groaned.

"What?" Cræosh asked.

"What's in Sularaam . . . Cræosh?" Katim asked pointedly.

It finally dawned on him. "Castle Eldritch. And Queen Anne."

The troll nodded.

"Shit!" Cræosh rose and began to pace. "Will she be able to sense us if we just pass through? I mean, she's probably pretty busy, right?"

"Probably," Katim agreed. "How much are . . . you willing to wager on that . . . particular 'probably'?"

"Not much," the orc admitted. "Okay, then. So what're our other options?"

"Isn't Tarahk Grond near Sularaam?" Fezeill asked him. "Couldn't we go through there?"

Cræosh shook his head. "Yeah, it's close. I have friends and relatives there. But Tarahk Grond's farther south in the Grieving Mountains. It's got no direct access to the Sea of Tears."

"Oh," Fezeill said. "Damn."

After a fairly lengthy moment of silence, Gork scowled. "I'm hearing a rather disappointing lack of creativity here, people."

"Oh, right," Cræosh said, "like *you've* got any better ideas."

The kobold shrugged. "Someone's got to supervise, right?"

"Jhurpess have idea!" the bugbear announced. "Jhurpess knows what squad should do."

"This," the orc said, "I've *got* to hear. I'm not sure I *want* to hear it, but . . ."

"Jhurpess will take squad through Trussus!"

"What?!"

"Trussus is bugbear village! Trussus near Sea of Tears!"

"Trussus on the Steppes!" Gork raged at the simian creature. "You want us to go back up into the Steppes? Into the tundra? You're not just stupid, Jhurpess! You're insane!"

"Trussus is warm," Jhurpess protested mildly. "Mountains shield Trussus from wind and snow."

"Maybe," Cræosh told him, "but that don't make it the slightest bit easier to *get* to the fucking place. Sorry, Nature-boy, but I've got no intention of freezing my ass off again. If I want it gone, I'll take my sword and cut it the hell off the top of my legs."

"To say nothing of the fact," Fezeill added, "that it would mean trusting our lives to a bugbear-made boat. Frankly, I'd rather have the raft of doors we made in Ymmech Thewl. I—"

The argument ended, or at least stalled, at the hideous sound of Katim running her talons thoughtfully down the flat of her axe blade. "What about the River . . . Krael?"

"What?" It came from three mouths at once.

"If we cannot get a boat . . . at the coast, we get one earlier. Then . . . we travel the Krael, which . . . takes us into the Sea of Tears . . . far north of Sularaam."

"Well, that's just fine, Dog-breath," Cræosh said—filing away, for the moment, the troll's *almost* unnoticeable faltering at the word "boat." *Just like she'd hesitated before stepping onto the raft. Trolly's got a weakness. . . .* "I suppose you've got a small ship stowed away in a belt pouch, right?"

Katim glowered until Cræosh began to fidget.

"All right!" he relented. "So you wouldn't have fucking brought it up if you didn't have some idea! So let us in on the secret, oh wise canine. We're breathless with suspense."

"If we've truly traveled . . . as fast as Gimmol claims," she said, "then we should . . . be fairly near Timas Khoreth. Since the . . . city sits on a tributary . . . of the Krael, it stands to . . . reason that they might have a boat . . . or two on hand."

"Wait a minute!" Gork exclaimed, horror dawning on his face. "Isn't the Krael *also* in the tundra?"

"Not precisely. It runs along . . . the southern edge." In fact, proximity to the tundra, and the poor quality of the frigid soil, was one of the reasons there *wasn't* a port city where the Krael met the Sea of Tears. But neither Cræosh nor Katim saw any pressing need to mention that fact to the irate kobold.

"No! No way! It's damn cold enough this far north already! Not a chance! I—"

Cræosh sighed and once again lifted the kobold off his feet, one huge palm wrapped around the struggling creature's head. "There are worse things than a little cold, right?

"Mrph!"

"I thought you'd see it that way." The orc dropped Gork to the ground.

"You know," the kobold snarled as he brushed himself off, "the next time you do that, I might just take a bite out of your hand."

Cræosh shrugged. "And I might just squeeze until your brains come oozing out of your ears like so much—"

Gork and Katim both turned away, determined not to hear whatever metaphor the foul-mouthed orc intended for "oozing brains."

Cræosh grinned briefly before turning his attention toward their pet sorcerer. "How about it, Gimmol? Can you speed up the boat the same way you've been accelerating us?"

"I'm afraid not, Cræosh. Creatures only. I might get us to row a little faster, but that's it."

"Ah, well," Cræosh sighed. "Doesn't really matter, I suppose. Taking the river's faster than walking anyway. All right, you losers! Let's get some sleep. Tomorrow, we've got a boat to catch."

It was an hour past noon, and the Demon Squad was huddled silently in a thick patch of brush and scrub just west of Timas Khoreth, watching the ebb and flow of traffic on the road.

Well, *most* of them were silent. Gork was still at the tail end of a snit and was grumbling all manner of profanities in Kobold.

"I thought you *enjoyed* being sneaky," Gimmol whispered to him.

"Oh, bite my ass, gremlin! I'm *finally* in a position to pull rank on the humans, and you bastards won't let me!"

Cræosh sighed. "We've fucking been through this. We can't afford to go through official channels to requisition a boat. Queen Anne—"

"Yeah, yeah, Queen Anne'll catch wind of it. But we'll be long gone by the time she does!"

"You want to count on that, Shorty?"

More profanities in Kobold. More long hours spent watching the constant river of humanity flowing through the gates of Timas Khoreth. Merchants entered, soldiers departed, horses and donkeys and mules wandered past, lost in their own equine thoughts.

"The problem isn't really getting in," Gork said, his attentions finally directed toward the issues at hand. "There are entrances besides the main gate, so we can enter in ones and twos. I haven't seen a *lot* of goblins in the crowd, but there are enough that so long as we don't try to pass all at once, we shouldn't stand out too badly. No, the real challenge is going to be getting *out*."

"I'm not sure I follow," Cræosh admitted. "Any particular reason that we can't just sail out?"

"Yeah. You wouldn't know this, 'cause you pretty much got to

Timas Khoreth just in time for them to assemble our little shindig, but I had some time to explore. There's a guard tower just north of the city proper. It sits right at the intersection of the Krael and the smaller tributary that flows through Timas Khoreth. We have to sail right past it to get out."

"Could we just make a run for it?" Fezeill asked. Then, when it appeared that Gork was ignoring the doppelganger, Cræosh nudged him in the shoulder.

"No," the kobold said. "We'll be fighting the current until we reach the Krael itself. And even with Belrotha paddling, that's going to slow us down. A lot."

"We could portage it," Cræosh suggested, though his voice was doubtful. "Have Belrotha carry the boat until we've reached the Krael."

The ogre's eyes widened. "But if me carry boat, me be under the water!" she protested.

Gimmol patted her reassuringly on the calf. "No, Belrotha. If we need you to carry the boat, it'll be *out* of the water."

"Oh." She beamed after a minute. "Me got it now."

"Good." The gremlin smiled.

"But if us out of water, what us need boat for?"

Gimmol gave up.

A brief discussion, however, proved that particular line of thought unnecessary. ". . . really don't think," Fezeill was saying, "that even Belrotha could carry a boat big enough for all seven of us."

"I've seen more than seven . . . people stuffed into some fairly . . . small boats," Katim said.

"No, he's right," Gimmol said, rejoining the main conversation. "If it was just a question of the river, sure. But remember, whatever boat we steal has to be able to navigate the Sea of Tears, too. That means sturdier, and *that* means bigger and heavier."

"Well," Cræosh said abruptly, rising to his feet and dusting off his hands, "there's no help for it, then. We grab the best boat we can, paddle like drowning dwarves, and hope we clear the tower before they realize what's happening—or that something better comes up in the meantime."

All told, it wasn't much of a plan, but it was all they had. The squad waited until the sun had just begun to caress the western horizon. Then, as one, they abandoned the dubious safety of their patch of scrub and dashed toward the walls of Timas Khoreth.

It was, as Gork had foretold, simplicity itself to actually enter the city. Fezeill, of course, had no difficulties whatsoever. The bulk of the squad, in ones and twos, just fell in with the regular traffic, now rushing to pass through the main gates before nightfall. Those who would stand out *too* much from the crowd—Katim and Belrotha, specifically—moved around to one of the posterns, meant primarily for refuse. Katim crept up on the single unwary guard and smacked him over the head. She'd decided (reluctantly) that she couldn't justify killing a fellow soldier under the present circumstances, and had pulled her blow accordingly. Nevertheless, when trolls hit people, they tend to stay hit. The guard didn't wake up for half a week, and to the end of his days, the poor fellow swore he could see a small flock of purple-winged hedgehogs fluttering at the periphery of his vision.

It took even longer for them to wend their way across town without drawing excess attention, forcing them to remain alone or in pairs rather than reassembling—the fact that Jhurpess and Belrotha both got lost on the way didn't help—but finally they'd gathered, crouched in an alley not far from the riverbank.

Slowly, methodically Cræosh, Katim, and Gork surveyed the area. Now that the sun had set, the pier was lit by a series of lamps hanging from eight-foot metal poles. Most of the vessels moored here, thumping hollowly against the waterlogged jetties in the shifting tides, were rowboats and rafts. Two, however—a small, flat-bottom barge and a single-masted fishing vessel—looked capable of surviving the Sea of Tears.

There remained, however, a problem. Two problems, actually, and they were both sitting beneath one of the streetlamps, using a wooden crate as a makeshift table. The staccato smack of cards being slapped down onto the wood reverberated softly in the night air, occasionally followed by either a chuckle or a grunt and the clatter of coin changing hands. Even over the damp scents of the river, several of the goblins could detect the tang of sour sweat and cloying pipe smoke.

"I'm still not entirely opposed to killing them," Gork said in a low whisper. "I mean, it's not as if there aren't more where they came from. My people have a theory that it was the humans who taught rabbits everything they know about breeding."

"Leaving aside the trouble that murdering two guards is gonna cause us if we're discovered here," Cræosh explained—again—"I'm not really sure how King Morthûl's gonna take it if he finds out we were killing his soldiers on our way to see him. I'd sort of rather he be in a good mood when we meet him."

"Amen to that," Gork agreed firmly.

"Good. Then shut the fuck up, unless you've got an idea that *doesn't* involve stabbing them in the back."

"Could Katim just bash them?" Gimmol asked. "Like the guard at the gate?"

The troll, however, shook her head. "I couldn't be certain . . . of getting them both before one could . . . sound an alarm."

Much to the horror of the rest of the squad, the bugbear grinned broadly. "Jhurpess has idea! Katim *can* go hit guards! Jhurpess will take care of the rest!" Before anyone could stop him, or even *think* of stopping him, the bugbear jumped up to the nearest second-story windowsill and scrambled onto the roof.

"I think," Fezeill said, "that the word of the day is 'shit.'"

"Shit!" Cræosh agreed. "All right, Dog-breath, I don't see that we've got any choice anymore. Nature-boy's gonna do whatever he's gonna do, regardless. Get out there and beat their heads in before all hell breaks loose."

Katim nodded and charged, keeping to the shadows almost as well as Gork could have. It was only when she reached the circle of light in which they played that the guards noticed her at all.

The first collapsed facedown on the table before he'd even managed to stand, the side of his head bruised and bloody. Katim lunged over the crate, grabbing the second soldier by the hair and slamming her other fist into his jaw—but not before he'd lifted the signal whistle that hung on a cord about his neck and loosed a deafening screech.

Just as they'd feared. It was a short whistle, aborted abruptly when the troll's fist drove the tiny device through the man's front teeth, but it was enough. Already, the faint sounds of running feet echoed from nearby streets.

The remainder of the squad broke cover, racing to join the aggravated troll. "So where," she asked, her raspy voice even darker and more dangerous than normal, "is the . . . damn bugbear? He—"

As though summoned, Jhurpess materialized from the flickering shadows directly beside them. "Jhurpess done," he announced happily. "Squad can go now."

"What did you do, you stupid monkey?" Cræosh asked. *This was not going to be pleasant. . . .*

"Jhurpess gave guards a better reason for the alarm," he said. "Squad *really* should go now."

"He's right, Cræosh," Gimmol called from Belrotha's shoulder, a perch he'd resumed while waiting in the alley. "The guards'll be here any second."

The orc stubbornly shook his head. "Not until we know what he did!"

The far end of the dock erupted into a towering fireball that could probably have been seen from the tundra, followed by a roar that could have been described as the angry growl of thunder's pet dog. Heat washed over them; a deluge of acrid fumes made their eyes water, their nostrils burn. Dark silhouettes raced toward or around the fire, shouting and flailing, utterly oblivious to the gathered goblins.

"Lamp oil?" Cræosh asked, shouting over the roar of the fire.

Jhurpess nodded. "Soldiers keep it in small shack at end of pier. Jhurpess smelled it."

"Did it ever occur to you," the orc snapped back, "that the pier's not gonna be the only thing to burn?"

"Jhurpess not worried. Squad has a few minutes before flames reach it; plenty of time to get on boat."

"*Boats* burn too, you asshole!"

The bugbear's face fell. "Oh," he said quietly.

Cræosh's sword hand twitched.

"As it happens," Gork said acidly, stepping between the arguing pair, "the fire hasn't *reached* the fishing boat yet. Do you want to be angry because the boat *could* have caught fire, or because it *did*? Besides," he added, pointing at Jhurpess, "do you really want to smell that much hair burning?"

With a final glare, Cræosh stomped away to board the vessel.

None of the squad had ever done any real sailing, but Gimmol remembered enough of what he'd read in the past to direct the others. After only a few false starts, the boat drifted steadily away from the pier. The current fought them every step of the way, and the wind was too limp to do much good, so Cræosh, Katim, Jhurpess, and Fezeill (having, to Cræosh's disgust, assumed the shape of an orc) set to rowing. Belrotha's help would have been welcomed, but the oars were situated belowdecks, and she just couldn't fit. Still, the four oarsmen—oarsgoblins—weren't precisely lacking in muscle, and the vessel moved steadily toward the River Krael.

They came *this close* to pulling it off. The soldiers, forming a bucket brigade and desperately struggling to quench the fire before it spread, might never have noticed the boat was missing. But it was not to be so easy. Perhaps the firelight reflected off something on the stolen vessel; perhaps a wayward creak reached their ears despite the crackling of the flame; perhaps someone had just happened to look the right way at the wrong time. Whatever the case, a barrage of shouts and pointing fingers aimed themselves at the boat.

"Well, that tears it," Gork muttered as he looked back over the spindly railing. "Next time we just kill the bastards and be done with it!" Of course, most of the squad was belowdecks manning the oars, and Belrotha stood by the wheel, steering under Gimmol's direction, so there was no one there to hear him. He continued to curse anyway.

"Hey!" Gimmol called to him, not looking away from the dark waters. "We're coming up on the watchtower!"

"So?" Gork shouted back.

"So get to the damn prow of the ship and keep a lookout!" the gremlin ordered him. "We're not moving all that fast. The soldiers may have had time to get them a message!"

Grumbling, Gork shuffled to the front of the ship and cast his eyes upward.

Not much more than thirty feet tall, the tower stood only a few paces from the bend where the tributary met the Krael. Torchlight burned in the narrow windows, but the kobold had no way of knowing what activity, if any, was going on beyond them, nor could he see, even at this distance, what might be happening behind the crenellations on the roof.

"Looks clear so far," he called to the gremlin, "but I can't tell—oh, dragonshit!" A sudden loud snap, audible even at their current distance, sounded from atop the tower, and something blotted out the glittering stars.

"*Catapult!*" Gork hurled himself, screaming, to the deck. Just beyond the stern, the water burst upward in a short-lived geyser, drenching everyone on deck.

"They're getting our range!" Gimmol cried, clinging desperately so as not to be hurled from his perch. Gork, for once, couldn't blame the gremlin for the panic he heard in Gimmol's voice, since he was right there with him.

"What the fuck's going on up there?" Cræosh's voice drifted faintly from below. The gremlin and the kobold both ignored him.

Belrotha craned her neck forward, staring thoughtfully (on a relative scale, of course) at the tower. Then, gently, she lowered Gimmol to the deck. "Can you handle wheel?" she asked.

The gremlin frowned. "I think so," he said. "Especially if Gork helps."

Belrotha snorted. "Gork not help with anything. Him selfish. Me be back soon." And with that she plunged overboard, sending up another drenching spray not much smaller than that caused by the boulder.

"What the hell?" Gork shouted.

"Shut up and come help me with this damn wheel!"

They couldn't actually tell if Belrotha had swum to shore or sunk to the river bottom and walked, but she reappeared swiftly enough. She rose from the water at the far bank like some emerging monster—which, come to think of it, she was. Two strides brought her to the tower's side. She didn't even slow to open the door, just ducked her head beneath the stone frame and plowed straight through the wood.

"Think she can get upstairs before they can get off another shot?" Gork asked nervously.

Gimmol shrugged, practically hanging from the wheel with both hands. "It takes a while to load those things," he said, "but not *that* long. I don't—"

They cringed as one at the sudden snapping sound from above. He and Gork tugged on the great wheel, struggling to turn, and Gimmol was convinced they were about to die horribly, or at least get very wet. Another missile streaked across the stars, and Gimmol clenched his teeth, bracing himself. . . .

Although, now that it drew nearer, did that look a little small to be a catapult boulder? And . . .

"Is it *screaming*?" Gimmol asked hesitantly. Gork could only nod.

A wildly flailing human, clad in the black uniform of Kirol Syrreth, plummeted from the sky and spattered messily across the deck.

"Well, they've obviously got our range," Gimmol said tonelessly, not trusting himself to speak further.

Again Gork nodded. The boat passed beyond the guard tower without further incident.

Belrotha rejoined them a few moments later, having jogged ahead and dived into the river. It was a matter of no small effort dragging her back aboard; Gork and Gimmol had eventually convinced the others that speed was no longer of quite so much essence, allowing Cræosh and Katim to come up and give the dripping ogre a hand.

"I'm almost positive we talked about the whole murder thing," Cræosh said once they were done, staring at the uniform that was now glued to the deck by an assortment of various bodily fluids.

"Couldn't be helped," Gimmol said happily, having reclaimed his spot on Belrotha's shoulder. "The guards were lobbing boulders at us. Damn near sank us, too. Belrotha, um, talked them out of it."

The ogre beamed. "Me can be convincing," she said quietly, as though letting them in on some long-kept secret. "Me find that most peoples very cooperative after me tear their friends' arms off."

"Yeah," the orc said, "I can see how that might end a debate or two." He sighed. "I don't suppose you thought to hide the evidence?"

Belrotha cocked her head to the side. "Too messy to hide," she said slowly. "But at least them won't be able to tell how *many* dead soldiers up there."

That may not have satisfied the orc, but it was enough to make him stop asking questions. He and Katim returned below, and the ship reached the River Krael just before dawn. At that point, the squad relaxed, taking shifts at the oars only in pairs and allowing the current to do most of the work. And slowly, the Sea of Tears drew near.

Cræosh, sprawled in a chair with his feet up on a crate and his head tilted back against the railing, chuckled as Gork staggered across the deck, lurched over to the opposite railing, and generously donated his most recent meal to the nearest hungry school of fish.

"You might want to do something about that," the orc said critically, eyeing the kobold as he stumbled from the edge.

"Go to hell, Cræosh."

"I'm just concerned is all, Shorty. I really don't think you're big enough to hold that much half-digested food. You may be missing some important organs."

Gork glowered at him.

"Tell you what," Cræosh said. "Why don't you head on downstairs and grab yourself a slice of fish. It's bland; it might calm you down a bit."

"Fish?" Gork squealed. "*Fish?!* We've eaten nothing but fish for a week!"

"Well, we've got a little yeti left. Seems Gimmol twiddled his fingers and cast some spell to preserve it when we weren't looking. A nice, greasy glob of yeti fat would slide down real smooth, don't you think?"

The kobold made a sort of gurgling sound and quickly dashed back to the railing.

He'd exaggerated just a tad, actually. It had only been a few days, not a full week, since they'd been vomited from the mouth of the Krael like one of Gork's meals and begun to cross the Sea of Tears. It *felt*, however, as though they'd been at sea for months. Not a single member of the squad was fond of fish, and half of them had been seasick at least once. Clothes were crusty with saltwater spray, and nostrils quivered with the unaccustomed scents of the ocean. It was something akin to a minor miracle that Cræosh had managed to let off enough steam by verbally abusing the kobold, rather than snapping and trying to tear someone limb from limb. Belrotha had taken to staring moodily out over the water. Even Gimmol had started snapping at anyone who spoke to him, and *nobody* dared set foot anywhere near Katim. From the instant the boat had reached the sea, the troll's ears had actually folded back along her head, and she'd planted herself in a single spot, unmoving, hands wrapped around the shaft of her axe. Everyone knew full well that it was as much as their lives were worth even to look at her cross-eyed.

Nonetheless, they'd survived those past few days, and they survived the ones that followed. Nobody was even permanently maimed.

The end of the journey was, by a wide margin, the easiest stretch. The isle of Dendrakis boasted a startling number of fishing villages, pockmarks blemishing the otherwise pristine coastline. They were—or this one was, at any rate—astonishingly, even frighteningly normal. Although it thrived in the shadow of the Iron Keep, the people there were friendly, even helpful. The fishermen scrambled to clear one of the town's only piers, and aided the goblins in tying up when it became obvious that nobody in the Demon Squad had the slightest idea of how to go about it. Cræosh, uncomfortably aware of their proximity to the Iron Keep, offered to pay a fair price for berthing; the villagers, in turn, accepted only half that amount.

It was, all told, more than a little disturbing. Cræosh and Gork both came near to spraining something, trying to keep watch behind them as the village disappeared into the distance.

The "main road," which was also the *only* road, was a pebble-coated path that meandered across the rocky terrain toward the mountains in the northwest. They came across no one once they departed the village, and in fact, they spotted no life at all: no wild goats climbing the rocky hills, no lizards scuttling through the scrub, no birds circling overhead. Thunder rolled perpetually from a bank of clouds that hovered low above the mountain peaks, but it—along with their own footsteps and occasional nervous voices—was all that broke the oppressive silence.

Another gradual turn over the path, around the edges of another hill of stone, and even the footsteps and the voices went silent.

They stood immobile, intimidated (even if some would never admit it) by the alien lines of the Iron Keep. Their eyes were drawn, all unwillingly, to the tips of the twisted spires, and then nearly blinded by the lightning that seemed deliberately drawn to those towers from the clouds above.

And still they saw no sign of life. No guards walked the battlements, nor peered from behind the ferrous crenellations. No footsteps echoed from the keep's outer halls; no torchlight flickered in the arrow slits. The Iron Keep looked as dead as its lord and master.

They finally psyched themselves up to approach, halting only at the massive gate: a solid slab of metal that smugly barred the only entrance to the keep. It was pretty much featureless—a notable sight amid the intricate runes filigreed into the rest of the iron—marred only by a single handle. This protruded from the precise center of the door, far too high and far too large for use by anyone even remotely human-sized.

"What do you think?" Fezeill asked, casting a glance at Gimmol. "Magic?"

The gremlin's scowl might have been more convincing had his lip not been quivering.

Cræosh finally shrugged. "We'd better knock, I suppose," he muttered glumly. Then, realizing that if they started arguing about who was to actually do it they'd be there until next autumn, he raised a hand to take care of it himself.

Barely had the orc's knuckles brushed the dull metal when the door opened, sliding upward with a muffled clanking of chains. And there before them was the first of the Iron Keep's halls. Here, the interior walls were made of a dark-hued stone, rather than the iron filigree common to the upper floors, and that fact imparted just the tiniest hint of normality, enough to convince the squad to step inside. The corridors were lofty enough that even Belrotha could stand comfortably, though Gimmol couldn't stay on her shoulder and had to walk on his own.

No one appeared to greet them, but they couldn't doubt which way to go. It was a simple enough system, really: So long as they were headed the right way, the corridors remained empty. If they made a wrong turn, they found themselves face-to-face with one of the Charnel King's rotting sentinels. Those walking corpses made no threatening moves, unless one counted the fact that they moved at all. Their presence alone, standing at attention in the hall's center, sword or axe or halberd in hand, was all the impetus the Demon Squad needed to try a different route. Slowly, the goblins made their way into the upper levels, drawing ever nearer the godlike king who held their lives in his long-dead hands.

"Now *this*," Gork muttered, his footsteps echoing hollowly on the filigreed-metal floor, "I don't like."

"Oh, right," Cræosh said. "As opposed to the rest of this trip, which has been a damn picnic."

"I don't know," the kobold said, glancing uneasily at the black iron walls. "This is different."

Cræosh snorted, mostly to cover up the fact that he agreed whole-heartedly with the nervous thief. It wasn't even so much the dead guards that bothered him; after running into the first eight or ten, one eventually grew numb to the whole experience (except, perhaps, the stench, to which there was no growing accustomed). No, it wasn't the presence of the dead but the absence of the living that was starting to utterly unnerve the already-jumpy orc.

"Doesn't anyone actually *live* in this damn place?!" Gimmol finally shouted, startling the rest of the squad halfway out of their skins. Obviously, Cræosh wasn't the only one disturbed.

Katim spun like a top, lashing out. Gimmol found himself lifted off his feet and slammed into the nearest wall. "Don't *ever* do that . . . again!" the troll snapped, her talons digging into the gremlin's leather armor. "Never!"

Belrotha's gaze fixed on the troll and she growled softly, one hand rising to the monster sword that protruded over her back. The others backed slowly away.

"Twenty silver on the ogre," Gork whispered to Cræosh.

Maybe I should take him up on that. I'd win either way. . . .

"Oh, really." The voice—a thick blend of amusement, disdain, and a bored arrogance—sluiced from the shadows of a nearby stairway. "I hardly think King Morthûl would have let you get this far if he didn't wish to speak with you. So he's not bloody well about to let you butcher one another, is he?"

Everyone in the hallway now faced the darkened stair; the ogre, the troll, and the gremlin shoulder to shoulder. (Well, shoulder to hip.) "Who are you?" Cræosh asked, half-drawing his sword. "Show yourself!"

"Spare me the clumsy theatrics, orc. I'm in no mood for jokes."

Katim advanced, putting herself between the orc and their unseen host before Cræosh could say something (read: anything) that would make the situation worse.

"You'll have to forgive . . . the orc," she said, wondering just how many times she was going to have to apologize for his behavior. "He doesn't mean . . . to offend." She paused. "Actually, he *does* mean . . . to offend, but that's because he's . . . too stupid to know better. I am T'chakatimlamitilnog, of the House—"

"Of Ru, yes I know. I know you all." Slowly, ignoring his own previous condemnation of theatrics, the figure slid into the light. He was tall for a human, and gaunt to the point of deformity. He wore breeches that were far tighter than his physique warranted, and his coat and cloak were foppishly ruffled and excessively bright. He was, overall, a man impossible to take seriously. Unless you knew who he was.

Katim and Cræosh knew. Katim held up both hands, palms outward—the gesture means something along the lines of, "I hold no weapons and will not try to kill you at the moment" and is the closest thing trolls have to a formal greeting—and even Cræosh had the grace to bow his head.

"My name is Vigo Havarren. If you'll follow me, I'll take you to see King Morthûl."

Their guide remained silent and aloof as he led them through the labyrinthine passages of the Iron Keep and finally made his excuses as they approached a single black door at the end of a long black hallway. (Cræosh was, by this point, getting mighty sick of the color black.)

"He waits through there," Havarren said, gesturing casually. "I'll not be joining you. It's you he wishes to see, and I spend enough time in his presence that I think I can tolerate being apart from him a little longer. I trust that whatever knowledge you bring is worth his while. Our lord is not a patient man; wasting his time is unwise." And with that rather melodramatic pronouncement, the skinny wizard moved to leave.

"Wait!" Cræosh called after him.

Havarren froze. "Wait, *what*?" he asked dangerously.

Cræosh nearly choked on it, but he wasn't *that* stubborn. "Wait, please."

The mage smiled. "Of course. What is it?"

"He knew we were coming, didn't he?"

Havarren's smile widened. "He became aware of your journey the moment your keel hit the waters of the Sea of Tears. He found it most curious that his own Demon Squad felt the need to sneak across the kingdom in a leaky fishing boat, so he ordered his forces to allow you to land, rather than to sink you outright, and to avoid disturbing or distracting you on your way through these halls. He's most anxious to hear your tale. Now, if you'll excuse me . . ."

Cræosh watched the enigmatic mage depart and then reluctantly turned his attention to the black door. He drew a deep breath, doubtless preparing some crude comment, and slowly exhaled as the door opened by itself.

"You'd think they'd get tired of that trick," Gork whispered, drawing another of Cræosh's patented Irritated Glares. Then, drawing himself up to his full height, the orc stepped across Morthûl's threshold.

The expansive chamber swallowed the sound as they made their way across the onyx-hued floor. Their footsteps landed with muffled thumps, and even their own breathing sounded somehow distant. Cræosh, as well as most of the others, examined the twisted cages that were wrought in the filigreed walls, wondering and worrying as to their purpose. Gimmol, however, glanced downward just in time to see a flash of movement beneath the supposedly solid floor. A brief tremor shook his body, and he found himself moving closer to the ogre, seeking a protection that he knew she wasn't equipped to offer.

And then they reached him. He was seated behind a mundane writing desk, poring over a large tome stained and cracked by centuries of use. One leathery finger reached out, slowly turning the page, and none of the squad could tell where the crackling of parchment left off and the rustling of dried flesh began.

Only after he had finished that final page did the Charnel King rise.

Cræosh had seen countless corpses in his life. He had faced the undead in the swamps of Jureb Nahl, and the skittering vermin of the Steppes creatures. Disturbing as it was, nothing in Morthûl's visage should have proved so overwhelming. And yet the orc swallowed hard, barely forcing a whimper back down his throat. His heart beat wildly in his chest, and for the first time, he truly understood Gimmol's horror at the notion of there ever being a second such creature. Now, beneath that sickly glowing gaze, Cræosh wasn't certain that the world could survive *one*.

As though reading his thoughts as easily as he had the book—a possibility that Cræosh wasn't willing to rule out—the flesh-covered half of the Charnel King's face contorted into a shallow smile. The bending and snapping of the desiccated skin sounded like cracking ice. "I understand," he said in a distorted voice, a voice all the more horrible for the fact that it had clearly once been human, "that you wished to see me."

Cræosh's jaw moved, but he found to his horror that he was unable to form the words. For a moment he gaped idiotically, and then he finally shut his mouth, trying to salvage some semblance of dignity. Behind him, the others shuffled, none willing to speak up, and Morthûl's parchment-like flesh creased in irritation.

It was Gork, actually, who stepped forward to speak—not because he was any less terrified than the others, but because he was *more* terrified of irritating King Morthûl. If the master of the Iron Keep chose to peer into their thoughts, rather than waiting for their answers, he'd learn *far* more than Gork ever wanted him to know.

"You-your Majesty," Gork stammered, "we did indeed wish to-to speak with you. You see, we discovered—"

The Charnel King raised a hand, and Gork choked on his own words. "I have been too busy to properly keep abreast of your activities," the Dark Lord informed them. "Perhaps that was an error in judgment. Start from the beginning. Start from your arrival at Castle Eldritch."

And so he did. Gork launched directly into the tale and, other than omitting any mention of the dakórren and his peculiar familiar, spared no detail. The others chimed in occasionally, when he neglected something or to clarify a point; and though he remained terrified, Gork found himself feeling slightly more relaxed by the time the tale wound to its conclusion.

"There are some who would suggest," Morthûl said softly, "that I should not believe a word of what you've just told me." Gork's nerves began to fray once more, to pound beneath his skin, perhaps seeking their own escape. He began to sweat, and dug his nails into his palms to keep from fidgeting.

"But," the Dark Lord continued, "I cannot imagine that you would come all this way, risk your lives and even your souls, to lie to me." He spun on his heels, the gesture flinging a small shower of thrashing insects from his tattered blue cloak. He either didn't notice, or ignored, the kobold's frantic efforts to dislodge them before they burrowed into his clothing.

"It seems that I have not been paying attention," Morthûl said, staring at something only he could see. "I have neglected my queen, and she has gone astray. And I fear there is little to be done for it now." He faced the squad once more, his sockets blazing with a profane yellow light. "I must act. And you will help me."

"M-me?" Gork squeaked.

"All of you." Morthûl returned to his desk and waved a hand over it, once, twice. A transparent image of Castle Eldritch materialized atop the wood, shimmering and wavering. For a time, the undead king studied it, as though attempting to breach its walls through will alone.

"Castle Eldritch was the home of King Sabryen," he said without looking up from the image. "He imbued it with many sorcerous protections, and Anne has expanded them further. Some, now, are nearly as potent as my own magics. Were I to waste the strength to batter through them, I would be forced to delay other preparations I must complete before Dororam launches his so-called invasion." Now he did look up, somehow seeming to meet each goblin's individual gaze at once. "It is time for you to serve your *true* master, my Demon Squad. You will return to Castle Eldritch, and it is through you that I will deal with my wayward queen."

"Um, Your Majesty?" Cræosh began, finally having regained his voice. Even in the midst of their overwhelming terror, the rest of the squad looked shocked at the discovery that the orc could, in fact, be polite. "May I speak?"

"You may."

"Well, I've been a soldier for more years that I can count, Your Majesty."

"More than three, then," Gork whispered very, very softly.

"So please understand," Cræosh continued, "that I'm not questioning orders. And if you order us to our deaths, that's your right, and our privilege to obey. But your Majesty, there's no way we can take on Queen Anne."

"I'm aware of that, orc." Morthûl waved a hand in a casual dismissal of his concerns. "I have no intention of having you attack my bride. I simply need you to deliver this." Something spun through the air toward Gork, who—with a loud "Eep!"—barely raised his hands in time to catch it.

It appeared to be a human skull the size of an apple, carved from marble. Gork opened his mouth to ask a question and just about fainted when the skull began chattering its teeth together and cackling softly.

"What . . . ?" Cræosh began.

"It's a talisman, orc. It should allow me to penetrate the barriers surrounding Castle Eldritch without breaking them down first. It will save me a *staggering* amount of effort.

"Of course, for it to work, it must be in immediate proximity to the source of the wards to be circumvented—in this case, the very heart of my dear queen's laboratory. I rather doubt she'll allow you just to walk in there, no matter how much she trusts you. But you're a Demon Squad. I'm certain you'll come up with something."

The entire squad stared stupidly at the Dark Lord as the marble skull continued its mindless cackle.

The booming echo of Morthûl's chamber door washed over them from behind, and with it a rapturous feeling of relief. Yes, they remained within the alien halls of the Iron Keep, and there was still enough tension in the air to chew on, but the worst was behind them. They hadn't felt this relaxed since their fishing boat had bumped up against the pier on Dendrakis's shore.

And of course, now that they felt more themselves, they were more than willing to argue. "We should have told him about Ebonwind," Fezeill said as they moved back down the hall. "I think he'd have wanted to know that someone's trying to gather information on his military movements."

"I didn't hear you suggesting it in there," Gork snarled. "It's real easy to think about it now, isn't it?"

"We were all . . . distracted," Katim interrupted before the doppelganger could respond. "Not a one of us was . . . thinking clearly at the . . . time. We're alive, and . . . we've delivered our news. Let's . . . call this a victory and leave it . . . at that."

Cræosh glanced around, noting that the human servants and living guards had finally chosen to make their presence known; obviously, Morthûl was no longer concerned with "distracting" them. That, too, provided a sense of normality and added to the squad's (relative) peace of mind.

Havarren awaited them on the lowest step of the first of many stairs they would have to descend on their way out. The squad stopped, falling silent in as close to a show of respect as they could muster. After the Charnel King himself, Havarren just didn't seem so intimidating.

"Are you ready?" the wizard demanded. "I haven't got all day."

"Ready for what?" Gork asked suspiciously.

"For your journey, of course." Havarren wiggled his fingers. "You didn't think King Morthûl would take the time to have you *sail* back to Sularaam, did you?"

"But," Gimmol said, "he told us there are wards in place to prevent—"

"Yes, yes, yes." The blond sorcerer was clearly growing impatient. "Around Castle Eldritch itself, not the entire bloody town. You'll appear just beyond the main bridge. You can walk from there, and it'll create the illusion that you've arrived by more mundane means. Now, if you're through asking stupid questions?"

Actually, Havarren clearly didn't much care if they were through or not. He twisted his hands, and it was done. The Iron Keep melted away like wax under the midday sun, and in its place appeared a familiar stretch of Tiehmon's Way. The wind blew cold, carrying the frigid bite of the Steppes. Beyond the next rise in the road, they all knew, stood the bridge that crossed the River Krom. And beyond *that*, Castle Eldritch, where Queen Anne waited.

But waited for what? Cræosh glanced over his shoulder at his companions. "Who's got the Tree of Ever?" he asked. Katim tapped the largest of her sundry bags and pouches.

"Good," the orc said, nodding. "Until we learn otherwise, we'll assume that Queen Anne's still waiting for the relic, and has no idea anything's changed." He frowned. "Keep your eyes open, though. If she *does* suspect something's up, she sure as fuck ain't gonna give us a lot of warning before she acts on it."

They crossed the bridge with little difficulty, receiving a shallow nod of acknowledgment from the guards as they passed. Most of the bustling throng cleared out of their path, and those who didn't were casually shoved aside. The constant low roar of the crowd finally faded just slightly behind them, and there they were. Castle Eldritch towered over them, gleaming white in the sun. The gates, however, were closed, and no line of petitioners occupied the lanes surrounding the walls.

Fezeill grunted and shifted back to his human form, abandoning the orcish body he'd worn for a while now. "Easier to hide in the crowd," he said in response to the squad's puzzled looks. "Should the worst happen, of course."

"Of course," Cræosh said.

"Should we knock?" Gimmol asked.

The orc shook his head. "I don't particularly like this development. Where are all the people?"

"Home," Gork said. "Which makes them smarter than us."

"Let's not announce our presence just yet," Cræosh continued. "The wall ain't so tall that we should have any real problem getting over it. If we're spotted, we'll just tell them that we got impatient. Hell, that's in character, right?" He grinned.

"For you, anyway," Katim said. "But it . . . will suffice."

"I'm so fucking thrilled you approve." He glanced down toward the kobold. "Grappling hooks are damn loud when they land, Shorty. Why don't you scramble on up there and secure a rope for us?"

Gork skittered up the wall, grumbling the whole way—more for the sake of being ornery, Cræosh thought, than because of any real objection. He carefully planted a grappling hook over the lip of the stone, then waved. Cræosh tugged it a few times, nodded, and the entire squad shimmied up to the top.

All, of course, save Belrotha, who was a whole lot more ogre than the rope could handle. Instead she backed up a few paces, raced forward, and leapt. Without hesitation and seemingly without difficulty, she vaulted the thirty-foot wall—her hands coming very near to squishing Gork in the process—and landed in a crouch on the other side.

Gork and Cræosh, still hunched atop the wall, gawped at one another.

The kobold was the first to speak. "Did she just . . . ?"

"No," Cræosh informed him. "She didn't. Now shut up and flip that rope over here so we can climb down."

All told, it took the Demon Squad less than two minutes to clear the wall. It was swift, professional, and relatively silent (despite the thump of the ogre's landing). Still, Cræosh found himself disturbed by the complete lack of attention. Sure, he'd hoped their entrance would go unnoticed, but he hadn't really *expected* it to. Queen Anne's guards might not be of the same caliber as the men (and other things) who patrolled the Iron Keep, but they couldn't be *this* incompetent, could they?

Which meant they had to be occupied elsewhere, with something big enough to draw every last one from his assigned post, or they'd been dismissed. Neither option was appealing in its implications.

Unlike the outer gate, the inner doors hung open, and the squad simply marched into the castle proper. Their feet once more trampled the lush carpeting; again, their hackles rose beneath the gaze of the poor inhabitants of the gleaming armor. They strode past the various murals and tapestries, each and every one of them steadfastly refusing to look up.

And then, the door to the throne room. Unguarded. Cræosh threw the portal open before him without slowing his pace.

The throne room was empty.

The queen's absence was one thing; she could hardly spend *all* her time in public audience. But the lack of guards, of servants, petitioners, sycophants, all pointed to something substantially more sinister than a slow day at court.

"I don't like this," Gork said.

"You've said that before," Cræosh reminded him. "In fact, last I checked, you didn't especially like much of anything."

"True," Gork admitted. "But I don't like this a lot more than I don't like a lot of other things."

Cræosh briefly reviewed that, trying to determine if it actually made any sense, and then decided not to bother. "Okay. I don't know if this means she's on to us or not, but there's obviously *something* strange going on."

"You have such a tight . . . grip on the obvious," Katim said dryly, "that I'm astounded . . . you haven't broken it so far."

"Shut up, troll. I'm not in the mood."

She grinned at him.

"So where do you suppose Queen Anne's laboratory is?" Fezeill asked. Every face turned toward Gimmol.

The gremlin frowned. "Well, I can't say for sure, of course . . ." he hedged.

"Say it anyway," Cræosh told him. "You've got a better shot at it than we do."

"If you say so. All right, let's see." The gremlin paused thoughtfully. "Magnificent as it is, Eldritch isn't really that big of a castle. We know that the second level consists entirely of sleeping chambers and the like, so that's out. We've already seen the main hall and the throne room. It *could* be elsewhere on the ground level, but that wouldn't offer much room. Or privacy. Privacy is a big deal with wizards; having an experiment interrupted is bad."

"I can imagine," Cræosh muttered. "One of the towers, then?"

"Yeah. Or else underground."

Katim shook her head. "No. She will not . . . be underground."

"And what makes you so sure?" Fezeill asked acidly.

"Queen Anne is a . . . woman of great power. And great . . . ego. She would have to . . . be to seek the kind of immortality . . . she covets. She will surely keep . . . her workspace somewhere that . . . allows her to look out over her . . . domain. Her pride will allow her . . . nothing less." She leered evilly. "It is a common failing . . . among those who rule."

"I'm not sure I buy that logic," Gork said.

Cræosh shrugged. "Look, we've got to pick one to start with, right? I say go with it. If anyone here knows about haughtiness and ego, it's Katim."

The troll snarled, and Cræosh permitted himself a brief grin. *Score one for the orc.*

"Up it is, then," Gork agreed, though he didn't sound one hundred percent convinced.

"Good!" the bugbear said from the back. "Jhurpess hates being underground."

"This is all well and good," Gimmol said, "but we still don't know how to get into the tower. If it *is* her laboratory, I doubt the door's going to be easily accessible."

"Then," Katim said, "I suggest that we . . . start looking."

"Just like that?" Gork asked incredulously. "Do you have any idea how long it'll take to search this entire castle?"

"And how long will it . . . take us to find the entrance if . . . we do *not* look for it?"

Gork shut his mouth, and the squad began their search with the throne room.

The throne room ultimately revealed not one, but *three* concealed doors strewn throughout the chamber. One led to the queen's garden, opening up far too near the evil-looking vines for the squad's comfort. The second led into a small observation chamber, apparently designed to allow the queen to unobtrusively monitor her soldiers as they practiced in the castle's training arena. And the third provided ingress to a small barracks, perhaps the sleeping quarters of Queen Anne's personal guard. It was as devoid of life as the rest of Eldritch.

So the goblins' explorations had continued, as had their discoveries. They discovered a hidden panel in the ballroom, leading to a dusty, cobweb-filled enclosure with murder holes drilled in the walls, providing a clear field of fire at the celebrants. They discovered that Queen Anne's library, while not remotely the equal of Ymmech Thewl, could nevertheless have kept Gimmol occupied for the next three years (not counting chamber pot breaks), had they permitted him to stay. As it was, they'd had to drag him out whimpering. And they'd found numerous supply closets stocked with tools, rope, ladders, lamps, torches, oil, extra dishes and silverware, and basically anything else required to maintain the smooth operations of a castle and its inhabitants. Not a one of them could figure out why *those* doors had been concealed.

By the time they'd fully scoured the entire ground level, they'd determined Castle Eldritch had as many secret doors as normal ones—but that none of them offered so much as a trace of any possible entrance to the central tower. They had also failed to find one single sign of human life; even the smaller guard towers were empty.

"Is anyone besides me starting to get just a tad nervous about all this?" Gimmol asked when Gork dropped back down from his check of the fourth guard tower.

The kobold dusted his hands off on the sides of his pants. "I take exception to your use of the word 'tad.' And the word 'starting,' for that matter. Anyone who's not already as nervous as a halfling virgin at a dwarven orgy is an idiot."

Cræosh, who had been staring intently down a nearby corridor, glanced sharply at Gork. "'Halfling virgin?'" He grinned widely. "You've been traveling with me too long, Shorty."

"Well shit, Cræosh, *I* could've told you *that*."

"I don't suppose," Katim rasped sourly, "that . . . I might impose on you to . . . take just a moment of your . . . time and focus on the reason we're . . . here?"

"Sure you can impose," Cræosh said. "Just as soon as you have the slightest fucking clue what we should do next, you can impose to your heart's content."

"Is there anyplace we haven't looked?" Fezeill asked.

"Are we in the . . . tower?"

"Umm . . . No, not really."

"Then I'd say there's at least . . . one place we haven't looked."

Fezeill glowered at her. "Wise-ass troll . . ."

"What was that?"

"Um, I said you're a wise troll."

"Yes, I know. It was . . . decent of you to point it out . . . however." The doppelganger continued to mumble.

"Queen Anne is wizard?" Belrotha asked suddenly.

"Yes, Belrotha," Gimmol said patiently. "Queen Anne is a wizard."

"Then why we look for door to tower? Maybe Queen Anne not build door to tower. Wizard not need door. Wizard can just go wigglety-poof with fingers and be in tower already."

"'Wigglety-poof?'" Cræosh asked mildly.

"She's got a valid point, though," Gimmol acknowledged, trying not to sound *too* surprised. "Queen Anne *could* make do without a door, at that."

"It don't wash, Gimmol," Cræosh disagreed. "Even if she's too out of her skull to care, it was King Sabryen who designed this castle, remember? And kings have to think strategically."

"Doesn't that make it *more* likely, then?" Gork asked, stepping up to join the discussion. "I mean, a tower with no doors is pretty safe from siege, wouldn't you say?"

The orc shook his head. "Yeah, but it also means that he can't move large numbers of supplies or assistants in and out. Plus, there's those wards King Morthûl mentioned. He'd have to lower them every time he wanted to move in and out of the tower, and that'd expose him to outside sorceries. Not a wise idea. There's *got* to be an entrance, even if only for emergencies."

"I hadn't thought of that," Gimmol admitted.

"But that puts us back where we started," Fezeill said. "Knowing it's here doesn't help if we can't find the damn thing."

"We haven't checked upstairs . . . yet," Katim reminded them.

"There's nothing but sleeping chambers and guest rooms upstairs, remember?" Fezeill said.

"So far as we . . . know. Perhaps one of those rooms is . . . more than it seems."

Gork wilted. "You mean we've got to search every one of the upstairs rooms?"

The piercing gaze of his companions was answer enough.

The kobold was still sulking as he stomped along the first of the seemingly endless upstairs corridors. It felt as though he'd spent the last ten years of his life doing nothing but searching through this and digging through that, and it was starting to wear thin.

Normally, Gork *liked* the opportunity to explore other people's homes and possessions, but the "risk versus reward" equation here seemed unduly weighted toward risk. He'd rather have been home, or in a nicely crowded city with lots of loose purses, or hell, *anywhere* else. Gork had never wanted to be a soldier, let alone assigned to a Demon Squad. The direction that his life had taken recently was starting to eat at him, a parasite in his gut that he couldn't quite ignore.

Thus it was that when the light went out—*all* the light, from the still-burning torches in their sconces to the dull sunlight penetrating the narrow windows—Gork reacted not as a soldier, but as a thief. With a stifled cry, the kobold hurled himself toward the nearest wall. He knew, from before the darkness had fallen, that he was only a few steps from one of the bedroom doors. His hands scrabbled across the stone, frantically seeking the knob, and escape from whatever was coming.

Gimmol dropped into a crouch, mouth and hands moving in the beginnings of an incantation. Belrotha and Jhurpess both put their backs to the nearest wall, arms stretched out in the hopes of intercepting anything that drew near. Fezeill shifted through a multitude of forms, hoping that the heightened senses of the elves or the catlike vision of the troglodytes might penetrate the unnatural shadow; the sporadic but vehement cursing suggested that they failed. Cræosh and Katim stood back-to-back. The orc's heavy sword methodically sliced through empty space, and Katim's *chirrusk* whistled menacingly in the dark.

It was a dark not merely of sight, but of soul. Thoughts came sluggishly, through a haze of forgetfulness. The hum of the troll's chain, the heavy breathing of the unnerved ogre, the distant thump of what sounded like a slamming door—all took on a low, muffled feel, as if the entire squad had been submerged in something cold and clammy. Cræosh's skin crawled, and he felt the hair standing up on the troll behind him.

The voice, when it came, was *not* distorted by the ebon blanket that covered the hallway, but rang out instead like a clarion.

"And a pleasant day to you all, my dear friends. I trust you find the accommodations satisfactory?"

"Rupert," Cræosh greeted him, eyes flickering madly in search of any sign of light, of life. "You might want to have a word with the servants. They seem to have let the torches burn out."

The dark-robed seneschal chuckled softly. "And to think, dear Cræosh, there are those who accuse you of being humorless."

"I'm not humorless. I've got lots of humor. I'm so full of humor that my bladder's about to burst. Why don't you do something about this darkness and I can actually show you?"

"I'm afraid that wouldn't be convenient," Rupert said with a sigh so melodramatic it really needed its own cloak to swirl about its ankles. "The dark should make it *so* much easier to slaughter the lot of you."

"Slaughter us?" Cræosh played up the shock, stalling for time. "Wouldn't that upset Queen Anne?"

"Queen Anne is aware of your betrayal, you miserable little orc!" Rupert's voice was suddenly ice. "If she weren't otherwise engaged, I'm sure she'd have loved to attend to you herself.

"But I'm glad she can't. I'm rather looking forward to doing this myself. And you can stop waving your sword about like a ninny, Cræosh. I can see quite well enough to avoid it, thank you much."

Cræosh's mind transformed every sound to tickle his ears, every touch of breeze on his face, into the precursor to an attack. He stabbed or parried desperately, striking only empty air. And all the while, he knew that Rupert lurked, laughing silently as he drifted nearer, nearer. . . .

And then Gimmol, hunched beside the ogre's calf, released his spell.

Everyone in the hallway froze, including the queen's startled seneschal. The gremlin hadn't the magic to *completely* counter the unnatural darkness. The torches shone as little more than beacons in the gloom-swaddled hall, and the windows glowed only faintly. As though standing outside on a cloud-dimmed night, the goblins could see only a few feet beyond their noses, stood in a world of abstract shapes and shadows.

But it was enough.

Cræosh slashed murderously at the brown-robed figure that had appeared only a few feet away. Rupert hurled himself aside, barely avoiding the whistling steel.

"Now ain't that interesting," Cræosh remarked. "I don't know what you are under all the wrappings, but you're as scared of a sword as the next man, aren't you?"

Rupert snorted and rose to hover several feet above the carpet. "You cannot possibly comprehend what I am, little pig. And your sword is harmless if it cannot land a blow." Sparks arced between the seneschal's outstretched fingers, then crackled across the hall. A loud sizzling, the pungent aroma of roasting meat, and Cræosh screamed in pain, flinging his sword away as though it had bitten him. Smoke rose from the palm of his hand, and several strips of well-cooked flesh clung to the weapon's hilt. A few sparks popped from the tip of the sword, and several tongues of flame flared on the carpet, only to die again just as quickly.

"Katim?" Cræosh asked, his left hand clenched around his right and his voice made hoarse with pain.

"Yes?"

"Whatever Rupert is, your collection doesn't have one, does it?"

"No."

"Perhaps you ought to rectify that."

Rupert pivoted toward the advancing troll. She grinned, her twisted jaw opening, her horrible teeth shifting roughly in their sockets. Her gums brushed against the insides of her lips, and a thin trail of saliva fell to vanish into the carpet.

"Attractive," Rupert said, raising his hands to point at Katim's chest.

"Yeah," Cræosh agreed. "And distracting, too."

Belrotha drove both fists into Rupert's robe from behind and began to tear.

An inhuman wail sounded from deep—far, far *too* deep—within Rupert's hood. His hands thrashed wildly, and even the ogre rocked back as they slammed against her. Cræosh could only wonder, marveling, at the strength contained within that flimsy robe. But Belrotha held fast, ignoring the deep mottled bruises, ignoring the streams of blood that slowly trickled down her face, dribbling over her lips. The form beneath that robe was *wrong*, gave impossibly as she twisted and yanked. No bones broke and no flesh tore, for whatever the robe contained, it appeared to possess neither.

Again Rupert reached out, but this time he was not striking at the ogre. A shimmering rainbow light rose from his palm to burst before Belrotha's face. Her eyes glazed over, pupils dilating, and her grip went limp. She stood frozen, staring deeply at nothing at all, or at least nothing that any of the others could see.

Rupert yanked himself free of Belrotha's slackened fists just in time to catch Katim's *chirrusk* across his head and Fezeill's blade in his back. Writhing, the robed figure twisted aside, hauling himself off the doppelganger's sword. Beneath the prongs of the hook, the left half of his hood tore completely off the robe.

Cræosh felt his jaw drop and saw Katim's do the same as the hooked end of her *chirrusk* fell unnoticed to the carpet. Vaguely, he thought he heard Gimmol gasp, and Jhurpess—who'd just been approaching Rupert with club held high—fell back whimpering.

Staring at Rupert's head, or rather where his head should have been, was akin to staring down an ambulatory hole. The hallway beyond was visible *through* him, but distant, distorted—like looking through the wrong end of a dwarven spyglass. Cræosh had to lower his gaze, to look at the robed torso rather than through that "head," lest he be overcome with vertigo.

"I do hope your curiosity is satisfied," Rupert said. "But it's dreadfully impolite to stare so."

The others snapped back to attention, but the phantasmal seneschal had taken advantage of their stunned immobility, drifting some way down the hall, putting himself well beyond reach of the Demon Squad's weapons. Already his hands were raised for another spell. Cræosh,

Katim, and Fezeill bounded forward; Jhurpess dropped his club and was desperately fitting an arrow to his bow; but none of them needed Gimmol's frightened shout to know that they could not cover the distance before Rupert unleashed his magics.

Behind Rupert, the door to one of the hallway's many bedrooms creaked slowly open, revealing a single gleaming eye.

Gork had no love for his companions—in point of fact, he hated most of them—but as the battle raged, two thoughts kept floating to the surface of his devious little mind:

If they all die, Morthûl's gonna be really *pissed at me.* And . . .

If they all die, I'm gonna be stuck facing Rupert and Queen Anne on my own!

And so, as he had against the yetis, the kobold waited until he was sure he could make a difference, and then he charged. His *kah-rahahk* remained firmly in its sheath; he'd seen enough to know that Rupert had no corporeal body to stab, and while Belrotha's tearing at the robe itself had clearly caused him pain, Gork knew that he couldn't shred it with his tiny blade, not before the creature roasted him like a kitten on a spit.

But thanks to the neatly made bed within the chamber he'd chosen as a hiding place, that jagged dagger was not the kobold's only weapon.

Gork burst from concealment, pounded down the hall in a matter of seconds, and leapt. Using both feet and one hand, he scrabbled and crawled his way *up* the strangely moving, almost viscous robe, appeared over Rupert's shoulder, and allowed himself to drop down in front of him. . . .

Dragging, the entire way, the quilt he'd hauled from the bed. The heavy wool draped over Rupert's head, or whatever it was he had in place of a head, forming a colorful, pastel shroud.

Gork was leaping again even as his feet touched the floor, passing under the robe and between where Rupert's ankles should have been. Clutching a corner of the quilt in one hand, he reached up and snagged the edge still trailing behind the flailing figure. For just an instant, as Gork clung tightly in the face of Rupert's bucking, the seneschal was well and truly netted.

Cræosh never slowed his charge. As his pumping legs carried him toward the disoriented foe, he dropped his own blade, reached out with his uninjured hand, and yanked Fezeill's short sword from the doppelganger's fingers. Ignoring the sudden yelp of protest, the orc lowered his shoulder.

His own wicked blade, after all, was meant for chopping. And just this once, that wasn't what Cræosh wanted. Roaring, he slammed the thrashing figure back a few steps, then shoved the smaller blade through the heavy quilt and through the nonexistent "face" below.

For an instant, there seemed no substance, no end, beneath the heavy fabric. On and on the blade continued without hint of resistance. Cræosh's hand tore through the rent in the quilt; every muscle tightened, as though he were stretching for something he couldn't quite reach. An impossible cold, worse than anything the Steppes had offered, brushed his skin.

Finally, though, the blade punched through the back of the quilt and into the heavy wood of the nearest door, pinning the seneschal down, a rare and dying butterfly. The wood splintered, squealing, as the sword, driven by the orc's powerful thrust, sank into the door to the hilt.

Rupert shrieked, and his voice was the roaring wind. On and on, whipping about them, sending clothes and hair to violent fluttering. His hands thrashed at angles impossible for anything remotely human, reducing the quilt to tatters—all save the patch he wore like a hood, nailing him to the door. Ribbons swirled about the hallway in a flurry of woolen snow.

The illumination in the hall flickered, dimmed, and then returned to normal as Rupert's incantation of darkness faded away.

"You know," Gork said conversationally, "he might just pull out of that eventually." Even as he spoke, the short sword shifted, the metal pressing against the surrounding wood with another teeth-grinding screech.

"He might," Cræosh agreed, kneeling to retrieve his own sword from the floor. "Gimmol?"

The little gremlin stepped forward, frowning. "It must be the robe that gives him substance," he offered, though he sounded hesitant. "I can't think of any other reason he'd have avoided your sword, or why Belrotha's attack hurt him."

"Me can hurt *anything*," the ogre said dreamily, only slowly awakening from her trance.

"I'm sure you can." For once, Cræosh was feeling somewhat magnanimous—perhaps because he'd already gotten the chance to stab Rupert in the face. "After you," he offered Katim, along with a shallow bow.

Her axe slammed into the twisting seneschal, splitting the door in two. She yanked it down, shredding fabric by the foot. Rupert's gale-force scream grew even more shrill, until every ear in the hallway throbbed. Ignoring the pain as best they could, the orc and the troll took turns, slashing and slicing with mechanical regularity. The door crumbled into so much rubbish—Rupert was pinned, now, to nothing more than a plank of wood, albeit a heavy one—and still they continued, never letting up for even a single heartbeat.

After a full two minutes of this, Rupert's unending cry finally wavered and faded away. After five, the robe was nothing more than random scraps of cloth, mixed in with the splintered heap that had been the door. Just for good measure, Gork reached up, swiped one of the torches off the wall, and shoved it into the pile. It caught instantly, and the kobold watched with a satisfied smirk as smoke began to stain the ceiling.

"Have I mentioned how beautiful today is?" Gork asked.

"How's Belrotha?" Cræosh asked Gimmol, who had gone over to check up on the bewildered giant.

"Definitely coming out of it," the gremlin replied, relief etched deeply in his face.

"Pretty colors," the ogre said, blinking.

"I'm sure they were," Gimmol commiserated.

"Can Gimmol bring colors back?"

"That, uh, wouldn't be a good idea, Belrotha."

Gork snorted from across the hall. "She can't *really* be that stupid, can she?"

Cræosh grinned. "Never overestimate the intelligence of the ogres, Shorty. I once saw one trying to wrestle a tornado."

Belrotha glanced up sharply. "Who win?" she asked.

The entire hallway shook as Jhurpess slammed his heavy club hard into the nearest wall. "Jhurpess tired of this!" he shouted, waving his arms, glaring viciously at the lot of them. "Jhurpess tired of talking, Jhurpess tired of wandering like lost cubs, and Jhurpess tired of castle! Jhurpess wants to find queen and leave! Now!"

"Ape's got a point," Cræosh agreed with a shrug.

"You think the entrance to the tower's up here after all?" Gimmol asked as Belrotha once more lifted him to sit beside her head. "I mean, Rupert's the first living thing—well, more or less—that we've seen. Maybe he was guarding the entrance?"

Katim's jaw curled. "I don't think so. Why . . . go to all the trouble of building a . . . secret entrance, and then go and . . . attack anyone who gets near? It . . . sort of ruins the secrecy, don't . . . you think?"

Cræosh nodded. "I'm inclined to agree with the troll," he said. Katim allowed her mouth to gape open, and she clasped both hands over her hearts and staggered.

"Funny," the orc continued, barely even glancing at her. "I think Rupert would've waited to attack us until we were *away* from the entrance, so as not to tip us off."

"Unless he *expected* us to think of that, and so he attacked us when we *were* near—" Gork began.

"Stop it, Shorty, or I'll have to hurt you."

"It was just a thought," the kobold said sullenly.

"Yeah? Well you can take that thought and shove it back up your ass with the rest of your brain!"

"Hello?" Fezeill said, snapping his fingers. "Entrance? Tower? Remember?"

"If we assume that . . . the entrance is not here," Katim continued, "then it only leaves one . . . place. The only place we haven't . . . searched. It really," she added, "should have been . . . our first guess, now that I think . . . about it."

"Oh, fuck," Cræosh said succinctly.

Katim nodded. "Indeed."

The squad, after a few brief stopovers in several of the castle's sundry supply closets, stood gathered at one of the doorways to the queen's unnatural garden. Each of them peered uneasily at the twisting plants and twisting paths—most of them because they'd seen the unpleasant varieties of vegetation residing therein, Belrotha because she still couldn't accept the sudden shift of seasons.

"Okay," Cræosh said, "what now?"

"We still have to find . . . the door," Katim told him.

"Yeah, I sort of know that. How do you propose we go about it? Leaving aside the fact that it really *would* be summer by the time we finished searching the whole place, I'm not getting anywhere near that damn ivy. I've already had to fight one homicidal shrub this month, and that's one more than my quota."

"I agree," Katim told him, a strange excitement coloring her tone. "That's why . . . I've got no intention of searching the . . . garden."

"So what are we doing?" the orc asked, clearly exasperated.

"*Clearing* the . . . garden. Why do you think I . . . insisted we stop on the . . . way?"

Cræosh glanced back at the haphazard collection of supplies and then grinned. "Queen Anne's not going to be at all happy with us."

"You know, I had that . . . exact same thought." Then, together, they both called for the ogre.

Belrotha was more than strong enough to ensure that the barrels reached even the farthest corners of the garden, and that they cracked open when they landed. Even five barrels of the stuff wasn't enough to coat *everything*, but the mess was spread wide enough to serve.

Cræosh began to tear up as the fumes washed over them. "Shall we?" he asked, his nose wrinkling. Katim began striking flint and steel over the end of a torch, a tendril of saliva wobbling from a wide, jagged grin.

"You're enjoying this," Cræosh accused.

The troll shrugged. "I've found very few problems that . . . cannot be solved with the proper application . . . of fire."

"I swear, you're as bad as the bugbear."

Katim's torch finally caught. "You may wish to . . . step back." The blazing brand hurtled over the queen's courtyard, vanished from sight behind a shrubbery. For a long moment, silence—and then, with a heavy *whumph*, the torch ignited the first puddle of the lantern oil in which they'd drenched the garden.

The fire spread quickly, and plants unlike those found anywhere else on the continent began to burn. Thick, cloying smoke rose from the center of Castle Eldritch, impregnating the high-floating clouds, meshing its dull, greasy black with their pristine ivory. A choking miasma—alien, even obscene—spread perniciously across the city of Sularaam. It crept through cracked windows and open doors, clung tenaciously to clothing and carpets and hair. It would take weeks, perhaps months, before the city could rid itself of the lingering stench. Across the tiny isle, hundreds turned to gawk at the smoke that was rapidly transforming from a column to an umbrella over the castle's towers. But the doings of Queen Anne had always lurked beyond the comprehension of mere mortals, and though many a curse was leveled at the choking aroma, not one soul dared approach the castle to investigate.

Within the castle halls, the goblins crouched or huddled in the corners, curled up to shield themselves from the waves of heat that poured through the open doorway, hands clasped tightly to ears, lips and teeth pressed together in grimaces of torment. For within that garden, many of Queen Anne's plants did not go silently as they burned. Across that unhallowed courtyard laired the clinging vines that had required so much more sustenance than soil and sun—and those vines lamented their deaths in a terrible keening that scrabbled at not merely the ears, but at the mind. On it went, and on, unhindered by any animal need to pause for breath, and only when nothing but ash and charred clumps of sticky fibers were left did it finally cease.

And it was long minutes after *that* that Cræosh found himself regaining some sense of hearing through the pounding in his ears.

"Is everyone all right?" he called, somewhat louder than he realized. Some of the replies were more coherent than others, but everyone was alive and not *totally* deaf. He could only hope that by the time the flames died away, they'd all have recovered enough to move on.

Indeed they did—although Katim complained of sporadic ringing in her ears—since it was two hours before the last of the fires sputtered and died. Embers glowed here and there from within heaps of coal-gray ash, and puddles of sap and other fluids bubbled and steamed, but it appeared safe to cross.

It wasn't even that hard to convince Belrotha to step through the doorway. Apparently, she'd somehow decided that burning down the garden was sufficient punishment for its refusal to follow the law of the seasons.

It was Gork, of course, who gave a victorious shout, perhaps twenty minutes later. Every one of the squad was coated to the elbows in black sludge, where they'd pushed and dug through the clinging detritus that had been the ivies, saplings, and other plants growing along the walls. Gork traced a few lines in the ash, revealing the outline of the door.

Directly behind where the man-eating vines had dwelt. "Of course," Cræosh said.

Gork peered at the latch, trying to determine if it was locked—and then threw himself back with a rather porcine squeal as Jhurpess, still impatient, slammed his club into the door. The portal flew open, very nearly wrenching itself from the hinges, and slammed against the wall of the corridor beyond.

"Well," Gork announced sourly, "I guess it's unlocked."

Jhurpess grinned at him, then grinned wider when Belrotha said "Good smash."

"Oh, great." The kobold shook his head. "They're encouraging each other."

The passage beyond the door led to a spacious spiral staircase winding its way up the center of what had to be the tower they'd sought. The stairs themselves were clearly well used and well maintained both. Torches, unlit but ready to go, jutted from sconces at regular intervals. The plush carpet—probably a deep red, though the light of the squad's own torches wasn't quite sufficient for them to be sure—remained firm, almost bouncy, and showed the impressions of many a footfall.

After enough winding about to make a wagon wheel dizzy—

Gimmol, when asked, estimated that they were probably a good five stories or more aboveground—the staircase finally deposited them on a landing. It boasted the same thick carpeting, and a single door, which Gork swiftly reached out and opened, silently, before Jhurpess could use it for a gong.

The squad gathered tightly around the doorway, staring at what could only be Queen Anne's bedchamber. Cræosh, literally leaning over the kneeling kobold so as to get a better view of the room, found his jaw dropping in amazement.

It was *ordinary*! Yes, the carpeting was deep enough that Gork could have gotten lost in it. Yes, the canopied, four-poster bed was larger than the hut Belrotha had flattened in Jureb Nahl and trimmed in silks expensive enough to pay, if not a king's ransom, then at least a baron's. But for all that, it could just as easily have belonged to any one of a hundred nobles in any of a dozen kingdoms.

Well, except for a single repulsive (but, thank the Ancestors, not erotic!) portrait of King Morthûl hanging beside the bed.

Cræosh scanned the room, as he was certain the others were doing as well. In addition to the bed, the chamber held a huge wardrobe, a table with a gold-framed mirror, and two doors—no, three, counting the one in which they stood.

Except that one of them couldn't exist. Unless he'd gotten *completely* turned around, that should be the outer wall of the tower itself! It took a moment for his mind to stretch back several weeks and dredge up the relevant memory. "The carriage," he whispered.

"What?" Fezeill asked.

"The carriage," Cræosh repeated. "There was a door in the carriage, remember? Rupert said that it led to the queen's private chambers." He shook his head. "That's a hell of a trick."

"Indeed," Gimmol agreed, nodding. "I couldn't even guess at the spells required to pull this off." He paused. "I wonder if it functions when the teleportation wards are active?"

"I wonder if it matters," Gork said sourly. "Can we just get this done with and worry about Queen Anne's parlor tricks later? I don't want to die here—and that includes of old age."

"Keep your testicles on, Shorty, we're moving."

A perfunctory search revealed nothing else unusual, and they quickly devoted their attention to the last of the three doors. "Queen Anne through here?" Belrotha asked.

Cræosh grimaced. "She fucking well better be. If not, it means we missed something. Else. I swear, this woman doesn't just have a thing for corpses, she's also got a bloody door fetish."

Gork shuffled forward, reached for the door, and promptly flew across the chamber, accompanied by a sizzling sound rather like a lightning bolt coated in bacon grease. Whiskers standing erect, wisps of smoke rising from his fingertips, Gork used the wardrobe to haul himself upright and fixed the others with a baleful grimace. "I think it's someone else's turn to open a door."

No one moved.

"Well, this is just fucking great!" Cræosh snapped. "After all this, we're not gonna let one damn door stop us, are we?"

"Of course not," Katim told him blandly. "You go . . . right ahead and open it."

"Um . . . Shut up, troll."

"That's about what I . . . thought."

To their credit, they certainly got creative. They tried everything, from bashing it open with Jhurpess's club (the wood somehow conducted the unnatural electricity, and Cræosh and Katim couldn't help laughing at the sight of the bugbear with his entire coat of fur standing on end) to standing back and letting Gimmol toss spells at it (none were strong enough to open the portal) to standing even farther back and letting Belrotha toss furniture at it (which bounced off).

"Gork!" Gimmol exclaimed suddenly. "The skull!"

"Gimmol!" the kobold replied in the exact same tone. "What the hell are you talking about?"

The gremlin sighed. "The talisman King Morthûl gave you, remember?"

Gork nodded slowly. "What about it?"

"He said it was a focus, to assist him in penetrating the barriers around the castle. Maybe we can use it here."

"I dunno," Cræosh protested from a few feet away. "Didn't he say that it had to be as close to the laboratory as possible? Are we close enough here?"

"No," Gimmol said. "But that's not what I meant. Gork, hold the skull up to the door."

"Not a chance! I'm not getting anywhere near that door again!"

The gremlin sighed. "So don't get too close, Gork. Just do it."

Mumbling, the kobold raised the talisman and held it about a foot away from the door.

"A little closer than *that*, Gork."

Grumble, grumble.

The skull suddenly began chattering and cackling, twisting in Gork's hand like a live rodent.

"Ouch!"

"What's wrong, Shorty?" Cræosh asked.

"It *bit* me!"

Gimmol's eyes went strangely unfocused. "Just hold it for another minute, Gork. . . ."

And then the gremlin cast his spell. It was a simple spell of opening, not much more than an apprentice-level incantation. It certainly wasn't powerful enough to open *this* door; he'd already tried it once, and failed.

But this time, speaking through parched and cracking lips now pursed in concentration, Gimmol cast the spell through the Charnel King's talisman, rather than at the door directly.

The skull ceased laughing. For perhaps a full minute, nothing else happened; and then it *barked*. There was just no other word to describe the abrupt shout that burst from the tiny marble mouth.

The door didn't open so much as it simply ceased to exist, revealing a narrower flight of spiral stairs, once more leading up.

Gork and Gimmol both stared at the skull, which was once again cackling maniacally, and then at each other. "If you've somehow used it up," Gork said, shoving the talisman back into his pack, "don't expect me to get between you and His Majesty."

This particular flight of stairs emitted an odd smell, one foreign to the rest of the castle. The closest that even Katim, with her acute senses, could describe it was as a vague olfactory echo of Queen Anne's own scent, combined with the dust of ages and just the faintest hint of decomposition.

"Um . . ." Fezeill stopped abruptly, his feet on two separate steps. "I'm just wondering . . ."

"What?" Cræosh asked, twisting at the waist to look back and down. "What is it now?"

"If we're here to stop Queen Anne's rite, or at least to let, uh, 'someone else' stop it . . . Do we really want to have the Tree of Ever on us? What if she gets a hold of it?"

Silence in the stairway.

"This," Cræosh grumbled, "is a *fine* time to think of that!"

"Could tree stay here?" Jhurpess asked.

"No way," Gimmol said before Cræosh could answer. "Leave it lying around the castle? Might as well give it to her."

"Okay, fine," Cræosh said, dragging it from his pack. "Belrotha?"

"Yeah?"

"This symbol said bad things about your mother."

The ogre, who had turned sideways to fit through the staircase, glowered at him. "Me not stupid, Cræosh. Little tree thing can't talk."

Sigh . . . "All right. I just wanted you to crush it."

"Why you not just say so?" The ogre reached out, plucked the Tree of Ever from the orc's hands, and ground it swiftly into sawdust. The squad began tromping up the stairs once more.

"Cræosh?"

"Yes, Belrotha?"

"Why us bother to go to woods and get little tree thing, if us just going to crush it?"

"Shut up and keep climbing, Belrotha."

"Okay. Cræosh?"

"*What?*"

"You not talk about my mother again."

The staircase finally opened up onto another landing, similar to the one providing access to the queen's bedchambers. Again a wooden archway sat in the center of the wall; no doorway, this time, but just an open space. Gork raised a hand, signaling the others to stop, and then crept silently to the gaping entryway. Crouched as low as he could, he peeked around the frame.

The laboratory—for surely this must be it—was perfectly circular, taking up the entirety of the tower's upper level. Shelves and hooks and cupboards and niches lined the walls, containing, it appeared to Gork, a bit of everything. Books, plants, fluids, stones, preserved body parts from a thousand different creatures, the tools used to extract said parts— these and more were scattered about, in no order that he could discern.

Standing in the center of the chamber was a platform of a rough stone, slanted at a steep slope. Carved into it was a human-shaped depression equipped with manacles of all sizes and shapes. And in the center of that hollow, looking ludicrously small, lay Shreckt.

He was locked down by the smallest shackles the contraption possessed, and he appeared weak and listless, his head lolling with the rhythm of his breath. Gork found himself wondering idly if they could afford to postpone their interference until after Queen Anne had finished with the aggravating little imp.

He tried to jump out through his own snout when Katim appeared beside him, almost as silent as he himself had been.

"Does it strike you as odd," he whispered, trying to cover until his beating heart slowed, "that we just *happened* to show up when her ritual was going down?"

"Not really," the troll said softly back. "She probably started . . . when she learned we were coming, in hopes of . . . getting it done before we . . . found her."

"Indeed, I'm afraid I had to rush things. Do you approve, sweet Gork?"

The kobold and the troll tensed at that measured, feminine voice.

"Oh, dear. I've startled you. How rude of me. I know you're there, of course, just as I know that your friends are crammed rather uncomfortably into the stairway. Why don't you all come in?"

Gork gave some brief thought to refusing, and then, with a small sigh, he rose and stepped through the door. Katim followed an instant later.

"Hey!" Cræosh hissed in a strangled whisper. "What the fuck are you two doing?!"

"She knows we're here, Cræosh," the kobold said in a normal tone of voice. "She's invited us in."

"Oh." Cræosh scowled. "I guess, in that case . . ."

The squad filed in on the kobold's heels, several of them aiming satisfied glances at the chained demon.

"It's a vivisection table," Gimmol whispered to the others. He held off on mentioning that the tiny straps holding the imp were probably intended for human children. He was afraid that that fact wouldn't bother his companions as much as it did him.

"How splendid!" It was Queen Anne's voice again. "It's so good to get together with old friends." Slowly, the Charnel King's bride stepped out from behind the curious stone table.

Queen Anne was completely nude, although it took the squad a moment to realize it. Her long, lustrous hair was gone, her scalp shaved bare, and every inch of her body was covered in swirling runes and intricate sigils. Gork, for one, couldn't begin to guess if they were painted on or actual tattoos.

"That must've taken a while," Cræosh commented.

"I am patient," she said simply. Then she frowned. "Up to a point. I'm afraid that after you'd been gone so long, however, I found my patience running rather thin."

"Yeah," Cræosh said, "I see you started without us." He glanced at the laboratory around him, ending on the items scattered by the queen's bare feet. "I see the bones," he told her. The others held their breaths, watching for her reaction. "And the flower, and the heart, and the cobwebs. You've got all kinds of herbs and shit here—that should take care of the more mundane ingredients. And right there," he added, pointing to Shreckt, "you've got a demon whose soul you can suck." He grinned. "But what about the relic? We've still got that, you know."

"I see you've discovered my little secret," Queen Anne breathed, and her voice was no longer friendly. "May I ask how you pieced it together?"

"Wasn't too hard. Hell, you sent us after most of the shit ourselves."

"But I never told you what for."

Cræosh shrugged. "Just lucky, I guess."

Gork heard Gimmol sigh in relief that the orc hadn't revealed his secret.

Queen Anne advanced on the impudent orc. "Do you really think you can hide the answers from me?"

"Maybe. Do you really think that's an appropriate fashion statement for this time of year? I'd think you'd be fucking freezing."

Keep talking, keep talking . . . Casually, desperate not to draw the queen's attention from the orc, Gork reached into his pouch for Morthûl's talisman. He winced in anticipated pain and shoved his hand into the skull's mouth to prevent it from chattering. It proved unnecessary, for the thing remained completely silent. *Stars, I hope Gimmol didn't really use it up*! Slowly he lowered it to the floor at his feet and then stepped forward, putting himself between the marble icon and Queen Anne.

". . . suppose it doesn't really matter all that much," she was saying when he once again began to pay attention. "So you figured out what I'm doing. Congratulations. Now what, my dears? Are you going to give me the relic?"

"Well, since you asked so nicely . . ." Cræosh began, clearly relishing what was to come.

But Gimmol shook his head, glancing up and down as he traced the symbols in their intricate ballet across the queen's skin. "It doesn't matter," he whispered. The others couldn't tell if he was speaking to them, or to himself. "It doesn't make a damn bit of difference. She's got what she needs."

Queen Anne smiled, a radiant expression, tinted by madness. "You didn't really think I would start a ritual I couldn't finish, did you?" she asked. Slowly she snaked one arm down behind the table. When she lifted it again, she held a wave-bladed dagger, less than six inches long, of tarnished bronze.

"And what god does that belong to?" Cræosh grumbled.

"Don't be silly, dear orc. If just anyone had heard of him, he wouldn't be forgotten, would he?

"When it became obvious that you weren't on your way back to me," she continued, "I was forced to send Rupert out to complete the job you'd . . ." Her brow furrowed. "Where *is* Rupert?" she demanded.

Gork glanced behind him and had to fake a sudden coughing fit to cover his startled yelp. The skull was gone! In its place, a deep hole, perfectly circular, had appeared in the solid stone of the floor. A hint of movement deep within tugged at his eye, but he swiftly looked away, still determined to avoid notice.

And just as well, since if he hadn't been paying attention to what happened next, he'd never have believed it.

"He got in our way," Cræosh said in answer to the queen's query. "So we killed him." He grinned widely. "That was right before we burned your entire garden right down to the fucking ground."

Gimmol put his head in his hands and moaned, Fezeill gawped incredulously at the orc, and even Katim whimpered. Not even *Cræosh* could have just said that, could he?

In desperation, Gork again glanced back at the hole—and saw, with a nauseating combination of revulsion and relief, that a small horde of roaches and beetles had begun to swarm from the shaft. "Come on," he whispered so softly even he barely heard it. "*Come on. . . .*"

Queen Anne stood petrified, the sigils dark against her suddenly bloodless skin. "You didn't!" she breathed. It was virtually a plea.

Cræosh scowled. "Actually, I'm surprised you didn't sense it, you're such a high-and-mighty sorceress." He blatantly leered down at the queen's naked form, then back unabashedly to meet her gaze. "Obviously, your body's held up to the years a lot better than your mind. Probably a good thing we interrupted before you could ruin *it*, too."

Cræosh should have died on the spot, his organs boiling away into steam, or his flesh putrefying off his bones, or any of a hundred other sorcerous deaths Queen Anne had devised over her many lifetimes. But as it was, so bestially enraged was the Charnel King's bride that she lashed out physically, backhanding the orc like a common brawler, shrieking enough to shatter glass.

Of course, enraged or no, she remained a sorcerer.

Cræosh's abbreviated flight across the chamber was not markedly slower than a ballista bolt. Wood, glass, and shards of far less readily identifiable substances sprayed out from behind him as his body shattered one of the shelves along the outer wall. (Painful, certainly, but that shelf actually saved him from splattering like a rotting plum against said wall.) Gork couldn't help but wince at the sight of the mottled bruise already spreading across the orc's jaw. Cræosh slid to the floor and looked blearily upward; a thick trickle of blood slowly carried a fragment of tooth down his chin.

"Next time," he wheezed at Gork, "you get to be the diversion."

Given the queen's expression as she advanced on the crumpled orc, fists clenched and ribbons of eldritch energy streaming from her pupils and from the sigils inscribed across her body, Gork felt that the notion of "next time" was unduly optimistic. She was snarling something as she neared—perhaps *ranting* was more accurate—but damned if he could make out a word of it.

The hole in the floor erupted, vomiting a torrent of black, clacking vermin into the ceiling. They sprayed and spattered from the stone, falling in a twitching rain throughout the room. In the heart of that horrid fountain, a silhouette gradually took shape as though approaching from a vast, incomprehensible distance.

"About time," Gork muttered, his heart pounding.

The power flowing from Queen Anne's body snuffed out like a candle. Her fists opened; her expression melted from uncontrollable rage to something near the very edge of despair—yet still tainted by a touch of the twisted lust that even now made Gork shudder just to contemplate it.

Hesitantly, she took a step toward the living column. "My love—"

"*Silence!*"

Queen Anne dropped to her knees, as did half the squad. A skeletal hand reached out from the fountain of insects and parted the deluge, revealing the twisted, enraged visage—well, half a visage—of Morthûl.

"Your Majesty," Fezeill said carefully, "we—"

"*Out!*" The Charnel King waved his flesh-covered hand at the door. The entire tower shook with the gesture, and hailstones of rock fell from the ceiling. The squad ran, Jhurpess stopping long enough to drag the battered orc to his feet.

Guess it was too much to hope he'd be left behind, Gork refrained—barely—from saying.

"Cræosh rest later!" the bugbear shouted into the swamp-green face. "Cræosh run *now*!" The two of them ducked through the doorway, hot on Gork's and Katim's heels. An enormous slab of stone slammed down beside the entryway, not *quite* blocking it; Fezeill shifted into a kobold between one step and the next and dove, his newly shrunken form slipping easily through the remaining gap.

Gork spun and looked back just in time to see Gimmol topple, clutching an ankle lacerated by rocky shrapnel. Only the kobold and the doppelganger were small enough to go back for him, and Gork, at least, had no intention of daring the rain of rock.

Nor was there any need; something enormous moved in the chamber behind the fallen gremlin. Belrotha gently lifted Gimmol from the floor, leaning forward to shield his body with her own, and tossed him underhanded toward the obscured doorway. Her throw was perfect, and the gremlin sailed through the gap just before another plummeting section of the ceiling sealed even that last tiny opening, totally and irrevocably burying the doorway.

"I've got him!" Katim shouted, snagging the gremlin out of the air before he could hurtle past them (and possibly over the edge of the stairwell). "Let's . . . go!" As though in emphasis, a trickle of dust sprinkled from above, scattering across the landing. Clearly, King Morthûl's fury was not confined to the laboratory.

"We can't!" Gimmol shouted, thrashing in the troll's grasp. "Belrotha's still in there! We have to—"

"Gimmol!" Katim shook the gremlin until his teeth chattered. "We can't get back in . . . there! We have to go!"

"No! I won't!"

Katim shook her head and then cracked Gimmol across the jaw with a closed fist. He stared at her incredulously for an instant, and then his eyes crossed and he fell limp. "Your loyalty becomes . . . you," she whispered. Then she casually slung him over her shoulder like a sack of halflings.

Gork wasn't sure if any of the others had even heard the comment.

He *was* pretty sure *he* wasn't intended to, and so made none of the various comments that sprang to mind.

The tower shook once again; the trickle of dust grew quickly into a flowing stream, and small rocks joined the downpour. The stairs creaked loudly, and several began to crack up the center.

"We'll never make it to the bottom in all this!" Fezeill shouted.

"We don't have to!" Gork said. "Follow me! I've got a plan!"

The tower shaking and buckling beneath them, the squad bounded down the stairs.

Belrotha hunkered down behind the largest of the slabs that had blocked the door and tried, for the first time in her life, to hide. She wasn't very successful at it.

Before her, in the room's center, Queen Anne knelt, staring up into the enraged face of her lord and love. Several times she opened her mouth to speak, and each time, as though deliberately interrupting, the tower trembled.

And then, for just a moment, the quaking ceased. "Did you think to supplant me?" Morthûl asked finally, and even Belrotha was stunned at the change in his tone. No more fury, no rage, no indignation; just cold curiosity, a weariness beyond all mortal comprehension—and maybe, just maybe, the slightest echo of what, in a past life, could have been pain. "Was it not enough to share my throne? You had to have it for yourself?"

"My lord, no!" Tears glistened in twin trails down the queen's face. Tears! From Queen Anne? "I wanted no such thing! I wished only to rule beside you, forever, as we were meant to be! I thought—"

"You thought what, Anne? That I would welcome this?"

"Yes," she whispered. "Now, of all times . . . With the failure of your great spell, and the coming war. I thought—"

"Not now. Not ever. Why do you think I never offered you this spell on my own? This was the one possibility, above all, that I wished to *avoid*."

Slowly, even gently, the master of the Iron Keep knelt and placed his hands on either side of his wife's face. Her eyes closed at his touch, and she moaned softly. "For now, you wish to sit beside me, my queen. But in time, it wouldn't be enough. I know, Anne. More than anyone can ever understand, I know. And be it now, or tomorrow, or centuries hence, I cannot let it be.

"There is power in this form, my queen. Power, perhaps, to rival the gods." The flesh covering half the Charnel King's face tightened almost imperceptibly. Anne's eyes opened abruptly, perhaps in sudden realization of what must come next. "But the thing about being a god, Anne, is that you are only safe—if you're the only one."

There was no sorcery involved, no spells, no magic. Morthûl simply tightened his grip, and twisted. The snap that reverberated throughout the laboratory was not merely the breaking of Queen Anne's neck, but of the Charnel King's last ties to the humanity he'd abandoned long ago.

Carefully, so carefully—as though, absurd as it seemed, he were afraid of injuring her—he lowered Queen Anne's head to the floor. He even took a moment to reach out with his leathery hand to close her staring eyes. Then, with a sound that might have been a sigh, he rose.

"Did you get all that, ogre?" he asked, his voice flat.

Belrotha emerged from behind the stone slab, clenched fingers digging into her palms to keep them from trembling. "Me see and hear," she admitted nervously, "but me not understand."

"Really?" Even as he spoke, Morthûl casually stepped across uneven heaps of broken stone to stand beside the vivisection table—or rather, where the table had been before being crushed to powder. He stopped for a brief examination of the rubble; then, apparently having learned whatever it was he needed, he turned back to the ogre. Behind his flapping cloak, Belrotha caught the tiniest glimpse of a crushed and mangled foot protruding from the stone. "And what didn't you understand?"

Belrotha, dense as she was, knew that she was treading on very dangerous ground here, but she wasn't about to ignore his question. "Why you kill Queen Anne?"

The Dark Lord's half-lips frowned. "Did you not hear what I told her?"

Belrotha took another deep breath. "Me rule Itho for two seasons. Me know what it mean to rule, to have power. Even though me not have as much power as you," she added in a rush. "But me not think Queen Anne could hurt you. You too strong, rule too well."

For a long moment, Morthûl stared. And then he laughed.

It was not the maniacal laugh of a mad tyrant, nor the cruel chuckle of a sadist, but a true, honest-to-gods guffaw, the laughter of a man who has finally gotten the joke.

"You," he said once his mirth had run its course, "are not nearly as stupid as you're supposed to be."

Belrotha wasn't quite certain how to take that. "Me can try harder," she offered tentatively.

"No, I think this will do just fine." The last of the grin faded from the Charnel King's face. "You're absolutely right, ogre. Queen Anne was no more threat to me than a newborn ogre would be to you. Oh, she could well have grown to be my equal, someday, but only if I chose to allow it."

"Then . . . ?" It had been hard enough to ask the first time, and Belrotha couldn't quite seem to spit it out again.

"Why kill her?"

The ogre nodded.

Morthûl frowned slightly. "I could tell you that it was for disobeying me," he said. "But I doubt you'd believe that any more than you believed the first. I could tell you it was for distracting me at this crucial time, but even you must realize that she could have proved *quite* useful in what's to come." He glanced sidelong at her. "I could simply kill you for having the presumption to question me. . . ."

Belrotha could no longer control her trembling.

"But that would be wasteful, and at the moment, the idea of further waste rather repulses me." The empty socket gaped hideously, its yellow glow nauseating. But there was something in the cracked and dried orb that sat beside it, and the ogre's jaw gaped as she recognized it as sorrow.

"Why did I murder my queen? Because this," and he gestured toward himself, two bony fingers pointing at a desiccated chest, "doesn't feel. I anger, I hate. I even, on rare occasion, rejoice. But it is only a shadow of what was, the dying echo of a long-forgotten song. For me, such sacrifice was more than worth it.

"But for Anne . . . My queen was a woman of passions, ogre. Perverse ones, perhaps; some of her more exotic aberrations appalled *me*, and that takes some doing. But whatever else her urges might have been, they were intense. They were the center of her world, of who she was. Had she truly understood what she must surrender, she would never have sought this out. And had she achieved it, it would have destroyed her."

Morthûl stepped back and once more knelt beside the body, gazing for one last moment on the woman who had shared his throne for six hundred years. "This was my final gift to her, though it was one she would never have understood. A last gesture." He gently took one of her hands in his own. "The final refrain of that forgotten song."

He rose again, and as though that were some prearranged signal, the tower again began to quake. "Come, ogre," he said, his voice once more arrogant, imperious. Empty. "Before you join my wife and your little sergeant as permanent residents."

Like a dissipating wisp of smoke, the Dark Lord vanished, taking the ogre with him. Now empty of the living, the room shuddered once, twice—and collapsed in on itself, beginning an avalanche of stone that would eventually consume the entire tower. Ton upon ton of stone crashed down, burying the tiny, broken corpse of a demon; the body of a woman who was perhaps the most twisted of any to have walked beneath the sun . . .

And burying, too, the closest thing to eternal love this world would ever see.

CHAPTER NINE

THE WORMS CRAWL IN . . .

"If I may say so," Havarren offered, "now was not the most opportune time for this sort of governmental upheaval."

Very slowly, the Charnel King raised his head from the map he'd been studying. He carefully rolled the parchment and returned it to its ivory scroll case. Only when that process was complete did he rise to his feet, turning to address his impertinent lieutenant.

"Do you think so?" he asked simply.

Anyone else would have been cowed into silence, and possibly into catatonia, by that icy tone. But this was the first chance Havarren had had to speak directly to his lord in the days since Castle Eldritch fell, and he'd been looking forward to it with sadistic glee. It was a rare opportunity, and the gaunt wizard was damned if he was going to let it pass.

Of course, he was pretty much damned regardless, being what he was, but that was beside the point.

"Indeed," Havarren said, his voice as calm as though they'd been discussing something utterly insignificant, such as the weather or the execution of a thousand elves. "With this war coming up, we need stability. Not to mention the fact that we must now do without one of our most powerful spellcasters." He was careful to keep his grin modest, rather than letting it spread ear to ear as it wished, when he added, "The next time you feel the need to murder your wife, perhaps you might consult with your advisors first. One of us might have suggested an alternative."

The scroll case in Morthûl's right hand shattered into slivers. Still he said nothing.

"Did the entire squad survive?" the mage asked curiously. "I would have thought—"

"The squad survived. Their trainer did not."

"Shreckt? Pity. He had potential. Of course, had Anne completed her spell, he would have died anyway, so I suppose there was no help for it."

And then the Charnel King smiled. "Yes, Shreckt would have died. As talented as my wife was, I fear her thinking was still bound by certain conventional beliefs. Everyone who attempts that rite seems to believe that the demon's *death* is required in order to bind its soul as part of the spell. You and I learned better ages ago, didn't we, Havarren?"

The wizard's smirk fell so abruptly that it almost made an audible thump as it hit the floor and skittered away into the corner. "Do not," the Dark Lord said in a voice barely above a whisper, "seek to taunt me about Anne's death. I may need you alive, but we both know what sort of agony I can inflict upon you at a whim. I own you; you are a part of me, for all time. Forget that again, and I will make your next thousand centuries a living . . ." He paused, considering. "Heaven," he concluded with a faint chuckle.

"Now," he continued, turning back to the desk. Carefully, he laid the map out once again and began brushing shards of ivory from its surface, taking care not to rip the parchment. "I assume you had reasons for seeking an audience other than your desire to make foolish comments about my queen."

"I did," Havarren said, shaking off his growing rage. His circumstances had been thus for hundreds of years; throwing a tantrum about it now would accomplish nothing. "There are several issues at hand, actually.

"First, Dororam's forces have ambushed another of our patrols."

Morthûl scowled. Ever since the foe had begun assaulting the new guard posts that were *supposed* to have been secret, General Falchion had become obsessed with outmaneuvering Dororam and had begun assigning wandering patrols to the passes. This was the fourth of his teams ambushed in the two weeks since the demise of Queen Anne.

"We have a spy, Havarren," the Dark Lord said, offhandedly examining a jagged sliver of ivory between his thumb and forefinger.

"I'd come to much the same conclusion."

"I was certain you would have. I assume we can rule out a leak at the top?"

Havarren paused for a moment. "I believe so. General Falchion and I are special cases, of course, and your other generals know what methods you would employ in questioning them were you to suspect treason. No price could make them risk it."

"Agreed. Someone of lower rank, then."

The mage nodded. "Someone who feels that he need not fear discovery, because he's not liable to deal with you or me personally." He smiled, though there was no humor in the expression. "Of course, that only narrows it down to about the entire army."

"Get on it, Havarren. These raids are . . . inconvenient. They're unlikely to matter in the long run, but let's not take chances. I want the spy found."

"Consider it done, my lord."

"No. When you hand me the traitor, I'll consider it done." Morthûl absently tossed the sliver of ivory to the floor. "You said there were several issues?"

"I did." For the first time in ages, Havarren sounded unsure of how to proceed. "We, umm. We seem to have lost Darsus."

"Lost it? The town's dying, Havarren, but I hardly think it's shrunk to the point where you might easily misplace it."

"As you say, it's dying. Most travelers on the highway bypass it outright. So we didn't learn of this immediately."

"You're stalling, Havarren."

"Sabryen took it. As best we can tell, every man, woman, and child in the town has been, well, wormed."

"Wormed?"

"So to speak, my lord."

"The whole town?"

"It wasn't that big a town, my lord."

"Why wasn't this news the first thing out of your mouth when you walked through that door?"

Havarren might have felt better if the Charnel King had screamed at him. The whole "calm and quiet" bit rarely boded well. "I knew it would consume all your attentions, and I wanted to make sure I had the chance to tell you of the spy."

"And take the opportunity to taunt me, of course." The Charnel King shook his head, sending a few stray beetles plunging to the floor. "I should have killed him," he muttered to himself.

"King Sabryen? Why didn't you?"

"I was young, Havarren. Relatively, anyway. I still maintained relations with others in the wizards' community, and curses were all the rage at the time . . ." Another head shake. "Ah, well. You know how it is." Skeletal fingers drummed on the desk with an idle clacking. "The timing on this is suspicious, at best. Sabryen just happens to awaken now, with sufficient power to spread beyond his tomb? I think not. I sense an outside hand stirring this particular pot."

"DuMark?" Havarren asked.

"Who else? I have to admit, it's clever. He forces me to split my attentions, waste my energies, without putting himself at risk. I wouldn't be at all surprised if we were to learn that he's responsible for our spy as well, and probably half a dozen other little inconveniences we haven't even noticed.

"Well, we'll have to deal with it. I didn't kill Sabryen then, but I certainly don't object to killing him now. Especially if he's chosen this moment to move against me, with or without duMark's prodding."

"Perhaps he hopes to take back his kingdom," Havarren suggested.

"No. Sabryen is no longer in any condition to rule; not a kingdom of men, anyway. He may be mad enough to turn the entire population into those creatures of his, though. In either case, he's a nuisance that I'd best rid myself of now—before the war, and before he grows into something much *more* than a nuisance."

"And you have a plan?"

"Havarren, haven't you learned by now? I *always* have a plan."

*

Cræosh slumped against the nearest vertical surface—the side of a coach, in this particular instance—and sank slowly to his knees, gasping for breath. He was exhausted, he was coated in blood (albeit mostly other people's), and his ribs ached from where they'd cracked against Queen Anne's shelving. He felt as though he'd started running then—as the tower came down around them, shaken apart by the wrath of the Charnel King—and hadn't stopped since.

Gork's plan of escape, he'd been forced to admit, had been a good one. Rather than try to race the collapse all the way to the bottom, he'd led them down a single flight, back to Queen Anne's bedchamber—and the mystical door to her Majesty's carriage. Whether it was designed to function despite the wards, or Morthûl's arrival had shattered those barriers, the Demon Squad neither knew nor cared. The fact that it worked, that it got them outside, was enough. Even then, though, it had been a near thing; with the queen's death, her magics had faded as well. Cræosh had just staggered from the carriage, falling prone in the royal stables, when the enchantments inside the vehicle collapsed. The interior instantly shrunk to its normal size, crushing the furniture and everything else within.

The goblins had remained within those stables for a time, mostly because Cræosh refused to move. They'd watched from across the wide courtyard as the people gawped in horror at the crumbling central tower, which took much of the keep proper with it. A few random stones had bounced as far as the stables, ringing loudly against the walls, but even that wasn't enough to entice Cræosh to get up, and the danger was sufficiently slight that the others chose not to abandon him.

A swift flash of sickly yellow light had blinded them, sending the already-skittish horses into a near panic, and Belrotha was there, hunched to avoid driving her skull through the ceiling.

"Uh . . . king say him not sure what to do with us just now," she'd reported. "Him say we work for General Falcon until him say different."

"General Falchion?" Gimmol corrected, climbing out of the

haystack into which he'd dived when the light first flared and moving to hug Belrotha's calf.

"Um, yeah," she said, patting the goblin (very, very carefully) on the head. "Him too."

Thus they'd spent the past days dashing madly across the length and breadth of Kirol Syrreth, alongside the steel-enclosed figure who stood at the head of Morthûl's armies. Inspecting this outpost, reassigning that garrison, collecting reports from those messengers, Falchion performed the sundry tasks necessary to prepare for the coming war. The Demon Squad, apparently out of favor for the nonce—*Right, like it's our fault Queen Anne was a fucking loony*, Cræosh seethed—had become little more than glorified bodyguards, a small fragment of Falchion's larger escort. The horses they'd been provided made the constant travel a little easier, but Cræosh still cursed King Morthûl—silently, of course—every evening before collapsing into his bedroll.

(The horse wasn't born that could carry Belrotha, and as the armies of Kirol Syrreth had apparently run short of elephants, the ogre had to walk. So far, however, she'd had no difficulties keeping up, and in fact she was a lot less sore than the riders every evening.)

Falchion, too, had proved something other than expected. During his years of military service, Cræosh had always heard the general described as a gruff loudmouth, tolerated only by the powers that be because he was damn good at his job. The orc had seen none of this for himself, though; during the twelve days they'd traveled together, Falchion barely spoke at all, save when necessary to growl his orders. His voice was hoarse, gravelly, not at all the bellow of a man accustomed to making himself heard across the battlefield. Most peculiarly of all, he never removed his bloodred mail, nor his jagged bucket helm, not even to sleep. Cræosh kept meaning to bring it up, ask his squadmates what they thought, but when evening came, he was always too tired, too sore, and frankly too uninterested in making casual conversation with any of them.

The attack came about an hour before noon on the twelfth day. The squad had been riding near the column's head, so Cræosh overheard Falchion launch into an uncharacteristic cursing streak. A messenger on a fast horse, both of them lathered and sweating despite the winter chill, had caught up with the column moments before, and it was pretty obvious that the news he brought was not good. Cræosh glanced over at Katim and Gork, both of whom were riding to his left.

"Something about some secret . . . patrols being ambushed," Katim rasped, her powerful ears swiveled toward their commander. "Dororam's men knew exactly where . . . to find them."

For reasons Cræosh couldn't begin to guess, Gork flinched.

The orc opened his mouth to say something, and that's when they were hit. A rain of arrows arced from a nearby copse of trees, and only the fact that they were mounted saved the three of them from becoming inverse porcupines. Reflexes honed by years of combat—or, in Gork's case, years of constructive cowardice—prompted them to drop beneath their horses. The unfortunate animals had taken the arrows in their stead, squealing and thrashing their death throes as they toppled.

Even as the next flight of arrows darkened the sky, the goblins surged from behind the fallen animals and charged, the surviving members of the column close on their heels. Abandoning their bows, the ambushers moved to meet them.

They wore no uniforms, no insignias, but Cræosh thought it bloody obvious that these were Dororam's men. With a sinking feeling in his gut, he realized that this suicide squad—for they must surely have known there could be no escape from the Charnel King's forces once they penetrated the Brimstone Mountains—would not have attacked just any random caravan. They had to have known exactly who they were waiting for.

Someone tipped them off to General Falchion's itinerary.

Falchion himself led the counterattack, slashing furiously with his curved blade. He seemed oblivious to any danger, taking blows on his armor that should have knocked a normal man off his feet if not broken bones and ruptured organs, but he never balked, never slowed.

In the end they won, but at a fearsome cost. In addition to the Demon Squad and Falchion himself, their column had originally consisted of sixty men. When the last of the attackers fell, his face split wide by Katim's axe, only eight of those men remained on their feet, and only seven of the ones who had fallen could be saved. The ambushers had planned perfectly; fully half of Falchion's men went down in the first rain of missiles.

Leaning against the provision-and-supply wagon, having finally caught his wind, Cræosh scanned the battlefield. For better or worse, the entire squad had survived relatively unscathed. *Say what you will about us, but we're some tough bastards, aren't we?* He actually felt proud.

Grass crunched beneath a heavy tread, and Cræosh snapped to attention, ignoring the twinge of protest in his ribs. His jaw opened—ready to offer some report or salute or whatever happened to emerge—and stayed open, hanging as loose as when Queen Anne had nearly broken it.

General Falchion didn't seem to have noticed, but a swath of chain had been ripped from his hauberk in the battle, and what lay beneath looked to have been scraped off a stove. "Burned" was woefully inadequate; the flesh was charred black, save for a few glistening cracks where it had split to reveal the muscle beneath. Even worse, there was a *smoothness* to it. It looked, Cræosh realized with a lurch, as though it had been literally melted and then allowed to jell into a form *almost* matching what it had held before. He could see, too, where rivulets of viscous flesh had oozed between the links of chain before hardening. Falchion never removed his armor because he *couldn't*.

Following the orc's gaze to the rent in his armor, Falchion shook his head. The movement was scarcely visible, causing the great helm to rotate only a bit. "I'll have to find a competent blacksmith in the next town," he said. "Unless . . . You're a smith yourself, aren't you, soldier?"

"Um, passingly, sir. But ah, I'm not sure I'd dare. Wouldn't I have to work on it while, um . . . ?"

"While I wore it, yes."

"Wouldn't that fucking *hurt*?" Probably not the proper language for addressing the general, but Cræosh was, well, Cræosh.

"What is pain to me now?" Falchion lifted a stray arrow from the grass at his feet and plunged it into the flesh exposed by the severed links. He didn't flinch, and no blood emerged—only a puff of fetid air, as though he'd punctured a pocket trapped somewhere within.

401

"Is *everyone* running this country already dead?" Cræosh demanded. Then, "Um, sir," he added. He'd heard rumors that the general had been badly injured recently—something about an incursion into the Iron Keep itself—but he'd never believed, never imagined . . .

"King Morthûl," Falchion said dully, "takes our oaths of fealty *very* seriously. You might do well to remember that yourself."

"I . . . Oh." Then, "I, uh, should probably see to gathering all the salvageable equipment off the field, sir."

"Splendid idea, soldier. Why don't you do that?"

Some few dozen yards away, Gork wandered from corpse to corpse, happily looting. He took only small items that wouldn't be missed—money and ornamental jewelry, for the most part—and he stole indiscriminately, regardless of which side the dead man had served. This was the part that made such skirmishes worthwhile, and the kobold found himself humming.

Until a hand yanked him off his feet and tossed him against the nearest tree. The breath exploded from Gork's lungs; his head rang like a drunken church bell, and the treasures he'd just collected slid to the ground from loosened fists. Gork looked up to see a trio of trolls, their features black, silhouetted by the noonday sun. He blinked, willing his eyes to uncross, and the trio of Katims merged back into one.

"What the hell was that for?" Gork mumbled, wincing as his own voice poked and prodded at the pounding in his head.

Katim bent down, putting her face inches from his. Gork fought the instinct to recoil from the troll's rancid breath. "Don't you think that this . . . has gone just about far . . . enough?"

The kobold focused past the pain to scrunch his face into a look of pure innocence. "What do you mean?"

The troll snarled, and Gork smacked his own head against the tree again as he flinched. "Don't play stupid with me, little . . . thief. You know damn well what . . . I'm talking about."

"It's a coincidence," Gork insisted.

"You told him about the . . . patrols. The ones that were . . . later ambushed."

"I only mentioned that I'd heard they were out there. I didn't know exactly where, so how could I have told him?"

"Once he knew to look . . . for them, it wouldn't have been that . . . hard."

"Coincidence," he said again.

"Four times?"

Gork looked away.

"And what of the battle . . . we've just waged?"

"Dororam's men were just looking for some of our soldiers to ambush," Gork protested, but it sounded lame even in his own ears.

"They were here specifically . . . for Falchion. Humans aren't so foolhardy . . . or fanatical that they'd throw their . . . lives away to destroy some random . . . force."

Gork opened his mouth to protest again, and then sighed as he saw the gold and riches promised by Ebonwind fading away. "Why? The dakórren have no reason to betray us! They hate the elves more than we do! Why would he have told Dororam *anything*?"

"Perhaps your friend is not . . . what he seems."

"What do we do?"

"That, little kobold, is the part . . . I'm still deciding. Pray to your stars . . . that I come up with something *other* . . . than turning you in."

One of the surviving soldiers interrupted them then—Gork could have almost kissed him—and announced that the general wanted to see the entire Demon Squad back at the supply wagon.

Where one of King Morthûl's messenger wraiths was waiting for them.

At the intersection of Kirol Syrreth's major highways loomed Fort Mahadriss, a bloated spider in a web of roads. Built of a drab and dirty stone, ringed by smaller keeps—one for each road—Mahadriss made no nod at all toward aesthetics. This was a bastion built for war, and it wore that fact as a badge of honor.

It had also, thanks to the collapse of a certain Castle Eldritch, just moved up from the third-most important installation in Kirol Syrreth to the second, behind only the Iron Keep itself. There was no way for the structure to actually appear smug about this, but it managed to anyway.

The Demon Squad was allowed entry only after proving their identities at no fewer than three separate checkpoints, and once they were in, Cræosh gave some serious thought to heading back outside to wait. The fortress halls were packed wall-to-wall with chaos that could only marginally be called "controlled." Soldiers, messengers, and servants by the hundreds shoved through dense pockets of other soldiers, messengers, and servants, each absolutely convinced that his own assignment was of far higher priority than anyone else's, and must absolutely be completed *right now*, and why couldn't everyone just "Get the hell out of my way before I start breaking faces!"? Bodies collided in the corridors, pressed close in unwitting parody of intimacy; equipment tumbled down stairs, chased by whoever had dropped it; and fistfights broke out at the drop of a hat. (Literally, in one instance, as a careless soldier knocked a page's cap from his head, for which the page jabbed him in the groin with a wooden scroll case.)

And yet, despite or perhaps because of that boiling anarchy, everything that needed to happen, happened: equipment stored, weapons checked, reinforcements assigned to this post or that. Despite how it looked to the uninitiated—or some of the initiated—Cræosh recognized, with some measure of respect, that the garrisons of Fort Mahadriss would be fully prepped well before Dororam's forces neared the Brimstone Mountains.

But he still didn't want to be standing around in the middle of it.

"Hey! Yeah, you!" It carried even over the crowded hall, a gruff tone clearly accustomed to making itself heard.

Carving a path through the throng with open palm and jabbing elbow, oblivious to the sullen glares he earned in exchange, was an orc. He was perhaps three inches shorter than Cræosh but a tad wider at the shoulders, with a touch of filthy gray to both his swamp-green skin and his mud-brown hair. He wore a blackened steel breastplate embossed with the silver crown of Morthûl, and an enormous warhammer at his belt. The beaked end of the weapon stuck out, drawing lines of blood on those who drew too near in the packed hall, but they proved unwilling to complain.

"What?" Cræosh barked back—and then, finally noticing the stripes of rank embossed on the armor's right breast, correcting himself to "What, *sir*?"

"Better. You Cræosh?"

"Yes, sir!"

"So this would be your Demon Squad then." The orc frowned at the others (and up at Belrotha). "Sorry-looking bunch, but I suppose you'll do. I'm General Rhannik."

Cræosh's spine went straight as an arrow, and the others snapped to attention as well—well, those of them who did that sort of thing, anyway. Widely considered to be among the top contenders to replace Falchion should anything happen to the steel-cocooned commander, Rhannik's was a name well known throughout the rank-and-file.

"What are we doing here, sir?" Cræosh asked. Then, "The wraith told us to come, but he didn't say why." He pretended not to notice Katim and Gork both staring at him in mild shock. *Yes, I do know how to be polite. Try not to faint, you fuckers.*

". . . away from this bloody crowd," Rhannik was saying as Cræosh turned his attention back to the officer, "before we talk about this. *Move!*" he bellowed into the mob. Soldiers and workers fell over each other clearing a path, and the general led the squad to a small, unobtrusive door. "Through here."

The contents of the room were few: a single round table, perhaps a dozen chairs—and Vigo Havarren, casually leaning back with his feet up on the table, sipping on a glass of what appeared to be brandy.

"Hello again," Morthûl's lieutenant said blandly. "I so greatly missed the sparkling conversation from our last meeting that I simply had to come and chat with you again."

"Sarcastic bastard, aren't you?" Cræosh asked as he selected a chair, as far from Havarren as the table would allow, and sat.

"Hardly a bastard. My parents would have to have been unwed."

"So?"

"So what makes you think I have parents?"

Cræosh chose not to dignify that with a response and settled for glaring and grinding his teeth as General Rhannik and the rest of the squad took their seats. Belrotha shoved several chairs out of her way and planted herself cross-legged on the floor.

The orc couldn't help but notice, even with most of his attention devoted to imagining the murder of the aggravating wizard, that the furniture had clearly been borrowed from the mess hall: the table, though recently cleaned, bore the stains of grease and beer. The room itself had been swept only moments before, as evidenced by a few heaps of dust in the corners, and smelled faintly stale. Clearly, the chamber didn't see a whole lot of use.

Cræosh felt a serpentine twisting in his gut. This briefing hadn't been planned in advance; they'd just grabbed the most convenient furnishing and the nearest empty room that could fit the entire squad. For Havarren and Rhannik to be present at what could only be an emergency meeting foretold extreme unpleasantness ahead.

"General?" Havarren said with a languid wave. "Would you be so kind?"

"Of course." Rhannik leaned over the table, his large hands flat against the wood. "Some days back, possibly as long as two weeks or more, King Sabryen's worms emerged, in force, from the Demias Gap."

None of the squad spoke, but a veritable web of meaningful glances wove itself between them. They'd never heard the things associated with the former king of Kirol Syrreth, but none of them had any doubt as to which worms were being discussed.

"At this point," Rhannik continued, "we've only lost Darsus. But we have *utterly* lost it. As near as we can tell, the entire population has been, ah, consumed.

"For the time being, they seem content to wait, most likely gathering their forces. None of our agents have returned from Darsus itself, but a few have gotten *close*. They report a slow but constant flow of worms, centipedes, and other critters coming over the lip of the gap. King Morthûl and General Falchion both feel that it's only a matter of time before they strike at other targets."

"As I'm sure even you cretins can imagine," Havarren interjected, "this couldn't have come at a worse time. We have less than a month before Dororam marches. We cannot possibly recall enough soldiers from the border to deal with this, not and return them to their posts in time. Further, His Majesty and I both need to conserve our powers for the war, until and unless we have no other option. Thus we find ourselves forced to turn to a third alternative." He wiggled his fingers at the goblins in sarcastic greeting. "Hello, third alternative."

"Listen, Blondie," Cræosh said, "I'm flattered beyond fucking measure that you think that highly of us, but there's no way we can take on an army of those things. Hell, we almost got our asses kicked the last time, and there were a *lot* fewer of 'em."

"Don't be stupid," Havarren snapped. Then he smiled. "As well tell the sea not to be wet, I suppose. Still, *try* to think for a moment. We don't want you to attack the worms."

"No?" Cræosh asked suspiciously. "Then what?"

"It's rather obvious . . . actually," Katim said from across the table. "They want us to kill King . . . Sabryen."

Havarren nodded as the others gawked at the troll. "Perhaps you're not *all* as stupid as all that," he admitted.

"What is he?" Gork asked. "I mean, if it's the same Sabryen who used to rule here, he's obviously not any more human than King Morthûl, is he?"

"You'd be surprised what's possible. But no, he's not human, not anymore." Havarren sighed. "Far be it from me to question our lord," he said, his tone bland, "but I'm afraid that this is one instance where he erred. Badly. Rather than slaying his foe outright, Morthûl cursed him.

"I don't know the exact wording of the curse, but I know that it was meant to play on Sabryen's greatest terrors." He smiled. "Sabryen was terribly disgusted by Morthûl's—shall we say, pets? He had a real horror of insects. Our Charnel King felt it poetic to curse Sabryen to an eternity in a similar state."

"He turned him into a bug?" Gimmol asked.

"Worm," Havarren corrected. "And I wouldn't say 'turned into,' precisely. Say instead the king was granted certain wormy attributes. He was supposed to wander off into a distant corner of the land and go slowly mad." The wizard shook his head. "I'm afraid His Majesty and I both rather badly underestimated the man's will. He went mad, yes, but not exactly as we'd intended.

"And he's obviously found a way to spread his curse. Hence, his invertebrate minions."

Cræosh, who'd been staring thoughtfully at the table, looked up. "Is this a coincidence, then?" he asked. "Or was this assault timed deliberately?"

"As in, does Sabryen know we're about to go to war?"

The orc nodded.

Havarren shrugged. "We don't know for certain, but . . ." He chewed his cheek, apparently considering how much to reveal. "It's no secret that we've been mobilizing, but we don't know how much rational thought Sabryen retains. King Morthûl believes that our enemies might even have *inspired* him to act now. Whatever the case, we must assume that he knows exactly what he's doing."

"Okay," Katim said, her nostrils flaring. "This is all well and . . . good, but it doesn't give us any . . . insight into how to go about killing . . . him."

"Ah," Havarren said with a smile. *"That's* where things get interesting."

"I really, *really* hate that word," Gork muttered.

The gaunt wizard snapped his fingers. The door creaked open, admitting a stooped, white-haired old man. He shuffled to the table, a wooden box clasped tight in palsied hands. Havarren took it without comment, and the old servant departed as swiftly as age would permit.

It was pretty mundane, that box: walnut brown, unmarred by any ornamentation, held shut with a simple catch. Havarren, however, caressed it reverently as he laid it on the table.

"The initial challenge, obviously, is reaching Sabryen in the first place. Our dear Lord Worm isn't the type to lead his troops from the fore. To get to him, you'll have to maneuver through a rather sizable force of his crawling soldiers."

"Define 'sizable,'" Cræosh demanded.

"Quite possibly all of them."

The orc started to rise. "If you think I'm gonna fucking sit here and—"

"Cræosh!" Rhannik snapped. "Sit down before I *put* you down!"

He sat. Katim leaned over toward Gork. "If I'd known it was that . . . easy," she whispered, "I'd have tried it a long . . . time ago."

"You!" the general barked across the table. "Shut up!"

Katim's ears laid back and her snout wrinkled, but she held her tongue.

"Perhaps I overstate the case," Havarren continued calmly. "It won't be *all* of Sabryen's forces, because a large population of his creatures are currently occupying Darsus. You'll just have to get through the remaining thousands of them in Krohketh."

Cræosh and the squad exchanged puzzled looks. Krohketh was yet another of Kirol Syrreth's ancient cities that had fallen at the height of its prominence. (There were, several of the squad couldn't help but note, a rather substantial number of those in the kingdom's history. It was one of the reasons so many of the goblin races tended toward the nomadic, or at least smaller communities.)

Krohketh's demise, however, had been rather more dramatic than the slow decay of Darsus or the gradual flooding of Jureb Nahl. Centuries ago, the city's citizens had awakened one morning to what originally felt like a mild earthquake. By that evening, the city was gone, and the Demias Gap—having grown by close to forty percent in a matter of hours—gaped hungrily where Krohketh once stood.

Cræosh, who had decided that nothing would ever surprise him again after the events of the past few months, said, "You think part of Krohketh survived down there?"

Havarren nodded. "Our studies suggest that large portions of the terrain actually *sank* as the gorge widened, rather than plummeting over the precipice. It's quite possible that a surprisingly large portion of the city remains partly intact."

"So you want us to infiltrate a ruined city filled with these worms, find their king, kill him, and get back out?"

"Well," the mage said with a slow smile, "if you find it all too much, I suppose getting back out could be made optional."

"Fuck you, Havarren."

This time, General Rhannik didn't bother to chastise him.

"There are two factors that might just enable you to succeed, orc—*and* return alive," Havarren said, his grin fading. "First is this." With a contemptuous gesture, he sent the wooden box sliding across the table.

Haltingly, Cræosh flipped open the catch and removed one of over a dozen ceramic vials, about three inches tall and as thick around as a small apple. "So what're these about?"

"His Majesty had me concoct these specially. It doesn't do us much good if our Demon Squad gets eaten and subsumed by the enemy, does it? Should you find any of those damn creatures burrowing into your flesh, you drink one of those. It should kill the, ah, *intruders*. Digging them out is up to you, but at least they won't keep burrowing."

"Wonderful," Cræosh muttered, eyeing the vial in his hand as though it were about to bite his fingers off. "And the other factor?"

"Not even you can be expected to deal with thousands of these things," General Rhannik said. "So that's why I'm here."

Fezeill snorted. "No disrespect intended, General . . ."

"He never intends any disrespect," Gork whispered to Katim. "It just comes naturally." The troll chuckled.

". . . but you haven't fought these things. When they take one of their humanoid forms, Sabryen's worms are nigh unstoppable. It takes an obscene amount of damage to kill them, they can hurl their worms for yards, and some even seem capable of casting spells. If you lead a brigade down there with us, all you'll be doing is feeding them. And while I have no inherent objection to watching a large number of the lower races consumed by worms, I'd prefer the dead didn't, in turn, rise up and come after me."

"Lower races?" the kobold asked sarcastically. "Gosh, Fezeill, does that mean we're not friends anymore?"

"I'm well aware of the situation, doppelganger," the general told him. "And I've no intention of wasting good men on your worthless carcass. No, I've cooked up something else entirely."

Havarren rose before any of them could ask for clarification. "Go get some sleep," he ordered abruptly. "You report to the gap tomorrow morning. Don't forget your drinks." And just like that, he was gone.

"Normally," Katim announced to the squad around her, "I don't have . . . much use for orcs." She paused as another of Rhannik's catapults launched its payload of flaming pitch and naphtha into the Demias Gap. "But I think I could get to . . . like the general."

The entire squad, along with Havarren, stood perhaps twenty yards from the edge, directly opposite the town of Darsus. They'd arrived to discover a legion of Rhannik's soldiers in the final stages of reassembling a sizable number of engines—mostly light catapults, but even a few trebuchets. The wizard and the general had consulted for a few moments, tweaking the weapons' trajectories until they lined up perfectly with Havarren's best estimates of Krohketh's location, and then Rhannik had begun a bombardment that was now entering its third hour.

The idea, as Katim understood it, was for there to be little left to oppose the squad when they finally descended.

"Of course," Havarren pointed out, "this will only take care of the vermin that are actually exposed to the flame. It's entirely possible that many will survive inside ruined buildings or in a lower level of the gorge. But this should, if nothing else, make your task simpler." He appeared even more distant than usual this morning, often staring into space and ignoring those around him completely. He hadn't even bothered to insult them, much. Clearly, he had issues other than King Sabryen's worms on his mind.

Katim stepped forward, placing herself directly before the wizard. "We know who the spy . . . is," she told him.

Instantly she had his full attention—not to mention the rest of her squad's. "What?" Havarren asked, his facade of bored contempt cracking. "What did you say?"

"Rumor around Mahadriss was that . . . you've been searching for a . . . spy. His name is Nurien Ebonwind. He is . . . one of the dakórren."

Gork was making very faint strangling noises.

"And how do you know this?" Havarren asked coldly.

"Gork has been feeding him . . . all his information."

The kobold stopped choking; the kobold, in fact, went completely silent. He might have tried to vanish, but with soldiers to every side, where could he go?

"Has he now?" The lanky face went as hard as Katim had ever seen it.

"Of course," she continued, her tone calm. "It was the only . . . way to trap him."

411

"What?" And now the expression was one of utter confusion. So, for that matter, was Gork's. "What are you talking about?" the wizard demanded.

"Ebonwind approached us in the . . . tundra. We knew if we rejected . . . his offer, he'd just find someone . . . less loyal in the ranks. But if . . . we could feed him just enough to . . . keep him coming back, we could . . . maneuver him into a position where . . . we could determine exactly who he . . . worked for. Then you or General Falchion could . . . capture him alive. Gork was . . . truly distraught at the lives lost . . . due to the information we handed . . . over. But better to lose a few . . . units now because of . . . this spy than to lose the . . . war. After the attacks on . . . the security patrols and the assault . . . on General Falchion, we could be certain . . . that Ebonwind was spying for . . . Dororam."

Havarren pondered for a moment, and then beckoned Gork to step forward. "Is this true?"

Gork shrugged. "It seemed like the right idea at the time."

"I will report this to King Morthûl. If you have indeed discovered the spy we've been searching for, you will be rewarded. You should have told us immediately, mind you—you haven't the authority to initiate an operation of this sort—but if it worked, I think we can overlook it. *This* time.

"I must go immediately; Rhannik will inform you when it's time to begin your phase of the operation." A wave of his hand, a few whispered syllables, and he was gone.

Slowly, Gork sidled over to stand beside Katim. Together they stared at the flaming barrels raining down into the chasm. "Why?" Gork finally asked.

"It seemed like the right . . . idea at the time."

The kobold scowled. "If you expect me to believe for one tiny, minuscule, insignificant second that you did this out of the goodness of your hearts, you must think I'm dumber than she is." He gestured in the vague direction of the ogre, who was trying hard to grasp Gimmol's patient explanation as to why they couldn't just fill the entire chasm with oil and light it all at once.

The troll grinned, a far nastier expression than Gork had ever seen.

"Just remember that you *do* . . . owe me, Gork. A great deal. That . . . fact might just be relevant someday."

Gork stared up at the face of the troll and wondered briefly if a torturous death at the hands of the Charnel King could really be all that bad.

Another hour died screaming before Rhannik decided that the bombardment had been sufficient, and a couple more after that until the flames below had diminished enough to make a sortie possible. The squad assembled at the edge of the chasm, beside both the general and an insanely thick rope that trailed down into the depths.

"Best guess is that it's three to four hundred feet down," he reminded them. "What with the various overhangs and the ruins of the city, there are certainly fires still burning that we can't see from up here."

Cræosh sniffed. "We're about to walk into the lair of those fucking worms from hell. I find myself less than concerned about a few stray bonfires."

"Hopefully," Rhannik continued with a glower at the other orc, "the rain of pitch was enough to wipe out most of the resistance. With a smattering of luck, and those elixirs, you might just find Sabryen himself and kill the bastard." He paused long enough to look each and every one of them in the eye. Katim found herself impressed, despite herself; very few beings—Morthûl notwithstanding—could hold her gaze for long. "This is important," he said finally, once he was sure he had their attention. "You're on deadline. You have three days to come back."

"And after that?" Gimmol asked nervously.

"Morthûl would prefer to have you kill Sabryen personally," the general said, "so we can *confirm* that he's dead. But if you aren't back in three days, my orders are to resume bombardment."

Something in the general's tone made the hair on Cræosh's neck stand tall. "For how long?" he asked carefully.

"Days. Possibly weeks, if we can spare the pitch and naphtha from the war effort. It's not a perfect solution; there'll be no way to be sure if we've gotten Sabryen. Nevertheless, if you don't make it back, my orders are to do what I can to basically cauterize the entire chasm like a fucking wound." His smile was utterly devoid of humor. "So you might want to consider hurrying."

Belrotha was unaccustomed to this sort of climb, primarily because she had never before encountered a rope capable of supporting her weight, and nearly lost her grip more than once. Each time, the entire squad would tense, and each time, she recovered only after slipping several feet down the column of hemp. After the third incident, Cræosh glanced up at Katim. "And you wondered why I insisted that she go first."

"I wasn't surprised that you wanted . . . her to go first," the troll corrected. "I was surprised that you . . . had sufficient forethought to think . . . of it on your own."

Still, while harrying, their descent concluded without major mishap. The bottom proved to be almost exactly 350 feet from the top, leaving an additional 50 feet of rope. Cræosh wondered idly what they would have done had the general misjudged the depth of the chasm, and then firmly decided not to think about it.

Without a word, the squad scattered, weapons in hand. Some crouched against the wall, some vanished into the shadows; all were prepared to meet just about any sort of resistance.

None presented itself. They'd very deliberately descended the chasm wall some several hundred yards south of Krohketh's ruins—or where Rhannik and Havarren had estimated them to be, anyway—but still, the goblins were half convinced they were going to find an army of singed and seriously pissed-off worms lurking in wait. Only after several tense moments did they meld together again as a group and, after a whispered discussion, set out slowly toward the north.

Before long, the burning embers and flickering flames of Rhannik's assault began winking at them coyly through the shadows of the chasm's depths. The light cast strange shapes, filtered through the stinking, oily, smoke-tinged air and the rubble of the outermost ravaged buildings. Ever nearer they came to the heart of Sabryen's domain, and still they encountered no resistance.

"Either that rain of fire was *really* damn successful," Gork said, "or . . ."

"I have an idea," Gimmol said from Belrotha's shoulder. "How about we don't dwell on 'or'?"

The squad finally reached the outskirts of Krohketh, and all thoughts of "or" now appeared excessive. Rhannik's bombardment had *definitely* been a success.

There could be no telling, from this distance, how much was a result of the initial collapse, centuries before, and how much a result of the attack. Most of Krohketh lay in ruins, piles of shattered stone and heaps of dirt that only vaguely resembled the structures they'd once been. Only against the edges of the gap did a few buildings stand—crooked, unsteady, supported by neighboring edifices that were equally precarious, or by the cliff-face itself. Every surviving wall was riddled with faults; the few expanses of stone not thoroughly coated in the dust of ages were now blackened with soot. Cræosh felt the grime permeating the air, settling into his pores. He found himself briefly longing for a bath, then quickly sublimated such thoughts before they could open the floodgates to other sissy desires that might lurk in the back of his mind.

He watched as Katim sniffed the air, her coarse fur bristling, but he didn't need the troll's sensitive snout to detect the multitude of competing stenches in the air. Smoke, of course, clinging to the walls and emerging in fits and coughs from the fires crackling away in unseen hollows. The earthy aroma of the dirt that lay beneath the rocks along the floor of the Demias Gap. That peculiar scent of age itself, wafting from the patina of years that lay across the ruins.

But there was something else, too, something alien to Cræosh's experiences—and, to judge by her puzzled look, outside the troll's as well. It wasn't until something crunched loudly beneath someone's foot—Jhurpess's, as the bugbear wandered off to the side—that Katim and Cræosh both realized what it was.

Worms. Thousands, perhaps millions of worms, maggots, millipedes—all spread throughout the city, all charred to tiny, twisted crisps. They covered the surviving roads, a sick attempt at paving; they clung to the walls, baked into the mortar and stone. Cræosh swallowed nervously, truly comprehending for the first time just how hopeless it would have been to fight through such a horde.

"Okay," he announced, his voice low. "Here's how this is gonna work. We have to split up."

"*What?*" Gork appeared fully prepared to go into one of his near-hysterical tirades until Belrotha leaned over and tapped him on the head. It was, to her credit, a very gentle tap, so it only stunned him into silence, rather than knocking him out utterly (and possibly causing permanent damage in the process).

"Thank you," Cræosh said.

The ogre shrugged. "Me want to know where kobold keep his voice, 'cause it too big to fit in such tiny body."

Cræosh couldn't help but laugh. "It is, isn't it? All right, then. General Rhannik's done a pretty good job of clearing out the critters, but you can be damn sure there's a whole fuckload left *somewhere*. So what we've gotta do is get eyeballs on as much of this place as possible. The place where the worms start reemerging the fastest, that's where we'll find Sabryen."

"Makes sense," Katim admitted, nodding. The others agreed—even Gork, though he was somewhat slow to chime in, and his words were slightly slurred.

"So here's what I'm thinking," the orc continued. "Jhurpess, find a perch somewhere—a ledge, one of the standing buildings, whatever—and get as high as you can without collapsing anything. If you see anything suspicious, or if you see one of the teams getting into trouble, you give a yell."

The bugbear nodded.

"Gimmol, you're with Belrotha. You work well together. You do the searching—eyes or magic, whichever you think best—and she keeps you alive to do it.

"Gork, you're with Fezeill. Hey! Shut the fuck up and deal with it. The two of you can squeeze into the nooks and crannies, where the rest of us can't reach."

"I don't remember anybody putting you in charge," Gork spat at him.

"That's because you were practically unconscious at the time." He crooked a finger at Belrotha. "You want a reminder?"

"Ah, no. I think me and Fezeill make a wonderful team."

"Splendid." Cræosh sighed. After that speech, he couldn't very well make too big an issue out of this next step. "Katim, you're with me."

The troll's snout twitched. "That must have . . . galled you."

The orc shrugged. "Ain't anyone else left, is there?"

"There is that," she said.

"Any of you find anything, sing out. We shouldn't be more than a few minutes away from each other. And for fuck's sake, don't take on the whole lot of them by yourself!"

They scattered, Jhurpess making for one of the structures that didn't look *entirely* unsound. The last thing Cræosh heard was Belrotha asking her partner, "Does orc care what song me sing if me find anything? Me not know any orcish songs."

Fezeill, in a decision that, though logical for crawling through tiny gaps, lacked all sense of tact, had once again taken the form of a kobold. Gork took that as a personal insult—which, to be fair, might well have been the intent—and for the first hour of their search, he refused to communicate with the doppelganger beyond the occasional grunt.

The pair of them had just twisted and shoved themselves into a rundown, rubble-filled structure. The spacious interior suggested this might once have been an official or government building of some sort, but the outer walls were so crumbled that ingress had proved nigh impossible for even their tiny frames. They both swiftly relit their torches and scanned the wreckage. Fezeill immediately resumed the diatribe he had begun moments earlier, and Gork realized that his fists were clenching of their own accord around both his torch and his *kah-rahahk*.

"It's the same thing I've tried to point out to you before," Fezeill told him, staring into blackness only slightly diluted by the torchlight. "You take things too personally. I thought you might have learned that after your brief stint in prison, or at least over the course of our travels. You're never going to make a good thief if you can't put your own petty feelings aside. Your attitude right now is a perfect example. Why it should bother you what I . . . look . . ."

The doppelganger's voice dribbled away as both he and Gork stared at the wall before them. A single worm poked its head through a tiny gap in the stones. It very carefully drifted from one side to the other, as though engaged in some reconnaissance of its own. Then it casually dropped off the wall to the dusty ground and began slowly squirming toward the intruders. A second worm emerged from behind it, a third, a millipede and two maggots, another worm . . .

It wasn't a large swarm, not compared to others they'd faced. But it was big enough.

Gork, accustomed to fighting alongside much larger allies, stepped behind Fezeill, putting the doppelganger between him and the approaching vermin. "Fezeill," he asked, a nervous quiver in his voice, "if you're injured, and you shift form, can you make your wounds heal or close up at all as part of the transformation?"

"I wish. This sort of thing would be much easier if I could." Even from the back, Gork could tell that he sneered. "Why, are you hoping I might protect your precious hide?"

"Something like that."

The pommel of the *kah-rahahk* crunched into the outside of Fezeill's knee. The joint separated with a loud pop and the doppelganger collapsed, screaming. His torch and his sword both skittered across the stone as both hands dropped instinctively to clutch at the terrible injury.

Gork glided across the uneven floor to the nearest wall. The building was in such a sorry state that even the tiny kobold had little difficulty knocking a section of stones loose, scattering them across the prostrate doppelganger—who, in his agony, had begun shifting back to his natural, repulsive form. They weren't as large or as heavy as Gork might have preferred, those stones, but they would be enough to account for the shattered knee if anyone were to ask. He added a few more anyway, just to make it look good, working quickly as the worms edged closer.

"Gork, what are you doing?!" The panic in Fezeill's voice was the most beautiful song the kobold had ever heard.

He didn't answer. Instead, he bent forward and, with the greatest care, plucked the lead worm from the ground. He squeezed it just behind the head, ensuring that it couldn't turn on him—but he held it

418

gently, taking great care not to injure the wiggling thing. And finally he knelt beside the fallen doppelganger, snout split in a wide grin.

"What . . . ?" Fezeill began again—just as Gork had hoped he would.

Gork clamped his palm over Fezeill's open mouth and let the worm drop. The doppelganger gagged and then started to spasm, the heel of his one good leg beating hard against the ground.

"Don't you worry now, Fezeill," Gork said comfortingly, patting his cheek and then rising. "I'll bring the others back in time to dispose of your corpse properly. You won't be coming back as a shambling mass of worms, I promise."

"Gork . . ." It came out choked, nearly unintelligible. A bubble of yellow ichor burst between Fezeill's lips and oozed down the side of his face.

"I could tell you that this is for getting me arrested back in Timas Khoreth. Or for any one of a thousand other slights." Gork's grin was so wide it was astounding the entire upper half of his head didn't simply topple off. "But you shouldn't really care. After all, I'm sure you're not taking this *personally*."

And with that, he was gone.

For long minutes Fezeill thrashed and squirmed as he felt that *thing* tunneling through his innards. Nearer and nearer the rest of the swarm crept, and there was nothing he could . . .

Yes, there was! The elixirs!

Each member of the squad carried two of Havarren's vials. If he could reach his, he might survive to repay the kobold for this treachery. Eagerly, questing fingers thrust themselves into the pouch at his side.

The pouch, he realized far too late, that Gork had deliberately smashed with some of those falling stones. His fingertips tore against shards of broken ceramic and came away coated in both ichor and the last lingering drops of potion that had not yet seeped through the burlap.

Around the tearing agony in his throat, despite the fact that many of his vocal chords had already separated, Fezeill howled his frustration, his fury, into the uncaring darkness.

He was still howling when the worms reached him, but Fezeill's final screams were not of rage.

"Well," Cræosh said, his face flickering in the light of the burning mass that, moments before, had been the remains of his shapeshifting companion, "I guess that's that. Anybody wanna say anything?"

Most of the squad just peered at him. A few shuffled their feet. Belrotha—who'd hauled away enough of the wall to allow them access to the structure and was now standing with her hands pressed against the ceiling to ensure it didn't bury the lot of them as it had partly done Fezeill—just grunted. Nobody spoke up.

"Yeah," the orc said finally, "me neither."

So far, nobody had questioned Gork's wide-eyed account of their battle with the swarming creatures, their lashing out with blades and torches both, the doppelganger's wild swing that had brought down a portion of loose wall right on top of him. Nobody questioned, for there was no cause to question—but Cræosh allowed himself to idly wonder. And the troll's narrowed gaze, fixed on the kobold even as she'd recommended burning the body to prevent it from rising again, suggested that he was not the only one.

Now that gaze swung side to side, as though Katim was determined to memorize every detail of the building. "This is the only place where . . . the worms have reemerged," she pointed out, speaking up over the roasting doppelganger. "Or at least the only . . . place *we've* seen them."

"True," Cræosh agreed. "All right, then. Shorty, which wall did you say they came from?"

Gork pointed.

"Okay. Belrotha?"

"What?"

"The worms on the other side of that wall insulted your momma. Let's get them!"

The ogre looked askance at the orc. "Us talk about this before, Cræosh. Worms not insult mother. Worms never *meet* mother! And you not supposed to talk about her, either."

Cræosh sighed. "Just get rid of the wall."

Belrotha sighed at Gimmol. "All him had to do was ask," she complained. "Him a very slow learner." Then, one hand firmly on the ceiling, she twisted so no shrapnel would strike the gremlin on her shoulder and slapped her other palm against the stone. The wall didn't so much crumble as simply cease to exist in any meaningful capacity.

"I *thought* this building looked official," Gork muttered as the dust settled and the last echoes faded away into the chasm's eternal night.

"What are you talking about?" Cræosh asked. "It's a fucking stairway. How can you tell what kind of building this was by looking at the fucking stairway?"

"This was the headquarters of the watch, Cræosh, or something similar."

"How do you know that?" the orc demanded.

Gork waved negligently at the steps. "Because those steps lead to a dungeon, you festering sore! No one builds stairs that steep or that narrow unless they lead to a dungeon. Trust me, I've seen enough of them."

"I'm not convinced. But let's find out."

"Um, Cræosh?" This from behind, as he set a foot upon the topmost step.

"It'll be tight, Belrotha, but I'm sure you can fit."

"Me not asking about stairs. Me asking about roof."

"Oh. Hmm."

Still, after some nerve-racking experimentation, they determined that the ceiling would remain standing without its load-bearing ogre. At least, it would for a time; the ugly creaking promised them they'd have to hurry, or be prepared to find another way out.

So they hurried. Cræosh remained unconvinced by Gork's logic until they reached the bottom of the stairs and found a solid wooden door, lying half off its hinges. It wore rusted brackets that would have held a dauntingly weighty bar.

"Okay," the orc finally agreed. "It's a dungeon."

"Told you," Gork said smugly.

Cræosh growled something unintelligible.

"Well I *did* tell you. You all heard me tell him, didn't you?"

"Why don't you scout ahead, Gork?" Cræosh asked, his fist closing tightly on the kobold's collar.

"What? I'm not going in the*aaaaagggghhhhh*!"

The kobold quickly sailed beyond the range of their torchlight. A resounding thump echoed back to them a moment later, followed by a brief whimper.

"I see why you enjoy doing that so much," Cræosh said to Katim.

"It's cathartic," she acknowledged.

"Anything to report so far?" the orc called cheerfully.

A low mutter came drifting through the darkness.

"What'd he say?"

The troll chuckled. "I believe he said . . . 'Just a very hard wall.'"

Cræosh laughed. "All right. Let's go scrape him up and keep moving."

As the squad ducked through the doorway, Gimmol leaned across his perch so he could whisper into the ogre's ear. "They're acting like nothing happened! Doesn't anyone care that Fezeill's dead?"

The ogre shrugged, once more coming near to dislodging the precariously balanced gremlin. "No one like Fezeill, so no one care that him dead." She smiled. "You not worry, though. Me like you. If you die, me care."

"Swell."

It was less than cheery, even as dungeons go. The entryway was dominated by all sorts of encouraging images carved in the stone: here, a masked headsman, axe raised high; there, a woman, also hooded, standing atop a gallows, noose dangling from her clenched fist. The cell doors were black, fastened by both a small bar and a sizable iron padlock half eaten by rust. They lacked even the tiny barred window common to so many prisons, denying the prisoners the least exposure to a world beyond their four tiny walls.

"What a nasty place," Gork observed to no one in particular. Appropriately enough, then, no one replied.

By the time they'd reached the end of the long hall, Cræosh had rather irritably made two observations. One was that the doors on about half the cells—perhaps five on each side of the corridor—were open, revealing the skeletons of long-dead inhabitants who had not survived Krohketh's fall. Two, and it was this that inspired the sudden darkening of his mood, was that there appeared to be no exit from this dingy hallway other than the way they'd come. Not even so much as a fist-sized hole in the wall.

So where had the bloody worms come from?

As if she'd read his mind, the troll appeared at his side. "We seem to be missing . . . something rather important."

"Gee, you think so? Whatever might make you think that?"

"If we had an hour or . . . two to spare, I'd explain it to . . . you."

"Obviously," Gimmol said from atop Belrotha's shoulder, "what we're looking for isn't in the hallway. So we're going to have to check the cells."

"Makes sense," Cræosh agreed, just as happy to avoid the upcoming argument. "We'll check the open ones first. I doubt the worms have been closing the doors behind them."

"Cræosh?" the crouching ogre asked, staring back over her shoulder. "Am dead humans the same as dead ogres?"

"Belrotha, what the holy bubbling fuck are you talking about?"

"Dead ogres stay dead."

"That ain't exactly unusual, Belrotha. Most dead things stay . . ." It finally dawned on Cræosh exactly what the ogre was implying. For just an instant, he squeezed his eyes shut and allowed himself a brief whimper.

Sure enough, several of the skeletons had risen to their feet and dragged themselves out into the hallway. They shambled, their movements slow and abrupt, tendons flexing as they . . .

Tendons?

Cræosh looked closer. Those weren't tendons!

"Ancestors . . ."

Some of the longest worms he'd ever seen had wrapped themselves about the bones, intertwining themselves through the various joints. They flexed, they stretched, and the long-dead bodies walked once more.

423

"Now that," Gork commented, *kah-rahahk* held out before him, "is truly disturbing."

"Innovative, though," Katim added.

The skeletons drew closer, bony feet scratching the stone floor with each step. They wavered like drunken sailors, threatening to topple to one side or the other, but they never did. Fleshless hands reached out, fingers prepared to rend whatever stood in their path.

Disturbing and innovative they may have been; they were not, however, particularly effective. Cræosh allowed the first of the shambling skeletons to draw near, and then he attacked. Bone and, more importantly, worms split beneath his heavy blade. Both arms fell limp, and indeed the left forearm fell with a clatter to bounce its way across the floor.

Katim and Gork returned the orc's evil grin, Jhurpess pounded his massive club against the floor, and Belrotha just grabbed the crippled skeleton and pulverized it against the ceiling. She held onto a single femur, wielding it as a club.

In a matter of instants, the skeletons were nothing but a carpeting of powder and the occasional chunks of bone, glued together by a thin paste that had once been several dozen long worms.

"That was fun," Cræosh said, kicking at the refuse.

"Easy," Belrotha grunted in agreement.

"Well, that was mostly because I disarmed him for you," the orc told her—and then began hopping and cursing as Katim stamped on his foot.

"Why?" Gimmol asked, frowning down at the bones.

When it became clear that Cræosh was too busy to answer, Katim shrugged. "Experimentation? To see what . . . techniques other than swarms might . . . function? Perhaps, after the bombardment . . . there weren't enough for more than . . . this? Or perhaps, this is . . . all they needed."

"Worm-bones not do good job at stopping us," Belrotha protested.

"No," Cræosh said, finally ceasing his frantic hop. "But I bet they know we're coming now. Get the hell back to searching."

In the second-to-last cell on the left—which contained one of the dungeon's skeletons that had *not* been puppeteered by Sabryen's worms—Gork discovered a segment of wall distinct from the rest. The mortar around those bricks had been chiseled out and several pitons driven into one side as crude hinges, transforming the entire affair into a heavy, primitive door.

"Who builds a back door in a prison cell?" Gimmol asked from out in the hall.

Gork shook his head. "Nobody. This is new. Well, newer than the rest of this place, anyway. This place wasn't a dungeon anymore, just part of the ruins."

"Oh." A long pause. "Why would worms need doors? They should get by just fine with holes in the walls."

"Because some of the worms are wearing human skeletons, remember?"

Again, "Oh." And then finally, "So what's behind it?"

The kobold stepped back. "Any two of those bricks weigh more than I do," he announced. "Cræosh?"

"Yeah, right. And this has nothing to do with you being worried the entire thing could collapse on your head?"

"I never said *that*. . . ."

The orc heaved. Ponderously, groaning like a constipated whale, the portal swung open. Beyond was a wide, shallow staircase leading even farther down. The steps, made of the same dark stone in evidence everywhere else, were completely free of dust.

"Worms," Gork announced after a quick examination. "If it had been humanoids using the stairs, there would still be some dust where the wall and floor come together. But even that's swept clean."

Jhurpess spread his arms, measuring the width of the stairs. "Take a lot of worms," he noted.

"What a coincidence, Nature-boy," Cræosh snorted. "There *are* a lot of worms."

"True," the bugbear conceded.

And unfortunately, as the squad discovered soon enough, a substantial number of them were lurking up ahead.

The staircase terminated in a long hall: a straight expanse, relatively featureless save for the sconces at regular intervals along the walls. The torches within, for no reason the goblins could fathom, were lit. The gentle glow revealed a thick layer of worms, millipedes, and maggots coating the floor in a restless rug.

A rug that had to be half a foot deep, if not more, since the squirming vermin were about even with the top of the bottommost step.

"Well, fuck me backward," Cræosh said. Then, turning to the troll, "You're the athletic one. Why don't you jump it?"

Save for the twitch of an ear, Katim didn't bother to acknowledge his existence.

"Gimmol?" he asked more seriously. "Anything you can do? Burn us a path, maybe?"

The gremlin swung down from his perch atop the ogre's shoulder, landing with a faint thump. "Not burn, no," he said, peering out over the worms. "Not with so many of them; they'd just fill up the spaces. I think I *can* get us across, but it won't be easy—not for *any* of us. And I might not be much good to you for a while afterward."

Cræosh shrugged. "If we can't get through, it doesn't much matter anyway. Whatever you've got to do, do it."

The gremlin nodded. "Okay. Be ready to move *quickly* when I say so. The path's not going to last long. And, uh, watch your step."

For a long moment, Gimmol chanted and muttered, lips rumpling around foreign syllables, fingers dancing like a flight of hungry mosquitoes. Then, wincing only slightly, he stepped off the stairway and into the hall.

Ice crystallized from the air around his feet at every pace, spreading not only out but down. Insects and invertebrates froze, encased in the spreading ice. The bulk of the creatures, fortunate enough to escape being entombed, instead flopped helplessly against the slick and frigid surface, lacking sufficient purchase to climb up and ravage the gremlin's feet.

His brow already damp with sweat, Gimmol moved toward the hall's far end. "The invocation was intended for creating bridges across slow-moving water," he muttered in response to his companions' unasked question. "Since there's no water to freeze here, the ice is fragile. Don't start until I say so, and when you do, for the gods' sakes, *be careful*."

426

"The cold didn't bother the worms when we were in the tundra," Gork said, a note of complaint actually evident in his voice.

Cræosh shrugged. "They weren't frozen inside it or trying to climb it, were they?"

Gimmol disappeared from sight, moving beyond the envelope of torchlight. He left a path of ice behind him, but even as the others watched, the first few inches were starting to bead with moisture.

"Why didn't we just walk behind him as he went?" Cræosh wondered.

"Why not ask him when you . . . get there?" Katim said.

"I'll just do that."

More minutes passed. Tiny rivulets trickled from the flimsy walkway, pooling in the corners of the hall. And finally, just as Cræosh was about to suggest they'd waited long enough, Gimmol's voice floated back from the corridor's far end. "Okay, guys. One—*only one*—at a time! Go!"

Katim was moving before the echo faded, skating as much as running across the ice, gliding across the churning sea of worms. Cræosh followed with rather less grace; three times he nearly lost his balance, and only frantic pinwheeling of his arms and wrenching strain in his back saved him from toppling over. Gork just put his head down and ran, and Jhurpess . . . Well, Jhurpess managed. Loudly.

It was, in fact, just as the flailing bugbear skidded to a halt beside the assembled group—who were themselves standing beside yet another dull, unmarked wooden door—that Gimmol's eyes went wide. He actually reached up and grabbed the startled orc by the breastplate.

"What . . . ?"

"*Why didn't you let Belrotha go first?!*" the gremlin screeched.

"I figured she might shatter the . . ." And then Cræosh's own jaw dropped, as he realized what must soon be barreling his way. "Gork! Get that fucking door open! *Now!*"

The distant torchlight darkened, obscured by a fast-moving shadow. Grunts and exclamations erupted from the passageway, and it finally dawned on the rest of the squad that ogre plus ice added up to a *whole lot* of momentum.

Jhurpess, in the midst of his unintelligible shrieking, decided that waiting for Gork to do something with the lock was clearly going to take too long. His massive club flashed over the kobold's head—close enough to rustle the hair Gork didn't have—and split the wood straight down the middle. There was plenty of room beyond for the entire squad, except that Cræosh, Jhurpess, and Gork had all dived for the opening at once and succeeded in firmly wedging themselves into the doorframe.

Katim leapt, digging her talons painfully into the crevices in the stone, clinging to the ceiling above; a vicious, malformed arachnid. Gimmol just cowered into a little ball as far from the center of the path as he could get without rolling off into the vermin beyond.

By the time Belrotha reached them, she'd ceased running at all, having already built up what even she recognized as an excessive amount of speed. The ogre held herself completely stiff, legs locked in a crouch, arms extended for balance, and still she slid rapidly across the ice, slowly rotating as she came. A look of bemusement plastered across her face, she glided beneath the quivering troll, past the cowering gremlin, and plowed full tilt into the flesh-packed doorway.

The sounds of impact finally faded, the dust and the splinters and the frost settled into a thin haze, and Katim allowed herself to drop to her feet, shaking her aching fingers as though to slough off the pain. She felt the ice crack beneath her soles and shivered as a spray of cold water splashed over the tops of her boots. Gimmol's spell was quite clearly giving out. She nonchalantly reached out, lifted the gremlin-ball, stepped through the now-vacant doorway, and promptly dropped him again.

Some yards ahead of her was a haphazard collection of limbs that Katim assumed accounted for the rest of the squad. Even as she watched, Belrotha rose and shook herself, sending more splinters—and also Jhurpess—into the air. Cræosh dragged himself rather more slowly to his feet: staggering, blinking owlishly, and leaning vaguely to his left.

And Gork—Gork lay, facedown and unmoving, on the hard stone floor.

Well, there was no blood, at least. Carefully, Katim knelt beside him. "Gork? Gork, you need to . . . get moving."

"Go away," the kobold muttered, his voice muffled by the rock into which his snout was pressed. "I'm dead."

"You're not dead. Now . . . get up."

"I'm dead," he insisted firmly. "I got run over by a herd of rabid wildebeests, and now I'm dead."

"You're not dead," Katim said again.

"I—"

"But you're *about* . . . to be."

"—suddenly feel a whole lot better," Gork finished smoothly, rising to his feet. His arms were mottled with fresh bruises, and he favored his right ankle just a bit with his first few steps, but otherwise he appeared remarkably unscathed by his collision with the "wildebeests."

Satisfied that the squad would be hindered by neither the kobold nor, after a few moments to regain his equilibrium, the orc, Katim examined the room around them.

"Room," as it turned out, was something of a misnomer. Apparently natural, to judge by the veritable forest of stalactites and stalagmites, the cavern must have been over a hundred feet on a side. Fires—not torches, these, but small bonfires—burned at seemingly random intervals. Large slabs, apparently leftovers from the formation of the Demias Gap, lay scattered throughout those various protrusions, creating a stone hedgework not dissimilar to Queen Anne's maze of plants.

"Katim, left flank," Cræosh barked. "Gork, right. I'll check the center. Belrotha, Jhurpess, and Gimmol will fill in the gaps and provide reinforcement should any of the three of us find anything."

"Are we giving orders . . . again, Cræosh?" Katim asked him. "I thought we'd broken you . . . of that particular habit."

"Do you have a better idea?" Cræosh challenged.

"As a matter of fact, I . . . don't."

"Then get the fuck moving, and save the arguments for some other time when I might give a shit what you think."

Katim flared her nostrils at that, but said nothing more.

Slowly, the squad spread out, moving carefully ahead. Most of the cavern looked just like what they'd already seen, but the far left portion . . . *flowed*.

"Ancestors," Cræosh exclaimed. The others could only nod in agreement.

If the hallway had contained a river of worms, this was the ocean to which it ran. Cræosh would not have believed that all the worms and all the maggots in all the world could have formed so large a mass. It possessed its own tides, that sea, caused by the individual writhing of millions of component creatures. It ebbed and fell, sometimes subsuming this rock here, other times disgorging that stalagmite there.

No, not the rising and falling of a tide, Cræosh decided reluctantly. The beating of some vast heart.

"So," Gork said, grinning through clenched teeth, "which one of them do you suppose is Sabryen?"

"NONE! *I* AM THY RIGHTFUL KING! *I* AM SABRYEN!"

The expanse surged again, the first half of that horrid heartbeat, but this time, when it contracted, it left a figure standing in its wake. Arms spread wide, King Sabryen emerged from the embrace of his loving subjects.

The Charnel King certainly hadn't stinted on his curse. From the waist up, Sabryen's flesh was pale, tinged with the faint blue of death, decorated with ragged tears that flapped like ghastly lips when he moved. A few strands of thick, stringy hair clung to his skull, and a thin film of maggots roiled in his empty eye sockets.

And this was his better half. His flesh was torn at the waist, jagged and uneven. The tip of a spine dangled obscenely from within, tracing random patterns in the dust. From beneath his dead flesh his innards drooped, intestines and strings of muscle and meat—only they were no longer organs at all, but unthinkably long worms that tensed and clenched and pushed his body across the floor.

Gimmol wretched. Jhurpess whined and covered his head. Even Cræosh looked somewhat greener than usual. "I thought King Morthûl was bad," he whispered hoarsely.

Katim licked her chops, a thin string of drool splattering the toes of her boots. "No troll alive has anything . . . like *that* waiting on them . . . in the next world," she cooed.

"Is that all you can think about?!" It was as near to panic as Cræosh had ever heard his own voice, but he couldn't help it.

"What else is . . . there?"

"PUT THY WEAPONS ASIDE!" Sabryen boomed at them, the profane thing that was his body sliding ever nearer. "THOU CANNOT HARM ME! AND I NEED NOT HARM THEE. THOU SERVE THE USURPER, BUT THOU ART NOT MY FOE." He spread his arms even wider and smiled, making his face even more obscene. "I AM A BENEVOLENT KING, AND I GRANT THEE THIS OPTION. TURN THY BACKS UPON THE FOUL USURPER OF MY THRONE! SWEAR TO ME THY ALLEGIANCE, THY FEALTY! THOU SHALL BE THE HIGHEST OF MY SUBJECTS. LAY LOW THINE ARMS, AND THOU SHALL BE EXALTED BEFORE ALL MEN. WOULD THY CURRENT MASTER, THY CHARNEL KING, PROVE SO GENEROUS?"

"He'd prove even less generous once he found out we'd turned traitor on him," Gimmol mouthed quietly.

"You know," Cræosh called more loudly, "you're the second, um, *person* to ask us to betray Morthûl."

"INDEED." Sabryen sounded less than impressed. "AND WHAT REPLY DID THOU MAKE TO THE FIRST?"

"We told him to pull his ass cheeks over his face and sing hymns."

"I don't remember anyone saying that," Gork said.

"Shut up!" Katim rasped.

"I SEE." The maggots contorting in Sabryen's sockets seemed to grow agitated. "AND WOULD THOU MAKE SO RUDE A RESPONSE TO MY OFFER AS WELL?"

Cræosh made a show of pondering for a moment. "We don't have to," he finally said. "Can you suggest a more polite way of saying 'Fuck off sideways'?"

"I SUSPECTED THOU WERE FOOLS, TO SERVE THY TREACHEROUS LORD SO WILLINGLY." The last traces of affability had dripped from his voice like the roaches cascading from the Dark Lord he so hated. "STILL DID I GRANT THEE THE OPPORTUNITY TO SERVE ME VOLUNTARILY, THAT NONE MIGHT CALL ME AN UNREASONABLE MAN."

"None might call you a man at all," Cræosh observed. "Spread out!" he hissed at the others, who were already doing just that.

"BUT WILLINGLY OR NOT, THOU WILL SERVE! ALL OF KIROL SYRRETH SHALL BE MINE AGAIN!"

"I think that's our cue," Gork said.

"FEAST, MY CHILDREN!" Sabryen cried, his horrific innards thrusting him across the ground at astounding speeds.

"Cræosh!" Gimmol shouted as the entire quivering mass of worms began to flow toward them, "we're going to have a hard time getting to Sabryen if we're covered in that!"

The orc glanced aside from the oncoming king long enough to curse. "Can you slow it down?" he called back.

The gremlin shook his head. "Even at full strength, I couldn't hope to affect *that*! I—"

"Gimmol, go help kill man with worm-guts," Belrotha said. "Me can stop worms."

"Belrotha, no! You can't—"

"Gimmol not argue, or me get mad!" she screamed at him. "Gimmol not want me to get mad at him! Me be very sorry after, but Gimmol still be squished into very small lump, and me not be able to undo!"

"I'll just go help with Sabryen," the gremlin agreed uneasily. Almost unwillingly, he turned away.

Belrotha offered a single grunt of approval and then calmly surveyed the onrushing tide of worms, maggots, millipedes, and other things for which she had no names. Even she was smart enough to realize that her fists and her sword would prove useless against such a foe. But not once in the entire history of her race had futility ever prevented an ogre from acting—and besides, Belrotha had a *plan*.

It was a new experience for her, having a plan; but she'd watched the others do it, and it didn't seem that tricky. What she had learned in her months of traveling with this motley group was that "having a plan" basically meant "finding a new way to kill whatever it was that had caused the need for the plan in the first place."

Belrotha took a step backward, bent down, and smoothly lifted one of the massive slabs that lay strewn about the cavern like the toys of a messy (not to mention exceedingly large) child. *Fist squish only a few. Sword squish only a few. Big rock squish* many.

The stone, taller than she was and equally as wide, crashed into the oncoming tide. Ichor and sludge spurted from beneath, and the ogre imagined she could hear the death screams of a thousand thousand worms. Grinning wildly, she reached for the next rock.

The others were faring somewhat less well. The instant Sabryen had shuffled into range, Cræosh leapt forward, sword raised high. With a vicious cry he brought it down, determined to cleave Sabryen's head completely in half.

It didn't happen that way. With a contemptuous twist of his arm, the hideous thing caught the blade in an open palm. Sword broke skin, but only a trickle of a thick, brackish sludge oozed from the wound. The shock of impact ran up the blade and through the orc's arms, very nearly enough to make him drop the weapon. Sabryen's other hand slammed into Cræosh's chest, and the orc found himself on his back a dozen feet away. Groggily, his chest screaming in agony, he staggered back to his feet. A massive palm print had been dented into his breastplate, and only the steel's protection, feeble as it had proved, had saved him from a new array of broken ribs.

Katim's *chirrusk* whistled, its razor-tipped barbs sinking into the flesh of Sabryen's extended arm. She twisted and yanked, the chain snapping taut. It was a traditional trollish maneuver, supposedly capable of toppling any opponent through a combination of agony and main strength. Katim had once seen it used to pull down an ogre even larger than Belrotha.

But here and now, she might as well have been trying to topple the Iron Keep with a skein of yarn. The chain reached the end of its slack and just stopped. Her mightiest tug couldn't so much as move the creature's arm, and he appeared perfectly content to ignore a degree of pain that should have sent any living thing into shock.

Sabryen flexed that arm in the opposite direction. Katim, snarling like a rabid dog, allowed the *chirrusk* to slide from her fist rather than find herself slamming into the floor at the worm-thing's "feet." The former king glanced curiously at the chain dangling from his skin and then, without so much as a flinch, tore the barbs loose from his flesh and dropped it behind him. Grinding her teeth so loud the others could hear it, Katim drew her axe.

The darkness cooked away, sizzling beneath bolts of flame that Gimmol, face squeezed tight with effort, hurled from his trembling fists. They were feeble indeed, thanks to the gremlin's fatigue, but Sabryen flinched, if only a little. Behind him, waiting for just such an opening, Gork struck. The *kah-rahahk* tore through the limp flesh of the worm-thing's back, just above the ragged edge.

It proved about as useful as the *chirrusk*. Looking more irritated than pained, Sabryen pulled away from the barbed weapon, leaving reeking gobbets of flesh stuck to the blade. The creature twisted, reaching a hand toward the kobold, yet Gork refused to run.

Had Sabryen actually *known* Gork, he'd have recognized that for the suspicious gesture that it was.

From the shadows to the left, Jhurpess lunged at his distracted foe. With every muscle in his simian body, the bugbear swung his heavy club into the side of Sabryen's skull.

The crack of impact reverberated throughout the chasm; Sabryen shuddered and fell, flopping limply on the stone. Jhurpess and Gork grinned at one another, perhaps pleased at having defeated their enemy, perhaps at having shown up Cræosh and Katim both.

Those grins dropped away swiftly enough when the cursed king, looking none the worse for wear save for a new flap of skin hanging loose from his scalp, rose smoothly to his full height.

"I GROW TIRED OF THEE." His lips quivered, his fingers twitched, and Gimmol hurled himself to the floor, shrieking *"Spell!"*

A wave of force, unseen but for a brief shimmer as it passed and the swirling dust in its wake, burst from the old king. Blood fountained from Jhurpess's nose and mouth; he was thrown back by a blow Belrotha could scarcely have matched, sliding across the stone until he fetched up against the base of a great stalagmite. One hand clasping his club, the other scrabbling at the stone, he struggled to rise—and for a few moments he failed, weighed down by muscles that refused to obey and a pounding ache that refused to fade.

Cræosh was slashing away at Sabryen once more, screaming at his allies not to let up for an instant. For long minutes, the battle raged. Cræosh and Katim and Gork slashed and stabbed, delivering wound after wound that should have slain any living thing. And Sabryen ignored each wound as he had the first, immune to pain, too mighty to fall. The goblins' only victory, if victory you could call it, was that they had so far prevented him from casting any further magics.

It was a losing strategy, and the orc knew it. Sooner or later, one of goblins would tire; not much, perhaps, but enough. Sabryen would cast another spell, or land a blow solid enough to put one of them down for good. And then the others would follow within seconds. So they continued to fight a battle they could not win—their efforts punctuated occasionally by the sudden report of one of Belrotha's stones landing across the chamber—because every other option was even worse.

Cræosh retreated a few steps, allowing Katim to dart across and open another rent in Sabryen's torso. The creature lashed out, not at the troll passing before him, but at the more distant orc. Worms, hurled by Sabryen as they'd been by his servitors in the tundra, pattered across Cræosh's chest in a stinking rain. He fell back, screaming, beating at the skin exposed above the steel of his breastplate, muscles already burning as the first of the parasites burrowed into his flesh.

And then Gimmol was beside him, thrusting a ceramic vial at the flailing orc. "Drink! *Drink*, dammit!"

The orc was already too far gone to recognize why he was being given such an order; clearly, it hadn't penetrated his gibbering mind that he should just have grabbed one of his own elixirs. Nevertheless, he obeyed. The bitter fluid sluiced down his throat, choking him, but the worms ceased their digging the instant the stuff reached his gut. One last instant of agony, as the dying creatures spasmed within his body, and then they were still. With a heartfelt nod to the gremlin, bulling through his lingering pain and a growing pall of despair, Cræosh struggled upright once more.

If dying on his feet was the last victory he could hope for, then by all his ancestors, die on his feet he would.

Clinging to the base of the stalagmite for balance, Jhurpess watched as his friend nearly fell to the terrible worms, as the tiny gremlin saved him in the nick of time. He gasped in grateful relief—he'd already put so much work into the orc, he'd hate to have to start over—and then froze. He watched, not as Cræosh hurled himself back into the fray, but as Gimmol's hand dropped to his pouch, fingering the last of his elixirs. And the bugbear's entire face lit up with inspiration.

Not, despite what his companions thought of him, as foreign a sensation to Jhurpess as it was to Belrotha. Sure, he was a creature of instinct, not intellect; his options were primarily drawn from the rather limited selection of "eat it, kill it, fuck it, or flee." A bugbear's life was, on the whole, not a complex one.

But while Jhurpess might not know much, what he knew, he knew *well*. And Jhurpess knew nature. He knew its ins and outs, its patterns, and—as Gimmol had learned to his chagrin the day they first met—he knew its hazards.

Slowly Jhurpess stood, shifting his balance from the stone to his own two feet. He forced himself to be patient, methodical, despite the raging battle; to ensure that each limb was pulling its own weight, that Sabryen's magic had caused no crippling wound. Only then, satisfied that everything worked despite the lingering pain, did he begin a wide circle around the fray.

Careful step after careful step; between one and the next, Jhurpess reached into the tiny pouch he wore slung on the same harness that bound his bow to his leather armor. From it, he removed the first of his own ceramic vials.

Sabryen struck, sending Katim staggering. Only her phenomenal dexterity kept her on her feet, and even then it was a near thing. Cræosh stepped in to fill the gap, offering Katim a few precious seconds to recover—and Jhurpess the instant he needed.

He was beside her in a flash, reaching out with a hairy hand. "Mouth," he grunted, placing the vial in Katim's palm.

"I've got my own, Jhurpess, I . . . do not need—"

"Not Katim's mouth. King's mouth! If gunk poisons *little* worms . . ."

Katim's eyes grew wide and her jaw actually gaped. "Then maybe it poisons the . . . *big* worm," she breathed. "I'm an idiot!

Jhurpess shrugged. "That okay. Katim has other redeeming qualities."

The troll nodded and flowed fluidly back into the fray. Jhurpess wrapped both hands around his club and waited.

"Cræosh!"

The orc spared a millisecond to glance at the approaching troll. "You alive?"

"Back off!" she commanded. "Take a moment to . . . catch your breath."

"That'll give him time to cast something, you idiot!" he shouted, barely interposing his sword in time to catch a dreadful overhand blow that threatened to cave in his skull.

"That's the point!"

"*What?* I—"

One of Sabryen's wormy innards swept low, nearly taking the orc's feet out from under him and leaving a swath of slime across his ankles. Cræosh staggered, and the cursed king smacked him aside with a casual backhand.

Come on—come on . . .

Sabryen raised his hands as she'd hoped he would and opened his mouth to begin the incantation that would have rained fire down upon his foes, or swept them aside in an eldritch wave, or dissolved the flesh from their bones.

Katim almost, *almost* wished she had someone to pray to as she cocked back an arm and threw.

The whiplike snap of Sabryen's jawbone dislocating was lost in the tinkling, musical sound of teeth raining in pieces onto the floor. He staggered, gagging, reaching up to tug the strange obstruction from between his jaws. His cheeks spasmed as muscles strained against one another, and it was only the vial itself—cracked but not shattered—that kept his unattached jawbone from flopping loosely this way and that.

And then Jhurpess stepped in and swung a devastating underhand blow, bringing the tip of his club up into Sabryen's chin.

The creature's head snapped back, the shattering ceramic audible despite the layer of muffling flesh around it. Shards of vial—and indeed, of bone—imbedded themselves in the roof of Sabryen's mouth, severing his tongue at the roots. Jets of Havarren's elixir spurted from between his lips, tinged black with Sabryen's tarlike blood.

Limbs flailing, broken visage tilted impossibly back, the ancient king of Kirol Syrreth screamed to shake the foundations of the earth in which they stood.

"You think one vial's enough?" Cræosh shouted dubiously, wincing away from the unending sound.

Gork popped up from the rocks behind Sabryen like some mad gopher. "Let's find out!" The kobold jumped, latching onto the fleshy torso. Claws clinging despite the creature's violent spasms, he scampered up until he could get a solid grasp around the king's head. He yanked back and down, clinging to Sabryen's forehead, forcing wide the blood-filled maw. "Who's first?" the kobold yelled, his legs dangling beneath him in mockery of Sabryen's own thrashing limbs.

Cræosh and Katim grinned, already reaching for their packs.

By the time they'd forced the fourth elixir down the creature's throat, the spasms had grown too strong for Gork to hang on any longer. The squad now stood and watched as the great King Sabryen lay twitching and frothing on the stone. Something about the wormy tendrils grasping at nothing in particular made the sight particularly revolting.

"Okay," Cræosh said finally, "he's not going anywhere, but he's still alive. Now what?"

Gork grinned his nastiest grin. "Belrotha!"

"Me kind of busy right now!"

In fact, the ogre stood ankle deep in the tide of worms. All about her, huge slabs lay where they'd fallen, puddles of spreading goo serving as testament to the effectiveness of Belrotha's plan. Nevertheless, she'd been unable to stem the tide. Blood trickled from her ankles and calves to vanish beneath the writhing creatures. Cræosh could only assume that she'd already drunk one of her own elixirs, considering that she wasn't in the throes of an agonizing death. She held another large rock over her head and was repeatedly smashing at the worms around her feet.

"Belrotha!" Gork shouted again. "We need you over here!"

"Me busy!" she repeated. "You come back after me kill all worms!"

Cræosh tapped Katim on the shoulder and whispered. She nodded, and the hulking pair moved toward Sabryen's broken body.

"Belrotha, you *can't* kill all the worms!" Gork shouted in frustration. "There's too many!"

"That okay! Me not counting!"

Gork gurgled in rage. Fortunately, before he could do anything stupid, the orc and the troll reappeared, carrying the writhing Sabryen between them. He was actually remarkably light; Cræosh supposed that missing one's legs and portions of one's internal organs would do that.

"Belrotha!" Cræosh shouted.

"*What?*"

Cræosh and Katim heaved, and Sabryen landed amid a splatter of worms at the ogre's feet. The creatures recoiled from the body of their king, perhaps sensing the poisons coursing within.

In an abnormal rush of awareness—perhaps her brain remained warmed up from the novel experience of having a plan—Belrotha offered the orc a crooked grin. "Him say something about mother?"

"Twice," Cræosh confirmed with a chuckle.

Belrotha allowed her latest rock to tumble into the horde of worms, killing several hundred with a loud bang. Then she lifted King Sabryen off the ground with one hand; with the other, she reached inside his gaping torso and began ripping out anything and everything she could grasp. The sudden stench nearly brought the goblins to their knees, gagging on centuries worth of rot, and the slow tearing sounds would haunt their dreams for years to come.

There wasn't enough left in him even to scream. Sabryen twitched a final time and fell limp. The maggots that had filled his sockets poured from his skull in a dreadful stream, putrefying before they hit the ground.

The sea of worms simply . . . stopped. Hundreds of thousands died on the spot, while others returned to their natural state, wriggling aimlessly or dashing for the nearest crevice. In less than a minute the swarm had dispersed, leaving behind only the dying and the dead.

"Has anyone else found these past few weeks just entirely too disgusting?" Gimmol asked.

Cræosh nodded. "I'll admit to a certain amount of revulsion."

Katim actually laughed aloud. "You are one of a hand-selected . . . group of soldiers who directly serves . . . a dead king with insects . . . crawling across his body and skittering . . . from his orifices on a regular . . . basis. I believe you may have to . . . redefine your entire *concept* . . . of disgust."

"Troll's got a point," Gork said.

Cræosh chose not to answer to that.

"Jhurpess has idea," the bugbear said.

"Well," Cræosh said, "I hate to admit it, Nature-boy, but your last idea was a pretty damn good one. Let's hear it."

"Jhurpess thinks squad should get the hell out of canyon."

"Ah," Gork said. "An even better one. Jhurpess, you're a genius."

The bugbear grinned happily. Then, a look of sudden concern on his face, he stepped over to stand before the troll.

"Katim not worry too much about being an idiot," he said in his most comforting tone. "Cræosh not very smart either, but Jhurpess still Cræosh's friend."

Cræosh, in the face of the entire squad's laughter, merely squared his shoulders and moved toward the exit.

CHAPTER TEN

THE WAR OF THE RUSES

"They actually did it, my lord," Havarren said to Morthûl's back. His normally bored tone was tinged with just a hint of incredulity. He paced rapidly, his footsteps echoing on the marble floor, as though looking for an angle from which the news would be easier to believe.

"So you've said," the Charnel King replied dully without turning away from the table. "Repeatedly. Don't let the fact that I have only one ear fool you, Havarren. I heard you quite clearly the first dozen times."

"My apologies," the gaunt wizard said, his voice completely unapologetic. "I'm just rather shocked. I thought—"

"You thought?" Morthûl finally turned. Was there just the slightest tightening in his cracking, half-expression? "You thought that I'd begun to lose it. You thought that I'd chosen a gaggle of incompetent half-wits as my champions. You thought that it was nothing shy of a miracle that they'd lived this long, and that sending them after Sabryen was a death sentence. Is that what you thought?"

"I . . . Perhaps something along those lines, yes."

Morthûl advanced, and even Havarren couldn't help but gag at the vague suggestion of slow rot that perfumed the air around him. He tried to meet the Charnel King's gaze but found himself distracted by the constant wanderings of Morthûl's various multilegged inhabitants.

"So many years, Havarren, and you still haven't figured it out." Morthûl spat each word, a rancid morsel accompanied by an explosion of putrid breath and, in a few cases, dust. "How long will it take you to realize that I do not make such mistakes? Another century? Two? A millennium? An endless life does not inherently encompass endless patience, and I grow tired of your constant questioning.

"For all their rough edges, for all their lack of anything approaching subtlety, this Demon Squad may be one of the best we've ever fielded." For just a moment, his clenched jaw softened. "Whatever else I might think of her actions, I owe my queen my thanks. The ogre has worked out admirably. And Anne's foolish quest has done a far better job of tempering them into a cohesive unit than any of our training missions could have."

"And if Queen Anne's efforts, or the fight against Sabryen, had killed them, Your Majesty? You'd have nobody left to accomplish . . ." Havarren let his voice trail away, since even he hadn't been told precisely *what* Morthûl intended for the squad to accomplish.

The Charnel King stepped away from the table without answering, hands clasped behind his back, apparently lost in thought. For the first time, Havarren could see just what the master of the Iron Keep had been working on. Sitting atop the table, lying in the midst of a rather haphazardly strewn pile of sundry components, was Morthûl's own tarnished silver crown.

Havarren frowned. Amid a few dozen items of lesser power lay the heart of an unborn faerie; over there, what had to be a jar of phantom's tears; and he thought he recognized, over the Charnel King's own pungent scent, the bitter aroma of the pagaera blossom. A flower even Queen Anne's late and lamented garden had lacked, pagaera sprouted only in soil fertilized with the urine of a Prince of Hell. The wizard wondered briefly where Morthûl could possibly have obtained such a flower and then decided he was probably better for not knowing.

No spell Havarren knew, none he'd ever heard of in his long millennia of sorcery, required the precise combination of components arrayed before him. He couldn't even begin to fathom what Morthûl was doing, but enough power radiated from that simple silver crown to tell Havarren two things.

One, this was the spell for which the Charnel King had been conserving his power for the past months.

And two, it scared the hell out of him.

"It will be some weeks before it's completed, Havarren."

The mage spun to face his lord, not having realized that his observations were themselves being observed.

"It's an *interesting* ritual, Your Majesty, from what I can see of it."

"It is indeed. Would you care to know what it does?"

To his shame, Havarren actually found himself hesitating. "Yes, I would."

Morthûl grinned. "Perhaps I'll tell you some day."

Havarren fought to keep the scowl (*and the relief*, a mutinous portion of his mind whispered at him) off his face.

Slowly, his own smirk fading, the master of the Iron Keep drifted to the nearest wall. It was constructed of solid stone, overlaid with wrought iron, and located in the center of the keep's uppermost floor. Despite all this, Morthûl reached his fingers into the filigreed designs and pulled open a window that hadn't previously existed. Beyond stretched many miles of the isle of Dendrakis.

"What do you see, Havarren?"

The wizard glanced disdainfully out at the impossible view. "I see a few mountain peaks covered in ice and snow. I see the road. I see a barren expanse of land. Same thing I always see when I look through the keep's more, ah, *traditional* windows."

"There are, though it batters the ego to admit it, some forces that none of us, however powerful we become, may ever hope to control."

"As you say," Havarren agreed, his voice neutral.

"And now you patronize me. But it is true nonetheless. There are such forces, and the most aggravating is time.

"We may make ourselves immortal. We may reach into the past, in an attempt to change what has been. But no man, no wizard, no god controls the process itself. And our time, Havarren, has run out."

A bony gesture encompassed the view beyond the casement. "You cannot see it here. Dendrakis is too far north; the isle will no sooner grow warm than the Steppes would. But were you to cast your gaze to the south, you would see different. You would see the snow starting to melt on the lower peaks of the Brimstone Mountains. Plants and flowers beginning to bloom again in the forests, crops to grow in the fields. The birds are preparing for their long flight back home, and the bear stirs in his cave."

This isn't good. Havarren carefully kept his face locked in a bored expression, but inside he cringed. This wasn't like Morthûl at all; it was too poetic, too overblown.

"Spring comes, Havarren. And with it, Dororam's army."

"True, my lord, but it's scarcely of any consequence. We—"

"Are not ready."

Havarren blinked. "What?"

"We are not ready. Had we another year to prepare, we still would not be ready."

"I don't understand."

Morthûl silently closed the window. It vanished completely, once more nothing but another stretch of wall.

"We lost too many of our soldiers last autumn, to duMark and his wretched allies. Dororam has assembled the largest army this continent has seen in recorded history. I wonder, for all your experience, if you are truly capable of understanding what that means. You think of humans, elves, and dwarves as little more than annoyances."

"It's what they are," Havarren said dismissively.

"To you or me, yes. In certain numbers, yes. But they face our armies, Havarren, not you and me. And they come not by the dozens or the hundreds, but the *hundreds of thousands*! Were our armies at the peak of their strength, as numerous as they'd ever been, we would be hard-pressed to hold our borders. As things stand now, all we can do is delay."

"Surely you're not giving up?" Havarren couldn't believe what he was hearing. Is *that* what he'd sensed in Morthûl's odd speech? *Despair?*

"Giving up?" The Dark Lord sounded truly shocked. "Don't be a jackass, Havarren! I didn't come this far, turn myself into what you see before you, so I could *give up*!"

"Then . . . What *are* you going to do?"

"Why, Havarren, I'm going to cheat.

"Summon my 'inept' Demon Squad. It's time for their *real* task."

It was a testament to King Dororam's powers of self-control that he merely scowled, holding his temper in check until the nervous messenger had bowed and scraped his way out of the war room. Only when the door had shut and latched did the King of Shauntille allow some semblance of his true feelings to show.

"Gods damn it all to bloody hell!" The scroll case he'd held when the messenger came knocking, a priceless antique ivory relic of kings past, shattered into fragments against the wall. DuMark didn't even flinch, of course; a casual wave of his hand, and the shifting dust that rained from above cascaded away from him and drifted slowly to the floor.

"Any closer," the half-elven wizard said coldly, "and I might have thought you were aiming at me."

"Maybe I should have," Dororam growled, stalking across the room and slamming his fists on the stone table. The various maps of Kirol Syrreth leapt and danced. "That's the third one in two weeks, duMark."

The mage shrugged. "Scouting parties get caught, Dororam. It's a risk of the job."

"Not this often. We'd gone weeks without a single unit running into trouble. Now . . ."

"What are you suggesting?"

Dororam sighed quietly. "Your precious informant is either incompetent or playing you for a fool—that's what I'm suggesting."

DuMark bristled. "How many times must we dance to this particular tune before you're satisfied? I've told you over and over, my sources—"

"Are reliable. Yes, you've told me. Over and over, just as you say." Dororam spun away from the table. Before it could even occur to the half-elf what was happening, he'd crossed the room and dragged the wizard from his chair by his collar. "*So why the hell am I losing my men? What are you here for, duMark?*"

The wizard's face went vampire-pale. "You will *never* touch me!" He smacked the king's hands away from his throat, his fingers twitching, perhaps in readiness to cast a spell. "I will not be treated like—"

Dororam's advancing years hadn't stripped from him the skills ingrained by a warrior's life. DuMark's tirade ended in a pained gasp and a rush of breath as the king literally lifted him off his feet and slammed him hard into the stone wall behind his chair.

Dororam knelt beside the wheezing wizard. His own cloak of office draped over them, forming a canopy to isolate them from the outside world.

"It is just about time," Dororam whispered, his voice quivering angrily, "to clarify a few matters, duMark. You are the greatest mage in the Allied Kingdoms. You are our greatest hope against that abomination who rules the Iron Keep.

"But *I* am king! I! And I am tired of you remembering that fact only when it suits you! There will be no more of this wasteful debate, no further argument from you. I am your king, and you will either do as I say—*exactly* as I say, when I say it!—or you will forswear yourself here and now and go your own way!"

"You . . ." The half-elf drew a deep, shuddering breath. "You cannot defeat the Charnel King without my help."

"Perhaps not. But I'll give it my all. I will have no more of this foolishness. Either you are with me, with all that entails, including obedience, or you are not. I'll not stop you from leaving, if that is your decision. I'll even wish you the best of luck in your travels, and I'll mean it. But I *will* have your answer, and I'll have it now."

Smoothly, wobbling only a little—*damn these old knees!*—Dororam stood, allowing duMark sufficient room to do the same.

"You make," the wizard said, one hand gingerly rubbing the back of his skull, "a forceful case."

"Your answer, duMark."

The half-elf sighed. "I am with you of course . . . Your Majesty."

Dororam smiled. "I'm glad. It would, as you say, have been difficult without you."

DuMark tried to match the king's expression, but it came out as more of a sickly grin. "And now that this is settled, what would you have me do?"

The king took the gesture for what it was and pretended he couldn't hear the wizard's teeth grating behind his lips. "Quite simply, duMark, I am not convinced of the reliability of your source."

"I believe I'd actually picked up on that."

"I'm afraid that your assurances are no longer sufficient. I'll not risk any more of my men on untrustworthy information, especially since the main body of the Allied Armies begin their march in a matter of days. I need you to obtain *confirmation*, either that the spy can be trusted, or that he cannot."

DuMark shook his head. "I still feel this is a waste of time, Your Majesty."

Dororam's eyes narrowed dangerously.

"But I will, of course, do as you wish."

"I'm delighted to hear it."

Just as the mage was reaching for the heavy latch with trembling fingers, the king called out from behind him. "DuMark?"

The mage's jaw twitched. "Yes, Your Majesty?"

Dororam waved idly at the pile of dust and debris that had once been an antique ivory scroll case. "Fix that before you go, would you?"

"Oh, yeah," Cræosh grumbled sarcastically, profound exasperation writ large across his face. "Join the army, fight for the glory of Kirol Syrreth and the all-powerful Charnel King. See exciting places, kill exciting people." He looked once more over the empty, unadorned grass that surrounded them on all sides, now painted a burnt umber by the last rays of the setting sun. "I'm just not sure I can take any more of this kind of 'excitement.' It's so thrilling, I could just snore."

"Oh, shut up," Gork groused from his sleeping blanket. "After the last couple of months, I could do with a few days of quiet."

Cræosh shook his head. "I just don't like the idea that there's a war going on out there, and we ain't invited."

"I'd hardly call this uninvited," Gimmol said from the other side of the small encampment. "I'd say we're more like the guests of honor."

Cræosh grumbled some more.

The squad had enjoyed a few days of rest and recuperation after their sojourn in the Demias Gap, and then it was "up and at 'em" once more. General Rhannik had again been the one to instruct them, although that meeting had at least taken place in an honest briefing chamber, rather than a rapidly swept-out supply room.

"Dororam's armies are marching," he'd said without preamble. "Obviously we've mobilized, but it's going to be a hell of a war."

"So where are we assigned?" Cræosh had asked (a bit too gleefully for his companions' tastes).

"You're not. You're going nowhere near the front."

The briefing had then paused while everyone worked at calming the enraged orc. Cræosh, in what Gork and Gimmol both took as a convincing sign of lunacy, had been eagerly looking forward to the spring thaw. Apparently, he'd gotten through the prior months by assuming everything they'd done was a mere prelude to the massive carnage to come. He didn't take at all well to the discovery that said battles would be waged without him.

"Now," Rhannik had continued, staring across the empty room (empty because Cræosh had reduced the table to kindling), "where were we?" Cræosh, held immobile by Belrotha's fists on his shoulders, had snorted. "Before we destroyed the furniture, I mean.

"Ah, right. Your assignment. As I was saying, you'll not be at the front . . ." Cræosh had growled again. ". . . because you'll be well past it."

That, finally, had gotten the orc's attention. "Do what now?"

"Ananias duMark is Dororam's greatest sorcerer, but he's far from the *only* one. Dororam's own entourage includes close to a dozen wizards, elven spellweavers, giloral enchanters . . . not to mention the rather sizable number of advisors and generals who are also part of said entourage."

"Sounds like it'd be heavily guarded," Gork had noted.

"It is. Which is why a full unit would never get near enough to do us any good. But a small group . . ."

Rhannik had grinned as understanding dawned on the faces of the

Demon Squad. "I'm so glad you see it my way. You understand, though, that we cannot afford to allow any hint of your approach to reach Dororam. Therefore, you are ordered, in no uncertain terms, to avoid *any* confrontation with the enemy until you've reached your objective. If that means running from a single human soldier with a rusty sword, so be it."

Scowls all around, at that, but no one had protested.

"If you have no other choice but to engage, it's as much as your lives are worth to let even one enemy escape and report back. Are we clear?"

The squad had nodded as one.

"Good. Understand something else, too. Get in, do the job, and go. Do *not* attempt to strike at Dororam himself. He'll be far too well guarded. More to the point, if you kill him, you make him a martyr. Your first objective is to take out as many of his damn wizards as you can. Secondary target includes his generals and advisors. After that, you get the fuck out."

And they'd been off.

That had been close to a week ago. They'd crossed through the Brimstone Mountains without incident, using passes so winding and tiny that neither side could be bothered to guard them, and were now well beyond Kirol Syrreth's borders. And since then, they'd done . . . nothing.

Time after time, they'd been forced to hide from Dororam's outriders. Any one of them would've been an easy kill, but the squad hadn't quite gotten impatient enough to ignore Rhannik's more-than-explicit orders. Not when there was a real risk of discovery by an entire army. Not even Belrotha was that stupid, nor Katim that psychotic.

Since said army consisted of hundreds of thousands of humans, elves, and dwarves, plus the occasional halfling and giloral, plus horses, supply wagons, and disassembled siege engines, the entire thing stretched on for days. It was larger, in fact, than some of the smaller nations that had contributed to it.

And somewhere, in the midst of all that, rode Dororam's own entourage.

"It shouldn't actually be all that difficult," Gimmol said the next morning. They were crouched atop a small hill, staring across an endless sea of flesh and steel. The people below scurried about madly, a hive of ants whose hill had been not only smacked with a stick but doused in oil and set afire.

"And how precisely do you figure that?" Cræosh asked irritably.

"Well, this is King Dororam we're talking about. All we really have to do is find the largest single concentration of guards and servants amid the soldiers, and he should be right there."

Katim snorted once, and Cræosh rolled his eyes. "Just fucking great, Gimmol. As a tactician, you make a wonderful scratching post. Did it ever occur to you that you can't see the whole thing? This fucking army stretches on for miles! If we can find a high enough vantage to see more than a sixth of it, I'll be stunned!"

"That doesn't take much," Gimmol muttered.

Katim finally cleared her throat. "If I may put forth . . . a theory?"

"Put forth anything you want," Cræosh glowered. "We don't seem to be going much of anywhere."

The troll's gaze met his. "Where did we get our orders . . . from?" she asked.

"What are you, stupid? General Rhannik."

"Very good, little . . . orc. So where do you suppose . . . those soldiers down there are getting . . . *their* orders from?"

Cræosh blinked, and then very softly began to curse.

"Me not understand," Belrotha admitted in a whisper that could've puffed down a small house. "Katim saying that human soldiers *also* getting orders from General Rhannik?"

"No, Belrotha," Gimmol explained. He couldn't even take pleasure in the orc's consternation, since he was feeling equally stupid. "She's saying that the soldiers get their orders from their generals, same way we do."

The ogre looked no less puzzled.

"What our little red mage is trying to spit out," Cræosh said, "is that all we have to do is backtrack any one of the runners who delivers the orders, and they'll eventually take us right back up the chain of command."

"To where king is!" she exclaimed, finally getting it.

"Very good," the orc said.

"But me not see any chain."

Cræosh very nearly sobbed.

Said reasoning, of course, still left the goblins with a fairly significant problem: namely, it seemed improbable, at best, that any of them could infiltrate Dororam's forces without being spotted more or less immediately.

"I never thought I'd hear myself say it," Cræosh admitted around noon, "but we could really have used Fezeill here." They sat atop that same hill, proposing and rejecting idea after idea as the army passed slowly below them.

"Eh," Gork said, waving one hand dismissively. "We don't need him. I can sneak through the crowd well enough to follow the messengers."

"I'm uncertain," Katim said—not the first time she'd objected to this particular suggestion. "Even at night, there . . . are a great number of guards you . . . would have to avoid."

"I can do it. Getting the lot of you past the outer guards is going to be more of a challenge, but as far as locating—"

"Perhaps this is the sort of situation in which *my* assistance might prove valuable."

Six heads rotated in tandem. Ebonwind stood behind them, one foot on a small stump, resting an elbow on his bent knee. His gray cloak floated serenely about his legs, despite the absence of any breeze, and his familiar sat upon that foot, preening one of its floppy wings.

"I thought we'd made our position clear, dakórren," Cræosh growled. "We don't need your kind of help. Not at your price, anyway."

"Me either," the kobold said, abruptly stepping forward. "Not anymore."

The mage's eyes bulged so wide, Cræosh briefly wondered if he wasn't turning into a toad for some unfathomable purpose. "Gork, what are you—"

"They know, Ebonwind. Katim and I told them everything."

Ebonwind's mouth twisted. "You!" he spat, pointing a quivering finger at the troll. "I knew you were trouble. I should have killed you up north!"

"Perhaps," Katim admitted with a slight shrug. "But you . . . did not."

"I can rectify that now," the dakórren threatened.

"Before you do," Gork said, "you may want to read this." He produced a thin ebony tube, capped with a plug of carved bone. General Rhannik had handed it to him as their briefing dispersed, with the cryptic mutter "Havarren says to give this to your old friend if he shows up again."

Reluctantly, Ebonwind took the case and began to unscrew the cap.

"Your little friend's being awfully quiet," Gimmol pointed out. "Little fellow catch a cold?"

"Ibrif! Nur erpin!" the thing squeaked.

"He's sulking," Ebonwind answered absently, working at the strangely stubborn case. "He's been running off by himself recently, so I yelled at him. He always sulks when I—" With a sudden pop, the cap came off in his hand.

No parchment or scroll slid out, but instead a blue-tinged, clinging mist. It poured to the ground, forming an almost liquid puddle of haze at Ebonwind's feet. Tendrils wafted that way and this, a newborn thing seeking to understand the world around it. And then, without warning, without any transition from one to the next, the mist was gone and King Morthûl loomed over them.

Most of the squad were scrabbling back like startled crabs, and even Ebonwind recoiled before the truth set in. Not the Charnel King himself, this, but an image formed of the shifting mists. Closer (and calmer) scrutiny revealed faint wavering in the frightening figure, subtle shifting of its component vapors.

"Greetings, Nurien Ebonwind." The voice, at least, was as solid and as present as the real thing. "For some time, I have been aware of a spy in our midst. And now, thanks to my Demon Squad, I know that you are he. So be it. You wish information? Then listen well.

"Many leagues south of Shauntille, in the midst of the elven kingdoms, sits a small town called Tirfeylan. As with many fae villages, it is currently inhabited only by women, children, the old and infirm; only those who could not or would not answer the call to ride alongside Dororam.

"The moment you opened this scroll case, you triggered an invocation. A particularly vile one, if I say so myself. I'm pushing things somewhat, spending power that could be useful in my other endeavors, but I think you'll agree it's worth my time. In the woods surrounding Tirfeylan, madness creeps through the minds of the wildlife. Rabbits, squirrels, sparrows, deer, owls . . . All irrevocably altered. They have become vicious, irritable, and quite, quite carnivorous.

"You may find the notion of a meat-eating squirrel, or a vicious sparrow, an amusing one, Ebonwind. But what of a hundred of them? A thousand? Even as you listen to this, a veritable tide of such creatures—all the innocent, peaceful dwellers of the woods—crashes down over the town. When next the gaze of the living falls upon Tirfeylan, it will be a bloody ruin, occupied only by the ravaged skeletons of its women and children."

A shiver swept through Cræosh's flesh at the words of the monster he so willingly served. He'd committed horrors of his own, borne witness to many more, but this chilled him to his soul. Women and children . . . This was not the way to wage a war.

"If you are who I believe you to be," the image concluded, "then this is ample punishment for your interference. If you are not, if the evidence has led me to an erroneous conclusion . . ." The Dark Lord actually shrugged. "Well, one can never kill too many elves, can one?" And just like that, the image was gone.

Ebonwind had indeed gone whiter than the snows of the tundra in which they'd met. "Why?" he whispered, gawping at Gork. "Why would you do this?"

"Call me crazy, Ebonwind, but I don't enjoy being betrayed."

"Betrayed? You imbecile! I would have kept my part of the bargain! You would have known reward your feeble little mind cannot comprehend!"

"Yeah, *after* you reported everything I said to Dororam."

"What are you *talking* about?" the dakórren demanded, and for the first time, Gork looked suddenly uncertain.

"If you really are dakórren," Cræosh snarled, "why the fuck is any of this bothering you?"

"Because some of *my* people are in the eilurren woods! That's why we were monitoring Dororam's troop movements, remember? So that we could strike at the elves unopposed! I have no idea how widespread Morthûl's spell may be. *Hundreds* of my people could be caught in it!"

Cræosh shrugged. "War's a bitch."

Ebonwind's hands rose, fingers wide—and instantly the squad spread wider, moving to encircle the raging wizard. "Try it, Ebonwind," Cræosh suggested, his sword held low. "You'll probably even get one or two of us before the rest have you spitted and carved up like a fucking roast. That'll really help your poor lost little soldiers, won't it?"

The air crackled with building ozone; the grass around the dakórren's feet curled and browned. And then, with an enraged howl nearly loud enough to be heard even in the chaos of the marching armies beyond the hill, he was gone.

For several long minutes, the squad stared at one another across an empty circle. It was Gork who finally broke the silence.

"You know," he said slowly, "he kind of sounded sincere."

"He did, didn't he?" Cræosh said.

"Could we have made a mistake?" Gork was practically vibrating as he grew ever more agitated. He must have been thinking of the reward he'd thrown away, and Cræosh's lip curled in amusement as the kobold actually clutched a hand to his heart.

"I don't think . . . so," Katim said after a moment. "We know that . . . the enemy was acting on . . . information given to Ebonwind. If . . . he was not the spy, then . . . someone he had contact with . . . *was*."

The squad returned to puzzling out some way to pass unseen through thousands of enemy soldiers, and—save for Gork's occasional nervous twitch—put all thought of spies and dakórren behind them.

The room was pretty blatantly intended for purposes other than comfort. The threadbare layer of carpeting over the floor was worn as full of holes as an old sock, and whatever hue it might once have boasted had long been trampled into an unassuming, colorless gray. A single chair, its cushion torn and hemorrhaging stuffing, its wooden frame bending beneath the weight of years, sulked in the corner. The bed frame, in equal disrepair and clearly not on speaking terms with the chair, would have long since collapsed if it hadn't been propped against the wall. Only the wardrobe and its contents—cloaks, leggings, and tunics on one side, breads and salted meats on the other—showed any sign of care.

All told, far less homey than the small cottage for which it served as inadequate replacement. But it was, if nothing else, far more secure, as neither window nor even door provided ingress.

A shimmer in the air, a dull pop, a breeze to stir the dust from the carpet, and he was there. Ranting, through twisted lips, the most profane epithets that a dozen languages had to offer, Nurien Ebonwind actually beat his fists upon the walls. Only once he'd run through each separate profanity two or three times, as well as several more that he made up on the spot, did he finally calm down sufficiently to think. The oddity that was his familiar fluttered from him to perch haphazardly upon the chair, which groaned once at this added indignity.

"Damn the Charnel King, and damn that wretched kobold. . . ." It was a final, petty snipe, followed by a loud creaking as the dakórren sank onto the shabby mattress. "All right," he continued, "how do we warn them?" It was an old habit, speaking to his familiar, since the little creature was his only constant companion.

"I can't just teleport to them. The eilurren have warded their woods against our magics since our last war." Narrow fingers drummed idly on the mattress, or would have if the mattress had been capable of producing anything approaching a drumming sound. More accurately, they "fumped" idly on the mattress. "I'd have to enter on foot, and by the time I could find them . . . Agh! Bastards!" He rose and began to pace once more, though this time the walls were spared the fury of his fists.

"Oh, they'll suffer for this betrayal, the kobold and eventually the Charnel King himself! Once the eilurren have fallen, they'll—"

"I think not, dakórren."

Ebonwind barely had time even to register the voice, let alone recover sufficiently from his shock to react to it, before the sound bowled him over. Thunder—thunder so weighty as to tangibly fill the room— burst over him. The walls shuddered, the wardrobe toppled to spill its contents across the floor, even the mattress exhaled its down with a feeble puff of breath. The dakórren found himself sprawled against the far wall. His head rang, his ears throbbed with pain; he struggled to stand and found his equilibrium so skewed that he couldn't even begin to rise.

And only then did the *real* pain wash over him. Agony climbed his body like a mountain, digging into him with blazing pitons. It chewed at his nerves, bit at his mind, shredded his concentration like wet paper. He thrashed, bit his lip in an effort to regain control—and gawped, in sudden, abject horror, at the charred, steaming ribbons of meat that had, not long ago, been his legs.

Of course. It was almost funny, somehow. *With so much thunder, there* had *to be lightning.*

Random flopping of muscles finally twisted him about, enough to stare at the chair in the corner and the creature who had launched the eldritch assault.

His familiar was no longer seated upon rickety wood, but upon the shoulder of a man who now occupied the chair. In his other hand, the cloak-wrapped stranger clasped a heavy staff. He peered at Ebonwind through features not all *that* dissimilar to Ebonwind's own.

"Well," the stranger said, idly scratching the cooing creature under the chin, "I'm glad I'll not be doing *that* again."

"Who . . . ?" Ebonwind's difficulty in finding his voice was not due solely to the physical pain. "What about my . . . ?"

"Oh, I'm sorry. Your familiar's actually been mine for quite some time. You cannot *begin* to imagine how subtly I had to balance the magics, not just to usurp the link but to keep you from sensing it. I lost my connection to a familiar once, myself. Put me out for two weeks. It's been exhausting, to tell you the truth."

"You—you're . . ."

"Ananias duMark, at your service." The half-elf bowed from the waist, so far as the chair would permit. The creature danced on his shoulder, trying to retain its perch. "Well, for a few more minutes. After that, even my services wouldn't do you much good."

"Why?"

The brown-haired wizard leaned back in his chair. "Because you were perfect. I could keep an eye on the dakórren—it was pretty obvious you'd use the war as cover to strike against us—and gather intelligence on Morthûl's armies, all at once. I'd really hoped to learn his plans for his Demon Squad, too," he admitted, "but you saw how well that went. Honestly, I think even they didn't know. Otherwise, the kobold would have said something about it."

"You . . ." Ebonwind took several deep breaths, struggling past the pain—both physical and, as his familiar fluttered its wings, emotional—and gathered the tattered remains of his faculties. "I'm surprised," he said weakly, "that you haven't set out to save Tirfeylan."

He had, at the least, the pleasure of seeing the smug satisfaction fall from duMark's face. "Because I know the bony bastard too well," the mage admitted sadly. "If he was willing to tell me about Tirfeylan, it's only because he knew I could do nothing about it. He probably triggered the spell long before you opened the tube, regardless of what his message claimed. He thought you were me, Ebonwind. He knew I had family there, and this was his punishment." The half-elf sighed. "Perhaps I can do nothing to save Tirfeylan, but I'll not subject myself to the pain of seeing the results."

"And what of me?" Ebonwind asked quietly.

"You? You, my friend, are dead. I don't know if any of your people are within the range of Morthûl's spell or not, but you'll ensure that at least one dakórren joins Tirfeylan in death. That, and I can't have you interfering in this war, or launching more attacks on the eilurren, can I?"

"Someone else will take my place," Ebonwind spat.

"Perhaps. And I'll do this to them, too." DuMark raised a hand and pumped a second levinbolt across the chamber. Ebonwind's head turned instantly to ash, though it was some moments before his legs ceased twitching.

It was all so *aggravating*! He'd put so much effort into this, ever since he'd learned through his eldritch spies and divinations that Morthûl was assembling a wartime Demon Squad. Uncovering the dakórren's efforts; appropriating the obnoxious, tiny creature; using the wizard's lingering link with "his" familiar to subtly influence Ebonwind's actions—from intercepting the initial teleport to focusing on the Demon Squad when other sources of information might've been easier or more forthcoming— it was absolutely grueling. It had distracted duMark from his other efforts. And all for what? The intelligence he'd gained had been useful, but none of it *vital*, none of it regarding the squad's own purpose, none of it anything he couldn't have acquired more easily through other methods.

"You're fortunate," duMark said bitterly, standing from the chair and nudging the corpse distastefully with his left foot. "You deserved a death as horrible as what was done to Tirfeylan. Give thanks from hell that I was feeling merciful. Or . . ."

Again, a tiny breeze flitted across the sealed chamber, making the ashes of the dakórren dance. DuMark began to fade away.

". . . at the very least, feeling rushed," he amended. And then he was gone.

The tiny creature tumbled, spreading its wings and gliding to a halt only inches above the floor. It felt duMark vanish, not just physically but mentally, felt the link binding them dissolve. It glanced about the chamber, spotting no avenue of escape.

And then its gaze fell on its former master.

"Ookt irpva!" It settled beside the smoldering corpse and began to chew.

Cræosh was absolutely livid. Bad enough that the rail-thin bastard had woken them in the middle of the fucking night, but now he had the gall to hand them this load of merry dancing horseshit!

"But we've actually got a fucking plan!" he protested. Again. "We were gonna start out tomorrow! We can do this!"

Havarren, sitting casually on Cræosh's sleeping pallet with his ankles propped up on Gork's backpack, shrugged. "And I commend you for your creativity, but your assignment has changed. You are not to attack Dororam's forces."

Cræosh growled as he introduced his fist to a nearby tree.

"It makes sense, Cræosh," Gimmol said carefully, keeping a weather eye on the orc's movements. (He wanted a good head start if he had to run.) "If Ebonwind was the spy—or had a spy in his own people—there's a good chance that they know we're here. I mean, he found us easily enough, right? Who's to say how long he was listening before he revealed himself?"

"I didn't say it didn't make fucking sense!" Cræosh snapped at him. "I just said I don't like it!"

Katim, who had been staring moodily off into the distance ever since being told that she would not, after all, have the opportunity to add a large handful of mages to her stable, aimed her snout at Havarren. "This was all quite . . . deliberate, wasn't it?"

"Why Katim, whatever do you mean?" He wasn't even bothering to hide his smirk.

That, at least, got Cræosh's attention. "Yeah, troll," he said, "what *do* you mean?"

"They never intended us to . . . complete this mission, that's . . . what I mean. This entire . . . damn exercise was a . . . lure."

Gork's own irises, gleaming evilly beneath the faint light of the moon, also locked on the mage. "You wanted to be sure that Ebonwind was the one," he said slowly. "So you gave us something to do that would draw his attention."

Havarren's smile widened. Cræosh put his fist back through the tree, ignoring the sizable smears of blood he was leaving across the bark.

"It had to sound feasible," Havarren explained blandly. "An assignment that was too obviously fake wouldn't have fooled anyone. There is some good news, though."

"Fuck you," Cræosh said.

"You haven't wasted your time out here. You've gotten a solid idea of Dororam's troop movements, so it'll be that much easier to avoid them. And since you're several days out of Kirol Syrreth, you're already that much closer to your *real* objective."

"And assuming you aren't lying through your fucking teeth again," Cræosh grumbled, "where would this 'real objective' happen to be?"

"Why, you're going to Shauntille."

To that, even Cræosh had no comment.

"The truth is," Havarren told them, after allowing them a few moments to settle down, "this is not a war we can win." He quickly held up a hand to forestall any protests. "Not through standard tactics, that is. Dororam's army is simply too big for us to confront head-on."

"So?" Gork asked, his tone suspicious. "You and King Morthûl together should be powerful enough to just, I don't know . . ." He waved his fingers about randomly. Then, glancing over at Belrotha, he shrugged. "Wigglety-poof. No more army."

"It's not that simple, kobold. It's possible to destroy an army this size with magic, but it would take a sizable portion of Kirol Syrreth along with it. You're right, though, that we *could* make a substantial difference—if not for one particular irritant."

"DuMark," Katim rasped.

Havarren bobbed his head once. "DuMark. Dororam has other wizards, certainly, but either myself or our Dark Lord could deal handily with them, leaving the other free to concentrate on more mundane foes. But duMark . . ." The mage scowled, and it was quite clear that he didn't care for the taste of the words to come. "DuMark is quite possibly my equal, and not too substantially weaker than even Morthûl. This impudent half-elven mongrel requires that one of us grant him our full attention; combined with Dororam's other pets, it means that neither of us can focus on the armies themselves."

"So why us not kill wizards as planned?" Belrotha asked, having managed (with Gimmol's occasional whispered explanations) to follow the discussion. "Then you not need to worry about them."

"Because only a few of the Allied Kingdoms' wizards are actually in Dororam's entourage. You could make a difference, but not enough of one. Not here. Thus, we need you to go to Shauntille."

"More cities!" Jhurpess whined unhappily. As had become the norm, he was quite soundly ignored.

"And what," Cræosh asked carefully, "would you have us do in Shauntille?" His muscles stood out from his arms and shoulders, etched against his skin, and the others slowly backed away at the realization that he was actually prepared to *attack Havarren* if he didn't care for the answer. "You don't fucking expect us to take on duMark, do you?"

"What would you do if I did, orc?" the gaunt human asked languidly. "Kill me? It might be an interesting attempt.

"But there is," he continued, "no need for such suicidal gestures. I've no intention of sending you to your deaths. Not in so futile an effort, anyway. You're good, but you've as much chance of defeating duMark as you have of lifting the Iron Keep from its foundations and sailing it across the Sea of Tears. Besides, duMark isn't *in* Shauntille."

"But there are . . . others," Katim said.

"Precisely."

"Others?" Gimmol asked. "Others you want dead, you mean."

"Scarcely surprising, is it? You weren't assembled for your social skills."

"Queen Lameya?" Gork guessed. "That'd do some nasty things to Dororam's state of mind."

But Havarren shook his head. "Dororam is quite upset enough at the moment. And we're not sending you into Castle Bellatine. Ever since the demise of Princess Amalia, it's far too well guarded, even for a group as creative as you've proven to be.

"But duMark has friends, or at least allies—national heroes all. It was they who assisted him in his prior efforts against King Morthûl; they who made this war necessary in the first place. They are the key to demoralizing not merely the populace, but duMark himself, and they, not the royal family, are your targets." He handed over a small scroll case sealed with wax. Cræosh, after a moment's hesitation and a quick flashback to the message for Ebonwind, accepted it. "It's taken us months to find them. DuMark warded them against all manner of scrying and mystical detection. But our mundane spies have finally located them.

"Which reminds me . . ." Havarren waved a hand, and a cloud of glistening dust wafted through the air. It sprinkled down across the startled goblins, making them glitter like fool's gold for an instant. Noses wrinkled against a vaguely peppery stench, and then it faded.

"What . . . ?" Cræosh began.

"A similar ward, for you," the wizard explained. "In case Ebonwind—or some other sorcerer, for that matter—gets it in his mind to try to find you again, or spy on you from afar."

Cræosh couldn't help but notice Gork's head come up a bit, as though he was surprised at what he'd heard—or had finally figured out something that'd been bothering him.

"Given the sorts of folk duMark is apt to hang out with," Gork interjected sardonically (deliberately changing the subject, perhaps?), "I'm starting to see why you didn't just send your typical cutthroats to deal with this."

"It might have proven insufficient," Havarren agreed. "There are four names discussed therein," he said, pointing at the scroll. "And you'll need to destroy that once you've read it, by the way. The first three, you are to kill, by whatever means necessary. The bodies are to be left public, displayed in the most grotesque, atrocious ways you can devise. We want to engender the greatest possible reaction."

"And the fourth?" Gork asked.

"The most important. Lidia Lirimas. A rather feisty woman, and a closer companion to duMark than are the others."

"A female?" Cræosh asked, ignoring twin glares from Belrotha and Katim.

"Easily the most dangerous of the four, orc, your prejudices notwithstanding. Even more so because we want this one alive."

Everything went silent, down to the shifting and grinding of the troll's teeth in her jaw.

"Alive?" It was actually Gimmol who found his tongue first. "You want us to carry duMark's favorite and most dangerous friend to you? From Shauntille? *Alive?* Havarren, it's over a month from Shauntille to Dendrakis, even *without* trying to control a captive or avoid an army on the way. And no, before you ask, I *can't* maintain my acceleration spell that long."

"Not alone, you can't." Havarren snapped his fingers, then opened his palm to reveal a plain copper ring. "This contains a portion of my own magics. Channel your spell through this, as you did your charm of opening through the skull talisman—a clever use of magic, gremlin, I must admit—and you should be able to make the journey in about a week."

"Great!" Cræosh said. "Hell, we can get there in a day or two with that, do what we have to do, and—"

"No. A spell of this power is child's play to detect. Activate it now, and duMark will be waiting for you in Shauntille with open arms. You use it on your way out, not before."

Cræosh glowered at him.

"Is all this particularly wise?" Gimmol asked, his tone uncertain. "Do you really want duMark any angrier than he already is?"

"Even wizards make mistakes, when they're angry enough. But more importantly, it keeps him occupied. He'll have to return home, figure out what happened. Even with his magics, a proper investigation should take him several days. By then, you should have delivered your captive to us. She becomes a bargaining chip, or at the very least, another obstacle to slow duMark down. Even if he's willing to sacrifice her, he can't allow himself to appear so cold-blooded." Havarren smiled. "Wouldn't do to sully the reputation, would it?

"And it takes four powerful enemies off the field. At the moment, they're not riding with the armies, but they'd involve themselves in the war sooner or later. Preventing that, and depriving duMark of their assistance, is worth the effort by itself."

"Just to make damn sure I've got this in a row," Cræosh said, "let's review. We're going to infiltrate Shauntille. We're going to take on, and kill, and publicly display the bodies of three of the greatest champions they have to offer. Then we're going to capture a fourth, and bring her back here alive. Does that just about sum it up?"

"Fairly succinctly, yes."

Cræosh laughed. It was an ugly, guttural sound, the voice of ridicule rather than humor.

"You find something amusing, orc?"

"Yeah. I can't believe Fezeill's still fucking haunting us."

Katim nodded. "He's right. I appreciate you trusting . . . us with such a mission, but wouldn't . . . human or doppelganger agents prove . . . more appropriate?"

"It would. In fact, we've already tried. An assassination team already made one attempt. One of the targets—Kuren Bekay, we believe—slaughtered the lot of them. And we simply haven't a second appropriate team available. Not many of our doppelganger or human operatives are good enough to take on these targets, and those who might are engaged in other, equally important operations. To put it bluntly, you're the only ones available who might be remotely good enough to pull this off.

"More to the point, these are King Morthûl's orders. You're welcome to march to Dendrakis to ask for explanations, if you want. I wonder what he'll turn you into?"

"Say!" Gork's face brightened. "Wouldn't that work? Couldn't you make us look human?"

"Disgusting," Katim muttered.

Gimmol, however, was shaking his head. "Illusions aren't that hard to detect, if you're looking for them. And if the wizards in Shauntille are on a war footing . . ."

"Your little friend is correct," Havarren confirmed. "I could *actually* transform you into humans." He smiled at the faint shudders running through his audience. "But it would defeat the purpose. Trying to fight, or sneak, or whatever it is you do with new muscles, newly shaped limbs . . . We'd lose the very skills we chose you for. Maybe if you had a few months to train . . ." He shrugged. "Well, you've got a long journey ahead of you. Plenty of time to come up with something. If it was easy, we wouldn't need a Demon Squad to handle it."

All eyes in the squad swiveled toward Belrotha. The mage sighed.

"Yes, that is something of an issue, isn't it? Belrotha, you won't like this, but I'm afraid that, in your case, there's truly no choice. I assure you that it's quite temporary."

The ogre blanched. "What . . . ?" she began.

Havarren chanted something, then reached out and tapped the recoiling ogre on the hip. For an instant, nothing happened.

An instant later, and Katim was the tallest member of the squad.

For her own part, Belrotha was staring wildly at the scenery around her, a thin sheen of sweat on her face. Finally she turned, desperately, to Gimmol. "How wizard make world grow?" she asked anxiously.

Cræosh, who was standing on tiptoe just for the novel experience of looking *down* at the ogre's head, decided he probably wasn't helping matters and stopped.

". . . a delicate balance to keep her shrunken without weakening her," Havarren was saying. "When you cast your hasting spell through the ring, the energies should be enough to overwhelm the spell and return her to her normal size. If not, however, it ought to reverse itself in about a month.

"And now, I have my own preparations to make, and you have a long walk ahead of you. I suggest you get some sleep."

"Do you think?" Cræosh asked him. "I figured we'd sit up until dawn playing tiddlywinks. I don't suppose you might bring us a set? I left mine in my other pants."

Strangely enough, Havarren ignored him. A casual wave, and he was gone.

"I've got to learn to do that," the gremlin muttered.

One by one, the others wandered back to their blankets and dropped off, leaving Gimmol to stand watch—and to try to calm the profusely sweating ogre.

Day upon day, mile upon mile upon mile, creeping along the coast of a flesh-and-steel sea set to crash upon the borders of Kirol Syrreth. They stayed well away from the main roads, did most of their traveling in the dark; nevertheless, the threat of discovery nipped constantly at their heels. Four or five times they'd been forced to shelter in a copse or a gully to avoid the army's scouts, and once they'd had no choice but to kill a lone outrider who stumbled upon them—actually *over* them, having literally tripped on Gork—in the dark. They buried the body, smoothed over the shallow grave as best they could, and pushed on throughout the night so as to be gone before he could be missed.

During the hours of daylight they slumbered, nervous and fitful, none able to sleep for more than a few hours straight. Tempers grew frayed with every passing minute, as misery gained ever more ground and patience was forced into retreat.

Belrotha was clearly having the hardest time of it. She never strayed from Gimmol's side, constantly glancing at her friend—now walking beside her, since she was too small for him to perch comfortably on her shoulder for any length of time. So accustomed was she to looking down at her companions that she spent most of her time speaking to their shoes, rather than their faces; she'd proved unable or unwilling to make the transition to what Gork had rather irritably referred to as a "shorter way of thinking." Gimmol spent every waking moment comforting and reassuring her, but it was anyone's guess how much good he was actually doing.

It was just after sunset of their sixth evening on the road when the traffic began to change. The last straggling soldiers and supply wagons of the armies had passed them by, and the byways were beginning to fill instead with farmers and merchants—sparse at first, but in rapidly growing numbers. The goblins breathed a sigh of relief, to be finally beyond the reach of that enormous army, for the changed demographics could only mean that Shauntille itself drew near.

And that revelation, in turn, drove home rather sharply the point that, given their snappish and unpleasant journey, they'd not taken the time to confront the most pressing issue facing them. Namely, how the hell were they to set so much as one foot inside the city without being swarmed over and torn limb from limb?

They clumped ever more tightly together as they marched, conversing quietly, proposing and then shooting down plan after notion after idea.

"Even if I was strong enough to disguise the whole lot of us for any length of time," Gimmol was patiently explaining, "it's not an option. They'll probably detect that sort of thing, remember? Havarren already went through this."

"But people don't usually notice the little things unless they're given cause for suspicion," Gork argued. "Trust me, I know. They'll only detect the disguises if we give them a reason to look for them."

The gremlin shook his head in frustration. "This is sorcery, Gork. It doesn't work like that."

"Eh," Gork said dismissively.

Gimmol sucked in his breath and held it for the count of ten. "Gork, my magics aren't all that powerful. Any wizard of halfway decent standing can actually *see* the magics I generate, including my illusions, with only the simplest of detection spells. And with the city on a wartime footing, I can *promise* you some of them have those spells constantly active. If I try to cloak us with an illusion, they'll find us as easily as you'd find a single burning torch in a dark cavern."

"Eh."

"Listen, you stupid—"

"I believe," Katim growled from behind (and above), "that we're . . . getting somewhat off topic. Since . . . magic is not an option, let's . . . think of another, rather than . . . arguing *why*."

"Sounds good to me," Gimmol said, glaring sidelong at Gork.

"Eh."

"Where the fuck is Nature-boy?" Cræosh interrupted suddenly.

The squad almost stumbled over themselves, so swiftly did they jerk to a halt. They had a decent amount of light yet; the sun had only just dipped below the horizon, dyeing the earth with a red-tinged aura, and the gleaming moon, just shy of full, had already begun its ascent. On both sides of the road, the land was barren of crops but overgrown with weeds and stubborn grasses, acre upon acre still fallow from the slowly diminishing winter. A few wildflowers sprouted here and there, reaching tentatively from those less pleasant weeds as though seeking escape. Obviously, with the armies on the move, insufficient laborers remained behind to work every field.

Cræosh stepped on one particularly lovely bunch of those wildflowers as the squad spread through the high grasses. If something had happened to Jhurpess, if he was laid out in that overgrowth, they might never find him. He was just about to call the goblins back together, suggest something a little more drastic than a simple sweep, when the missing bugbear's shaggy visage popped up from the weeds a few yards ahead. Cræosh very nearly took the simian head off its neck before he realized who it was—and even afterward, a part of him was seriously considering it.

"What the hopping three-legged fuck are you *doing*?!" Cræosh shouted, only *just* keeping his voice pitched low enough not to carry on the still air. "You don't sneak the hell off by yourself, and you *sure* as hell don't sneak up on me like that! Ancestors, are you *trying* to get yourself beheaded? 'Cause if you are, all you had to do was ask!"

As the others gathered, Jhurpess slowly rose from his crouch, casually picking the worst of the leaves, burs, and twigs from his matted fur. "Cræosh finished ranting now?" he asked.

The orc scowled. "Let's just say I'm taking a breather long enough for you to explain."

The bugbear shrugged. "Jhurpess was just walking along with squad, not doing much of anything."

"Like usual," Gork muttered.

"Then, Jhurpess noticed a strange smell. Smell like burning wood."

"Probably a campfire," Gimmol suggested.

"Jhurpess thought so too. But smell was coming from other direction, not from the road. Jhurpess knew that if whole squad went to look, whoever was there might see. So Jhurpess went alone to find out."

Katim grinned at the look of consternation slouching its way across Cræosh's face. "Go ahead and say it . . . Cræosh. You know it's true, and . . . it's just going to eat you until . . . you spit it out."

For a long, frozen moment, the orc scowled as fiercely as his face would permit, hating everyone and struggling to figure out whom he hated most. Then, with what sounded very much like a sigh, he turned back to the bugbear. "That was actually pretty decent thinking, Jhurpess. Good job."

The bugbear beamed.

"Still should've fucking told someone you were going, though," Cræosh reminded him.

"In any case," Gimmol quickly interjected, "you obviously found something, didn't you?"

A nod. "Yes, Jhurpess find big human house."

"Well twiddle-dee-shit," Cræosh said sourly.

"A house?" Gork asked incredulously. "All this for a *house*?"

"Have you ever considered meditation?" Gimmol asked. "This temper can't be doing your heart any good. . . ."

Ignoring him, the kobold reached up and snagged two fistfuls of bugbear fur. "All you found was a house!" he repeated, seeming unable to wrap his mind around the concept.

The bugbear cocked his head. "Why Gork upset? It not Jhurpess's fault that smoke was coming from house."

"Well, no, but . . . but . . ." Gork trailed off, his expression helpless.

"Besides, Jhurpess did not just find a house. Jhurpess found a *big* house."

Cræosh and Gork both opened their mouths to comment—or, in the kobold's case, perhaps to scream—when Katim spoke. "Jhurpess knows the difference . . . between a large house and any . . . other type of building."

The bugbear nodded. "Jhurpess been in lots of cities lately. This was not castle, or barn, or anything. This was built like house, just big."

The troll nodded. "Sloped roof?" The bugbear nodded. "Chimney?" Nod. "But bigger." Vigorous nod.

"What the fuck are you doing?" Cræosh demanded.

"It's not a house, you . . . dolt. And nobody's going . . . to build a mansion way . . . out here. He's describing a . . . church."

Cræosh pondered a moment. "Could be. Humans have some strange ideas of what churches are supposed to look like. I haven't seen one yet with a halfway decent spike pit. So what?"

"So if there was smoke . . . coming from the chimney, it . . . suggests that the church is . . . occupied."

"At the risk of repeating myself, so the fuck what?"

The troll grinned widely, a thin tendril of spittle wobbling in the breeze. "I'm willing to wager that . . . we might just find ourselves a . . . few nice, voluminous hooded . . . monks' robes."

Slowly, Cræosh too began to grin.

"Who calls?" As fast as his arthritic knees would permit, Brother Elton shuffled down the hall toward the front door. Whoever stood without hadn't bothered with the tarnished brass knocker, and the old monk had barely even heard the faint tapping at the wood. Uncharitably, he wished he hadn't—tomorrow they were patching the holes in the thatch, and his back ached from his efforts today at restoring the herb garden for the new season, and he really pined for his bed—but he dismissed such thoughts. If someone had come to the abbey so late, they must surely be in need. He called out again as he neared the door. "Why are you not at home abed?"

For a long moment, silence. And then, a peculiarly hoarse voice called from beyond. "Father? (cough) Can you help me, Father? (cough, cough) I'm lost, and (cough) sick."

A child? "Abide just a moment!" he called out, fumbling at the locks. *What was a child doing out here alone? He can't live nearby, or he'd know my proper title. This damn war; everything's in such chaos out there. . . .*

Brother Elton hauled the door open and got one brief glimpse of the "child"—a short, scaly, lizardy thing—before everything *inside* was in chaos as well.

The moon and stars, glowing merrily now that they no longer had the setting sun competing with them, were put abruptly to shame by a new rival from the earth far below. Glass shattered with a musical tinkling as wood, thatch, and tar ignited in a fearsome conflagration. In moments, the old mortar began to crack and flake from between the bricks; the stones to lean outward, ready to topple. The smoke loomed high and orange, illuminated from beneath, otherwise invisible against the night sky. By morning, this house of faith and comfort would be just another heap of loose rock and charred earth.

Some distance away, proceeding along the main road, a small train of monks trudged toward Brenald, capital of Shauntille. This late, the road was empty of other traffic—and just as well it was, since the monks didn't quite have their act together.

"Me not like robe," Belrotha complained, her voice surly. "Me can't move right. Arms trapped. Me feel like a fish."

"At least she's consistent," Cræosh muttered to no one in particular. "She smells like one, too."

"Ah, you're just pissy because you can't move either," Gork taunted him.

The orc responded by stomping his foot on the rather prodigious train of cloth that followed the kobold through the dust—the robe was, after all, made for someone almost twice its current owner's height—and held it there until Gork reached the end and tumbled to his face with a sudden lurch.

470

"I hope," Katim sighed, "that we can . . . make this a little more convincing . . . by the time we reach Brenald."

Gimmol glanced at her. "Um, Katim?"

"What?"

"Your snout's showing."

Katim cursed, trying unsuccessfully to tug the hood far enough forward to hide the offending visage. "Stupid humans. How do . . . they smell at all with . . . those tiny things, anyway?"

No one answered her, because Jhurpess chose that moment to fall headfirst beside the kobold, having once again tripped over the massive club that he insisted on keeping under his robe. It was, to put it mildly, something of a travesty in the annals of disguise. When the weapon wasn't tangling his legs, it was protruding obscenely from his collar or forming a huge hump across his back. Cræosh's and Belrotha's swords weren't proving much more cooperative, either.

"All right, that's it," Cræosh announced. "We camp right here, and we don't move from this damn spot until we've hashed this shit out."

There was, thankfully, no argument.

"Gork, Gimmol," the orc continued, "cut those stupid things down to size." A thought struck him. "Try to remove the extra lengths of cloth intact. I think we can use them." The two small soldiers looked puzzled, but each drew a knife from somewhere or other and quickly complied.

"Okay, great. Um, anyone here know how to sew?"

Silence reigned, disturbed only by the constant—and, in Cræosh's opinion, rather maddening—chirp of background crickets. Finally, looking vaguely embarrassed, Gork raised his hand.

Cræosh blinked at him. "Really?"

Gork shrugged, his expression sheepish. "Kobolds live underground, remember? Lots of jagged rocks and sharp edges. Sewing's something of a universal skill."

"Whatever." Cræosh tossed him back the extra cloth. "Think you can make a large—and I mean *large*—sack out of that? Something Belrotha could carry? Something that might just fit a couple of swords and a really big fucking stick?"

Jhurpess looked wounded at the description of his favorite weapon, but held his tongue. Gork laid the various strips of cloth out lengthwise and then glanced critically at the weapons in question.

"Yeah, I think so," he said dubiously, "but there's not a lot of room for error."

"So don't fuck it up."

"And it won't be comfortable or easy to carry."

"That," Cræosh said sagely, "is not my problem." Belrotha glared at him.

"And it's going to look pretty weird," Gork warned.

"Stick a holy symbol on the end of it," Gimmol suggested, fingering one of several pendants they'd "borrowed" along with the robes. "Make it a ceremonial bundle or something."

The orc nodded. "That should work. Now, about—"

The bugbear raised a hand. "Jhurpess's club is taken care of, but what about Jhurpess's bow?"

"Shit," Cræosh responded thoughtfully.

But Gork shook his head. "An unstrung bow shouldn't take up that much room. I can probably squeeze it into the pack. As long as we don't need it without a couple minutes' warning, we're gold." He scowled. "Even the swords won't be accessible all that easily, you know. If we're attacked suddenly . . ."

Cræosh shrugged. "We've all got knives on us. Anything unexpected comes up, they'll have to do until someone can get the pack open." He gave Gimmol a slap on the shoulder that sent the gremlin staggering. "If we're doing okay without your magic, that'll be your job," he said.

"Oh. Glee."

"Katim, short of some quick surgery, I don't have a clue what we're doing about that damn snorter of yours."

The troll shook her head and uttered a gurgle that probably passed as a trollish sigh. Carefully, she removed a handful of bandaging from her pouch and began to wrap it around her head and snout. She also leaned into a steep huddle, giving herself a stooped, even hunchbacked appearance. Once her snout was fully wrapped, she craned her head down, tucking her nose beneath her collar. The resulting shape was crippled and deformed, but more or less human. Thanks to her steep hunch, the hood hung over most of her head, allowing only tiny glimpses within—and those revealed only a swatch of bandage.

"That can't be comfortable," Gork said.

"You have no . . . idea," Katim replied, her voice heavily muffled.

"Can you see anything besides your feet?" Cræosh asked.

"Barely. One of you gets the . . . honor of leading me. And the disguise . . . is gone to hell and back if I . . . have to fight anyone." With a supple twist of her neck, she pulled her face up and out. She kept her snout bandaged, however, for quick concealment.

The remainder of the night passed in preparation. Gork stitched the excess cloth into a passable sack, which proved just a hair too small for the gathered weapons. So he unraveled it and started over, cursing loudly the entire time. Then, when the loop proved too small to sling over Belrotha's arm—even at its current, reduced size—the kobold actually screamed. Fortunately, with the aid of a short length of rope (suggested by Gimmol), he found a way to adjust that loop without having to disassemble the entire bag once again, and thus was a severe emotional breakdown, followed by murder in the night, narrowly avoided.

And then, finally, there were no excuses remaining. It was time to get back on the road.

Every nerve in the squad was stretched to the breaking point as they sauntered calmly out onto the highway, wandering past and through an ever-growing flow of traffic. Katim was forced now to keep her head perpetually down. The discomfort, the fact that she had to rely on the others to guide her, or both made her even edgier than usual. The others had to keep their faces covered too, of course, but at least they weren't functionally blind.

"Have I mentioned," Cræosh groused, "how much we could use Fezeill right now?"

Even through the bandages and the hood, he could *feel* Gork's glower.

For every pair of human eyes that lit upon them, the orc felt a surge of adrenaline flow through his arms and chest, felt his hand twitch of its own accord toward his hip and a sword that was no longer there. Each time, he was convinced that *this* weakling human would be the one to penetrate a disguise that felt ever more feeble, ever more futile, with every passing mile.

But each new traveler reacted just as the others had, either waving a friendly greeting or, more often, ignoring the "traveling monks" completely, far more concerned with the road ahead than with being cordial to those who shared it. The trek to the gates of Brenald was nerve-racking and hideously uncomfortable, but it never did cross that fine line into dangerous.

And then they were there. Walls taller but less robust than those of Timas Khoreth blocked the bulk of the city from sight, allowing only narrow glimpses through the main gate—a main gate that was manned only by a pair of soldiers and which stood wide open, beckoning all travelers to enter. This was a city that *could* be fortified to withstand siege, but hadn't prepared itself to do so. Dororam must have figured that the presence of the Allied armies between here and the Brimstone Mountains rendered his own lands safe from a major counterattack.

The goblins of the Demon Squad were really looking forward to proving him wrong.

"Jhurpess," Cræosh hissed as they stepped nearer the guards, "I want to make something abundantly clear."

"Yes?" the bugbear asked.

"You pull any of your cowering, whimpering shit here, I'm gonna yank out your tongue. Via your ass."

"Jhurpess understand."

"I'm *so* glad." They waited patiently while the guards asked a few casual questions of a small merchant caravan that arrived just before they did. Cræosh pointed over the travelers' heads to a large building visible between the gates. "If we get separated, meet there.

"Gork," he continued, his voice dropping even lower as the line shuffled forward, "if we need any scouting, you get to do it. Your Manspeak is up to it, and you enjoy skulking anyway."

"I'm tired of skulking," Gork whispered. "I thought I might prowl for a change. Maybe even lurk. Is it okay with you if I lurk?"

"Gork . . ."

"Because I wouldn't want to ruin any of your plans. How set on this are you? The skulking versus lurking thing, I mean."

"Are you through?" Cræosh asked irritably.

The kobold pondered that. "Probably not."

The last of the merchant's carts trundled through the gate, and it was now the goblins' turn.

Captain Sirribeth of the Brenald Capital Guard and Lancers had long since ceased berating her men for slouching and bantering while standing post. The processes of gate duty were mind-numbing, capable of boring even the most attentive sentry into insensibility; so long as they remained aware, and asked each entrant the questions they were required to ask, she wasn't about to yell at them for a little unprofessional fraternization.

But she was heartened to see them straighten, snapping to something approximating attention, as the procession of monks, the hems of their robes coated in road grime, approached the gates. The guards knew when to pretend a certain element of respect. Sirribeth stepped in to handle this one herself, plastering her lips into a welcoming smile, and then almost tripped over her own boots as the passing wagons offered her a clearer glimpse at the brethren.

"Is that a child?" asked one of her subordinates, one Corporal Dennis.

Her lips struggled to turn down of their own accord. The lead figure looked no taller than her own son. "If it is, they're recruiting a lot younger than we are," she replied.

In fact, the entire bunch appeared more than a little odd. There was another child or midget, only a tad larger than the first, while three of the others were taller than Sergeant Boldryn, the biggest man in her unit. Only one of the lot looked to be of average height, and he walked with a shifting, arm-swinging gait more animalistic than human. The first trickles of suspicion began pooling at the base of her skull.

Still . . .

"Greetings, Brothers," she said formally, advancing into their path. Unsure as to whom, precisely, she ought to be addressing, she rested her gaze neutrally between the first two monks. "May I inquire as to your business in Brenald?"

"You may," the short one answered, his words hoarse. She'd heard similar tones in the voices of men too much enamored of their pipes. Sirribeth shuddered slightly. She'd never cared for the habit herself. Wretched-smelling stuff, that.

She craned her neck downward, focusing on the spokesman. "My apologies, Brother," she told him. "It's just—"

"Just that you expected someone tall enough to have experienced puberty."

Sirribeth made a faintly strangled sound, somewhere between a gasp and a chuckle. "Well, um . . ." *This isn't exactly what I expected. . . .*

"It is of no moment, Captain. My brothers and I hail from a specialized order. Our members, as you've no doubt already surmised, are drawn from the ranks of those who are, let us say, atypical."

She nodded wordlessly.

"There is little place in this world for the deformed, Captain," the monk continued. His hood tilted in what might have been a nod as the captain blanched. "Even the word disturbs you, yes? We are grown used to it. In fact, we revel in it, for we are living proof that all mankind may honor the gods, no matter what shape they may have seen fit to grant us."

"You shame me with your words," the captain said. Cheeks flushing, she bowed her head. "Your appearance . . . I've been rude."

"Humanity means making mistakes, my friend," the short monk offered sagely. "Mend your ways, and all will be forgiven."

"Of course, Brother."

"We have come," the monk said, changing tack, "so that we might pray, at the greatest and most resplendent temple in all the Allied Kingdoms, for the safety and success of our brave warriors who go forth to battle the heathen minions of the Dark Lord." A slight hitch marred his words at that. *He despises even speaking the creature's title,* Sirribeth thought in wonder.

"But," he continued, "we have never been to your great city before. Might you direct us to your temple, friend Captain?"

"Of course, Brother. I . . . That is, the roads in and around the marketplace are confusing in the extreme, practically labyrinthine." She smiled ruefully. "Brenald still thinks of itself as the small town we once were.

"I fear," she said, falling unconsciously into the monk's own formal cadence, "that if I attempted to provide you detailed directions now, you would find them meaningless by the time you arrived at the market, and already, I see looks of impatience cast our way from those who await entrance. Let me instead direct you to the marketplace. Once there, you should have little trouble in finding someone to show you the way."

"That will do," the hoarse voice agreed. "And I thank you."

"No, Brother. Thank *you*."

Directions were given, and the motley procession finally proceeded through the gate. "All right!" Captain Sirribeth yelled, responding to the mutters coming from those next in line. "Keep your shirts on; it's your turn now!"

She moved to question the next band of travelers, but her mind remained on the peculiar monks. Their leader's words had struck her hard, but already she felt better about herself, knowing in her heart that she would indeed mend her ways when dealing with those less favored by birth.

To her credit, Sirribeth maintained her new attitude for two full seasons—far longer than most would have—before drifting back into her old habits. Simply for the sake of posterity, it ought to be noted that she struck her head on a loose cobblestone and died seventeen years later, almost to the day, when a one-legged beggar, aggravated over the soldier's lack of charity, stuck out his cane and tripped her.

"That," Cræosh said as they pressed through the shuffling crowds, "was impressive." He was unable, despite his best efforts, to keep the admiration from his voice.

It was hard to tell beneath the thick folds of his robe, but he thought Gork might have shrugged. "It's really just a question of character," he explained as they walked. "Get yourself in the mind-set of the person you're supposed to be, it's pretty easy to come up with the right answers."

"How him know so much about human priests?" Belrotha asked.

Cræosh, though no one else could see it, raised an eyebrow. "How about it, Gork?"

"Does it really matter?"

"No," the orc admitted. "Tell us anyway."

The kobold sighed. "If you must know, we ate one a few years ago."

"We?" Gimmol asked.

"My tribe. It was in the middle of winter, and we encountered a small procession of pilgrims near the Brimstone Mountains. We were pretty full after eating their mules, so we saved the humans for later. One of them was a monk on his first pilgrimage in ten years. We spent a few days talking to him. Idiot thought that by educating us about the glories of his gods, we'd come to see the error of our ways and accept our places as their servants—albeit less well favored than their *human* servants, of course."

"Okay," Cræosh said. "Then what?"

This time, Gork's shrug was obvious. "Then we got hungry again."

"Let's try to restrict ourselves . . . to more human conversation," Katim suggested from deep within her robe, her voice almost inaudible. "Wouldn't want to . . . be overheard."

"You know," Cræosh said, "Gork just sounds hoarse, and me and Gimmol can pass if we have to. But that croak of yours is a dead giveaway. Not to mention the fact that, with your snout tucked in like that, your chest bulges when you talk."

"So I'll be mute. We're . . . all deformed anyway, remember?"

"Mute." A beatific grin spread over Cræosh's face. "These robes *are* holy."

Their first sight of Brenald's bustling marketplace was revealing, perhaps even profoundly revelatory. Not because it was sparklingly clean, or overflowing with the joy of carefree, happy patrons, because it wasn't. It was very nearly identical, in fact, to the bazaars at the heart of Timas Khoreth.

Sure, it differed in the specifics. Fewer of the humans were clad in armor or military uniform. None of the goblin races could be found, but here a dwarven beard wagged as the little man argued with a merchant;

there, a willowy elf glided through the streets, her graceful steps unimpeded by the roiling mass of humanity; and once, they even spotted the head of a halfling, bobbing through the throng.

(Gork, for all he loathed the annoying, childish race, couldn't quite suppress a grin when he realized what the halfling was doing. His technique needed a bit of work, but several humans were going to find themselves greatly perturbed—not to mention rather more impoverished—in the next few minutes.)

But those were mere details. The atmosphere, the feel, the *souls* of the two markets were the same. Unwashed bodies rubbed moistly against one another, spreading their sour miasma over the streets like a plague. Merchants shouted, trying to make themselves heard over the mob; customers shouted, trying to make themselves heard over the merchants. They were barely people at all, these creatures, but organs in the greater living body that was society—just like in Timas Khoreth.

And that was the problem. This was Brenald, not Timas Khoreth; Shauntille, not Kirol Syrreth; the realm of Dororam, not Morthûl. Argue and debate and war over which was better, but they should, at least, have been *different*. For all the proclaimed weakness of the living king, all the whispered evils of the dead one, the subjects of both lived the same lives. They woke, and worked, and ate, and breathed, and slept, and died the same.

As revelations go, it disturbed Cræosh's sense of the world far more than it should have.

Okay, enough of this shit! He shook his head, setting his entire robe to rustling. He could ponder the intricacies of life some other time; right now, they had a job to do.

"So who do we ask?" he muttered, directed not so much at the others as at himself.

Gork responded anyway. "I'm sure one of the watch could help us. But honestly, I'd just as soon avoid them if possible. Call it a habit. I almost broke out in hives just talking to the captain."

"I can respect that," the orc said. "Okay, so what? Pick someone at random?"

"How about her?" Gimmol asked, pointing.

The gremlin's finger guided them to a nearby kiosk apparently belonging to a fruit merchant. She was an older woman, worn by the toil of years. Her hair was wrapped in a scraggly babushka, and she wore a slightly less scraggly dress. She was, at the moment, arguing—and blatantly growing ever more exasperated—with a customer.

And it was to this customer, in particular, to whom the gremlin had directed them. She was short, for a human. Her hair was a lustrous black, although how much of that luster was natural and how much from a buildup of oils was impossible to tell. But what had attracted Gimmol's attention was not her hair, or her size, but her intellect—or her apparent lack thereof.

". . . don't understand," she was whining at the merchant, absently fingering a gently bruised and surprisingly pungent cantaloupe. "Why are they so much more expensive this year?"

The merchant sighed, and launched into an explanation that she'd clearly repeated a goodly number of times already. "As I've said, m'lady, it has to do with the weather down in Gorash. They had an unusually long winter, so they couldn't begin their planting season as early as usual."

"But *we* didn't have a long winter!" the woman protested. "Why should *we* have to pay more?"

The merchant's eyes began to glaze like a pastry.

Cræosh glowered at the peak of Gimmol's hood. "Any particular reason you want to saddle us with an idiot? If her brain were any smaller, it'd fall down her throat and be digested."

"She won't ask too many questions," Gimmol countered, "or make a fuss about our, uh, deformities. Or wonder why we don't know how to get where we're going."

"You're assuming *she* knows how to get to the temple."

"Eh, she's obviously a citizen here. I think even she probably knows the landmarks."

"Jhurpess will talk to woman!" the bugbear announced brightly, and was off into the crowd before his words had fully registered.

"Oh wise and mighty gods," Gork intoned, "please, in thy mercy and grace, ensure that our misguided companion comes to no harm, nor brings any upon his brethren."

"What the fuck was that?" Cræosh asked.

"I'm staying in character," the kobold replied, his voice tight. "Jumping up and down and screaming at the top of my lungs might look suspicious."

The orc glanced apprehensively at the merchant's stand, bedecked in multihued produce, and at the robed form that drew ever nearer to it. "You could always claim to be possessed," he said dubiously. "I'm sort of feeling the need for a little judicious hollering and screaming myself."

"Don't tempt me," Gork told him.

Had Jhurpess been aware of his companions' reactions, he'd have been crushed, since the whole point of his peculiar decision was to impress them. The bugbear was determined to make up for his previous weakness when it came to bustling cities, and though he quailed and quivered inside, though his fur stood on end beneath the heavy robe, he was determined to prove that he could function just as well here as in the depths of the woodlands.

As he crossed the bustling market, he realized, in a show of foresight that would have stunned those selfsame companions, that he probably ought not call himself by his real name here. Not that anyone in Brenald knew who "Jhurpess" was, but it didn't sound like any human name *he'd* ever heard.

He steadied himself with a single deep breath as he approached the woman's side. Her scent—ripening fruit, a human's typical tang, and a mixture of various pheromones that meant nothing to the bugbear—was cloying.

"Pardon," he said, struggling to force his voice into something resembling a human tone.

The woman jumped, startled by the growly, heavily cloaked creature. "Y-yes?" she asked hesitantly. "Who are you?"

"Jhu—umm, John."

"John?"

Jhurpess nodded quickly, relieved she hadn't detected his misstep. "John."

The merchant, by this point, had taken immediate advantage of the woman's distraction and moved on to other, less aggravating customers.

"What do you want?" she asked.

"John needs directions to temple. John wishes to pray." Hey, this wasn't going so badly! Who needed Gork?

"Why are you all wrapped up?" she asked breathlessly.

"John a monk!" Jhurpess said, pounding a fist against his chest for emphasis.

"Really?"

The bugbear frowned inside his hood. He couldn't read her well enough, didn't know if the question was purely rhetorical or a genuine expression of disbelief. If she was getting suspicious . . .

But then, Jhurpess had overheard *two* good stories used to fool humans in the last few days. And if one was good, then both together must be better!

Lowering his voice even further, trying to remember exactly how Gork had sounded when he'd knocked on the church door, he said, "Not just because John a monk." He hacked out a gurgling cough. "John also has bad sickness. When John—"

And then he could only watch, puzzled, as the woman dashed away into the crowd with a terrified wail.

He was just giving some serious thought to chasing her down and asking what was wrong when a thick, meaty hand closed on his shoulder. "You ever do that again," Cræosh hissed in his ear, "I'm going rip your testicles off and choke you with them! You got that?"

"Yes," Jhurpess said sullenly. "John understands."

"Good! Now let's get the hell away from here! We're drawing attention."

The large monks quickly retreated from the marketplace. As they neared the remainder of the squad—all scowling at Jhurpess beneath their hoods—Cræosh stopped short, his nose wrinkling as confusion wafted before his face like a foul odor.

"Who the fuck is John?"

While Belrotha clutched the back of Jhurpess's neck in a firm (and moderately agonizing) grip, Gork wandered in search of another potential guide. This particular encounter went a great deal more smoothly, possibly because Gork refrained from mentioning anything about plague, and within moments, they were on their way once more.

"Left at Rolly's clothing shop, then a right at the building with the big stain on the wall, and then . . ." Gork muttered as they trooped through the milling crowds. "I hate locals. I don't care where you go, the locals are idiots."

"Wouldn't that sort of make *everyone* an idiot?" Gimmol asked. "By definition?"

"*Now* you're catching on," Gork said.

Finally, with only a modicum of further grousing, they arrived. The grandest, most venerated temple in all the Allied Kingdoms rose up majestically before them . . .

Well, not *too* majestically.

"That's disappointing," Cræosh muttered.

"Why do you care . . . what a human temple looks . . . like?" Katim rasped from within her robe.

"I expected this to be something I could make fun of. But it's *practical*. Since when do humans do anything practical? My sense of the natural order just took one on the chin."

"Shall we?" the troll asked dryly.

Heads bowed as piously as they could feign, their steps slow and shuffling, the train of "monks" climbed the wide stone steps.

Cræosh, somewhere in the back of his mind, was battling shock. They were here. Despite the apparent impossibilities inherent in a group of goblins infiltrating Shauntille's capital and making their way to one of the most well-known spots in the entire city, they were here. It had been almost *easy*.

Glumly, the motion barely ruffling his hood, the orc shook his head.

Great. Okay, we're here. Now what the fuck do we do?

CHAPTER ELEVEN

WAR AND PIECES

Slowly, methodically, Havarren climbed.

The steps were sadistic, bordering on murderous. Each was a foot and a half above the previous, stretching the muscles of calves and thighs into so much taffy. The staircase was claustrophobically narrow, making it impossible for a climber to fully extend even one arm before smacking against the stone walls. And the steps themselves were only a few inches deep, forcing climbers to make the entire ascent on their toes—just in case the calf muscles weren't already battered enough. Few human beings, even among the hardiest of the breed, could have made it from floor to pinnacle of this particular tower.

For Havarren, it was just one more annoyance.

A familiarity born of years allowed him to navigate the stairway's abrupt turns and switchbacks with nary a sideways glance. Although disorienting in the extreme, the strange, sharp angles had not been intended as another obstacle. Rather, it was an architectural requirement, since the tower itself was less than ten feet in diameter. For it to pierce over a hundred feet of darkening sky, a needle protruding from the highest roof of the Iron Keep, was a physical impossibility.

But then, who the hell would notice one more of those here?

Step, step, step, step, curse, curse, step. It wasn't exhaustion so much as impatience that spawned the wizard's ire. He could, with a moment's thought, have teleported to Morthûl's side and been done. But no, the Charnel King himself walked the steps to his uppermost sanctum, rather than allow his magics to carry him, and none of his underlings would do otherwise.

In fact, those underlings were normally forbidden to enter at all, but Havarren had been summoned. And so, reluctantly abandoning his meal—damn, but he hated letting an innocent soul go to waste!—he climbed.

"I'm here, my lord," the mage announced as he pushed through the trapdoor at the top, his tone perhaps more tart than was entirely wise. "What did you wish . . . to . . ." He blinked, finally caught off guard.

The great minaret offered, as it always had, a splendid view of the isle of Dendrakis: a vista of frozen mountain peaks in one direction, a rocky and largely barren plain in the other, both vanishing eventually into the waters of the Sea of Tears.

But today, superimposed upon that scenery, an ephemeral image no more substantive than a fever dream, was a chamber of comforts far larger than a dozen towers this size could have supported. Gorgeous tapestries and ancient works of art hung grandly in empty space, mounted on insubstantial walls. Bookcases leaned cordially over a velvet-cushioned array of sofas and chairs, scattered haphazardly across the nonexistent floor. Havarren thought he could even smell the musty fragrance of ancient pages.

Morthûl sat upon one of the largest sofas, this one trimmed in red and gold. He held a large tome in his rotting hands, although it was impossible to tell if he was truly reading or just staring off into the distance over its pages.

"Ah, Havarren," the wavering image said, turning his head to observe his lieutenant. "There you are." His voice was distant, muffled, somehow small.

"My lord?" the mage said, puzzled. "What . . . ? That is, where . . . ?"

"Why don't you join me, Havarren?" The Charnel King waved a bony hand.

Havarren felt the faintest of pressures, as though a bubble of something soft and pliable pressed, then burst, against his flesh. The huge "chamber"—though still lacking in walls, floor, and ceiling—was suddenly solid. It was now the tower-top that wavered, phantasmagorically, when he peered down at it.

The vistas beyond had changed as well, and even the jaded Havarren couldn't smother a gasp. No longer did he peer out over uneventful Dendrakis; now he saw before him, in minute detail, the entirety of Kirol Syrreth. From the Sea of Tears to Ymmech Thewl, the Northern Steppes to the Brimstone Mountains and beyond, every part of Morthûl's kingdom revealed itself before him, the ultimate map.

"Welcome," Morthûl said simply.

"How?" Havarren asked, his voice strangled.

"What, the view? A simple twisting of light and—"

"No!" The mage seemed angry at the not-quite-room in which he stood. "All of this! How could you have kept this hidden from me? I should have felt something, sensed that *something* was here! It's not possible! It—"

Havarren's jaw snapped shut with a clack as the Charnel King raised his single eyebrow. "Still, after all these years, Havarren?" He sounded disappointed. "*Still* you underestimate me, because I had the misfortune of coming from human stock. I have powers you've never seen. You *know* this, and yet you're surprised every time. Hiding this from you was hardly the easiest thing I've ever done, but it wasn't all *that* difficult." He frowned, then, and damn if it didn't resemble true sorrow. "I don't come here often. It was our little sanctum, until she took to spending most of her time at Castle Eldritch. . . ."

Havarren, cradling his injured pride, slumped into the nearest chair. With his arms flopped limply over the sides, he looked less like one of the world's greatest wizards than just another tired, middle-aged man with very poor fashion sense.

"Why have you summoned me here?" he asked, his voice weary. "Was it just to gloat?"

"Gloat, Havarren? I find precious little to gloat about. Look." The Charnel King pointed over the sprawling expanse of Kirol Syrreth. For an instant, their view wavered, and then lurched. The earth raced along beneath them, growing as they descended. When the shifting images finally steadied, the two watchers were several hundred feet above the watchtowers guarding the Serpent's Pass.

"Fort Rohth," Havarren identified. "And Fort Jhikinian. What of them?"

"Look," his lord commanded again.

Havarren looked—and saw, now, a bustling carpet of activity coating the pass and the surrounding lands. As though responding to his own urges, the view shifted once more, moving ever nearer, so the mage could see clearly.

"Dororam . . ."

"Indeed. His soldiers reached the border some hours ago. The war has begun in earnest."

Havarren nodded slowly. "All right, I can see why you might wish me informed. But it's not as though we haven't been expecting it. We—"

"Look."

The blond wizard stifled an exasperated sigh as he obediently looked back at the magnified vista. He hadn't the vaguest notion what Morthûl expected him to see, but if his lord wanted him to watch, he'd watch.

His bored gaze landed on a particularly vicious battalion, a unit consisting of equal parts human and orc. They tore through one of Dororam's columns from the left flank; humans, elves, even horses fell before their bloody onslaught. The Allied soldiers in the vicinity began to fall back.

Havarren was preparing to comment on their soldiers' efficiency—obviously there was *something* here he was supposed to note—when the air behind the advancing unit shimmered, something seeping up from the earth like a morning mist. It parted down the center, a heavy curtain of haze, revealing an entire legion of Dororam's knights. They fell upon the Charnel King's soldiers from the rear, crushing them under a steel tsunami bristling with spears and blades.

Havarren turned from the disturbing sight, even as the Dark Lord allowed the image to retract back to its nationwide view.

"DuMark?" he asked quietly.

Morthûl nodded, the movement sending a pair of roaches tumbling from his empty socket to land with a series of clicks upon the invisible floor. "It seems, Havarren, that you are not the only one with an unfortunate penchant for underestimation. I was convinced—absolutely convinced—that the half-breed would hold back, saving his strength to counter any moves you or I might make. The notion that he would involve himself in the day-to-day business of the war itself . . ." The Charnel King chuckled, a sound without humor.

"We told him ourselves, you know," he continued. "When we risked sending the Demon Squad to deal with Sabryen, rather than finishing him more swiftly and certainly ourselves, he must have realized we were saving our strength for greater things. And he realized he could afford to expend some of his magics early, for we would be reluctant to counter him."

"But then . . . has he left Dororam defenseless?" Havarren asked incredulously. "Teleporting so many troops must take so much out of him. . . ."

"He has left the other wizards in charge of the king's protection." Morthûl closed the book he'd held this whole time. "A foolish, posturing bunch of old men and women, but putting their minds to cooperation, they can accomplish some noteworthy results. Still, the lot of them together aren't worth duMark."

Havarren pressed a finger to his chin, staring off into space. "I wonder if our half-elven friend might not be getting a tad less protective of his favorite puppet."

"From what I've learned," Morthûl said, "the puppet's been tugging back on his strings of late. I doubt duMark would be thrilled if something unfortunate were to happen to Dororam, but I agree that he seems less concerned with the man's safety.

"Unfortunately, that actually makes our position *more* precarious. With duMark tossing soldiers around the map like darts on a board, I find our time growing short far sooner than I'd anticipated."

"Not even duMark can teleport an army a thousand miles!" Havarren protested.

"No. But he can hasten their advance. We should have had months before Dororam's forces could try for Dendrakis itself. Now, we may have only weeks."

"Then let us deal with Dororam," the mage demanded. "If he's less well-defended than we expected, let's take advantage!"

"To what end?" the Charnel King asked. "To settle a personal grudge? I have greater concerns at the moment. Cut off the head of the army? Dororam is a capable leader, but there are others among his compatriots equally as capable. He would become a martyr, a banner to be trotted out before the army as an impetus to fight 'the unnatural evil of the Iron Keep and its half-dead master.'" That last was spoken in near-perfect imitation of Ananias duMark.

"The armies?" Havarren asked halfheartedly.

"Would never have been able to hold Dororam off indefinitely, even under optimal circumstances," came the matter-of-fact reply. "We've had that discussion already, as I recall. With this new stratagem—"

"You and I could counter it," the gaunt man pointed out.

"Perhaps. But my energies must remain devoted elsewhere—now more than ever, with this acceleration of Dororam's timetable. And you, well, perhaps you *could* take duMark. Perhaps not. But to take him and Dororam's other wizards at once, without my assistance? Suicide, even for you."

Havarren nodded in reluctant acknowledgment. "Then we depend entirely on your Demon Squad," he said, clearly not happy at that prospect. "If they get back in time—"

"I think it unlikely, with the armies moving so quickly how. But truth is, it never *mattered* if they got back in time."

Havarren stared incredulously at the creature before him. "*What? I*—"

"Even you are not meant to understand all my plans. I know full well what I'm doing. For now, you must content yourself with that."

"But—"

"Kindly close the trapdoor on your way out, Havarren. Consider what you've seen, and if you come up with any means of slowing them down, even slightly, let me know. Until then, leave me be. I have work to do." Another sudden pop, and the mage found himself once more standing on the tower, Morthûl's opulent chamber barely visible around him. Cursing, Havarren returned to the twisted stairs and took only a sliver of petulant pleasure in not merely closing, but slamming the trap-door behind him.

Absently, Morthûl reached up and lifted the tarnished argent crown from his brow. He held it before his face without really seeing it, then turned it over and over in his hands. Long he sat, motionless save for the dancing of dead fingers across the silver, staring at nothing—or, just perhaps, at a view beyond even the magics of the mystic chamber. Perhaps a large stone edifice, an ancient temple in the center of a bustling city . . .

Finally, having seen all he wished to see, or perhaps merely rousing himself from deep reverie, the master of the Iron Keep laid the crown carefully on the table beside him, out of the way, and resumed his work.

Okay, that chant was *really* starting to get on Cræosh's nerves.

It had begun when they first passed through the temple's doors, squirming and flickering through his ear canals like the tongue of a drunken, lecherous toad, and it hadn't ceased since. Low and sonorous, it hung somewhere between a hymn and a dirge. The orc couldn't see the singers, nor did the echoes reverberating in the cavernous chapel allow him to pinpoint them by sound. A fortunate occurrence, that, for their anonymity was the only thing that kept the orc from bending them over and wearing them as gauntlets. Each time the chant wound to an end, the singers paused just long enough for Cræosh to hope that maybe this time it was over. And they'd start it all up again.

"So beautiful," Gork whispered.

"What?" Cræosh whirled, the hem of his robe twirling around his ankles. "Beautiful?! That *noise?*"

"No," Gork breathed, his face vaguely slack. "Every time the chant comes to an end, I picture myself smashing them in the face with some-thing heavy. It seems to help."

Cræosh tried it. It *did* help, but only a little.

Hoping to distract himself from the maddening acoustic deluge, he resumed his abortive inspection of their surroundings. His initial assessment of the building as "functional" remained intact, but the interior was at least a little more opulent.

They stood at the rear of an enormous chapel, filled primarily with long pews. Thick stone columns, ringed with carvings that presumably depicted important events and figures from human mythology, supported an arched ceiling about three times Belrotha's (normal) height. Stained-glass windows leaked puddles of shifting, multicolored light across the floor, and the air was equally polluted with what Cræosh could only assume the humans considered to be incense.

At the far end of the chamber, a raised dais held a simple stone altar flanked by fonts. One held water, the other some sort of wine or nectar that was providing heaven on earth to a thick cloud of fruit flies. On the wall beyond hung a shape, about the size of a small wagon wheel, that couldn't quite decide if it was a stylized sun or a compass rose. The orc couldn't tell right off if it was actually made of gold or simply gilded, but either way . . .

Without even looking, he snagged Gork by the collar just as the kobold was stepping forward. Gork's feet flew out from under him and he hung limply from his heavy robe.

"No," Cræosh said simply.

"But—"

"No."

"Cræosh—"

"No."

The kobold sighed. "You're a bastard, Cræosh."

"Yes." He returned the kobold to the floor with a faint thump and then firmly guided the little creature to turn around and look at something else.

It was but a few moments later that someone, finally, arrived to greet them.

He was an older man—forty to fifty, if Cræosh was any judge—but in good health. His slow pace was that of the contemplative, not the infirm. His robe was not terribly dissimilar from their own, except it was an eggshell hue rather than brown; it looked pure white compared to the iron gray of his hair.

"Can I help you, Brothers?" the man asked, his voice deep and yet somehow gentle, soothing. "You appear lost."

"We seek Father Thomas," Gork said, advancing a step.

The older man nodded. "I am Thomas."

Excellent! It was why they'd chosen the temple as a starting point—they knew Thomas would be easier to locate than the others—but finding him first thing was a stroke of fortune.

"My name is Brother Gerald," the kobold told him. "My brethren and I have traveled many leagues to be here with you."

"Did you now?" Thomas asked, his voice neutral.

Gork hesitated. This one wouldn't be so easily fooled as the gate guards, not if their conversation touched more than briefly on theology. But this wasn't exactly a functional place for murder: too many parishioners scattered throughout the pews, flipping through holy books or chatting with each other; too many members of that unseen choir. No choice but to bull through.

"We did, Father. We're a . . ." Thomas wouldn't be so quick to buy the "deformed monks" story, but neither would he be so quick to panic. "We're a leprous community—no longer contagious, I assure you. We keep to ourselves, mostly, but with all that's going on, we've come from the south, in order that we might enter into this very temple and contribute our own prayers for the victory and safe return of our armies." Gork swallowed, shivering slightly, repressing the urge to look behind him. *It's part of the disguise; even if he somehow hears, he'll* know *it's part of the disguise. . . .* "And to petition the gods to lend our good soldiers strength and glory in crushing the forces of the hell-spawned abomination who dwells in the Iron Keep."

Cræosh erupted into a violent coughing fit.

"Are you well, Brother?" Thomas asked, real concern in his voice.

"Fine," Cræosh croaked. "Just a bit of road dust, aggravating the— uh, my weakened lungs."

"And where are my manners?" the old priest said suddenly. "You have, as you say, traveled far, and I'm quite certain that you could use some time to recover from your journey. If you'll follow me, we have extra sleeping cells for visitors. They possess little in the way of comforts, I fear, but then I imagine that you're accustomed to even less. You are welcome to them for as long as you wish."

"You are too kind, Father," Gork said courteously, trying to repress a snicker. All they had to do now was get him into one of those cells and . . . "We are indeed weary. And I'm certain that whatever accommodations you provide will be eminently acceptable, in our eyes and the eyes of the gods as well."

They followed, some few steps behind, as Thomas led them around one of the massive stone columns and into a tiny side passage that might well have gone completely unnoticed without his guidance. Torches in sconces burned cheerfully, shedding more than sufficient light to brighten the windowless corridor. They passed several younger priests on their way out, greeting each with a simple nod. Fortunately, as it was afternoon, the sleeping chambers were unlikely to be occupied.

"So, my brothers," Thomas said conversationally as they walked, "what order do you hail from?"

Gork's expression grew momentarily alarmed beneath his hood and bandages. "My brethren and I serve, ah, the Church of Saint Ignatius," he said, pulling from his memory the first religious figure that captive priest had mentioned.

"Indeed," the Father said. "Truly a steadfast brotherhood, yours."

Unsure how to respond, the kobold kept his mouth shut. He noticed, between the sounds of footsteps, that Gimmol was mumbling to himself. He wanted to reach back and smack the gremlin—monks, Gork was fairly certain, didn't mumble unless they were praying—but doing so would probably be an even more obvious infraction than the gremlin's idiocy. Gork gritted his teeth and stayed silent.

Father Thomas finally led them to a line of doors, simple and unadorned. Given the narrow expanse of stone between each, the rooms must have been tiny indeed.

Thomas opened the nearest, then stepped back. "Does this meet with your approval, Brothers?"

Gork made a show of looking the minuscule cell over. "It does indeed, Father. I . . ." He stopped, curiosity slowly giving way to a sinking feeling of dread, as a gentle tickling wafted across his nostrils and he smelled the faint scent of herbs. He spun and saw the priest's hand extended and the last traces of dried and powdered leaves settling through the air.

Oh, Stars, what's he done? He was already moving toward the old human, several of the others falling in beside and behind.

"All-Seeing Divine," Thomas prayed, backpedaling before their advance, "gods of my ancestors, gods of my children, gods of my soul, I beseech thee now to shield thy servant from danger, from those who would corrupt thy house, those measured as both his enemies and thine."

Okay, the man wasn't retreating that quickly, had even slowed down as his prayer reached its end, so why couldn't they seem to catch him? Why did everything seem to be . . . slowing . . .

Oh, dragonshit.

Gork's limbs simply went away. He could *see* them, and he wasn't feeling particularly dizzy or sleepy or anything; he just had no feeling anywhere in his body. He teetered, frozen, keeping his feet through exquisite balance and sheer luck. He heard some of the others toppling behind him, but couldn't even look to see who'd fallen.

"Foolish creatures," Father Thomas announced. "Did you think I couldn't see through so transparent a charade?" His robes swishing around his boots, the priest stepped forward and placed his hands on Cræosh's hood. "I know already what you are not. I would know what you are." And with that, he yanked cloth and bandages back, revealing a swamp-green face and squinting red eyes.

"Orc!" the priest hissed, again retreating a pace. He sneered in growing comprehension at the other "monks" arrayed before him. "The Dark Lord has far more gall than even I gave him credit for. To send goblins into Brenald, into my temple!" He smiled, then, and it was not the kindly smile of an elderly priest. "Well, if you don't mind waiting here a few moments, I'll be back with the King's Watch. I'm sure they're going to have all sorts of interesting questions for you to answer." With a dramatic flourish, Father Thomas moved to depart.

✳

The instant the man's back was turned, Gimmol advanced, as casual as a summer stroll, and plunged his short sword into Father Thomas's back. The pristine white of the old man's robe became a deep, rich red. He gasped once, staggered, and toppled.

"Well," Gimmol said, practically sauntering back toward his companions, "that should about settle that." He knelt beside Cræosh and Belrotha and cast his spells. Flexing fingers and twitching feet were evidence enough that they would recover within seconds.

He'd just risen, in fact, to move toward the next of the fallen goblins, when a shadow flickered across Gork's face. Thankfully, Gork wasn't the only one to see it, since he couldn't even move to shout a warning.

"Down!" Cræosh shouted, wobbling unsteadily to his feet, far too late to do any good.

Father Thomas, his teeth clenched so tightly against the pain that his jaw creaked, had arrested his fall, bracing one hand against the wall. With the other, shaking but strong, he yanked a hand-axe from within his robe and swung at Gimmol's unprotected head.

And then Belrotha was there. With a banshee howl, standing tall against the drug that hadn't yet faded entirely from her body, she hurled the gremlin clear of harm's way—not to mention a good twenty feet up the corridor—and took across her ribs the blow meant for Gimmol's head.

Had Thomas himself been uninjured, the blow might have penetrated both her leather jerkin and her thick hide—but he wasn't, and it didn't. Belrotha staggered, grunting once at the pain. Then she exhaled a single hot, pungent breath into Thomas's face and crushed his skull against the wall.

"What were you saying?" Cræosh asked casually as he helped the battered gremlin back to his feet.

"That . . . should about settle it," the gremlin repeated painfully. "Sorry about that."

"Sorry?" the orc asked, amazed. "We'd all be fucked if you—how did you do that, anyway?"

"Magic," Gimmol said cryptically, kneeling so he could attend to the others.

"Well, no shit, magic. But we were frozen. I thought you had to move and talk and all that to cast a spell."

"That's true. Actually, I had a protective spell going *before* the old man paralyzed you."

"*That's* what you were doing!" Gork burst out as the gremlin's magics sent feeling coursing back through his muscles. "I thought you were just talking to yourself."

Gimmol shrugged. "I try not to talk to myself. There are so many more interesting conversationalists about."

"But how did you know he was going to do that?" the kobold insisted.

"Well, I didn't know, exactly. But you saw what Havarren's list said about him. 'Herbalist and alchemist.' *Some* of us know to take that stuff seriously."

Cræosh and Katim both stared at their feet, seeing as how they'd laughed and scoffed at that when first studying the scroll they'd been given. "So he's a *healer*," the orc had snickered. "That should take about half a minute."

"So," Gimmol continued, "I cast a spell to cleanse the body of poisons. It's not all that potent, really—I normally use it for sobering up—but I figured that anything he could throw at us would either be pretty weak, or at least take a while to fully work its way—"

"I think," Katim said before Gork could explode, "that he meant . . . to ask how you knew that Thomas . . . had seen through our . . . disguises."

"I'm kind of curious about that myself," Cræosh added.

"Oh." He sounded a little crestfallen. "Well, it was sort of Gork's fault, actually. Don't get me wrong," he added quickly, sensing the coming diatribe. "I mean, obviously you had no way of knowing. But I've read up on a lot of this, of course, so I knew—"

"Knew *what?*" Cræosh demanded.

Gimmol smiled ruefully. "Ignatius is the patron saint of health and beauty. There's no way they'd ever accept a colony of lepers, or the deformed, into their order. The instant you used Ignatius's name, Father Thomas only had to look at us to know you were lying."

"Oh," Gork said after a moment's pause.

"Yeah," Gimmol agreed.

"Well," Cræosh said, glancing around, "it's done. This corridor's pretty well abandoned at the moment, but it ain't gonna be too long until someone finds him. We want to be out of here before that happens. And we still have work to do here." He shrugged philosophically at the others' puzzled expressions. "We're supposed to 'display' the bodies, remember? This is messy, but it's just a start. Let's get to it."

Nobody paid much attention to a procession of monks wandering through the temple; or rather, they were noticed as newcomers, but otherwise went unremarked. And thus unremarked, the Demon Squad remained also unmolested as they proceeded from the tiny hallway, through the chapel, and on toward the front doors. It took every iota of control to maintain that steady, plodding pace when every instinct screamed at them to *run*, to be well and truly gone before their handiwork could be discovered.

But when the huge temple doors boomed shut behind them and the midday sun prodded ardently at the heavy fabric of their robes, they still heard neither hue nor cry from behind, no alarm of any type. They were clear.

"What now?" Gimmol asked.

"There." Cræosh pointed. A small crowd was gathered alongside the temple's side, and not a few clerical robes—both the white of priests and the brown of monks—bustled within. The various clergymen handed out small bundles of dried meats and loaves of a hard bread to the assembled citizens. "See if you all can't find a loaf of something to hand out."

"Growing charitable in your old age, Cræosh?" Gork asked sourly.

The orc snorted. "It's a place to hide. And I'd rather stay near the temple."

"Gloating over your handiwork?" For some reason, the kobold seemed more bound and determined than ever to pick a fight.

"Okay, oh genius, you tell me how the fuck you were planning to find Brookwhisper, Lirimas, or Bekay."

"Well, I was . . . That is, I thought we, umm . . ."

"Uh-huh." Cræosh shook his head. "Such planning. Such fore-thought. Tell me something, are you this meticulous when planning your thefts, too, or do you prefer to trust those to luck?"

"Your point?" Gork asked, his voice sullen.

"My point is that once word of what happened to Father Thomas gets—" The point, then, was made far more eloquently than Cræosh could have managed by the sudden scream from within the temple. Some peculiar property of the hall's acoustics magnified it until it burst in a torrent from the doors and windows, flooding over the crowd. Voices petered out; hands froze in awkward poses; even the noisy chewing of tough, cheap viands ceased midbite.

The crowd—a living, amoebic thing—drifted a single step toward that holiest of structures, only to flinch away as a second scream, even louder and more distorted than the first, escaped the edifice. Several of the throng's more excitable citizens began babbling about ghosts and demons, and some few actually turned tail and bolted.

"The watch is gonna be here in seconds," Cræosh hissed, already drifting toward the shifting crowds, staring as though he, too, was focused morbidly on the source of the screams. "Get the fuck over there, and spread out!"

They sifted into the crowd, subtly, deliberately—not that it mattered overmuch. Cræosh and Katim could have stripped naked and waltzed through the streets, and no one would have noticed, so fixated was the crowd on the temple.

Gork, though he followed, seemed oddly reluctant, his feet dragging stubbornly beneath the hem of his robe. He glanced up only when Belrotha brushed past him.

"What Gork's problem, anyway?" she snapped quietly at him.

"It's just . . . I think I'm allergic to charity."

"Me understand," the ogre said sympathetically. "Me allergic to honey. Me get hives wherever me touch it. Lucky that honey not common in Itho."

"Ouch," Gork said, commiserating despite himself. "I can't imagine what getting hives on your mouth and tongue must feel like."

"Mouth? Tongue?" Belrotha stared as though he'd just sprouted a tuber of some sort from his forehead. "What you *do* with honey?"

"Uhh . . ." Gork couldn't help but feel that now wasn't really the time for this. "We eat it, same as anyone else."

"*Eat?!*" Belrotha's voice touched registers that the kobold would never have believed she could reach. Several people in the crowd glanced momentarily her way before returning to the drama being played out— or rather, sounded out—before them.

"Well, yes. What do *you* do with it?" His mouth formed the words, even as his face tightened in obvious horror of whatever answer he might receive.

"Not *eat*," she avowed. Gork had never heard her so revolted. "In Itho, we—"

"Hey!" Cræosh interrupted with a hiss, reappearing before them. "Keep the fuck up, will you?"

Belrotha offered Gork a single shrug and moved to follow the orc. Gork trailed behind, shaking his head and keeping rather more distance from the ogre than was strictly necessary.

And not, as it happened, a moment too soon. Barely had the squad insinuated themselves throughout the crowd when a small contingent of the city watch—perhaps half a dozen, hands clasped tightly on the hilts of their swords—dashed around a nearby corner. Even as they pounded up the steps, their boots clacking dully against the stone, the doors burst open, unleashing a small tide of parishioners. Rather than try to fight their way through, the guardsmen leapt aside at the last minute, allowing the sudden flow of humanity to play itself out. Only then did they proceed through the towering double doors.

A handful reappeared only a short while later, their faces bloodless, one or two wiping vomit from the corners of their lips. (Katim had been particularly proud of her idea to tack Thomas's entrails to the wall in the starburst pattern of his temple's holy symbol, and later insisted on taking full credit for the humans' obvious discomfort.) The soldiers took up post at the base of the stairs, presumably to keep any curious bystanders from barging in. A few of the more belligerent tried anyway, spouting off about the temple being "the people's property," but when a particularly irritable watchman clubbed one of said belligerents over the head with the pommel of his sword, the others decided the guards had made their case and backed off.

People shifted, voices muttered, feet scuffed, soldiers scowled, minutes passed with all the alacrity of an insomniac sloth. Cræosh began to worry; the longer this took, the more likely someone would pick one of the "new monks" out of the crowd and associate them with what had happened. . . .

A deafening bellow from behind dug into the crowd, a nigh physical presence parting them down the center to allow a singularly imposing figure to approach the doors.

"See?" Cræosh whispered to his nearest companion—Katim, as it happened. "I knew if we waited long enough . . ." He paused as the figure passed him by, the ground seeming to shake beneath the newcomer's sandaled feet. "He's a big one, ain't he?" the orc noted.

The man in question was actually only about Cræosh's height, but his chest, his arms, his legs, even his neck bulged with flesh-wrapped boulders masquerading as muscles. His dark-toned skin—largely exposed to the air, for in addition to his sandals, he wore only leather leggings and an X-shaped baldric on which hung a mighty axe—bulged with every step, every movement, seemingly every *thought*. His goatee, the only hair on his head, bristled ahead of him as though it, and not his voice, were carving his path through the assembly.

This, then, unless Havarren's description was dramatically flawed, would be Kuren Bekay. Titan among men, ally to the enigmatic Ananias duMark, one of the great heroes who'd thwarted King Morthûl's previous efforts, and, of most immediate importance, longtime friend to one Father Thomas. The guards, after exchanging a terror-filled glance, fled his path as swiftly as the crowd had, allowing him unfettered access to the temple. No one protested the inequity; no one dared.

"How long, do you think?" Cræosh asked casually, his voice still low.

Katim shrugged, a gesture he was aware of only due to the rustling of her robe. "Two minutes or so to . . . reach the room in which we . . . left Thomas. Almost a full minute . . . of shock and grief. I'll say three . . . for him to rail against fate . . . and the gods, and to threaten . . . the watch if they do not . . . quickly find the killers. One more . . . to get back out here."

"You gave him two to get in," Gork reminded her.

"But he'll be enraged and . . . he'll be running on his . . . way out." She played the numbers back in her head. "Seven minutes."

Cræosh shook his head. "Nah, don't think so. I know his type; he's gonna skip the shock and grief and go straight to the shouting. Six minutes, tops."

"Eight," Gork said, appearing briefly at Cræosh's other side before vanishing once more into the crowd, lest they be too easily spotted together. "Just for variety."

It was, in fact, six minutes and forty-three seconds before the large man reappeared in the temple doorway. His fists were clenched so tightly that Cræosh swore he heard the knuckles creaking over the crowd. One of the watchmen appeared behind Bekay and whispered something, only to vanish back into the chapel's shadows—completely off his feet—with a single shove from the mountainous fellow. Then, staring straight ahead, the warrior descended the shallow steps and, knocking aside anyone who didn't clear the path fast enough, made for a nearby thoroughfare and disappeared.

"Gork," Cræosh whispered as loudly as he dared. "Gork!"

The kobold again materialized from nowhere, crinkled the hood of his robe in what must have been a nod, and slipped away after Bekay.

The traffic on this, one of Brenald's major streets, was less tightly packed than the temple's surroundings, but heavy enough in its own right. People still scattered from Bekay's path; even those who hadn't yet heard rumors of the horror at the temple recognized his expression as an indicator that this was a man better left unimpeded and undisturbed. Gork, however, was finding it difficult to keep up, for while there were fewer legs for him to scramble over, around, or between, those legs were in constant motion. Worse, the farther he got from the temple, the less his robe served as adequate camouflage.

But then, this was Gork—Gork the clever, Gork the formidable (in his own mind, at any rate), Gork the stealthy-as-an-embezzling-rat—and there wasn't a crowd in the world with enough eyes to keep him from sneaking wherever needed to be snuck. And so, despite being the recipient of the occasional curse here, being smacked in the face by the occasional hanging scabbard there, and finding himself tangled in flowing skirts a time or two, he succeeded in keeping Bekay in his sights until the big man finally moved off the road and bulled through the door of a short and stubby establishment.

Run-down, filthy, and apparently assembled by a drunkard with delusions of carpentry, the building crouched on the side of the roadway as though begging for scraps. The door didn't entirely fit in its frame; the windows were a greasy parchment that looked to have been used to polish old chamber pots. Through that dull opacity, Gork saw an amorphous shape—presumably Bekay—drift in from the direction of the door and seat himself at the counter that ran the entire length of the far wall.

Gork stepped back, glancing around for any sort of signage, and located it above his head: a thin wooden plank hanging from a rusty metal pole.

It depicted a stylized figure that, if viewed through a tight squint at just the right angle, bore a very faint resemblance to Gork himself. It was capering about, one knee raised above its waist while it balanced on the toes of its other foot. Beneath the image, the name was spelled out for that portion of the citizenry who'd actually learned their letters.

He, of course, couldn't read a word of it, but it didn't take more than a few minutes of loitering before he heard the name spoken by passing customers.

The Capering Kobold.

Gork's left eyelid developed a violent twitch.

His internal debate, as to whether he should go in there and start slitting throats or just burn the place down, was fortuitously curtailed by a barrage of shouts from within. While most was far too distorted to be intelligible from his vantage, he had little difficulty identifying the word "*Out!*" The door flew open, clinging to its cheap hinges by finger-nails it shouldn't, as a door, have possessed, and a crowd of half-drunk patrons exploded from the tavern in a mad rush, the combined weight of their breath sufficient to make Gork himself tipsy. When the *bartender* joined the fleeing crowd, carrying the tankard he'd been cleaning, Gork couldn't help but grin.

They keep making it so easy *for us. . . .*

He watched and waited for a few more minutes, blending into the shadows of a doorway across the street. The fuzzy shape that had to be Bekay remained at the bar, what appeared to be an entire ale barrel standing on the counter before him. Every so often, a potential cus-tomer—either frightfully unobservant or catastrophically stupid—would step through the front door and move toward the seated warrior. Gork still couldn't make out more than a few words, but he recognized the questioning tone, inevitably followed by an animal bellow, even more inevitably followed by said customer scurrying back out the door in search of someplace less suicidal to drink.

Finally, when he was thoroughly convinced that Bekay wasn't going anywhere for a good long while—except possibly under the table—Gork wove his way through the packed streets back toward the temple. Several times a ripe, plump coin purse hove into view, and he felt his fin-gers twitching of their own accord. And yet he forced himself to hold off, cursing every step of the way. He couldn't afford to take the risk. Getting caught swiping someone's pouch or picking someone's pocket, however improbable, would be far more strain than his already delicate disguise could handle. He tossed the coin purse from hand to hand, the repetitive gesture easing his frustration, helping him concentrate so as not to . . .

Coin purse? Gork stared with a sinking feeling in his stomach at the leather pouch in his fist. Where had this *come* from?! How dare his hands make that sort of decision without consulting him? A look of unease scribbled across his face, the kobold walked the remainder of the way with his arms firmly crossed inside the folds of his robe, each hand clutching a purse to keep it occupied. . . .

Each hand? *Oh, dragonshit!*

It was a profoundly disturbed Gork who finally rejoined the squad, where they'd assembled a block or so from the temple. There they'd stood for minutes on end, occasionally muttering the name of this or that god and making various pious gestures toward the temple and the guardsmen who were scurrying all over it like ants on a dead raccoon.

"It's about fucking time, Shorty!" Cræosh snarled, waving politely at a nearby citizen. "You get lost?"

"I need help," the kobold murmured, his gaze slightly unfocused, clearly having heard not a word the orc said.

"Well no shit, Gork. I could've told you that. You wanna tell me where the hell Bekay's gotten to?"

"Bekay?" Gork asked, glancing up for the first time.

"Yeah. You know, Kuren Bekay? Big man? Muscular? Bald? Dark skin? The man you were supposed to be following? Any of this ringing a fucking bell?"

"Oh!" Gork shook his head. "Right, Bekay. He's in a tavern about a mile off. By himself, no less."

"By himself?" Gimmol asked, stepping closer to better hear the kobold's report. "In a tavern in a city this size? How'd that happen?"

"It may," Gork said sagely, "have had something to do with the fact that he pretty much walked in and told everyone to get the bleeding hell out. Only a lot less politely."

"Yeah, that might just do it," Cræosh agreed. "That's one big son of a bitch."

"So you've said," Katim rasped. "Gork, what's the . . . name of this tavern?"

Gork's eyelid twitched again. "Didn't catch it. I can find it again, though."

"Good enough," Cræosh said. "Let's go. Uh, not too quickly, though. Might as well give the man a chance to get good and soused first."

They set off at a sedate pace, arms crossed, heads bobbing up and down in "silent prayer." Citizens nodded from afar, or expressed whispered condolences as they passed. But they remained relatively undisturbed, and no one impeded their progress.

"How long you think these disguises are likely to hold up?" Gimmol asked as they walked. "Right now everyone's running around in blind panic, but sooner or later someone with half a brain is going to associate the 'deformed monks' with what happened."

"Not long," Cræosh acknowledged. "So we'd better make damn fucking sure this doesn't *take* too long."

For all their impatience, however, the orc and the gremlin both had to pause for a few moments to recover once they'd finally spotted the tavern and, more importantly, the sign. Katim chuckled slightly, and even Jhurpess and Belrotha, who could see the picture if not read the words, grinned widely.

"Didn't catch the name, Shorty?" Cræosh asked when he'd finally gotten his mirth under control.

"Shut up."

"Oh, come on, Gork," Gimmol said, his grin threatening to split his face wide open. "You're flexible. I'm sure you can do better than *that*. Come on, let's see! Dance for us, Gork!"

Slowly, ignoring the fact that Cræosh had again exploded into helpless laughter, Gork approached the smiling gremlin. "Have you," he asked, his voice low, "ever considered a career as a eunuch?"

"Thought about it," Gimmol said slyly. "But I decided I don't really have the balls for it."

Cræosh howled, bending double and holding his gut. Only the realization that his "persona" was in jeopardy, that people were starting to stare at the strange, laughing monk, finally calmed him down.

"Are you through?" Gork asked coldly. Cræosh snorted, his lips quivering, but he held his mouth firmly shut. "I'm so glad," the kobold continued. "Were we planning to actually accomplish anything here, or did you all just come to see the show?"

"Okay," Gimmol said, also sobering up. "So what's the plan?"

Jhurpess peered askance at the building. "Squad could burn it down," the bugbear suggested. Unlikely as it was, Cræosh chose to believe that his hairy companion was joking.

"Anything else?" he asked.

Katim shrugged. "The man is in there alone . . . and it's fairly private. Let's just . . . walk in and kill him."

"Works for me," Cræosh said. "Any objections?"

"I don't know," Gork said. "According to Havarren, he's supposed to be seriously strong, remember? *Magically* strong, even, thanks to his association with duMark."

Belrotha cracked her knuckles. Cræosh was fairly certain that he couldn't have reproduced that sound with a pickaxe and a granite wall. "Me stronger than human," she announced.

"Belrotha," Gimmol said seriously, "Bekay's strength is magic. He actually might be stronger than you are."

The ogre shrugged. "Me doubt it. But if him stronger, that okay too. Me just outsmart him."

"I think," Cræosh said, a truly odd hitch in his voice, "that we better do this already."

They slipped into a nearby alley—not entirely sure whether it was the thick shadows or the thicker miasma of rotten food and dead rats that concealed them from casual view—and began passing out the heavy weapons from Belrotha's sack. The robes did a piss-poor job of hiding said armaments, but it should be sufficient for a quick dash across the street. Jhurpess even took a moment to restring his bow, though nobody thought he'd have the chance to use it in the close-quarters melee to come.

"Wait a minute," Gimmol said. He muttered a moment, fingers twisting around one another, a ball of russet slugs. Then, ever so slowly, he faded away.

"Where he go?" Belrotha asked, her jaw slack.

"I'm right here," the gremlin's voice replied. And now that they knew where to look, they could indeed see him again, though he looked somehow fuzzy, as though their eyes refused entirely to focus.

"I don't get it," Gork said.

"I can't do real invisibility, but it's sort of a mental camouflage," the gremlin explained. "If you're looking for me, you can find me okay, but if you're concentrating on anything else, you just kind of fail to notice I'm here."

"That might've been a useful trick to show us earlier, you know," Cræosh complained. "A few times, even."

"I can't do it for more than a few minutes, tops, and it pretty much wipes me out. I have to concentrate harder than everyone around me can look. This is just in case Bekay does prove too strong for a head-to-head fight. Gork's a good sneak and all, but . . ."

"But," Cræosh agreed. "And we can't just send you in to kill the bastard by yourself, because you need us to make sure he's distracted enough for the magic to work. Right?"

Gimmol nodded, or he seemed to. Cræosh couldn't be sure.

"All right, then," the orc said. "Are we ready?"

"We better be," Gimmol muttered. "This is starting to hurt."

"One more thing," Katim said, stooping to retrieve a small stone—or actually, a chunk of brick—lying nearby. She paused a moment, feeling the weight and heft, and then hurled it down the street. An old man, returning home with an armful of produce from the market, cried out sharply and collapsed, his head bleeding. Everyone nearby immediately focused their attention on him.

"They might have found it . . . odd to see a group of monks . . . wandering into a tavern," Katim said. "Let's go while . . . no one's watching."

They had no time for subtlety, not with a juggernaut like Bekay. The orc slammed the door open and charged, his massive sword swinging before he'd even reached his target. If the alcohol had slowed the man enough, this could be over in a single burst of blood.

No such luck. Roaring, the huge man rolled smoothly off his stool, his grace belying both his size and the copious quantities of ale he'd consumed. He didn't even reach over his shoulder for the titanic axe he carried, just smacked Cræosh's sword aside with an open palm against the flat of the blade.

Well, it *looked* like he'd just used an open hand, but it *felt* like he'd parried the attack with something far larger. Such as, say, a rhinoceros. The sword struggled to vibrate itself clear out of Cræosh's numbed fingers, and only mule-headed determination—and the fact that he probably couldn't have relaxed his grip if he'd wanted to, until he regained some control over his digits—allowed him to retain the weapon.

He tensed, recoiling, watching for a counterstroke, and found himself facing an empty expanse of wall and window.

Window? No bar? No Bekay? What the . . . ?

He realized, only then, that Bekay's parry had spun him completely around; had his companions not engaged the enemy, he'd have been left absolutely open to any imaginable counterattack.

His shoulders hunched, his steps careful, Cræosh advanced once more upon the foe. Havarren's scribbled warnings and all the various tales hadn't done Bekay justice, and the orc was starting to wonder if he really *was* stronger even than Belrotha herself. Cræosh sidled around the tavern's furniture, his mind racing, watching for any sign of an opening.

It was not, he observed grimly, going well for his companions. Belrotha was picking herself up amid the splintered wreckage of one of the tavern's large tables. Blood coursed down her face from her split forehead, but even through that mask of crimson, her astonishment was easy enough to read. Clearly, no matter Gimmol's warning, the ogre had been unable to grasp the possibility of a human stronger than she. Her flight through the tavern, and the tavern's table, had finally taught her otherwise.

Jhurpess vaulted the bar, his long limbs spread, reeking of spirits spilled from shattered bottles. Howling and gibbering, he brought his gargantuan cudgel sharply downward, determined to introduce Bekay's chin to his own pelvis.

A single ground-eating stride carried the human just beyond the bugbear's reach. Even as the bludgeon swept past his face, he grabbed the weapon with both hands, halting it as firmly as though it were frozen in ice. It was impossible—indeed, as Cræosh had suspected, even Belrotha couldn't have pulled that off, at least not without a lot more strain than Bekay evidenced—and yet, he'd just seen it happen.

Bekay shoved, driving the narrow end of the club back as though it were a spear. It shot from the bugbear's intertwined fingers and punched into his gut. A semisolid mass, equal parts air and the remains of his most recent meal, exploded from Jhurpess's mouth. He fell to the ground with a limp thump, curling into a hairy, shuddering ball.

Katim slid past the crumpled bugbear, her axe swinging. Bekay bent double into a sideways V, angling his stomach out of the path of the wicked blade. It was precisely what Katim had expected, and even as the weapon passed a fraction of an inch from the human's skin, she twisted. Not even the troll's phenomenal control could turn it into a killing blow, but she angled the blade upward so it scraped viciously against the base of Bekay's rib cage, rather than slicing empty air where his gut had been.

It wasn't a deep wound; wasn't even particularly incapacitating, costing Bekay little more than a wide strip of skin. But for the first time, the blood that flowed was human. The goblins scented the pungent, metallic tang, saw pain in the set of Bekay's jaw, and their spirits rallied.

He retreated, cursing, one hand pressed to the shallow wound, the other reaching over his back toward his mammoth weapon.

"Watch the axe!" Cræosh shouted—probably unnecessarily.

Bekay was already outside the reach of Katim's own blade, but that didn't make him safe. From her left hand, her spinning *chirrusk* arced toward him, moving to snag his arm before he could draw.

But again the impossible human surprised them. The bloodstained hand with which he'd grabbed at his wound—lulling them, Cræosh saw now, faking some measure of his pain—blurred into motion. The chain ceased its high-pitched whistle, and Katim's nostrils flared at the realization that her enemy now clutched the barbed hook of her favorite weapon in his unbreakable grasp.

She must have known—she *had* to know—what was coming next, and *still* she could not react fast enough, could not release her own grip before he hauled her forward.

Staggering, stumbling, Katim raised her own axe, not in any attack but in a last-ditch defense. Bekay's own weapon plummeted toward her skull, the prodigious blade seeming to crush the air, rather than slice through it. The troll's arm shuddered at the impact, her ears laid back at the terrible screech of metal on metal, and she flinched away from the shower of sparks raining over her snout. Her knees buckled, her arm trembled, and the rounded edge of the human's axe hovered less than a hand's span from her scalp.

All of which left her completely helpless to avoid the fist, wrapped in the links of her own *chirrusk*, that plunged into her gut like the head of a frenzied boar.

Katim staggered, dropping the other end of the *chirrusk* and very nearly her axe along with it. The breath billowing in and out between her shifting teeth as she struggled to replace the wind Bekay had knocked from her carried flecks of blood. She glared at the orc, her expression demanding to know why he hung back, accusing him of the cowardice she'd always suspected he harbored in the depths of his soul.

Was Cræosh frightened? Say, at the least, that he'd developed a healthy aversion to Bekay's proximity. But call it cowardice or call it wisdom, that was not the reason Cræosh held back. No, he lurked at the periphery, creeping but never closing, so that Bekay would eventually have to move, or at least turn, to follow his movements. Would have to move to put his back to the bar.

And to the faint shimmer in the air *behind* the bar.

When the man *finally* turned his way, exposing a broad expanse of naked back to the hidden gremlin, Cræosh struggled to repress a grin. Kuren Bekay could be as strong as he fucking well wanted; it wouldn't do him any good with a short sword jammed through his spine.

Later, throughout the days to come, the squad would discuss it over and over, replaying every second time and again, desperate for some sense of understanding, of what could have gone so terribly wrong. Maybe Gimmol made some accidental noise the rest of them missed in the heat of battle, something that alerted Bekay to his presence. Perhaps the man's battle-honed instincts, forged over a lifetime of combat, perceived something his conscious mind never registered. Or maybe, in addition to his phenomenal strength, duMark's magic had granted his ally an enhanced awareness as well.

But for all their pondering, all the possibilities, all their theories, the goblins knew that, ultimately, they could never be sure.

All they knew for certain was that as the gremlin clambered up atop the bar, unseen sword ready to strike from unseen fist, Bekay spun away from Cræosh and whipped the back of his fist into Gimmol's skull.

A wet snap, like a rotten branch cracking from a dying tree, echoed across the confines of the Capering Kobold. All other sound ceased as every eye in the squad fixed on the brown-robed gremlin, now clearly visible. The befuddled look on his face was almost funny, in its way; he seemed to watch, all uncomprehending, as his sword slipped from slackened fingers and bounced, point first, upon the floor. A sliver of Cræosh's mind, incongruous as the notion was, insisted on pointing out that such treatment couldn't possibly be good for the blade.

Limply, his head flopping at an angle that not even a serpent could have duplicated, Gimmol crashed to the floor in a graceless heap.

Somewhere across the common room of this tiny, run-down tavern, the gates of hell must have torn open, for the agonized wails of the damned blasted their ears, their organs, their souls—a torrent of sound the goblins could never have imagined.

No, Cræosh realized, an inexplicable shiver dribbling along with the sweat down his back. *Not hell. It's not the damned screaming, it's . . .*

Belrotha. The animalistic bellow peaked even as the orc recognized its source, descending—devolving—into a guttural, mindless snarl. Cræosh looked into the ogre's face, and he cringed.

No sentience remained in the *creature* staring back at him. Whatever awareness, whatever limited intelligence was normally to be found in the visage of an ogre were gone, washed away in a primal deluge.

Cræosh, however, had *not* lost his mind, and was therefore wise enough to get the hell out of her way.

The tavern shook beneath her tread, the charge of a maddened beast. Glasses and mugs tumbled from shelves to shatter across the floor; dust snowed from the rafters. Bekay, his own expression uncertain for the first time, raised his axe for a beheading stroke that the ogre was clearly in no position to avoid. Cræosh, shaking free of his fugue, darted toward them, even knowing he was too far, that he could do nothing to stop the blade's inevitable fall. . . .

But something else dropped loose from the ceiling, along with the clouds of choking dust. Something—some*one*—that Cræosh, once again, hadn't even realized was missing.

His short muzzle twisted in lunatic rage, Gork plummeted from the rafters of the Capering Kobold and drove his *kah-rahahk* into the human's beefy arm.

Flesh tore beneath the jagged blade, naked bone glinted in the lanternlight, and spattering blood beat a rhythmic tattoo on the floorboards. Bekay howled, an overdue sign that he was, for all his might, only human. The monstrous axe slid from his slackening fist.

Gork tumbled from Bekay's shoulder, rolling skillfully as he hit the floor—uncomfortably near that falling axe—and came smoothly to his feet halfway across the room. Blood trickled across the *kah-rahahk*; from its barbs hung decorative streamers of flesh and muscle.

"Not bad, Shorty," Cræosh cheered, glancing at the gaping wound on Bekay's arm. "But couldn't you have picked a *lethal* spot?"

"No," the kobold told him, his voice far more serious than Cræosh had ever heard it. "He's not mine to kill."

Belrotha, who'd retained *just* enough presence of mind to pause long enough for the kobold to clear her path, was unyielding as an avalanche when she finally slammed into Gimmol's slayer. And all the strength in the world didn't make Bekay any *heavier*.

A length of the bar disintegrated as the stampede of two crashed through it, through the barrels and bottles behind it, even partly through the back wall. Blood and alcohol spilled over them from a dozen decanters and a hundred lacerations.

The rotted-meat stench of her hot breath blasting Bekay's face, Belrotha wrapped her arms around his chest and heaved. His feet left the floor; his ribs creaked audibly beneath the pressure; he gasped raggedly, struggling to regain the breath her charge had knocked from him. Over and over, he drove his good fist into Belrotha's head and neck. Cartilage cracked as her nose flattened and spread across her face; teeth fell from their sockets; bruises formed across her collarbones, outlining sharp-edged fractures. Cræosh and Gork, Katim and the newly risen Jhurpess, flinched in sympathy with every blow. And still Belrotha would not let go, seemingly oblivious to the damage he was doing her.

For what felt like minutes but must have been the span of only a few breaths, she seemed confused, as though unsure what to do with him now that she had him. And then, a final roar sent beads of blood-flecked saliva across Bekay's face. He tensed, clearly prepared to be dashed to the floor, or squeezed until he broke, rallying his strength for a final effort.

Belrotha did none of these. Belrotha craned her head forward and ripped through his jugular with her rotten, blackened teeth.

Her head vanished entirely into the eruption of crimson bursting around her lips. Bekay's sandaled feet kicked in a gruesome dance, and then the mightiest warrior in a dozen kingdoms went finally limp. For some minutes, Belrotha clung to the body, savaging the ruined throat, squeezing the ribs until the entire torso resembled a mealy apple. Only then did some light of sanity begin to shine through the mask of blood, and she allowed the corpse to slither noisily from her arms.

Cræosh, uncomfortably aware that he had played a smaller role in this battle than perhaps he ought, gave the body a few solid kicks, luxuriating in the sharp sounds as the last surviving ribs snapped. No one else appeared at all impressed, though, and after one last kick for good measure, he reluctantly turned his attention to the tavern's *other* corpse.

Slowly—even, Cræosh would have said if he wasn't sure he knew better, *respectfully*—Katim and Jhurpess lifted the broken body of the gremlin from the debris of the shattered tables. His empty eyes were wide, glassy; his head flopped obscenely as they carried him. But for the first time since Cræosh had met the brightly clad gremlin, so many weeks ago in an overgrown courtyard in Timas Khoreth, the nervous squint was gone from his face. Gimmol—terrified of failing his companions, failing in his duties, more than he'd ever been of the enemy—was terrified no longer.

And never, not once, had he failed them.

His footsteps crunching in the detritus, the orc approached the surviving length of bar on which they'd lain the body. As gently as he knew how, Cræosh placed a hand on Gimmol's shoulder. "Ancestors and Stars watch over you, Strawberry." He grinned weakly. "You did good for a little turd." It was as affectionate as he could get; he was pretty sure that, somewhere, the gremlin understood.

He glanced over, puzzled, as Katim began tearing the monk's garb from the small shape. "This is not who . . . he was," she said, holding the robe up for inspection and then tossing it aside. She gestured at the brightly hued armor that waited beneath the drab cloth. "If he is to remain . . . here, so many miles from his . . . home, let it be as his . . . true self."

Stunned, Cræosh could only nod. He couldn't begin to guess if she meant what she said, or if she was just going along for the sake of the others, but either way it was the most respectful thing he'd ever heard her say about anyone she wasn't planning to enslave in the afterlife.

Jhurpess limped up next, still slightly doubled over. For a long while he hesitated, staring at the brilliant red that had come near to getting Gimmol killed the first time they met. Timidly, he stretched out a hand and laid it, briefly but firmly, upon the gremlin's chest. Then, his eyes downcast, he stepped away.

And finally, Belrotha. Tears streamed openly down her face, washing furrows into the blood that clung to her cheeks, and she made no move to wipe them off. A sob racked her heavy frame, and a single tear flung itself from her chin to land glistening on Gimmol's cheek.

With a shaking hand, she drew a tiny, thin-bladed knife from the back of her belt. Made, to all appearances, from a random scrap of metal, crudely heated and beaten into something resembling a blade, it could only be meant as a tool, not a weapon.

"Him always sit on shoulder," Belrotha told them, her voice quavering. "Him say it a better way to see the world, than to always look up." With the knife held tightly between her fingers, she reached down and carefully removed both of Gimmol's eyes. She then pressed his lids shut, hiding the empty sockets from the world. "Him always travel with me now," she declared, solemnly swallowing first one mushy orb, then the other. "And maybe him watch over me . . ." Her voice cracked, and the tears flowed once more. "Even though me could not watch over him!" Belrotha wailed once and then collapsed in the corner and wept.

For a time, the silence of the tavern was broken only by the ogre's wrenching sobs and the occasional shout filtering in from the street. Cræosh stared into space, unsure of what to do next. They couldn't stay much longer. Obviously, word had gotten around that Bekay had usurped the tavern for his own use, but sooner or later, someone who hadn't heard was going to pop by for a tankard. The warrior's body had to be "displayed" by then, and they had to be gone. Nor could they just leave Gimmol's body; bad enough to have a murderer loose in the city, but if the authorities learned of a goblin presence, they'd crack down *hard*.

Now if he could just find politic means—by which he meant "non-suicidal"—of convincing Belrotha that they had to move on. . . .

And the Ancestors, blessed be their names, provided.

"Kuren?" From the front door, creaking slowly open, rang a melodic voice, its notes made sour by worry and grief. "Kuren, we heard about Thomas. Are you . . . ?"

It was somehow awkward, that shared moment of stunned immobility as everyone took in the sight of everyone else. The newcomer, as tall as Katim but far more slender, boasted revoltingly lush locks of golden-brown hair, irises to shame the deepest ocean, intricately embroidered leathers, upswept ears, and a recurved bow strapped to his back. Thanks to Havarren's descriptions, he might as well have been wearing a six-foot tapestry embroidered with "Erris Brookwhisper"—but even had his identity not been obvious, the goblins would have demanded his bloody death on aesthetic principles alone.

"Do you fucking mind?" Cræosh snarled at him. "We're in the middle of a funeral!"

Brookwhisper, to his credit, was fast. He'd almost gotten his bow unslung when his efforts were interrupted by a loud *twang*. His obnoxiously deep eyes crossed as he struggled to focus on the primitive but extremely sharp arrow now protruding from the bridge of his nose. One step, a second, and he flopped bonelessly to the floor.

Cræosh glanced first at Kuren Bekay's body, and then back at Brookwhisper's. "Not that I'm complaining," he said, "but that was somehow anticlimactic."

"Convenient, though," Katim pointed out.

"It was that." The orc shrugged philosophically, then offered Jhurpess a grin. "Nice shot."

"Jhurpess thanks you," the bugbear replied, raising his own bow in a half-salute. "What squad going to do now?"

"Hmm . . . We should string the bodies up there, and, uh, *there*." Then, when nobody objected, he approached the ogre in the corner, ready to run at half a second's notice. "Belrotha, we can't take Gimmol with us. There's just no way to hide him."

"Me know," she sniffed. "Him have to stay."

"We can't just leave him, either," the orc clarified. "We can't let the humans know we're here."

"What you want to do?" she asked suspiciously.

"We're gonna have to burn the place down," Cræosh said.

For a moment, Belrotha pondered that, then nodded. "Him would be okay with that."

"Cræosh?" Katim asked. "If we burn . . . the tavern, we'll destroy the other . . . bodies as well."

"I know. That's why I want them as obvious as possible. I figure if we put Gimmol in the back, behind the bar, and then start the fire *there*, it'll take a while to engulf the whole room. A few people will have seen the other bodies by then, if only when they run in to see what the smoke's about."

The troll's nose wrinkled in distaste.

"I don't like it either," he said, "but I don't see that we have much of a choice."

"I'm not real good at hauling corpses around," Gork piped up. "I'll take care of getting the fire ready to go." He glanced briefly toward one of the parchment windows. "It's too bad the surrounding buildings are mostly stone," he commented absently. "It'd be nice to take the whole neighborhood along with the tavern. Ah, well . . ."

The kobold sauntered toward what was left of the bar, ignoring the sounds of dragging, cutting, sawing, ripping, heaving, and hammering (mostly in that order). He expertly surveyed the jugs and carafes that had survived the battle unbroken, hopped up onto a rickety stool, and selected a wide assortment. These he poured in a shallow layer across the bar, the floor, and Gimmol's body. Every scrap of loose wood from the broken tables and chairs he placed strategically throughout the spreading alcohol. To this he added a pile of rags he found tucked behind the bar (presumably kept for washing the glasses on what, judging by the encrusted scunge, must be a monthly basis at best).

"Ready when you are, Cræosh," he called.

"Just about, Shorty. Just one more coil . . . there!" Cræosh meandered over to stand beside the kobold.

"You've got to drape the intestines just so," he commented critically, "or they just slide off and land in a heap on the floor." He tilted his head, examining their handiwork. "Does it look to you like we nailed Bekay's right hand a little crooked?"

"It looks fine, Cræosh."

"I suppose so." The orc sighed. "There's never enough time to do a really good job with these things."

"Cræosh . . ."

"All right, all right. Don't get your testicles in a clinch." Carefully checking his robe for any rents and tears too large to be easily hidden, the orc raised his hood and moved to join the others, who were already shuffling through the door. "You coming, Shorty?"

"Just let me kick over the anthill."

Cræosh nodded and slipped out.

His snout burning as the vapors of the alcohol permeated the air around him, Gork stood beside the gremlin whom he'd spent months tormenting. The gremlin who'd then saved all their lives more than once—well, who'd saved *Gork's* life, since Gork wasn't so concerned with the others—using a power with which he could easily have slain Gork a dozen times over, had he chosen to do so.

Ignoring the frightened seconds as they skittered away, the kobold turned to search the wreckage behind him. It took only a moment to find what he sought; he'd a pretty good idea of where it had fallen, after all.

As gently as he'd ever filched a coin purse, Gork lifted Gimmol's stupid-looking porkpie hat from beneath a jagged table leg. The feather was creased sharply across the middle, and try as he might, Gork couldn't make it straighten out. Giving that up as a lost cause, he ran his hands over the hat itself, shaking the dust and splinters from it as thoroughly as he could. And then he placed it, ever so slightly crooked, atop the gremlin's head.

The night air was already redolent with smoke, made pungent by the sharp tang of alcohol and the disturbingly appetizing aroma of roasting meats. From his new vantage atop a nearby baker's—a perch easily enough obtained, despite the encumbering robe—Gork watched not only the growing flicker of his handiwork, but also those others who watched it.

Heads were beginning to pop through various windows, and running footsteps could be heard in the nearest side streets. A few quick-thinking souls were shouting for their neighbors to form a bucket brigade, and already one brave citizen had torn a hole through one of the parchment windows and begun to scream at what he saw within.

And of course, there was the rest of the squad, huddled once more in that alley. Expression and identity were difficult to determine from above, thanks to the thick hoods, but their postures and gestures suggested that they watched the growing conflagration with some concern. Gork briefly considered waiting to see how long it would take for one of them to go look for him—but he quickly decided that he didn't want to know, since it was entirely possible they'd never bother. Instead, he pried a chunk of shingle from the roof and winged it into the alleyway, smirking as it careened off the orc's head. Four gaping hoods tilted his way, and he waved.

Cræosh's return gesture was somewhat more crude.

"You may want to get out of that alley," the kobold called in a loud whisper. "It's going to get pretty smoky, and I think we want to be gone before it gets too crowded.

"I'm going to take a look around from up here," he continued. "I'll catch up in a few minutes."

The robed procession ambled into the street, skirting the edges of the throng that was already forming around the edges of what had been the Capering Kobold.

The *non*-capering kobold flinched as a contingent of the city watch came running along the street, then forced himself to relax. They'd never spot him way up here, and they'd probably be fixated enough on the building, spitting flames like a stuttering dragon, so as not to notice the others, either. And even if they did, the disguises should hold up for a little longer. Hopefully . . .

Ignoring them for the moment, then, Gork scanned the rest of the gathering crowd. The ugly man there, wringing his hands and pleading with the guards in almost eunuch-high tones to do *something*, was probably the owner of this not-so-fine establishment. Nothing of import there. Wait, that man there in the back! Was . . . ? No, he was nobody. Just a tall, thin human who bore a passing resemblance to Nurien Ebonwind. (Gork remained a tad jittery at the thought of the dakórren coming back for revenge.) And there . . . Oh, yes.

The flailing arms and strident demands coming from the witness who'd peered in through the tavern's window had finally managed to divert one of the guards from the fire. Gork watched the soldier's expression ripen from aggravated impatience, through disbelief, to utter horror; saw his cheeks go white even in the ruddy glow of the burning building. The kobold couldn't hear a word, but he knew very well what the witness was describing.

The guard, in turn, went to fetch his commanding officer from farther along the street, and Gork scrambled over the rooftop, desperate to worm his way near enough to hear. Again, fortune and the Stars smiled upon him, for against the noise of the crowd and the flaming timbers, the guard had to shout at his captain to make himself heard. The lurking goblin couldn't make out *everything* that was said, but he heard enough.

He heard the captain tell his subordinate something that sounded an awful lot like "You'd better go tell her."

Unless Gork was woefully mistaken as to who "her" must be, their final target was within their grasp. Practically galloping on all fours, he crossed the roof's deep shadows once again, cursing with every gasp of exertion. He had to tell the others, let them know what was going on, and get back before the messenger was too far gone to tail.

At the far end of the roof—the near end of the roof? *Oh, Stars blast it all, the* squad *end of the roof!*—Gork saw his companions shuffling slowly away, only a few buildings along, determined not to draw attention. Determined, but unsuccessful. Another of the city guards, her hands clasped on the bucket she'd just emptied with a steaming hiss onto the fire, was scrutinizing the "monks" with undisguised suspicion. She, then, turned to the nearest members of her squad, muttering and pointing.

And Gork's memory began whispering in the back of his mind, placing her among the guards who had appeared at the temple after Father Thomas's murder. Again the kobold cursed, louder and longer;

someone was finally doing the math and coming up with "monks" for an answer. The soldiers—who, despite their best efforts, could really do precious little good until the fire-wagon arrived with its larger barrels—laid their buckets on the ground and advanced, hands on hilts.

Gork, running dolefully short on any better ideas, yanked another, heavier shingle from the roof. He cocked his arm back and threw, his entire body snapping like a mangonel. The tiny projectile sailed down the street and completely missed its target (the orc's head again, naturally), but its impact against the cobblestones did the trick anyway. Cræosh and the others spun, seeking the object's source, and saw instead the team of guards headed their way.

"You there!" one of them called, realizing they'd been seen. "Halt!"

The squad, of course, declined. All pretense of stealth and subtlety abandoned, they charged headlong for the nearest intersection, half a dozen of Brenald's finest in hot pursuit.

Scowling, Gork returned to his own pursuit, hoping it wasn't already too late for him to catch up with the other soldier—and hoping, as well, that Cræosh or Katim would remember where they were supposed to meet.

Because dammit, if he had to spend days tracking them down through this stinking, aggravating, *human* cesspool of a city, then by the Stars he was going to take it out on somebody's organs!

The "monks" dashed past startled passersby, ignoring shocked and puzzled glowers, shoving the slow-moving from their path or deliberately knocking them prone to entangle the legs of the pursuing soldiers. But this was no blind, panicky flight, for all its chaos. Cræosh wasn't running *from*, but *to*, if only he could find what he needed in this city he didn't know. . . .

There! Grinning beneath his hood, the orc led his companions around the rough corner of a dilapidated warehouse. As he'd surmised from the road, they found themselves in a cul-de-sac, really little more than a wide alley with a wall at the far end. They'd cornered themselves, yes, but more importantly, they'd also stepped out of sight of the city's citizens.

The guards pounded around the corner, weapons drawn to meet

what must surely be the final stand of cornered, desperate fugitives. These were Brenald's finest, expertly trained, and they outnumbered the enemy six to four.

They never stood a chance. The last one died, Katim's *chirrusk* buried in his throat, before the first, his head mashed to paste by Jhurpess's club, had even ceased twitching.

"That was fun." Cræosh said.

"But dangerous," Katim pointed out. "This city's . . . already lost three of its most . . . hallowed citizens. And now an entire . . . patrol of the watch as . . . well. If we keep this . . . up, we'll have the entire city . . . locked down before we can get . . . out."

"True," the orc admitted. "We need to get this done with, then."

"Are disguises still good?" the bugbear asked, though whether due to real concern or just hoping to shed the uncomfortable cloth was anyone's guess.

"Well . . ." Cræosh nudged an unrecognizable hunk of flesh and muscle with his boot. "The guards who recognized us are, um, indisposed. But there's no telling if any of the others were suspicious, or how quickly news spreads in this fucking human-hive. I'd say as long we don't run into any more guards, or anyone we just tossed out of our way, we're good for a *little* while longer . . . but not much. Let's find Gork."

Find him they did, though it required half an hour of waiting, cursing, waiting, idly scuffling feet, and waiting in the shadows cast behind the ostentatious structure. (Clearly designed to impress anyone passing through the front gate—that was why it had stood out, why Cræosh had picked it when they first arrived—it was probably a city office of some sort, though the goblins never did find out for certain. Regardless of its intended purpose, it served well as a conspicuous landmark for visitors lost in Brenald's winding streets.)

"Took you fucking long enough," Cræosh barked as Gork finally materialized from the darkness.

"Gee, I'm ever so sorry, Cræosh," the kobold replied. "Next time I'll only follow the target *half* the way. I mean, that's close enough, right?"

"Okay, fine," the orc said, somewhat grudgingly acknowledging that Gork probably had a point. "And you're sure it was her?"

"Unless the guard had reason to visit some *other* scar-faced redhead and report what'd happened to Brookwhisper and Bekay."

"So where is she?"

"Home," Gork said simply. "Or it's *someone's* home, anyway. It's a stone house on a hill at the outskirts of the city."

"City has a skirt?" Belrotha asked.

Gork sighed. "Outskirts," he explained slowly, through clenched teeth. "It means the very edges of the city."

"Oh. Me understand."

"I'm *so* glad."

"Gimmol would explain to me nicer, though," she said with a loud sniff.

Cræosh distracted the kobold with a light cuff on the shoulder before he could retort. *I really hope he's fucking smart enough to watch his mouth around her.* If Gork made even one disparaging comment about Gimmol where Belrotha could hear him, Cræosh planned to wash his hands of the whole situation and just try to avoid the blood as he dove for cover.

"Just how far out are we talking about?" the orc asked. "'Far out' as in no neighbors?"

"A few," Gork corrected, his brow and muzzle wrinkling as he envisioned the area. "But none on the hill itself. It's a really big property, far bigger than the house warrants, actually. Guess she really does love her some natural surroundings. Neighbors *could* see something amiss, but they'd have to be looking up and making a point of it."

"Well, that's a help," Cræosh muttered, his brow creased in thought.

"It also," Katim pointed out, "means that anyone . . . in that house is probably . . . going to see us coming."

Cræosh shook his head. "I was sort of hoping to hold off until later. Maybe after midnight, make sure everyone's good and asleep."

"No," Gork said firmly. "Cræosh, it took me over an hour to make my way back here through those damn streets. Kobolds don't build in straight lines, but that's because we have to make do with caverns. I don't know what the humans' excuse is.

"But the point is, I can't swear to you she's even at home *now*, let alone where she'll be in a few hours. If she decides to hunt down whoever killed her friends, or if she realizes she's the next target—and I sort of got the impression from Havarren that she's not a complete moron—there's no guarantee she'll wait till morning before going Stars-know-where."

Cræosh chewed his tongue. "All right, you're making sense for some reason. Don't know what the fuck this world is coming to, but there it is. We'll go now."

Again they marched at a stately pace, arms crossed piously before them and heads bobbing to a rhythm only they could hear.

"You can get us there without taking us back past the Capering Kobold, I hope?" Cræosh asked. "I'd rather not run into anyone who remembers the jogging monks."

"Relax, Pork-face. We don't have to get anywhere near there."

"Pork-face?"

"What I want to know," Gork continued, "is how we're planning to get her out of this damn city, if and when we do manage to grab her."

"Yeah, well . . ." Cræosh hedged.

"Actually," Katim rasped from behind, her robe bulging as she talked, "I believe I have . . . an idea about that. . . ."

"What do you think, Gork?" Cræosh asked once Katim had spoken (and rasped) her piece. "Anyplace on the way you can grab the gear?"

"Quite a few," Gork said. "We'll have to make a detour to get the bodies, though."

Cræosh shrugged. "Unless someone happened to wander in, the guards should still be in the alley where we dumped 'em. We'll have to get a little closer to the Capering Kobold than I'd prefer, but I think we can pull it off."

"Then let's pick up the pace a little," Gork whispered. "There's a lot to do. And Cræosh?"

"Yeah?"

"The tavern is gone. We burned it down. So stop looking for excuses to say the damned name, would you?"

They stood now at the base of the shallow hill, gathered alongside the property's fence line. Streetlamps flickered at every nearby intersection, but the pockets of shadow were more than thick enough to hide in. Stacked at their feet were several man-sized bundles, just beginning to smell.

"If Havarren's to be believed," Cræosh muttered, his tone indicating quite clearly what he thought of *that* idea, "this one's supposed to be more dangerous than any of her companions."

"Yeah," Gork said, somewhat less than enthusiastically. "Great." Both were clearly thinking of Bekay and Gimmol, though neither spoke either name. If Lirimas was worse . . .

"I never in my whole fucking life ever thought I'd say this," the orc said, "but I think I've had enough fighting for the day. Anybody got any bright ideas as to how we ought to go about doing this?"

"Jhurpess could set the house on fire," the bugbear offered. "Squad could wait outside and hit Lirimas on the head as Lirimas comes out."

"You know something, Nature-boy?" Cræosh said. "You've got an unhealthy obsession with fire for someone as flammable as you are."

"It may not, however, be such . . . a bad idea," Katim pointed out.

"Uh, hello? Dog-breath? That's a *stone house*."

"The tavern was stone, too. The . . . furnishings inside still burned well . . . enough, yes?"

"Maybe." Cræosh was clearly unconvinced. "But we did that from *inside*, and we had time to work. You're talking about doing it from out here, and fast enough that she's got no time to react except to run. There's a word for this kind of plan, and it ain't fit for polite company."

"When has that ever stopped you?" Gork asked.

"Couldn't tell you. Near as I can figure, I've never been in polite company."

"Cræosh . . ." Katim warned, gesturing toward the moon as it sailed slowly across its sea of clouds and stars.

"All right, all right. I suppose I haven't got any better ideas. I still think this one is bloody fucking stupid, mind you. I just can't think of anything less so. Gork, make a quick circle of the house and find out—"

"Did it when I was here before, Cræosh. Two doors: one on the north wall and a smaller one leading into what looks to be a vegetable garden on the south. Four windows big enough for a small human to climb through, one on each side." He shrugged. "It's a pretty simple design, really. If it weren't built of stone, on a property big enough for a small manor, I'd call it a cottage more than a house."

Belrotha frowned in concentration, one finger of her right hand counting the fingertips of her left. "That . . . one, two, three, four, five, uh, six exits. There am only, uh, five of us."

"The ogre," Cræosh remarked, "actually has a point."

"Besides the one on top of her head?" Gork asked. Then, quickly raising his hands, "Okay, okay, don't get snippy. The window in front is right beside the door. One of us—one of the larger of us—can probably cover them both."

Cræosh nodded. "Belrotha, that'll be your job."

The ogre shook her head. "Me not as big as me supposed to be. Me not know if me can cover door and window together."

For a moment, the orc repressed the need to squeeze his head, fighting back the incipient headache. "Belrotha, you *do* understand that I mean to watch them both and knock Lirimas on her head if she tries to come out, and not to *literally* cover the door and window, right?"

"Oh. Yeah, me can do that."

Yep. Headache. "Katim, east window. Jhurpess, west. Shorty and I'll take the door and the window in the garden. Any complaints?"

"Yes," Katim said. "There a great many more . . . fleas this far south than there . . . are in Kirol Syrreth. I find . . . especially given the irritation caused by . . . these heavy robes . . . that the fleas are . . ." She broke off at the look that had fallen over the orc's face. "Yes? Was there . . . something?"

Cræosh's jaw twitched.

"Ah. You meant complaints regarding . . . our upcoming endeavor. No, it . . . all looks fine to me."

Twitch.

"You might wish to have that . . . examined by a healer when we return . . . home," the troll suggested. "Gork's eyelid was doing that earlier . . . in the day. Perhaps it's . . . contagious."

Cræosh, who was beginning to regret having ever developed language skills, retrieved his sword, a skin of oil, and an unlit torch from the squad's newly augmented supplies. The others quickly followed suit, each pretending not to notice the self-satisfied chuckle floating softly from beneath Katim's hood.

Cræosh, scowling in contemplation, sat atop the eastern slope of the small hill and looked out over the twinkling lights that were the night-time city below. Absently, he clenched his left fist around a ragged gash on his right bicep, efficiently bandaged but throbbing angrily. *The bitch was fucking* fast, *gotta give her that.*

"You seem remarkably cranky, all things considered," Gork said from his usual nowhere, dropping down to sit beside the glowering orc. "What's your problem now?"

"It was . . . Well, it was too easy," Cræosh said slowly, trying to corral his jumbled thoughts into some kind of order. "I mean, okay, so she was no pushover." He flexed his injured arm in testimony, "but shit, Bekay was a lot worse."

"Cræosh, Jhurpess hit her on the head when she dived out the window. That club's enough to loosen a constipated dragon; of *course* it slowed her down!"

"Yeah, maybe." The orc didn't seem convinced.

Gork's eyes suddenly flashed, nearly as bright as the torches below. "I know what this is about," he said abruptly. "You're just pissed that the plan worked! You thought it was stupid, and you're angry that we pulled it off!"

"No," Cræosh said then—though, to his credit, he'd taken a moment to think about it. "No, not pissed. Worried."

"Worried? About what? The plan worked!"

"*That's* what bothers me. It worked. Totally, completely, one hundred percent, went off without a fucking hitch. One of *our* plans. Without a single fuck-up." Cræosh shook his head. "It ain't natural, Shorty."

"Stars," Gork exclaimed, bouncing to his feet. "I thought *I* was paranoid! Come on, Cræosh, we've still got to get her, and us, past the walls and all the way back home. There's plenty of time to screw up if you really want to."

"Put that way," Cræosh said, also rising, "maybe I can do *without* the usual fuck-up."

"I thought you might."

"Just this once, though. Don't let it become a habit."

Gork grinned. "Us? Fat chance of that."

"If you two are finished . . . playing," Katim called from around the corner of the (smoldering) stone house, "we're ready."

"Keep your tits in a row, Dog-breath! We're coming."

They found the others in the midst of the vegetable garden, along with their parcel. Lirimas, her hideously scarred face now a mask of bruises, was trussed up with more knots than you'd find on a two-masted galleon. Hands and ankles had each been tied together, and then to each other, and then both to the prisoner's neck, bending her back like Jhurpess's bow. A wadded rag, tied with string, made an effective gag. She'd then been wrapped in a second layer of rope, an amorous constrictor coiled around her entire body, and on top of *that*, she was covered with a number of bedsheets. (The linen closet, thankfully, had been closed up and hadn't suffered unduly from the sudden rain of burning oil that drove Lirimas outside.) No *way* was their prize escaping them at *this* stage of the game!

Of course, there remained the issue of getting her out of the city and on the road to the Iron Keep. *Boy, the fun never stops.*

"Wheelbarrow?" Cræosh asked.

"It here," Belrotha told him, gesturing behind her.

Cræosh eyed it warily. "Couldn't you have found a bigger one, Shorty?"

The kobold snorted. "These are humans we're talking about. Their wheelbarrows don't come much larger than this. It'll do."

Working together, Cræosh and Belrotha pulled aside the tarp that hid the bodies of the six dead guardsmen and then lifted a few of the bodies themselves. Katim and Gork carefully rearranged those that remained, leaving a faint hollow. The unconscious prisoner—after Katim gave her an extra whack on the head to ensure she stayed that way—they dumped atop the heap, and then swiftly replaced the bodies they'd just moved. Arms and legs spilled haphazardly over the sides, and the uppermost corpse wobbled dangerously each time the wheelbarrow moved.

"This isn't going to work," Cræosh groused.

Gork grimaced up at him. "You're such a pessimist. I told you before, people don't look hard unless you give them reason to."

"And a night of murders and fires isn't reason to?"

"Oh, give it a rest. It'll be fine."

"Yeah, we'll have plenty of time to rest when they throw us all in—"

Katim's fist slammed down between them, emphasized by the crack of bone. Had the guardsman not already had bigger problems, such as being dead, that leg would never have been the same again.

"Let's just *go!*" she spat through grinding fangs. "Unless . . . you *want* to prove yourself right by . . . getting caught?"

And since no one really had a better option, they went. Trusting one last time to their increasingly worn disguises, they shuffled down the hill and onto the main streets. Cræosh and Belrotha pulled the wheelbarrow awkwardly behind them. Gork led the procession, a lit torch in one hand, a tiny bell he'd picked up from Ancestors-knew-where in the other. Every minute or so he'd chime it softly, announcing their presence without disturbing the majority of citizens who had already taken to their beds.

"Are you sure you know where the fuck you're going?" Cræosh hissed.

Gork sighed. "For the hundredth time, yes! I saw a cemetery off this way when I was following the guard."

"This isn't gonna work," the orc muttered again.

"Why are you so damn paranoid about this?"

"Because our *last* plan went off perfectly! Now we've got twice the bad luck waiting for us!"

Gork shook his head, rang his bell, and kept walking.

Late as it was, a city the size of Brenald was certain to have something of a nightlife. Here and there on the otherwise vacant streets, small groups paused in the midst of their own nocturnal wanderings to watch the passing procession. As before, Cræosh was certain that one of them would sound an alarm at any moment, that the entire watch would come crashing down on the squad's head like . . . like a head-crashing thing. (Cræosh was tired, and more than a little jittery, and can perhaps be excused for lacking the mental wherewithal to formulate an appropriate metaphor.) But though their expressions were often puzzled, every citizen stepped aside, bowing or tipping a hat, when the streetlights revealed to them the sad contents of the wheelbarrow. Some recognized bits of armor and saluted the fallen soldiers; others were, perhaps, merely offering respect to the recent dead on the way to their eternal sleep.

And so, ever more apprehensively, they continued. The wheels of the pushcart clattered over every nook in the road, announcing their presence far more loudly than the kobold's tiny bell. The bodies, just starting to ripen, poked at their nostrils with tiny daggers of scent. Limbs flopped about, smacking Cræosh or Belrotha in the arm, doing even more damage to already frazzled nerves. By the time the cemetery gates hove into view, most of them would have happily traded places with those bodies in exchange for a few hours' relaxation.

"See?" Gork chided, perhaps a bit louder than he needed to. "What did I tell you? There it is."

And even better, like so many graveyards, it bordered the outermost wall of the city. They should finally be able to get the hell out of this wretched place unimpeded, since any potential witnesses were already premurdered.

They'd passed beyond the more traditional tombstones, woven their way between most of the aboveground mausoleums of the rich and powerful—trying not to notice how much some of the gothic statuettes atop them resembled the late and unlamented Shreckt—when their hopes of an easy escape were firmly planted in a grave of their own.

"Hey!"

As one, the entire squad craned their necks upward, though not so high that their hoods might fall off.

"Yes?" Gork asked politely.

A lone sentry peered at them from atop the outer wall, crossbow cradled low but steady in his hands. "What are you doing in the graveyard after dark?"

Cræosh began to curse in a very unecclesiastical manner. Gork stepped back and "accidentally" trod on the orc's foot. "We are strangers to your city, good sir!" he called up. "We just wished to do our part to help."

"Help? Help with . . ." They could hear a faint creaking as his hand tightened around the stock of his weapon. "Are those dead *guards* in that wheelbarrow?"

"Yes, sir," Gork said, making no attempt to sidestep the issue. "They were found, brutally murdered, in an alleyway this afternoon. I am afraid, what with the tragedy that has recently befallen your heroes, that these brave souls would have been forgotten amid the chaos. Though my brethren and I do not know Brenald that well, we recognized that these good men should not be left to the mercy of the elements. Thus, with the blessings of the church, we took it upon ourselves to transport them here, to their final rest, while the city deals with more weighty matters."

Even before the kobold finished, the watchman's face clearly signaled his utter lack of credulity. Cræosh, who was furiously wishing that this sword and the other weapons were somewhere more accessible than wrapped in Belrotha's satchel, allowed one hand to drop casually into the wheelbarrow. The soldiers' swords wouldn't prove all that accurate at a distance—javelins they most assuredly were not—but he had nothing else to hand. . . .

"So how come," the guard challenged, "I haven't heard a damn thing about this?"

"My good man," Gork said, his tone tightening, "I certainly wouldn't know. Perhaps, out here at this lonely post, the word simply hasn't reached—"

The crossbow rose, the heavy bolt now aimed squarely into the darkness of the kobold's hood. Cræosh was sure that he could actually *hear* Gork start to sweat.

"I just went on duty a half hour ago, friend," the guard said coldly. "I should have heard about this. I think we're going to have to get to the bottom of this before anyone proceeds any further."

"But sir—"

"Shut up! I—"

Throwing caution to the winds—after all, it wasn't *his* face sitting in the path of the bolt—Cræosh yanked the narrow sword from beneath the corpse of its owner, hauling back for a desperate throw.

Someone beat him to it. Jhurpess took to the air, bouncing first from the edge of the wheelbarrow with a dull clang, then from the roof of the nearest mausoleum, and then he was near enough the top of the wall for his lanky arms to haul him over. The crossbow thrummed, but the startled guard had started back; the bolt hurtled over Gork's head, rather than through it. The human drew a single, croaking gasp before Jhurpess reached out with two broad hands and snapped his neck.

The bugbear caught the body as it fell, then dropped into a crouch, lowering the guard carefully to the pathway atop the wall. His robe bunched and twisted as he swept for any further foes.

None yet, no, but soon. Quiet the altercation had been, but not *silent.*

"Could you have cut that just a bit closer?" Gork ranted up at him, his voice hovering just below an actual shout. "I have enough holes in my face already, dammit! I don't need any new ones!"

"It was perfectly safe, Shorty," Cræosh answered on Jhurpess's behalf.

"Safe? How the fuck was it safe? The man had a crossbow aimed up my nose!"

"Yeah, but I was fairly sure he was gonna miss *me*," Cræosh said sardonically.

"*What?*"

"Jhurpess sure, too," from above.

"Why you lumbering behemoths, I—!"

"Alec? Alec, you over there?"

The entire squad froze, Gork's mouth hanging open in mid-diatribe. They had *maybe* a minute before the rest of the patrol came into view, not enough time for them all to clear the wall—certainly not while lugging a captive.

"Jhurpess!" Katim scurried forward, tossing the bugbear one of their coils of rope. "Leave it hanging on . . . the *outside* of the wall! Dump the . . . body next to it and get . . . back down here! Belrotha! Get the prisoner . . . out of the wheelbarrow! Gork!" She pointed one taloned digit. "Get that . . . door open! Your way, not . . . mine."

Gork followed her finger and nodded, perhaps in sudden understanding. Cræosh, who did *not* understand, could only count heartbeats as the squad rushed to do the troll's bidding, and pray to the Ancestors that she knew what she was doing.

The citizens of Brenald were up in arms, the commander of the city watch was forced to resign (and to go into hiding, lest he find himself lynched), but they never did catch the blackguards responsible for the horrors of that night. The guards had handily spotted the dangling rope, and the corpse lying just outside the wall. Instantly they'd mobilized, scouring the roads, the woods, *everywhere* for the fleeing fugitives. They seized every wagon, searched every farmhouse, beat every bush, even climbed every tree, within *hours* of the wall. Nothing.

They found the wheelbarrow of corpses, of course (though it contained only four; the other two guards were never found, and presumed lost somewhere in the city's back alleys). Between that, and the tales told by various soldiers and citizens, the authorities recognized that the assassins had moved through town disguised as monks and had used the bodies as cover to make their way to the cemetery and escape. The watch conducted a search of Brenald itself, in case the murderers had accomplices, but since they'd obviously escaped the walls already—the rope and the body were evidence enough of that—it was a cursory effort.

The city's reeve, left in charge in the absence of King Dororam, called for five days of mourning: one for each of the great heroes, and another for the guards who had fallen. Black tunics, black dresses, and black banners transformed the streets of Brenald into a net of darkness. Dirges sounded from street musicians, and tavern owners offered everyone a free drink in honor of the lost (and then, of course, raised the prices on every subsequent drink, turning a healthy profit). Priests read lengthy sermons, but never at the central temple. It was closed for the days of mourning, in honor of Father Thomas.

But finally, on the sixth day, life slowly edged back toward the routine. People dressed normally once again, businesses kept normal hours, and the extra sentries on the walls returned to their normal duties.

And only then did the Demon Squad—who had passed those six hellish days in the cramped, crowded, and rapidly suffocating confines of the graveyard's largest mausoleum, surviving on the flesh of those two missing corpses—emerge from hiding. None of them were speaking, for that was the only way they'd kept from killing each other, and they reeked of decomposing flesh, body odor, spilled blood, urine and feces (they'd used the coffin as a chamber pot), and the vomit of their prisoner, whom they'd had to force feed. They crept out in the middle of the night, sent Gork to scout and make *sure* there were no guards on the wall nearby, and then scurried over another rope and ran as though the ghosts of the men they'd eaten were nipping at their heels.

The following days, though exhausting and not precisely pleasant, proved both uneventful and far more comfortable than being cooped up in that damn crypt. They kept their distance from the main roads; though there were no soldiers to be seen, the entire army having gotten much farther ahead, the highways remained crowded with farmers, merchants, and other wanderers. Cræosh cursed every extra moment their circuitous routes and constant hiding cost them—especially now that, without Gimmol, they had to make the return journey in normal time—but it was better than being torn apart by a mob of angry humans.

Lidia made only a few abortive attempts to escape. Her struggles with her bonds were apparently enough to convince her that they hadn't left her any slack, and a vicious snarl from the troll made it clear that the goblins didn't appreciate her efforts. Twice per day, they loosened her bonds enough for her to choke down a few gulps of water and morsels of food, as well as to relieve herself. Under full guard, of course. Cræosh and the others couldn't give a halfling's ass about human notions of privacy or propriety, but neither were they interested in lugging a captive covered in her own wastes.

Cræosh saw her eyes flicker from Katim to Belrotha a time or two, and wondered if she was going to appeal to them in the name of gender unity and sisterhood. *Yeah, good luck with that.*

The squad forced themselves to maintain a punishing pace, sleeping only a few hours at a stretch, pushing onward even as calves ached, sides split, lungs burned. Day after day after day, until vision went bleary and tempers frayed even shorter than normal—but eventually, with agonizing sluggishness, the Brimstone Mountains began to peek over the horizon ahead.

And still they spotted no sign of even the straggling tail end of Dororam's armies. The orc started to fret, and he actually grew more alert, his fatigue digested by the worry now roiling through his gut.

"We need to start being careful," Cræosh said that afternoon. "We've no fucking clue how the war's going so far, but it looks as though Dororam's already gotten farther than he should have. If we don't run into his men between here and the mountains, you can fucking bet that we'll meet them in the passes. Keep your eyes open."

"Eyes open," Gork said. "Got it. Anything else we should know, or did you want the rest to be a surprise?"

"Gork?"

"Yes?"

"Shut your fucking hole."

The kobold looked innocently around at the others. "Touchy today, isn't he?"

Very deliberately, Belrotha placed one enormous fist over Gork's face. It was a move she'd seen Cræosh pull more than once. Normally, her hand would've enveloped his skull entirely, but since she hadn't resumed her normal size, it was just the proper width for a good, solid grip.

Of course, it was still a long *stronger* than the orc's.

"Me not remember," she said, and Cræosh wouldn't have laid odds on whether she was exaggerating for Gork's benefit, or honestly confused. "Do me lift? Or just squeeze?"

"Mmph! Mpfrm rmf!"

"Actually," Katim observed laconically, "I believe that you've . . . done quite enough."

Belrotha nodded and released her grasp.

"Air!" Gork croaked.

"Are we through now?" Cræosh asked the gasping kobold.

Gork nodded, panting.

"Good. Then let's move." He glanced over at the bundle slung over the ogre's shoulder. "Somebody tighten those ropes."

Another few days, equally miserable and, if anything, even more arduous, finally brought them to the Brimstone Mountains themselves. And there, it became apparent that something was, indeed, very wrong.

Moving carefully, the squad picked their way through mounds of corpses in various states of dismemberment and decay. Humans lay beside orcs, elves beside trolls, each and every one of them the victim of violent death. The Charnel King's troglodytes, ancestral guardians of the mountain passes, were scattered among them, lying where they'd fallen defending their homes. Flies buzzed in swarms thick enough to darken the sun; buzzards circled above in quantities large enough to be considered swarms themselves. The stench made their eyes water and their stomachs heave—this from creatures who had, short weeks before, subsisted on a pair of rotting bodies without hesitation. Katim spun and lunged toward the startled ogre, barely ripping the gag from the captive's mouth in time to prevent her from choking on her own vomit.

Of course, the carnage, although perhaps somewhat more prodigious than they might have anticipated, was only to be expected. What proved far more worrisome was not the presence of the dead within the passes, but the absence of the living. Even had the Allied armies somehow taken the passes swiftly and easily, an unimaginable feat at best, they most assuredly wouldn't have left them unguarded! The Serpent's Pass, as well as the smaller byways, were vital for messengers and supply trains, easy targets for counterattack. The only way anyone could *possibly* justify such a peculiar decision, according to Cræosh's understanding of basic strategies . . .

Was if Kirol Syrreth had already fallen.

"Impossible!" Katim protested when the orc hesitantly explained his assessment. "There's no way the armies . . . could have crossed even a fraction . . . of Kirol Syrreth. They must be . . . *months* from the Sea of Tears!"

"I know that!" Cræosh snapped back at her. "I know how fucking slowly armies move, and how this whole fucking war is supposed to work! I'm just telling you what I see!"

"Watch your tone . . . orc," the troll rumbled, scarcely more than a whisper. "At this stage in our . . . mission, one sword, more or . . . less, will not matter. And one more . . . corpse on the field wouldn't even . . . be noticed."

Steel sang against leather as Cræosh's sword leapt from its scabbard, severing the last feeble strands of his patience. "Now, is it?" he asked, his own voice turned to gravel. "Fine, then. Whenever you're ready."

He never found out if Katim would have backed down or followed through, for Belrotha reached out, lifted a random corpse off the bloodied field—an orc, as it happened, one whose ribs had been caved in by a mace—and used it as a bludgeon to knock the orc and the troll both from their feet. Slowly, gasping for breath and wishing his head would stop ringing, Cræosh dragged himself back up. He was heartened, at least, to see that Katim was moving as hesitantly as he.

"It *not* now!" Belrotha raved, her hands literally waving over her head, the stench of her breath blotting out the surrounding miasma of decay. "Cræosh and Katim want to kill each other, them do it later! Us have other things to do now!"

"Now, look Belrotha—" Cræosh began.

"You shut up!" the ogre yelled, shoving her face so close to Cræosh's own that her broken nose actually slapped against his. The orc recoiled violently. "That better!" She spun and jabbed a finger at the troll. "You not say anything either!" She stepped back, lowering her fists to her hips. "Until us know what happening, you not fight with each other! You not *talk* to each other unless me there to listen! You not listen to me—you try to fight again—me kill you!"

"I think she's serious," Gork muttered to the stunned combatants.

"You shut up too!" Belrotha screamed.

"What? But I didn't do anything!"

"Me not care! Me not like to hear you talk! Shut up!"

Silence fell, broken only by Belrotha's heavy breathing, the caws of startled vultures, and the smacking sounds of Jhurpess, off by himself, chewing experimentally on one of the less rotted bodies.

"What us wait for?" Belrotha finally asked, her voice now empty of any trace of anger. "Us have places to go."

Bewildered expressions on their faces, and tongues clenched firmly between their teeth lest they be tempted to comment, the others followed the ogre north.

"Hey!" Cræosh blinked rapidly, trying to squeeze the light of the dawn and the crust of sleep from his lashes. "You're big!"

Belrotha, who had reached all the way down from her newly restored and *proper* height to nudge the orc awake, sighed loudly. "Yes, me know." She turned to the bugbear, who was waving a chunk of meat vaguely in the direction of their small fire, his only concession to the cooking preferences of the others. "Him not very bright, am he?"

"Jhurpess had noticed that," the bugbear confirmed.

Grumbling, Cræosh rose and wandered off behind a tree to relieve himself before it was time to face the next in an endless parade of really, *really* bad days. He didn't even bother to ask his companions *why* Belrotha was towering over them again, choosing to assume that if someone had cast a spell on them as he slumbered—as opposed to the enchantment on the ogre simply having worn off—they'd get around to telling him eventually.

And then he'd see if he could be bothered enough to care.

The sights hadn't grown any more encouraging as they made their way through the wilds of Kirol Syrreth, and as Cræosh had anticipated, today proved no exception. Columns of smoke, thick and uncountable, stretched from all horizons, bloated worms emerging from a corpse. Grasses and plants were trampled flat, marked by the passage of thousands upon thousands of feet that should never have come this far. What little wildlife remained fled at the slightest disturbance; crops were crushed, burned to the ground, or savagely harvested for use by Dororam's troops.

The squad did detect a few sporadic signs of Kirol Syrreth's defenders. Pieces of black leather armor, boot prints clearly made by the twisted foot of a troll, corpses hacked by heavy orcish blades—all lay strewn across the roads and fields, easily spotted by those who knew what to look for. But only twice did the Demon Squad actually see anyone who might have left such signs, and those fled before the squad could draw near enough to identify themselves.

Far more frequent were their encounters with soldiers of the other side. As well as the goblins knew the territory, they were able to avoid the *bulk* of the invaders. They crept through woodlands, dashed along back roads, waded through shallow streams, or poled scavenged boats through deeper waters. Much as it galled them, they hid from the enemy when they could, ran when they must. On several occasions, circumstances forced them to engage this unit or that patrol, and then they took a tiny sliver of retribution for what had been done to their nation. The battles were swift, vicious affairs, over in less time than it takes to recount—but while the goblins were never in any danger, not against small handfuls of mere humans, each time they picked up just a few more nicks or scratches, earned a few more scars, left behind a few more drops of blood. They dared not even go *near* the major cities or fortresses en route, for all had clearly been overrun and occupied. Days accumulated into weeks, strides built up into miles built up into leagues, and the members of the Demon Squad grew ever more haggard.

"This can't be fucking happening!" It was far from the first time Cræosh had said something similar, since they'd begun creeping and sprinting their way across the massive nation that had once been home; but now, as they stared over yet another burned husk of what had once been a goblin town, he sounded more plaintive than ever. "This isn't a war! It's a fucking rout!"

"The Charnel King's got a plan," Gork insisted, staring nervously at the darkness around them, deliberately looming just beyond the pale ring of light shed by the village's last smoldering fires. "All we've got to do is get to Dendrakis. We'll hand over Lirimas, and things'll turn around. You'll see."

Gork, too, had repeated the sentiment more than once. Cræosh was pretty sure, at this point, that the little kobold was struggling to reassure *himself*, not his companions.

But there came a point, some days later on, where even Gork could no longer pretend.

The squad had been making better time, for they'd stolen a skiff from an occupied fishing village and practically flown along the River Krom. Propelled by the currents and Belrotha's mighty rowing, they were faster than any pursuit the humans could have offered, even had they been spotted. Finally, they were nearing their destination: The Sea of Tears loomed ahead, just beyond the island city of Sularaam.

Or what had been the island city of Sularaam. Now, though the bulk of the homes remained, the larger structures, the temples and government buildings, were as shattered as the central tower of Castle Eldritch.

"It isn't possible," Cræosh insisted once again, but much of the fire had gone from his voice. "Even if they'd been marching *unopposed*, Dororam's army couldn't have made it this far, this quickly. They . . ."

A brief shimmer, visible even in the light of the afternoon sun, flashed across a street near the outer edge of the once-great city. Like a curtain parting, a hole opened in the air itself. Through it rode a small platoon of Dororam's knights, dragging prisoners—human soldiers of Kirol Syrreth, judging by their battle-worn armor—behind them.

"Ancestors," Cræosh whispered. And then, more loudly, "Son of a bitch!"

"They . . . They cheated!" Considering his own proclivities, Gork seemed surprisingly offended by the notion. "They used magic! That's not fair!"

"It makes sense . . . though," Katim rasped, her attentions fixed on the newly arrived soldiers. "King Morthûl was probably . . . prepared to counter any . . . direct threat from duMark and . . . the other mages. But this tactic . . . may have caught him by . . . surprise." She shrugged slightly. "After six hundred years . . . it might become difficult to . . . react to unexpected—"

"No!"

Cræosh and Gork, perhaps remembering the ogre's *last* outburst, took a step back.

"Charnel King not surprised!" Belrotha insisted. "Him know what he doing! Him rule for lots of years!" She shook her head, and her voice grew softer. "Me rule Itho for only few seasons. But that long enough for me to know that nothing ever go right. Everything always changing. Charnel King rule Kirol Syrreth for long time, so him know change."

"The ogre may have a point," Cræosh admitted. "But we're not gonna know either way until we talk to him."

"Then I suggest we move," Gork offered. "Unless you want to hang around here until those soldiers notice us, it's still several days to Dendrakis. Probably longer, since we need to be circumspect. I'm sure Dororam has ships in the water by now."

"And we're going to get . . . a boat from where?" Katim asked. "This skiff wouldn't last . . . an hour on the open sea."

"Same place we always do," Gork said, his fingers twitching slightly. "Wherever we can."

She could see nothing at all, not through the layer of dusty, filth-encrusted sheets in which she was constantly wrapped. Nevertheless, she knew where she was. The jostling of the ship had been replaced by the far more familiar jostling of the ogre's shoulders; the tang of the sea washed away by the more arid scent of the mountains. They must be almost to their destination, and she was damned—possibly literally—if she let herself be taken any farther.

Long, hellish weeks of constant pounding against the ogre's back, of near starvation, of constant thirst had left her a parody of what she had been. But they had also granted her time, plenty of time, to study her captors: their patterns and behaviors, their actions and attitudes. Even better, they'd watched her far less acutely during their days at sea. She wasn't sure if that was because they knew she had nowhere to go, or if they were too busy sailing the vessel and (from what she could hear) being violently ill. Regardless, she'd taken the opportunity to study the ins and outs, the loops and the coils, of the many knots that bound her. And if she was not, now, what she had been, then by all the gods she was still *who* she had been. And Lidia Lirimas, hero of the Allied Kingdoms, was nobody's pawn. Winning free on the isle of Dendrakis was a frightening thought, but far less so than allowing them to carry her to the keep itself.

Her only regret was that, succeed or fail, escape or perish in the attempt, she would be unable to wreak her vengeance on the creatures who had done this to her. But from what she'd overheard, they suffered over what had happened to their lands, and that—at least until she was stronger, until she could hunt them down on her own terms—must suffice.

She waited, flopping loosely within the sheets, slowly working on those many knots, and watched for her chance.

"It's over." No despair, no grief in Cræosh's voice, just simple, matter-of-fact acknowledgment. He no longer possessed the strength for anything more.

"But . . . but . . ." Gork, for the first time in a great while, was truly at a loss for words.

Nobody else spoke, though Belrotha was making a vague strangling noise in the back of her throat. The others stared in silence.

Stared at what had once been the Iron Keep.

Whatever magics duMark and Dororam's other wizards had called from the heavens had surely been beyond anything ever seen, beyond what even the Charnel King was prepared to repel. The wrought iron had become slag beneath the blast of some incomprehensible furnace, hardened into a jagged carpeting across the broken stones. Great pinnacles, the skeletons of towers, jutted from the wreckage. Blackened by smoke and soot, they leaned precariously at impossible angles, held aloft only by the grasp of the hardened iron pooled around their base. A few bits of half-charred furniture poked from the debris here and there; the stench was the unholy progeny of smithy and abattoir.

A pitiful legacy for a demigod who had ruled unchallenged for over half a millennium.

"We're dead," Gork whispered.

"No." Cræosh finally looked up from the ruined keep, the symbol of everything he'd fought for all his life. "No, we've lost the war. We're not dead."

"It's just a matter of degree now," Gork insisted.

"No! You fucking listen to me, you little shit! We're alive! And I don't care how thorough Dororam's armies think they were, genocide ain't easy! There are more of us out there, a lot more! All right, fine! We'll hide, for now. We're going to go find them, and we're going to survive! And if it takes me to the end of fucking time, I'm gonna see Dororam's entire fucking kingdom dead! You got me?"

"Yeah, Cræosh," Gork said, uncaring. "Sure."

"Where did prisoner go?" Jhurpess asked suddenly. And indeed, where Belrotha had dropped her, all unnoticed, at the sight of what was left of the Iron Keep, now remained nothing but a pile of sheets and loose coils of rope.

"Should we bother to hunt her . . . down?" Katim wondered aloud.

The orc scowled. "No point. We need to be gone before any of Dororam's soldiers find us." He looked around, then pointed toward the mountains of Dendrakis. "We can get lost there, find shelter, and plan what happens next."

He'd already turned away when Katim nodded, so he didn't see her eyes, flickering from him to the mountain passes—and the precarious mountain ledges.

Slowly, despondently, their thoughts their own, the goblins of the Demon Squad filed away from the wreckage. All, that is, but one.

Her face twisted in despair, Belrotha couldn't drag herself away, not yet. For long moments, as her companions moved ever farther away, she gawped, uncomprehending, at the mess before her.

They were strong! The Charnel King was strong! They were supposed to win! They *had* to win! It wasn't supposed to end this way!

Belrotha didn't know much, and there were times when she even *recognized* that she didn't know much. But her knowledge of the Dark Lord's power was absolute, her faith in his abilities unshaken. This could not have happened; he would have seen it coming. He *would*! Any minute now, he would appear from the air before her, explain that this was all a part of his master plan. Any minute now . . .

"Belrotha! You coming, or just breathing hard?"

The ogre crashed to her knees. It *was* real. No Charnel King. No plan. No victory. They'd fought for nothing. Gimmol had died for nothing. The ogre dropped her head to her chest in grief, and blinked.

She could have sworn that something *moved*, the iron slag rippling aside like a wake.

Hesitantly, afraid she might get burned or bitten, she reached out. How it had survived the raging inferno, she had no idea, let alone how it had come to her from the midst of the ruins. True, it remained half encased in melted iron, but that was hardly an inconvenience to her. A loud snap, and it had come free in her hand.

She could only gawk at the tarnished silver crown. Had it truly been drawn to her, as she'd imagined, or was it pure, dumb luck that she'd found it? Minds far wiser than Belrotha's would have wondered; she knew only that it had to be a sign.

It had survived, somehow, even where its owner had not. And so had they.

Yes, the Charnel King had failed, but Gimmol hadn't died for him, not really. He'd died for Kirol Syrreth, and Kirol Syrreth would one day rise again.

The crown clenched tightly in her fist, Belrotha rose and scurried after her companions, before she lost them in the distance. Broken rock passed beneath her feet, rocky plains and then the first low foothills to her right and left. But time and again her gaze was drawn away from her surroundings, back to the silver circlet in her palm. Despite the tarnish, despite the clouds, it gleamed; casually, Belrotha wondered if, despite its size, it might not balance on her own head.

Of its own accord, her hand moved upward . . .

From atop the nearest peak, a distance so great that he should never have been able to see them, Vigo Havarren watched the Demon Squad depart the ruins of the Iron Keep. He saw their expressions and heard their conversation. They might, he realized, even have half a chance of surviving. Assuming they didn't kill each other.

Turning his back on the goblins, Havarren reached over and stripped the flesh from his left arm in a single, sudden yank. He sighed blissfully, wiggling his fingers. Hell, he thought he'd *never* escape that stupid man-suit!

He focused, gathering his will as he hadn't done, as he *couldn't* do, for six hundred years. And he laughed, nearly crying tears of genuine joy, as he felt the sudden flare of heat around him and heard once more the musical screams of the damned. All he had to do was step through . . .

His face, still masked behind a facade of mortal flesh, twisted in puzzlement. For just an instant, he'd felt a familiar tug. It was weak, oh so weak, scarcely an echo of the bond that had kept him bound to the undead creature who'd owned Havarren's soul. It certainly wasn't strong enough to hold him any longer, but that he felt it at all was troublesome. With Morthûl gone, the bond should have shattered completely. He should feel *none* of it now, however feebly.

Havarren shrugged, then, the last human gesture he planned to make. Some residual energy left over from the spell, perhaps. They'd been linked for a very long time, after all. It was of no moment, and all the comforts of home awaited him.

With one final glance around him, one final farewell to the planet-sized cage that had held him, the creature that men called Vigo Havarren departed. Nature itself seemed to sigh in relief as the weight of a demon prince was lifted away; and somewhere else, somewhere *deeper*, the damned began to scream just a little louder.

EPILOGUE

Ananias duMark, half-breed, greatest wizard alive and greatest hero of the so-called Goblin War, slammed the door and loosed an audible sigh of relief. If he had to sit through one more flowery, sputtering speech, one more song composed by the "finest minstrels of the land" in tribute to their victory, he was going to either vomit or start turning random passersby into something unpleasant. And probably viscous.

And to think, he would have to endure this every year! Gods in Heaven, enough already! Today was the third anniversary of the Allied Kingdom's defeat of Kirol Syrreth, and to judge by the celebration, you'd think the war had only ended last week. Oh, how these humans could natter on; for such a short-lived species, one would have thought that they'd have shorter attention spans. But every year on this day, duMark was paraded up on a ribbon-festooned podium with King Dororam, his simpering queen, Lidia Lirimas (and gods, what had he *ever* seen in her? Wouldn't shut up about what *she* had suffered through, as though it was somehow *his* fault), and a dozen others. There they forced him to stand for hours on end, waving genially and smiling until his jaw threatened to rip itself off his face. So far he'd managed to mollify his own impatience by picturing himself crushing the whole lot of them underfoot like bugs, but it was getting to the point where his aggravation wouldn't be assuaged by imagination.

He hated to admit it, but he was starting to understand where Morthûl had been coming from. They really weren't much in the grand scheme of things, were they?

Slowly, his back pressed firmly to the door, the half-elf opened his eyes. This had been his house for longer than Dororam had been king of Shauntille. It hadn't changed, not in all that time, but somehow it had never quite felt the same after the end of the Goblin War. That damn Demon Squad had soiled it; no matter that he'd fixed everything back the way it had been, he could never forget what they'd done. A ripple of anger shook the wizard's frame, for not only did this time of year mark their victory, it also commemorated the day he'd learned of the hideous fate that had befallen his companions.

He *had* learned, of course. Had learned how Cræosh and Katim and the rest of those subhuman ruffians had infiltrated his city. Had learned how they'd slaughtered gentle old Thomas, Bekay, and Brookwhisper—though he'd been gladdened to learn that Bekay, at least, had taken one of the foul creatures with him. And he'd learned, too, of Lidia's ordeal, when they'd taken her from this house that they'd thought was hers.

Oh, had he heard about that, over and over.

Those goblin bastards had sullied his victory. Thomas and the others had been heavily associated with him in the minds of the unwashed masses, and loved almost as well as he. That he couldn't protect them from the ravages of Morthûl's slaves had been a fearsome blow to his reputation. Yes, he was most directly responsible for the Allied victory in Kirol Syrreth, and that overshadowed everything else; nevertheless, he couldn't help but wonder if the adulation he received each time he set foot in the streets of Brenald was less than it might have been. *Should* have been.

Nor had the years been kind to his friendship with Dororam. His anger spent, the king had finally permitted himself to grieve for the death of his daughter, and his age had begun to catch up to him since the war's end. To duMark's mind, this was the perfect opportunity to expand the borders of Shauntille, to formally annex the fertile lands of southern Kirol Syrreth. But Dororam had refused to consider it. Kirol Syrreth was free, he'd argued, and would have to find its own way. Shauntille's resources were better spent elsewhere. DuMark had called the king a doddering fool before the royal court, and though they'd publicly reconciled in the months since, it was all for show.

Slowly, the mage sat on the edge of the large, unadorned bed. He sighed again as he took his weight off of feet that had supported him for hours in front of an unending stream of gawking yokels.

"Maybe it's time for some new rulership," he said to the room at large, reaching down to unlace his right boot. It was a habit he'd gotten into over the past years, when he realized there was nobody else particularly worthy of his companionship. He sometimes wished he'd kept Ebonwind's tiny familiar for company. "Dororam's old, set in his ways. He needs to be replaced with someone more . . . dynamic." The half-elf sat up, floppy leather boot clenched in his right fist. "King duMark. The Wizard King. I think I like the sound of that."

"It does have a nice ring . . . to it, doesn't it?"

The world exploded in agony and flashing lights before duMark could so much as turn toward that hideously familiar voice. He felt himself toppling, felt the blood running down the back of his skull, matting his hair into thick layers.

His thoughts began to clear moments later, and he found himself strapped to his favorite chair, hands bound tightly behind him. Even his fingers had been individually tied, each to the next. A heavy pressure rested on his shoulders, and it took him only seconds, focusing through the throbbing pain, to recognize that he was restrained by a pair of large, hairy hands as well as by the ropes.

"Jhurpess," he guessed. The hands tightened briefly in acknowledgment.

"And I take it it was my good friend the troll who hit me on the back of the head?"

Katim materialized from the shadows. The same leather and uneven furs adorned her wiry frame, the same hideous axe and needle-barbed *chirrusk* hung from her hips, and the same bloodthirsty, lunatic gleam brightened her eyes. The half-elf locked stares briefly with the troll and found himself forced to turn away. He'd thought she was bad *before*; now, there was nothing even resembling a soul behind those bestial orbs.

Gork, the miserable little thief, appeared from yet another corner of the room, idly tossing his *kah-rahahk* hand to hand. And following him came almost half a dozen others he did not recognize: two kobolds, two gremlins, and a man. They couldn't *all* have remained hidden from him in this small room, not via any natural means. Grimly, duMark began scanning for the wizard that he knew must accompany them.

"How did you get here?" he demanded, stalling for time. He'd find a way out; he always did. He just needed the chance to clear his mind of the pain, free his fingers . . .

"Come on, duMark," Gork said. "This is the biggest holiday in the Allied Kingdoms. *Lots* of travelers coming into Brenald this past week. Lots of wandering priests, too." The kobold smiled. "I'm starting to like monks, actually. I swear, *nobody* looks twice at them."

The mage smiled back. "You seem to be short an orc," he commented.

Katim's grin grew impossibly wide, and duMark thought he saw strands of some unidentifiable meat caught in the gaps of her back teeth. She said nothing.

Gork answered in her stead. "You mean Cræosh? He, uh . . . had an accident. On the Dendrakis cliffs."

"Seems a strange sort of place to get careless," duMark noted, still searching.

"Yeah, well . . . What're you gonna do?" Was Gork actually fidgeting? *Good.* If he was frightened of Katim—and given the implications, he had reason to be—that was something duMark could use.

"That doesn't sound like the troll," he noted. "Not to face Cræosh directly? Why, can you even be *certain* he's dead?"

"It's a long drop," the kobold muttered. "And it's been three years . . ." Katim's grin faded just a bit.

You keep telling yourself that, kobold. What he said instead was, "Wow. Really no telling who's next, with a troll *that* unpredictable, is there?"

But to that, Katim only chuckled. "Transparent, duMark. Perhaps I'm . . . not the only one in whom you should . . . be disappointed.

"So what's this about, Katim?" duMark asked with a forced casualness. "You're too smart to risk coming after me on some personal vendetta."

"That's *General* Katim to you, shithead!" the lone human grunted.

"*General?*" DuMark barked a dismissive laugh, and even bound, his body language screamed condescension. "And who precisely gave you that lofty title, hmm?"

In reply, a tall robed figure stepped through the front door, ducking to avoid the frame. It strode purposefully across the floor, stopping an arm's reach from duMark, and slowly lowered its hood.

Another laugh, more flippant than the first. "The *ogre?* You're taking your orders from the ogre? You . . ."

And then the laughter died, so that duMark could scream.

"Belrotha," flakes of dead and rotting skin falling from her face, shook her head and leaned over duMark, her eyes glowing with an unholy light. "Are we quite through now?"

"No!" It came out as a sob. Tears flowed down the half-elf's face; snot trailed from his nose. "You're dead!" he insisted, his voice hovering pitifully close to a wail. "You're *dead*!"

"I've been dead for centuries, Ananias. What's another death, more or less?"

"That's why you didn't interfere with the war," the wizard whispered, finally piecing together the puzzle that had confounded him for three long years. He gestured almost impudently with his chin, indicating the tarnished circlet atop the ogre's brow. "You were preparing for *this*!"

Belrotha smiled. "I haven't lived this long, so to speak, by being stupid, Ananias. I knew full well that we couldn't stand up to Dororam's armies. This was the only viable option."

"And you didn't care a damn thing about killing my friends, either, did you?" the half-elf spat. "You just wanted your precious squad away from Kirol Syrreth!"

"There were others who'd have served, had the squad perished during their exploits, but yes, I wanted my squad to be the ones. Still, I'd hardly say that killing your companions was something I 'didn't care about.' It's their fault as much as yours that this war even happened. If my squad's survival had been my *only* concern, there were safer places I could have sent them."

"Your Majesty," Gork hedged, twitching nervously. "The time . . ."

"Ah, yes. My little thief reminds me that we are deep in enemy territory. I'm afraid we'll have to cut our visit short."

Despite his predicament, duMark suddenly smiled. "You're running out of time in more ways than that, Your Majesty." His gaze flickered to the rotted flesh that decorated the floor around the ogre. "When your body died, you lost your claim to your pet demon's soul, didn't you? Without it, a mortal body can't maintain your sort of 'life.' Look at you! You're decomposing away into nothing, aren't you?" His grin, if anything, grew wider—even if it was largely bluff. "Kill me if you must, but you're following not long after."

The undead creature sighed theatrically. "It's true. Ogres are abominably strong, but even their bodies can only handle so much. The troll and the bugbear would do for a while, of course"—DuMark saw several goblins shiver at that—"but they, too, would fail."

"And you can't just summon up another demon," duMark taunted. "A spell of *that* power, with the strain you're already under, would destroy any body you have available."

"I fear you're quite right," the dead ogre said sadly. "What I need," Morthûl mused, as though the thought had only just occurred to him, "is a new body. One more adept. One more accustomed to channeling the sorts of magics I require."

"No . . ." DuMark broke out in a sudden sweat, his throat clogging. A wet warmth trickled down the inside of his thigh. "*No!*"

"My dear Ananias, some dignity, please," the Charnel King implored, slowly removing the crown from the ogre's scalp. Her face began to rot away, even as the others watched. "Look on the bright side." The crown drifted forward, held by quivering, near-skeletal arms, toward the half-elf's brow. The mage thrashed as much as the heavy ropes would allow, but Jhurpess's iron grip held him in the chair. He began screaming, incoherent now, tears raining down his face. "Did you not just say that you wished to rule? You will, Ananias. Kirol Syrreth *and* Shauntille. You will rule a kingdom larger than anyone has ever dreamed."

The crown settled gently atop his head, and he couldn't even scream anymore. He sat, immobile, as Belrotha's flesh sloughed off her body and liquefied in an accelerated caricature of decay. The stench that filled the room was horrifying.

Like flower petals drifting in the wind, the ropes surrounding duMark's hands fluttered to the floor. Jhurpess relaxed his hold, and the half-elf slowly stood.

"Well?" the wizard said, glaring at the others. "Don't just stand there gawking. Let's be off. There's so very much to do."

The last thing Ananias duMark ever saw, before his psyche blissfully drifted into the darkness of never-ending night, was his own familiar room—tinted, be it ever so faintly, by a nauseating yellow glow.

ABOUT THE AUTHOR

ARI MARMELL is a fantasy and horror writer, with novels and short stories published through Spectra (Random House), Pyr, Wizards of the Coast, and others. He has also worked as an author of role-playing game materials for games such as Dungeons & Dragons and the World of Darkness line. His earliest novels were written as tie-in fiction for the games Vampire: The Masquerade and Magic: The Gathering. His first original (that is, non-tie-in) published novel was *The Conqueror's Shadow*, followed by a sequel, *The Warlord's Legacy*. Although born in New York, Ari has lived the vast majority of his life in Texas—first Houston (where he earned a BA in creative writing at the University of Houston) and then Austin. He lives with his wife, George; two cats; and a variety of neuroses.

You can visit Ari online at www.mouseferatu.com.